*This book is a work of fict*
*haps more truth than fi*
— Anonymous

HLTCPB1
First Edition 2021
ISBN: 978-1-8381625-3-5
Published by BenGalley.com
Editing by Sarah Chorn
Map Illustration by Ben Galley

# ABOUT THE AUTHOR

Ben Galley is a British author of dark and epic fantasy books who currently hails from Victoria, Canada. Since publishing his debut Emaneska Series, Ben has released a range of fantasy novels, including the award-winning weird western *Scarlet Star Trilogy* and standalone novel *The Heart of Stone*. He is also the author of the critically-acclaimed *Chasing Graves Trilogy* and *Scalussen Chronicles*.

When he isn't conjuring up strange new stories or arguing the finer points of magic and dragons, Ben enjoys exploring the Canadian wilds and sipping Scotch single malts, and will forever and always play a dark elf in *The Elder Scrolls*. One day he hopes to live in an epic treehouse in the mountains.

Follow Ben on social media to stay up to date with new books, competitions, fantasy stuff and news:
WWW.LINKTR.EE/BENGALLEY

# BOOKS BY BEN GALLEY

THE EMANESKA SERIES
*The Written*
*Pale Kings*
*Dead Stars - Part One*
*Dead Stars - Part Two*
*The Written Graphic Novel*

THE SCARLET STAR TRILOGY
*Bloodrush*
*Bloodmoon*
*Bloodfeud*

THE CHASING GRAVES TRILOGY
*Chasing Graves*
*Grim Solace*
*Breaking Chaos*

STANDALONES
*The Heart of Stone*

SHORTS
*Shards*
*No Fairytale*

*To all the fellow questers, adventurers, and those*
*unafraid of paths untrodden*

For a closer look at the Emaneska maps, go to:
WWW.BENGALLEY.COM/MAPS

MAP OF
*Emanesha,*
*Paraia*
&
*Easterealm*

MOGADON

THE BITTER SEA

HARTLUND

BLUE MOUNTAIN SEA

CAPE PLUMMET

QOLTUR
VINSK
DATHAZII
EAGLE HOLD
DESTRIX
BEGRAD
NORMONT
ARSMIRE YAWN
THUNDER SHORES
CHANARK
HASPIA
AFFLIA GULF
BAY OF SOULS

SHOULDERS OF THE WORLD
RIVEN PLAINS
LILEROSK
BYTARA
DUELLING SEVI
DIAMOND MTS
KHANDI
METISKO
NONAME BAY
AZANMUR
BOISLI
FORBIDDEN COAST
KIRAXA BAY

NYR'S DAGGER
EAST JORP
SUMTER ISLES

THE SILENT SEA

HAMMER HILLS
THE SPINE
ICE FIELDS
TAUSENBAR MTS
OSEFENN MTS
VOHAUG
JORPJUND
SOUTH SPIT
KANI
SHATTERED ISLANDS
HERST SOUND
CAPE OF NO HOPE
BAY OF DRESSH

SCALUSSEN
ARKA
KROPPE
ESSEN
SKAT ISLANDS
KRALSHUNG
EUIAR
TROACLES
PHENOPS MTS

MARGARA
IRON BARRENS
NELSKA
CHAOS SOUND
JORMUNN SEA
HALORN
BELEPHON
ROLLA
LAKE HEXIS
LAKE UQRIA
JAR KHOUM

THE EMBERTEETH
THE DOOMSWELL
THE LONELY SEA
CRAWN
SACTATH
ALBION
BERN SEA
PARAIA
ASPHA
CAPE OF GLASS
PHORA
KALEUS

# heavy lies the crown

SCALUSSEN CHRONICLES BOOK TWO

# part one

## ADRIFT

# CHAPTER 1
## IN THE SHADOW OF IRMINSUL

*Magick is not a force to be harnessed like the muscle of a beast, or coastal gales to be captured in sails. Magick is beyond force. Vast and limitless though it may be, it is a mind in its own right. Few but the gods have glimpsed the true face of magick, and known its thoughts.*
FROM WRITINGS OF JEKOL THE HERETIC

'Hook the bastard, Dabbage! Don't let him escape now!'

Savage cries fought to be heard over the rushing river.

The dun steel hook came swinging, impaling the firegill right below its doleful black eye. Dabbage felt the sear in his muscles as he braced the weight of the fish.

Uncle was there. Line discarded, he dug his trusty knife deep between the firegill's copper scales. Bleeding as it struggled for its life, tail thrashing in the swollen river, it was a battle to wrest the monster where the air could exhaust it. Dabbage was slick with mud and crimson by the time uncle extinguished its struggles with another blow of the knife, right between its brows, if fish could be considered to own brows at all.

Dabbage felt a sharp sting in his ankles and he collapsed to the mud with a cry, arms trembling from the effort of the catch. He eyed the majestic fish and its slowly gasping mouth. It was a fattened shield of copper, half a man across any way it was measured. Its razored fins had carved right through his trews to his shin. He had been cut almost to the bone.

'Smear some of that river clay on it, boy, and you'll do well to stand a little closer to its nose, next time, won't you? Least you got some iron in those little arms of yours.'

Uncle was also bleeding from the shoulder, but Dabbage kept silent on the matter of hypocrisy. The man had a strong distaste to any form of cheek, backchat, and, if Dabbage was honest, general conversation. Uncle preferred the sound of his own voice.

He slapped a muddy hand across his expansive forehead, staining white hair dark. 'By empire's bones, think this might be the largest firegill I landed yet. This is a lake fish. No river fish. That flood must have driven it down to our narrower waters.'

As if the answer lay in the morning's fog, uncle looked across the river to what little could be seen of the far bank. The floodwaters of previous days had gnawed and swallowed what they desired of the riverbanks, finding a new level a yard higher than before. Birch trees, half submerged, still stood proud yet shivering in the waxen waters. The sodden ground crunched with a frost. A mire of wet ash sat atop it. Even now, it fell in faint flakes.

'Think we'll see the sky again today, Uncle? Been days of ash now. Father said—'

'Your father knows as much about the sky as he does about coaxing a single sprout from his fields. Bugger all, is what, boy. Why my sister insists on…'

Dabbage had learned to deafen his uncle's tirades with his own absent pondering. It was now the third day since thunder had shaken their farmhouse. Since fire had filled the sky and the flood had burst the river. The sun had yet to show its face. The smell of sulphur failed to die. The black clouds rising above the Tausenbar had only grown darker. As well as ash, grains of black stone had fallen upon the fields, and pale pebbles that had the texture of bone. The thunder refused to die. Dabbage had lost track of dawns and evenings. Only the village's trusty water clock kept his unease at bay, letting him know that at least the days still passed.

'...your drunken fool of a father's only good for one thing, I tell you, and that's helping us carry this catch back to the cottage. There's a week of eating in this fish and I'll be damned if I'm letting it spoil in this mud and foul ash. Hurry, boy. Fetch your father, swift and mindful now.' Uncle flourished his trusty knife. 'I'll get started.'

'Yessir,' Dabbage agreed, setting off back through the knitted mass of undergrowth to the barren sprout field. The fog kept the field's edges hidden. The world was wrapped in cotton, and yet Dabbage, not even nine years of age, could have run the path blindfolded. Even though tricksome wooden stumps and stones sought to trip him.

A distant yet unmistakable wolf's howl caused him to turn as he ran. Nothing pursued him, but he scanned the feathered boundaries of his field, nonetheless.

The boy faced ahead too late. A figure stood before him. Dabbage skidded to the frozen ground and felt his wounds open afresh as he scrambled to all fours.

A man stood in the centre of the field, imitating a scarecrow in both stillness and dishevelled nature. Broken, black armour hung from limp limbs. It was only when the man pivoted on scuffing feet and stared over Dabbage's head that the boy saw his burns.

One half of the man's face was charred black and blistered. The eye was melted clean out of its socket, now a tear-like smear across his cheek. He clutched at a ragged stump of a wrist with his one good hand.

Muttering, 'Hel has opened,' over and over in a hoarse whisper, the man stumbled onwards in his journey. He was aimed vaguely south.

While Dabbage hunched there like a startled cat, he saw more shadows emerge from the fog. First a handful, then a dozen. Then a score. Not one of them moved faster than a dazed shuffle. Most were mere shapes in the haze. Those that came close enough bore more bloody clothes and wounds, green and gold cloth soiled black with char and dirt. One had a beard full of frost and shivered uncontrollably. They carried the stink of sulphur with them, and a sour scent that lingered in the boy's nostrils.

Strong arms grabbed Dabbage from behind. A hand reeking of fish clapped over his mouth. He struggled until he saw the notched and runed knife before his face. His uncle's trusty blade, trembling in the faintest way.

'Stay still, lad,' he whispered, and together they watched more silhouettes appear. 'Smell that on them? That's the reek of death's hand. They're not right behind the eyes any more.'

No ranks held them. No orders accompanied their quiet yet seemingly determined shuffling. One decided to slump over a stone wall and stay there, giving in.

'Who are they, Uncle?' Dabbage breathed.

It took the man some time to answer, as if it made little sense to him either. 'The empire's soldiers, lad. The same ones that marched through here not a month ago.'

Dabbage remembered the endless hordes trooping past. He and his family had hidden within straw bales and a dry well to avoid the mages that put half the nearby village in chains for refusing to fight for their emperor. Now, on the heels of the red skies and thunder, these ghosts of men and women had returned in their place, drifting across the fields like the floodwaters that preceded them.

'D—did they win?'

Uncle shook his head. 'I don't think so, lad.'

There was a note of shock in uncle's voice Dabbage couldn't ignore.

A scream came from somewhere in the fog. Somewhere close to the village.

'Killed us all,' said a voice nearby.

A woman stood beside them. She was so pale as to be already dead. Half a sword quivered in her hand. A cut across her head showed skull.

'Killed us all,' she said again, as she reached for uncle's coat.

'Get away!' he yelled.

Steel clashed with a harsh ring. Blood spurted across Dabbage's face. He fell to his arse, stunned, pawing at the sudden warmth on his cold skin. In his peripheries, uncle fell to the ground. The bloodied fur coat peeled from him as he slumped, writhing to the floor.

'Killed us all,' the woman spoke to the frozen Dabbage as she reached for him, too.

# CHAPTER 2
## BEYOND MAPS' REACH

*They say war, trade, and curiosity forge roads. The former has left nothing but wary borders where the old Skölgard Empire once pushed its intentions. Trade and curiosity have long been the true architects of exploration, and have kept roads open even in the darkest times.*
*Three paths of note spear their way into the strange eastern lands. To the south, many run the dangerous Silent Sea by ship from Kroppe, Rolia, or Essen. Others take the Merchant's Bridge from Jorpsund, crossing Nyr's Dagger. The northernmost take the Sunder Road from Trollhammerung and Lack.*
FROM 'THE MAPBUILDERS', BY THE EXILED SAGE OLE WRUM, YEAR 912

With naught to endure but monotonous similarity, boredom sets in as quickly as the fever of a festering wound. The mind becomes prone to an anxious cycle of asking questions without answers. Change was the medicine, but the body was numb to fetching it.

With a claw of limestone, Mithrid scraped yet another cross on the wall. *Up, stoke the fire, eat, stare, sleep.* And repeat. Boredom sat upon her shoulders like a stone gargoyle.

For three days the storm had kept them cowered in the cave. The strange forest roared and creaked ceaselessly. Yet even without the howl of the winds that used leaves and twigs like biting ammunition, or the freezing nature of the rain, or the fact they had no idea where they were, their comatose charges would have forced them to stay put.

Farden and Durnus still had not awoken. Exhaustion had kept Aspala and Warbringer slumbering, nursing burns and a dozen other injuries from the final battle of Scalussen.

Frustration kept Mithrid defiantly awake and quite literally clawing at the walls. When she did close her eyes, all the girl could see was dark fire, hungry for flesh and bone and rock, consuming body after body until she wrenched herself awake. The faces of Bull and Hereni remained as shadows in her mind.

Mithrid scratched another cross on the wall.

'Quite the collection,' Aspala whispered from her makeshift bedroll of leaves and less pointy pebbles. She had not moved, but her amber eyes were open. Her broken horns and the purple bruises across her crooked snout gave her a roguish – if not unfortunate – look. She hadn't let go of her broken golden sword since Durnus' spell had whisked them... *somewhere.* The answer of their where-abouts was still trapped in the unconscious vampyre. Or out in the forest.

'Mmph,' grunted Mithrid.

Aspala took some time to push her weary bones up. 'Better than death.'

Mithrid offered her a tired scowl. 'I'm doubting that.'

'Wherever we are, no matter what state we're in, it's better than being dead.'

It was dismal comfort, but it counted.

Aspala tottered to the mouth of the limestone cave they'd stumbled upon after a day, dragging Durnus and Farden through the forest. Even with Warbringer, it had been hard toil.

The Paraian sniffed at the wild air, stared at the silver trees with their flat, russet gold leaves. The smells rising from the sodden soil had a strange scent. Offensive only through their difference to the pines and salt Mithrid found herself missing so dearly. She felt the same as she had that gloomy morning outside Troughwake, kneeling before Arka mages with her hands bound.

'Don't smell like Emaneska. Smells… bitter. Like almonds,' Aspala was whispering. 'I hate almonds.'

'As you've said. Still doesn't answer where we are, and what we're doing here,' Mithrid suspired. She pushed herself from her stone seat and brushed the dirt from her legs. Stepping over the slumbering minotaur and the circle of embers she curled around, Mithrid examined the vampyre and mage for the dozenth time.

Farden was in a coma of his own making. As not even Warbringer's strength could pry the scarred Scalussen armour off him, they couldn't do much but keep him propped up and listen for his breathing between the slits in his helmet.

As for Durnus, no bones seemed broken. At least, none they could tell from poking and prodding. The vampyre had awoken briefly once to take water and yet dribble it out again. He was so pale between the scabbed burns Mithrid could almost see the bones of his skull.

She pressed a hand gently to his thin arm and tried to wake him. All she got was a murmur. It was, instead, Farden that awoke, and with a lurch so sudden and violent it tested the fortitude of Mithrid's bladder. She recoiled in a panic, narrowly avoiding the fire and collapsing against Warbringer's hoof. Farden instinctively raised his hands, one clawed in magick, the other as if he held a sword.

'Farden! It's us, you idiot!' Mithrid yelled at him. Shadow swirled around her fingers.

Warbringer was now awake, half-upright and growling low in her throat. The copper rings in her snout jangled softly. Between the wounds she wore without care, large patches of her charcoal fur had been burned away. Her horns were whole but scarred with fresh notches carved by blades. Her armour, scant and unnecessary though it had been before, had been reduced to a kilt of mail and crisscrossing leather bandoliers. She clutched at the necklace of bones as if fearing it had been lost.

Panting breathlessly, Farden clawed at his helmet, raising his visor to gulp in air before wrenching the steel from his head. The metal scales that normally interlocked so finely scraped as they came loose. At last, the king was revealed. Sweat and dirt muddied his face. Eyes red with burst veins stared wildly at Mithrid and the others.

Only when he had caught his breath did Farden try to speak. 'Did we... Did I...?'

'Win? Is that what you're asking?' Mithrid asked, teeth clenched. She struggled to forget the mage had almost scorched them to dust. 'Without a doubt.'

'Arka naught but ash and bone.' Warbringer thumped her bare chest. 'Fine deaths for my people.'

'Scalussen was destroyed, too,' Mithrid muttered. 'And almost all of us, if it hadn't been for Durnus and me.'

Farden seemed to deflate, eyes gazing past the mouth of the cave as the memories of the battle flooded his mind. 'I couldn't stop it,' he whispered. 'Irminsul was too powerful. Too full of... *rage*, for want of a better word.'

Aspala nodded. 'It took your armour almost a whole day to cool down.'

'My—' Farden flinched again, patting himself down with frantic hands. His face turned to horror as he saw the state of the blackened gold and crimson, and the bent scales of the cuirass. The design of the snarling wolf upon his breastplate was charred across one side of its face. Of the two rubies that lay embedded as eyes, one was missing.

The mage took a moment to remove his gauntlets so he could probe at the steel. Some scales seemed unnaturally loose, others twisted into new positions. His fingers trembled with either anger or fear, Mithrid couldn't yet tell. It was then she realised Farden's left hand was lacking its smallest finger. It seemed an old injury, decades healed.

'I can't feel it,' the mage was muttering.

Aspala was concerned. 'Something wrong with you, Farden?'

He looked up as if he had already forgotten his concerned audience and his murky surroundings. 'Where in Hel are we? What are we doing here?'

Mithrid pointed to the vampyre. The question had burned in her mind for days. 'Only Durnus knows, but unlike you, he hasn't woken up yet.'

Farden didn't reply. Much to his increasingly frustrated growling, he took an age to push himself to his knees. Aspala moved to help him but he waved her back.

'Durnus,' he yelled in the old vampyre's ear. 'Durnus!'

Mithrid sighed. 'We've tried that.'

Farden began to shake him with the sense and level of force not to injure him further.

'Tried that too,' rumbled Warbringer.

Farden reached for the warped, half-molten Weight that still lay trapped in Durnus' hands. The metal refused to part from his claw-like fingers. 'Where have you taken us, you old fool?' Farden growled.

'All he managed to say before he fell into his malady was "east",' said Aspala.

'East?' Farden stared at the quiver in his hands.

The mage got to a shaky version of upright, face scrunching as though every muscle in his body complained vociferously. It took him several stumbles, but Farden prised his cuirass and greaves from his burned skin. He pushed himself to the cave mouth, where he braced against the storm winds. He reached to wet his hands and vambraces in the pummelling rain. Whatever sun shone on this odd land was now falling to dusk behind leaf and copper canopy.

'There's no ice in sight,' muttered Farden. 'No snow. Don't recognise these trees. Doesn't smell right. Birds are too quiet.'

Mithrid pinched the bridge of her nose.

Farden staggered deeper into the storm. His simple trews and tunic were soaked within moments, but he pressed on, staring into the wild forest and scouring the thick weave of branches for a trace of sky. The storm was all-consuming. Around and around he turned, a wobbling top, until he staggered back to the cave and slumped onto the stones next to Durnus' charred satchel. The one that had no right to weigh as much as it did.

Farden's shivering hands grasped at the satchel's straps and something within. Aspala tried to help again, much to the mage's irritation, but at last, he dragged a huge tome into the open, one covered in grey and ancient leather. He scratched at its clasp and heaved it apart with a creak and what Mithrid swore was an irritated whisper.

The pages were decrepit, weathered at the edges. Mithrid blinked as two bright sparks of orange light emerged from the book's gutter. After her last experience with a spellbook, she recoiled instinctively against the stone. She was not alone. By the amount of sharp teeth she bared, Warbringer looked deeply disturbed by the tome.

'Death magick,' she whispered.

Only Aspala leaned inwards.

'Show me Elessi,' Farden blurted. Not to any of them, but to the book. His fingertips clawed at its blank pages.

The lights spun around each other like duelling flies, unsure. Wherever they moved, they left smoky amber trails of light behind, drawing half-hearted shapes. Mithrid made no sense of their efforts but Farden bowed his head, breathless in relief.

'Eyrum,' he whispered, and again the lights appeared broken.

Mithrid, half-expecting a sabrecat to come bounding from the spellbook at any moment, spoke up. 'What is that thing? What does that mean?'

'It's called the Grimsayer, and it means they're not dead, girl. Alive and hopefully well, somewhere,' Farden pressed his head against a boulder. He heaved with a deep sigh.

The others bowed their head, grateful. Warbringer whispered to some god of her kind. Mithrid was still staring at the lights, still uneasy. 'What of Hereni? And Bull?'

'If the others are alive, then—'

'Ask it. Please.'

The lights looked as confused as before. Mithrid felt her heart give up its rapid pace. She shook off the fears that lurked in the darkest corners of her mind.

Farden half-closed the book, but paused to argue with some inner impulse.

'M—' Farden stopped himself, unable to say the third name. He had to physically spit it out. 'Malvus.'

Once more, the lights drew nothing. The mage's comfort turned to disbelief. He pushed himself up, lip curled in anger. 'Loki!' he hissed at the spellbook. The orange lights died away as if bored of failing.

Mithrid flinched. She had heard that name before in the emperor's tent, but other matters were more pressing. 'Wait. Does this mean Malvus survived?'

'Yes, it fucking does.' Farden grimaced so severely his lip had begun to bleed.

An uneasy silence settled in the cave. Their victory, it seemed, was not so complete after all. Such sacrifice. Such sweeping death. Mithrid scrunched her eyes shut. Once more, the flames of Irminsul greeted her, along with the screaming of the countless Arka.

Farden slammed the tome shut and shoved it back into the vampyre's satchel alongside other tomes. His armour grated on the stone as he sprawled, exhausted. 'We'll wait for the storm to pass. Leave at first light. Find a vantage point to see where we are,' Farden muttered, while he stared at his scarred vambraces. His movements were fidgety, as if he tried to quell an inner panic. That, or he desperately needed to piss.

Far beyond the mouth of the cave, something screeched pitifully. It commanded their attention until something else silenced it.

'It's raged for three days already,' said Mithrid.

'Then surely it should be over soon. Failing that, we'll wade through it,' Farden growled. He clenched a fist to still his quivering hands. 'Are you injured? Can everyone walk?'

Aspala's voice was hoarse. 'Bruised, but I can travel.'

'I can walk,' said Warbringer, staring beyond the cave. Her bearded chin and jawline ruffled in the bothersome winds.

Mithrid simply nodded.

Farden reached for the ashes and half-burned wood of their fire. He spread his fingers over the shimmering embers. It took no time for Mithrid and the others to notice there was a problem. The mage strained harder, narrowing his bloodshot eyes. Farden was nearly grasping the embers by the time he gave up, hunched over his hands. He looked at them as if they had just inexplicably strangled a loved one.

Mithrid seized a handful of kindling and a log from the meagre store they'd gathered, and began to stoke the fire the old fashioned way. The wood was a faded silver. Bronze knots ran through it like rivets, and when it burned it gave off a fragrance of almond and cloves. Aspala could be seen wrinkling her snout, but the heat was too enticing.

Farden caught Mithrid's eye as he inched closer to the fire. It was too narrow a look for her liking, too full of suspicion and unspoken words. But he did not look at her again. His gaze remained fixed on his scorched armour for the remainder of the evening. At least until Mithrid's eyes drooped, too heavy to keep lifted. Too exhausted to fight the boredom and fatigue.

She was escorted into dreams of a fiery dark by a sound she at first presumed was snoring. A lone, sighing horn, quiet through distance. Yet sleep already commanded her.

Morning found Farden kneeling over puddles, furiously scraping the soot from his Scalussen armour, piece by piece. Slumber was a realm he had left the others to enjoy fitfully. Three days of sleep was more than enough. Any more felt like tempting death.

The mage's body ached awfully from scalp to sole. Farden was convinced a rib was cracked. The night's flames had kindled his raw skin, flushed with heat from a dozen burns where both magick and flame had scorched him.

The jagged cave entrance was dark, four still figures huddled within. A faint stream of blue-grey smoke rose from its mouth, the last breaths of the fire. It mingled with the morning drizzle the storm had left behind.

Massaging raw fingers, Farden stacked his armour in a neat pile, crouched with his head in his hands, and surveyed it with a grimace. Not in forty years of battle and narrow scrapes had his armour ever seen such damage. Not since it was forged for the Knights of the Nine over a thousand years before.

Several sections of gold and red scales were buckled. One small portion had even melted together. The cuirass was warped. One pauldron wore an alarming dent. Scratches and stubborn black scorch marks were an added eye-watering garnish. A muscle above Farden's lip began to twitch sporadically. A damning thought struck his mind like a hammer to a bell.

*His armour was broken.*

When he at last could look no more, the mage thumbed the black tattoos on his forearms: black skeleton keys, jagged of tooth and running from his wrist halfway to his elbow. Whatever wounds broke the rest of his skin, not a scar or scratch dared to cross their ink.

The forest around him was silent save for the patter of nodding, dripping leaves. Stepping out of sight of the cave, Farden walked along the short limestone cliff until he found a natural basin of trapped rain. With much grunting, Farden pulled his tunic free of his scorched skin and let the morning air cool him. He could feel its cold breath keenly against every swirling line of script running along his shoulders and back. It was not the effort of his tired muscles that brought the sweat to his brow, but the persistent notion that his armour was irreparably damaged. Farden snarled it into silence and began to douse himself with icy water, too tired to flinch.

Eyes glassy, unfocused, he thought of Irminsul's fire as he bathed. The battle with the blaze had left his memories patchwork after the moment Modren had fallen to Gremorin's claws. It felt unbearably recent, as if his old friend had died yesterday. Inwick, too. The grief had been stolen by war, but now it swooped upon him. Farden choked as his throat clenched. He splashed water on his face to calm his itching eyes, pooled some in his hands to drink. He choked on that, too.

Crackling leaves betrayed Mithrid's approach. A wild mess of red hair poked around the rock. 'Thought you'd left us here. Snuck off,' she said.

Much to his guilt, the heartless thought had crossed his mind not long before. 'Look away, girl,' ordered Farden, hastily donning his tunic. It stank of sweat and smoke.

'Never took you for the bashful type,' Mithrid replied. She did not smile, but there was no scowl on her face, either. Aside from the char on her armour and pale skin, the few cuts and gashes, she looked remarkably untouched by the chaos of war. There was no hint of Irminsul's fire in her emerald eyes. Not that Farden could see. She merely paid him a cautious attention.

'Funny,' he said. 'Not while my Book is on view. It's too dangerous even at a glance.'

Mithrid lifted her face to the drizzle instead and closed her eyes. 'Even for me, do you think?'

'Even for you.'

Farden slid the Scalussen vambraces over his wrists and waited to feel the icy prickle in his veins that normally accompanied the magick of the Nine's armour. Godblood in the steel, so the legends spoke. To Farden's dismay and continuing underlying panic, he felt nothing but cold, damp metal, devoid of its subtle powers. The word *ordinary* had rarely – if ever – been applied to Scalussen armour, but there it was. Plain, ordinary steel.

'I should thank you,' Farden said hoarsely, donning his greaves and gauntlets.

Mithrid crossed her arms and leaned against the rock. 'I reckon you should.'

'Not only for coming back, but for stopping me from…' Farden paused. 'Doing something regrettable. My memories are broken, filled with naught but flame, yet I remember you reaching for me. Yelling at me. I thought I could wield it, but in fact I was powerless to stop it. I saw a face of magick I've never seen before. It used me, and now it's betrayed me. And here I was, beginning to believe the notion I was invincible,' Farden muttered. 'That I was the Forever King.'

'I'm just glad somebody was there to stop you. The saviour needed saving, it seemed. Durnus said you could have wiped out half the north if I hadn't done something. Perhaps all of Emaneska. We're fortunate you didn't.'

*Saviour.*

Farden winced at the notion of destruction. The shadow of his actions was a sickening worm gnawing at his stomach. The fact the others were alive was the only fact keeping it from consuming him.

'Was it worth it, do you think?' Mithrid spoke up, hesitant and unsure for the first time.

That was one thing Farden was certain of. He steeled himself. 'It will be,' he asserted. 'And you said it yourself: the Arka chose their side.'

'And yet I can't stop thinking about Malvus' grinning face somewhere, happy to be alive. I can't stand that we went through Irminsul only for him to escape. All I seem to care about is him dying,' Mithrid spoke up. 'Can that grim book of yours tell us where we can find him?

'First, we have to find out where *we* are. And be careful of that obsession, Mithrid. It can harm you in ways you can't imagine.' Farden cleared his throat. 'I have to ask you something.'

She looked at him at last. 'What is it?'

'Did you do... something to me?'

'What, by Hurricane, are you accusing me of?' she asked, immediately insulted.

'My magick, my armour. They're not as they were. They don't...' He forced out the words. 'They don't work any more. Did your magick do something to me?'

Black smoke curled around Mithrid's fist. 'I did what I had to do to save us. From you, *Forever King*. The one wielding the inferno of a volcano. Maybe look to yourself before you seek to blame others.' Mithrid tutted, and left him to scratch at his stubbled chin. Farden could at last see the pain in Mithrid's eyes, one beyond Farden's infamous way with words and his thin accusations. The pain of being lost lay in the helplessness of the soul, not of the body. Farden knew it well, because he felt the very same. By the molten walls of Scalussen, were they lost.

'Well done, Farden,' the mage sighed to himself.

Looming like the troll who owned the limestone burrow, Warbringer was waiting for them, looking impatient and disturbed by the constant dripping of the forest canopy. The Paraian woman, Aspala, was holding one of the fallen leaves, shaped like a bronze star with sunlit veins. She wiped her thumb across the leaf and it came away grimy.

'Soot?' she asked of Farden.

'Or ash.'

'A promising sign, no? The mountains must be close,' War-bringer said. She raised her giant warhammer Voidaran as if it weighed no more than a wheat bushel. A faint and wistful moan accompanied the weapon's every movement, however subtle.

'Would you help me, Warbringer?' Farden asked, standing over Durnus. It wounded him to see his friend so helpless, yet for the moment, he was most concerned with the pungent waft coming from the hulking minotaur. Warbringer moved the mage aside, scooped Durnus up with surprising care, and draped him across her unarmoured shoulder.

'Like a feather,' she said.

The satchel Durnus had rescued from Scalussen was another matter. The weight of the tomes and the Grimsayer within were nothing short of sadistic. Farden got a corner of it off the ground before his arms and back protested. He bared teeth as he paused to try again.

'You're not yourself yet, King. You'll need time,' Aspala said as she hoisted the satchel over her shoulder. He saw her grimace with the effort and tried to take it from her, but she was already out of reach.

They gathered at the cave mouth, each peering in a different direction. Farden listened to the heavy breathing of his companions: a Paraian, a minotaur, a half-dead vampyre and a… Mithrid. He still hadn't figured whether she could be called a mage. He realised they were staring at him.

'Where to then, King?' asked Mithrid.

A sweat prickled his skin. 'Don't call me that. I don't deserve that title any longer.'

An awkward silence hung before he spat in the loam.

'I say anywhere but this fucking forest,' said Farden, choosing the only direction that made sense to his tangled mind. *Onwards*.

It took them half the day to notice, but it turned out the forest was a carnivorous beast. Its spoils were not of meat, nor of bone, but of soul and spirit.

The scant amber light the treetops let through offered the survivors of Scalussen no sun for a compass. They could only guess at the passage of time. Only the thump of their boots in the damp loam counted the moments. The wet air felt so thick as to be an unwanted coat around their shoulders. Throats and nostrils itched inexplicably, and another sharp, unpleasant smell now pervaded the forest, like that of witches' powders and tinctures.

The monotony of their arboreal prison was bewildering. The trees never crowded or encroached on each other. Hardly a single tree was crooked or fallen. And though the tree trunks were twisted and woven, each was still painfully alike. Only the scars across their silver trunks told them apart, as well the gouges Mithrid and the others cut in their wood to mark their way. Crimson sap dribbled like blood, which made them all the more noticeable when they crossed upon their own marks again and again.

On the fourth occasion, Farden slammed his armoured fist into the tree. His guttural yell scattered the few ground-birds that dared to break the forest's silence. Mithrid was inclined to agree. Being so enclosed made her yearn for the flat face of the open ice flats. She throttled her axe.

'We could cut one down, get some damn air.'

'We should climb one,' Aspala offered. 'See what's beyond.'

Farden was too busy inspecting the threads of sticky pale sap that came away with his gauntlet to offer an answer.

When nobody moved, Mithrid rolled up the sleeves of her cloak, showing the scorched black armour on her wrists. 'A fine idea, and I'll bet there isn't a better climber here than me.'

Rubbing the damp from her fingers, Mithrid eagerly reached for the first branch. With a lurch that almost made her yelp, Farden seized her wrist. Only one of her fingers had touched the branch. He dragged it back, dragging a single strand of sap with it. Mithrid twitched as it stung her. It felt like a knife slicing down the length of her finger. Black shadow swirled around Mithrid's hand as she clenched it.

'It's no magick, Mithrid,' Farden said, drawing her away from the tree. 'Poison, maybe.'

'Poison? Shit…' she seethed, immediately bending to wipe her finger across the mud and scrape it in a puddle. The panic died with the pain.

Farden pointed at another nearby tree with an irregular trunk. 'Look. Can't figure how I didn't notice it before, but it's right there.'

It took a tilt of her head, but she saw it: the vague shape of a deer in the silver wood, wrapped around the tree trunk. One leg and antler remained protruding as skeletal branches. No wonder not a scuffle of hoof or paw dared disrupt the silence. No wonder the bird-song was so meagre and haunting. The trees were truly carnivorous after all. Mithrid felt betrayed by every plant she had ever tended.

Warbringer snorted in anger, as if the mere existence of the trees was an affront. She glared at every branch or trunk within a swinging distance of her warhammer. 'Meat-eating trees? We are in the Dark Fields, Farden. Is that where vampyre brings us?'

A frantic screeching of some bird trapped upon a branch spurred them onwards. A smattering of its feathered friends burst from the forest floor and took wing. With no more than a collective nod, the whole group seemed to agree at once to follow them, hoping the birds would flee the forest and lead them to light.

With the sounds of a tortured creature ringing in their ears, they dashed across the loam until their legs turned to fire. Ever on-wards, they pressed, even when a wailing horn echoed through the forest. It was no creature, but blown by human breath. A gust of sick-ly wind blew around their sweating, stumbling forms as they chased its direction. The trees rustled overhead, and still they ran.

*Sunlight.*

A glorious blotch of it speared the oppressive, endless trees. Mithrid outpaced the others, though it was terrifying to see War-bringer bringing up second. For a moment, the soggy ground was sand of grey and black, and it was not the remnants of a war behind her, but Remina, and Bogran. And Bull.

By the time her legs were becoming gelatinous, Mithrid could spy the edge of the cursed forest. Where the loam ended, timid grass of yellow grew glowing in the sunlight. Baring teeth, Mithrid threw herself towards it and escaped the forest in a sprawl of limbs and tangled hair. She tumbled into a heap and let her lungs heave, drawing in a mouthful of dry grass but also a lungful of the freshest air she'd ever tasted.

Hooves skidded next to her. The minotaur's rump colliding with the ground reverberated through Mithrid's ribs.

'First,' she whispered, out of old habit.

Warbringer seemed put out. 'Not race, girl.'

Aspala brought Farden across the threshold with her, the mage leaning heavily on the woman's arm as they ran. They were the first to notice they had an audience.

Mithrid gradually pushed herself from the ground, eyes shifting from a powder blue sky and mountains so yellow they looked like sand dunes, to the sweeping plains leading right up to the grass still sticking to her face. The same faded grass that, not a stone's throw away at the edge of the forest, a score of incredibly angry-looking strangers stood upon.

From their yellow and blue fur pelts to the scythes they brandished, to the grinning skull masks they wore, nothing was familiar about these people. Especially not the man standing at the centre of their huddle, who had deer horns affixed to his mask of silver.

It appeared as though they had interrupted some kind of ceremony. A body wrapped in white cloth lay before a huge specimen of the foul trees. Another figure stood kneeled before the trunk. The wood had swallowed his arms up to the elbows. The rest of his skin was turning a mottled silver. With his head back, mouth agape to the sky, thin green tendrils had sprouted from the man's long-dead eyes.

Barging through his fellows, the silver-masked leader marched towards Mithrid and the others. He used the staff of his tall scythe like a walking stick while he bellowed in a dialect of the Common-tongue, the words so thick they were almost another language.

'Who dares to defile the Bronzewood?' he demanded in furi-ous tones.

Farden raised a hand in greeting. 'Our mistake, sir! We are in-credibly and undoubtedly lost. We meant no disrespect. As you can see, we wanted to leave the forest as quickly as possible.'

The man halted before them.

'I am the High Cathak Tartavor, and I demand to know who defiles the Bronzewood! It is sacred Cathak land. Give me your names so I can have the Dusk God curse you for your flagrant sins.'

Farden cleared his throat. 'And as I said, we are lost. If you could tell us where we are—?'

The man spluttered. 'How does one forget the path they took to be here? One does not simply stumble into the Bronzewood!' By now, the others in Tartavor's pack had begun to form up behind him. His stern expression softened. 'Yet our god is not cruel. Forgiveness for the fools, we preach. Instead, you shall pay the Dusk God a toll for your disrespect and trespass.'

Mithrid decided it was a fine time to stand at the mage's side. As did Aspala. Warbringer stayed on her arse in the dust, looking bored by the whole affair. Durnus was still slumped over her shoul-der.

Farden crossed his arms. 'Really? A toll?' He spoke sideways to Mithrid. 'The oldest trick of bandits and waylayers. And I imagine it won't be cheap.'

The High Cathak removed his silver mask to reveal a righteous grin smeared like honey across tanned and hairless features. A black crescent moon had been tattooed on his forehead, like the closed lid of a third eye. 'You imagine well, for the price of trespassing upon sacred Cathak land is high indeed. A toll is necessary so the Dusk God may dispense his glorious forgiveness upon your shoulders. Unless you wish to make a sacrifice in blood. As is customary, of course.'

'Of course.'

'The religious kinds of bandit really are the worst,' Aspala muttered under her breath, eyeing the others fanning out past their leader, scythes raised in two hands. 'A plague on the desert paths of Paraia.'

Farden nodded. 'Aren't they just?'

Tartavor attempted to look humble, almost discontented with his holy duty. 'Your arms and armour would satisfy the Dusk God's needs, I am sure. All of it. Even your half-sword, child of the Burnt South.'

Aspala thumbed the jagged edge of her gold blade, where the metal had been notched and broken. 'And that will dispense enough justice, will it?' she hissed.

'Perhaps that ungodly pig-beast's crude hammer as well, and the Exalted One's wrath might be appeased.'

That got Warbringer's attention something fierce. Putting Durnus aside, she arose and stretched to her enormous height before brushing past the others. Warbringer made no noise, no grunt of effort as she calmly approached the Cathak. Her "crude" hammer Voidaran screamed like a tortured ghost as she swung it, breaking a man beside Tartavor in two before driving his shattered corpse through two others. It was so barbarically abrupt it stunned half of the bandits immobile. Those who didn't run, the minotaur broke like kindling. One man was decapitated so rapidly his body cartwheeled before landing in a headless heap. Another whose legs failed her found Voidaran dropped on the back of her skull with a whine.

Though the ease of which the human body was reduced to pieces turned Mithrid's gut, she nodded appreciatively to see the

High Cathak scarpering. Pelts flailing behind him, scythe forgotten, Tartavor had outstripped the half-dozen survivors and was dashing along the border of his precious Bronzewood. He soon disappeared over a rise in the grassland. His antlered helmet lay nearby in the dry soil.

Warbringer snuffled. Cheated of further spoils, she wiped her gruesome hammer across a patch of trampled grass and patted it. 'Called me pig-beast.'

Farden shrugged. 'No explanation needed.'

'I think you made quite the impression,' Mithrid said.

Warbringer smiled through sharp teeth. It was a brief moment of levity, and as their boots squelched through the blood, their minds turned back to serious matters, such as why in Hel the dead bundle of cloth was now trying to move.

Before Mithrid could point, Aspala was already hobbling towards it. Her sword made short work of the cloth, and she had to jump aside as a young boy exploded upright. Even gagged and bound, he managed to wriggle to his feet and hop madly around in a circle. He was barely dressed in sackcloth, covered in bruises and the bleeding marks of brands. The Cathak had sheared his head. Whatever he screamed under the gag was indecipherable, and Farden cuffed him lightly to keep him still. The mage tugged the cloth from the boy's mouth while Aspala held his bonds.

'Please don't kill me! I have nothing to offer you! They took me as sacrifice. They were going to feed me to the Bronzewood—'

'Shut it,' Farden snapped. 'Just tell me where in Emaneska we are and we'll be on our way.'

'Ema... Emeska?'

The way the boy questioned the name made Mithrid abruptly aware of the heartbeat pounding in her head.

'You're not in Emeska, sir.'

Farden shook him. 'Where? Where then?'

'You stand on the Rivenplains, sir.' At their blank looks, he elaborated further. 'On the S—Sunder Road. North of Lilerosk. Or west of Dathazh, you could say. That's a proper city.' The boy fussed with his hands.

The mage had his answer, but clearly not the one he wanted. It caused him to physically stumble. Sweat beaded his forehead. Farden looked to the plains and the sky, blinking owlishly as if he only just awoken.

Mithrid was still trying to make sense of the words when Farden began to totter away from the Bronzewood.

'Where are you going?' she called.

He shouted his answer to the cloudless blue. 'South. Home.'

Mithrid chased after him. 'Are we just going to leave that lad behind?'

'At least he knows where he is.'

It was a coldness Mithrid had only seen Farden reserve for Arka. 'Don't you care?'

Farden whirled on her, temper soaring unexpectedly. 'Of course I don't, Mithrid! If I have to deal with one more problem right now my skull will simply explode. My mind is currently full of grander matters, as it happens. Such as the terror that we are the only survivors of Scalussen, lost in a land I've never seen. Or the fact I cannot feel my magick beneath my skin, and my armour seems inexplicably broken. Or that, despite my hopes of crushing Malvus and his ideals once and for all, despite killing thousands, hundreds of thousands with my own hands, despite sacrificing everything I've built, including my oldest friends, he still lives. And now, as if that wasn't enough, a greater evil plays his games with Emaneska, and I am right back where I fucking started!'

Mithrid stared at him wide-eyed and breath held. Despite the rising fire in her chest, her armour, and wild hair, she felt the same Hâlorn girl who had stood before Farden atop the Frostsoar: unsure, untrusting, cowed. It was as if the last months had been wound back, and counted for naught.

Farden pinched the bridge of his nose. 'I'm sorry. I—'

A noise distracted him. A moment passed before Mithrid heard it also: a slight yet rumbling tremor in the ground. She searched for clouds but saw no culprits of thunder.

'I don't think we've seen the last of our gods-fearing friends,' Farden warned in a low voice, at the precise moment a small copse of crooked scythes appeared over the rise. Two score of them, all wearing the same skull masks. Half of them sat astride muscular piebald cows. The rest ran, and, as they charged, their low and disturbing chants filled the air.

Warbringer readied Voidaran gleefully. Aspala began to hiss, half-blade low and backwards like a dagger. Farden reached for his sword and found it lacking. Mithrid caught his eye as it moved to her axe.

'Not a chance,' she said, sweeping it from its sheath and holding it fast.

'Fuck it,' growled Farden. He stretched for the ground, grimacing at his shaking arms. Mithrid was torn between watching the mage struggle and the charging Cathak rapidly close the distance between them. Worse, she felt no swell of magick in the air. None of their attackers were mages. Mithrid swallowed against a dry throat as she took a pace forwards, axe raised.

'Look!'

A shadow crossed the bright afternoon sun that hung above the Bronzewood. Mithrid winced in the glare. Before she could shield her eyes, fire spewed from the sky. The bandits' charge was enveloped in a blazing cloud of flame. Those who weren't turned to cinders ran screaming with flames and smoke streaming from their furs. Cows bellowed and scattered in fear. The two score immediately became a dozen, and by the looks of the remainder, they had no wish to fight. In their panic to escape the fire, some even sprinted into their sacred Bronzewood.

A turquoise dragon brushed the grass with its wings before crash-landing in a heap. Mithrid and the others recognised its colours and pattern immediately.

Farden galloped ahead. 'Fleetstar!'

Clouds of dust mingled with the smoke of Fleetstar's laboured breaths. 'Two thousand...' she was gasping, huge, forked tongue lolling like a hound's.

'Two thousand what?' Farden looked around, expecting an army marching into sight at any juncture.

'Two thousand fucking miles,' she cursed.

Farden had to put a hand on her warm scales to steady himself. The sweat ran down his cheek.

Mithrid stood close by. She was struggling to imagine such distance. 'Where is that? Where does that put us?'

The dragon wheezed. 'East of Trollhammerung. At least five hundred miles past what I'd safely call Emaneska. Past the old Crumbled Empire of Skölgard.'

'How in Hel did you find us?'

Fleetstar blinked at the sun, distracted and abruptly quiet. 'I just looked for trouble,' she growled. 'I spied a town further south.'

'Lilerosk,' interrupted the boy. He spoke in a whisper, transfixed by the dragon. It took him a moment to realise they were all staring at him expectantly. 'It's my home. It's not far. A day or two's travel.'

Mithrid sucked her teeth. 'Well, Farden?' She seized the chance at clinging onto a spot on the map.

While the mage pondered, the boy leaned closer to Aspala. 'What is that thing?'

'A dragon, boy.'

'Never seen one before. Or whatever you and your... husband are?' The lad looked to Warbringer, who promptly lifted her hammer. Aspala stayed her hand.

'Two thousand miles,' was all Farden could say to it all. He reached for the helmet that dangled from his waist and shoved it over his head. Grumbling at the crunch of metal, he patted Fleetstar between the spines of her neck.

'Can you walk?'

The dragon rumbled somewhat inconclusively. 'Not now,' was all Fleetstar said, and she closed her eyes as if it were a fine moment and place for a nap.

'Walk where, Farden?' Mithrid interjected, but Farden ignored her. The mage levelled a gold finger at the rescued lad.

'And you, boy. You have a name?'

'Kursi, sire.'

'Then in return for saving your life, Kursi, you can take us to this town of yours,' Farden ordered. 'I'm tired of being lost. We should gather our thoughts and fill our bellies. Supplies. Weapons. A healer for Durnus. Anything we'll need for our journey back to Elessi and the other survivors.'

Mithrid squinted to read his eyes behind the visor, but Farden turned and merely began to trudge, keeping the sun on his right. With a tired nod to the others, agreement was reached, and they followed the mage south.

The boy hop-skipped alongside her as if he couldn't decide between walking or running. 'So!' he said, cheerful merely to be alive and not tree-fodder. 'Who are you people?'

# CHAPTER 3
## ALL SPARKS

*It is not gold nor military might that is most valuable in all the world, but
souls. Not their belief, but their raw power.*
FROM ANCIENT WRITINGS OF THE CULT OF EVERNIA

The first hawks from the north had arrived in the eyries of quiet
Krauslung.

The rumours of scribbled, bloody missives, telling tales of
mountains of fire and utter defeat had spread as a plague from the
messenger towers to the streets, from one household to the next, until
a fever of unrest claimed the empire's capital. Crowds coalesced in
markets. Streets turned quiet by war were filled by a press of bodies.
The need for answers vomited the residents of shuttered houses onto
the streets.

Under a sunset of red and bizarre green, Krauslung had
gathered at the mighty walls at the valley's mouth. There they
flooded the wall-tops to wait for sons, daughters, fathers, and wives
to come stumbling home through the pervasive, chilling shadow that
had enveloped the Össfen Mountains. Most watched in silence, suffering the ailment of waiting. Others found company for their own
fear by stoking those of others. Fear deteriorated into anger. Fights
broke out between city guards and citizens. Before long, mobs
stalked the streets, demanding answers of a city that could produce
none. The emperor was as absent as his hordes.

It was then that the first flakes of ash began to fall under a cold
northern wind.

❧

For all their gilded achievements, their towers of marble, their silken finery, humans had never strayed far from their animal natures. The gods had given them two thousand years, and they were no closer to true improvement. It was like dressing up a hound and sitting it at a banquet table. All it would take was a whistle or a grab of its scruff, and all too quickly the dog would show its fangs.

Loki raised his pale hand to a sky of umber torchlight, and let a fat wafer of ash land on his knuckles. All it had taken Krauslung to show its fangs was fear. The shocking realisation that Malvus' Arka might not be invincible after all, and that the price for such knowledge was the people's to pay. Like animals indeed, they had scented defeat in the air like approaching rain.

Loki drew a dark line across his skin with Irminsul's ash and smirked. To know Farden was behind it all was simply delicious. Surprised as Loki had been by Irminsul, he was more shocked at how easy the mage had made this for him.

The god continued his journey. Loki was feeling brazen. He wore no other face besides his own. His trademark coat, streaked by the ash, curled around his legs in breezes pinched by the narrow streets. Boots scuffing through the patina of ash that had gathered, he kept his gaze wandering.

Along an adjoining street, a portly man was being dragged from his stately home. He was not alone. Plenty of the merchants and magistrates had paid Malvus to keep their sons and daughters from the war. This didn't sit well with those of lower status and lighter pockets. Loki saw the fists and staves descend upon the man while his crying children shivered in the ash nearby. The smart ones had either joined the mobs in their protests or sealed themselves in the Arkathedral.

Loki watched a band of Street Legion guards deflecting rocks from their shields, stubbornly and stupidly upholding Malvus' orders.

The gutters beneath their feet were already stained red from a fallen guard, curled around a spear.

Some animals are smarter than others, of course. The clever ones were calling for calm and strong leadership. Not for any reason as preposterous as altruism; that belonged to the idiots. Loki knew, just as they did, that if the rumours of utter defeat were true, Krauslung was now a treasure trove to be claimed. Not merely of wealth, but of power.

A fine example was the cults of various gods. Long oppressed by Malvus' opposition to worship of anything beyond him, they now gathered in their throngs. The bright colours of their varying robes and cloaks had washed monochrome. Each of their preachers blamed the other for not praying in the right way or to the right god. In the Arkathedral, it was no different. Loki had wandered many places that night, and had seen plenty of ex-councillors, guard captains, and even a foreign duke arguing for even the most temporary grasps at control of the headless empire. Loyalty was always self-serving.

Loki's boots scuffed against a broken lantern, already smeared in grey ash. He paused at a junction where a familiar face was emblazoned on the wall of a bakery. In the flickering light, Loki stared at the narrow eyes enshrouded by a hood, fist raised in defiance. Farden's face, now smeared in cow shit, by the reek of it. The word "believe" had been defaced. "Traitor" replaced it, written in something that look remarkably similar to blood. Loki had to smile.

As he climbed the incline to the walls, he noticed the growing crowds, afire with discussion and theories over the Arka's apparent massacre. Chants for answers and explanations assailed the gatehouse, where figures of rank had likely holed up. There again, he saw ash-covered speakers upon carts and boxes, proclaiming this and that as a guise for leadership. If Emperor Malvus' reign had proved one truth and one truth alone, it was that Krauslung's – and Emaneska's – power was anybody's to seize. Loki was planning on it.

Chatter ran through the people, fed by a woman of considerable years and a crown of rags about her head. 'Enough!' she was shouting. 'Enough, I say! This is our land. Our city, built by our hands. Why should we bleed for those who won't bleed for us!'

It was a fine sentiment, irkingly similar to Loki's ideas but a satisfactory sign that the people of Krauslung yearned for change. Loki slipped through another crowd enraptured by a man denying the rumours as a hoax, and weaved a path to the top of the walls.

Loki had barely put a foot to the mighty stone when a shout froze the crowds.

*Daemons.*

Even in the steel blizzard of ash, they shone like beacons. Several ignited upon the slopes of Hardja and Ursufel, the shoulders of Krauslung's valley. Others upon the rooftops of Manesmark's towers. They perched and waited as crows would.

Washed onwards by the gawkers, Loki found himself at the parapet, eyebrow raised. Even the daemons had come to stake their claim on the Arka.

'Right on time,' Loki whispered.

A clap of thunder punched a momentary bubble in the haze of ash. In full view of Krauslung's walls, Gremorin appeared in a blaze of fire. He stood with his black sword outstretched and a flaming crown rotating over his horns. He surveyed his onlookers with four eyes of brimstone.

There came a crash of armour as the Imperial Guard emptied from the gatehouse and formed shaky ranks along the battlements. Loki was curious whether it was mere habit, resilient obedience to the absent emperor, or the fact that every mortal in Emaneska shat themselves before a daemon that brought them to action.

'What now?' somebody along the wall wailed. 'What new Hel must we face now?'

The cry stirred equal parts resentment and fear in the crowds. The impromptu leaders like the rag-woman charged up the stairs, leading cries of, 'Nevermore!'

Those who had any sense were already backing away from the walls. Loki saw one man fleeing at a speed that only a brick wall or the sea would stop.

The daemon prince snarled at his reception. 'Hear me, mortals! Your emperor lies dead alongside his murderer, the one they called Forever King. Both armies have been laid to waste by a mountain's fire. They are no more. It is likely their very remains fall upon us now.' Gremorin raised dark claws to pinch at the ash. He flashed a smile of far too many fangs while a collective moan filled the air. 'I am Prince Gremorin, Orion's Shadow, ruler among daemons, and you will all bow to me. Surrender, or we will take this city by our own means.'

A mass exodus had begun behind the walls as the crowds fought to return to the city. Frustrated yells broke out over the clamour.

'What can we do?'

'Face them!' yelled the old woman.

'Face them... are you mad or plain stupid? We have no mages! No soldiers!'

'Barely a thousand Imperial Guard protect the city.'

'You mean the ones your cult are currently fighting?'

Loki had to drive a nail into his palm to keep himself from pouncing too early. He manoeuvred into position while the tension rose to breaking.

'We should surrender! What else is left to us?'

'We should run! Get to the ships!'

'This is our home, Evernia curse it!'

Loki forced the grin from his face. 'Evernia?' he cried out, his magick carrying his voice far and wide. 'The gods have abandoned you, friends, if this is to be your fate. Slaves to daemons. Prisoners in your own city. Fodder. No better than beasts.'

The wall around him had hushed momentarily. Loki stood upon a crate. 'Isn't it time the power of this empire resided with the people that *make* the empire?'

'What empire?' a man yelled. 'Malvus is dead.'

'The emperor lives!' Loki shouted. He was in danger of enjoying himself too much. He had crafted these words as a carpenter works upon pine. 'He lives in each and every one of you. In the pride of the Arka! In the stubbornness that founded this city a thousand years ago and has kept it standing, even now, when all seems lost. The time for fighting is over. It is time for discussion and calm.' Loki turned to look down upon Gremorin. 'I will talk to the daemons.'

It took a moment for his words to make sense to the crowd. Gasps came.

'You'll... what? Talk to them? About what?' demanded the rag-woman, glaring at him for stealing her light.

'I will get them to leave this city alone.'

'You're a madman!'

'A fucking fool!'

'Why should we listen to you? Who are you?'

Loki approached the gatehouse and guards, nonetheless, demanding they let him through.

'If you long to be the first to die on that daemon's blade, then be my guest, young man,' said a grizzled guard with one eye.

Loki kept his head high as he was given passage through the crowd. Too shocked, too morbidly fascinated, hopeful, or just plain vacant, they all stared at him as he approached the humongous wall of black steel and granite. He was shown to the stout wicket gate embedded in one half. To say he was shoved would have been alarmist, but the gate slammed shut all too quickly.

Loki walked confidently across the dirt and ash. He left nothing but footprints. No glances back, just a head held high enough to cause whispers along the wall. When Gremorin recognised him, his shoulders flushed with fire.

'I thought you dead, little god,' the daemon rumbled.

'Not so lucky, Prince Gremorin.'

'Have you come to face me? To fight for this city?'

'Please,' Loki laughed. 'I am no fool.'

A curious smile spread across the daemon's charred lips. 'You wish to treat with me, then. Another bargain.'

'I delivered on our last bargain, didn't I? I gave you war.'

'Not enough. The glory was stolen from us by the mage. This city and its people will do as a fine replacement.' Saliva dripped from the daemon's fangs and sizzled in the ash.

Loki tutted. 'I imagined you had bigger dreams than that, or are you truly Orion's mere shadow?'

The black blade of charred steel rested a foot from Loki's throat. He could feel the heat of it on his skin.

'Speak carefully, god,' Gremorin warned.

Loki stepped closer to the blade. 'The emperor takes breath. And not only will he deliver us Farden if the bastard still lives, but much, much more. The very sky itself.'

Gremorin's four eyes blinked independently.

'Are you sure the mage survived?'

Loki stared to the dark smear across the sky. 'I know the girl lives, but that is all. I have come to doubt the mage can be killed, but we will test that notion, Prince. You can trust me on that. Give me the city and enough time, I will give you the rest. Emaneska. Hel. Haven. Everything Orion ever wanted will be yours.'

Gremorin blew flame. 'Why? Why would a god stand by while we burn this world back to ash and fire?

Loki already knew the deal was done. He turned and sauntered back to the walls, speaking over his shoulder. 'Because,' he said, 'what better a light to show the look on Farden's face when he finally fails.'

It took three steps before the air battered him from behind in the concussion of Gremorin's departure. Echoes of his kin following suit echoed through Krauslung's valley. Ash billowed around Loki, and it was to silent whispering that he stood before the gates. He stopped in their golden sea of torchlight, hands wide. His gaze scanned the mosaic of confused, shocked, and grateful faces that spanned the mighty walls.

'All it takes is talking,' he called to them, speaking honestly. 'No more fighting is necessary. You will finally know peace with me at your helm.'

The rag-woman screeched. 'And what is your name? Who are you?'

'Me?' The god smiled broadly. 'They call me Loki.'

❧

Malvus dropped his beaker of bark and twine with shock. Dust and cobwebs swirled around the black silhouette of Loki, standing against the farmhouse's filthy boarded windows.

'Fuck it all!' Malvus snapped, agitatedly wiping at the full measure of cold wine now sitting in his lap. 'How many times have I asked you to refrain from doing that? Look at the mess you've made of me, you bastard! And that was the last of the wine!'

Loki was hiding a smirk. 'Expediency is key in such times, my dear Malvus.'

Malvus put his unsteady feet to the floor. A vexing shake had taken up residency in his thighs and hands since Farden had scorched the Arka from the north. It was easier to blame the mage than the thirst for daemonblood that plagued him constantly. Malvus raised a finger, found it quaked too much, and threatened the god with a fist instead.

'Expediency, you tell me? Then why have I languished in this abandoned shack for almost a week, feeble as a foal while you galli-vant who knows where? You have left me in silence, forgotten!

Forced to shit in a corner, no less. It has been days since you left for Krauslung, curse it, and now I have run out of bloody wine!'

Loki was too busy brushing ash from his coat to meet his gaze. 'I've been busy working on your best interests, Emperor,' he assured him.

'Look at me!' Malvus shrieked.

Loki regarded him with those damned golden eyes, bewilderingly deep, yet giving away nothing of what hid behind them.

'I am still the emperor of this land! You will speak when I tell you to.'

Loki bowed, slow yet shallow. 'As you request.'

'What of my horde, god? My army. How many have survived?'

'All gone, as I feared, Malvus. *Obliterated* to be more accurate. The ruins of Scalussen still burn with the volcano's fire. The north is black with ash and floodwaters from melted ice. The few that survived are hundreds at most, scattered across the north and Össfen mountains. Toskig betrayed you, of course. Saker is either dead or gone. The dukes of Albion squabble over Wodehallow's throne. Gremorin has disappeared with the wind.'

'Does he live?' growled Malvus.

'You mean Farden?'

'Who else?' Malvus snapped. He could not rid the sight of the mage from the dark behind his eyelids. Farden, burning black against the endless wall of fire. Farden, laying waste to everything Malvus had built. Toskig had been wrong. It had been the mage that ruined them. Not the emperor.

'I haven't seen any trace of him, living or dead. The remainder of Scalussen sails south in their grand bookships.'

Malvus pushed himself from the stinking bed of hay and blankets. He had no choice but to seize the god's arm for balance. 'Then I must return to my city soon, before Farden's forces put their detestable fingers on it and steal it from me.'

Loki's gaze turned beyond a crack in the window boards. There was a grimace on his face.

'What is it, damn you? What of Krauslung?'

'Its people have rejected you, Emperor. The survivors might not have returned bloody and burned yet, but news of your defeat has. They revolt in the streets. The Arkathedral plays host to every magistrate and dignitary. Cults preach a dozen sermons on street corners. Even the daemons came to lay claim. The crowds speak of ruling themselves once and for all.'

Malvus fell back to the bed, head spinning. The dampness across his lap was beginning to seep down his legs. He clutched at the ragged blankets and threw them at the god. 'I said I have run out of wine!'

Finally, Loki fished within his seemingly endless coat and brought out a slim bottle. Malvus snatched it, smashed its waxed neck against the wood, and poured it liberally down his gullet. He didn't care for the way the glass cut his lips, or how it scraped against his teeth. He forced the fire of the alcohol down into his souring belly, shards and all.

'Farden has not just burned me from the north, but from my home,' he hissed, dribbling wine. 'Stolen everything I have ever worked for.'

'You might be pleased to hear that Krauslung curses his name, too. His glory has turned to ash. They will turn the Scalussen ships away, just as they turned away the daemons.'

The words stung Malvus' ears. 'With what force?'

Loki shook his head. 'No force, but with words.'

The emperor scoffed.

'A man of the people has already stood before the gates and treated with Gremorin. A bargain was apparently struck. The daemons departed without incident.'

'Lies! How can that be?' Malvus protested with thin hope. Despite the sour taste in his mouth, he already believed the god. How else had he risen through the Arka echelons but via a golden tongue? He knew the power of well-timed words, and here he was, being outmanoeuvred by some unknown peasant or cultist.

'Though I am known for my lies, I speak the truth,' Loki told him. He moved to the window and drew a pattern in the filth. 'I could hardly trust my eyes, but Krauslung chant for him even now.'

'Tell me his name.'

Loki paused halfway through drawing a noose and its wretched victim. 'I didn't catch it.'

The emperor pushed himself up once more, almost falling. The absence of the daemonblood had wasted his muscles, and brought his sickness rushing back to him. 'All the more reason to return. And swiftly!' he rasped.

'You are in no state, Malvus.'

'You doubt me, god? Dare to defy me?' The emperor babbled as he searched for fresher clothes. There were none. All were soiled with sweat or blood or wine. 'My remaining officers will still be loyal to me. Watch Captain Foarl of the Street Legion would die at my feet if I commanded him to do so. I will show myself atop the Arkathedral. Yes, once they see me alive, this upstart will be forgotten. Then hanged...' He pointed to the window.

Loki sucked his teeth.

'Instead of standing in my way, perhaps you should be helping me as you vowed to. Gah!' Malvus snarled as a trembling leg crumpled beneath him. His muscles had withered. In the absence of his fine surroundings, with the daemonblood lacking in his veins, his sickness had returned to ravage him.

'I told you, Malvus you're too we—'

'You promised me daemonblood. Give it to me!'

'And not several days ago you cursed it for clouding your mind in the north.'

Malvus had cursed half the world and more during the first days he'd languished and rotted in the farmhouse. Anything but his own rash decisions of war, of course. The emperor bared his teeth, but a cough took him before he could speak. Swallowing the bitter taste of blood and phlegm, Malvus extended a palm. 'I feel hooks in my skin. Barbs in my eyes. Every day I am without that blood, the weaker my body becomes. You poisoned me, god—'

'I warned you of the consequences.'

'—and you will pay for that one day. Now, however, you will do as I command.'

The god took his time searching his pockets. The emperor inched closer, almost falling again before Loki showed him a blue vial stained dark purple by what sloshed inside. He held onto it while he watched Malvus grow more irate.

'Give it to me, Loki!'

'There is another way to win your empire back.'

'Enough games!'

'Farden.'

'Don't you say his name!' Malvus felt the sweat running down his cheeks. He wiped it away, and left a palm print on his trews. He loathed the glint of mischief in Loki's unblinking gaze. 'What of the bastard?' he relented.

Loki tapped the vial with a long nail, his voice set to the rhythm. 'If Krauslung has abandoned Farden because of the chaos he wrought in the north, perhaps the Forever King's head on a spike might just win you back Krauslung's hearts and minds.'

Malvus hated how much sense the god made. 'And just how, exactly, do you propose we kill a man like him? I saw that mage wield an entire volcano against me.'

'All sparks die out eventually.' Loki pressed the vial into Malvus' palm and then patted his ashen coat as if a precious treasure hid within. 'You regain your strength, Emperor, trust in me, and then I promise you, we will see about the death of a mage.'

Malvus needed no encouragement. The thirst had become un-bearable. He drank every drop the vial had to offer, and, when the shadows began to rise from the floor, when the needles started to pierce his insides, Malvus had no choice but to submit to the fire blazing behind his eyes. He sank into the spinning void that yawned before him, grinning.

*The death of a mage.*

He liked the sound of that.

# CHAPTER 4
## OF HIGH SEAS & LOW HOPES

*They say a fire burns in the west. A great rift blown open in the world, burning with an endless flame, whose winds and ash fall upon our lands. A sickness spreads with its touch. A plague has crept from the ice of the north, infecting us with raw magick.*
FROM A REPORT TO KING BARREIN IV OF THE LUNDISH

Uncertainty was a slow wound, bleeding life and patience. Unlike the Jörmunn Sea, which had thrashed the Rogue's Armada from the moment they had broken free of Chaos Sound, the survivors of the war were silent and stoic. Even the sailors toiled automatically, their shouts as cold as their calloused hands.

Hereni stood defiantly at the bow of the *Autumn's Vanguard*, cupping a flame between her hands. She stared vacantly at the rush of black sea beyond her fingers. The hurried snowflakes that dared to land on her melted to drips, snatched away by southerly winds.

The lad must have thought himself sly, but she could feel Bull inching ever closer every few moments. Despite his size and bulk, he was swaddled in two fur cloaks and still looked cold.

'There's been no word of Mithrid or Farden, Bull,' Hereni sighed. 'Still nothing.'

Bull nodded solemnly. 'I know. I asked Kinsprite already. I'm just here to watch.'

The dragons and Ilios had exhausted themselves flying ever longer sorties to Scalussen and back. Half of the armada still held their breath for the Forever King's return. The other half had seemingly resigned themselves to grieving, or staring blankly into space as if the volcano's fire still surged towards them. Stubborn, Bull and Hereni belonged to the former.

Hereni expanded her orb of fire, making the lad recoil. 'We'll find them. Don't you worry,' she reassured him. Beneath her boots, she felt the bookship hammer through a wave as the *Vanguard* gathered even more speed. The mage raised an arm to deflect the ensuing spray. Bull was not so quick and spat seawater. She kept her eyes to the east, where above the formidable Hâlorn coasts, a scrap of sky had been painted with faint streaks of purple and green, like the First Dragon's Wake. It was a peculiar omen. Bull stared long and hard, no doubt trying to spot what was left of his home.

'You miss your home?' Hereni asked. She had done the same the evening past, as the armada had passed Dromfangar's Spit.

'No,' he admitted. 'Yes. It might sound cruel, but Scalussen was my home. I became... something there. I was different. I liked it. At least before the fighting started.'

She smiled. 'It's called growing, not that you notice until you've already changed. War ages you quicker than most. Loss does the same thing, too. Ever since the night my family was taken, I've felt ten winters older than I am.'

Bull ground his knuckles against the bulwark. 'All I can think about is Mith and the others.'

Hereni knew the feeling. Mithrid had barely left her thoughts since the fire had filled the sky. 'Me too.'

There were shreds of hope to grip onto besides the possibility Farden and the others had perished: *Durnus was also lost, and either he or Farden could use the Weight. The dragon could have already flown them south. Perhaps they found shelter in Scalussen's forges.* There was even an optimistic suspicion making its way around the ships that Farden was actually waiting for them in Krauslung, and would already be lounging on the Blazing Throne.

And yet every hope, like a coin, always had the reverse: the pervasive doubt that Farden and Mithrid had died in Irminsul's inferno. Speculation without proof was painfully cyclical. The race to Krauslung was for answers as well as securing Scalussen victory.

Hereni clapped her hands around the fire and folded the magick back into her bones. After spitting over the railing, she pointed ahead to the Arka warship trying with all its might to outpace the armada.

'Think they'll try us, Bull? After what Farden did?'

He gripped the haft of his stout longbow, lashed across one shoulder. 'Is it bad I want them to try?'

Hereni looked across the armada spread in a tight arrowhead around the *Vanguard*. At her side, the two identical and colossal bulks of the *Summer's Fury* and *Winter's Revenge*. Each of the bookships had piled every scrap of black sail onto their masts. Despite the added weight of extra souls aboard, the gales were snapping at their heels and the wind-mages were hard at work. Their iron bows crashed through the Jörmunn rollers with defiant ease. Beyond them, a dozen warships, carracks, and barques fitted for battle. Even a Siren warship, too: the *Jaws of Nelska*, scaled with plates of bronze and green copper like a dragon. Fifteen vessels carried all that was left of Scalussen: thirty-thousand souls in all.

They held tight to the railing as a particularly large wave shook the *Vanguard*. 'It's time to find out,' she hissed.

Letting Bull trail behind, Hereni marched across the crowded decks. Sand-scrubbed wood rasped beneath her boots as she weaved between mages and climbed the enormous aftcastle.

Eyrum and Admiral Lerel stood with their arms crossed several paces behind the ship's wheel, hoods and cloaks littered with snow and spray. Their expressions were ones the entire armada shared: abject boredom and a brow furrowed with worry. Hereni spent a brief while gazing at the dozen dragons that hung aloft behind the ship, enjoying the wind chasing their wings. Their scales shone dully in the grey weather. Ilios was perched on the very edge of the ship, eyes closed, feathers and fur drenched. From the low hang of his head, and the way his claws sprawled on the deck, the gryphon looked spent.

'Has she come out yet?' yelled Hereni.

Lerel shook her head. The woman's piercing, feline eyes were rimmed with red. Her greying hair was slick to her forehead and skull. Even the tan shade of her Paraian-born skin looked pale from the cold. Yet she had determinedly battled the wheel for days now.

'Still in her cabin, mage,' said Eyrum, deep voice almost inaudible over the waves and wind. He had foregone his usual bulky armour for a Siren robe over leather scales.

Hereni ground her fist into the railing. 'Well, it's high time we changed that!'

'Hereni!' Lerel called after her.

Ducking into the aft stairwell, Hereni passed the dragon nests and pushed her way through the crowded Siren survivors to where the officer cabins resided. Guards only stood at one door: the cabin where the general had sequestered herself for almost a week now. At first, the two lumps of armour stiffened at Hereni's appearance. One even tried to wave her along.

'Oh please, Sergeant,' Hereni scoffed. 'Don't make me put you flat on your arse again like I used to in the training yards. Repeatedly, if I remember right.'

'Captain, I—'

'I need to see her. Open the door. That's an order.' Hereni's tone was loud and sharp. Bull cleared his throat menacingly for good measure.

The older guard sighed. 'She said no admittance to anyone, and her orders matter more than yours do.'

'There's an Arka ship out there that I think she'll want to know about. And within another day we'll be in Krauslung.' Hereni barged past the soldiers and rapped on the door. There was no reply.

'Back up, Captain!' the sergeant barked.

Concentrating, Hereni let a fire spell trail around her hands. The heat of her magick spread fast through the narrow corridor. It made the guards lean backwards as she pointed a fiery finger at them. At her side, Bull cracked his knuckles.

'Move, or we will move you.'

'Bloody Hel! This is mutiny,' accused the other guard. His armour scraped on the bulkhead as Bull muscled them out of the way

'This is for your own good, man,' warned Hereni as she knocked again. 'General!'

Still no answer.

Hereni found the door locked. *She had come this far*, she thought. Might as well press forwards, as Farden had always taught her. Gods, did she feel uneasy without the mage around.

The fire spell melted the handle into a sad lump of metal. It took a stout shove from both her and Bull, but within moments, they were standing in the cabin's doorway.

'General?'

The cabin was a temple to gloom. Shutters clad the windows. Aside from the stench of burned wood and metal, the scent of spoiling food was strong. Clothes and broken objects lay strewn across the floor. Hereni and Bull carefully stepped around them as they walked deeper.

'Elessi?'

Hereni's gaze roamed from a torn mattress with a dagger protruding from it, to the rear of the cabin, where a desk piled with scrolls and nautical objects cast a silhouette against the scant light. A figure was huddled in furs, hunched over a book of green pages.

'What do you want?' it asked.

'It's been almost a week since we've seen you, General. The admiral and others are asking after you.'

There was a rustle of cloth as the silhouette hunched over further. 'I'm busy.'

'We're a day from Krauslung.'

'Are we, indeed?' Elessi's question needed no answer. Instead, Hereni stepped closer to the desk. Her vision was still adjusting to the dark. She could make out shining eyes beneath a fringe of untamed, ashen hair. Half a dozen blankets and furs must have been wrapped around her.

'Any news of Farden or the others?' Elessi asked.

'None yet.'

The laugh was cold as a snowball to the face 'Yet.'

'Anything in the inkweld?' Hereni asked, nodding to the thick green book on Elessi's desk. She held onto it with white knuckles. The inkweld looked as blank as Hereni had last seen it, a day after they left Chaos Sound.

'Nothing.'

'I know you're grieving. But you are still in command, General.'

'So it would seem. But you've got several admirals and another general up there, all of them more used to leadin' than I am. Put them in charge.'

'Eyrum has declined, and so has Queen Nerilan. You're the highest ranking out of Farden's council. After Durnus, you were closer to Farden's dream of freedom than any of us. You've been at his side for decades. Helped him build Scalussen into a city, not just a fortress. It was you that led us to the ships—'

'And for what? My dream of freedom had my husband in it. Alive and well, not ash on the breeze! Why bother to fight for that dream now?'

'Elessi, you can't mean that.'

'Stop telling me what to think! Leave me be!'

Hereni lit the gloom with a flame. Elessi shrank from it blinking. 'And for how long? Are you going to stay in this cabin forever? Hope didn't burn with Scalussen, you said. Where's your hope gone now?'

'Everything I had vanished along with Modren. I have nothing left. No place here.'

'You'd give up on Scalussen that easily?'

Elessi didn't answer.

Hereni shook her head. 'Then Modren died for nothing.'

'He died to save us!' Elessi snapped. She reared from the desk, furs falling in clumps.

Hereni held up a hand. 'That he did. To save the idea of Scalussen. To keep Emaneska from darkness. You're still a part of that, Elessi. Why bother to fight on? Because we need you, that's why. We believe in you. And because he would have wanted anything else for you than succumbing to grief. To give up means he died in vain.'

'Stop!' Elessi screeched. Her long nails clawed splinters from the wood as she took breath. 'Stop saying it. How dare you use my husband against me.'

Hereni found Bull's hand on her shoulder. The big lump came to stand by her side. He looked at Hereni with his forlorn eyes wrapped in a frown. The meaning of his look was a wise and simple, "shut up".

Hereni bowed her head. 'I'm sorry, Elessi. I didn't mean to. I've always dealt with my grief by doing. Never stopping to think. I'm still learning we aren't all the same.'

'No, we ain't.' Elessi sighed, dejected. She poked a finger through the shutters, half-blinding herself with daylight. Despite its overcast nature, the light was startling compared to the gloom.

'There's just one more task,' Hereni encouraged her, seeing hope in her movements. 'Then, we can have peace that we've all fought so long for.'

Elessi made her way around the desk. She took a moment to collect herself. But when she spoke through gritted teeth, halfway to sobbing, Hereni knew it was useless.

'Leave me be,' she ordered.

Hereni nodded slowly and backed away from the desk with Bull at her side.

☙

'Grief isn't something you can just turn your back on like a bad town. It's a journey,' Lerel intoned as Hereni joined her and Eyrum at the wheel. 'You should know that as well as we do. Elessi is in the middle of her journey, mage. Don't worry yourself that you didn't manage to get her on deck. She needs time is all.'

'Time we're running out of,' Hereni told her. A light rain had sprung up in place of the snow, mixing with the spray to create a constant downpour. 'She's the one Farden would want to lead.'

'But if she doesn't want the command, then we have to do this without her,' Lerel looked to Eyrum, but the Siren was trying his hardest to stare out to sea. He was never comfortable with the kind of confrontation that required words and emotions. Not unless there was some mörd around. He preferred to settle most of his arguments with an axe.

Lerel continued. 'Whatever happens, we have to finish what Farden, Durnus, and the Hâlorn girl—'

'Mithrid,' Hereni interrupted, beating Bull to it. 'Her name is Mithrid.'

The admiral sighed. 'Finish the job they, and Mithrid, started no matter what. Even if they're gone for good.'

Hereni wondered if it was that notion or the salt waves that had reddened the admiral's eyes. She knew faintly of a past between Lerel and the Forever King.

'Eyrum? What say you of taking charge now?' Lerel nudged the huge man with her elbow.

The Siren crossed his arms. 'No. I still would not,' he said openly. 'It was never my calling to lead. I cannot presume to give orders to the Old Dragon or Queen Nerilan any more than I would to Farden.'

'It would be easier if Towerdawn and Nerilan took charge, but they will only speak for the Sirens.'

Hereni looked to the dragons. If she peered into the haze of rain, she could just about make out the great dragon high above, shimmering gold in the light that didn't reach the sea. 'Same can be said of Ko-Tergo for the snowmads and Wyved for the witches,' she said. 'Besides, they're too worried about being too far south as it is. All they know is the north.'

'We can all go back to our homes when this is over,' Lerel sighed. 'What about you, Bull? Want to be in charge?'

Bull visibly shuddered.

'Looks like it's you, Admiral,' suggested Hereni with a shrug. 'You'll have to speak for us in Krauslung.'

'Gods,' Lerel hissed.

'No need, Lerel,' proclaimed a voice. Elessi stood upon the deck, swaddled in a giant cloak, face puckered in the rain. Her guards stood beside her. Eyrum offered an arm but she shook her head.

'Though she could learn some tact, Hereni's right,' Elessi said. 'As much as I want to crawl into a dark hole and forget you all exist, there's not the time for it. I can't just sit in the dark. Modren would be chiding me if he were here. Yellin' at me to get up off my arse, and he would be right.' She found the faintest of smiles. 'We don't owe this just to Modren, we owe it to all those who died for us to be here. Like Inwick. Even if that means Farden, and Durnus, and Mithrid. Even if that means the Arka too. There's been too much death to fail now. If it's left to me then fine, I'll lead. At least I won't 'ave any guilt in my heart. It's already too full of sorrow as it is.'

Elessi took Eyrum's arm then and leaned heavily on it. 'So what this I 'ear about an Arka ship?'

Lerel pointed along the *Vanguard*'s expansive deck. 'Single warship. No dragons, no daemons. A straggler that must have bolted the war early. She's coming up fast with all our wind mages on deck and a southerly gale. What do we want to do?'

'I say we take no chances,' Eyrum growled.

Elessi took a while to answer. Hereni saw the sharp angle of her jaw.

'No. We leave it alone,' she replied. 'Like I said, there's been too much death already. This is no time for petty revenge, as much as I want it.'

Orders bounded down the aftcastle and spread through the bookship as an echo. Lanterns were hooded and unhooded to tell the rest of the armada to give the Arka a wide berth and no trouble. Sailors, mages, and soldiers gathered at the railings and in the rigging to watch the warship draw closer. The *Vanguard* approached on its port side, the *Revenge* on its starboard.

Hereni stood with Bull at the bulwark. He had an arrow nocked on his bow, likely for the same reason the veins of Hereni's hand glowed. They stood ready, just like the rest of the armada.

They were close enough now to look their old enemy in the face. Their decks were as crowded as the Rogue's Armada. Archers sat in the crow's nests of their masts, bows also drawn and waiting.

The *Vanguard* and *Revenge* were drawing level with the ship now. Hereni could make out its name on its hull: the *Essen's Jewel*.

So large were the bookships in comparison, it must have seemed to the Arka as though a canyon had swallowed them. Over the crash of waves, Hereni could hear yelling. A fight had seemingly broken out aboard the *Jewel*'s aftcastle. The ship careened to starboard, looking close to ramming the *Revenge* before it came swinging back to port in an over-correction. Whatever had happened aboard the *Jewel*, it resulted in several men being thrown into the sea.

'Somebody stop that man!' came a dire shout from the Arka decks. It was followed not moments later by a heavy snap of ballista ropes. An iron bolt as tall as a Hereni burst from one of the *Jewel*'s open ports. It struck a lucky hit, glancing inside one of the *Vanguard*'s ports and eliciting a round of screams from the decks far below.

Admiral Roiks aboard the *Revenge* abandoned his patience and ordered a volley from ballistae and mage alike. Fireballs and bolts peppered the *Essen Jewel*'s starboard side. It began to list within seconds.

'Hold!' cried Lerel and Elessi, but the orders came too late. The Arka were now firing in sheer panic and desperation. Arrows peppered the bookships' decks. One dug into the bulwark next to Bull's arm, and he did not hesitate to fire back. Neither did the *Vanguard* officers below. A burst of fire and lightning exploded from the ship's ports. Hereni watched a man that looked like the captain skewered against his deck by a ballista bolt.

Cheers were soon rising up from the bookships as the *Jewel* was dealt a final blow by Towerdawn himself. Raining fire upon the ship, he broke the crow's nest from the ship's mainmast to add insult to injury. As the armada left the Arka in its churning wake, the *Essen's Jewel* was already tipping stern up.

'The stupid fools!' Elessi was cursing them. The silver curls of her hair were sodden. The aching of her heart swelled as she watched sailors thrash in the water. 'We would've let them live.'

'They had no way of knowing,' Hereni replied.

Elessi's face had hardened. She swiftly hoisted her hood and aimed for belowdecks. 'Let me know when we reach Krauslung!'

Three hours later, Hereni did precisely that.

The cabin was still full of gloom, but the blinds had stayed open. Elessi had put on fresh clothes and furs. Her silver hair was tangled by salt, and with her stubbornly red eyes, she looked decidedly witch-like. All she needed was a few finches hopping across her desk and she would be one of Wyved's witches.

'Is it time?'

Hereni nodded. 'We're in the Bay of Rós. Rain's cleared somewhat. You can see Krauslung mountains.'

'Have you ever been to the city?'

'Me? Once. On a mission with Farden before Kserak. Didn't like it much. Too crowded.'

'You should've seen it when Durnus and Farden's uncle Tyrfing were in charge. Not perfect, mind you, still a city with far too many people crowded into it. Tends to drive folk a bit mad without them knowin', or so I saw. But it was as close as it's ever been to peace.'

'Reckon we can take it back to those days?'

'Here's hopin' that's possible, girl. Frown all you want, Captain. Until you're my age and grey as an Albion winter, then you'll still be a girl to me.'

'You sounded like Farden, is all.'

'You miss him?'

'As if I've lost a father all over again.'

Elessi shut the inkweld on the desk and covered it with a cloth. 'No news is good news, Durnus used to tell me.'

'And how long does it take until it stops being true?'

'We'll see,' said the woman with a sigh. She stumbled against the table, enough to make Hereni dart to help her.

'I'm all right. Just tired, is all.'

'Have you eaten today? Yesterday, even?'

'Somewhat.'

A horn blew across the armada, deep and sonorous in a way that Hereni could feel it in her gut. 'Looks like it's time.'

Elessi leaned on her arm more than expected. Because of her fierce nature and sharp tongue, Hereni often forgot Elessi's age. This was the first time she had witnessed the woman wearing her years. She had not dealt a single blow, but the war had ravaged her all the same.

High on the aftcastle, the rain had been reduced to a resentful spitting. Ahead of them, the Bay of Rós was largely empty of ships. Smaller faerings and fishing skiffs were hauling in their crab pots and nets, eager to flee back to harbour at the sight of the Rogue's Armada rounding the headline. Now in a line, the fifteen Scalussen ships plied the deep, black waters silently, as if their captains and admirals savoured the coastline. After all, it had been decades since a Scalussen ship had sailed the Bay of Rós free of challenge.

The ocean swell died here. The water broke beneath the iron keel of the *Vanguard* like a sheet of glass. Every soul had squeezed onto deck. Some had never seen the bay and Krauslung before. Many others stared upon a home they had left behind long ago, and had been promised ever since.

The black mountains of the Emaneska mainland stood bold and steep against the sea. Sharp islands caused the ships to take a wide arcing course towards the Port of Rós, Krauslung's mighty harbour. With minor vessels scattering before the *Vanguard*, they rounded a cliff to finally look upon the city.

In the deep valley between the twin mountains of Ursufel and Hardja, Krauslung sprawled. Hereni had forgotten how large the Arka capital had grown. The complicated mess of white marble and granite shone in the afternoon light. The mighty Arkathedral, propped against the eastern wall of the valley, took on a golden shine at its layered peak. Buildings clambered over each other to prove their worth. Pillars of smoke and steam drifted up to the clouded sky in their scores. Beyond the city, the land stretched up to Manesmark, where smog hung over sharp rooftops of pine and slate. Hereni could smell the char of its factories and smiths. Ravens and vuleguls wheeled high above as if the city was a corpse on its way to dying. It certainly would explain the silence. Not even the gulls and rimelings squealed.

Hereni remembered a constant roar to the city of Krauslung, noon and night. If it wasn't the constant marching or fighting of soldiers, it was the fighting, the whoring, and the drunken songs of countless ale-sodden reprobates drinking away the sorrows of

Malvus' rule. On that day, there was a silence to the capital, as if cotton clogged the mage's ears.

'Hear that?' Hereni asked.

Elessi looked confused. 'What?'

'Exactly.' Hereni snuck a look at the sharp scars that marred Elessi's neck. 'Any daemons?'

'None that I can feel.'

They soon realised the cause of the stillness. As they sailed closer to the city, they saw how crowded the port was. Not just the boats, arranged as a thick barricade made of mast and hull, but every inch of deck, flagstone, walkway and jetty was taken up by people. The entire population of Krauslung, what was left of it, stood in silent welcome for the Rogue's Armada. There were no flags or pennants flying. No horns blaring. No applause or cheers for the returning victors. To Hereni, it looked more like a battle line.

'What are they doing?' Lerel hollered. Her voice sounded unnaturally loud.

'Something is wrong,' Elessi whispered, eyes widening. She slapped her hand on the railing. 'Stop the ship, Admiral.'

Elessi's boots drummed upon the stairs and deck. Hereni followed as dutifully as a guard. The crowds of Scalussen parted for them while Lerel called for the sails to be furled and the mages to halt their wind spells. At the bow they found Peryn, Wyved the High Crone, and Ko-Tergo standing waiting. Their faces were blank, their lips pursed. The witches' sparrows were silent.

'So this is our prize?' the yetin asked. 'Krauslung at last?'

'It is indeed.'

Ko-Tergo sniffed the salt air. 'I preferred the snow.'

'So did I,' muttered Elessi. She took a deep breath and patted Hereni's arm. 'I can take it from here.'

Hereni hoped the general was right.

# CHAPTER 5
## THE VULTURE

*Beware the Goddess of Reflection, for she will show you everything you want to see, and everything you don't.*
EASTEREALM PROVERB

Elessi climbed as high on the bowsprit as the stairs and railing allowed. The bookship still drifted under momentum and power of the water mages. Her gaze scanned the crowds. The bulk of them were a featureless mass at that distance. She could only see the faces of those piled upon the ship barricade, or on the towering lighthouses that marked the harbour entrance. It was between them that the *Autumn's Vanguard* came to a halt.

A lone boat emerged from the barricade. It had no sail nor mast, just a simple longboat lined with men working oars. A single figure stood on its bow in mimicry of Elessi.

It took some time for the longboat to cross the gap of water. The silence grew deafening as she spent every moment trying to identify the man. It was not Malvus. Too plainly dressed. Not General Toskig. Too short. It was Eyrum's Siren eyes that recognised it first. He called the name out like a curse.

'It's Loki.'

'What?' Elessi whirled, performing a complete circle before she turned back. She felt needles across her brow. Even the name put a cold breath on her nape. 'Here?'

She had only met the god in passing, more than twenty years before. Despite such time, his likeliness had stuck in her mind like a splinter.

Elessi saw Loki now: that smug air that forever ruled his face, the shade of his dirty flaxen hair, the leather coat that reached his knees. There were some differences. A sword hung at his side. Fine silver mail shone on his chest and forearms.

Elessi raised her chin to watch the longboat draw close. In the shadow of the *Vanguard*, it stopped. It was small comfort that Loki had to crane his head to meet her eyes. Elessi's head was still spinning. She had expected a city in mourning, perhaps in turmoil. Not a city of organisation and simmering calm that had already chosen its new leader. Elessi gripped the railing to stay the tremble in her legs. *They were already too late.*

Loki called out to her. 'General Elessi of Scalussen, originally of Leath. Our paths cross once again, as I expected!'

'And much as I'd hoped they wouldn't, here we are.'

The little god examined who else stared down at him. 'I see Admiral Lerel. General Eyrum. Queen Nerilan and the Old Dragon. Strange, I had expected King Farden to be standing on the bow of that ship. Or Undermage Modren, perhaps. Am I to assume they have all perished?'

The bones in Elessi's hands crunched as she gripped the railing. Her reply was quiet, barely restrained. 'They are elsewhere.'

Loki's golden eyes were ashine. 'Is that so?' The god roamed the broad bow of his boat. He began their duel of words, raising his voice so that it echoed across the waters like the stirring beat of a war drum. 'How many there are of you, compared to the few survivors of the Arka that have returned to their homes!' he crowed. 'Those that do are barely alive. Dead in the eyes. Wounded in their souls. Have you come to drown Krauslung in blood as you have the north? Have you come to finish us off for good?'

Loki might not have had a Book on his back, but he weaved spells with his voice just fine. His rhetoric worked its subtle magick. A low and dissenting moan spread throughout the port. Angry cries came from the lighthouses and wallowing boats nearby.

'Murderers!'

'Traitors!'

'Down with the Outlaw King and his kind!'

Even from the mouths of strangers, the words cut her deep. Elessi shouted as loudly as she could muster. She pleaded with clasped hands, hoping they could make out the shock and insult on her face.

'People of Krauslung! Whatever this man has told you is a lie. Every word that comes from his mouth is a lie! He wouldn't know how to tell the truth if his miserable existence depended on it.'

Her words were not well received. Krauslung decried her. Amongst the masses, somebody screamed, shrill enough to reach her ears.

'He has come to save us!'

Loki held up his hands for quiet as stamping feet and voices momentarily gave Krauslung back its old roar.

Elessi felt the heat in her cheeks. Not embarrassment but rage. *Inwick and Modren had not died purely for Loki's gain. How dare this creature claim what they'd won with death and toil?*

'A liar, you call me? Blood does not lie, Elessi!'

Elessi hated the way her name sounded in his mouth.

Loki pressed on. 'Where are our brothers and sisters, mothers and fathers? Where are they? Murdered by you, is where!'

'They are lying right next to our own soldiers! It was Malvus who sent them to the deaths, not us. He's the one who took your parents and children from you. We fought for the same peace you now preach and defended ourselves as anyone would.'

'You play wounded when it was you who lit the north on fire. It was your Forever King that almost consumed us all in flame. Look around you. Look at the ash on our rooftops. How the waters have risen already.'

Now that Elessi looked, she saw the marks of the war in the north all around her. What she thought was granite was actually grey ash streaking the buildings. Some of the lower piers and boardwalks were awash with detritus and bilge from high tides.

'Farden is no saviour. Neither are you. Even though you sail into this port as victors, come to claim your spoils,' Loki dictated.

'We haven't come here to fight, but to return to Krauslung in peace as we've wanted for years.'

Loki scoffed. 'Really?'

'Truly!'

'How is it, then, that during your voyage here you destroyed a defenceless Arka ship, simply trying to return home from war? Where is the peace in that!'

'I...' Elessi could not lie. Even if she had been able, her silence was already damning. The blood drained from her face. 'They attacked us!'

A torrent of boos and curses assailed her.

'A single ship attacked an armada like yours? With your ironclads, your dragons, and your and mages?' Loki bared a reptilian smile. 'Come now, you embarrass yourself, Elessi.'

More cries rang out from Krauslung.

'We are prepared to defend our city, whatever it takes,' said Loki. 'If you must conquer us as well, then I invite you to try. We turned away the daemons, and we will do the same to you. Krauslung no longer bows to any emperor or king. Especially not to a traitor Forever King. He is the true liar. Where is he, I wonder? Why does he send you instead, Elessi? Tell me he didn't perish in those flames...?'

Cheers of defiance now. Elessi saw weapons in the hands of the crowds.

'You foul worm. Farden was right about you. Malvus was a petty criminal compared to the evil in your heart.'

Silence reigned. Loki's smile spread like butter over toast. He held his hands wide. 'We have traded enough words. Attack us, if you dare.'

Elessi wanted nothing else to do with the god. She turned to the others. Hereni, standing with hands glowing and face a storm. Eyrum, eyes narrowed as if he were measuring the distance he'd have to throw his axe into Loki's face. Wyved the High Crone and Ko-Tergo swapped glances. Elessi could imagine their thoughts. They were likely echoes of hers: all this effort. All this death. All this way for nothing.

Queen Nerilan hissed between lips of gold scales. The steel of her glaive somehow shone even in the overcast ceiling of clouds. 'I say we take them,' she growled. 'They'll soon cower if the Arkathedral burns with dragonfire.'

'We cannot let old grudges rule us, my Queen,' Eyrum said with a bowed head. 'The old war between Arka and Nelska is long dead. We need not start it again.'

'*Finish it*, General. Finish all of this,' Nerilan corrected, and Eyrum said no more.

'We'd only prove Loki right, and that seems like the most dangerous thing in the world right now,' Elessi confessed. 'There won't be a Krauslung left if we fight. And think who Malvus would've left behind? The young and the old and the sick is who. You really want to burn them alive? Is that winnin' to you? Damn it if that blasted god hasn't got a point. We would be the murderers after all, and I won't 'ave that. That's not Modren's or Farden's legacy.'

'Or Mithrid's,' muttered Bull.

'Then what, Elessi?' Lerel spoke up. Arms crossed against her leather admiral's tunic.

Elessi looked down at her strange council and tried desperately to produce a coherent thought.

'We can't possibly surrender to Loki,' scoffed Hereni, eliciting similar reactions in Ko-Tergo and Wyved.

'I've no intention of doin' any such thing,' protested Elessi.

'Then what?' Lerel's voice rose higher.

'We should kill him,' Nerilan suggested. 'Drag him from that city like a wyrm from a hole and make an example of him. End his lies and tricks.'

'Kill a god?'

'End this!'

The bickering of the council spread down from the forecastle to the deck. The crowds of survivors and crew were swiftly in a constant murmur of confusion and doubt.

Elessi felt like barging through them, finding her cabin, and slamming the door. She could not lead these people, not against empires and gods, and yet her promise called to her. She stuck out her chin, refusing her nervous legs. She expected more of herself. All she was hearing was madness, and she would not stand for it.

It was then she heard a thought as clear as day. Far too clear to belong to her knotted rosebush of a mind. Far too loud.

*We can forge a new Emaneska.*

Elessi stared around, demanding with her eyes to know who had spoken. She looked up to the dragons perched high in the crags of Hardja and Ursufel, or in the great masts of the bookships like multicolour hawks in a tree. Only one wore golden scales, and he hovered on the high winds of the mountain peaks. *The Old Dragon.*

'Admiral Lerel!' Elessi yelled over the tumult. It took two attempts for the decks of the *Vanguard* to fall silent. 'Lerel!'

Lerel grazed past Nerilan, cutting the queen off from a tirade about dragonfire and superior forces. The look on the Siren's face was murderous.

'Aye, General?' Lerel barked.

'I want a league put between us and this spineless city.'

'Aye!'

Orders began to ricochet across the deck. Sailors stumbled into action, though they worked with furrowed brows of confusion and dismay.

'If Krauslung doesn't appreciate what we've done and the blood we've shed for it, then we'll either wait for them to come to their senses, or leave them to their madness,' Elessi spoke, surprising herself with her volume. 'If we have to, we'll forge a new Krauslung.'

Nerilan spun her narrowed stare on her as if she had heard those words before. 'And leave our home? Our rightful lands?'

Elessi didn't reply. She returned to the bowsprit and looked down upon the god. The crowds of Krauslung's docks had begun to stamp their feet in rhythmic unison.

'What say you?' Loki called out.

Once more, Elessi let silence loiter. They didn't deserve her breath. Instead, she stared back at Loki with as little rage as possible showing in her expression. The power of the wind mages behind her blew her silver hair around her face. The clank of contraptions unfurling black sails spoke for her.

To the cheering of Krauslung and the slow yet resounding clap of Loki's gloved hands, the *Autumn's Vanguard* slowly backed from the harbour until Lerel showed the city her giant stern.

The other two bookships lingered until the *Vanguard* had passed between them, menacing the port with their bulk as a parting warning. Only then did they follow, and with their lanterns lit against the encroaching evening, they withdrew deeper into the bay. The dragons left their perches, either disappearing into the clouds or swooping down to follow.

Somewhere between the flat islands of Skap to the south and the mocking cheering that still filled the air and black waters of Rós, the Rogue's Armada dropped its anchors.

Loki lifted his arms to the thunder of the crowds. Behind him, the rowers drummed their callous hands against their oars and said his name, over and over.

'You've done it again, sire!'

'Showed them what for!' they yelled.

The power of their adoration and belief felt like waves coursing over Loki's skin. Enjoyable to any god, of course. Strengthening, naturally. Emboldening even, but their adoration was not what made this a moment of victory.

No, his pride was all his fault. And gladly so. With little but words and threats and promises, Loki had stolen the heart of a city and broken the hopes of Scalussen in the same week. Hopes and dreams two decades in the making. What glee it gave the god to guide his foes astray, if only to see the torment on their faces.

And how simple it had all been! How wonderfully the unexpected trick of Irminsul's fire had only played into his hands. To turn the last Arka warship into a frenzy of fear had only taken one sailor's borrowed face and barely an hour. How slow they were. How easily he had plucked Farden's Emaneska from beneath him.

For an instant, Loki's smile wavered. *All a little too easy*, in fact, he thought.

Reinforcing his smile, Loki waved to the crowds. It was not enough to cripple them, he realised. They remained a threat. His success was proof of how the forgotten and ignored can forge the downfall of their so-called betters. Like the daemons, who would one day know their own downfall at Loki's hand, Scalussen had to be crushed.

Loki knelt at the edge of the longboat, where the weight of those on board forced the water close to its flat deck. Into his endless pockets, dug his hands. It took him a moment to summon the trinket from the dark void within his coat; his hoard of the lost, trapped beyond the dawn and the dusk, known only to those who truly know what it is to be forgotten.

Into the light of evening, as torches were lit upon the layered boardwalks behind him, he withdrew a small silver bell. The trinket was a tapering pyramid, somewhat similar to a cowbell. All manner of markings had been engraved across its three faces, then scratched out, then rewritten in a different language, and so on. Parts of it bore marks of repair, as if somebody had once tried to destroy it. The only markings that survived were of curling, scaly heads poised on each face.

Ever since he had found it, lost in the depths of Essen's markets, Loki had always wanted to ring the Serpent's Chime. For years he had highly suspected its powers were nothing more than a merchant's rumour. There was no better time to test it than now.

Much to the muttering conversation of the onlookers, Loki held it above the water, shook its weathered handle and let the piercing tone of the bell ring loud before he plunged it into the dark, polluted waters.

The tone continued underwater, growing and deepening. The water around his submerged hand danced in peaks and crowns. Loki watched the note ripple out across the waters. Other than the distant roar of a dragon above, a quiet fell on the harbour. An uneasy silence, charged with questions and curiosity.

The note died, and, out of the water, the bell returned to a silent piece of silver. With a tut, Loki spun the bell in his palm and slid it back into his pocket. Perhaps the bell was a lie after all. The chime was another useless, worthless artefact. 'Alas,' he said aloud. 'Would have been quite the evening's entertainment.'

'What's that, milord?' asked one of the nearest men.

'It is a shame is all, my good sir—'

'Sorry, sire, but I meant that noise. What is that?'

Loki's disappointment was stifled by the distant moan of a horn or trumpet. So distant it had almost gone unnoticed. Another joined it, louder.

'More trouble, sire?'

Loki grinned as he felt the wind shift. 'Not for us. Not for Krauslung.'

The Serpent's Chime was not a fake after all.

❦

'Where, Elessi? Where are we to go?' Roiks demanded.

Everybody wanted answers. Half the souls aboard had hollered questions as they had hustled below. Even the other ships had sent admirals and captains on rowboats to the *Vanguard* to discuss what in Hel was going on. Even the Warbringer's second in command: a bloodmonger with a name apparently only pronounceable by minotaurs, much like dragons' true names. He filled the doorway. He snuffled continuously at the dust and the smell of magick in the room.

Elessi now sat on a high-backed chair of wood, elbow to knee and chin cupped in her cold hand. It was gloomy in the libraries deep within the bookship. The smell of old pages and salt was thick in the air. In the brief moments between bursts of avid conversation, the sound of blue moths pattering against their glass lanterns ruled.

Elessi had expected a round table to be just what she needed, and yet somehow they still stared at her as though she alone sat at the table's head. 'Wherever we go, the north is ruined. There is Albion, maybe…'

Half the crowd groaned. She shook her head, tutting at the suggestion. She was still repeating Loki's words in her head, desperately figuring where the god had outwitted her. Her homeland was out of the question.

'We would have to fight the dukes tooth and bloody nail,' said Roiks.

'Then we go south, or continue east.'

Lerel spoke up. 'The empire might still reign in Paraia. They might need our help. We'll be warmer, too, for once.'

The northerners of the room, particularly Ko-Tergo and Nerilan, growled at that. Having spent half her life in a land of precipitation, Elessi knew the feeling.

'We minotaurs go home to Efjar, the land our Warbringer fought for and your dead king promised.'

'Farden is not dead,' Lerel hissed. 'Not until we know for sure.'

'What is that noise?' Peryn asked. High Crone Wyved was shaking her head back and forth, knocking her ears with her palm.

'A roomful of people not able to make a single decision?' Hereni grumbled by Elessi's side. Her comments drew narrowed stares. 'What?' she challenged them. 'We put the general in charge, didn't we? Then we should bloody listen to her. Let her decide.'

Peryn snapped. 'Quiet, Captain!'

Hereni slammed a hand on the table. 'I've got as much of a right to speak here as you do, witch—'

'Captain!' Elessi barked.

Wyved was reaching for the nearest shelf of books, hands outstretched, her long black nails quivering. One of the many tiny birds stowed in her layers of rags and matted hair hopped down her arm and perched upon a fingertip. It pecked at the spine of a book, and between its intermittent cheeping, Elessi heard it: like the cry of a pack of wolves, haunting despite how distant they sounded.

'What is that?' she asked.

Lerel was staring between her fellow admirals and captains, eyes creeping wider with every passing second. Elessi watched the blood drain from her face. 'No…' she was whispering.

The scrape of Roiks' chair set half the room flinching.

'Fuck me!' he bellowed before sprinting from the library without explanation.

'TO ARMS!' Lerel roared as she chased him.

'What is happening?'

With Eyrum and Hereni forging a path for her, Elessi bustled upwards through deck after deck. Lerel's orders had turned the uneasy mood of the ship's bowels into manic activity. Mages stood by the portholes and hatches. Crews loaded and cranked ballistae. Sand and water scattered the deck in preparation for fire and blood.

'Admiral!' Elessi yelled to Lerel as she breathlessly ascended to the forecastle. She scanned the skies, seeing nothing but whirling dragons. The city was as calm as ever. Not a sail besides those of the armada's broke the horizon. The night was creeping in from the east, where the noise was coming from. The shadow of the mountains betrayed nothing.

'What's happening?' she yelled.

Lerel seemed to be having trouble spitting out her words. Roiks and Sturmsson were too busy bellowing orders to their captains back aboard the bookships. It was from Roiks that Elessi finally got an explanation.

'A leviathan, by the bleeding gods!' the admiral roared. 'To arms!'

The word ignited further energy and panic. Standing like a rock in a river of action. Elessi wracked her brains to make sense of it. *Leviathans.* They were nothing but creatures of fairytale. She saw the same uncertainty on Hereni and Bull's faces. Then again, Loki was in their vicinity, and nothing was for sure with that god around.

'East!' came a cry from the lofty crow's nest. 'A league out and closing!'

Elessi was swept towards the port bulwark. Her heart pounded to the tune of fear even though she had only a name to be afraid of. In the gloom past the headland, white water frothed. She saw no shape, no body, only the water displaced as something surfaced momentarily.

'Lights!'

Lanterns bloomed in a wave across the Rogue's Armada. The lights turned the water glossy green, like the surface of fluid and ancient copper. Silver fish scattered from beneath the keels.

'Dragons, with me!' yelled Queen Nerilan, standing upon the edge of the aftcastle. As Elessi watched, Towerdawn appeared from beneath the bookship, seized the queen in his claws, and soared over the *Vanguard.* In a pirouette of colour and scaled armour, the dragons of Scalussen climbed into the air. For a dreaded moment, it looked as though they were abandoning the armada.

'I want answers, Lerel!' Elessi shouted.

'There's nothing a ship fears more than a leviathan, Elessi,' Lerel snapped, making a rapid path for the wheel. 'And I'm pretty sure Loki just summoned one. In all my years on the waters, I've never heard of ship surviving a direct encounter with a leviathan.'

'Even a bookship?' yelled Elessi in hope.

Lerel flashed her a petrified stare. 'I don't want to find out. Raise anchor! Mages at the ready! Ballistae stand by!' she hollered at her crew.

Barely half a mile beyond the anchored armada, the surface of the sea exploded into white and black water. A wave arose, surging towards them. A dark, serpentine form coursed through the sea beneath. Two broad fins, spiked as a dragon's crest and an ultramarine blue, pierced the waters. Each of them was a tree's height. They broke the water with white froth, creating bow waves like the keel of a ship. From their size alone, Elessi found the fear in her heart utterly valid. She remembered the primordial terror she had felt first meeting a dragon. That memory paled now.

The fear only increased as the leviathan swept towards the armada. Elessi found herself breathless as the wave crashed against the hulls of the bookships. No impact came. No rending crash. It seemed, for a wonderful moment, as if the leviathan passed them by. It was then she saw the dark shape barrelling towards the surface.

'Fire!' cried Lerel and Eyrum in one voice.

The *Autumn's Vanguard* rocked as the starboard side unleashed its volley. The sounds of crashing spells and a ballistae unloading was a thunder that temporarily deafened Elessi.

The water roiled with bolts, fire, and lightning. The surface of the sea steamed within moments. When the last spell had been unleashed, a dread silence settled over the armada. Every neck craned over each bulwark and railing, staring down into the waters to see what their barrage had done.

The short answer was nothing.

In the vacuum of the volley, with a detonation of water, the leviathan at last emerged. Elessi swept back from the edge of the ship, stumbling in her panic.

Seawater coursing across its teal diamond scales, the leviathan's head alone rivalled some of the smaller vessels in size. Its neck was as thick as a tower, built of scale and sinew instead of stone. In slow, deliberate movements, it kept rising from the sea until its gaze drew level with the top deck of the *Vanguard*. Serpentine in nature, its head sloped like the blade of a pickaxe and bristled with webbed fins. Its eyes burned a piercing blue. Serrated fangs bristled from its mouth, each competing to poke as far from its gums as possible. And when it opened its dire head to emit a deafening roar, its jaws opened in quarters rather than halves. Thick, blue spittle soaked the decks between sailors clutching their ears. Wherever the saliva touched, the wood bubbled and smoked. Holes began to appear in the deck. Flesh melted like wax before a fire. Excruciated screams of the crew joined the leviathan's roar.

'Fire again!' Lerel yelled. Elessi could hear the desperation in her voice.

The onslaught collided with the leviathan. In panic, a good portion of the volley overshot the leviathan and landed upon the rest of the armada. Screams unfurled alongside sails as the ships tried frantically to set sail.

The ballistae bolts that found soft places between the leviathan's scales only served to anger the colossal beast. Fire, while it seemed to stall the monster, failed to elicit any damage but anger. As it unlocked its jaws, the leviathan reared backwards to add weight to its strike.

'Hold!' bellowed the officers across the *Vanguard*, but it came too late. The leviathan smashed its giant head into the bookship's port side. Bulwarks and railings splintered into sawdust before its strength. A dozen sailors and mages' screams were silenced as the jaws came crashing down. Bloody smears were their only eulogy.

Elessi heard the stuttered impact of the volleys from the other bookships colliding with the *Vanguard*. Bellows of pain and panic came from below.

'I need speed and sail, damn it!' Lerel was baying at her officers. Wind mages tried desperately to go to work between the chaos. The *Vanguard*'s clockwork spars let loose their sails, but as the leviathan withdrew, half the rigging became entangled in its spines and bladed fins.

'Fire at bloody will!' yelled the admirals to their ships. Spells exploded against the leviathan's hide one after the other, barely making a scratch. Spears and arrows clattered uselessly against its scales.

In a burst of fire from the heavens, Towerdawn's dragons made their attack. Jaws and fire assailed the leviathan. Blue blood spattered like rain across the *Vanguard*'s decks, causing more injuries. Elessi could hear the decks hissing.

The leviathan submerged as rapidly as it had appeared. Somehow, despite its terrifying appearance, the notion of it being hidden was much more unsettling.

'We need to move!' Lerel was screaming.

The panic struck Elessi again as a huge impact shook the *Vanguard* from deck to keel. Elessi heard the iron and timbers of the ship groan in complaint.

Elessi watched the other ships of the armada buck and shudder as the leviathan tested them, too. 'Get us out of here, Lerel!'

'I'm trying!'

The *Vanguard* shuddered as the sails filled with wind spells. The bookship started to move, setting a course that swung around the rest of the armada.

The leviathan surfaced again, not to attack this time, but to unhinge its quartered jaws and utter a blood-curdling scream. To her horror, Elessi heard an answering screech behind her. She whirled, catching sight of two more leviathans lifting out of the water. She saw their serpentine shapes: sinuous bodies arcing between the huge bow-waves they created.

'What about three of them, Lerel?' Elessi yelled. 'Anyone ever survived that?'

By the gaping whites of Lerel's eyes, she had seen them too. The admiral unleashed a barrage of orders as she swung the *Vanguard* around. Ballistae and mages fired at will, lashing at anything that moved beneath the waters.

Dragons became a constant hail, swooping in their dozens to bathe the creatures in their fire. It was perhaps the only deterrent that kept the leviathans at bay. But while their jaws stayed below the waves, their serpentine tails wreaked just as much havoc.

Elessi stared wide-eyed as an enormous blue tail reared from the sea and collapsed upon one of the armada's warships. It was the *Waveblade*, an ironclad veteran of the Last War and one of the oldest ships in the fleet. Seawater swamped its sides as the ship was forced down under the weight of the impact. Sailors and soldiers flew in all directions under the force. The sea was peppered with bodies. The leviathans churned the water into a bloody frenzy as they feasted on the fallen.

'Move, damn it!' Lerel yelled to the sails, urging the bookship on.

Elessi seized the railing next to the wheel, holding tight as another wave rocked the bookship from side to side. 'Where do we go?'

'Anywhere but here!'

Roiks deafened them with his opinion. 'West, damn it! The leviathans came from the east.'

To Elessi's nod, Lerel did exactly that, driving the ship at such an angle half the deck almost slid into the sea. All the while, the ballistae and mages belowdecks fired incessantly at anything that moved in the water.

'Hold!' yelled Roiks. Elessi barely stayed upright as the three leviathans arose as one from the sea. With the *Waveblade* frantically bailing water, it made an easy target. The three monsters struck as one, crushing the decks of the ironclad warship as if they were tack biscuits. Screams filled the air beyond the crash of wood and iron between jaws. Elessi tried to shut her ears to the sounds of the dying, but they filled the air and bled into her mind.

'Sail, damn you!' Lerel screamed.

At last, the admiral's orders took effect. The *Waveblade*'s sinking corpse distracted the feasting leviathans long enough for the rest of the ships to turn their keels and break west. To the ring of haunting echoes, Scalussen tucked tail and ran. It was a sore sacrifice, stolen rather than offered, but it saved the rest of the armada.

Unable to stare upon the carnage or the monsters, Elessi faced forwards, as if willing the armada into safe waters. It took some time for her to peel her hands from the railing. When she did, she found Lerel in a similar white-knuckle state, clinging to the wheel for all her worth.

The admiral's words ground out like a pestle on spices. 'That god needs to die.'

# CHAPTER 6
## LILEROSK

*The Arka Empire, though far-reaching, was not the pinnacle of Emaneska's
dominions. The Skölgard Empire held sway over the frozen lands for centuries before its fall at the closure of the Battle of Krauslung, in 890. Thanks to
the hard, cruel, and irascible nature bred into the Skölgard people, their
empire claimed all of Emaneska bar Nelska and Albion. It also stretched
deeper east than most in Emaneska knew. It was the first Skölgard kings that
forged the Sunder Road east, into Nyr, the Rivenplains, Golikar, and beyond.*
FROM THE DIARY OF VIKR ENLY, NOTED EXPLORER AND MERCHANT

A timid snow was beginning to fall across the plains when, at last, the
town was spotted.

At great volume and with much repetition, Kursi had spent the
journey boasting of the many so-called wonders of his town. They
had walked through the night and half a day, and Mithrid could
barely remember hearing the boy take breath.

By his accounts, Lilerosk was home to not one, not two, but
three taverns. Great ogin bones, whatever they were. There was pur-
portedly even a fountain in the town square, too.

Now that the rest of the exhausted, dishevelled band stood
upon a hill and looked down into Lilerosk's valley, Kursi was proved
to be either utterly naive or a liar.

Lilerosk looked like a boil festering upon the pea-green com-
plexion of the grasslands. Sitting upon a squashed hill, its slanted
walls alternated between clay brick and wood painted red and yellow.
White arches spanned a gate. Conical rooftops of woven grass and
clay tiles formed a swollen blister of construction that culminated in

a crooked tower poking up like a skeleton's finger. Faint paths through the grasslands speared the town from all degrees.

Carpeting the undulating plains for miles around Lilerosk were tiny white specks. She thought them farms or orchards before she saw them moving like flocks of white starlings. On the winds, Mithrid could hear a shrill cawing and the whistles of the figures that herded them.

Aspala must have seen her slitted, curious eyes. Mithrid caught her staring. The Paraian was smirking. Crystals of snow clung to the edge of the hood that disguised her horns.

'You never seen sheep before, Mith?'

Hâlorn's coasts were known for many things, but rich farmland and beasts of burden were not one of them. Fish, crab and birds' eggs were the only bounties cliff-folk farmed. Mithrid listened to the wailing tones of the nearer creatures. She decided they looked like a goat that had tangled with a dirty cloud. The small ones that tottered about, she had to admit, were rather adorable.

'I know what a sheep is,' Mithrid said. 'Just never seen one, is all. Hâlorn trades with Albion for its wool.'

Aspala shook her head in disbelief.

'Taste good, too,' rumbled Warbringer as she thumped her way down the hill. 'Almost as good as you pink-fleshes.'

Mithrid found that to be a distinctly disturbing recommendation.

Over the last few hours, the minotaur had become more impatient to reach the town than the mage. The journey had barely tired her, whereas it had exhausted Farden, which culminated in Warbringer now leading the way. Farden dragged behind, now limping.

Kursi was still babbling on incessantly by Mithrid and Aspala's side.

'And as I said, Lilerosk being famous for its wool and its mutton means that lambing season is a great festival where—'

To Mithrid, Kursi's chattering had become featureless noise, a backdrop for her repetitive thoughts. It seemed, however, that Aspala had heard plenty from the boy.

Quick as a snake, with her thumb and forefinger, Aspala seized Kursi by the lips. The boy squirmed, but Aspala pinched only harder. 'Enough babble. Where I am from, young ones are seen and not heard. Learn the beauty of silence, child.'

The silence Aspala was rewarded with was golden but short-lived. Striding through the snow-speckled grass, Kursi was soon pointing out whose flock belonged to which town clan, what the painted runes on the beasts' flanks meant, and sharing all manner of shepherd gossip. It was deploringly uninteresting.

For all her intrigue, Mithrid never got close to a sheep: War-bringer's presence disturbed the flocks greatly. The sheep scattered from their path. A few of the shepherds yelled in a foreign tongue, to which Kursi hollered back.

'They don't like you,' said the boy.

Warbringer blew steam from her copper-ringed snout. 'Then the feeling is mutual.'

'You scare them, is all.'

'Then it's fortunate that Fleetstar agreed to stay out of sight. Hopefully she has the wherewithal to listen to me and stick to the plan.' Farden sounded far from convinced.

A gathering of townsfolk had emerged from the gate: an arch-way of two curving white struts bound together in copper wire. Mithrid angled her cheek to the breeze. There was a thin thread of magick in it. Magick, inert and minuscule, but power, nonetheless, coming from the arches.

Mithrid trailed along with Farden. The mage's shoulders were sullen but his steps were determined enough.

'What if the men at the gates don't like us either?' she asked

'I've talked my way around many a guard and magistrate in my time, Mithrid. I'll think of something.'

'Durnus was right. You're not the best with plans, are you?'

'The Written weren't trained as strategists. We were the teeth of the beast, not the mind.'

'That explains a lot,' Mithrid whispered, catching a side-eye from the mage.

'You forget, girl. Words are some of the sharpest and most terrible weapons in the world. As a wise yet foul man once told me, words can't hammer in a nail, but they can start a war.'

The others had reached the foot of the town's hill. Lilerosk sat above them, an ugly crown. The sheep penned around the converging paths baaed woefully.

'Let's see what your silver tongue can do then, King,' Mithrid waved him ahead.

With a creak of metal, Farden removed his helmet. Despite the scattered snow and cold winds sailing over the grassland plans, the mage was drenched in sweat. His dark hair was plastered to his scalp and forehead. Even as roasted as he appeared, his skin remained pale, wan.

The moment Farden set foot to the hill, a plump man encased in knitted drapes emerged from the gathering and held out his palms.

'That's far enough, stranger!' he yelled in the same thick Commontongue Kursi used. The townsfolk at his back looked on, speaking behind their hands.

With a lot of creaking and grunting of pain, Farden bowed. 'We mean no harm. We are merely travellers from the west. Far from home.'

'And what brings you to Lilerosk's gates?'

Mithrid snorted. *Gates was a bold stretch.*

'Food and shelter,' replied Farden. 'A healer and armourer if you have them.'

It was clear to see that most of the wool-clad inhabitants of Lilerosk had eyes only for Warbringer.

'We have no food for strangers who have no names. No shelter neither. Grave dangers walk the Sunder Road. In all... shapes and sizes,' said the man.

Farden glanced to the growling minotaur, as if to silently beg her for patience and to not reduce any townsfolk to bloody jam, no matter what insults they had for her. Clearly no minotaurs existed beyond Emaneska's reaches.

Mithrid yelled out instead. 'We hear you are famous for your fine wool and mutton! Perhaps we can trade?'

'With what? You have no wares. No flocks nor herds. Unless you have coin?'

'Hmph,' Farden grumbled.

'Looks like you've lost your touch,' teased Mithrid. She meant only to jest, to ease the awkward tension, but the look Farden shot her was severe.

In the end, it was Kursi that bought them entrance into Lilerosk.

'But they saved me!' blurted the boy, pushing past Farden and Mithrid and running up the hill.

A shrill voice cut the cold air. 'Kursi!'

'Mother!'

Before Mithrid knew what was happening, a woman burst from the crowd of townsfolk and sprinted so rapidly down the hill it looked as though she would fall and fold in two at any moment. Kursi raced to meet her, and in the dusting of snow and worn grass, they embraced tightly.

Soon enough, she was rushing to clasp the hands of the strangers, babbling something that Mithrid assumed translated to "thank you". To the mother's credit, she even grabbed Warbringer by the arm in gratitude. Not once did she stop talking at them, and Mithrid knew precisely where Kursi had learned his wagging tongue. Nonetheless, the reunion was satisfying to see, but all it did was remind Mithrid of the miles between her and the others. Between

Hereni, and Bull, of course. *And Elessi. Akitha.* The name of Malvus tolled like a bell in between her ears.

After ushering her son up the hill, chattering every step of the way, Kursi's mother quickly turned her verbal barrage on the fat man. His bluster was no defence for her demands, and within moments, Kursi came halfway to fetch them. He waved his hands, urging them onwards.

The leader of Lilerosk, whatever his title was, stood beside the gate looking utterly terrified of the ragtag creatures he was admitting to his town.

Warbringer had no interest in enduring the townsfolk' stares. She was busy staring up at the white arches. 'They're bones,' she grunted to the others as they passed beneath them.

'What?' Mithrid followed her gaze. The milk-white struts were lashed together at their points at least twenty feet above them.

'Bones. But the bones of what?'

The beast these spurs of bone came from must have once been enormous. She wasn't sure whether it was the bones themselves or the foreign runes that gave off the magick, but the sensation was noticeably stronger here. Still intermittent and faint, like a winter's sun, but there, nonetheless. She watched Farden closely to see if he felt it, but the mage was preoccupied with the leather-armoured militia standing nearby.

'The bones of Garyon of the Burnt South, last of the ogin,' boasted the town's leader.

'Very... impressive,' said Mithrid. Or at least it would have been, if she understood any of it.

'They lay a blessing upon all who enter here with pure intentions and a curse on those that would be our enemies.'

'Blessing it is, then,' Farden said. He sketched another bow and joined the others in looking around the abject mess that was Lilerosk's town square.

Sheep ran freely in and out of adjoining streets, either herded or chased by skinny shepherd children. Whatever building wasn't dedicated to the shearing and spinning of wool was either a butcher's or a tannery. The fountain that Kursi had boasted of existed, but it was a dubious greenish colour from the people washing tools and boots in its brick pool. It was not a charming sprawl but a loud, confusing, and muddy tangle.

Their leader puffed out his ruddy cheeks. 'The Dawn God welcomes you to Lilerosk. I am Flocklord Boorin, master of this town and vassal of Dathazh.'

It took Farden a moment to reply. 'I'm sorry… *Boring*, was it?'

The flocklord wore the exasperated glare of a man who had never said his name only once in all his life. 'Bo-orin.'

'Ah. And I am Farden of Scal—Emaneska. Might I introduce Mithrid Fenn of Hâlorn, Aspala of Paraia, the unconscious fellow is Durnus, also of Emaneska, and this is Warbringer of Efjar.'

Boorin cleared his throat. 'And what, pray, is it?'

'It speaks for itself,' Warbringer interrupted. 'A minotaur, or so you call my kin in pink-flesh tongue.'

'You are strangers indeed, far from home. You will obey our rules while within this town. We will have no trouble here. You have our gratitude and hospitality for saving Yurit's boy from those foul, kidnapping, murderous, cow-piss-drinking, Dusk-loving, Cathak heretics!' Boorin cleared his throat as he remembered himself. 'You may stay for the evening, that is. You will be gone before morning prayer.'

Mithrid raised a hand. 'What time is that?'

Boorin looked markedly insulted. 'Our god is the Dawn God. I shall leave you to figure that out.'

'Charming.' Farden asked once more about an armourer, making Boorin scoff.

'Armourer, you say? Do you see grand castles and knights anywhere around us? Armour of your kind is a luxury beyond most purses in Lilerosk. A healer, however, you will find along that street. Mind yourselves.'

With that, Boorin bid them a good day. Not in so many words, but in the waddling strut with which he marched away from them.

Farden sighed. 'Guess that means no decent weapons, either.'

Aspala sniffed at the air: a curious mix of sheep dung and bubbling stews. 'Should have found another boy to save from bandits. Could have earned ourselves two nights.'

Mithrid snorted in amusement.

The choice of Lilerosk's three taverns was a sliding scale of tolerable, filthy, and hideous. Despite their lack of coin, Farden put his faith in the town's hospitality and thankfully chose the tolerable tavern.

Some unimaginative dolt had dubbed it *The Shepherd's Rest*. It had the look of any usual tavern besides its pointy roof of thatched grass. Three huge, puffed-up sheep with curled horns were lashed to a railing outside the tavern's glowing windows. They were nearly as large as cows, and a small patch had been shaved in their thick wool to allow for a simple saddle. The rams were far from bothered by their approach. Even Warbringer went unnoticed. The sheep were staring avidly at the middle window. It was slightly ajar, and a hand kept sneaking out to sprinkle morsels for the mounts.

If Mithrid had hoped to evade the stink of the town and countless sheep, the innards of the *Rest* was no escape. If anything, the concentration of sweaty shepherds and their pet beasts within a smaller room enhanced the smell.

'I'm sensing a theme to this town,' Farden growled to Mithrid and the others.

Everything that was made to sit or lean on was crafted of wool or leather. The heads of prize-winning sheep graced the walls. Horns bristled around the central fireplace. Even the tankards were made of horn.

Though the flocklord's bidding had been passed around town over the past few hours, the staring had not decreased. The roar of voices all but died at the sight of the strangers.

'Evening,' Farden greeted the tavern as one. 'We don't mean to interrupt. We simply need a room. One with a fire, if you have one.'

The innkeeper was tending to a nearby table, his fists full of a dozen horns of ale. 'As you wish, strangers. Flocklord said you might be coming. Dawn's luck, I have kept one spare. Though it might be a touch... small. Or there are the stables.'

Warbringer was already stalking to the stairs that curved up into the inn's upper reaches. The wooden boards creaked ominously under her hooves.

'A room it will be,' Farden repeated.

'Right you are,' babbled the innkeeper.

Mithrid was busy watching the people from beneath her brows. She assumed they would be interested in the minotaur or Farden's armour, but there was plenty of stares for her. Her scarlet hair and Scalussen plate were apparently just as foreign to these sheep-people. She felt a deep desire to vanish into her hood. It took a different kind of bravery to greet such attention without a care. Even after Scalussen, Mithrid couldn't grasp it.

Farden and Aspala seemed used to it. They paid no heed to the conversations now brewing, and simply climbed to the second floor as assuredly as if the *Rest* was their own home.

The innkeeper was not wrong: the room was small and sparse, yet it was comfortable enough. The thatch sat high above their heads. Tallow lamps burned in glass bowls, mutton-fat by the strangely enticing smell. The mud bricks drowned out much of the incessant baaing of the flocks and the conversation from down below.

'Does your kind take ale and stew?'

Farden bowed politely. 'We do. We are famished from our travels.'

'I will bring some horns and bowls of mutton.'

The minotaur emitted a snarl. 'We take a barrel. No stew for Warbringer. Meat. Raw. Any beast will do.'

The innkeeper searched his mouth for spit and came up dry. 'A barrel...?

Nobody said a word. Those of weak constitution will always seek to fill a silence, rather than let it grow deafening and crushing. The man crumbled, adjusting his woollen jerkin as he scurried from the room. 'Bless me, a barrel it is!' he called back to them.

Warbringer shut the door. 'Think little man might have shit his trews.'

Mithrid took the bed by the thin window and collapsed into it with a dry laugh. Her muscles sang with relief. Exhaustion sank its claws into her.

Farden saw to Durnus, who Warbringer had lain on another wool-stuffed bed. The vampyre remained utterly comatose.

The healer they had found in Lilerosk's market didn't speak the Commontongue, never mind understand what was wrong with the unconscious Durnus. A few tinctures had been offered. Blessed sheep's blood, of course. The word curse was muttered a few times. Rather than risk suspicion over a vampyre in their midst, the strangers had moved on. Otherwise, all the healer had given them was an idea. One that Farden explored without wasting any time.

'It's time you woke up, old friend,' Farden was muttering. 'Aspala, your sword?'

Mithrid was curious. 'What are you doing?'

'The only thing I can think of. Durnus is a vampyre, after all. Perhaps he needs blood.'

With the golden blade in one hand, Farden positioned his other over Durnus' lips. The broken sword cut a neat line across the mage's palm. Clenching his fist, he dripped the blood into Durnus' mouth until the cut ran dry.

They waited, listening to the screech of a fiddle that somebody in the tavern thought fit to play. Durnus did not stir.

Mithrid watched Farden's shoulders slump. The rest of the room seemed to follow, with Warbringer settling into a lump in the corner and Aspala hanging her head.

Farden stalked to the window, standing at the foot of her bed while he gazed at the strange little town of Lilerosk. 'Dusk and dawn gods. High Cathaks. Flocklords. Vassal of Daz-something. I feel more lost than I did in the woods.'

'At least we know the others are alive.'

Farden flinched as if stung. He shifted to the heavy satchel Aspala had been lugging around. It took him considerable effort to drag the thick black tome out onto the blanket. Warbringer snuffled in judgement and busied herself picking burrs from her hooves.

The ancient pages were painted yellow in the glow of the tallow lamps. Amber sparks appeared once more, twirling in a dance about each other until Farden spoke the name, 'Elessi' to them.

The sparks stuttered. They drew faint lines that crumbled instantly. As before, nothing appeared, and Farden seemed to relax.

Mithrid watched the meandering lights. 'What does it do when somebody is dead?'

Farden took a while to answer. 'It shows you their soul—'

A loud knock on the door interrupted. Farden threw a blanket over the Grimsayer before it swung open. Two wide-eyed lads, full-grown but with fluff on their chins came in bearing a pot of stew and a barrel. The innkeeper followed them up, ushering them out of the room before they could dawdle and gawp. He held a tray of ale-horns and cutlery, and waited politely while the mage and minotaur made some space for a table by upending a bed.

'I trust lamb will be all right, for you, er, *fine guests.*'

Warbringer tore into a raw steak of sheep and the blood drained from the innkeeper's face. He hovered between the strangers, tray rattling in hand.

'And wh—what brings you past Lilerosk? Don't get many Emaneskans in these parts after the Skölgard left. You lot keep to yourselves and your own borders. Heading onto Dathazh and Golikar for the Tourney, I expect?'

Farden had propped the barrel up on the bed and was staring expectantly at the innkeeper. 'No. South, back to Emaneska.'

'Back home, is it? I see. Well, word is you saved Yurit's boy from the Dusk God's clutches. Bless me, glad you were around.'

'The idiots in fur coats? They didn't like us trespassing in their wood.'

'Cow-riding heathens who have tormented us for decades,' said the innkeeper with sudden vigour. 'They disguise themselves in our colours, kidnap us, feed us to their cursed trees or sacrifice us in the name of their foul Dusk God. Took my darling Skisvel a decade ago now. We've got no warriors like you. No soldiers, see? We are but humble shepherds and craftspeople. And innkeepers, of course.'

Farden and Mithrid both nodded politely. That had been painfully evident in the lack of any weapons in the Lilerosk market. Beyond a pitchfork or shears, at least.

Warbringer chewed noisily until the innkeeper became too uncomfortable to linger further.

'Bless me,' he breathed. 'I shall bid you a good eve—'

The tray was a hairsbreadth from the table when Durnus chose to awake.

The vampyre sat bolt upright, roaring hoarsely. He did both with such speed and volume that the innkeeper almost embedded himself in the thatch ceiling before falling on his backside. The horns of ale and cutlery fell like rain while the tray clattered over the man's head. His two lads were at the door in an instant, braced for a fight, fists raised and quivering.

Panting and eyes near popping out of his head, the innkeeper shuffled from the room on his arse. Mithrid didn't blame him. She had quite nearly soiled herself in surprise, too.

'D—do let us know if you need anything else. Anything at all!' he yelled.

The door had barely slammed by the time Farden wrapped Durnus in a blanket. The vampyre's eyes bulged, red raw as if still burned by smoke. His momentary outburst over, he collapsed back to the bed.

'Durnus! Can you hear me?' Farden shook him lightly.

Durnus' blood-stained lips moved in small increments. 'Got to stop him. Before he kills us all,' he whispered, over and over.

Farden made him take some water between his mumblings. The mage even cut another line in his palm to give the vampyre more of his blood. Durnus' consciousness was short-lived no matter what they tried, and before long, he was once again a limp bundle of blanket and grey skin.

The others ate in silence, too focused on filling mouths and desolate stomachs to talk. Now that the sun had dipped below the strange western hills, tiredness and the allure of sleep had Aspala and Warbringer snoring within the hour.

Mithrid wasn't immune, and after she choked down some of the thick, sour ale Lilerosk brewed, she clutched her swollen stomach and found her eyelids inescapably drooping. The last she saw was Farden standing at the window, watching the fading light.

It was a faint orange shine that awoke her. Not the tallow lamps of the town, now fallen still and asleep, but that of two firefly lights over the Grimsayer. Mithrid shifted surreptitiously beneath her blankets so she could watch the mage.

Farden was hunched over the Grimsayer like a child devouring stolen sugar. Hooded by a blanket, his face was ghoulish in the glow, eyes fixed on the figure that the lights had weaved. His armour was stacked beside him. All he wore were his scaled vambraces. They had little gleam to them.

The figure was Modren, barely the height of her thumb, his scarred head held high as he marched across the page without ever travelling. He still wore most of his armour. His eyes shone white between the orange threads that weaved him.

He looked so real that Mithrid couldn't help but sit up and reach out to touch him.

'Just a reflection of a soul, nothing more, Mithrid,' Farden whispered, voice cracking. 'He died saving Scalussen. Without him, we would be all that's left.'

Mithrid looked up to find the mage had been watching her instead. She sat up, feeling her back click and crunch. She felt as though she had seen seventy winters, not seventeen. She nodded solemnly. The loss of Modren was a raw wound for her also. Modren was there, behind her eyes, falling out of sight over and over, a daemon prince arched over him.

'I always wonder what and where I'd be if Modren and Kinsprite hadn't arrived that day. Hadn't killed the Arka mages and taken us north. I would be dead, most likely. That feels like years ago now. It's been barely months.'

'That's what Modren did: saved people. Over and over.' Farden sighed. 'He's in my uncle's care now. And that of the gods.'

'Your uncle?'

'His name is Tyrfing. He practically raised me.'

No sooner had Farden spoken the name did the Grimsayer's lights begin to draw another man. An older version of the mage, standing with arms crossed and with a defiant glare that proved him of Farden's blood.

'He was a mage like Modren and I. Now he serves the goddess Hel in her domain, deep beneath the world in endless caverns full of journeying souls, where the edge of the void lies. A bridge used to carry souls to the other side, but it was broken not long ago. Since then, the souls gather in their multitudes, both below and above us in the stars. Hel and Haven.' Farden pointed beyond the grubby window, now fogged with their breath. His voice had become guttural.

'Souls stored like grain, feeding the gods with their belief, just like mortals' prayer.'

'You speak as if you've seen such a place,' Mithrid whispered.

Farden stared at her from beneath the hoods of his brows, as if balanced on the edge of a story.

When he spoke no more, Mithrid worked her tongue around the sharp edges of her teeth. 'Could I use it? Your Grimsayer?'

Farden considered for a moment, more unwilling to leave his uncle behind than give up the book, she supposed.

'It's heavy,' he said. 'And it's grown heavier and thicker since the battle of Scalussen. Since...'

Mithrid knew very well what he meant. Since the obliteration of hundreds of thousands. War, they called it. Mithrid heard its other name in her mind, over and over. *Murder*. With Malvus still alive, it all felt increasingly senseless, even though she had agreed wholeheartedly to the plan. Having lit the fuse of Irminsul, Mithrid felt a guilt groping at her. It was perhaps why she had found herself glaring at Farden in the passing moments. That, and the blame he had laid at her feet for losing his magick.

'Wait,' she replied. 'Grown, you say?'

Farden's face was painted dark as the tome was passed into Mithrid's hands. She underestimated the weight and almost dropped it immediately. She swore she heard a whisper from Aspala or Warbringer as she picked it up.

'A page for every soul who's passed into the death, and gone to Hel or Haven.'

Mithrid shook her head, confused. 'I don't know these things. All I was ever taught was stories of Njord the sea god. Hurricane was who we worshipped and burned our dead to. Quietly, of course, seeing as belief in anyone but Malvus was banned by the empire. My father worshipped the memory of my mother rather than any god.'

The pages of the Grimsayer were much thinner than expected. They turned with what sounded like breath. Voices, perhaps. She shook her head, blaming the mutterers of passersby outside the window instead. She let its weight sink into the blanket before speaking the name.

'Gammer Fenn.'

The orange lights went about their art and spun a man standing with shoulders hunched yet head proud. His arms were raised as if grappling. There was a cut above his brow, but otherwise his teeth were bared in the half-smile, half-growl of a man in the middle of winning a fight.

Mithrid choked. She leaned closer to study her father's glowing features, shocked and shamed at the details she had already forgotten.

'I haven't let myself dwell on him since I stepped aboard the *Winter's Revenge*,' she admitted in a whisper. 'Too painful.'

Farden nodded. Only the street lamps of the slumbering town showed his features. 'I never told you at the time in Scalussen, but my father was also a woodsman. He died along with my mother in an avalanche when I was six winters old. She was a wind mage. You and I are not so different in our beginnings, it seems.'

'Similar, but the man that killed my parents still lives,' Mithrid answered him, gaze fixed on her father. She felt a dagger of emotion between her ribs. It was a different kind of guilt. One that reminded her she had failed her promise of revenge.

Farden took some time to answer. 'Too many have died because of Malvus Barkhart. Now Loki. I won't let Durnus join them,' Farden muttered before chuckling drily. It dragged Mithrid's attention away. 'You know, it's a shame that it's Durnus that's injured. Out of all of us, he's the healer. He'd know what to do. Even if it's wielding that necromancy he insists on using.'

Mithrid shuddered as she recalled the fallen rising to seize the living, wreathed in blue light and foul magick like she had not yet felt. Before she could reply, a familiar voice croaked from the bed next to Farden.

'It is not necromancy, godsdamn it. And it has saved our backsides more than once now.'

Both of them snapped around to see Durnus' eyes glinting from between the blankets, open at last.

Farden was kneeling beside him in a blink. 'By Evernia, you're awake!' he hissed, rousing Aspala from her slumbers. Warbringer continued to snore.

'And speaking of necromancy, I feel like death,' the vampyre rasped. He angled his head to the Weight still clutched in his hands, and with a faint moan, broke his fingers from its warped surface. Bones clicked. Skin tore. Durnus clutched his hands to his chest and shivered. 'Where are we?' he asked.

'I could ask you the same bloody thing. Don't try to get up.'

But Durnus ignored him and shakily pushed himself upright anyway. Farden helped him until he was slumped against the brick wall. He looked fit to faint again at any moment.

'I…' The vampyre moved his tongue across wrinkled lips. 'I had to get us on the path, Farden.'

'What path, old friend?'

'Is everyone alive? What is this place?'

'Elessi and the rest are alive for now. As for us, we're cooped up in an arsehole of a town called Lilerosk. Past the Hammer Hills in a place called Rivenplains.'

'Then it worked.' The vampyre's head lolled for a moment before Farden lifted his chin. 'We've begun.'

'What?'

'I had to get us—'

Durnus blinked as a brief glow lit his face. Mithrid noticed it too, in her left eye, beyond the window pane. It was gone as quickly as it appeared but it roused distant shouts from the town walls. She and Farden rushed to the window. The snow was still falling in faint specks, lit only by the sparse lanterns. As torches blossomed across the walls, they saw it again: a lance of fire illuminating half the grassland valley. And there, in the flurries of snow, they glimpsed the unmistakable shadow of a dragon. The night's silence was filled with the baying of sheep and their apoplectic shepherds.

'That blasted reptile!' Farden cursed. He was already gathering up his armour. 'I told her to stay unseen, far beyond the town!'

Lamps lit across the town like sparks scattered by a boot. The streets were quickly filling with figures rushing to see what calamity was befalling them. Shouts of, 'Daemon!' and 'Dragon!' filled the air. Half the folk were prostrate on the ground, praying for their Dawn God to bring an early light.

Farden shut his eyes, mouthing silent words for the dragon to stop terrorising Lilerosk's flocks. He murmured darkly as he shoved on his gauntlets. 'She says they have far too many sheep, and she's doing them a service,' said the mage. He seized Durnus by the fore-arm. 'You should've known better than to trust the Mad Dragon, old friend.'

'There is no faster beast in Emaneska. And I had not expected to bring so many of us.'

Farden wagged a finger in his face. 'You have a shitload of explaining to do come morning, Durnus. For now, let's get out of here.'

Warbringer hoisted Durnus aloft and followed Farden, Aspala, and a bewildered Mithrid still trying to affix her cloak around her shoulders. Half her armour was stuffed into her haversack.

'Why the haste, Farden?' she hissed.

'A bunch of strangers arrive the same night a dragon roasts half their flocks? You tell me whose necks they'll be keen to put a noose around.'

Mithrid shrugged. The mage had a fair point. Her feet hurried down the worn steps of the tavern. The drunks who had fallen asleep at their tables were staggering about in confusion. The innkeeper and his lads crowded the doorway, staring at the distant fire. There ap-peared to be some kind of group gathering on the doorstep. Voices were raised. As the clatter of the strangers on the stairs turned everybody's heads, there was a pregnant pause in which everyone froze, eyes locked in accusing stares.

'It's *their* doing!' came a shout. It was the spark the mob needed.

For all his injuries and weariness, Farden pounced terrifyingly quickly. He seized the innkeeper by the throat, dragging him away from the door while Aspala played along: menacing the man's neck with her golden blade. His lads raised stools and clubs as the other townsfolk fought to squeeze into the door.

Mithrid was pushed along in the chaos, deeper into the tavern. Warbringer scattered tables and wool-clad chairs before them.

Durnus' voice was shrill from upside down over the minotaur's shoulder. 'It would be a fine time for some magick, Farden!'

But Farden ignored the vampyre. 'Got a back door, innkeeper?'

'Please! I'm but a humble—'

'Answer the question!'

No!' he wailed. 'Just the one door!'

'Warbringer!' roared the mage.

'A pleasure!'

The minotaur swung Voidaran at the tavern's back wall. The poor bricks stood no chance. Half of them were reduced to powder as the warhammer's blunt face collided. The rest exploded into the night, leaving a hole big enough for them to squeeze through.

Mithrid lingered, spinning her power between her hands to leave trails of black shadow behind them. The superstition of the townsfolk did the rest, halting them from chasing.

'Dusk God!' they yelled.

In the confusion, Mithrid and the others managed to escape too much scrutiny as they dashed for the southern wall. At the chokepoint of a street made of clay and thatch buildings, they found themselves once again at the mercy of Warbringer.

After pressing the limp vampyre into the arms of Farden and Aspala, the minotaur began to swing Voidaran in a wailing arc. She charged, whirling the weapon overhead until, half a dozen paces from the wall, she let it fly. Voidaran split the wall of brick and wooden scaffold asunder. It was closely followed by Warbringer, who lowered her horns and drove her charging bulk into the gap. The wall collapsed, leaving her to roll almost comically down the hill on the other side.

'Who needs a locksmith when you've got a minotaur?' Aspala yelled as they scrambled over the wreckage.

'It's all fun and games until you're fighting against them,' snapped Farden as he stumbled and rolled.

The townsfolk and their ramshackle militia had noticed their escape. As the strangers sprinted into the darkness, snow stinging their cheeks, a dozen flaming arrows drew streaks in the sky. They landed wide and short, but they still spurred them to greater speeds.

'Dawn curse you!' came the cries.

'Bandits!'

'Whores of Dusk!'

More arrows soared into the sky. One landed with a thud and a hiss close to Mithrid's feet, and she yelled to Farden.

'Their aim is getting better!'

Farden didn't answer. He was busy searching the skies. 'Fleetstar, you damnable swine!' he yelled.

It took an arrow clanging against Farden's armoured shoulder for the dragon to answer their pleas.

Her black shape skimmed so close, Mithrid swore she felt scales brush her hair. The dragon tore clods of grassland up as she skidded to a halt. Her eyes were cold crystal points in the gloom. Dangerous and wild. She said nothing as Mithrid, Aspala and Durnus clambered aboard her saddle. Farden and Warbringer braced as her claws closed around them. With several inconsiderately lurching wingbeats, the dragon was aloft and skimming the grasslands into a cold and flurrying night.

Mithrid clung on for dear life, having lacked the time to strap herself in. The biting wind sealed her eyes shut. All she could focus on in that rushing darkness was the overwhelming smell of roast mutton.

# CHAPTER 7
## MONSTROUS THINGS

*Beyond storms, pirates, and sharp rocks, the sailor fears the leviathan the most. What does the leviathan fear, you ask? The giant and fearsome keraken, if any still exist.*
FROM THE 'WET LETTERS' OF MASTER WIRD'S SEAFARING EXPEDITIONS

It was with the screams of the Bay of Rós fading in his ears that Loki ascended the steps of the Arkathedral. The Scalussen armada was speeding west, hurried by the sailors dying behind them as a ship sank into the dark night's water.

Half a mile of steps had already passed before his feet, and yet he trod them just the same: an inexorable climb.

The fawners had fallen away, too tired to keep up. Even the guards struggled, and still Loki climbed. He had the peak of the Arkathedral in his mind, and he would be damned if anyone stopped him.

With strength unknown to mortals, Loki reached the hall of the Marble Copse, where the magick council and Malvus had once issued their orders and decrees. Past the unlit Blazing Throne, Loki walked. Curving up the stairs until he felt the chilling breath of evening air on his warm skin, he emerged into the Eyrie. Here Malvus had trodden amongst the vulegul nests and stared down upon the core of his empire.

Loki did the same, daring his feet to the edge of precipices that had no balustrade or iron railing. Below him, the white marble tiers of the Arkathedral descended one by one, until the walls became fused with bridges to mansions and inflated watchtowers. The streets were afire with lanterns and torches, held by citizens parading in celebration. Not just for the victory over the Scalussen fleet. Not merely for the leviathans he had summoned. But for the god that resided amongst them.

As he stood tall against the wind, Loki heard his name chanted across the city. He basked in it, hearing, as well as feeling, the adoration from below. It fuelled him, and he twisted his face into a mask of haughty satisfaction that even he was unused to. He remembered himself at last, smoothing his smile across his cheeks with his forefinger and thumb before chuckling. It was time to gamble some more.

*And this time with higher stakes.*

Loki made sure he moved out of sight before he vanished from Krauslung. The people thought him a saviour; they were not ready to know a god walked in their midst. *Not yet.* He needed them to adore him willingly, and so he left them to suspect and wonder at his nature.

Snow scattered around his boots. Loki looked upon the farmhouse that sat lonely amidst a frozen field of stumps. Its windows had been boarded up in panic. The thatch looked one stout storm away from collapsing. There was a loneliness to it that Loki appreciated. A defiant kind of existence much like him, immune to the grinding change of the world around him.

Above the farmhouse, the night sky was full of colours. Great swathes of dusty light, blue and green, duelled with each other lazily. Above the black Tausenbar, fire still burned in the northernmost mountains. Half hidden by clouds of smoke and ash, a pillar of cobalt light dominated the dark. It reached high into the heavens. Loki felt the swell of Irminsul's power in the air, pulsing as a heartbeat.

Already creatures had come to gather. On the edges of the field, in the misted darkness, Loki spied the diamond shine of the eyes of wolves, and their larger cousins, fenrir. Trolls, too, of charred wood and stone. Ghouls and ghosts aplenty, some freshly wrought. he ignored them all.

Stepping over the half-frozen corpses of an old man and boy, Loki's boots crunched on the hoarfrost. He could hear shouting inside the farmhouse. Something crashed against a wall. Loki tutted.

*Humans.* They could never be trusted to sit still.

Within the gutted abode, dark figures stood hunched and hooded around a single candle. These were the scrapings of the wilds; Arka survivors that Loki had found lost in the mountains or stuck halfway to Krauslung.

A lone surviving Scarred stepped upward, light threading between her fingers before realising it was Loki. Two particularly burly figures watched over a shivering huddle of prisoners. One twiddled a dagger between his fingers. The other tended burns that Loki could still see glowing with magick.

'It's time,' he ordered. To the whimpers of the prisoners, Loki climbed the rickety stairs to the upper room amongst the thatch.

Another crash came from the other side of the door. Loki let his hand hover over the handle a moment before clasping it. Light spread across the cracks of the wood as it unlocked.

In the gloom within, lit only by the night sky creeping through the boarded windows, stood a heaving, raging shape.

Loki slammed the door behind him at the same time as bringing the glass cube of Jurindir's Candle into the light.

Malvus looked wild. The daemonblood Loki had left him with was gone. The bottle lay in pieces at the foot of the far wall. Malvus' feet had trodden upon the shards, it looked like, and dragged bloody footprints across the floorboards. His shirt was ripped and soiled. The pillowy body of an emperor whose habits were mostly sitting and shouting and coughing up blood was evident. Though a potbelly remained, he had grown gaunter in the chest and arms even in his short stay in the farmhouse. A sandy beard had sprouted across his face.

Judging by his physical appearance, his gaze had no right to burn so brightly. Loki smiled. 'Good!' he announced.

'Good?' screeched Malvus from behind his hands. The light blinded him.

'I can see the rage in you once more. The strength. You're more yourself than ever before. You've healed well.'

'You fiend.' Malvus choked on a cough and wiped his lips. Loki saw the faint smear of blood on the back of his thumb. The god trusted he had not dallied too long.

'You accursed fiend. W—who do you think you are to keep me prisoner? Days, I have waited here. All the while Krauslung betrays me and that fucking mage keeps drawing breath! I will have you flayed for your insolence.'

'Just like the loyal soldiers beneath us, it was for your protection, Malvus.'

'You will refer to me as Emperor, damn you…!'

Loki gestured for him to sit on the bed. Malvus remained standing. 'You needed the time, and so did I.'

Malvus said not a word. His breaths came rapid and heavy. 'You made me a promise when last we spoke.'

'That I did.'

'Then speak. How exactly do you propose to kill Farden?'

'Me?' Loki patted the emperor on the clammy shoulder twice before Malvus pushed him away. 'Not I, but you, Malvus Barkhart.'

The level of scorn on Malvus' face was almost impressive. 'With what weapon?'

'Why, you, of course.'

The confusion was not amusing to the emperor. Somehow the scorn deepened. It was then Loki saw the sliver of glass in Malvus' other hand, clutched so tightly that blood pattered on the floor.

'You toy with me,' he growled.

'I wouldn't dare, my good Malvus.'

Loki rapped a knuckle on the door. The hooded, pale Scarred appeared. The prisoner in her clutches was babbling a constant stream of apologies and promises of silence. Other dark figures lingered in the stairwell. Loki removed the sack from the man's head and let him blink in the light of the Candle.

It took him a moment to recognise his emperor, and when he did, he fell limp in the Scarred's hands. 'Your Majesty,' the man gasped.

Malvus gestured to the man's robe. Once a clean grey, it was now soiled with mud and piss. 'A scribe?'

'Astute! Your wits have not failed us yet.' Loki explained. 'Only a score of them survived creating the Scarred. Half of those we left behind fled Krauslung. The other half were dutiful enough to remain in the Arkathedral, where I found them. They did not come willingly. It took time, as I said. Quite the opposite, in fact, with much screaming and vomiting, as it happens. The way I travel is not for everyone's stomachs, I suppose.'

Malvus grunted in agreement. 'And what do you propose to do with them? Make more Scarred? Even if we had your Hides of Hysteria—'

Loki swept the grotesque tome from inside his coat and thumped it on the straw bedding. Malvus narrowed his bloodshot eyes.

'—then the Scarred would still be useless in the face of Farden. Hundreds have already failed to defeat him. No Book is as strong as his.'

'Fortunately for us, we have a copy of his Book.'

Malvus laughed in Loki's face.

Once more, the god summoned a prize from his pocket. He slapped the folded sheaf of leather down atop the Hides and crossed his arms.

'You liar…'

'Stolen from beneath the mage's nose not one moment before your Arka charged Scalussen for the last time.'

Loki watched the emperor's dishevelled face cycle through a range of emotions, slipping from scoffing hilarity to confusion, outrage, and finally to awe. Not of Loki, much to his irritation, but of the Book that lay within arm's reach. Malvus reached towards it, then stumbled backwards.

'Farden's Book...' he breathed. 'By the gods. What have you done? How did you get this?'

Loki could hear the guards whispering, even as stunned by Irminsul's fire as they were. 'With this and the other Books, we can at last create a mage worthy of opposing Farden. A mage the likes of which Emaneska has only seen once before. In Samara, Farden's dead daughter.'

'The girl who brought the sky crashing down...' Malvus rasped, reaching again for Farden's Book. 'Yes. Yes, god. You have proven your worth once more!'

'And tenfold, I'd say.' Loki motioned to the Scarred. The scribe prisoner was thrown unceremoniously to the floorboards and left there to whimper. He had already guessed his fate. A hundred scribes had died or gone irretrievably mad from the rushed effort to forge the Scarred. He could not tear his wide eyes from the Hides of Hysteria.

'You had best prepare yourself then, Malvus,' Loki suggested.

The emperor's head shot around. 'We are leaving?'

'No, Your Imperial Majesty. You should prepare yourself for the ritual.'

'Ritual?'

Loki was far from impressed by how long it took Malvus to realise what the god was suggesting. Perhaps it was not the stress and disease that had dulled his mind, but the sheer preposterousness of what Loki had just implied.

'Nonsense!' Malvus blurted. 'You can't mean that I... that you want me to—'

'Ah, but I do.' Loki went as far as to wink. The human expression had never suited him.

The emperor brandished his sliver of broken glass as a dagger. 'Then you mean to murder me, Loki! More than half the mages we turned to Scarred died during the process, and they were trained! You know I have no magick in my veins. Even if I were a mage, the ink and needle would destroy me! Soldiers, seize this traitor—!'

'You have something else in your veins now, Emperor.' Loki presented him with a glass bottle of red liquid. It filled his palm. Black wax sealed its stopper.

'None of our mages ever had *this* to keep them alive. With daemonblood, with your stubbornness, with the sheer determination of entitlement I know burns within you, you can survive.'

Loki flicked open the leather sheaf, baring the slimmest corner of Farden's Book. Just enough to glimpse a flowing line of black runes. Malvus and the unfortunate scribe recoiled. Loki watched them closely. Malvus battled with every fibre of his being not to look, tendons stretching on his neck, eyes white on the corners. The god smirked. He could see the intrigue in the emperor like a hook in a fish's mouth. Yet it would take skill to reel him in.

'And not just one Book. Two, perhaps. Three.'

Malvus stumbled backwards with horror. 'Do you seek to torture me for your own pleasure? This is pure madness! I will not do it.'

Loki stamped his foot. His kin had not blessed him with height but he used his gods-given magick to fill the room with his presence. Shadows crept along the walls. 'Madness is precisely what is needed to defeat Farden! The mage is a brute force that has foiled you every step of your journey. With these Books you can fight him on his own level. Head to head as never before. That is the defeat you always wished for. I dare you to tell me I'm wrong. I saw it on the ice fields.

Saw it in your eyes as you watched your soldiers throw themselves against Farden's walls. That's how Farden dropped your guard the day his steel dragon came out of Scalussen.'

There, Loki paused, examining his trimmed fingernails in the darkness. This world incessantly soiled his hands with its dust and filth.

'Unless, of course, you have a better idea? Or, if you are done with your lust for conquest and revenge, Malvus Barkhart, then this conversation is moot. Let Farden and his ilk disappear into the sunset as they no doubt always wanted. Let Krauslung govern itself. You can build a quiet life here once the ash stops falling and the frost melts. You could till the fields, even. Live out your remaining days until your illness takes you at last. I could provide as much daemon-blood as I—'

'ENOUGH!' Malvus roared.

Loki had cornered him. Now, he had broken him. The god tilt-ed his head as Malvus began to pace forwards and back, left to right. Fear was an emotion of many faces.

'Farden will be no match for you. Nothing will stand in your way. And when you are done, while holding the mage's severed head in your hand, you will show Krauslung you are their true emperor.'

Shaking like a winter pine, Malvus Barkhart sat upon his straw mattress and dragged his shirt from his back. He spoke to the dark corner. 'And if this fails, then you will pay with your life, Loki. Even if I have to come back from Hel to wring your neck.'

The god waved a hand at the Scarred and her prisoner. 'Bring him forwards. No better time to start than now.'

The scribe, whose head had volleyed back and forth as the god and emperor argued, now fought tooth and claw to be free.

'No! No!' he howled, until the Scarred walloped him in the face and singed him with a palmful of fire to keep him quiet.

'Hush now,' Loki soothed the man, stroking his sweat-soaked mop of hair.

'Just kill me now. I'm dead either way!' he threatened.

'Dear me,' Loki pulled a face. His stroke became a grip, not on the man's locks but on the soul within him. His eyes turned up in their sockets as he screamed. Even the Scarred recoiled until Loki had released him.

Loki chuckled as he rode the rush of power. Even the smallest taste of it was intoxicating. *Prayer and adulation be damned.* 'There are many things worse than death, my good man. Worse than what we want from you. This?' From his jacket, he brought rare ink, and a long, slightly curved whalebone needle. 'Take it from me. This is the easy way out.'

The man reached, whimpering, for the needle. Another soul broken.

'Just do it,' Malvus growled from behind them, before smashing the neck from the glass vial of daemonblood. Both it and the blood from his own sliced lips ran down his neck. 'I won't die here. Not like this.'

'That's the spirit.'

Loki closed the door shut behind him and crossed his arms. He smirked. What he did was heresy to both god and human, and he revelled in it. He hoped his fellow gods were looking down, wondering at the shadow he had made of himself, and that they shivered in the cold dark of their void.

# CHAPTER 8
## RIDDLES

*The great ogin once roamed the lands of Golikar and Easterealm. Nobody remembers what killed them, except that the giants vanished during one final battle, west of Dathazh. All that remained of them was their bones and their mighty swords, dug deep into the earth. The bones, of course, were pillaged for trophies and medicines, but the swords remain on their battle-field as if they would curse any that touch them.*
FROM THE DIARY OF TREASURE-HUNTER BALEO THE SQUEAKY,
FOUND UPON HIS CORPSE

If the Dawn God sought to avenge the worshippers in Lilerosk, he was a frail and ineffective deity, defeated by mere clouds.

Fleetstar flew until the earliest hours of day before she set her passengers down upon the mountaintop. It was a scant and feature-less place, an angled dustpan of broken orange shale that crunched underfoot. Not a single tree or shrub dared to grow. Here and there, stone tors and cairns had been erected. Some were huge, looming as ominous shadows between the drifting clouds.

'We'll spend the night before carrying on,' Farden ordered qui-etly, as they stared across the desolate peak with listless energy. There was no wind, thank the gods, but the wet air left dew on their clothes and steel.

The mage set a course for a larger boulder, wind-smoothed like the narrow features of a hawk. He hunkered down behind it where a hollow had been carved between rock and mountain slope, and wait-ed for the others to join him.

'Fleetstar, would you give us some heat?' he asked, gesturing to the pile of shale before them.

The dragon considered him for a moment, almost suspicious in the way she narrowed her great blue eyes. Her turquoise scales looked utterly out of place on the mountainside.

Fleetstar bent her head to a nearby boulder. Flame poured from her pursed lips. The heat of the dragonfire alone drew the others closer and sat them down. After several prolonged breaths, Fleetstar withdrew, chest heaving deeply. The flat boulder glowed, giving off a mild heat that they put their hands to.

With care, Warbringer and Aspala propped Durnus up close to the makeshift fire. The cold flight had withered him somewhat, and it took time for him to come fully awake. Farden and Mithrid handed out several of the supplies they had purchased at the market: dried mutton, good on long roads; sausages meant for proper fires; green-veined cheese; bread that looked stiff as oak and suspiciously full of seeds; hardy beetroots and sour apples; and blue lumps that the merchant had sworn, three times, were potatoes.

Tired and shivering, they dined on dried mutton, the apples, and silence. Uninterested in the food, Warbringer disappeared beyond the great boulder to stand watch and likely quell her hunger or boredom. It was only when Durnus spoke up that the mountainside's quiet was broken.

'How far beyond the Hammer Hills did you say we were?' the vampyre hissed. 'Rivenplains, did you say?'

'Do you need anything, Durnus?' Aspala asked. 'Meat, water?'

'Food turns to ash in my mouth, child, but thank you,' Durnus croaked. 'Unless there is wine? No? Then I shall take a blanket. And that skinny, broad book of mine from my satchel.'

As Aspala found him the book, Farden offered up his cloak and hunched over the vampyre. Within the book was a faded map spread across two pages. It was upside-down to him, but he recognised the edges of his homeland: the claws of the Spit; Emaneska's far-flung eastern border. That was this map's beginning, and Farden barely recognised a single island or shore beyond that. The name of Easterealm was splayed across the opposite side.

'You've had a map this entire time?' the mage shook his head, wondering why he hadn't looked deeper in the satchel.

'Of course I did. One of the few accurate maps of the east. For centuries, Emaneska has largely been content to keep within its own borders. Keep to its own problems. The cartographers of the east seem to be few, illiterate, or eager to overestimate their own countries,' Durnus lectured, wheezing softly. 'An answer to my question if you please, Farden. How far?'

'Two thousand miles from Scalussen, according to Fleetstar.' Farden looked to the dragon. She was still quietly smouldering after the escape from Lilerosk and subsequent scolding by Farden. Apparently, the lambs she had snatched and roasted in mid-air before their shepherds' very eyes had not sated her hunger. Eyrum had always jested about a famished dragon being a dangerous dragon, and Farden saw that anger now in Fleetstar's glowing eyes. It made him feel cold to his gut.

She flashed a row of sharp teeth, speaking as she too disappeared into the haze. 'Five hundred miles past Trollhammerung. Four hundred further than you said you would be, vampyre.'

Farden's head turned so swiftly he hurt his neck. 'And what exactly does she mean by that, Durnus? Did you... Did you plan this?'

The vampyre's pale eyes avoided their eyes, tongue poking at a fang. He closed the map with a sigh.

Mithrid spat out an apple seed. 'You're saying us being here wasn't an accident? I thought it was a problem with the Weight. A lapse in concentration or something.'

'From what I'm hearing, I would wager not,' Farden spoke with jaw clenched. 'You said in the tavern "it worked". What exactly worked, Durnus? Talk quickly.'

With much wincing, Durnus held his scarred hands closer to the fire. 'It was the only way to make you come with me. When Skertrict revealed himself as Loki and snatched your Book, I knew the battle of Scalussen would not be the end of this war.'

Mithrid held up a blade of dried mutton. 'I'm sorry, did you say the scholar Skertrict was Loki?'

'You know that name?' Farden demanded.

'A man named Loki was in Malvus' tent. That's what the emperor called him. Always lingering in the background. And in the battle when you rescued me. He...'

'He what?'

Mithrid just shook her head. She wore a pensive frown. 'But the gods aren't real, are they? I mean, in flesh and bone, at least. I thought they were all up there. Trapped in the sky for two thousand years.' She pointed past the swirling clouds.

Durnus nodded. 'You are mostly correct, Mithrid. Emaneska was once a battleground of fire and ash. God and daemon, human and elf, we fought for tens of thousands of years. That was until the gods sacrificed themselves in one last grand attack, two millennia ago, and dragged the daemons from the world and Hel beneath us into the heavens. That is where most of them now remain, in their towers of shadow and light. Even Gremorin's numbers pale in comparison to the daemons that still stare down at us. The elves, too, though I have come to believe another story, that they were banished forevermore to another plane beyond the fabric of this world, but in any case, Evernia, Njord, Jötun, the Allfather, Thron, they're all up there—'

'The short answer is, yes, they're real, and Loki is a very dangerous specimen.' Farden glared at the girl for causing such a tangent of discussion. 'You were saying, Durnus?'

The vampyre was more concerned with Mithrid's question. He waved his hand feebly at the mage. 'Loki was hiding amongst us in

Scalussen as that stammering scholar all along in an effort to steal a copy of Farden's Book. His tattooed spellbook.'

Farden clenched his teeth so hard his jaw popped. He recalled the battle upon the rooftop in his mind's eye, and Loki's smirking face, aching to have a blade driven through it.

Aspala and Mithrid were trading wary glances. 'A god,' they repeated in chorus. 'In Scalussen?'

'Yes, one that betrayed us in the Last War. A god who fell from the sky. A god who is now in possession of one of the greatest magickal artefacts known to history. With Farden's Book, Loki can—'

'DURNUS!' Farden snapped. 'Answer my question. Come with you *where*?'

'Along the path to victory, King. Or so I hope.' Durnus blinked owlishly. 'Forgive me for my doubt, old friend, but I knew Irminsul would consume you, just as it almost did. I saw the very same thought in your eyes the last we parted. I had already chosen to disobey your orders; to return and use the Weight to save you from yourself. Yet, with Loki's plan revealed, I knew more had to be done than simply surviving to reclaim Krauslung. We need a weapon against him. Not just you. Not just Mithrid. And I knew that unless I forced you, Farden, you would never embark on this journey with me to find it.'

Durnus uttered a rasping cough. He brought the cracked and warped Weight from his nearby satchel and let it fall in the shale. 'I told Fleetstar to join us east of Trollhammerung before we left for Irminsul. But the Weight is dangerous enough without worrying about perfection. We were in the height of battle and I forced too much power into it. Broke it in doing so, unfortunately. But it worked, and despite it being to my detriment, overshooting the Hammer Hills has saved us many days of travelling. The road to finding the Spear of Gunnir will be long and no doubt arduous.'

'The what?' Mithrid piped up again.

Farden tilted his head while the words fell into place. 'That fucking *spear*, Durnus?! That is why you brought us here?'

Durnus was trying to dig another book from his satchel, but his raw hands proved too painful. Aspala set to helping him.

'If the accounts I've found are true, then it could be the weapon capable of defeating Loki. It is a spear of great power, made by the ancient elven clan of Ivald. A clan of fabled smiths. It is said to have been able to carve the peaks from mountains, that it shines with the light of a sun.'

Farden was not done. 'But "if" is not good enough, Durnus! You've forced me to abandon the rest of Scalussen in the time they need me most, based on a bloody hunch you found in one book! An elvish book, no less!'

'Speed is of the utmost importance, Farden. We cannot wait for Loki to act. He was two steps ahead of us in Scalussen. We are now ahead of him. What Elessi and the others need most is for you to seek out the spear.'

Farden's mouth hung slack. 'In all the decades I've known you and that vast mind between those pointed ears of yours, I've never once thought you a fool. This moment right here, Durnus? This is a first for me.'

'Your doubt is astoundingly blind, mage. Fool, you call me? I have researched the Spear Gunnir thoroughly. I believe it is no myth, but history, the same as the armour of the Knights of the Nine. How many times did people scorn you for believing in its power? Your uncle and I included?'

'Don't talk about my armour.'

As if Durnus noticed for the first time, his eyes examined the charred marks and scars across the mage's armour. He reached to touch it, but Farden deflected his hand.

'What has happened?'

'Irminsul's fire is what happened, Durnus,' he snapped. He had no wish to speak of his armour now. Nor his magick. Nothing but the cursed spear. He remained stubbornly silent.

'Here, General,' Aspala said, assisting Durnus further upright.

'You do not have to call me that, madam. We are not in Scalussen any more.'

'Thanks to you,' muttered Farden.

Durnus looked around, fang over one lip and eyes twitching. 'Do you all... Have I offended you in some way?'

Mithrid shook her head. 'If being here can help kill Malvus as well as this Loki, I don't see the problem.'

Farden found himself snarling. 'Because you don't understand, Mithrid. This is beyond you.'

'So was magick and war when I first arrived in Scalussen. Look how that turned out.' Mithrid might have shrugged, but there was a dangerous glint in her eyes. Her scarlet hair billowed like a fire around her stern face. 'You aren't the only one who wants to get back to Emaneska. I miss and fear for the others just the same as you. Same as Warbringer. Same as Durnus. And the fact that Malvus survived burns in my heart, too. I haven't given up on my revenge. Somehow, I want it all the more. If there's a weapon that can kill both him and Loki, who you all say is worse, then what's wrong with finding it?'

Farden stood. He fought to keep his finger from thrusting in the vampyre's face. 'Because,' he whispered, 'if I remember correctly, the idea of the spear was first raised to us by Scholar Skertrict. Wasn't he the one who told you to look deeper into that elvish book? Or am I wrong about that, old friend?'

As expected, Durnus took some time to answer. 'Yes, he was.'

'So if Skertrict was Loki in disguise, then surely it's *Loki* that wants us to find that spear. This is no more than another of his lies. He conned you into coming here, thinking we'd be desperate enough to try once Malvus closed his noose. It is a trick, and you've fallen for it. If I were you, Durnus, I would forget about the spear and concentrate on finding us a way back to Elessi and the others.'

Shale broke under Farden's boots as he sought the silence of the drifting mist. To be alone with his dismay and frustration. In his mind, Loki had just landed yet another punch to Farden's gut.

❦

Durnus stared at the whorl of mist where Farden had vanished. Mithrid flicked a tongue around her teeth as she watched the vampyre. His shoulders slumped, dejected. His raw hands rested on the spines of the book in his satchel.

'He hasn't been himself since we came here,' Mithrid tried to explain.

'How long have I been unconscious?'

Aspala answered between chattering teeth. She looked interminably cold. 'Four days, perhaps five. Warbringer carried you most of the way. There was a forest that tried to eat us. Religious bandits. Lots of sheep. It has been a strange time.'

'Farden gave you some of his blood,' added Mithrid. 'Seemed to wake you up.'

Durnus' red eyes stretched wide. 'With the magick in his blood, I do not think that was wise, but I am grateful. Did I hurt any of you? Weight magick is not the most accurate. And in the pressure of the fire—'

'We're all fine. It is simply hard being lost,' Mithrid said.

Durnus patted his tomes. 'I have a path, young madam. You need not worry.'

But Mithrid did. The name of Loki was an echo in her mind that refused to die. She watched Aspala help Durnus to his feet. The old vampyre seemed set on following the mage. He tottered something awful without his walking stick, but he managed to stay upright even though Aspala followed him with arms spread and ready to catch him.

As the vampyre left, the minotaur rejoined them. She had found a handful of some purple tuber with tough leaves, and a kind of snake that had armour like the shale around them. Though Aspala nodded appreciatively, having the appetite of a hound and a stomach for inedible items to match, Mithrid wrinkled her lip.

'Where is mage and vampyre?' asked Warbringer. She placed the snake down on the hot rock, still roasting from the dragonfire. Mercifully she had already beheaded it.

'Talking somewhere. Hopefully not killing each other.'

The minotaur crouched in the shale. Voidaran she laid before her. Her stubby claws traced its runed surface fondly. 'Talk is useful,' she said. 'Many Warbringers that come before me do not realise this. There is battle in talk. Too much talk, however, is waste. We must move soon. Wind changing.'

The presence of the giant minotaur was calming, much like the presence of the dragons Mithrid had grown used to in the Frostsoar's eyries. A presence that could crush any enemy that could wander from the mist.

Mithrid felt exhaustion weighing heavy on her, but a lone thought kept her from falling into sleep. Aspala and Warbringer exhibited the same tiredness, but they were too entranced by the sizzling snake. It was hissing as if still alive. Aspala poked at it with her broken sword.

'Doesn't look poisonous, Mithrid. Don't worry,' Aspala assured her, noticing her furrowed brow.

'It's not that,' Mithrid answered, looking over her shoulder for Farden and Durnus. The vampyre had also disappeared from view.

'What is it then, girl?' Warbringer asked. Mithrid found it hard to escape the minotaur's eyes. Dark brown, almost black, but ringed and flecked with a blood red. Hot air drifted from the creature's nostrils.

Mithrid shook herself, realising she was staring at Warbringer without answering. 'You know the god they were talking about?'

'Loki.'

'He saved my life.'

Warbringer and Aspala stared at each other for a moment. The latter spoke first.

'When?'

'In the battle to save you and I, and Bull. When Farden tricked Malvus. Littlest came at me with a knife. She caught me off guard. I was on my back, helpless, when Loki appeared.'

'What did he do?'

'He dropped a knife on my chest, did this,' Mithrid put a finger to her lips, 'and disappeared.'

The mood was uneasy.

Aspala thumbed the healing stubs of her smashed horns. 'Why save his enemy?'

'Because he not your enemy,' Warbringer suggested.

'Malvus wanted me alive for his own purposes,' Mithrid said. 'But if what Farden said is correct, Loki doesn't serve Malvus. Maybe the opposite.'

'Which still makes him our enemy,' Aspala muttered.

Mithrid wanted to speak up but knew better than to argue. It wasn't the god who had dispatched the Arka mages to her Trough-wake door. Malvus was that man. The fact that Loki meant evil was a fact passed along by hearsay. At least for the time being. It was that uncertainty that befuddled her.

'Are you doubting Farden?' asked the Paraian.

'No,' Mithrid said, shocked. 'I don't doubt his hatred for the god. Just Loki's intentions. To be honest, I'm still struggling to be-lieve gods exist in the flesh.'

'If they're flesh, they can be killed,' Warbringer replied.

Aspala shuffled closer, conspiratorial. 'Where is that knife now?'

Mithrid had barely thought about it until recently. She had tucked it into the folds of her cloak the day she returned to Scalussen.

She still had it strapped to her armour, and held out its curving silver blade. Its gold and filigree handle shone even with no sun.

Warbringer's big fingers grazed Mithrid's palm, still dusty from digging in the shale. She took the knife, examined it for a moment, and promptly hurled it into the fog. Mithrid was horrified to think how far it must have flown. She started after it, but the minotaur seized her wrist to the point of pain.

'Leave it, pink-flesh. It is gift from a god you want no gift from.'

The words sounded ominous. 'What does that mean?' asked Mithrid, cautious.

'Do not accept it. Leave it behind. It has power to it. An evil I can feel.'

Mithrid wanted to scoff. She had felt nothing in the knife, but her memories told her to mind the sensations of magick. Even those that were imperceptible to her. She bit her tongue once more.

'I would not tell Farden,' advised Aspala. 'At least not yet. That mage has too much on his mind at the moment.'

Mithrid nodded, letting her head rest on her arms as she scanned the mountainside. The rock was losing heat, but Warbringer had decided the snake was ready. Mithrid shook her head when it was offered, and listened to the crunch of tough skin and bones around her while she pondered what a god would want with her.

With a stumble, Durnus accidentally drove a fang into his lip and cursed. He tasted his own blood, and with a wince he opened up a dozen others across his mouth and face. Only twice in his millennia-long life had he felt such weakness and pain. Every bone felt bruised. Every muscle stabbed with needles. Every step across the tilted landscape a wobbling, uneasy placing of the foot.

'I can hear you coming, old man.'

Durnus struggled to make the mage out. There was a certain presence along the slope, a line of shadow that he headed towards.

'How the tables have turned. It is I sneaking up on you for a change.'

Farden didn't reply. Durnus saw the shadow hunch.

The mage was perched on a chunk of rock that had a hollow rift cut down its length. Even in the gloom and mist, the innards of the rock glistened with the prickly clusters of purple gems. Amethyst, if Durnus identified correctly.

'I am not angry with you,' Farden said, beating him to speaking. 'I am shocked. Disappointed at the risk you've taken.'

'Do not pull that trick with me, mage. That guilt is how I kept you in line for decades.' Durnus collapsed against the rock and dragged himself to where Farden sat. 'I hear you gave me blood.'

'I did. Wondering whether I should regret that now.'

'Hmm.' Durnus kept a distance from the mage. 'It has barely scratched the surface of healing me. Roused me and nothing but. Something is amiss.'

'Do we need to find you some unwitting shepherd or prisoner to feed on?'

A wash of concern ran through Durnus' innards. He was reminded of the prisoner within the Frostsoar, and the soul he had accidentally dragged out of her. More so, the energy that it had fed him, whether he wanted it or not. Like his death magick, it had called to him ever since, begging to be explored like an unread tome. And it had called with a daemon's voice. The half of his ancestry he had thought buried in the vampyre's curse.

'That may help,' Durnus confessed. 'But what of your armour? And do not think I have not noticed the absence of your magick. What has happened?'

'I don't know. Perhaps Mithrid's magick.' Farden glared at him.

'But without the magick in your armour, you'll—'

'Begin to age? Die? I know that all too well. It's already start-ed. But I told you: not now, Durnus. I can't cope with any more than being here and your damn spear. Your betrayal.'

'Is that what you think of me?'

It took the mage far too long to answer. 'No.'

'I did this to help us. Especially after Loki played his hand atop the Frostsoar.'

'That's what he wants you to think. You didn't ever spend time with him. That god is not the god of the first light and the morning star, as the other gods say. He is the god of trickery and lies. Every-thing he does is for himself.' Farden sighed. 'Are you not worried why Loki wants us apart from Elessi and the others? Or what he and Malvus will do with them while we're stuck here?'

'Do you doubt yourself, Farden? You speak as if Loki has al-ready beaten you,' Durnus implored. 'Skertrict—Loki—was obsessed with the spear. He hounded me constantly, which might suggest he cannot reach it himself, or he would have done so already. He needs us to find it. And let us say we do? Is it not better to have the spear in our possession than Loki's? Surely we could secure such a weapon—'

'If it exists, which makes this all conjecture.'

'Yes, *if* it exists, Farden,' Durnus snapped. He knew how to fight the mage's obstinance. 'Consider how long would it take to travel back to Emaneska with or without Fleetstar. We are closer to the spear.'

'How do you know?'

Durnus pointed into the mist, already confused as to where he had come from. 'As I told you in the Frostsoar, the elvish tome sug-gests to us that the Spear of Gunnir was never hidden in Emaneska but far to the east. That is why I planned to start at the Hammer Hills, where the map begins.'

'There is an actual map to the spear? You never mentioned that.'

'Well, not so much a map as a set of instructions.'

'Instructions?'

'Well, riddles.'

'Oh, good. Riddles.'

'A riddle. Only one, to be precise.'

Farden fixed him with pleading eyes. 'Can you promise me you aren't wrong?'

Durnus thought about it, second-guessing every moment of Skertrict in his presence, every word the god-imposter had uttered. 'No,' he said. 'I cannot. But as I have already said, the god wants this spear. If we can turn it against him…'

'Enough,' Farden said. 'I am no king here. I will bow to my council. Even if that is a minotaur, two people I've only known for months, and you.'

Durnus was pleasantly – if not bewilderingly – surprised. 'Really?'

'It's not just me that's stranded here.'

Durnus was caught staring. Farden looked offended.

'What? I'm old and wise enough to understand this isn't just my decision.'

'Then you've never been more kingly, Farden, old friend.'

'You misunderstand. When I make decisions people seem to die. Krauslung, decades ago. Kserak. Now Scalussen. You were right, Durnus. I chose the siege.'

'And from what we know, you also not only defeated Malvus but saved half of Scalussen.'

Farden didn't answer. They sat in silence. Durnus shivered beneath his blanket. He tensed his weary muscles for warmth, only to find pain shoot across his body.

'Modren sacrificed himself to save the others. He made his decision. His death was not your fault, Farden. We all chose war. We chose to make a stand. Perhaps it was not the wrong decision, but it simply did not work as expected because of Loki's interference.'

It was hard to see beneath the tendrils of his dark hair, but Durnus saw the moisture that brimmed upon Farden's eyes.

'Both that god and Gremorin owe me a death.' Farden seemed to catch himself, stiffening suddenly and knuckling his eyes. 'And as for you, Durnus, you still have a lot to make up for.'

Without another word, the mage got up and tramped back into the mist. Durnus did his best to follow him at his own speed, but the mage was too fast. The vampyre seethed at the ache in his bones. He felt as frail as dry parchment and just as thin. Hollow. The copper residue of blood lingered in his throat, but it did not stir his hunger.

By the time Durnus returned to their makeshift camp, Farden was already standing over the rock, with the others in concert spread around him. Fleetstar had rejoined them. Barely. She sat upon the edge of the rough camp, barely visible and somewhat terrifying to the uninitiated.

'I'm not going to order anyone to do anything or go anywhere. You may decide for yourselves,' Farden announced. 'Durnus believes in this fabled spear. Apparently, so does Loki, and it appears we may be closer to it than Emaneska. If Durnus is right, this is a powerful weapon, and possibly why that blasted god wants us to find it. If we could keep it from Loki: a god who can change shape and flit where he pleases, we could destroy him. If this sounds to you like madness, as it does to me, then we will return to Emaneska, either by foot or by dragon, depending on what Fleetstar decides.'

The dragon rumbled, eyes closed as if bored.

'Those are your options. Back to the mess I made of Emaneska and our friends, who may be in need of our help. Or deeper east, into unknown and frankly bizarre territory, in search of a weapon that may or may not exist.'

Farden's armour clanged as he let his hands fall by his sides. He leaned against the tall rock and angled his face to the breeze. Faint yellow sky, full of mountain dust, began to show through tears in the clouds.

Durnus spoke up, wincing at the creak in his voice. 'I vote for the spear.'

'Of course you do. Aspala?'

The woman's golden eyes were fixed on the mage's. 'I came to Scalussen because I vowed to fight the Arka. That task is not yet done, and so I shall remain fighting beside its king until it is.'

That appeared to nettle Farden but he nodded all the same. 'Warbringer?'

'You and girl helped save last clan in Efjar. You gave us fine war. Fine deaths like you promised. Those of my clan who not reach Bright Fields now safe on your ships. Clan survive your fire. Now, when Warbringer return, we take back Efjar.'

'So that's a vote for Emaneska.'

'No,' replied the minotaur gruffly.

Farden scratched his head. 'What?'

'Not finished. I trust my bloodmongers and silver-hair general to keep clan safe until their Warbringer return. But I owe vampyre life debt for saving skin. If enemies still exist, like this pink-flesh god, then I follow Durnus to god's death. Or vampyre's. Whichever first.' She shrugged her great shoulders. 'Spear sound like fine weapon. Fine fight. So speaks the Broken Promise, Katiheridrade.'

'Two for the spear, then.'

'Mithrid?'

She held a piece of brown shale in her fingers and picked the flakes from its edges. 'I've been torn over this question. I worry for Hereni and Bull and the others. The strange lands out there worry me, I'll admit. Being lost does not sit well with me. But Malvus isn't dead yet, like I said before. That's what I promised myself and my father, and that's the simple fact of the matter,' she growled. 'I don't know about Loki's hand in all of this, but I vote we search for the spear. Especially if it gives us the chance to kill whatever we need to.'

Durnus clenched his teeth. He remembered his first meeting with the girl, the day she had passed out in the testing lines. She had been lost before Modren found her, and she had stayed lost for many weeks before she had found her place in the world. That place had just so happened to be one of war and death, and it had changed her deeply. He now looked upon a different girl – a woman – one defined by vengeful purpose. Brazenly confident, yet blinkered, he feared. Blinkered by the fact she knew she was a weapon. And all weapons have a purpose until there is no more blood to spill. It reminded him too much of a certain young mage he had first met long ago; the mage nodding slowly beside him. Durnus had yet to decide whether that was a good thing.

'Three for the spear,' Farden said quietly. 'Fleetstar, you want a say in this?'

The dragon bowed her head. With the clearing cloud, they could see the edges of her wings, held high and proud as if she rode air currents. 'You are all fools if you think I can – or will – carry you back to Emaneska. We go forwards, not backwards.'

The reply was brief, abrasive as usual, and yet decidedly in favour against Farden. The Mad Dragon had spoken.

Though the mathematics were simple, the mage took his time in deciding. 'So it shall be. It is decided. We go for the spear. Not Emaneska.'

Mithrid's shoulders sagged. 'Feels good to have purpose at last.'

Farden grumbled something that didn't sound remotely agreeable. 'Where to then, Durnus? Where does this strange map of yours say the Spear of Gunnir is?'

'There's a map to the spear?' Mithrid asked.

'Not a map,' Durnus admitted. 'A riddle. A poem, if you will, but it is the key to uncovering the spear.'

With Aspala's help, Durnus slid down the rock next to his satchel, and dug out the Grimsayer to reach other tomes. The vampyre swore he heard a mutter from the book as he thumped it unceremoniously on the slope.

With shaking, weak hands, he dug out the other volumes he had saved from his library. First came a book covered in bands of copper and leather.

Farden was abruptly at his side. 'You have the inkweld, too?'

'I do.'

Farden opened it feverishly, showing off green pages. 'Give me ink,' he demanded.

'I have none.'

The mage stared at the empty pages. Nothing broke their virgin paper. Inkwelds only worked if both twin books were open at the same moment. Timing was of high importance. Farden snarled, performing an angry circuit of the rock before making peace with another disappointment. He brooded over tightly crossed arms. The vampyre felt completely to blame.

'More magicking?' Warbringer asked, snout creased in a grimace.

Mithrid and Aspala looked remarkably more curious than the minotaur's judgemental expression.

Durnus explained. 'It is a way to speak to Elessi and the armada, and your clan, Warbringer. Each book is part of a pair. A twin. This book should still have its sibling aboard the *Winter's Revenge* or *Autumn's Vanguard.*'

'The riddle, Durnus.'

Durnus produced the elvish tome, a purple, moth-eaten block of ancient pages. Suspicious eyes graced it as he laid it on the shale. The elvish runes within swam before his tired eyes, but with much blinking and the help of his scarred fingertips, he traced page after page until he tracked down the words.

'This book was written almost two thousand years ago, at the dawn of the Scattered Kingdoms: the darkened ages before our civilisations emerged, when the stars were new and Emaneska still reeled from the last war between gods, dark elves, and daemons. The book's language is old, a strange dialect of elvish runes written not by elves, but by servants of the Allfather. Cultists, you might say. It is largely a chronicle of the times, but there is one story hidden within that says the cult was entrusted with hiding a powerful weapon from the greed of flourishing humanity.' Durnus showed off the rough sketch of the spear in the book. 'They call it the Teh'Mani Spear, which translates to Skyrender, or God-Corpser, or just Gunnir, depending on the translation. The cultists went to every length to smother every trace of its existence. All the cult left behind was this tome, which holds – hidden amongst histories of the elves, and the clan of Ivald – one clue of its final location: several short lines of a riddle signed simply, "Doom".'

'Then out with it,' said Farden.

'*Three tasks every god and mortal fears to face await. Three duties yet fulfilled of blood, breath, mind, and soul. Three cursed keys to three doors to be left locked evermore. If that be your fate, your errand, the first task lies in Eaglehold's roots before the serpent's shimmer, by Gunnir's last blood. Hear the last breath of retribution's lesson. Follow its call to your screaming end.*'

The silence was palpable.

'That's it?' Fleetstar snorted. Her scales flushed a sandy red in an echo of the emerging sky. Durnus wished he could fade into the rock at his back as easily as the dragon.

'Gunnir is the spear. And the spear's last blood suggests Sigrimur. It is the only part of the riddle I understand so far,' he said.

'Who?'

'Sigrimur was a figure of the early world,' he explained. 'I have found conflicting stories of him in my research. Most paint him as a chosen hero of the gods, a precursor to the Knights of the Nine. Others, a murderer. When the gods sacrificed themselves to drag the daemons into the sky, they chose a noble-hearted mortal to protect humanity in the dark years before the Scattered Kingdoms. Sigrimur was that hero. He was gifted the Spear of Gunnir by the Allfather, who had claimed it from the clan of Ivald in the last and final war of gods and daemons. There are many tales of Sigrimur's deeds hunting down creatures and elves that escaped the gods' justice. According to the eastern eddas, however, Sigrimur fell to his own pride and betrayed the Allfather, who then killed him with Gunnir. It was lost from the world shortly after, hidden by the cultists at the behest of their god. If Sigrimur was the spear's last blood, we might need to find where he died.' Durnus poked at his map of the east. 'Eaglehold is not mentioned here, but the Sunder Road leads on further east to a land called Golikar. We should head in that direction.'

'Three tasks, three keys, three doors,' Farden muttered. 'Seems straightforward to me. We just find somewhere called Eaglehold, a shiny serpent, and some dead fuck named Sigrimur.' Seizing the inkweld from the earth, he began to climb at a parallel angle to the summit. Shale tumbled from around his boots.

'Now?' Mithrid shouted. 'Shouldn't we rest?'

'Mithrid's correct, Farden.'

'No, she's not, Durnus,' Farden called over his shoulder. 'You rest if you wish. But the cloud's wasting and we'll soon be exposed. We can get off this mountain by sundown. Find the Sunder Road and follow it east before trouble catches up with us.'

'It's highly irritating when he has a point,' said Mithrid, dragging herself to her feet.

Even with Aspala carrying his satchel, Durnus was soon reduced to a shuffling heap. He found the rough paws of the minotaur under his ribs. He tried to push her away.

'Madam! I do not need you—'

'Grey-skin need to stop whining. Five days I already carry you. One more not matter.'

'Hmph.' His complaints trampled beneath her hooves, Durnus found himself carried to the ridge of the mountain in the most dignified of manners: as limp as a sack of flour under Warbringer's uniquely pungent armpit. And yet, even that exhausted him. He felt like a shadow before the rise of dawn, soon to be burned away.

It soon became apparent that Farden was nowhere to be seen. While Durnus would never, for a moment, believe the mage would abandon them, the suspicion did slink across his mind. The lower cloud had burned away, but nearer the ridge a canopy of vapour enveloped them.

The vampyre called out. 'Where has he gone?'

'Bloody vanished.'

Mithrid was just cupping her hands to her mouth when a hooded figure appeared amongst them.

Farden seized Mithrid's wrist and motioned for her to be silent. Taking the finger from his lips, he pointed ahead, to where the ridge knifed away into the half-lit murk of cloud. Had they paid no heed whatsoever, any one of them might have gone tumbling down the severe drop.

'What in Hel are you doing?'

'It's called scouting ahead, Mithrid,' Farden whispered. 'Keep your voices down and wait for a gap in the cloud. You'll see. Down there.'

The others hunkered down around him. Though his eyes ached with the light, Durnus stared hard and waited.

It did not take long for an updraft to blow the cloud aside momentarily. Long enough for Durnus to see a swathe of rubble leading to some sort of quarry. Littering the slopes below were conical tents of leather and bright yellow and blue furs. They battled for space between pens stuffed with cows. Figures sat around camp and cook-fires, scythes or spears piled around them. Though far below, they were close enough that Durnus could make out the glitter of silver and copper jewellery, and count the tangles of elaborately matted and braided beards.

'These again,' Aspala sighed.

'Thought I caught the scent of campfires a while back. I thought this would be a quick way down the mountainside. We could have stumbled across each other far too easily.'

'That wouldn't have been a friendly meeting.'

Durnus interjected. 'Clearly I missed something while I was unconscious. Who are they?'

'We crossed paths with these folks before. Call themselves Cathak. Servants of a so-called Dusk God, apparently. We interrupted one of their sacrificial rituals a short while ago. They weren't pleased.'

'Why do I get the feeling that means you have killed some of them?'

'They demanded a toll. We disagreed.'

'Only you could insult the local populace so quickly and thoroughly, Farden.'

Farden shot him a dark look. 'None of this is my fault,' he hissed.

Faint but harsh laughter ricocheted up the slope to their ears. If Durnus squinted, he could make out four-legged creatures in smaller wooden pens. They were the size of hay bales, sprouting fur between leathery, ochre scale, as though a goat had relations with a lizard. Their backs were ridged with stubby spines running down to short tails.

'What in Emanes—what are they?'

'They look delicious,' Warbringer whispered. The sound of fangs grinding from behind them suggested the dragon agreed.

'We'll take a longer path north along this ridge until we're out of their territory,' ordered Farden gruffly. 'No point getting ourselves into scrapes we can't afford to get into. There must be several hundred down there. And Fleetstar…?'

Hunkered down, it was rather difficult to make out where the dragon's scales ended and the mountainside began. 'Mage?'

'Not a claw out of line. The rest of you keep quiet and watch your footing.'

Farden made it one step before they heard the faint echo of voices. They were smothered by cloud and breeze, but approaching, clear enough. 'Curse it!' he hissed.

The vampyre crouched down and almost stumbled flat onto his face. The mage ignored him and looked between the others instead. His teeth were bared in frustration. Weapons had been drawn. 'Too risky,' he was muttering.

Durnus put a hand on the mage's vambraces, confused as to his hesitation. 'Can't you hide us with a spell, Farden?'

'Come here, fools,' Fleetstar growled.

The sky turned dark as the dragon's wing swept over them, clouting Warbringer in the horns in the process. Under the scaly canopy, they scuttled and slid into a clump down from the ridge, and let the cold skin of the dragon envelop them. Durnus watched Fleetstar's turquoise colours fade, not as changeling as Shivertread's scaleshifter powers, but a pale grey that was enough to blend with the thick cloud at a distance. A thin strand of light crept under the edge of her wing, and Durnus crawled towards it.

'Stay still,' whispered the dragon before she sucked in a great breath.

The scent of the winged reptile was somewhat overwhelming when one was squashed flat under their very wing, but still not as unsettling as Warbringer's musk. Durnus endured, took in a lungful of air, and with the others, waited pensively for the interlopers to pass.

The voices were barely audible over the crunch of rock.

'I'm keeping it.'

'Tisn't for you to decide!'

'It is so!'

The footsteps drew nearer. Durnus angled his head to the shale, glimpsing beyond their hiding place. One figure could be seen between the haze. A coat of yellow and blue furs dressed him from head to toe. A mask shaped like a picked skull hung at his neck. The rest of his face was beard and pox-scar. He was busy prodding himself in the chest with assured confidence. In his other hand was clutched a knife of silver and gold. A fine piece of weaponry for a man wearing skins and holes in his boots.

Another figure in similar furs trailed after him. Fortunately, they were far too deep into an argument to notice the lump of grey dragon not a stone's throw away.

'The Dusk God gave it to *me*,' the bearded man was complaining. 'Fell right from the sky at my feet, did it not?'

'At the first light of dawn, you heretic! Tis no gift but a curse of the Dawn God. The High Cathak must see it.'

'You are wrong. A storm brought it, perhaps. Dropped by a magpie. Perhaps that fire-breathing beast—'

'Don't! Speaking of it will draw it near.'

Curious gazes spread beneath the gloom of Fleetstar's wing. Mithrid held her axe tightly and bit her lip. Warbringer looked ready to explode into the light. To the sounds of crunching feet, Durnus saw the boot of the second man tread closer to Fleetstar. Dusty, ragged trails of furs dangled in view. His voice was far too loud.

'Look at it. That is no Golikan smithing. That is rich silver. Gold of the Burnt South. A strange knife falls out of the clouds days after foreigners emerge from the Bronzewood. Dire omens!'

The second closed the gap on the bearded fellow. 'You give it up, you hear?'

'You'll do no such thing. It is my knife. I will tell the High Cathak myself.'

'I don't trust you. Give it, Durlok. You've got no business with it.'

You're a damn thief! Back away!' Durlok slashed the air with the knife as the other fought to get close.

'What's gotten into you, man? Give it here!'

The second Cathak retched as Durlok stabbed him high in the chest. Shale sprayed as their feet tangled. Durlok stabbed again and again until his face was spattered with blood.

'You...' The man's last words went unfinished as he teetered backwards. Wide-eyed with shock, Durlok gave up the knife at last, leaving it in his friend's throat.

Durnus tensed as the body came toppling onto Fleetstar's wing.

The Cathak might have been in a daze, but not enough for him to ignore the strange colour and bend of the rock beneath the corpse, and, at last, the wing of a dragon pressed against the shale.

'What by Dusk?' he spluttered. He recoiled, bloody hands raised, and shuffled precipitously close to the edge of the ridge.

'He has seen us!' Durnus warned.

'Fuck it!' Farden hissed.

Daylight flooded their hiding place as Fleetstar's wing retracted.

'Grab him!'

Farden's call went unheeded. The dragon swung her tail like a whip; a whip that weighed as much as a wagon for all the muscle and strength Fleetstar put into it. The crack of ribs and sternum was audible as the tail collided with the man's chest. He did not fall. He *flew*.

Instead of tumbling down the cliff to horrid injuries, he soared outwards from the mountaintop like a slingstone. The piercing pitch of his wail fell with him as his body disappeared into the clouds, no doubt to land somewhere highly inconvenient below.

'Curse it, Fleetstar! Why did you do that?' Farden raged. 'We could have done that quietly.'

The dragon shrugged her giant shoulders. 'He was already falling. Might have survived and told the rest of his clan about us.'

On the wind came a rising and incredulous roar from the Cathak camp somewhere below. Durnus could not see where exactly the body had landed, but he bet it was somewhere inconvenient.

Farden pointed down the slope. 'I think they might have some clue now!'

Warbringer slammed her hammer against the shale. 'He did fly pretty well for a two-legged pink-flesh.'

Farden pressed his fingers into his forehead. At first, Durnus thought he was cursing them all beneath his breath. It took some time to realise he was chuckling. It was a dry laugh: an exasperated surrender to the dark comedy of the situation.

'That he did,' Farden said as he shook his head, prompting the minotaur and Aspala to begin laughing aloud. Mithrid joined. Fleetstar bared teeth and belched smoke. Even Durnus cracked a weak smile. It was a brief medicine, but much in need. Their path felt like a pit of gnashing teeth for all the uncertainty it held. To find mirth built a bridge, however frail and brief, across it. How better to dull the gloom of dire predicaments, lest one submit and lose themselves to them. Upon that shattered mountainside, they remembered themselves and their humanity.

Farden dragged the strange, ornate knife from the dead body. He whipped the blood on the corpse's furs, spun it in his hand, and put it through his belt. Durnus caught Mithrid and Aspala exchanging curious glances, but no words came.

Hood already up and boots forging a path down the western slope, Farden ordered their departure. 'We'd best make ourselves scarce. This mountain will be swarming in no time.'

The others needed no encouragement. Fleetstar took to the air and disappeared into the whorls of cloud. Only Durnus trailed behind. Warbringer hovered momentarily to offer help, but he waved her on.

'As you please,' she grunted.

With the horns of the Cathak beginning to fill his ears, Durnus stood by the corpse. Although his fangs and the animal within him ached to feed, it was not the blood still seeping from the man that lured him, but rather the persistent thought of the prisoner in

Scalussen. The memory of her soul seeping into his veins in place of blood. The lingering charm of the power that had suffused him.

Even now, he felt the soul lingering behind dead flesh. It called to him. He extended a trembling hand, sharp nails crooked and bent. Before he knew it, his hand was inches above the man's bloody chest. Faint blue vapour emerged from his furs, chased by another wind than the one that blew across the ridge. Durnus felt its icy touch permeate his fingers. He went rigid as power seized him.

'Durnus!' came the shout.

He opened his eyes, snatched his hand back, and stood there quivering. Blue vapour trailed from his fangs. He could not ignore the fresh and unusual strength burning in his limbs. It felt far more furious than the effects of mortal blood he was used to. It was more intoxicating than before in Scalussen. He was barely healed, but at least now he could take a step without wanting to crumble into the dirt.

'Durnus!'

He could make out the rough shape of Farden in the cloud. 'Coming! Slowly but surely!' he yelled back.

Overwhelming repugnance brought a sweat to his cold skin as he made his way down the slope. There was only one creature in the lands that drank upon souls in such a way.

*Daemons.*

# CHAPTER 9
## DEEPER EAST

*Thieves, the lot of them. The Golikans learned their trade from the Destrix to the east. Scruples do not exist in these lands, but thieves, con-artists, and liars there are aplenty.*

OVERHEARD IN THE SPOKE TAVERN

The scramble from the mountaintop was completed with little grace and even more haste.

The horns of the enraged Cathak chased them all the way, thankfully growing fainter with every step.

Below the clouds, the survivors of Scalussen found a sloping wasteland of broken rock and timid grass peeking through the rubble. Their legs thrashed it aside as they ran north. Immovable boulders the size of small cottages made them swerve this way and that.

Trying to spit but lacking the moisture, Mithrid slogged on across the vexatious ground. Three times now, she had almost snapped an ankle in the dreaded shale. She wished Fleetstar hadn't disappeared; she had a powerful desire to be carried at the moment.

It had only been hours, but Mithrid was already exhausted. The brief respite she had gained in Lilerosk had all but disappeared. Her muscles were aflame, her joints hot coals. She stared at the mage ahead, wondering how in Hel he kept going in his injured, weakened state. His steps were dogged and stiff, like those of the dead Durnus had animated. That memory never failed to drive a cold shiver down her spine.

By midday the clouds had drawn back, leaving faint trails across a sky suspiciously tinged with pink and yellow in the west.

'Smoke,' Farden uttered.

Aspala was not convinced. 'Ash from Irminsul, perhaps.'

Warbringer did not stop long to look. 'Strange lands. Stranger skies.'

Durnus had nothing to say on the matter. In fact, now that Mithrid considered it, the vampyre hadn't said a word and had managed to keep up for most of the escape, but now he struggled most of all. For some reason, he refused Warbringer's help, flinching away from her touch.

Mithrid shielded herself from the sun with a hand. Though they were beyond the mountain slopes and halfway around the northern side of the range, they still stood upon their shoulder. The rolling grasslands were below them. From their height, she could see for leagues upon leagues. Mithrid looked west for the first time. She could see faint flocks and herds in the distance, moving like cloud-shadows. Further, plains of grass and earth, spreading to a silver streak of distant water, spearing the thirsty land. Dark mountains formed the very edges of their world, filling the far north and west. Darker clouds hung above them. Colossal, sweeping anvils of charcoal and yellow that had conquered a sizeable portion of the sky.

'And I did that,' Mithrid muttered to herself.

Before she turned away, she caught another cry of a horn, so faint as to be a whisper. She scanned the mountains behind them. They had already put twenty miles between them and the ridge. There was not a scrap of blue and yellow fur to be seen. She put her worry to the back of her mind.

As Mithrid's feet longed for grass and soil instead of bothersome rock, Farden had quite literally stumbled upon a road. An old road, unkempt, polluted by grass and occasional litter, but a road, nonetheless. They followed its path around the northernmost tip of the mountains to a broad, flat table of sandy rock. The pass between the scrub mountains was broad. Ochre grassland surged through it like a river bursting a dam. Their path pressed down and north, cutting across a broad road of dirt and primitive flagstones. The Sunder Road, no doubt. It forged east to an impressive mountain that notched the horizon.

However, it was not the views of sweeping golden lands that stunned them, nor the mountain, but the sword that stood standing on the edge of the plateau.

Ancient, rusted red and weathered black, it stood as a cold and colossal silhouette against the sky, with its point buried and pommel to the heavens. Whomever once wielded it – if that were even possible – would have regarded even Warbringer as nothing more than a pest. Mithrid had to crane her neck to take it in. Its crossbar alone would have made a fine spear.

Long moments passed before she realised it was not the only one. Beyond the plateau, where the earth plunged down into grassland, a veritable forest of the giant swords stood silently along the old path. Some of them spread east along the wide road. There were hundreds, perhaps thousands of them.

Mithrid approached the nearest sword slowly. She dug a fingernail into its blade, weathered beyond bluntness. Flakes of rust came away in her palm and stained her pale skin orange. The blade was so old even the graffiti carved into it had been lost to weather. She felt no magick in them. Just a solid, immovable cold.

Not all were as grand as the first, but even the least was twice her height. Every one of them had been buried deep into the earth. Some of the blades had been broken through time's teeth or vandalism. Their hilts lay half-buried in the dry soil. Grass had overgrown them.

'Whose swords were these?' Mithrid asked.

'I dread to know,' muttered Farden.

Aspala knelt by the tallest of the ancient blades. 'There is a sword in Belephon like this one. Perhaps as big. The sword of Shareste. It used to attract crowds long ago, but no more. Half-forgotten, it is a pilgrimage for those who remember the old tales of rathcata.'

Farden was digging into one of the swords with his new knife. Mithrid ground her teeth. 'What are they?'

Durnus spoke for the first time in hours, so hoarse barely audible. 'Similar to our trolls, but more of muscle than of wood and stone.'

'They are stories we hear as children,' Aspala asserted. 'I still remember the great ones. Of Neringaë and Paranis who fought the cyclopes and the rathcata back to their caves. And Orestus, who slew the last greatwyrm at the gates of Belephon.'

'And I thought our stories and eddas were strange,' said Mithrid.

'All your pink-flesh stories are strange,' muttered Warbringer.

Farden fought a yawn. 'The bones we saw at Lilerosk. Master Boring called them "ogin".'

'Well, let us hope there are none left alive in the east.'

Mithrid's gaze followed the road that coursed through the undulating grasslands. The huge, lonely mountain was black with the sun sloping behind it. Clouds haloed its crooked peak. A faint hint of snow could be seen atop it. In its shadow, there was a glimmer of water, perhaps a river. Upon the road, specks of wagons and beasts inched slowly to and fro. She could almost make out a settlement or a village far in the distance. A flash of blue showed her a distant Fleetstar breaking through the clouds, staying out of sight but always watching.

It was with a quiet reverence that they slowly descended from the plateau. They followed the path through the forest of swords as one would move through a battlefield littered with dead. There remained a chill amongst the blades that kept the hairs on Mithrid's arms at attention. It reminded her of the old burial mounds that lay north of Troughwake, where father told her ghosts would steal the souls of travellers and – conveniently – misbehaving cliff-brats. *Barrows*, he'd called them.

She was disconcerted to find the feelings still raw, even after glimpsing him in the Grimsayer. Mithrid distracted herself, attempting to imagine the size of the beasts that once swung such weapons. *If* that was to be believed. The youth in her marvelled. The older and darker side she had found growing within her since Troughwake whispered doubt; told her it was an elaborate hoax by these sheepfolk. Or the Cathak.

'Mithrid,' Farden called to her. 'You're slacking.'

She caught up, shins aching from the slopes behind them. 'Aren't you tired? You haven't slept in days.'

'Yes, but we are on a quest, are we not? Time is always wasting on a quest.'

Mithrid looked around. She had the mage to herself. Aspala and Warbringer were chattering about old myths. Durnus trailed behind as per usual. She spoke honestly. 'I know what you did back there, you know. On the ridge.'

Farden regarded her with an impassive stare. His eyes had lost some of the green within them, looking greyer than usual. A fraction more salt to his black pepper hair, too. 'And what is that?'

'Letting the rest of us decide for you, instead of making the choice yourself. I didn't peg you for that kind of coward. Is it so you can blame us if it all goes wrong again? Because I can tell you want the spear as much as we do.'

The mage did not scoff. His expression barely changed at all. 'Can you, indeed? Do you know me that well already? Maybe I just want Loki dead badly enough to believe in a fable.'

Mithrid felt as though she did. 'Though at first you were, now you're not so hard to read. My father taught me all about how emotions rule a man. Whether with his words or his fists.'

Farden worked his teeth across his dry lips. 'You're not the timid girl with all the questions any more, are you Mithrid?'

'Helping you incinerate half a million people tends to change a person, I've been told.' Mithrid admitted. 'I only care about the next step. About making that sacrifice worth it. You can build your kingdom. I want Malvus. Who, by the way, you seem to have forgotten about. You're too focused on Loki.'

'Only because he has my Book, and that is a greater weapon than I, Durnus, or you. That's why not even Malvus worries me as much as what Loki is planning. The spear, if it does exist, secures a victory we currently have no chance of. It's a blind hope and a gamble, but we've faced odds like this before. Taken greater risks,' Farden replied, his voice trailing off. He took a moment. 'Do you regret it, then? Irminsul?'

Regret was a strong word. It admitted fault. Mithrid stayed silent.

'They chose their side,' Farden said, as if reassuring her thoughts. His voice was low, tough as rock. 'I only regret it didn't take them all, as planned, and finally put an end to this.'

Mithrid remembered the feverish power behind Littlest's eyes.

Farden must have noticed her frown. 'And I regret dragging you into the war. I regret putting that weight on your young shoulders. You don't deserve that. Nobody does.'

'You didn't,' Mithrid sighed. 'Malvus did. Father said the mantle of being an adult would rest on them one day.' Mithrid held out a hand, letting power swirl in her palm. Farden looked upon it with something like jealousy.

'All I want is that life back,' she said. 'I know now that's impossible. It makes me angry to my core. So much I don't know what to do with it. I find myself so furious, I am not nearly as horrified as I should be at what we did on the ice fields.'

Farden nodded. 'Now you know how I feel. At least you had a taste of normal. I've been fighting so long I've forgotten almost everything else. Though it's all I've fought for, I wouldn't know what to do with peace.'

They walked in silence for a time, cutting a corner from the road to save time. The gold grass swayed about their legs, almost reaching their waist. The swords around them were diminishing in size and number. Several wide holes suggested a few of the ogin blades had been stolen. Mithrid's eyes strayed to the knife at Farden's side.

'This Loki, then. There's no way he could be tricking all of you? That he actually has good intentions. How sure are you that he is so evil?'

Farden fixed her with a fierce stare and then spluttered with laughter. 'I'd stake my life on it. If you knew him, you'd never even question it. He needs to die, both him and Malvus. You think I've forgotten about him, Mithrid? Malvus has done much worse to me for longer than you've been alive.'

'I wasn't aware it was a competition.'

'Just in case you doubt my conviction.'

Farden stumbled upon a hidden rock. He cursed beneath his breath.

'You need rest. You don't seem yourself,' said Mithrid.

Farden held out a hand. Not for rain: the clouds were not dark enough. Not for her hand or to steady himself, but presumably he tested his magick once more.

'No, I don't,' he muttered.

'Ever run out of magick before?'

'Once, but that was because I'd spent years purging it from my body with the nevermar drug.'

'Why?'

'I blamed my magick for my problems. For everyone's problems. I saw it as dangerous and wanted it dead. That wasn't my fate, as it turned out. Yet now I feel like I'm reliving those old memories. That I'm to blame, once more, for all of this.'

'You are,' Mithrid said. She made to sure to smile when the mage's head whipped around. 'You saved Scalussen, don't forget.

You almost killed us and everyone we know and love in the process, of course, but you defeated Malvus' hordes. As much as I can't dwell on the lives we took in case it crushes me, you did what you set out to do.'

'Wagon!' Aspala called out.

Between the hills, the forest of swords, and the thick grass, it was occasionally tricky to see who or what was walking along the Sunder Road. Sure enough, a wagon led by a fat beast had risen over the next hill.

Given the Cathak morons, Mithrid's first instinct was to hide behind a blade or flat in the grass, but the beast made no charge towards them. She could make out red cloth around its driver instead of yellow and blue. His cargo was a large mound covered in sacking.

Farden took a stand at the side of the road in the shade of a sword. Warbringer found a rock to sit upon so as to appear less threatening. Durnus stayed on the road, hands clasped in his best impression of a diplomat.

'You talk, Durnus. You know this land and that "doomriddle" best,' Farden hissed.

'Doomriddle.' The vampyre tutted. 'Leave this to me.'

The wagon slowed once the travellers were spotted. The driver pushed his beast and the wheels of his wagon as far over the edge of the road as they could go. The beast was a mound of muscle covered in grey flesh. Its feet had the thickness and shape of tree trunks, and they thudded against the earth in ponderous rhythm. Blinkers covered its eyes. A leash ran from the giant horn in the middle of its wedge face to the driver.

'Good afternoon, sir!' Durnus called as the wagon and driver came close.

The most remarkable feature of the rotund driver was his nose. Or lack thereof. It ended abruptly, as though it had been cut off in the past. That, and his bulbous eyes gave him a hoggish look. Mithrid could see there was a short bow of some kind sitting on his lap.

'Don't carry no silver nor gold on me,' he called. 'Just a farmer, I am. Beetroot and taters is all I got. You can check if you like, but if murder's your game then you'll have an arrow in your throat—'

'There must be some misunderstanding. We are also travellers, not bandits or thieves.'

'You look like 'em. Many are old soldiers like you. Got armour and blades like you. You from the south?'

'West. Emaneska.'

'You are far from your borders,' stated the farmer.

'And looking to be further still. Perhaps you can help us. We're trying to find a place called Eaglehold.'

'Eagle—' The gleam that took over his eyes was terribly hidden. 'Well, now. Eaglehold. That information must be worth something to you.'

Farden spoke up. 'Or worth something to you, friend.' He patted his knife. 'We're not bandits, but we're also not stupid.'

The farmer huffed and jerked a thumb over his shoulder. 'That mountain's Eaglehold. Got many names. Most call it the Rainmaker. But there are a few who know it as Eaglehold still. Old name.'

'And where would you find the mountain's roots?'

'Its roots?' The farmer clicked his tongue, moving his beast and wagon on. 'I... Hmm. That'd be Dathazh most likely. Somewhere in its old town. Never heard it called that before, though. Farewell, strangers.'

'And you,' Durnus called after him.

'Dathazh,' Farden repeated, giving the vampyre a chance to dig out his map. 'That Lilerosk runt mentioned the same place. So did the innkeeper.'

'The Sunder Road leads right to it. According to the map, Dathazh lies on the border of Golikar and a city labelled Venis, or Vensk. We seem to be going the right way.'

Aspala nodded. 'He also mentioned a tourney of some kind.'

Mithrid was already walking, trudging up the hill and earning shooting pains up her legs for her troubles.

At the hill's modest summit, the settlement she'd seen before was now in plain view. It had the shape of no building she had seen before, and was every colour beneath the sun. But by the look of the wagons and beasts going to and fro, it was a place to find more answers. Perhaps rest and hot food, at very least.

Durnus appeared silently at her side.

'What is that place?' she asked.

'No idea,' he answered, and turned to yell hoarsely to the mage. 'Farden. We should rest.'

'We keep going.'

'You'll walk yourself into the ground, Farden.'

Farden did not listen. Instead, he kept walking down the road.

As always, Warbringer had some of her wisdom to dispense. 'Mage is trying to prove something to somebody. Men like that don't live long as they should.'

❧

A signpost spoke its name before any voice did.

*The Spoke.*

The closer they drew to it, the more popular and bizarre the structure seemed. There was no architectural plan behind any of it. If Mithrid had to guess, she would have wagered ten different houses had been thrown together, crushed into one, then dragged out into different shapes.

What was most disturbing was how top-heavy the building was. Its base was a sprawl of tents and awnings that spread into the grassland. A thin neck of wooden foundation preceded the rest of the building: bulbous and tangled like swollen shoulders. Half-built towers leaned against one another. Doors opened into nonexistent balconies, with only half of them nailed shut. Steam and smoke came from some central core of the building, and with it, the smells of roast meats and the grain smell of something fermenting. One section thumped along to music just like any fine tavern, while another rang with screams and cries. Mostly ecstatic, though, with the occasional snap of a whip and a yelp of pain. Mithrid furrowed her brow. She was not exactly clueless as to what cathouses and brothels sold, but she was still confused.

Farden and the others were equally bemused by the mess. The Spoke looked fit to tumble to the grasslands at any moment. Durnus even forbade the minotaur from leaning on any part of it.

'Information only. We won't be staying here long.'

'We can spend *some* time on our backsides, Farden,' Durnus chided him. 'We need rest.'

Farden looked at the rest of the group before he realised he was the one the vampyre was talking about.

'I'm fine,' he said, but as he turned, one of his legs weakened. He tottered before steadying himself. He muttered darkly. 'All right. We leave at sundown, no arguments.'

He threw one last look at the skies as if he had spied a dragon, but the streaks of clouds were clear. Wherever Fleetstar was, she was not there.

The Spoke was aptly named. The Sunder Road might have been the largest, but it was not the only path to meet at the Spoke. Roads running in all directions wandered from the grasslands to connect at this strange watering hole. Mithrid saw the Lilerosk sheep folk in abundance. While their flocks remained beyond the Spoke, the shepherds came to water, drink, and swap gossip with their kin. Their loud conversations were strangely heated. Talk of more sheep disappearing, or piles of burned bones, if Mithrid heard right.

It seemed all manner of kinds converged at the Spoke. Even a herd of piebald cows like those of the Cathak. So diverse were its customers and residents that Aspala and Warbringer received half their usual measure of fearful glances. Mithrid also saw tall women in pastel cloaks. Their porcelain masks were featureless except for holes for their odd, purple eyes. Others walked about proudly shirt-less, wearing nothing but tattoos and loincloths and leaning against more of the leathery, horned beasts. Mithrid heard their name above their ruckus. *Coelos.*

Aspala was at her shoulder. 'We have such beasts in Paraia. To the south of the Dune Sea. They are too revered to be hunted, as it should be. If they can be tamed, they make great steeds for warriors. Their hides are already armoured.'

'Not to mention they come with that horn.'

Aspala tutted, looking proud. 'They are smaller in these lands. Not as large as Paraian coelos. Ours are not covered in shaggy hair, either,' she said as she pointed to a woolly specimen that grazed further out in the fields. A man daubed in yellow clay lay upon its back, arms clasped behind his head as if fast asleep.

Within the Spoke, the same level of tumult from outside reigned within, just concentrated between mismatched walls. Corridors changed shape every corner, from claustrophobically thin and triangular between two sloping bulkheads, to the next moment emerging into an inner courtyard with a huge willow tree bent over a pool of water and a sputtering fountain. The courtyard seemed to be one large open tavern. Tables filled the strange cavern. Windows were few amongst the press of jumbled buildings. Candles sitting atop thrones of old wax, dubiously adjacent fireplaces, and lanterns stuffed with glowing moths lit the space. Stewards weaved to and fro holding trays of ale and roast lamb racks.

Instead of getting lost or trapped elsewhere in the Spoke, Farden claimed the nearest empty table, tucked away by a merchant asleep in his stall. The last arse had barely met the seat before a steward appeared. His hair and beard were so long both were tucked into his belt, and he was polite enough to keep his gaze from lingering on Warbringer too long.

The man spoke so quickly it took Mithrid a moment to realise he was saying the same greeting in several different languages. At last, she heard Commontongue. His accent was incredibly thick but just coherent enough to understand.

'No fighting, no gambling, no murderin'. The Spoke is a sanctuary on the Sunder Road. If you keep the rules, then we're welcome to all and closed to none.'

'The Spoke, you say?' Durnus piped up, ever the curious one.

The steward sighed with an emotion that might have once been pride. 'That's right. Four hundred years we've been here.'

'Impressive. And wh—

Farden cut Durnus off. 'Do you have any armourers or swordsmiths in this maze?'

'No, sire. Farriers and minor smiths only. Now, sires and madams, drinks or vittles or both?'

Farden upended a burned coin-purse on the table. It was far from a spectacular fortune. Two gold coins rattled out. Farden slid one onto the steward's tray. 'Both, and plenty of it.'

The man tested the coin by biting it. 'This'll get you room and board and stable, y'know.'

'I'd rather it buy us some quiet and privacy.'

The man grinned. 'Right you are, sires and madams.'

They were left to stare around the constant bustle and oddness of the crowds that surrounded them. No doubt they looked the strangest there, but it seemed far more acceptable in a place as strange as the Spoke. There was a bard in the corner who rivalled them. He was dressed head to toe in a costume of moons and suns, capering about between tables with a flute.

'Durnus, the inkweld if you please,' asked Farden.

Aspala saw to that, having chosen herself as the book-carrier of this expedition. She thumped the inkweld on the table and slid it to the mage.

'Worth trying,' Durnus agreed. He signalled for the steward, who speedily attended them. 'If you have ink and quill we would most appreciate it.'

'Don't have none of that here, sir. Might want to try Edna's Glyphs, over there.' He pointed past the pool to a woman hunched over a stall as vacant as her gaze.

Mithrid snagged the other coin from the table. 'On it.'

Wandering a path that avoided every occupied table, Mithrid passed a bar packed with stewards pouring ales from spout after spout. Kitchen steam enveloped her before she stood at this Edna's stall. She had scrolls for sale, along with old parchments on all manner of topics Mithrid couldn't translate. Blank papers, too.

'What is it, miss?' she asked. She seemed a woman who had far too many wrinkles for the age of her voice.

'I need a quill and ink, if you please.'

Edna rolled her eyes as if serving a customer was some great inconvenience, yet rummaged behind her stall until she produced a battered quill and a half-empty pot of ink.

'A silver.'

Mithrid put the gold coin on the counter.

Edna poked at the Emaneska seal on the coin: the irksome face of Malvus Barkhart. 'What is this?'

'More than enough, is what it is.'

'Mmph. I'll give you two silvers back. Your coin ain't worth the same in the Rivenplains.'

'Four. I might not have seen a lot of the world, but I know gold doesn't stop being gold based on what's stamped on it.'

'Three.'

'Fine.'

Edna emptied the three silver coins in Mithrid's hand, crossed her arms, and turned away in a mood.

With a shake of her head, Mithrid headed back to the table. Wrapped up in looking at the dirty smear of ink within the little glass vial, she didn't realise how close she was to a group of drinkers until one of them snagged her cloak.

Mithrid snatched herself away, looking down at a man with pockmarked skin and a shaved head. He had stars tattooed across his forehead, just like each of the three louts that shared his table. Each was clad in a riding cloak of chestnut fur and chainmail.

'Don't see many like you around these parts,' he said over the rim of his flagon. 'Not with hair of fire like yours. Nor armour, either. Never seen that kind before. Must be a rich lady to afford such plate. What's your name, lady?'

'None of your business is what it is.'

'By the Dusk God, she is fire herself! I like that,' he brayed to his friends.

It was then, with a last glance, that Mithrid saw the skull masks balanced face-down on the table between their ales.

She hoisted up her hood and led a meandering route back to her table, fortunately poised just out of their sight around the willow's fronds.

A flagon of ale for each of them had come, two bowls of bread, melted butter, and a clutch of sausages sizzling on a stone. Mithrid sat alongside the mage, watching the others filling their stomachs.

'You look concerned, Mith,' said Aspala, spitting crumbs.

'I think there are some Cathak here. Didn't recognise us but they have the same masks. Dressed in brown fur instead of their usual colours,' Mithrid said.

'We'll be swifter here than planned, in that case,' the mage ordered.

While each of them surreptitiously stared over their shoulders, and while Farden saw to the ink and quill, Mithrid drank the dust from her tongue. The ale was crisp, somehow freezing cold, and only had the lightest of scum floating in it. Mithrid sipped as she examined the walls of windows, and the stairwells and walkways crisscrossing the roof. The tree had a scent that was much more preferable to the tobacco smoke and ash of the fireplaces. It did not smell like wood they were burning, but dung.

Farden bent over the inkwell, staring at his simple message of:

Elessi. We are all alive.

Please tell me you are the same.

F

'Please,' he was whispering. Perhaps even praying. 'Please.'

Mithrid sipped away, eyeing the table of Cathak while they waited, and rested their weary bones.

❦

'Brace!'

The roar barely preceded the strike of the mountain of a wave. It rammed the *Autumn's Vanguard* sideways as it broke against its starboard side. Seawater flooded the top decks, sweeping even more of the wind and water mages from their posts. Lanterns extinguished as they were smashed apart by the fierce waves.

Though the rain tried its hardest to hammer her into submission, Hereni stood obstinate at the railing of the aftcastle. Lerel was roaring orders behind her. Hereni did not care for the wicked rain, nor the wind-driven waves that sought to drown them. She stared, unblinking into the roiling ocean, dreading to see scales and fins at any moment.

'Hereni!'

The bellowing of her name was a timid, faint wail in the storm, but Hereni at last heard it. Elessi stood beside the wheel, holding onto Eyrum for dear life but insistent on seizing the mage's attention.

Hereni let go of the railing. The wind was savage, blowing her back across the deck until she caught hold of the Siren. There was no fear in their eyes. None of the crouching terror that Hereni felt, but instead soaked and wide-eyed faces.

'It's Farden!' Elessi cried.

'What? Where?'

'In the inkweld! He's alive!'

'Thank the bloody gods! And Mithrid?'

'They all are!'

Hereni practically raced them belowdecks. She stumbled into the cabin and rammed her ribs into the desk.

Elessi had left the inkweld open on her desk. Low and behold, a scrawled message was slowly vanishing. Hereni tilted her head to read it.

'We're all alive,' Elessi uttered. 'That's what it says.'

Hereni collapsed at the desk with relief. 'Where are they?'

After wrapping a towel around herself, Elessi sat down at the desk and scrabbled to dip the quill. 'I was just about to ask them that exact thing.'

'Yes!'

Farden's exclamation drew stares, even the frowning attention of the bard by the pool.

They all drew inwards around the inkweld. 'What? Is it them?' Mithrid asked.

The inkweld answered for her. Script appeared upon the empty green pages. Slow, steady, and in flowing scribble.

'That's Elessi's hand, if I'm not mistaken,' whispered Farden.

ALL ALIVE, FOR NOW AT LEAST.
FLEEING KRAUSLUNG AND LOKI. HE'S CLAIMED THE CITY.
LEVIATHANS SUMMONED. WE HAD TO SAIL SOUTH.
THE WAVEBLADE HAS BEEN LOST.
WHERE ARE YOU? ARE YOU INJURED?

E

'Loki has claimed Krauslung?' Durnus breathed. 'How?'

Mithrid spluttered. 'After all we did? Why would the city do that after we won? Freed them from Malvus?'

Farden fixed Mithrid with a sour look. The quill bent in his fist. 'What did I tell you about that bastard god?'

Mithrid was too busy trying to figure whether Hereni and Bull could be counted in "all". She hoped with all he heart it did. She was about to ask Farden to clarify when the minotaur spoke.

'Leviathans? What are these?' Warbringer looked perturbed.

Durnus explained. 'Great creatures of the sea. Rare but incredibly dangerous. Sometimes known to menace ships and eat the occasional small boat.'

'The Waveblade is not a small boat, Durnus.'

Farden dipped the quill in the diminishing ink.

## WE ARE ON THE SUNDER ROAD, FAR TO THE EAST...

' "...Not injured but locals aren't the friendliest",' Elessi read aloud, even though Hereni watched the script move from poised over her shoulder.

'Where in blood-drenched Hel is the Sunder Road?' asked the mage.

'I haven't a clue. Eyrum? Do you?'

Eyrum shook his head, brow a deep trench of frown. 'Far to the east does not sound helpful.'

Elessi ran the quill against the ink-pot. 'Durnus must have accidentally taken them there with the Weight,' she was muttering.

A deep boom shook the ship. Hereni sought the comfort of a bulkhead. She could feel the tremor of the storm-waters running across the hull. At least, Hereni hoped it was merely the storm.

'Unless he took them there on purpose,' she voiced.

## WHEN ARE YOU COMING BACK TO US?
### E

Mithrid watched Farden's hand hesitate for a moment before replying.

'We're not,' he whispered as he wrote. 'Even if we wanted to, we are trapped here without a quickdoor. The Weight is broken and Fleetstar cannot carry us all. We are searching for something to help us. A weapon we will need to destroy Loki.'

Elessi had barely understood the script before a lurch of the ship sent her ink pouring over the inkweld's green pages, utterly flooding it.

'Gods curse it!' Elessi yelled. Despite her attempts to wipe it with the towel, the inkweld was ruined.

'I need more ink!'

In desperation, she scratched the word *tomorrow* into the mess of black ink with the quill and hoped Farden would see it.

'Leviathan on the port side!' came the roar from the hallway. The *Vanguard* bucked under a heavy blow, as if the bookship had run aground. The screech of something against the iron hull plates was spine-crawling.

'Ink, damn it!' Elessi yelled.

But Hereni was too transfixed by the shout. Eyrum was already out of the door.

'What did they say?' shouted Hereni.

Elessi slammed the inkweld shut. *Trapped.* Staring at the quivering bulkheads, she knew the feeling all too well. 'No help is coming, mage. We are on our own for now.'

'Haven't we always been?' Hereni growled. Her question needed to answer. The air crackled as flames spread from her fists to her shoulders.

🐦

'What the...?' Farden recoiled as a black blotch of ink spread across both pages of the inkweld.

With the meat of his fist, Farden tried to rub it clear but the ink on the pages was dry as dust. The blotch began to fade away, leaving a faint ghost of the word, "tomorrow" in the ink.

'Ever seen that before?' he demanded of Durnus.

'Never. Though I would wager some kind of ink-based accident on Elessi's part.'

Mithrid heard more hope in the vampyre's voice than certainty. She met Farden's wide, blood-rimmed eyes.

Farden wrote Elessi's name across the page three times. The ink did not fade this time. It lingered on the page, despised as a confession.

'Leviathans,' snarled the mage. 'How did Loki summon Leviathans?'

Mithrid had heard stories of the sea monsters. Colossal serpents of scale and fang. She could feel her heart beating faster. 'Will they be all right?'

Durnus' hands spread across the table. 'Calm, both of you. Fear only grows without facts. Trust in your allies, as you struggle to do so often. Elessi has the Rogue's Armada. She has Eyrum, Hereni, and not forgetting Towerdawn and the Sirens. You might argue they are safer than us.'

Again, the vampyre's voice wavered. It could have been whatever malady of weakness still affected him, yet he seemed stronger since leaving the mountain ridge.

Farden looked anything but. Mithrid could see the white of the knuckles in the mage's hand as it wrapped around his borrowed knife. To her surprise, whatever inner monologue raged within his skull, stayed there. Instead, Farden closed his eyes, took a breath through his nostrils, and held it.

'I trust them,' he said at last. 'I do not trust Loki.'

'Tomorrow, mage. We will try them again.'

Farden slid the inkweld across the table and shoved himself back in his chair. 'The sooner we leave, the sooner tomorrow will come.'

Mithrid's heavy eyelids, the cold sensation of ale in her stomach, and the ache of her muscles made her want to do nothing but to stay sitting. Perhaps even to graduate to lying down. Yet Mithrid felt the same frustration and restlessness that Farden felt. She knew all too well how desperately one will scrabble for control in situations bereft of any. So it was that Mithrid half rose, but the others stayed still.

Durnus shook his head. 'We fear for them as much as you do, mage. But how much use will we be to Elessi and the armada if we walk ourselves to death before we find the Spear of Gunnir? We are, all of us, exhausted.'

Aspala nodded.

'Speak for yourselves, weak ones,' chuckled Warbringer. She had already drained her flagon and was looking menacingly at a haunch of meat roasting across the hall.

Durnus rolled his eyes. '*Except* for our good Warbringer here. You are half-dead, Farden. I see it in you. Hear it in your heartbeat, smell it in your blood. Do not forget what I am.'

'Is nothing in my control any more?' he muttered. With Loki's knife, he began to carve an idle pattern in the table.

Mithrid's tired bones were secretly glad for the vampyre's complaints. She settled back in her chair and seized her tankard. She suffered guilt for it, especially knowing that at that moment the armada was fighting to survive, but Durnus was right. And, somehow, the more she sipped her ale, the more leaden she felt.

'Steward!' called Durnus.

He appeared momentarily. If he was expecting more gold, he was disappointed.

'Another round, sires and madams?' The steward's eyes lingered on Warbringer as if to wonder if either of those salutations were correct.

'Have you heard of Sigrimur, my good man?' Durnus asked.

The steward laughed so immediately, Mithrid thought he had suffered a surprise sneeze.

'You might as well be asking if I have heard of the sky, sire. I mean no offence, but everybody in the Rivenplains and beyond has heard of Sigrimur. At very least, they've heard of his head.'

'His *head*?'

'You really are far from home, aren't you?' The steward now looked more shocked than full of mockery. 'You don't know the Head of Sigrimur? By the plains, what else would they give as a prize for winning the Scarlet Tourney? Champions travel for leagues for a chance to hold that head. All other tourneys – even the pits of Lezembor – pale in comparison. There's nothing like it. The fights, the blood, the cheering. And the Golikan ale!' The steward scratched his neck, remembering himself. 'I assumed that's why you were passing through. Armour and weapons like yours…'

'This Scarlet Tourney, where is it?'

'Why, in Vensk, of course. The capital of Golikar? By the plains. The procession begins in Dathazh in a few days. Just follow that. Now, more ales or not? I don't get paid as a guide.'

Farden set the man free from Durnus by thanking him with another silver. 'We will take those beds after all.'

'Fine. With company or without?'

'Without.'

The steward tutted as he left. 'Foreigners,' he huffed.

His interest in his customers and their coin squashed, he took his sweet time with the second round of flagons. Mithrid spent the wait watching others over her vessel. Drinking was a pastime she could easily get used to.

The bard was now entertaining a table for a coin, singing something dire about a shepherd crying about wolves. Mithrid found herself thinking of old Grey Barbo's wheedling tone, something he had only broken out on Highfrost's Eve. Home, she realised, was not about a hearth or a roof, but about safety and comfort. And she had been missing plenty of both since Troughwake. Since Scalussen, even.

'We should find that healer for you, Durnus. You still look awful,' Farden was saying, filling the silence.

'Speak for yourself, mage.'

Farden shook his head. 'I told you, I'm fine. All I care about is my armour and finding somebody who can fix it. Hopefully this city of Dathazh will be more than a scratch of wood and sheep shit. Civilisation, instead of these endless plains.'

' "Three tasks every god and mortal fears to face await. Three duties yet fulfilled of blood, breath, mind, and soul. Three cursed keys to three doors to be left locked evermore," ' Aspala recited the Doomriddle. The words had rattled around Mithrid's head, too, but in a misremembered order.

'Why's it always three?' she asked.

Durnus nodded sagely. 'One for each of the cultists that hid the Spear of Gunnir on the Allfather's command. They went to every length to hide it.'

'Why not destroy it, as the Knights of the Nine destroyed their armour?' asked Farden.

Mithrid looked at the mage's armour beside her. Hereni had told her of it in Scalussen: thousand-year-old armour made of the blood of gods. It sounded as ridiculous as the spear, but here it was, right in front of her. It made the world even larger, and made her knowledge of it more pitiful.

'Perhaps it cannot be destroyed.'

Warbringer scoffed. She was already halfway to her hooves, her big brown eyes still fixed on the meats roasting across the hall. 'All things are broken and built again,' she asserted as she left.

Mithrid watched as gazes followed the minotaur as she stamped her way across the mix of boards and bare earth towards food. As Mithrid turned back, she caught glances of another figure. This one came bustling from an entrance and pushed his way through the tables, no matter the complaints he received from other patrons. His colours caught Mithrid's attention: yellow furs trimmed with blue. A dishevelled owl clung to the man's right shoulder, wings splayed for balance.

As she watched, the fellow made a beeline for the Cathak men that had bothered Mithrid before. A cold prickle ran up her nape.

'Farden,' she said quietly.

But the mage was distracted. '...then we will destroy it when we're done, Durnus. Finish what these cultists failed to do.'

At first, the Cathak dismissed the newcomer with sneers and waves of their sausage-greased hands. The more the man pressed them, the more they began to listen. The leader's stare turned, swivelling across the hall to find Mithrid, staring right back.

'Farden!' she snapped.

'What?'

'Trouble,' was all she said. The others traced her gaze until they too met eyes with the Cathak men.

The squeak of chairs against boards confirmed her fears. The table of Cathak got to their feet. Three of them donned their skull masks before approaching. The flaxen-haired leader had a sword beneath his furs. He rested his palm on its pommel as he strode towards them.

In the corner of Mithrid's eye, Farden lowered his knife to his side, kept it close. Her hand strayed to the head of the axe balanced against her leg.

'Strangers!' called the leader when he was close enough. Far too close for his chosen volume.

He was met by a table of flat stares and silence. The four of Emaneska waited, poised and wary.

'If you have not been welcomed to the grandness of the Riven-plains, then I wish you welcome.'

Farden stayed silent. Jaw bunched. Durnus spoke for them.

'We are grateful.'

'What are your names, strangers? What brings you here?' Before anyone could object, the leader grabbed a chair and added it to their circle. His cronies stood close behind, all of them still, watching with unblinking stares.

'Our business is in Dathazh.'

'Come for the Tourney, is it? A lot of you strangers come through here. Keep themselves to themselves in most cases.'

'As do we.'

'Is that so?'

Mithrid heard a trap. Remina had once favoured such a trick: leading Mithrid into a conversation only one side knew the script of.

'I should hope so!' brayed the man. He ran a hand through his stripe of yellow hair and sighed. 'Alas, not all strangers are like you. A rumour is travelling the plains. A rumour of strangers who aren't so respectful of our lands and laws. Strangers wearing strange armour. Pale faces from the west. Strangers who come with trespass in mind and murder in their hearts. Strangers the Dusk God knows as enemies.'

'A shame,' Farden grunted. 'If we see any of them, we'll be sure to let you know.'

'That would serve you well,' the Cathak warned. 'A price has been put on their heads, you see.'

'How high a price?' Mithrid asked, curiosity overcoming her caution.

That sickly grin of the Cathak's showed itself even wider. 'Well, my lady of fire. The greatest price of all: death.'

'How inconvenient. For them, of course,' replied Mithrid.

'Of course.'

'Well,' Durnus surmised. 'It was a pleasure to make your acquaintance...?'

The man stood quickly, stretching as tall as he could muster. 'You will call me Lord Oselov. Son of the High Cathak Tartavor himself. And you will remember my name.'

'Curse it. Already forgotten it,' Farden teased.

The man's sword came halfway from his scabbard. Mithrid tensed, but Farden, Durnus, and Aspala barely flinched. Mithrid's eyes darted around the table, waiting for them to pounce. They seemed far too relaxed. The opposite of the Cathak cronies, each a hair from lunging with their blades.

Lord Oselov dropped his act. 'You insult me as you have my father. Enough play! I know who you are.'

Farden was so calm he sipped from his flagon. 'Oslo, was it?'

'Lord Oselov! You have a debt to pay the Dusk God. I will do what my father has not and collect that debt.'

Farden held the lord's gaze until the man could be seen turning the colour of beetroot.

'Sorry,' said the mage. 'One more time, then I'll have it.'

Oselov's curved sword flowed from the scabbard, drawing shouts from the stewards and drinkers alike. Whatever strike Oselov had planned, he halted in midair. It took Mithrid a moment to realise why.

Without her – or possibly anyone – seeing, the mage had switched his knife between hands. Much to Oselov's surprise, as soon as he drew his sword, Farden hooked the tip of the knife between the very soft and tender area between his legs. Oselov stood on tiptoes trying to avoid its point.

'I would think about that very, very hard if I were you, Lord Oslo,' Farden warned. 'It would be a shame to break the Spoke's rules now, wouldn't it?'

Shaking with outrage, Oselov's eyes darted around, trying to find a solution to his problem. While he clearly hoped it would be a violent solution, the arrival of a dark, ominous shadow behind him drained the fight out of him.

'Speak more, pink-flesh, and I will have fresh meat at last,' spoke Warbringer. Her sharp teeth moved very close to his ear.

Oselov visibly swallowed, making quite the trembling show of sheathing his sword.

'We will keep the rules. You can't stay here forever, strangers.'

With much cursing and pounding fists on his cronies, Lord Oselov made a hasty exit from the Spoke's tavern.

'Curse these Cathak,' Farden muttered.

'He is right, you know, we cannot stay here forever.'

Over the bustle of the tavern and the bard's hastily resumed wailing, Mithrid could hear a familiar wail of a horn. One that she had heard in the Bronzewood. It sent a shiver running down her spine.

Aspala heard it too. 'I get the feeling there are more of them outside.'

'Me too,' Mithrid affirmed. All eyes lingered on them. The stewards were huddling together, whispering like a nest of snakes. 'And I don't think we're welcome in here any more.'

'Looks like we'll be leaving before sunset. No rest for the wicked.'

'Is that what we are?' Aspala asked.

'To the Cathak.'

'And Emaneska, apparently,' added Mithrid.

Farden growled quietly. The subject of Loki and Krauslung must have weighed on him, too.

Aspala put her half-sword on the table. 'What is the plan?'

Farden signalled for a steward. 'We keep moving. If these Cathak want to stop us, then let them try.'

'You must be mad,' their steward greeted them, standing as far as possible from their table while still being in earshot. He did not look impressed. 'Do you know who that is? They are Cathak! That is the son of—'

'No, and I don't care. Where's the back door to this place?'

The steward pointed irritably past the willow tree and towards a dark hole between the misshapen architecture. 'There. Now, please go.'

'With pleasure,' Farden replied.

Whether it was the violence or the fact that they were leaving that stirred Farden, Mithrid didn't know, but the mage was already striding through the tables, not caring for the chairs he knocked over. Warbringer didn't delay following him. Durnus neither.

Aspala and Mithrid looked to each other. Mithrid felt a lack of breath in her lungs.

'Do you ever stop being nervous before a fight?' she asked.

'No,' Aspala replied. 'If you do, you're not doing it right, or so my mother taught me.'

Mithrid muttered a curse beneath her breath and got to her feet. Her axe felt heavy in her hands as she followed Farden and the others out of the Spoke.

Twisting this way and that through the confusing hallways, weak sunlight called them outwards, where the baying of the beasts around the Spoke was strangely silent.

Mithrid emerged into the fading daylight behind the others and wondered what had stopped in the doorway. She soon saw why.

The coelos, sheep, and various other beasts Mithrid didn't recognise were being led quietly away from their stalls and troughs. Out of sight and out of the way. Beyond the tangled foundations of the Spoke, Mithrid saw them: a swathe of Cathak waiting outside the Spoke. Browns, yellows, and blues, their colours were unmistakable.

Every one of them wore a confounded skull mask. Their numbers were considerable. Mithrid guessed at perhaps a hundred. A score of them sat upon their prize cows. Their horns had been dyed blue and filed sharp. Leather armour draped them.

Lord Oselov sat astride no cow. To Mithrid, the beast looked stuck halfway between a sabrecat and a salamander. She briefly pondered what animals had lain together to create such a monstrosity. It had broad scales down its flanks and ridged back, yet coarse, matted hair covered its underside and stout legs. Saliva dripped from its bared fangs.

There was now a scythe in Oselov's hands. It was firmly pointed at Farden.

'You spat in the face of the Dusk God one last time, strangers! You have insulted our lands. Our brothers. Our Bronzewood. My father will exact the Dusk God's righteous vengeance upon you.'

'You were right, Aspala,' Farden sighed. 'The religious ones really are the worst. If you're going to be a bandit, just be a damn bandit.'

'Surrender now or suffer our holy wrath!'

'You know we have a dragon, right?' Farden called out.

Half the heads of the Cathak immediately pointed upwards. But the sky was awkwardly clear.

'Somewhere,' Farden muttered so only the others could hear.

'Where is she?' whispered Mithrid.

Farden closed his eyes, reaching out with his mind. 'I don't know.'

Lord Oselov was not as dumb as his bearing suggested. He soon cottoned on. 'I see no beast other than that great thing beside you. You seem all alone to me.'

'What's the plan, Farden?'

'Fight,' he said.

'But we have no dragon and you have no magick.'

Durnus' gaze snapped around, flitting between Mithrid and the mage. 'What did you say?'

'I am quite aware of that,' Farden replied sharply.

'Surrender your weapons, your armour, and yourselves, and we will see the Dusk God's glorious mercy visited upon you.'

Farden held Loki's dagger to his forehead, the blade and hilt up. 'For Modren,' he hissed, as he started walking towards the lines of Cathak.

'Farden?'

'But there's too many, surely?' said Aspala.

'Not likely,' Durnus snorted. He took a deep lungful of air as he tested his own magick with a clench of his skeletal fist. Mithrid felt it billow around her as a breeze. 'Even I do not dare imagine how many souls that mage has taken with a blade or his bare hands.'

Warbringer seemed to relish the thought. She kept her palms flat and her hammer upright and followed behind the mage.

They approached the lines at so gradual a speed it did not seem to be a charge. With Farden's knife out in what looked like surrender, most of the Cathak began to chant in premature victory. Only a few stepped up to seize him.

Oselov was already grinning. 'Wise, to submit so willingly! That armour will look just fine on my arms, methinks!'

Scythes, Mithrid would soon learn, were cumbersome weapons. Due to their reach, they needed a lot of room to swing. They also required speed, and the right angle to be of devastating use. Up close, the beaklike blades were more dangerous to their owner than a foe. The Cathak wore curved shortswords, but Mithrid saw only a few drawn. Their confidence was their downfall, and the mage mocked them harshly for it. She watched on with mouth agape as Farden went to work.

Farden raised the knife so casually, the Cathak fighter looked utterly confused as it passed his open hand, flipped tip over pommel, and abruptly punched a bloody hole in his throat. After breaking the nose of the next man with his vambrace, Farden stretched, aimed, and threw. Loki's knife was a gold blur that ended abruptly in Lord Oselov's stomach. He howled with pain, toppling from his saddle and unleashing his strange beast.

Two more Cathak charged Farden. He bent a knee to duck their scythes. As they clanged above his head, he seized the swords in each of their belts and drew them into the daylight. Their steel blades were sharp enough to lop the arms from both men. They fell screaming. Farden stepped over them, swords wide and ready. Mithrid had, of course, seen him fight before, but without magick, the Forever King was a different beast. Savage.

Behind him, Warbringer entered the fray. Cathak flew over the heads of their comrades and landed with screams and sickening crunches. A mist of blood arose as she twirled Voidaran in her hands, the hammer screaming a war song.

Mithrid charged. Aspala ran at her heels, half-sword levelled at a now panicking crowd of enemies. The girl felt heat wash over her as Durnus began to unleash his magick. Forks of lightning lanced through the crowds. The cries of the Spoke joined the howls of the Cathak. Mithrid got the impression mages were far and few in those lands, especially those of the calibre of Durnus.

Mithrid ruined her first swing. The Cathak woman she had aimed to behead caught a glancing blow instead, still spinning to the ground but alive. Aspala dispatched her with a vicious boot to the face. That counted for a lot when Aspala's foot was more hoof.

'Steady, Mith!' she warned. Her blade flashed, spilling a fellow's guts to the grass.

Mithrid steeled her stomach, put the revulsion and panic behind her, and fought like she had learned to on the walls of Scalussen. Eyrum and Hereni's staccato orders filled her mind. *Pivot, parry, strike.* Her axe bit deep into a man's chest. She twisted it free with a crack of bone and brought the momentum up between another's legs. A blade dug into her armour. Before Mithrid could turn around to deal with the bastard, the Cathak was riddled with lightning. Blue light burst from his eyes. He fell, revealing Durnus weaving his spells. He spared her a moment to nod before unleashing his next spell.

Mithrid found Farden in the chaos. He was a blur of gold and blood-red who was determined to reach Lord Oselov. The man's cronies were trying to keep him upright. Several of them had already begun to flee. Their cows galloped through the crowds with abandon.

It was then that Oselov's strange beast came raging through the ranks. It slavered as if rabid, and the mage had captured its frenzied attention.

'Farden!' Mithrid warned.

Fortunately, he had already seen it coming. Steel clashed against its claws as he fended off its charge. Mithrid looked for an opportunity to hurl her axe, but she kept needing it to stay alive.

Warbringer roared something unintelligible as she barrelled through the fray towards the beast. The thing never saw her sharp horns coming until they had punctured its scales and were buried in its ribs. Warbringer kept charging, pushing the beast a dozen feet until rearing upright. Blood painted her horns.

That moment broke the Cathak. A good number of them ran for the sanctuary of the Spoke, while the rest broke across the grasslands. Those who rode upon beasts knocked their brethren aside as they scarpered. But not before Farden had found his prey.

Mithrid had at last caught up with him. The mage had a fresh cut across his cheek. A curtain of blood ran down his jaw. He was too focused on Lord Oselov to notice Mithrid by his side.

Oselov gurgled in pain as Farden withdrew the knife.

'You fucking bastards,' the Cathak cursed. Bloody spittle decorated his chin. Despite all the pain, he had a gleeful shine to his watering eyes.

'You don't know what you've done. You don't know who I am! What my father and I will do to you when we find you. You'll see me strutting in that armour of yours before we cook you alive.'

'And that,' Farden said between grit teeth. 'That is what you shouldn't have said, because now I can't trust you to stay put and not follow us, can I?'

Oselov chose foolishness instead of understanding what Farden was offering. 'I'll see you die slowly for your insult! The Dusk God will devour your soul for a thousand years!'

Farden pointed the knife close to his face. The light vanished from the lord's eyes as he realised Farden's intentions.

'You wouldn't dare,' he said. A spiteful final curse balanced on his lips, but it was never voiced. The mage dragged the blade across Oselov's throat.

Farden didn't stay to watch Oselov gurgle. He stood up and began to wipe the blood from his knife. 'Do you have a problem with my lack of mercy, Mithrid?' asked Farden as he put the blade back through his belt.

She was asking herself the same question. She watched the lord drift into death.

'Take it from somebody who's lived long enough to know,' added Farden. 'Loose threads need cutting. We seek to save these people from Loki as well as Emaneska. This lord's revenge would have hindered us.'

'Let's hope you haven't caused something worse by killing him,' Mithrid said as she sheathed her axe. 'All of this better be worth the kingdom you're fighting for, Farden.'

The threat was a lie. Mithrid walked away to hide her shaking hands. She couldn't deny the thrill of survival. The same dark love of battle she had first experienced in Efjar had returned.

It was under hundreds of watchful, narrowed eyes of man and beast that they departed. Their shadows long against the blood-soaked grass, the strangers took their leave of the Spoke and its troubles. Mithrid hoped they wouldn't follow them.

# part two

## PATHS CHOSEN

# CHAPTER 10
## THE HUNTED

*It was on this day the Noose God gifted intrepid Sigrimur his mighty spear, and the task of protecting humankind after the departure of gods and daemons. But Sigrimur was beset by envy on all sides. His family slain by a covetous king, he turned to the wilderness, lying in wait like a beast for his vengeance. At last, Sigrimur's patience was rewarded. After slaying his avowed enemy, he prospered for many decades, becoming rich and proud off his own legend. In return for wasting his gods-given mantle, the Noose God, in his anger, took Sigrimur's spear and struck him down. The fate of the world was instead entrusted to the ancient Scalussen smiths, who forged the armour of the Knights of the Nine.*
FROM THE 'TRUE TALE OF SIGRIMUR', A LESSER-KNOWN EDDA OF
EASTEREALM

They had washed the decks with bucket after bucket of seawater, yet still the stains of blue leviathan blood remained, mixed purple with the ichor of sailors, soldiers, and mages. Beyond the stains, the rest of the decks were a mess of broken rigging, smashed wood, and corpses still to be hauled away. A dragon lay dead and broken over the midships of the *Summer's Fury*.

Elessi stood above the carnage with Lerel. Both of them were hollow-eyed, exhausted, and tired of keeping watch. Slowly but surely, the citizens who had spent the escape from Krauslung deep in the bookship's hold were emerging for sunlight and fresh air. Their faces were aghast. Full of fear. Children and those who had lost loved ones cried pitifully.

There was something deeply wrong about so much danger being present on a day as fine as this. Over the flat ocean, the cloudless sun cast its diamonds of shimmering light. To their starboard, nothing but water ruled for as far as the eye could see. Storms like false mountains sat low on the horizon. Barely any swell divided the endless blue. White birds wheeled alongside the dragons that kept watch as far from the seawater as possible.

To port lay a sharp hook of coastline that was peculiar, to say the least. Each cliff and shore was made of perfect columns of basalt rock. Between them, giant thrusts of quartz crystal jutted like spears from a shield wall. Hidden beaches of white sand and crushed crystal sat between these great upthrusts of oddly organised rock.

The leviathans had disappeared for now. Hopefully sated upon the three ships they had broken over the last day and night. Four vessels destroyed altogether, including the old *Waveblade*. Elessi winced. It felt horrible to feel such a thing, yet still preferable to the dread she felt for the return of the monsters.

'Do you think they're done with us?'

'I fucking hope so,' Lerel muttered. 'We can't fight those creatures every league around the Paraian coastline.'

'Is that where we are?'

Lerel nodded. 'Just turned around the Cape of Glass. Looks like we don't have any choice but to go south now. Not with those bastards somewhere behind us.'

For the thousandth time, Elessi scanned the horizon, her heart flinching every time she saw a shadow in a wave. 'How did Loki summon them?'

'I have no idea,' Lerel replied. 'I've only seen two in my entire lifetime, never mind three together. The first was dead, like a dead log as long as four ships end to end. The second passed Chaos Sound once. Somehow, the orca chased it away. But Loki is a god. He has his ways.' Lerel sounded resigned to simply being outmatched.

'A god that's got a poisonous tongue and has had too much time on this earth for my liking,' said Elessi.

'You want to go back and face him?'

'No, I don't. Farden said he was in search of a weapon to defeat him.'

'Can't Farden do that on his own?'

The question fell on distracted ears. The general was deep in thought. 'We may need to meet up with him, help him, even…' Elessi stared to what she believed to be south, with the sharp coastline to port jutting into the endless blue without end. It chilled her to think of such vast empty places and the depths that lurked beneath them. Not to mention the vile beasts, too. 'How far south does Paraia go?' she asked.

Lerel sucked her teeth.

'How long to go around it and meet with Farden on the other side?' Elessi pressed her.

'Weeks, months maybe. Few sailors bother unless they have to. That's why Krauslung, Skap, and Essen are busy ports.'

'Tell me you or Roiks have made such a journey before?

'Around the Cape of No Hope? Only once for me.'

'What a charmin' name.'

'You better believe it. Apt, is what it is. Shoals, unpredictable storms, strange currents, pirates. What more could you wish for? And that would just be the halfway point, if the Rogue's Armada makes it that far. The Silent Sea beyond is just as perilous. We don't have the provisions. And I gave my word a long time ago to protect these books and these ships. Not sacrifice them. Durnus told me that they are what our civilisation has built, not cities and Arkathedrals, but knowledge.'

'Question is, Lerel, which would you rather us face? That god, those leviathans, or the prospect of leaving that mage to perish, or all that you just said?' Elessi asked. 'I 'ope you've got an answer, because I'm bloody clueless as to what to do.'

Lerel's eyes left the waves to meet Elessi's gaze. Her catlike eyes were wide, yet still buried in dark rings.

'You really doubt he'll make it back to us?'

'It's not that I doubt him. He's my friend, as well as my king. I can't help but worry. He and the others are alone in foreign lands.' After Modren was snatched from her, she knew the fragility of life as a keener edge.

'So are we,' Lerel replied.

'General!' Towerdawn boomed from above. Two dragons, Kinsprite and Shivertread flanked him.

Enduring the gusts of their wings, Elessi met the Old Dragon at the stern edge of the forecastle. Queen Nerilan sat atop his back, hunched in the saddle. Her sharp claws of fingernails tapped a musical pattern on the blade of her glaive.

Towerdawn's great golden head swivelled to eye his queen. She hissed through her teeth but slid from the dragon's flanks. She stalked across the ship, shooting Lerel a foul look before going below to the dragon eyries.

'What did I do?' called the admiral.

Towerdawn rumbled deep in his chest as he settled down upon the deck. He looked grateful for the rest: wings and legs folded, claws outstretched and head high like a cat. Even his great bladed tail swished restlessly. Smoke drifted from his nostrils as he spoke.

'Nothing, Lerel. Nerilan has not slept in many days.'

Before they had ever heard the names of Malvus and Loki, before magma and fire had claimed Nelska, Elessi and Lerel had spent months in the company of dragons. Towerdawn had been second to his predecessor Farfallen then. It had given her a deep insight into the beasts. They were far more emotional than their scaled faces betrayed. They contained deep wells of feeling. It leaked from them like their heat and reptile musk, and rushed through their riders' veins as it did theirs. Looking at the Old Dragon now, alongside the sorrow and exhaustion, Elessi saw the worry behind his eyes. She would not dare to call it fear.

'I'm sorry for your loss,' she offered, staring to the green dragon being reverently lowered into the sea.

'I had hoped the death of my dragons and people was at an end, General.'

'So did I, Old Dragon. But without Farden and his gamble we might have lost everyone.'

'I wish I could be as optimistic as you, Elessi. We dragons and Sirens are once again homeless. And now worse: pursued by beasts beyond any of us.'

Elessi stepped closer. The dragon bent his head so that his orbs of eyes were level with hers. They were hypnotic: glass spheres of swirling gold flecks and a black iris that was a void that called to her.

'It was you, wasn't it, who spoke to me in Krauslung?' she asked.

Towerdawn bowed. 'That it was.'

'And was that you or your queen speaking?

'It was I. Changing Krauslung's mind would have been a hopeless endeavour. We must find a new Krauslung. A new Nelska. A new Scalussen. Nerilan believes our place is in the north, alone and apart from the strife of Emaneska. It was how we once lived, and for years we prospered that way. I cannot deny that. Many other Sirens believe the same. I, however, believe remaining in Emaneska would be a bandage to a festering wound. Loki would not stand any challenge to his rule. His greed will grow. He may be a god, but he still walks in the shape of a human. War would come again.'

'So you're divided. Must be difficult for you when you and Nerilan share a mind.'

The dragon nodded. 'A soul, to be more accurate. That is why a dragon dies should their rider die, but not the other way. And yes, our arguments are… interesting.'

Elessi forced herself to ask. 'What will you do? Will you leave the armada?'

The Old Dragon looked away. 'I hope it will not come to that. Many of my dragons and riders feel the same. Half of us survived Scalussen. Our eggs are on these bookships, and as such, the very future of dragonkind. We cannot protect them and ourselves at the same time. If we must choose…'

Elessi bowed her head. Of all the tribes and kin of Scalussen, Elessi's hopes for keeping them alive lay mostly with the Sirens. This was just what she needed to pile onto the mountain of shite she already teetered over. She felt crushed.

It was then that Captain Hereni and Bull had appeared on the forecastle holding the inkweld. Half of the book's cover and spine still bore the black marks of ink.

'It's the same hour as yesterday,' said Hereni, swaggering up and sketching a short bow to the general and Old Dragon. Bull bowed so low to Towerdawn he almost toppled onto his nose. The boy had been obsessed with the dragons as soon as he came to Scalussen.

'Think it still works?' Hereni asked, patting the inkweld.

Eyrum grunted grumpily. The Siren had a deep injury to his shoulder. He still insisted on trying to wear his armour over the lump of bandages. 'Let's hope.'

'What happened?' asked Lerel, who had come to investigate.

Elessi scowled. 'You try scribin' on this stupid book in the middle of a storm.'

Nerilan had returned, and had apparently been busy summoning others. High Crone Wyved and helper Peryn. Ko-Tergo, too. The queen's northern allies in the argument to stay put. The thumping on the deck announced the arrival of the bloodmonger and several of his fellow minotaurs. Dried salt ran across their giant forms in stripes. One of them had been scorched by the leviathan bile. He wore the twisted burns as proudly as a new tunic. Elessi tried not to look too closely.

'We not safe at sea,' the bloodmonger began to order. 'Seasnakes too powerful. Drowning no fine death.'

Elessi resisted the urge to shut her eyes. *Not them too.*

'I agree completely,' Nerilan also chimed in. 'If the leviathans strike again, who knows what we might lose. We have to find a safe harbour.'

As Elessi held up her hands for silence, a shout from a nearby vessel made everybody present freeze. It turned out to be merely some cry at a sword falling overboard, but it showed the knife-edge the armada's patience teetered on. Elessi let go a ragged breath.

'Farden's alive,' she told the small council once she had their attention. 'As is General Durnus, Fleetstar, Aspala, Mithrid, and your Warbringer.'

The minotaurs hammered their fists against their chests, making their chains of teeth and bones rattle. 'The Bright Fields are poorer for it.'

Elessi had little to no idea what that meant. Instead, she watched Bull trying to imitate them. He thumped Hereni's arm with a big grin on his face. The mage scowled and promptly punched him back so hard he dropped his longbow.

'Quiet,' Lerel tutted.

'Where are they?' asked the Old Dragon.

'They're far to the east. Somewhere in a place called the Sunder Road.'

'I can spare dragons to fetch them.' Already, Towerdawn's wings were spread, testing the air.

'No,' Elessi said.

Ko-Tergo flexed, testing the seams of his tunic. His white skin shone under the light. His cheeks had been scorched pink by the sun. 'Explain,' he grunted.

'He's chosen a quest instead of returnin' to us. He's looking for a weapon that can supposedly kill Loki. To put an end to the god's meddling and bring peace once and for all.'

'We have a weapon. Its name is Farden,' Peryn said.

Hereni piped up. 'Not forgetting Mithrid.'

'He clearly believes we need another.'

Towerdawn had been staring at the Cape of Glass. Small skiffs with white sails drifted around the quartz and basalt columns, half-following the fleeing armada in curiosity. Hawks and vultures wheeled.

'What is in your mind, Elessi?'

The general took a breath. 'I think we should sail south and east to meet them. Farden and the others may need our help.'

'East?' Peryn questioned.

Nerilan's scales were blushing almost a copper. 'How long would that take?'

'Weeks.'

Nerilan's scales were blushing almost a copper. 'Through one of the widest, most uncharted, and dangerous seas on the map.'

'Yes,' Elessi replied, holding fast,

'You would risk us all?' spluttered the dragon queen.

'How do you know of this?' demanded the bloodmonger.

All eyes turned on Hereni as she thrust the inkweld into the air. 'How else but magick?'

Elessi nodded. 'We're waitin' to hear from Farden now.'

Hereni strode to a nearby map table that had gone mostly un-damaged and thumped the inkweld down. As the council gathered around it, Elessi spread the book's green pages wide. The spilled ink had disappeared, much to her relief. Quill and ink were placed at her side.

Taking a moment to dip the quill, she prayed Farden would be there. Not to give her answers, but to answer those that looked to her. Her dark cabin called to her once more. It was all so much easier to hide behind a locked door.

Elessi began to write.

WE'RE STILL ALIVE. ARE YOU?

E

The script lingered for a moment and then soaked into the page to vanish. Elessi hated the way everybody leaned in, shrinking the iris of sunlight shining on the green pages. She had never been so conscious of her frankly passable penmanship.

Then came the reply, as if written by a ghostly hand. Farden's scratchy runes.

SEEMS THAT WAY. DESPITE OTHERS' BEST EFFORTS.

F

She thumped the table with her palm. 'Thank Jötun. Told you.'

'A question,' Nerilan growled.

Lerel crossed her arms. 'Another?'

'How do we know this isn't another one of Loki's tricks? How do we know this is actually Farden?'

It was an annoyingly good point.

Elessi thought for a moment before writing something down. She shrugged. 'Why mince words?'

HOW DO WE KNOW YOU AREN'T LOKI?

E

As Farden's profanities continued to cover the page, the chuckles spread between Elessi, Towerdawn, and Lerel.

'Loki may be the god of lies, but he's not the god of cursin'. That's the mage I know,' Elessi decided.

'Roiks would be proud,' Lerel muttered.

And so, the two halves of Scalussen conversed for as long as they could.

WHAT HAS LOKI DONE TO KRAUSLUNG?

F

HE'S SOMEHOW TURNED THE PEOPLE AGAINST US.
THEY LINED THE PORT, SHOUTING LOKI'S NAME. THEY
THINK US MURDERERS FOR WHAT WE DID IN THE
NORTH. LOKI TOLD US THEY WOULD FIGHT TO THE
DEATH FOR EVERY INCH OF THE CITY. THE EMPEROR IS
NOWHERE TO BE SEEN.
MAYBE DEAD AFTER ALL.

E

NO. NOT DEAD. GRIMSAYER SAYS OTHERWISE. AND
THE LEVIATHANS?

F

THE BASTARD SOMEHOW SUMMONED THREE OF THEM.
THEY PURSUED US DAY AND NIGHT. WE'VE LOST A
DRAGON, THE WAVEBLADE, THE ETHER, AND THE
BLOODY DAGGER. THE LEVIATHANS HAVE DISAP-
PEARED...

Elessi paused, unwilling to write what she wanted due to the eyes
watching her. *For now*, is what she almost scribbled. She dipped the
quill to cover her stalling.

...WE ARE SAILING SOUTH AND EAST TO MEET YOU.

Murmurs came from all around her. The witches looked at each other
in silent conversation. As did the Siren queen and her dragon. Elessi
heard their disgruntlement. She kept writing.

DO YOU NEED OUR HELP?

E

The pause was uncomfortable. Elessi stared at the empty green paper, trying to imagine what Farden was doing on the other end. Was he cursing Loki's name once more, close to dashing the book on the ground, or was he the silently simmering Farden she knew? Had something happened? She ached for confirmation that what she had decided was right.

The wait had almost become too much by the time the mage replied. It was not fuming, nor damning, but it did nothing to slow Elessi's heart:

THE BOOKSHIPS, SCALUSSEN, THE SIRENS, THEY ALL
NEED TO BE KEPT SAFE. ALIVE. SAILING EAST WOULD
PUT YOU IN DANGER.
SURVIVAL IS ALL THAT MATTERS.
NO REST 'TIL FREEDOM SERVED.

F

Elessi echoed the words as her husband had spoken many times before donning his armour, or stepping from their chambers. 'No rest 'til freedom served,' she whispered.

Elessi couldn't shake the shame of letting the mage down. 'Something's wrong with Farden, I can feel it. He needs our help.'

Nerilan thumped a fist on the table. 'You are blinded by your devotion. The mage has spoken. Survival is what matters most.

'What are you afraid of, Queen?' Elessi snapped.

'I fear nothing except the extinction of my people and my dragons, Elessi.'

The witches and Ko-Tergo hummed in agreement.

Elessi wondered why she should feel so ashamed. 'As do I, Queen Nerilan. I haven't been to my birthplace since I left it forty years ago. I thought my home was my husband. I thought Scalussen was my family. But now that has been taken away from me too.' Elessi looked around at her council. 'As such, this armada is now all

I have. All that's left of *my* people, so don't you dare lecture me on what it is to fear extinction. Maybe you should fear Loki instead. If Farden is right about him, then he's ten times the evil that Malvus was. Ten times the threat. He's our extinction, Queen Nerilan. If Farden says we need a weapon to beat him, then I believe him, and I will do anythin' I can to help him attain that end. That is what matters,' Elessi ordered. 'And I think you'll find it's *General* Elessi.'

Elessi slammed the inkweld shut and stepped from the table. Nerilan stared daggers at her, but her lips stayed pursed. Elessi quietly counted that as a win.

'Admiral Lerel, take us south. Those are my orders.' The words sounded so foreign in her mouth, but they were not difficult. She had heard Modren, Farden, and Durnus speak them countless times. 'We're not letting that bloody god or his pets drown us. Not now. Not after what I – we – have been through. We trust in Farden and we stay alive. This armada is our home. We're not witches and snowmads right now. Not minotaurs and Sirens and Paraian, we're all Scalussen. And seeing as you've chosen me as your leader, then let me bloody lead. If you got a complaint about it, want to discuss it, or shout at me, then you'll find me in my cabin.'

Hereni leaned against the bulkhead beside Bull and Kinsprite.

'Well, shit me,' she said, pursing her lips. She watched Elessi cross the forecastle, trailed by Eyrum. At the map table, Nerilan seethed, scales copper and skin red. 'I feel sorry for your queen after that tongue lashing.

'Elessi's been a leader all along,' said Kinsprite in her deep tone. 'She's just never been given the chance before. Except the time she almost saved the world with only a dagger, but she'll tell you about that one day, I'm sure. I was barely ten years out of my egg at the time, but Modren told me the tale once. Elessi doesn't need magick to be dangerous.'

The dragon closed her eyes. Her scales turned a deeper blue, as a human might blush. Not like the scaleshifter Shivertread was, who was currently switching between green and orange.

Hereni felt the same sorrow. Modren had been an uncle to her, as responsible for her place in Scalussen as Farden. Hereni knew the stiffness of Elessi's jaw, the shine to her eyes, and the way the ink-weld's cover strained beneath her white fingers. Beneath her calm facade, she mourned and raged with every stirring of her heart. It had broken free for a moment, now she fought to restrain it. Hereni knew that all too well. She had never stopped mourning her parents.

'If Elessi had magick in her, she would be aflame right now,' Hereni said.

The mage had to steady herself while the *Vanguard*'s sails billowed. The bookship yawed, taking a closer route to the shoreline. She could feel the force of spells in the air as the wind mages made patterns with their hands and went to work. Her gold hair whipped about her face. Seawater sprayed past the lower bulwarks.

*Grieve by doing.* The Rogue's Armada unwittingly followed Hereni's advice. The fear of the leviathans and the stress of being stuck on strange waters weighed less when there were spells to hold, rigging to climb, and currents to ply.

Together with Bull and the dragon, Hereni silently watched the Cape of Glass disappear behind them. Her eyes were narrowed, her mind busy. Rings of fire snaked around her fingers.

'Ships like I never seen!' Mephin cried for the dozenth time. The skiff swayed back and forth as the dolt continuously moved about on the skinny mast.

Fifty years spent on the Cape's waters as a fisherman, and the motion was still beginning to make Fletcha sick.

'He's your wife's brother. He's your wife's brother,' Fletcha muttered to himself. He clung to his mantra. Once more, his eyes crept to various items around the boat he could solve his problem with. *A fish-club. Several oars. The knife. A rock. Even the ocean itself.* 'He's your wife's—'

'Surely the lobster pots can wait, Fletcha. Come now, let's chase them! You never seen a ship like that before. Must have been as tall as the cliffs.'

Why Fletcha had agreed to take the bald moron out on the skiffs that day was a confusing combination of spousal blackmail and a wild promise made while far too drunk. He stared after the huge bulks and their retinue of warships. He had seen plenty. Their wakes made his job even more troublesome.

Mephin prattled on. 'Arka maybe? Look like they been in a fight. I don't see no green flags or hammer…'

*The man needed a job*, Fletcha's wife had said. *A skill. Something to get him out of the town and out from under people's feet.*

'Black sails look like pirates though, and they got dragons too…'

*It used to be peaceful on the skiff alone.*

'Come, let's follow them, Fletcha! Everybody else is!'

Fletcha gripped the tiller so tightly, some tendon in his forearm twanged in protest. His restraint unravelled the more he spoke. 'Well, they look to be leaving now, and they're much faster than us, so why don't you do me a favour, if you would be so kind, and do your bloody job, Mephin!'

The man was stunned to silence. Leaning out from one hand around the mast, he stared down at Fletcha with a child's pout.

'Seris said you'd be mean.'

'You also said you'd listen and stay quiet.'

'But the ships.'

'I don't care about the bloody ships! I care about my pots and getting the lobsters out before they escape or begin to eat each other. Before I don't make any coin at market. Before I beat you blue because my family's got nothing to eat tonight.'

'You know what?' Mephin began to climb down the mast. He couldn't even do that right, falling the last third with his foot tangled in a line. 'You know what?'

Fletcha was on his feet before Mephin was. 'What? Go on. Spit it out. See where complaints or insults get you on my boat.'

'I'm tired of everyone thinkin' I'm stupid, or calling me idiot.'

Before he could stop himself, Fletcha found himself shoving the man against the mast. 'Then stop being one!'

'Get off me!'

Fletcha saw a fist swinging. He sprang away and raised an oar, ready to bash some sense into the fool.

Mephin truly was an idiot. He raised a pointing finger, face aghast at something conveniently behind Fletcha.

'How old do you think I am, man? You stupid dolt. I'll be doing your sister a favour—'

Between the waves crashing along the cliffs of glass and rock, Fletcha heard a rising roar of water.

'Look!' The shrill horror to Mephin's voice and the way all colour had vanished from his face told Fletcha this might not be a trick after all.

The fisherman turned around just in time to see the horizon blotted out by a gaping maw of crowded fangs, each longer than the oar that dropped from his shaking hands. Darkness enveloped them. The skiff was swept into a torrent throwing Fletcha and Mephin into the air, screaming. Just as it looked as they might escape the monster's maw, as though only the skiff might be swallowed, the other half of its jaws burst from the sea and closed around them with a rending crash. Fletcha was still in the midst of drowning when he was swallowed.

The leviathan barely slowed to enjoy its meal. Burrowing beneath the waves to the screams of other fishermen, it set a course south. The two sinuous giants followed in its wake.

# CHAPTER 11
## DATHAZH

*If you enjoy the wide rolling plains and clear views of the open ocean, then*
*don't come to Golikar. The place is infested with trees. The forests creep*
*about, I tell you. Trees appear in places they never stood. Paths close up*
*around you. Tis a place of madness that the irascible Golikan seem to*
*pleasantly endure. I will not travel this far north again.*
A LETTER TO THE LADY RIRK OF NORMONT, WRITTEN BY HER HUS-
BAND. THIS WAS THE LAST MESSAGE SHE RECEIVED FROM HIM BE-
FORE HIS DISAPPEARANCE

'Out of my way, curse you!' roared the rider to the guards barring the
gates of ogin bone. There was torment in his voice. Every thud of his
cow's hooves on the grass was a shuddering pain through his arse
and back. The struggle paled in comparison to his task. A cloud of
seed husks and dirt fled behind him. The rider clung on, slavering
just as much as his beast through bared teeth.

'Fucking move!' the rider yelled once more, shortly before
sending a guard flying with a barge from the cow's thick shoulder. 'I
have business with the High Cathak!' was the only apology he
offered.

The tent-lined path through camp swiftly cleared a way for
him after that. The day was still dawning. Fur-clad figures with sleep
in their eyes scattering before his cow's horns. The rider bent towards
the grand pavilion in his saddle and urged the last scraps of energy
out of his piebald mount.

Utterly spent, the cow collapsed in the dust, its scaled snout
coming to a rest on the steps of the pavilion of canvas and leather.

Crows squawked as they gathered in curiosity. The rider tumbled from his saddle and sprawled in the dust. He pushed himself to his knees, clutching a shoulder that felt suspiciously out of its socket.

Cries and yells from the rider's mad dash had brought High Cathak Tartavor from his sanctum and to the pavilion's door. With a savage burn still healing across the right side of his face, the High Cathak looked even more threatening than usual. His black and silver scythe towered above those of his guards. Their blue, woad-daubed faces were scrunched in concern.

'Who are you?' Tartavor demanded.

The rider prostrated himself on the sun-bleached steps. 'Vhazar, milord! One of your son's guards.'

'What news? Does he return with the sinners?'

'I'm... I'm afraid not, High Cathak.'

Swift boots closed the gap between them. Strong hands hauled Vhazar up by the collar of his sweat-damp coat. 'Speak! Or I shall have the Dusk God curse you!'

'He killed him, milord!' Vhazar blurted, all tact forgotten in the pain of his shoulder. 'The man in red and gold you wanted, he cut Oselov's throat without mercy.'

Tartavor's grip tightened, beginning to strangle the rider. 'You lie.'

'I wouldn't dare, High Cathak! Dusk God swear it. We found them at the Spoke. Your messenger arrived after them. We told them to surrender. Had them surrounded...' Vhazar trailed off. His own memory of the events were a blur. All he recalled was seeing the plains turn red and turning tail at the earliest opportunity. He had watched Oselov's murder from shamefully far away, but that detail didn't need to be admitted to the High Cathak, of course.

'And then?' The High Cathak's eyes had strayed to the gates, where other Cathak were hot on Vhazar's tail. Their dust cloud was a column in the eastern sky. The lowing of their cow mounts was constant. 'What of the dragon?'

'No dragon, milord. The foreigner threw a knife. A foul trick. He knocked Oselov from his firn. Before we could reach him, the man of red and gold...' Vhazar didn't want to say the words again.

The rider was summarily dropped on the steps. The High Cathak stumbled past him to the dirt as other riders thundered through the camp. Crows scattered in their dozens.

'High Cathak!' hailed the head rider.

'Is it true? My son is dead?'

With reverence, the riders dismounted their cows and slowly lowered a body wrapped in a blood-soaked cloak to the earth. Tartavor fell to his knees at his dead son's side. His hands pawed at the cloak, revealing just a portion of Oselov's white face and one bloated eye. It was all Tartavor could bear.

The rider had taken a knee, but was staring flatly at Vhazar.

Vhazar scowled back as he listened to the rider's explanation with growing trepidation.

'The foreigners have dark magick in them, milord. They were too strong. They killed Oselov and his firn. Half of the herd fled in fear and left your son defenceless. Just like Vhazar over there.'

'You filthy liar, Novod!' Vhazar spouted.

But Novod continued. 'After the foreigners escaped, those of us who fought on returned to fetch Oselov's body. We knew you would want to give him to the Dusk God, High Cathak.'

To Vhazar's horror, Tartavor stood and turned to face him. The unburnt side of Tartavor's face had turned as red as the scorched side.

'It's not true, I swear!' Vhazar exclaimed. His knees struck the dust once more. Before he could explain himself, he found the hands of Tartavor's guard gripping his shoulders. He writhed in pain.

'You were my son's guard, were you not?'

'Yes, sire,' answered Vhazar truthfully.

'Then you failed not only my son, but yourself, and your god. May the dusk feast upon your soul for a thousand years!'

Tartavor let fall his scythe, driving the blade through the top of Vhazar's skull and cutting his screech viciously short. He left the weapon in the corpse and staggered up the steps to the darkness of his pavilion. His voice was a broken roar.

'Ready the herd! We go east!'

In Troughwake there had once lived a fellow named Able. He'd earned the name from being a smart chap, capable of fixing most things and suggesting solutions half of Troughwake would never think of. An oddball, Mithrid's father had called him. Able had worn spectacles he built himself from polished seaglass. Always with a book, was Able. He would read constantly, even as he walked, head down and deep in concentration. This ultimately proved his undoing the day he accidentally marched off a cliff, book in hand and eyes lost in script. They found his body in the surf, somehow his spectacles still intact.

Farden was Able in that moment. The mage had walked for a day straight with the inkweld open in his hands. Every now and again, he would look up from the blank pages to notice their surroundings, and down his head would go.

'Anything else?' Mithrid asked once more.

'No. Elessi has gone silent,' came Farden's usual response.

Silence passed between them for a time before Mithrid broke it. 'Are they sailing east to meet us?'

'No. I told them to stay put. Stay safe. Sailing east would threaten them all. Without them, there's no Scalussen.'

'But can they beat these leviathans? Or outrun them?'

'Why do you care so much?' he asked gruffly.

For all the challenge she heard in Farden's voice, she saw the simple question on his face.

'I told you. Scalussen was my home. For a short while, of course, but despite that, it felt like home. Bull and Hereni are my friends. I don't want any harm coming to them.'

'Hereni,' Farden chuckled. 'And I thought she was the strong-willed one. You proved me wrong.'

Mithrid posed the question she had been working towards. 'Can I speak to her? Or Bull?'

'Tomorrow, maybe.'

Farden dismissed some inner worry with a shake of his hand. He looked up from the inkweld at the mountain that stretched before them.

Mithrid followed his gaze. Alone, the mountain sprang from the grasslands suddenly and without the polite introduction of foothills. Its sheer sides ascended from the plateau of golden grass at a sharp angle. Small settlements like barnacles covered its slopes, abodes of grass thatch and rock. Smoke curled from their chimneys and brought more of the dung-fire stink that had now become almost comforting. More sheep and goats peppered the rocks.

'So this is Eaglehold. Now all we have to do is find its roots and the shimmer of a serpent,' Durnus said from behind them. The vampyre had improved much since the Bronzewood. He barely hobbled now. His pale eyes, although ringed with red and set in dark hollows, were sharper than before, and his face had less of a sickly sheen to it. His Weight-burned hands were beginning to heal.

If only Farden had shown such healing. If anything, the mage worsened with every encounter and dying sun. His skin had taken on a grey pallor. His stubble had turned into the scraggy beginnings of a beard. Mithrid knew his age exceeded his looks, thanks to his immortal armour, but much to her concern, the years seemed to be catching up.

The grasslands changed around the foot of the mountain. The Sunder Road curved around its edge and between meandering fields of tors sprouting from the grass. They followed it on, filling their eyes with sun until it began to die beneath the yellow mountains behind them.

As they turned around a bluff of stone, they found themselves stumbling to a halt with wonder. A giant pine tree stood in the scree of Eaglehold's slopes. The tree had roots that stretched over the rocks for hundreds of yards. A whole village had been built in its branches. Rooftops extended above its foliage at severe angles. The tree had bent under the pressure over the years, but it was still tall enough the reach halfway up the Frostsoar, if that tower still stood.

'What in Emaneska…?' Durnus stopped himself. 'What in the world is that? I have heard tales of the giant eastern forests, but until now I did not believe them. That tree must be two hundred feet tall.'

'In the far south, beyond the tip of Paraia, they talk of trees this large and even larger,' Aspala said breathlessly. 'Trees large enough for whole cities to roost in, boughs as wide as roads.'

'Just a tree,' surmised Farden, continuing to walk into the pine's shadow.

'Not impressed?' Mithrid asked.

'No,' said Farden flatly. 'You've seen one tree, you've seen them all.'

By the time they had drawn level with the giant's trunk, the light of sunset had become strangely coloured, a mishmash of green and gold. Night's dark gradually ate into every colour.

'Where go you?' cried a voice from a watchtower clinging onto a flimsy branch. 'Here for the Tourney?'

'We search for Sigrimur!' Durnus yelled back.

The laughter was loud and mocking. Even the branch bobbed ever so faintly.

When the guard had recovered himself appropriately, he shouted, 'You're several thousand years too late, but if you've come for the homage…'

The guard, barely a thumbnail in size, pointed them on their way. East, past the mountain's scree and on to the forest. There, the mountain slopes spread into rumpled lowlands. A broad, silver slick of river cut a meandering path through the grasslands. They had been too fascinated by the tree to notice it. To the south, it stretched into a sprawling estuary that ended in what appeared to be a sea, bathed in orange sunset. Ahead, the Sunder Road led to a glittering smear of dark buildings. It huddled against the only bridge to cross the river's expanse. Beyond the river's banks lay a forest of the giant pines, stretching up like a plateau of sage green and umber wood.

Their stillness suggested to the guard they had no idea what a homage was, and he would have been right.

'You've got no idea what I'm saying do you? Dathazh. That city right down the mountain where the Sunder Road ends? That's the capital of the Rivenplains. You might want to start there, where the Scarlet Tourney begins. Ask around and you'll soon find the homage. Now move along, stop clogging the road!'

'So that is Dathazh,' said Durnus as they turned away to face the city lights.

'And it sits before a serpent's shimmer: the river,' Aspala added. Her finger traced the weaving of the river. Mithrid tutted at herself for not realising.

'Then we'll spend the night in the city and see about this homage. Hopefully it'll lead us to where Sigrimur died, and then we can move on,' Farden decided for them all. His voice was low and empty of tone. His eyes flitted between the copper skies and his un-armoured hands. He kept clenching and flexing them. Mithrid swore she could count more wrinkles in his hands.

'Aye,' Aspala agreed, stepping ahead like a scout. Mithrid wondered how she was still so loyally determined. She never had a single question for her proclaimed king.

Warbringer was the one who seemed reticent. 'Pink-flesh cities like this don't like minotaurs. Never have,' she grunted when asked. 'Uncomfortable. Dangerous.'

'Dangerous for anyone who means you harm or insult, more like,' Farden told her.

The minotaur shrugged. Mithrid had never seen her act in such a way before. Warbringer followed, shoulders stooped and Voidaran low in the grass, muttering in the harsh tongue of her clans. Mithrid only heard the word, '*Efjar*'.

All she could think of was another crisp ale and something sturdy beneath her arse instead of her feet. She willed the city closer with every step.

❦

The architects of Dathazh appeared to be an unimaginative bunch, both in ancient times as well as modern. Though it appeared a cramped town at a distance, the closer the Sunder Road led them, the more they realised the sprawl and height of Dathazh. And yet, there was a tedious uniformity to the place. Almost every building was of the same design and made of the same grey wood or brown clay brick, only varying in size and age. Square, was the rule of architecture here. Square edges and square bricks. Square roofs of square wooden slates and tiles of dry river clay. Square streets each meeting at perpendicular crossroads.

Only five buildings dared defy tradition. They reached above the slate rooftops at sharp angles. One was the elaborate fort that sat on the hill overlooking the river. The others looked to be temples to various gods. Golden symbols crested their spires, so thin that they couldn't serve any purpose except reaching taller than their rivals. The closest looked to be the crescent symbol of the Dusk God.

Farden imagined that some found it pleasing to the eye. The sort of mind that found happiness in order and perfect degrees. Farden found himself missing the tangle of Krauslung, where a city lived and breathed and grew like a great beast. The city weighed heavy on his mind. All he could think of was how Krauslung spoke the name of Forever King now. Cursed it, no doubt. Spat it out like poison.

For all Dathazh's jejune architecture, its citizens refused to remain as bland. Even before the square walls of Dathazh enveloped them, it was clear from the ruckus filling the evening air. The city roared with song and conversation. Great streamers of red and gold had been attached to the wall-spikes. They floated in the breezes above the heads of the crowds all vying to enter the city through a single diminutive gate. Which, of course, was no more than a block of square brick and sharpened stakes.

The crowds were divided by the roads they came in on, but also by their attire and the flags they waved incessantly. Farden recognised only one crest, which looked similar to an old Skölgard Empire flag he had once seen. Wagons and litters and carriages squeezed between the two-legged travellers. Cows, coelos, more of the lizard creatures, and tall persnippen lowed and shrieked at each other. Songs came from some of the more gilded carriages; battle songs that made the onlookers on the walls cheer. Names Farden had never heard were yelled in adoration. Rich and poor folk bustled alongside knights and priests of religious orders. It all seemed too much for the city to cope with.

*And it was.*

An hour, it took Farden to realise that half the damn people in the crowd were not queuing, but instead setting up their own camps and impromptu fighting rings.

'At last,' the mage huffed when they reached the glowing mouth of Dathazh.

Painted wood signs had been hung all around the gatehouse. Half of them were in Commontongue, and in yellow and red script they proclaimed the rules of Dathazh. For those in doubt, the guards checking each traveller spent every breath yelling the rules over and over.

'Fighting is for the Scarlet Tourney only!'

'Thieves will be skinned alive!'

'No warring here! Peace reigns no matter who or what you are!'

'No tricksters or frauds! All traders must be licensed by the Vassallord!'

'Absolutely no magick allowed in the city!'

'No vandalism!'

'Business and origin!

The last shout was directed at Farden and the others, who were focused on their monotonous shuffle. A guard in leather armour made of overlapping square scales was staring at them over a scroll. So large was the scroll two other guards held it in the crook of their arms.

'Er... Travellers from the Hammer Hills. We've come for the Tourney?' Farden tried to keep the question from his voice.

The guard looked Farden up and down, noting the armour and the two swords thrust through his belt. 'Fighters, I take it? Where's your retinue?'

'No, we're not fighting.'

Even the two guards flanking him rolled their eyes. 'Spectating, trading, gambling. Which is it?'

Impatient shouts from back in the crowd heckled them. 'Hurry up there! All the best whores will be gone by now!'

'They went days ago, you idiot!' cried another.

Farden growled. 'Spectating. Though we are looking for where Sig—'

'Next!' yelled the guard scribe. The other two guards pushed them onwards, much to Farden's rankling.

'In you go. Mind your rules and mind your coin.'

'What little we have of it,' Durnus muttered in the mage's ear as they stepped into the city. A square of trampled dust lay before them. The crowds spread outwards in all directions, filtering into the parallel streets as if there was a rush to take in as much of Dathazh as possible. All manner of acrobats, jesters and jugglers cavorted across the square. Skinny men on stilts blew fire above the crowd. Figures in all manner of over-polished and absurdly impractical armour stood on boxes or makeshift daises. They waved their swords and posed in ridiculous shapes. One pretended to duel with a fellow in a poorly-made dragon costume. At their feet, their retinues brayed their praises in theatrical verse. Heralds read long lists of how many princes and princesses they had rescued, or warlords and beasts slain. The less talented bellowed out branch after branch of family tree.

Aspala and Warbringer were busy looking around at the array of acrobats and jugglers. Warbringer had a strange smile on her face. No thanks to the glaring colours and roar of voices, but because in this mad circus, filled with every corner of a foreign world, she seemed to fit right in.

Mithrid stood beside Farden. 'Do we rest first or find this homage the tree-man spoke of?'

'No rest. We keep moving.'

Her sigh was audible.

'Are you sure, Farden?' Durnus asked.

Farden looked around the group, noting all the baggy eyes and slumped shoulders. 'We find this homage and Sigrimur. Then we can rest.'

'He'll push himself to collapsing at this rate.' Mithrid's whisper to Aspala wasn't as lost in the noise as she thought. Farden shook his head as he looked for an avenue that made sense in this mad city. *Mithrid was correct.* Farden would push himself, if that was what it took. He had gone that far and further before. He would do it again.

Even as that notion added some weight to his feet, Farden forced himself through a throng of bare-chested and over-perfumed people who led a cheering procession through the crowds. They had piles of leaf garlands in their hands, tied with red and yellow ribbons. One tried to put a garland over the mage's head, but the speed with which Farden seized the man's hand made him rethink his decision.

He placed the same wreath over Durnus instead. The vampyre wore a tired and bemused smile.

'It has been some time since I saw such joy without worry hiding behind it,' Farden heard the vampyre say.

'The last time I saw a place this festive it was Scalussen's feast before Malvus arrived,' Aspala hummed as if longing for that night again.

'Dear friends! Strangers! Halt there if you would.'

Farden turned, expecting a guard or some authority. Instead, it was a man in a hat so large and bulbous it made the rest of his body look like a silk thread hanging from an apple. The mage had to dodge to avoid being struck in the face by the fabric orb. He held it with both hands as he scurried to catch up with them.

'What do you want?' asked Farden.

The ludicrous fellow laughed heartily. 'A man of little time. I like it! I shall be swift. You are here for the Tourney, yes?'

'Actually—'

'I thought so! I know proud warriors when I see them. It is my business to see such things! You are aware that if you wish to join the Tourney at this late hour in the chancer's slots, you need a patron, and I just so happen to be the finest around! How lucky you are to run into Antor!' The man rapped his many silver and copper rings on the wolf of Farden's breastplate. The mage glared.

'Oof! Would not like to come across you in a dark alley, sir!' Antor laughed again, utterly unaware how close he had come to losing his hand. 'Tell me you have not agreed to fight for Fetharl or the other swines.'

'No, I don't know who that is—'

'Wonderful! Wonderful indeed. I've seen far too many fighters sign with the wrong people. You've done well. Intelligent souls, I can tell. Now, time is wasting to enter your names. The chancer's places are fading fast.'

The man spoke in a way that made Farden feel at fault for not understanding a word he said.

'And so, if you have the coin, I can promise you a place in the Tourney.' The man beamed a wide smile. Several of his teeth were painted green.

Farden tried to move past but the man blocked him from escaping.

'Look, Antor, was it?' Farden asked.

'Antor of Nyrdwell.'

'Well, Antor, listen here. I'm not interested in fighting in the Tourney, so if you could let us pass, I would—'

'Oh,' Antor said, looking shocked at such a suggestion. 'Not you, good sir. No, no. I am sure you can swing a sword with the best of them. No, no. I am more interested in you, madam.' Antor's gaze swivelled to Warbringer. 'Does this man speak for you?'

'I speak for myself,' the minotaur growled in reply. She put a protective paw on Durnus' shoulder, who almost crumbled under its weight. 'But I am bound to this one.'

'Good! Good! Let us discuss terms! How much coin *do* you have?'

Farden looked around. He saw no guards looking their way, and a convenient corner free of stalls or people hanging around. While Antor was still babbling, he seized him by the throat and drove him backwards until the stone knocked the breath from him.

'To touch one as me is death in Dathazh! Especially during Tourney week!' the man garbled.

'Me? See, I don't care. I'm new to this city. The rules don't apply to me. So you better tell me where the homage is before I snap your neck and leave you here in this gutter.'

'The h—homage?' The man looked confused, as if he had expected a demand for coin or some other favour. 'It's, er, in the first canals. At the statue of Sigrimur.'

'There's a statue?'

'How foreign are you? Where else would the homage to Sigrimur happen?'

Farden squeezed tighter, making Antor croak. A few of the other sponsors looked on. One crossed his arms and grinned at the display.

'Farden.' Durnus' hand alighted on his arm. 'Let him go. We are strangers here. Their rules are not ours.'

The mage relented, leaving Antor to scuttle off nursing a sore throat and promising all kinds of harm and worry.

'Another enemy made,' said Mithrid. When Farden turned to glare at her, he was surprised to find her glaring right back. The girl was not joking.

'What? I'm right, aren't I?' she continued. 'You seem like you're intent on making every enemy you can. We've got enough of those behind us. At very least, you're making every step of this journey harder than it needs to be. You're not the Forever King I know. Or is this the real Farden?'

'Mithrid,' Durnus hissed.

'Am I not right?'

'Let's find this bloody statue,' was all Farden said. Mithrid was right, but he refused to admit as much.

Deeper into Dathazh, they wound. The streets grew only marginally quieter than the city square. Taverns and kitchens bled into the thoroughfares. Some of the taller towers hosted loud parties. Men with long, double-ended flutes played on balconies. Where different fighters of the Scarlet Tourney had set up camp around their chosen taverns, demonstrations of strength and skill drew crowds where men and women glittered in armour. It was a market for flesh. People had their faces painted in the colours of their chosen fighter. Hagglers sold their tokens by the dozen. Fighters posed to attract attention.

Again and again, they were approached by patrons with glorious offers of a place in the Scarlet Tourney. And again and again, almost every one of them wanted a piece of Warbringer. One even offered a slot for Mithrid. Farden kept his hood low and his lips pursed, and blamed his scarred armour.

Dathazh's monotony held fast with every step. They did not meander through the streets, but followed a busy thoroughfare for a mile without taking a turn. The idea of a curve must have been more foreign than they were.

Halfway through the city, the cobbles grew encrusted with clay mud. The faint smell of salt and dank filled their nostrils. Before long, river water began to swallow street after street. Cobbles fell away to form canals. Gutters turned into paved banks. Every street running north or south became a bridge. Wagons and carriages were replaced with tiny coracle boats and long barges that were curiously jointed in the middle so they could turn the sharp corners of rigid Dathazh without trouble. Lanterns and candles floated on lily pads that spun and scurried – or sometimes drowned – in the wakes of the boats. They turned the water to gold and lit the faces of the stark buildings that leaned slightly over the waterways.

It reminded Farden of Tayn, a small town in Albion that no doubt still loathed the mage's name. He had found that place and its canals somewhat peaceful. Simple, if anything. But Dathazh insisted on being its riotous self. Instead of wagons and stalls in the street, the fighters of the Tourney sailed back and forth on their painted barges. Pigeons feasting on the scraps of the giant festival weaved through the buildings in tight, blizzarding flocks that made everybody duck. There was nowhere for the eye or for the feet to rest.

Aspala and Durnus were asking directions to the first canals and the homage. Most of the passersby they snagged were too drunk or unfamiliar with the Commontongue. From a vantage point at the peak of an arching bridge, it was Mithrid who saw the procession first. She nudged Farden and pointed.

His tired eyes took a moment to see them through the torchlight. A line of what looked to be priests snaked through the crowd. Their faces and torsos were painted grey with dust and clay so as to look like people of stone. Their grey loincloths were the only clothes they wore. Few bothered them with jibes. Most of the members of the crowd reverently touched the priests as they passed, daubing their necks or wrists with paint.

Farden worked his way through the crowds to meet the priests on their way through the crowd. The painted individuals had built up a small following.

'Is this the homage?' Durnus called from behind.

'You are correct, stranger,' said a chap with sun-kissed, scarred cheeks. He was clad head to knee in a shirt of chainmail. 'Though many have forgotten, it is good luck to pay respects to the ancient hero Sigrimur the night before the Tourney. Do you fight?'

'No,' Farden replied.

'I meant her.' Of course, he pointed to Warbringer. 'You, beast of the Burnt South.'

'No, I do not fight.' Warbringer flared her wide nostrils as she shook her head. The rings in her broad snout jangled. 'And I am of Efjar.'

'I have not heard of such a place, but I have seen your kind south and west. Beyond your lands, Paraian,' He said this to Aspala. Her broken horns had already started to grow. Her hood did little to hide their sharp stumps.

The minotaur shook her head. 'Not true.'

'Then tell me how one skewered me,' the man patted his side. 'And left me for dead.'

'See? Man lies,' Warbringer said before flashing her sharp teeth. 'True minotaur would have eaten you.'

'Then I am glad you do not fight in the Tourney! You may cheer for me instead.' Abruptly distracted, he pointed ahead. 'Behold, strangers of Efjar. The first canals and Sigrimur's Rest. Farewell and good luck,' he bade them, quickening his step to see Sigrimur sooner.

Even in his exhausted state, Farden could have cheered. Lo and behold, Dathazh broke form at last.

Ahead of them, the fort rose up out of the city and loomed over the river. Here, in the oldest canals, the buildings looked older, stretched taller. The purple sky was a jigsaw piece between their square-cut roofs. Not a star could be seen. And here, as if the architects experienced a moment of madness, lay a small, round clearing.

The buildings crowded around and leaned in like a blank-faced council. Wooden walkways ringed the circle, threaded with strings of mushrooms that shone with a soft rosy light. Sandstone pillars rose up around them like a temple, yet bore the marks of initials and graffiti. Water filled the centre of the clearing, shallow across a moss-covered floor of stone. Lanterns in iron cages sat in a concentric ring before the statue of Sigrimur.

Farden wasn't sure what he had been expecting, but perhaps something... taller. The sculptors hadn't made the so-called hero as large as Warbringer, but he would have made Eyrum or Bull stand on tiptoes. It was a modest statue compared to his supposed legacy.

They had carved him from silver granite, and he was unbelievably lifelike even for the artisans and sculptors of old. Where armour didn't cover Sigrimur, his muscles bulged. He wore no sword. He did not stand proudly or heroically, but humbly, almost in what looked like the moment of his death. His knees were half bent, One hand clenched and defiant by his side, the other clasped to his chest as if wounded.

Most notable, however, was the complete absence of Sigrimur's head. Maybe that was why he wasn't as tall as Farden expected. A stone stump of a neck was all that was left. If Farden's tired eyes could be trusted, it hadn't even been cleaved cleanly.

'Durnus?' Farden said. 'He is missing his head.'

The vampyre flapped his mouth. 'I guess that steward was not joking when he said the prize of this Scarlet Tourney was the head of Sigrimur.'

Questions burning, Farden and the others moved closer. The dust-daubed priests had gathered on the opposite side of the circle.

They sang slow and softly in a language Farden didn't recognise. Looking around, it was a far cry from the rest of the city. It seemed this world had taken Sigrimur's head and forgotten the rest of him.

A few groups of people stood about in quiet prayer or conversation. Some lit candles or tossed coins into the shallow water to make ripples in the red glow. It was almost peaceful. Farden found himself leaning against the wooden railings and staring at the hero. For a moment, he forgot the others, forgot why they had even come there. He wondered if there would be a statue of him like this one day: forgotten, alone, frozen in a moment of a final failure.

'Well, Durnus?' he said, cross-armed and contemplative like the others. 'Ideas?'

' "Gunnir's last blood",' Durnus whispered to himself while he ran a tongue around his fangs. He made his way around the walkway, walking his hands over themselves along the railing. 'Look there,' he called. 'They even carved his mortal wound, do you see?'

Farden and the others followed. They now stared at Sigrimur head-on. Where his hand clutched his chest, a hole pierced the stone. By the faint light shining from the other side, it ran him through. Once again, the detail of it astounded Farden. He could even see whorls in the headless stump that looked almost like bone and windpipe.

Durnus was fidgeting. There was an excitement in the vampyre that belied their exhaustion. Farden truly wished he could feel the same; some of the spark of his younger self when his world consisted of hunting down problems for the magick council. He had been free, then. He was growing tired of the feeling that every step he took, a thousand hands reached from the dust and held onto him.

' "Hear the last breath of retribution's lesson." What is usually the outcome of retribution in this world of ours?' asked Durnus.

Aspala spoke true. 'Death.'

'Then that means Sigrimur himself is retribution's lesson,' hissed Farden.

'So the first task is listening to… his last breath?' Mithrid thought aloud. 'How is that even possible?'

Before anyone could answer her, they noticed a woman of purple cloth and black hair further down the railing chuckling to herself. A heavy shawl covered in a complicated yellow pattern hung over her far shoulder.

'Something amuse you, madam?' asked Farden. No wonder she had overheard them; she had large, pointed ears on either side of her partially shaved head. Her hair ran in a tight tail between her shoulders.

'Retribution, I thought I heard you say,' she said. Her accent was of the same thick Commontongue of the east.

'And how is that amusing?'

'Because you, like most foreigners I meet, have obviously listened to far too many eddas written by the wrong bards and skalds. It wasn't retribution that killed Sigrimur, but jealousy.'

Sensing the presence of another scholar, Durnus stepped forwards. 'I understood it was the Allfather himself that killed Sigrimur. In return for his pride and betraying the gods.'

The woman smiled bright teeth almost matched her clear eyes, almost devoid of colour save two circlets of green. 'You must be of the west to use that name for the Noose God. And as such, you've likely only heard the false tales of Sigrimur; the ones the ancient scholars would have us believe is a moral lesson of pride and devotion. Lies. It was not Sigrimur's pride that killed him, but the Noose God's jealousy. Sigrimur was hailed as a god in his own right by the time he built the first of the Scattered Kingdoms. He built this very city, as it happens. Jealous of the adoration the people paid to a mere mortal, the Noose God took revenge on Sigrimur, not retribution. He killed him with Sigrimur's own magick spear. Many say he had a sword instead, broken into nine pieces, but that is wrong. The Noose God – your Allfather – then stole the spear and destroyed it. According to some songs, he threw it in the ocean. Here is all that is left of

Sigrimur's legend; his name celebrated but the man forgotten. Hundreds used to make the pilgrimage. Now only handfuls come.'

'Might I ask who you are to know so much about Sigrimur?'

'Because I,' she said, standing tall and haughty, 'am his daughter by bloodline.'

Taking a moment to adjusted her shawl, the woman brought forth an arm of polished and intricate grey wood. Unknown runes had been carved into its surface from shoulder to elbow. A contraption sat on her forearm that looked very much like a miniature crossbow bent back on itself. A small bolt sat ready and waiting to kill. She proffered her wooden hand to the vampyre, who didn't hesitate to shake it. His intrigue was far from subtle.

'I am Durnus Glassren of Emaneska.' Durnus said, admiring the forearm far too closely. 'And what a fascinating appendage, madam, I must say. Forgive me for staring but I have never seen the like.'

'They call me Irien, the Lady of Whispers,' she replied with a winning smile. 'And this is nothing but Golikan wood and Haspia magick to cover for an incident years ago.'

It was hard to pin down how old the Lady of Whispers was. Her skin was alabaster and she was more scars than wrinkles. Yet she had an assuredness to her that spoke decades. Farden found himself staring.

'What brings you to Dathazh, ladies and gentlemen? By the look of you I would say the Scarlet Tourney, but few of the fighters make pilgrimages to Sigrimur's Rest any longer. You are curious, to say the least.'

'We're just passing through,' Farden grunted. 'Spectators at the most.'

Durnus elaborated. 'We are explorers, in truth. Historians and scholars. We have journeyed here looking for relics related to Sigrimur, if possible.'

'Explorers, you say? How fortunate! In my spare moments, I am somewhat of a collector myself. And as a daughter of Sigrimur, Golikan and Easterealm art and trinkets are my speciality. If you are looking for something in particular, I might just be the person to help you. It merely depends on what,' Irien said, cocking her head.

'That it does,' Durnus replied, letting the silence drag before Irien changed the subject.

'And who might your companions be? By the look of them, Durnus, you must be looking for something dangerous, or at very least looking in dangerous places.'

Durnus flashed a smile. He had remembered to fold away his fangs. 'Sometimes both! These are my cohorts. Guards, if you will.'

Farden flashed the vampyre a scowl.

Irien laughed, making the others look uncomfortably between themselves. 'Three knights alone would have surely sufficed, Durnus, no? You alone must have cost a pretty pouch of coin, madam,' she said to Warbringer. The minotaur just thumped her warhammer on the walkway.

'This one owes me a life debt, fortunately,' Durnus answered quickly.

Irien tittered. 'Shame. I imagine you would do well in the Tourney.'

'Is this where you tell us you're a patron and have a chancer's slot for us if we have the coin?'

Irien held Farden's glower with her sharp eyes. Her smile spread ear to ear. 'You've been harassed all the way here, I imagine, sir…?'

'Farden.'

'Sir Farden. I am no patron. Like you, I am merely an intrigued spectator.'

'Well, it has been a pleasure—' Farden began, but he was quickly interrupted.

'Which inn have you managed to squeeze into tonight?' Irien asked.

Durnus shook his head. 'Er, we have not. Not yet.'

'We were actually heading to an armourer first.' Farden crossed his arms with a clank.

Irien laughed once more. Humour seemed an easy habit to her. 'Then you'll be queuing for hours and then sleeping in the streets with the other drunkards. I can offer you a place for the night as well as an appointment with a smith. I'm bound across the river tomorrow for the Tourney. Vensk armourers are famed throughout the Easte-realm. I can introduce you to a reputable man.'

'How much?' asked Farden.

Irien looked shocked. 'I would not be a good host if I asked for your coin, now would I? Come now. Follow me, it's not far.'

Sweeping her hand beneath the shawl, the Lady of Whispers thumped her way across the walkway in sturdy, heeled boots. Durnus was beginning to follow when Aspala held him back.

'Do we trust this woman?' she asked.

'I don't trust anybody,' Mithrid muttered.

'You said we need information, did you not? She might have it,' Durnus said. 'You heard her claim. Who better to ask?'

Farden was not convinced. 'And who else better to know what we're talking about, and want to tag along? Or worse?'

'One night, Farden. She would be a fool to try anything. She knows as little of us as we do of her.'

Farden was about to complain when an unusual wave of dizziness struck him. He sagged against the railing, making it groan. Mithrid grabbed him, but something about her touch worried him. He shrugged her away, accepting Aspala's arm instead.

'I'm fine. I'm fine,' the mage muttered.

Irien called back to them. 'Something the matter? I know all the finest healers and apothecaries if necessary.'

'It won't be, thank you,' lied Farden as he stood upright again. His knees protested with two loud clicks. Thankfully it sounded like his armour had made the noise. These were not just the echoes of injuries, but aches and pains that had no reason or cause. Instead of healing over the last few days, his body was doing quite the opposite.

'This way, strangers. Peace and quiet awaits.'

No longer able to argue with Mithrid's narrowed stare, and leaning on Aspala more than he liked to admit, it was with muttered curses that Farden followed the Lady of Whispers back into the maelstrom of Dathazh, to gods knew what and where.

All Farden knew for sure was that something was deeply and worryingly wrong with him.

# CHAPTER 12
## VENGEANCE'S POISON

*Compared to the elemental mages of the west, the magicks of the Easterealm
are far subtler. It resides in the manipulation of the mind or the alteration of
the self. It is coveted, held deep within religious orders or secret bloodlines.*
FROM 'THE COMPENDIONOMICORUS: A LIST OF ALL THINGS'

Three days had passed. Soldiers and Scarred alike spent it hunched in
the farmhouse's kitchen, holding their ears against the noise above,
quivering with the horror.

The first day had been filled with roars of pain. The unfettered
volume of a tortured man. Curses spewed from the farmhouse. Every
god was cursed until their name became a guttural cry. Loki's name
most of all.

Every few hours, the shrieks of the scribes would rise to join
the noise, until they were dragged away and thrown from the house.
There they raved in the wilds until the madness burned their minds
from their skull or they were taken by the gathered beasts.

By the second day, the roars had turned hoarse and desperate.
Pleas to halt and for mercy replaced vehemence. When at last those
calls went unanswered, the cursing began again as the sun fell; a
screeching rage those present had never heard from a grown man before.

*Farden.*

*Farden.*

*Farden!*

The mage's name was screamed at rafter and thatch until the creatures in the dark gathered beyond the farmhouse door. They had not left when the tattooing started, only grown in number.

Wolves howled to the ritual's dirge. Trolls thumped their chests in a stuttering rhythm. Beasts of shadow raised their hands to the tortured night.

Silence fell upon the third day. Only those in the house were privy to the senseless babbling of a man drunk on pain and the poisons in his veins. The occasional yelp cut the air as the whalebone needles cut too deep, or the magick gripped too strong. Constant and disturbing was the tirade. Again and again, the mage's name came, like a bell marking the hours of the sun.

When dawn came on the fourth day, the frozen scratch of earth and farm knew true silence. Not a sound emanated from its upstairs. Even the last scribe had fallen silent.

Loki had been there to listen to it all, avidly enduring.

He had not dared to witness the ritual. He had glimpsed through the crack of the door as often as he dared. Entered only to replace ink, daemonblood, a blunt whalebone needle, or a maddened, twitching scribe. Only once had Loki stood before Malvus and his work, and uttered the single word of, 'More.'

Even gods were not immune to the work of the original Scribe, and the power he wrought in the Books of Written mages.

And so, in glimpses, Loki had watched a body broken and built again. Watched a soul crushed by pain, only to be lifted by power. He had not left the doorway except to fetch another scribe, or ink, or another needle to replace the blunt ones. He could not tear himself away if he had wanted to. Years of planning unfolded gradually before his wary eyes. And now, he stared upon his creation.

Malvus Barkhart was no longer the man he had been before. He was possibly no longer a man.

The door creaked as Loki entered. The squat room stank of blood and sweat and shit. A lone candle, close to death, gave it light.

The last scribe was a limp heap on the floor. The man's neck was still crushed in Malvus' grip, several inches off the floor. A blanket soaked with blood and ink covered most of his body. Around his neck, Loki could glimpse the ragged, bleeding lines of script and runes. They stretched beneath the blanket and emerged again on his arm, reaching all the way down to his fingertips. The skin beneath was pale, sweaty, oozing with pus around the wounds the scribes had carved into him. There was now a bulk to him that didn't exist before. The veins in his skin were swollen purple between the misshapen muscle. Bunched shoulders lay beneath the soiled blanket, swollen with magick and daemonblood. The bottles of it Loki had supplied lay either empty or smashed about the room. It seemed the daemonblood had lent as much to this new creation as the raw magick in the Books.

'Malvus,' Loki breathed.

Malvus heaved with an inhale, rising slightly. He turned to show Loki his cheek. It, too, was carved with script. Blood streaked his pallid skin. This was no Scarred. No Written. Not one, but five Books – including Farden's – lay across his skin from thighs to arms. Another gamble on Loki's part, but once more, it seemed the luck of the gods was with him. The others of Haven frowned on the power of luck. To Loki, it was as strong as magick.

'I remember you,' came the reply. Malvus' voice had fallen several octaves while sounding like stone scraped against iron.

'I should hope so,' the god replied.

Another heaving breath. At last, with a crunch of bone, Malvus let go of the dead scribe. The corpse slumped to the floor.

'What have you done to me?'

'What you wanted. I gave you the power you've always wanted over Emaneska. The power of daemons. Of the greatest mages to ever walk these frozen lands. You are more powerful now than—'

Malvus arose shockingly quickly. His bulk cast a shadow over Loki as he turned. His bleeding, inked hand sought Loki's throat. Loki could have moved, could have fended him off, but he stayed still. Malvus' hand was simultaneously cold yet burning. The god could feel the magick coursing through the man's every vein. The strength testing the bones and cartilage of Loki's throat was of steel. Half of Loki wanted to cackle with accomplishment. Avoiding looking too long at the tattoos, Loki stared into Malvus' eyes: bloodshot, swollen; a yellow iris staring back at him. There was more daemon to him than human.

'Where is Farden?' Malvus growled.

The single-mindedness of Malvus' question caught Loki. He had expected questions. Complaints. Curses, at very least.

'To the east. Far to the east,' he replied.

'How?'

'Durnus took him there using a Weight.'

'How do you know?'

'Because I planned it. And one who is with them – the Hâlorn girl – carries a token of mine. One that calls to me.'

'The girl,' Malvus intoned. He stared around the foul room. 'She will die as well.'

'Leave her to me.'

Malvus' grip tightened. Loki tried to swallow and found he couldn't. His throat bobbed against Malvus' knuckles.

'She will die for standing against me.'

Loki swallowed his complaints. He was wise enough to recognise an issue that didn't need to be pressed. After all, the tool did not need to know what it was building, just merely to work.

'She will die indeed,' Loki affirmed. 'But first we need to fetch armour and clothes for you. A weapon.' If only to keep him from turning everything about him mad from magick, Loki thought.

Malvus released him. He flexed as if stretching new skin. The muscles rippled across his shoulders. White light shimmered across the tattooed, bleeding runes, as Loki had seen in Farden's Book once upon a time. However, here and there, some runes glowed a fierce red. Red as daemonblood. Waves of heat emanated from Malvus' arms and shoulders. The magick in him fought to be free.

Loki finished rubbing his throat. 'Shall we begin?' he asked, gathering up the Hides of Hysteria before he forgot. The foul book's weight faded into his coat.

Malvus dragged the blanket over his head like a makeshift cloak and said nothing. Loki forced a smile and wondered, just for a moment, whether he had made a rare mistake. A mortal error. *Only time and spilled blood would tell.*

After struggling to squeeze through the diminutive door built for peasants, Malvus took one look at the stairs and decided to break his way through the wall with his fists. Loki's hair blew in the shockwaves from the magick in his fists. Fresh night air flooded into the rank atmosphere. Malvus dropped from the farmhouse. The shudder from his landing could be felt through the stairs. Loki hurried his way out into the cold night. The trellises and shadows were stirring. Wolves' howls began to fill the air. Screeches and cries created a spine-chilling chorus.

Shoulders hunched and heaving, Malvus stretched to his full height. He would have rivalled Toskig had the fool of a general kept his mouth shut. To Loki's intrigue, Malvus raised his voice too. It started as a growl and rose as a wretched roar in unison with the creatures that had come to worship the magick.

Loki watched the rivers of light in the sky above tremble as if shaken by his voice. Far to the north, thunder rolled as Irminsul spoke. It was as if it roared for its champion. A monster of pure magick and hatred.

The god watched Malvus test his bare feet on the snow. The frosted ground couldn't break his skin. Faint steam came from wherever he stepped.

'Do you know what the roots of your name mean, Malvus?' Loki asked. The emperor looked at him over his shoulder. 'In old Commontongue it means "hammer". No longer do you have to rely solely on your silver tongue. Now, you are your name's true meaning. Test your powers, Malvus Barkhart. Test the magick I've given you.'

As light burned beneath his makeshift cloak, fire began to sputter around Malvus' fingers. Sparks grew into flames. Those flames began coursing up his skin. At first, Loki saw fear in his eyes. He flinched at the heat, and then as soon as it proved harmless to him, Malvus grinned. Magick unfurled from him in fiery arcs. Loki stood still, arms crossed, even when the fire lashed the snow a foot from him.

'Soon, you'll be able to bring the very sky crashing to earth. Once the daemons see your power, even Gremorin will bend a knee to you. Farden will be a worm under your boot.'

Malvus' foot thumped in the thawed mud, spraying not just grimy water but a shockwave that shook the pines and mountainside for a mile around them. Loki held his smile secure as Malvus whirled on him.

'East?' Malvus boomed.

'East.'

Malvus spent a moment surveying the forest's edge before marching towards a fenrir. The giant wolf skipped away from his touch for a moment before coming to sniff his bleeding hand. Loki heard the sound, but it took him a moment to realise what it was. It was Malvus chuckling.

Seizing its mane, Malvus jumped upon the fenrir and hunkered against its back as the creature clawed at the snow. The magick eking from the monstrosity seemed to dizzy the giant wolf for a moment.

'East it is, god!' he bellowed, before bounding into the dark.

Loki hung back while the other creatures raced after him. The night fell silent before he tasted a scent in the wind blowing past his shoulders. A cold he had not felt since his form had fallen from the stars.

'What have you done, child?' breathed the goddess of magick.

Loki turned on Evernia. She stood so close he could have grasped her throat. The goddess was full of form for a shadow of her true being. Mist drifted from her gossamer robe of silver. Her stern face was masked by hair of woven light, drifting independently of the night's breeze.

'You've found me at last. It only took you a decade or two,' Loki greeted her. 'I had expected you to come admonish me much sooner.'

'Even in the stars, in Haven, we felt the winds of magick change. I came here to see for myself. Instead, I see you, as Farden warned me, betraying not only your god-kin but the world itself.'

Loki smiled. He had rehearsed this conversation for many years. Yet now Evernia stood before him, he felt no need to laud it over her. He felt a pity for his kin instead. He laughed.

'Kin? You call me kin and yet I am nothing like you.'

'We made you from our own blood. My blood!'

'And so I should owe my all to you? I realised long ago that you call yourselves gods, and yet you are nothing but half-remembered lights in the night sky. We were the first sparks of this world! You created the humans to fight for and worship you. You gave them magick, and yet they turned their back on you. You sacrificed all to save them, and now the mortals use your name as curses. And somehow, you are still happy to subsist on their whispers and prayers, when all along you miss the true beauty of your creation. Their souls, Evernia.'

'You speak like a daemon.'

'Do I? Because I recognise the potential of the soul? There is untold power within your grasp, yet you refuse it. You could escape the dark void of Haven in a day, rule as you meant to rule, and yet you don't. That is what I've done: what you cannot. And let me tell you, Evernia, you are missing out.' He smirked. 'I have tasted that power.'

She stepped back, harrowed. 'Then you not only speak as a daemon, but act like them. You have betrayed your very nature.'

Loki flexed his fingers, spinning dust and frost around them. 'If you ask me, the daemons and elves had the right idea all along to enslave the mortals. They are not warriors, worshippers, not children, but cattle. Their souls are our right. Our spoils.'

'What have you done, Loki?' Evernia asked him again, her pearl brow furrowed in disbelief.

'I've done nothing different than what you did millennia ago when you gave the gift of magick's song to the mortals. Didn't you realise it was never yours to wield, Evernia? Not yours alone to give? You treated magick like a tool. Like wind in your sails, or a beast to harvest, and you gave it to mere cattle. That mistake of arrogance will cost you and Haven more than you ever expected.'

Evernia stared into the forest after the noise of crashing branches and the whining of creatures. Loki circled her.

'I've done what you always feared. Daemonblood and magick entwined. Farden's daughter almost managed to bring down the sky, but now I will succeed. I will bring this world to the wrack and ruin the daemons could never accomplish, and when every mortal scream cries my name, when the flames rise so high that you are choking on them in Haven, then you will see how pathetic you have become, and you will kneel before me, the god of gods.'

'You are no god,' whispered Evernia, already fading to dust.

Loki lashed out at her with his own magick. Petty, perhaps, but her frown had not given him the satisfaction he had expected. Pure power lashed the frost and torched the earth, but Evernia was gone.

Loki stood alone in the silent night once more, and snarled.

*Between the stars above, where the wind had no breath and time had no meaning, narrowed gazes fell upon the glowing world below.*

*There, in the faint parapets and castles of Haven, faint as gossamer, gods watched on in their multitudes with their wings folded and hands clasped. All of them wondering what it was they had felt wash through the endless void. What that taste of magick had meant. The word went unspoken, but it hovered on every godly tongue. Every lip.*

Doom.

# CHAPTER 13
## THE LADY OF WHISPERS

*Barons, satraps, merchants, peasants. All cheer for the fighters of the Scarlet Tourney. All are made equal by their adoration of death.*
FROM THE INSCRIPTION ON THE TOWER OF THE VISCERA

*In the dream, Mithrid stood upon a mountainside black as coal. The endless slope trembled beneath her. Pumice and boulders tumbled past her. Beneath her lay an endless void. Ahead, a peak that never came to a point. She alone climbed while everything else fell.*

*Ahead, Mithrid saw a doorway cut by fire into the rock. Smoke billowed from it. Song, too. Deep and earth-shaking. She couldn't begin to understand its words, spoken by no human mouth, in a language spoken before the world formed.*

*Her feet moved inexorably. Mithrid watched them shuffle through the ash and saw skulls amongst the rubble of the mountainside. A child-sized scalp glared eyeless from the dust. Her armoured boot crushed it before she could avert her step.*

*Thunder drew her eyes up to where tongues of flame now billowed from the doorway. The eye of a furnace burned beyond that black rock. She had seen that eye before. Its heat sought to envelop her. Mithrid felt the skin of her cheeks and arms sizzling. She cried out. Whether she had no voice or it was stolen by the roar of the mountain, she did not know. And still she approached the fire.*

*Mithrid reached for the fire, even as it burned the flesh from her fingers. Her shadow was a black shield before the fire. She reeled as the mountain paused its onslaught to take breath. She stood, shield ready and axe in her skeleton hands. She felt the heat raw on the bare bones of her cheek.*

*The volcano's inferno swallowed her, but even as she was scattered as dust, Mithrid found herself standing before a ladder. The kind that had hung from the walkways of Troughwake like tails. She heard a sea breaking in the thick darkness behind her. In her hand lay a small, frosted cake in the shape of a beetle. Before her eyes, it burst into flame. Formless, devoid of breath or time, she stared down at the flame until she became aware of a presence in the gloom opposite her.*

*Mithrid's gaze crept, inch by inch, until she saw the grinning visage: A face wreathed in fire and wild hair. A face covered in white shining runes. Mithrid recoiled in terror. Once again, fire consumed her. She was nothing but ash on the breeze. Forgotten. Trodden upon. Tilled with soil generation after generation. Stars spun around her in an endless dark.*

Mithrid awoke with a yelp she would later regret the pitch and volume of. The first thing she saw was the head of a giant moose with a golden apple clutched in its mouth. She pressed herself into the velvet couch in fright. Her eyes desperately searched the gloom. A skull with a huge horn loomed above her. Beside it was a painting with a puppet emerging from it. That, strangely, was the thing that reassured her. She had fallen asleep staring at the grotesque object, wondering what kind of person would buy, let alone make, such a thing.

Mithrid exhaled. She was in the house of the Lady of Whispers.

A gruff bark made her flinch. Beside her, upon another couch, Farden flew upright. In the dim candlelight, Mithrid saw the sweat on his brow. It also took him a moment or two to recognise his surroundings. His eyes locked onto Mithrid.

'Nightmare?' he asked.

'Yeah. You?'

Farden's brow furrowed. He stared at the moose for a while before speaking. 'What did you see?'

'Fire. Irminsul, I think.'

'Hmm.' The mage shook his head. 'I saw a face covered—'

'In runes?'

Farden's gaze came rushing back to her. The sound of shuffling shoes approached, along with the light of a candle. The artefacts covering the walls threw grotesque and daemonic shadows.

Durnus appeared. 'Did you two feel that?' he asked.

'We both dreamed the same thing.' Farden nodded. 'A face covered in runes. You?'

'A wind is all I can describe it as. Blowing through my soul and my veins. A wind from the west.'

'Whatever it is, why do I feel Loki is at fault?'

Mithrid pushed herself from her couch. 'Because you're probably right.'

'We cannot worry about that now. We must focus on Sigrimur and finding his breath.'

Farden pointed to Durnus. 'Where are the others?'

'Warbringer is standing watch over the Lady of Whispers. She is warier than you. The minotaur drinking horns on a table might have been something to do with it. Or she doesn't trust carpets. Aspala and I were swapping tales and knowledge by a fire with wine, spending an evening how it should be spent. How do you feel, Farden?'

The mage sighed as he knuckled his face. Mithrid stared once more at the gap of Farden's missing finger. 'Like I only slept for two hours.'

'If you ask me, you still look like shit,' Mithrid said, trying a smile although she couldn't help but notice a streak of silver in his hair she swore hadn't been there before. To her surprise, she actually coaxed a weary but matching smile from Farden.

'You should talk,' replied Farden. His eyes crept above hers. Mithrid put up a hand and found her unruly hair had rebelled once again. It was stuck up like a cliff-face. She shrugged. 'Still look better than you.'

Farden snorted as he arose. He had slept in his armour, with his helmet clutched on his chest.

'Do you trust this Lady of Whispers, Durnus?'

'She has given me no reason not to.'

'Those are the ones you have to worry about,' Farden sighed. 'What have you told her?'

'Nothing, yet. I have merely expressed an interest in relics of Sigrimur. You still think me a fool, old friend? I was not born yesterday. I know the value of secrets. I was once an arkmage, you know. After being your superior for many years.'

Farden tutted. With a series of grunts and curses, Farden removed his armour piece by piece. Even though it was clearly broken in some way, Mithrid still marvelled at the way its scales slid over each other, as if they had a life of their own. The tunic beneath was verging on threadbare where the armour had worn. The mage smelled road-weary. Mithrid was about to mention a bath until she took off her own armour. She caught a whiff of herself and winced.

'I wonder if the Lady of Whispers has a bucket and soap. Or a bath.'

Durnus' nose was firmly wrinkled. 'I hope so.'

Mithrid had never known such cleanliness. Even in Scalussen, when she had at last washed the salt and blood and dust of Troughwake and the *Revenge* from her body, she swore bathing had not felt this good.

The Lady of Whispers was clearly rich. Mithrid had never seen such a house for one person. She had seen a guard or two, but the only servants in the house were children half her age. Some even younger. They looked as filthy as peasants. A small girl with pigtails showed Mithrid and Farden to the baths. Otherwise, it seemed Irien was largely alone with her collections.

The things even spread to the bathing room. The glazed tiles of the wall were festooned with more trinkets and paintings. A range of varnished serpents sat rearing on plaques. Mithrid stared daggers at the strange things while she doused herself in bucket after bucket of warm water. The soaps tingled her nose with their fragrances, deftly treading the edge of being unpleasant. When Mithrid emerged from the steam, she found a robe-like dress and trews waiting for her. She had seen similar fashion on Dathazh's streets. It felt vaguely like putting on a disguise. It remind her of the time Bogran, Remina, and the others of the crew had dressed in dry seaweed all day to avoid the old ones of Troughwake.

The thought stalled Mithrid's hand an inch from the door handle. She shook her head, swallowed the emotion as always, and marched from the bath.

Farden was in the corridor. The beard had been cut from his chin and cheeks in uneven patches. He was trying to adjust his shirt, which for some reason came with laces and vacuous cuffs. 'Why in Hel there are laces on this thing, I don't know.'

He quickly gave up on chasing the folds of fabric and ripped the sleeves clean from the body. Arms bare but torso covered, he threw the sleeves down the nearest stairwell. Mithrid sputtered with laughter.

'You know, it's good to know that I'm a peasant girl, yet I've still got better manners than a king,' she said.

Farden hoisted his pack of armour over his shoulder. 'Let's see how this Lady of Whispers can help us.'

'She looked intrigued by you earlier, you know,' Mithrid smirked.

'Did she, indeed.' It wasn't a question, simply a reply to avoid silence.

Mithrid walked in silence up the stairs. Yet again, they were lined with all manner of relic and bauble. If it couldn't be stuck to the wall, it was displayed in glass cases, or on tables that intruded on the stairs or corridors.

They found the others in a grand sitting room. It was an opulent affair that was at complete odds with the stark Frostsoar, or the poorness of Troughwake. Mithrid had never seen such frivolous use of gold and silver. Columns and chairs were painted with it. Suits of opulent armour of the metals lined the walls between columns bearing tapestries and heads of beasts. There were even a few human heads in Irien's collection, with names in strange runes hanging from them. Swords and spears too. Nothing matched. Everything demanded her attention.

The only light was a fireplace that crackled and spat. The Lady of Whispers herself sat in a chair of striped hide. The back of the chair stretched twice her height into the gloom.

Aspala and Durnus sat upon a low bench lined with more velvet. Aspala's lids were half-closed. She clutched a goblet with two hands and stared into the fire, only smiling when Mithrid sat opposite her. The armchair was covered in the softest fur she had ever touched, decorated in the shape of stars. Its cushions were so soft, Mithrid swore the thing tried to eat her when she sat down.

'Ah, they have awoken, bathed, and returned!' Irien greeted them as they entered. 'The night is young. Come and enjoy the fire. Wine, if you take it. The city will not wake before midday tomorrow. Your master Durnus has been full of questions. What can I answer for you, lady and sir? Or will you tell me of your lives instead?'

Aspala had purple lips from the wine. She held out her goblet and Mithrid took it without comment. It wasn't a cold ale, but it was sweet enough to give Mithrid the same shiver. Within moments, she felt the sugar creep from the back of her tongue into her temples. She felt warm, and reclined in the chair.

Farden didn't hold back. 'Why do they call you the Lady of Whispers?'

Durnus nodded knowingly while Irien tittered. She plucked a cork from a flagon that rested at her side and poured a liberal slog of wine into her crystal goblet.

'The same question Durnus asked,' she said, staring boldly at the mage. 'Whispers and the secrets they carry are a currency in cities as old as complicated as Dathazh and Vensk. I trade in them as a merchant might trade in jewellery or silk, and have done for more years than I will admit. It is a craft that is despised by some, and not without its dangers.' Irien waggled her wooden fingers. 'But I have proven myself against great odds, worked hard, and I have succeeded. People come to me to learn things that my children – my eyes and ears across the plains and Golikar – bring me. You see, a whisper's worth is only what somebody will pay to buy or keep it. Some will pay the world to protect their secret.'

Mithrid piped up, wanting to appear involved. 'Vensk is the city across the river?'

Irien's gaze tore away from Farden and alighted on Mithrid. There was a constant gleam of delight in the woman's bewitching eyes. 'It is, indeed, young lady. The capital of the queendom of Golikar. It is where the Scarlet Tourney is held year after year, in an arena as old as the roots of the trees that form its foundations. We call it the Viscera. Countless warriors have lost their lives there over the course of centuries. Only champions emerge.'

'You sound proud,' said Farden.

Irien stared straight at Farden. 'It is a tradition, Sir Farden! Of course I am proud. It brings trade, notoriety, and honour to the two cities. And it keeps peace between our fractious nations and those of the east and south. Did you know that the Rivenplains and Golikar spent decades at war? Vensk and Dathazh were in constant siege. Now, thanks to the Tourney, the idea of war has become preposterous. We've had almost four hundred years of peace because of it.'

The lady took a moment to raise and finish her glass. She emptied the drips onto her carpet without care. 'I would rather have a pint of blood spilled in the Viscera than thousands die in war.'

Mithrid felt an unexpected twitch of guilt. The fire of her dream haunted her still.

To the burble of pouring wine, Irien continued. 'And, naturally, it introduces me to all manner of interesting people. A question of my own, now that you are all awake and partially rested. I wish to know more about you. Durnus has been rather quiet about the type of protectors he's hired.'

The ruse amused Mithrid. It appeared to needle Farden, and yet he played his part.

'As he should be,' replied the mage gruffly. He reached for some wine of his own, forwent the goblet, and took a gulp. 'There is nothing to tell. We are sellswords driven out of the Arka Empire by war. I was a mage once. This fiery-headed one has some skill with shadow magick. Durnus hired us all to protect his bony arse.'

Irien was listening in the way that Remina used to: as if she heard some mistake in Farden's words that nobody else noticed. The fire crackled while she pondered.

'It intrigues me why a hired knight should speak so openly. I have seen many a retinue, many a sellsword and mercenary from parts of the world the maps don't have names for, and none of them have acted as you do in front of their masters. I wager you've told me lies.'

Before anyone could respond, Irien flashed her trademark smile as she rubbed some of the purple from her lips with her surviving hand. Mithrid had not noticed the tattoo on her knuckles before. The word, "Live" in Commontongue.

'As I told you, I am the Lady of Whispers. Little happens in these lands without me knowing about it. My craft is to hunt out whispers, and many have reached me of a red-gold man, a minotaur, and a dragon no less, charging across the Rivenplains. It's said they appeared as if from nowhere, heralded by smoke and strange sunsets in the west like an omen of the Dusk God. Said to have burned half of Lilerosk and slain the High Cathak's son outside the Spoke. Oh yes, I've heard of you. Why you should be surprised is another question. You aren't exactly conspicuous blazing a path right to Dathazh's doorstep in fire and blood. I'm surprised the guards let you in at all. Lucky for you it's Tourney week, and they were probably half-blind with exhaustion.'

Mithrid drank more of her wine so as to keep from saying something she might later regret. Farden was looking at her sidelong, waiting. She watched Aspala instead, who now had her eyes closed in drunken meditation. Even so, Mithrid saw her hand was now rested on her sword. Mithrid's axe was elsewhere, but she longed for it all of a sudden.

'You are of Emaneska, that much is true,' said Irien. 'Mages, a knight of Paraia, a minotaur, and a vampyre, yes. Yet I know enough of armour to see that is ancient Scalussen steel you wear, Farden. That is not the armour of a sellsword. Neither is that hammer in your hands, Warbringer. And you, Mithrid the shadow mage, though your armour isn't as rich as Farden's. I have only seen nobles wearing such metal. None of you are mercenaries, that much is plain, so I'll ask again: who are you?'

Farden dribbled wine down his grizzled chin as he drank. 'We're fleeing the Arka Empire.'

'I'm not surprised. Not least because of the cruelness you westerners enjoy, but I hear whispers the emperor has gone to war. Raised the greatest army Emaneska or Easterealm has ever seen and took it north against a warlord mage. A single warlord, of all people! Would you believe it?' Irien laughed.

'Might I ask what you were doing at Sigrimur's statue?' Farden asked, swiftly changing subjects. Mithrid knew he had no love for subterfuge and betrayal, not even the faintest chance of it. After

Savask and Trenika's lies, she felt the same. Farden had the sense to be calm about it. 'Were you following us?

'Come now, Farden,' tutted Irien. 'Fortunate happenstance is all. You interrupted my vigil at my ancestor's grave. You piqued my interest the minute you clomped into Sigrimur's Rest. Like I said, you're quite the conspicuous bunch. I wanted to know who it was that's been causing such ruckus. The fact you were seeking Sigrimur is what interested me. The last breath of Sigrimur is what you said at the Rest, wasn't it, Mithrid?'

Mithrid watched guarded gazes turn to study her.

Irien tapped her pointed ears. 'You needn't fear my interest, my new friends. I would not be the Lady of Whispers if I did not know the need for discretion when I see it. That's why I keep no allegiances, no political leanings. Your secrets are safe with me.'

Farden leaned forwards, hands towards the fire. 'All for a fee or a favour, I imagine. I may not have travelled far beyond Emaneska in my lifetime, but I know that such kindness isn't free no matter how far you travel. There's always a price.'

'Perhaps there shall be,' Irien sipped her wine coyly. 'But sating my curiosity is enough of a payment for now. Particularly because I have never heard of Sigrimur's last breath. Not as a Lady of Whispers nor as a collector, nor even as a descendant. I fear whatever edda or song you followed here has fed you nonsense.'

Durnus sucked at a fang. Irien looked the least perturbed by a vampyre in her house. Mithrid wondered if they were commonplace in these lands.

'We are hoping that is not the case,' Durnus said. 'A question, my Lady: I am curious of your mention of a "grave". Does that mean that Sigrimur is entombed beneath the statue?'

Once again, the Lady of Whispers grinned as if the answer to Durnus' question was written on the walls. *Somewhere between her ghastly mounted heads and paintings that looked as though the artist had vomited their paints upon their canvases,* Mithrid snorted to herself. To her dismay, her goblet was already empty.

'My dear Durnus! That is no statue, but Sigrimur himself, turned to stone!' She took a moment to watch them while that sank in. 'When he was killed by his own spear in the Noose God's hands it turned him to stone. What you see in Sigrimur's Rest is the very form of my ancestor, almost two thousand years later. Now headless, you see. Which poses a problem for you.'

'How so?' asked Farden.

'Because, if I were seeking the last breath of Sigrimur, where more obvious a place to look for it than the Head of Sigrimur? Your problem is that my ancestor's head is currently the prized trophy of the Scarlet Tourney, as it has been for the last four centuries.'

The silence was awkward. Mithrid felt the floor crumbling beneath her boots. She felt lost once more, as if she were still hunched in a limestone cave, staring out at an unholy forest. All purpose bled away.

Irien grinned. 'If I were you, my new friends, I would be enormously glad our paths crossed!'

While the others quietly tried to decide if that was true, Irien found her flagon empty and clicked her wooden fingers with a sharp crack. Another child servant appeared, this one filthier than the one Mithrid had seen. Without an order, the little boy ran off into the dark with the empty bottle and returned in moments with a full one.

'In my years, I've learned that the why of a matter is not important. Say a woman comes to me seeking proof of her husband's supposed infidelity. She pays me to know which woman he's tickling the insides, not why he's gone astray. The why is between wife and husband. The Lady of Whispers deals in the who, the what, and the where. As such, my new friends, believe me when I say I do not care *why* you wish for the Head of Sigrimur. However, I can help you with where it is and how to get your hands on it.

'The most obvious way is no secret at all: you win the Scarlet Tourney,' Irien said, as if it was no matter at all. 'It would be your trophy. It would be yours to do what you wish with it.'

Durnus looked uncomfortable. 'It would be too great a risk. Even for our friend Warbringer here. Risky and needless.'

Warbringer rumbled as if disagreeing, but she made no further complaint.

Once again, Irien's eyes found Farden and stuck there. 'What of you, Farden? You look used to a sword.'

Farden shook his head. 'Durnus is right. Too great a risk.'

Irien chuckled. 'Then you are left with two simple choices. You either wait for this Tourney's champion to emerge victorious and bargain with them. Or, you steal the Head of Sigrimur before it can be won, straight from the vaults under the Queen of Golikar's nose.'

Mithrid could think of other ways to describe their choices than simple. Their decision was between wasting time and spilling blood, she could see it plainly.

For a time, nobody spoke. Each mind chewed away on its own thoughts. Only Irien looked aloof and unbothered, still watching the mage.

'Am I the only one,' Mithrid spoke up, 'that is wondering how a stone head can breathe?'

'All things are possible through magick,' Durnus said, attempting to be positive.

Irien flexed her wooden hand as if it ached. She smiled at Mithrid as she spoke. The girl found herself staring into those odd eyes, trying to figure the woman behind them.

'Indeed they are,' Irien said softly. She arose. 'And on that notion, I'll bid you a fine evening. Enjoy the wine. I will have food brought for you. My children will see to your needs. And in the morning, you will see the Scarlet Tourney with your own eyes.'

Farden stopped her as she turned. 'You still haven't mentioned your price, Lady of Whispers.'

Irien laughed disarmingly. 'Farden, Farden. Are you sure you were not a merchant back in Emaneska, instead of a mage? My price is simple. I wish to meet your dragon. Don't look so surprised! I believe the whispers. I have seen plenty of this world and its beasts but never a true dragon of Emaneska. I wish to meet it.'

'Is that all?'

Irien shrugged. 'Not all worth is in gold and silver, is it now? Besides, I am not, shall we say... *fond* of Queen Peskora of Golikar. Whether you compete for the Head against her prize fighters or you steal it from her grasp, any embarrassment to her is a delicious bonus for me.'

The Lady of Whispers said nothing more. With her robes of silk dragging on the floor behind her, she left them to the crackle of the fireplace and the sweet wine.

'I can fight. I can win,' Warbringer said. Mithrid could hear her voice in the arm of the chair.

Farden grew comfortable in his chair, stretching out his feet. Yet there was still a tension to him. Mithrid saw the creasing of his face every time he moved.

'I don't doubt that, Warbringer, but I won't risk you. It would be throwing you into a fight blind. We don't know anything about this tourney. Even less than we do about the Head, which is close to nothing.'

'You trust this pink-flesh now?'

Durnus hummed, quietly tapping the rim of his goblet against his fangs. 'She seems trustworthy.'

'Is that the wine talking, or you Durnus? Or the fact you've found somebody with as many stories as you?' scoffed Farden.

'What do you say then, old friend?'

Farden drank until his flagon was drained. He looked like he drank it as a medicine rather than a treat. 'As lost and as clueless as we are about these lands, I'll take what help we can get until we can walk the path to the spear ourselves.'

Mithrid found herself smirking. 'And are you sure that's not because of those green eyes of hers?'

Farden rolled his eyes. 'You go easy on that wine, shadow-mage.'

Mithrid flexed her hand, accidentally imitating Farden earlier. It was more difficult with her head tingling from wine, but she coaxed the dark shadow from her. 'I personally like the sound of that. Better than being called nevermar incarnate, at least.'

'Do you trust her?' Farden asked her.

As Mithrid considered the question, she swore she heard tiny feet padding through the gloom of the sitting room. 'I like to think I can see the ugly in people, and I'm struggling to do so with her. She speaks plainly. I get the sense she looks out for herself and herself only. And if she's powerful and rich, then she's not desperate enough to cross us, surely.'

'You sound like you admire her, Mithrid,' Durnus whispered.

'I just know we've got little choice in the matter. And I'm glad I can rest for a bit without you burning the place down, Farden.'

The mage snorted, but Mithrid caught the betraying smile. She knew she was right. It was good to forget where and who they were for a moment.

'I'd ask Aspala but I think she's asleep.'

The Paraian was far from it. 'Simple. If she crosses us...' Aspala's voice trailed away, but they all heard was the tap of her coarse fingernails on her gold sword.

To the thump of hooves, Warbringer loomed from the shadows to stand over them. The firelight cast dark shadows across her stormy face.

'Did I hear talk of food?'

# CHAPTER 14
## THE SCARLET TOURNEY

*A hundred men made the journey,*
*a hundred men to fight the tourney.*
*When dust fell still, just two survived,*
*half-dead and breathless, defiant, alive.*
*Palms out for trophies, their hope was broken.*
*Instead, two knives and one single token.*
FROM THE 'TOURNAMENT TALES'

'One hundred fighters from across the known world of Easterealm. Ninety-nine fights back to back over five days. Ninety-nine die. One emerges victorious. Simple.' Irien beamed as she explained. Her arm moved across the span of the river from north to south.

The trumpets blasted again. From Irien's balcony, Mithrid scowled down at the nearest group of them, standing like baby birds in a nest of red and orange, their trumpet mouths faced to the sky. A nest like this sat upon every one of the bridge's squat towers. One by one, the other groups of trumpets carried the fanfare across the bridge and into Vensk.

They had not stopped blaring since early that morning. Well, it had been an hour before midday, but after spending the evening drinking before a fire, it felt like dawn to Mithrid.

Farden and Durnus looked worse than she felt. Durnus was drawn and haggard once more, as if his mend had stalled. The mage had deep bags under his eyes. Back in most of his armour once more, the mage walked slowly and stiffly as if pained. Mithrid had found him asleep upright in an armchair, but Mithrid got the sense the mage was used to such a thing. In the sunlight, the silver threads in his black hair shone.

'Have you anything like this in the west?' asked Irien.

'No. We settle things the old way,' replied Farden.

'With war.'

'Sadly so.'

'They say the south brews with war. But they are only whispers. The Viscera continues to bring us nothing but peace. There is a savage nature in all of us, they say, and why we crave war. The Tourney sates that desire for blood and battle, and it only costs ninety-nine lives a year.'

Farden was not convinced. 'It's the spectating. The cheering. The revelling in it that turns my stomach. There's no entertainment in death.'

Irien flashed her smile. 'If you can tell me with a straight face you've never taken pleasure in killing, or seeing a foe meet his comeuppance, mage, then I'll believe you.'

'He can't,' Mithrid piped up. Farden was too tired to give her the usual glare.

'Hold onto your opinions until you see the Viscera for yourself. Shall we?' Irien said.

Without waiting for a reply, the Lady of Whispers swept into the perpetual gloom of her sitting room. The others followed in silence.

Her children scattered around her, bringing pieces of jewellery to try. The woman was already festooned with it but apparently she needed more. She wore silver bracelets up to her elbows, gold earrings that hung against her chest, even pearl beads that ran through her stripe of hair.

Mithrid had found her armour polished and waiting for her. Her axe too. When and by whom, irked her, but she couldn't deny it shone more than the day Akitha had first made it. Mithrid shone.

When Irien noticed her staring at her jewels, she shooed her children towards Mithrid. They approached her with hands glittering.

'It is a day to celebrate, Mithrid. How better to celebrate by wearing the finest? Please, help yourself. What's mine is yours. Gentlemen? Any finery for you?' A clap of hands brought more children in bearing cloaks with Golikan pattens.

The sense of it was simple, and Mithrid felt rude to refuse at least trying. The finest jewellery she had ever seen in Hâlorn was polished seaglass. Her mother had a quartz ring that father had gifted her. It had been left on his smallest finger.

Mithrid took a silver tiara from a pouting child and slid it into her mess of hair. Irien showed her an ornate mirror that hung beside the fire.

'You look like a lady of Vensk, my dear,' Irien told her, hands clasping Mithrid's shoulders. Mithrid surprised herself by not flinching away.

It was not the shine of the trinket. It was not even the fact it was silver in a cliff-brat's hand. Wealth had never mattered to her. It was almost as if she put on a disguise. The reflection staring back at her had her wild scarlet hair, even her black armour, but it was not Mithrid Fenn. For a moment, she was another person, with none of her troubles or past. None of the blood in her hands and a strange power in her veins. A blank canvas. And a formidable one at that.

Mithrid matched Irien's smile. 'Thank you. I'll look after it until—'

'It is yours, Mithrid. It was a gift from a goblin of a man many years ago. It looks better on you.'

Aspala looked well-used to the weight of jewellery on her arms, as if it wasn't an escape for her, but a reminder of a life long lost. She stuffed bracelet after bracelet onto her wrist until she smiled. Durnus took a cloak and a curious pair of spectacles that had black crystal lenses. Farden thanked the children but didn't move a muscle. His armour hadn't left his side. Even in its damaged state and lack of polish, he still somehow looked a king. At the very least, he smelled better.

'Are you all right, mage?' Mithrid asked him quietly.

'Tired, is all.'

'You don't seem yourself.'

'As you told me yesterday,' he said, with no malice in his voice.

'I was tired,' she whispered. 'I didn't mean it. Now that Malvus has survived, I feel so much pressure on us to succeed my entire being is focused on it. Not Loki. Malvus. That's why when I see you endanger this quest, I can't understand why, and it grates me.'

'You'll see, Mithrid,' Farden said. 'You'll see why I do what I do. This is why I never wanted to put this on your shoulders. This life of being a hero is no life to lead.'

'And yet I want it. I feel that's my calling. You said you've never been one for believing in a god of fate. And that something brought me to Scalussen. Irminsul is not all I can do. I know it.'

The mage took a moment to hover a hand over her shoulder as if to say thank you, but he merely nodded and walked on.

Mithrid watched him go, mentally railing against everything he had said. She wanted that life. *Desperately.*

Aspala was standing beside her. 'Trust him, Mithrid. We have to trust him,' she said. 'Are you going to talk to him about Loki's knife?'

Mithrid flashed her a look as if to tell her to shut up. She had forgotten about the damned knife. 'I'll tell him. If it means anything at all.'

'I get the impression whatever Loki does is not at random, and all for Loki's gain.'

A traitorous thought popped into her mind. It had not been the first time she had considered whether Loki was the villain everybody hailed him as.

Irien summoned them with a clap of her hands. 'Out into the world we go, friends! You will soon see why Vensk is famed the world over.'

❦

In the light of day, their surroundings looked stranger and more unfamiliar than they should. The fire of torches and lanterns had died at dawn, and now the sunlight showed them a different city. One that seemed in the grip of a mass, if not colourful and cheery, exodus.

Every crowd had coalesced as one, filling each of the plain streets like floodwater. Where last night they had been full of revelry and debauchery, today they all shared one goal. One direction, to be precise. *Vensk.* With so many people trying to move at once the pace was slow, but unchanging. Fortunately, they passed the time by blowing horns, hammering drums, and throwing handful after handful of red and orange petals into the air.

Irien had a number of guards in wooden armour waiting beyond her door. They held a perimeter around them to fend off the more excitable members of the crowd. They raised their fists and roared. Some screamed. Others appeared to be having fits of excitement as their group passed by. Mithrid saw one man perched on another man's shoulders. He was practically naked, covered only with paint. On his back was drawn the crude likeness of a fighter ahead of them. Mithrid had seen them from above: the contenders of the Tourney. Their retinues ranged from dozens to hundreds. Some had their own musical bands. Some warriors sat astride beasts while others marched amongst hosts of guards.

Irien pointed them out one by one.

'There we have Hrishnash of the Huskar. She is a famed krasilisk hunter. Ahead of her is the curiously named Night Knight. Her people come from a place of caves and caverns. There, you see the plumes of purple ostrich feathers? Rovisk Dal'Bvara. He is last year's champion and a favourite to win again this year. He is the son of a past champion from the southeast, nephew of a warlord. Whispers tell me he's killed a hundred men with his bare hands and never been beaten in a fight. He is Queen Peskora's favourite.'

Mithrid tried to pronounce the mouthful of a name Irien had spoken. Her gaze found Rovisk's retinue between the crowds. The man stood atop a dais that was supported by a whole swathe of sweating servants. Rovisk was shirtless, painted in colours of turquoise and purple. His southern skin shone with gold dust and oil. Between flexing his muscles, he stared leeringly at his adoring fans, of which their seemed to be countless numbers. Mithrid wasn't sure why, but she realised her lip was curled.

'Makes quite the impression, doesn't he?' Irien smirked. 'Some fight for others. Some fight for their country. He fights for himself.'

Farden was not impressed. 'Looks like a buffoon. I've seen plenty like him. No brains but plenty of brawn to throw about.'

Irien explained the Tourney as they slowly paced their way alongside the crowds.

'The Scarlet Tourney is the culmination of three events, or seasons of the year. The three champions of those tourneys are given automatic entry to the Scarlet Tourney. The rest either fight their way in or pay for their places. A hundred Golikan gold leaves to enter. Otherwise you find a patron who pays for you. There's a lot of gold and fame to be made as a patron. They take a share of the bets made. That's why smart fighters bid on themselves, just in case. It's not uncommon for patrons to take half or more of the winnings. As you said, Farden: brawn, not brains.'

'And if we want to place a bet? asked Durnus.

'You don't look the gambling kind, Durnus,' Mithrid answered.

'When you have lived as long as I have, you get good at gambling, my dear.'

'You will see huts and stalls around the Viscera. Any of the bet-takers baring the Golikan flag are legitimate. There are plenty more that aren't. Wherever there is coin to be made, a bet will be taken. If you should change your mind about fighting, you have until the second day to enter.'

At last, they reached the bridge. Wide enough for three fighters and their retinues, the bridge was made of stone that looked foreign to the clay of Dathazh. It wore the scars of old battles beneath the streamers and flower garlands and crowds of colourful people. At every one of its pillars, one of the infuriating nests of trumpets sat. Now even closer to them, their notes made Mithrid wince.

Over the walls of the bridge, she could see boats and barges covering the silty water. Flocks of green pigeons and doves scattered between their squat masts and giant flags. There wasn't a ship in sight, owing to the height of the bridge, but the barges of the river were bigger in length and width.

Irien was divulging all manner of history and gossip of the two cities. Durnus and Farden paid attention, but Mithrid found her attention wandering. Particularly to the fringes of Golikar, and the city at the end of the bridge.

'...the bridge itself is called Ogin's Ford. Or the Og, as the bargemen call it. Three miles long, it spans the River Torsa from city to city. Vensk, like most cities in Golikar, is built in both on the ground and in the trees.'

And what trees they were.

Even at that distance, Mithrid's neck was struggling to take them all in. The colossal pines stretched up, blade-like, scoring the sky jagged. Their boughs were as thick as roads, bursting with foliage. Their needles and bark were a lush green and brown, the exact colours of the Golikan flags that fluttered above Mithrid's head. The gardener in Mithrid was entranced. She did not know trees could grow so large.

The trees soon towered over them. The city of Vensk sprawled in two directions: across the riverbank and up through the forest's boughs. It gave the city an hourglass shape. It reminded Mithrid of Troughwake, and the way their cottages had clung to the cliffs. In Vensk, spherical buildings of wood and leaf thatch sprouted from the trunks and branches. Walkways hung suspended from cables spread like cobwebs between the giant pines. Lifts of complicated pulleys played a constant game with each other of how much cargo they could hoist and lower and how fast. Citizens filled every balcony and walkway she could see. They cheered just as loudly. The keen wail of wooden pipes joined the trumpets. The blasted things were now following behind the fighters. All one hundred of them were now upon the bridge.

As they crossed the threshold of the riverbank, petals rained like an impromptu blizzard. They had a perfume Mithrid had never known. Coins scattered underfoot, thrown by richer fighters to make the peasants scramble. Several Vensk women even held their infant children up high so that some of the fighters might touch or bless their spawn. Beggars sprawled on mats or hopping on crutches reached just to be seen by their heroes. More and more, Mithrid noticed a mania to the crowds. She saw plenty pointed ears, too, presumably a sign of Golikan blood.

'Welcome to Vensk,' she was saying. 'Oldest city in Golikar. Not the biggest, mind, but fine enough. The Queen Peskora of Golikar resides here for half the year. A distant cousin of mine, as it happens.'

'Lady of Whispers!' crowed a tall man dressed in black feathers. Irien spared a moment to greet him over the arms of her guards.

Durnus and the others were meanwhile fascinated by the rust-brown branches that reached over them, two hundred feet above or more. She didn't blame them. Mithrid could hardly help but stare either. That was until a petal poked her in the eye.

Mithrid found that Farden was the only one distracted. He was looking towards the distant echoes of a hammer and anvil. Irien had finished with her friend and had noticed the same look on the mage's face.

'Where did you get your armour, might I ask?' she asked him.

Farden jumped as if he had forgotten they were there. He spoke as they walked, barely audible over the crowd's roar.

'Gathered over years. Took a lot of time. A lot of struggle. A lot of blood.'

'Understandable. I've known entire dowries given for a full suit of old Scalussen armour. Even the *new* Scalussen armour is fine work that no doubt would fetch plenty of coin.' Irien's gleaming eyes crept to Mithrid's armour. Black steel trimmed with gold and crimson to match her axe.

'This, though.' Irien's wooden finger poked at the intricate design of the lone wolf on Farden's breastplate, between the damaged scales. Mithrid was surprised how still he stayed, merely giving her a narrow-eyed look, no doubt trying to figure her out.

'This is unlike any armour I have seen. The motif alone is unusual. Scalussen designs are normally plainer, elegant in their simplicity. Decorations are reserved for runes and whorls. If it had any magick in it, the collector in me might assume—'

'Lucky me,' Farden cut the sentence dead. 'Where is the smith you mentioned. Can he work with this kind of metal or just the wooden armour Golikans wear?'

Irien laughed. 'What do you take me for? I know everybody in the twin cities. My recommendations are worth gold.'

Mithrid decided to test her. She pointed at a man standing at the edge of the procession. He looked officious enough in his patterned robes of Golikan green. 'Who's that then?'

'Somebody not worth knowing,' Irien replied with a wink.

Mithrid was curious. 'You can sense magick, then?'

'Your magick in the west, at least, has a certain... *edge* to it. I have never found the word to describe it, but I can feel it like a cold draught.'

'I understand that completely.'

'Where is this smith, then?' asked Farden in an impatient tone.

Once more, Irien laughed him off. 'Have a little more patience, Farden, we are close.'

Mithrid chuckled with her, and found herself staring up once more at the branches and the falling petals in wonder.

"Close" was another hour of the procession weaving its way deeper into the tangled nest of Vensk.

The further into the city they walked, the fainter daylight became. Where the foundations of tree trunks were at their thickest and strongest, a grand city of thin spires and globular buildings had been built. The core of Vensk perched upon a great platform between the huge pines. It towered upwards to rival their tips. From its body of palaces and halls, swathes of buildings reached out and clustered around trunks. The architecture was everything Dathazh refused to be. There wasn't a straight line to be found. Every arch and roof and walkway flowed together. Even the sparse sections of clay and stone Mithrid spied was shaped and carved.

She was just pondering what damage a lone fire might do to this city when they crested a rise in the thoroughfare and looked upon the Viscera.

The Viscera hung beneath the city's centre. It had the appearance of an enormous dead spider on its back with its legs curled inwards. Its fat bulbous body was the Viscera itself, black and brown. Its foundations and walkways reached upwards and peered into the arena. Beneath the Viscera was a dark layer of buildings that pierced its belly. Smoke and commotion alike poured from that area. They were too far away to make up much detail, but Mithrid saw swathes of fighting yards, animal cages, kitchens, armourers, and bulbous clockwork machinery that the Viscera needed for some reason. It reminded her of the forge beneath the Frostsoar.

This was where the procession split. The fighters continued on to the Viscera's bowels while the gamblers, spectators and large retinues made their way into the walkways and towards their seats in the arena.

'Your choice, friends,' Irien said. 'We can join the others to watch the beginning of the Tourney, or find a smith within the Viscera's staging areas.'

Farden was already drifting after the fighters. Several guards had gone with him. 'You go on,' he said to the others. 'I will see about the smith. I have seen enough fighting to last more lifetimes than my own. I don't need to choose it.'

Aspala, who had been even quieter and shade paler than usual that morning, edged after him. 'I wish to see somebody about my sword, as it happens.'

Warbringer bowed her head and horns as if to agree.

Irien put a finger to her lips in thought. 'You will need me. Durnus, Mithrid, you can follow my guards. They will lead you to my private seating area. The Queen of Golikar will present the Head of Sigrimur shortly.'

Durnus pushed his black spectacles down his nose. 'Be safe, mage. If you could refrain from making any more enemies for us, that would be preferred.'

Irien bowed in mock grandeur. 'I will keep a close eye on him, Durnus, fear not!'

After the others, she swept, leaving Mithrid and the vampyre to press on with the spectators.

'And how are you this morning, Durnus? I forgot to ask.' Mithrid made conversation.

'My head is heavy with wine, I shall admit,' he replied. Even as he spoke, he took Mithrid's arm and leaned upon it. 'And my body is weak with all this walking and lack of... sustenance.'

Mithrid gave him a sidelong glance. 'By sustenance, you mean the vampyre thing? Blood.' she whispered.

Durnus shook his head with a smirk. 'Yes, the vampyre *thing*. I do not see you this disturbed when Warbringer eats.'

'It's different. You don't look like a... I forget what you are half the time.' Even when she saw his fangs, it took her a moment.

'That is what makes my kind so dangerous,' he joked. 'But alas, unlike the minotaur, I cannot eat anything else to sate my hunger.'

'Do you need to eat now?'

'Not yet,' Durnus breathed wistfully. 'What fills my mind is my concern for Farden. Without his armour's spell, the man only weakens rather than strengthens. If I did not know better, I would guess he is the vampyre of this group. Not to mention the lack of his magick. It puts us all in danger.'

'I have been wondering if it's my fault,' Mithrid confessed. 'What if I did something to him or his armour in Scalussen? Before you pulled us out of the fire?'

'And into the frying pan, it would seem.' Durnus thought for a moment before patting her forearm. 'I think not, child. And if I am wrong, then I have seen Farden lose more than his magick and still walk away the victor. Give him trust and time. Perhaps distraction will help him.'

'Do you mean the Viscera or the Lady of Whispers?'

Durnus cackled along with her.

'Too busy. Sorry!' barked the portly chap.

Irien flexed her wooden arm. 'You and I both know there is no such thing as too busy to an entrepreneurial soul such as yours, Krugis.'

'It's the damn Tourney week, Lady Irien! Not some treetop noble wanting to re-armour his guards.'

'Again, you present this as a problem, and yet it's your fault for producing such wonderful work, Krugis. I can't be held responsible for that.'

For a brief moment, Farden watched the flattery wear down the portly smith's puckered face. A yell from another nearby forge snapped him out of it.

'No! No more favours,' Krugis yelled in a whining pitch.

Irien leaned over his workbench, to her credit enduring the spittle on her cheek. 'A whisper for you then, Krugis. Hmm? I happen to know Queen Peskora is looking for a new ceremonial suit for her eldest son. The handsome one, not the newest inbred mutt she parades around. I can have your name added to the royal list. You know how well they pay. Open two new forges, kind of well.'

'Damn it, Irien!' Krugis threw his hammer down, startling the hound that slept beneath the bench. 'What do you need?'

Aspala held up her golden blade. 'This sword reforged.'

'Is that it?' spluttered the smith.

*Thunk.*

Piece by piece, Farden lay his helmet, gauntlets and vambraces on the workbench. The smith's eyes widened in increments as if they were being cranked open.

'Ever heard of Scalussen armour before?' asked the mage.

The man's heavy brows grew heavier as he fixed Farden with a glower. 'The lady should have told you; I'm not like these other smiths. Bloody shields and spears are all they're good for.'

Irien was dabbing at her cheek with a kerchief. 'I told him.'

'Then can you work with it?'

Krugis' sooty fingers picked up the vambrace, examining it reverently and from angle after angle. 'What happened, you throw it down the Rainmaker? I… this looks melted here, too. You know how hot a fire has to be to melt Scalussen armour? Either you've got yourself a fake or you had a run-in with a dragon.'

'No fake, sir,' Farden answered.

The smith smudged dark streaks across his face as he blew out more spittle and a deep sigh. 'I... I could work with it. Unpin and reforge the scales, if that's even possible on this cuirass. The helmet is tricky...'

'Can you do it?'

Krugis levelled a sausage-like finger at Irien. 'You,' he grunted. 'better get me that commission. And a hundred silver leaves for my trouble.'

A silk purse of coins landed on the workbench before Farden even saw Irien dip into a pocket.

'It'll take me some time,' said Krugis.

'How long?'

'All this? Three days, maybe more to reforge the sword as well.'

Another handful of coins joined the purse.

'Make sure it's two.'

As Krugis began to examine the armour in more detail, the others left the forge and escaped into fresher, cooler air. All except Farden. He found a tree stump nearby and perched his weary bones on it.

'What are you doing?' asked Irien.

'You think I'm going to leave my armour here, with a stranger, in a city I've never seen before?'

Irien scoffed. 'Krugis is a reputable smith, famous for leagues around.'

'I trust nobody.'

Irien chuckled and stared instead at the central tower that speared the Viscera's underbelly. A passerby caught her attention instead. 'If it isn't Antor Sleck! Always a displeasure,' she cried.

Farden and the others turned to see the man with the bulbous hat once more. The man Farden had throttled against a wall. The mage glared at him.

Antor sketched a bow. 'The Lady of Whispers. It's nice to see you in Vensk for once. You must enjoy the one week a year you are allowed into your own city.'

Irien admired the crossbow on her left arm, checking the bolt and tensed strings with a musical note. 'I enjoy it as much as I can with the riffraff they allow in these days. It seems anyone can be a patron. Who is it you've entered this year?'

The question made Antor's throat bob up and down. 'I am still considering several fighters.'

'Time's running out while the price goes up, Antor,' warned Irien. 'You'll get the hang of it one year.'

Crushed, the man muttered something impolite as he and his sour-faced guards wandered off into the maze beneath the Viscera.

'I am somewhat... banished from Vensk and most of Golikar. The Tourney week is open to all. It's the only time I am allowed back to my home,' Irien explained. It was the first time she had appeared irked by anything.

Farden nodded, not wishing to pick at that scab of conversation.

'Will you not watch?' Irien asked of Farden. 'Or do you plan to sit here for three days? You know I can vouch for this smith.'

Farden shook his head. 'I don't mean to be rude. I trust nobody with that armour.'

'Then forgive me, but watching the Tourney is the high point of my year. I must head above,' said Irien. Farden caught her eye before she turned. She looked disappointed.

Farden arched his shoulders and leaned his elbows on his thighs. Drums thundered above them in the Viscera, so loud he felt their throb in his ribs.

Aspala sat beside Farden. Now awake, Krugis' dog came out from under the bench to sniff at his master's customers. He was the kind of hound with drooping eyes and jowls, and with a slow shuffle to his walk. Aspala held her hands out and let the hound lick her fingers. 'Are you really going to wait for three days?' she asked.

'If I have to. I've never had much trust for smiths. Something to do with a fake silver mirror decades ago.'

'Then I will stay too.'

Farden nodded, thankful for company for once. He made conversation. 'What does that golden sword mean to you?'

'Perhaps not as much as your armour means to you.' Her dark skin creased as she smiled. 'It is a symbol of freedom. You know what Malvus did to Paraia. He enslaved half of us to build his roads and his armies. The rest he persecuted for their rebellion and forced to fight in arenas just like this one. At least these fighters choose their own fate.'

Farden finally understood the curious scowl that had sat on Aspala's face for most of the morning.

'We are a free people, as you know,' she said. 'No queen or king has ever ruled over Paraia, not from Troacles to Galadaë. Our gods do not even rule us. So it was, I rebelled.' The Paraian wrinkled her nose in disgust as if the memories offended her. 'This was my mother's sword. She was the captain of a rich trader's guard, the kind of woman born with a sword in her hand, and she taught me all she knew of blades and spilling blood. I could put up a fight before I could walk. Useful on the long caravan journeys to the rich south. I was a woman myself when Malvus started to worm his way into Paraia. When he started levying taxes on merchants and markets, the trader refused. He was arrested and beaten. My mother was a loyal kind, and she stepped in to defend him.' Aspala turned to face Farden. 'They executed her along with the whole caravan, along with the raider's family, too. They took my mother's head right there in the market square. Before the axe reached my neck, I managed to escape and spent the next few years getting my sword back from the Arka executioner who had taken it as a prize. I took his head as payment and began to journey north to Scalussen to fight for you. I will never forget the day I saw Modren's bookship off the Cape of Glass. The rest, as you Emaneska say, is history.'

The mention of Modren had thrown Farden off. Sharp needles of emotion prickled his eyes. 'He saved so many,' he whispered. 'Including me.'

Scraping a line in the dirt with his heel and clearing his throat, he pointed to the minotaur. 'And you, Warbringer. How does a minotaur come by a hammer like yours?' asked Farden. 'One that captures souls? I've never heard anything like it.'

The ghosts within Voidaran screeched as Warbringer swung it with little effort. 'It came to us from the stars. From gods.'

'How so?'

Warbringer's big claws drew a sharp line through the air. 'Fell one night from the sky. Onto head of oldest and first Warbringer. He was in middle of execution. The bloodmonger that was saved named hammer Voidaran. Means Dark Saviour. Realised it stole souls every time it killed. He was first to unite the clans. We say it come from our god Dotharadine. Every Warbringer of my clan carry it since. Now me, like mother before. This is why I understand you, King. To die so far from Efjar would mean clan loses Voidaran.'

'Where are the others?' Mithrid yelled over the roar of the Viscera. It filled her ears, rattled her bones. She had tried several times to take it all in and failed. The crowds were a colossal whirlpool of motion around the main bowl shape of the Viscera. Streamers and petals filled the air to such a degree Mithrid couldn't make out the far side of the arena.

Irien had to lean close to be heard. 'Your mage trusts my smith so little he has stayed to watch him finish the job.'

Durnus tutted. 'Gods, does he love that armour.'

Mithrid dared once again to look over the edge of Irien's private balcony within the masses.

They sat upon a shelf that encircled the Viscera. There was nothing but a disgustingly long drop and the sea of people. Beyond them, another drop to the floor of the arena: a vast oval of dust and peach-coloured clay. A broad pillar sat at its centre. It was so tall to be level with Mithrid, and at its top, a flat platform surrounded. Banners plastered its battlements. A varnished wooden bell hung above the platform. And pride of place beneath it, on a pedestal surrounded by flowers, was what looked to be the resemblance of a decapitated head, made of stone.

'Is that...?' Mithrid began to ask.

'The Head of Sigrimur? Yes indeed,' Irien confirmed. 'Your prize is gifted to the Queen of Golikar by last year's surviving champion. It is blessed with the soil of the Viscera and raised to the pillar. It stays there alongside the royalty until a new champion emerges.'

Durnus seemed content with that explanation, but Mithrid was not. She still had questions, but the Viscera had begun to fill with the fighters, one by one.

Men and women entered the Viscera to thunderous roars. Most ascended by lifts embedded in the clay. The others walked in via an archway at the far side. The first of the fighters were human. Several beastpeople like Aspala followed. One immense woman was covered in scales like a dragon-rider. Mithrid wouldn't have been surprised if she was Eyrum's long lost sister.

'Only one wins, right?' asked Durnus.

'Correct.'

Mithrid chimed in. 'Aren't they worried about the odds?'

'No, child,' Irien said. 'Because they think they're the best and they're willing to bet their lives on it. It's solely down to the Viscera to teach them whether they're right or wrong.'

It sounded too great a risk to Mithrid, but even then, she scanned the growing lines of fighters. Women and men with fierce faces and more scars than could be counted. She silently matched herself against each of them, and wondered – with a cold feeling in her gut – whether she could have survived the Viscera. Even without her dark magick.

❦

The roar of the Viscera verged on deafening. Even without it, the ringing hammers of the smiths and general hubbub beneath the arena would have done the job.

With their conversation muted, Aspala and Warbringer stared up at the Viscera's foundations. There hammering of feet and fists and clapping hands made the ground tremble. The chips of bark and leaves quivered around Farden's feet, where the hound had decided to curl up. He only stared at the smith, watching him as he examined the mage's vambraces. Farden's jaw clenched but he kept himself still.

Another wave of dizziness came, and he fought it off bitterly. Farden kept brushing his arms as if the rough feel of his own skin was foreign to him. He stared down at his hands and found them trembling as he clawed his remaining fingers back and forth. Perhaps it was his tired eyes, but he swore they had never looked so gaunt. Scarred, yes, but wrinkles bunched at his knuckles. His veins looked black in the low light at the roots of Vensk. He felt beaten by the quest already. He could not wait to have his armour fixed, and rid himself of the hideous feeling of time gnawing at him. Taking greater chunks of him each day. Farden caught the smith's eye over the red and gold scales of the vambrace. Krugis glowered before turning away, a hammer in one hand.

It took a moment to realise what the discomfort was. He was nervous. *Scared*, even. The armour and its magick had been one of the few dependable constants in his arduous existence. He feared losing it more than he feared losing a limb. He had avoided the crushing wheels of time for so long that he was now petrified of them. And now, to his horror, it seemed they were seeking to catch up with him. There was no ignoring it: the magick of his armour was fading slowly but surely. Time was his enemy now. Farden snarled and pushed the worry deep within as he always did, as if he were stone instead of flesh. Stone had no heart to ache. Farden clenched his fists, and fought back the tear that threatened to escape down his cheek.

Farden looked up to see Warbringer was licking her lips. She was looking at a small flock of sheep corralled between the forges and factories. They constantly circled their pen in an off-white circle.

'What is it, Warbringer?'

'Hungry.'

'You're always hungry.'

Warbringer smacked a fist against her stomach. The muscles beneath her matted charcoal hair barely flinched. 'Bigger than you. And I am starved of pink-flesh. Not the same.'

The minotaur was already taking steps to where steam and smoke drifted, from kitchens further into the gloom of the tree trunks.

Between the smell of hot steel and charcoal, Farden could taste something enticing. Something with spices and roast meats. It caused his insides to growl, but he stayed put.

'I could eat,' Aspala shouted over the noise.

Farden shook his head. 'You two go hunt down some food if you wish. I'm staying right here.'

Patting their stomachs, Aspala and Warbringer began to drift away. Farden closed his eyes.

❧

*Fifty… fifty-one…* Mithrid counted as each fighter entered.

Once they had taken their place in the growing lines, they turned to the pillar at the centre of the Viscera and bowed, saluted, or knelt in honour. That was where the royalty of Golikar sat, or so Irien informed them. The queen of Golikar and her princely-looking harem were hidden somewhere between the streamers and petals. And now orange and red smoke, lit by spectators far below her. It was a riot of colour and noise, not diminishing for a moment.

*Sixty-four, sixty-five.*

❦

Farden's stomach rumbled for the dozenth time. There was nothing like the power of hunger after a night of wine. It had become painful.

The mage was torn. Krugis hadn't turned around in a while, busy at work with fine tools and layers of spectacles.

Farden cursed quietly to himself. The noise from above was beginning to grate on him. It only seemed to get louder. Contender after contender was fed into the core of the Viscera. Farden could see them rising up in winch-lifts into the arena's belly. Crowds were now milling around the workshops, making arrangements for the week. It reminded Farden of Scalussen Underspire and the forges that never slept. It certainly sounded like them.

Again, his stomach protested.

'Damn it,' Farden hissed as he got to his feet. Boots crunching on the dry loam and dirt and taking nothing but the ornate knife, Farden walked in the direction Aspala and Warbringer had disappeared. He felt strangely light without his armour encasing him. His pale tunic moved too freely. His trews felt baggy. Farden felt as if he jumped he'd end up on a rooftop.

There were makeshift streets through the mess of low buildings. Beasts bayed from pens and paddocks. Children scampered about, running errand after errand, only stopping to clamour around the fighters. And still no sign of horns above the crowds.

'Aspala!' Farden called out, voice useless again the roar of the Viscera. 'Warbringer!'

An old woman bent over an anvil whistled to him. 'Looking for that cow creature?'

Farden glared. 'A minotaur, you mean?'

She shrugged. 'Guess so. My husband took 'em to the sculleries.' As the woman pointed, Farden glimpsed Warbringer's broad back disappearing between smoke.

Farden left without thanks, eager not to lose them. Had he lingered or bothered to turn, he might have questioned the woman's wolfish smirk.

Instead, Farden pressed on.

'Aspala!'

❧

*Eighty-seven...* Though the crowd of fighters now seemed huge, the Viscera was still vastly empty.

Durnus' voice cracked as he tried to be heard. 'Are any of these fighters mages, or wizards, Irien?'

The vampyre's question snapped the Lady of Whispers from her reverie.

'You Emaneskans and your magick. It does not solve everything, and there are plenty in Golikar and the Easterealm who see it as a problem to be solved,' replied the Lady of Whispers. 'No magick whatsoever is allowed in the Scarlet Tourney. No charmed or magick weapons, either. Only sharp edges, strength, speed, cunning. It is a true fight, and that is why there are only two fighters to a bout. See those bars around the edges of the Viscera? Those are the cells where the fighters stay for the next five days under the queen's guard. They are tended by their retinues, fed, healed, have their armour and weapons repaired, and even have whores delivered, but they may not leave the Viscera once they enter it. The tradition is supposed to keep them from cheating or killing each other, really. Most of the time it works.'

A fanfare of trumpets cut Irien short and deafened Mithrid. Durnus clamped his hands over his ears. Even shut his eyes, if that would help.

'What's happening?' Mithrid yelled.

Irien put on a beaming smile. 'The Scarlet Tourney is about to begin! Just watch, my dears, and you will see.'

'Aspala!'

Farden ducked through a waft of steam that smelled vaguely of rotten cabbage. Wincing against the light of a lantern, he could barely see them ahead, but they were walking fast, and Farden was still weak. Or hungover. Possibly both, he cursed inwardly. He spared a moment to catch his breath, and realised that they had wandered past the edge of the buildings, along paddocks of nervous cows. Machinery for the Viscera clanked loudly. Water ran through puddles and rivulets here, making the ground boggy. Hardly a soul could be seen except the unmistakable figure of Warbringer, two more smaller silhouettes by her side.

There, Farden saw them: shapes emerging from the herds of cows, dressed in black and baring clubs. Farden tried to shout, but the machinery was too loud. The bandits, whoever they were, had chosen a fine spot to strike.

Farden drew his knife and begun to catch up when the first figures pounced on Warbringer. There were at least a dozen of them, sprawled across her back and arms like cats on a curtain. Their clubs hammered at her skull. For every one she plucked off with her claws or crushed senseless with Voidaran, another two pounced on her. Aspala was mobbed in moments, driven into the ground. Even so, she managed to break the necks of one and kick one so hard in the face his nose had disappeared.

Farden ran all the faster, ignoring the aches that stabbing him in the back and legs.

They had somehow dragged Voidaran from Warbringer's fist. Her roars grew in ferocity, overriding the machinery and roar of the Viscera. One man she simply bit the face from before using him as a makeshift hammer.

A score of dead lay around her, and yet still more of the attackers appeared. Ropes had appeared. They lassoed the minotaur's horns first, then her arms and hooves. Warbringer managed to gore two of the bastards with her horns before they dropped her. Writhing and bellowing, they began to drag her and Aspala onto a sloped wagon. They worked painfully fast. The mage ran breathlessly for them.

Farden was a spear's throw from them when the trumpets sounded. The fanfare was ear-splitting even outside the Viscera. When Farden's looked back, he found a dozen shadows blocking his path. All of them hovered on the edge of the nearest lantern, casting an arc around him. Their faces were plain wooden masks, two black eyes punched in the middle to make them ghoulish.

'Get him!' one hissed, conveniently driving his fellows forwards before him. In pairs, they came at the mage, clubs raised.

Farden instinctively flung out his hand, aiming to drive a spell right through the pack. Nothing but pain lanced up his hand. A mere spark popped between finger and thumb. No magick came. Only the bandits, shuffling at him.

'Fuck it!' Farden yelled at the tremor of nerves that ran through him. He seized the hand of the first man to strike and twisted it so viciously the attacker somersaulted onto his back. Mud spewed. A swift kick to his jaw stopped his wriggling. Farden swept his club from his limp grasp as the next man came at him: sailing through the air in a mad attack. Farden blocked his strike with a loud crack and simultaneously plunged the knife deep into the man's neck before his feet had touched the ground. The mage drove him to the floor so hard he felt the knife punch through bone to dig into the grit beneath.

If Farden had hoped it would stun the others into thinking twice, he should have remembered they had just captured a minotaur. A weakened soldier – not a mage – like him was easy prey.

A fist clocked him hard on the brow. Farden staggered but managed to slash across his attacker's belly as he recoiled. The blade was keen; the man howled as blood and a string of guts spilled from him. He sank to the mud, clutching at his insides. The stink of bloody copper and shit mingled with the dank smell of loam and wood. Farden felt his heart hammering alongside the machinery, heard his breath roaring in his ears.

The attackers were only marginally stalled by the horror of the man's death. Just enough time for Farden to kick the knees from the next two, sink the knife into the back of one's skull, and seize the other in a headlock. He wrenched viciously, and another body met the dust. He clawed for his magick between every moment, straining so hard his jaw burned.

A club almost took his leg from beneath him. Another cracked the bone of his right arm. Farden yelled, spinning low and high, slashing across throats and chests and unarmoured bellies. Another fist glanced from his cheek, stunning the mage. A rope seized his foot and quickly hauled the world from under him. Farden slammed the knife into the earth to stop from being dragged, but before he could slash the rope, the blows came raining. Boots and clubs pounded Farden from every side. Mud choked him. Blood filled his eyes from a kick to the head. Farden roared as he felt a rib snap. A dread cold had seeped into one of his arms. He flung every limb in a desperate retaliation, but he was rewarded with only pain.

It all came to sudden a halt. A jarring peace after the beating. Farden stayed huddled, protecting his head with his arms, but not another blow touched him. He wiped his eyes of rasping muck and warm blood. Not a single attacker stood around him. They had scarpered into the paddocks and gloom. Farden had been left alone in a scarlet puddle of his own blood, with only the dead and dying around him.

With his clothes ragged and soiled, and with dirt and blood smeared across his face, Farden hauled himself to the nearest one. He was too busy muttering about his insides to notice the mage until Farden seized him by the throat and rammed him down into the nearest puddle.

'Who are you?' he shouted.

He hauled the man up, but all he had was religious babbling for him. Farden understood none of it. Beneath his mask was a tanned face and a pale eye. Farden drove him into the water once more.

'Who are you? Tell me!'

Whether it was death or drowning that gave the man a severe desire to live, Farden would never find out. All he knew was the man seized a fistful of the mage's hair and began to thrash. He struck a lucky blow on the mage's chest, catching the broken rib and sending Farden reeling.

'Gah!' spat the man. His face was a mask of dark mud punctured by two wild eyes. He reared up and fumbled for the mage's neck. Farden felt thumbs trying to gouge their way into his windpipe. Punches failed to dislodge him. Spitting mud, Farden's flailing hand caught the nearby knife. It sliced his palm as he seized it by the sharp edge, but it was all he needed.

Farden drove the silver blade into the man's eye. Once, twice, thrice, until the death throes had come to a halt. He slid the corpse into the mud, and lay staring at the Viscera, listening to its thunder. And below, in the tower that speared it, Farden saw Warbringer and Aspala rising up on one of the winch-lifts.

'No!' he yelled.

The fire of battle dulled much of the pain from his injury, but it was fading fast. Agony swooped in as soon as he had made it to his feet. Others had been drawn by the screams. Farden could see them running across the mud to investigate. Like the mage, they had arrived too late.

Farden could only stand and stare as the minotaur and Paraian disappeared into the Viscera.

'NO!'

# CHAPTER 15
## OLD FRIENDS

*If you like your head attached to your shoulders, it's best to stay on the good side of a Written mage.*
STANDING ORDER AT THE OLD SPIRE OF MANESMARK & WRITTEN SCHOOL

*Ninety-five…*

The fanfares blew once more to signal the arrival of the final and remaining fighters. The dark pits in the clay floor were filled once again as the lifts arose. Smoke billowed around them as if the arena was aflame. The cheers of the crowd took on a strange tone for a moment. One that sounded suspiciously surprised. Even some of the fighters turned. Mithrid could see some of them raising their hands in protest.

Durnus approached the edge of the balcony, eyes narrowed and peering.

Mithrid ripped a streamer from her hair. She pushed Irien aside as she too surged to the railing. There was something peculiar about the final fighters, and it set a stone weight in Mithrid's heart.

'What's the matter?' cried Irien.

Mithrid stared hard, willing the view to clear. She got her wish moments later.

There, on the far side of the arena, standing bleeding, battered, and with arms bound in chain were Aspala and Warbringer. Two hooded and masked fellows attended them.

Mithrid whirled on Irien. The lady did a fine job of looking surprised. Mithrid's axe was already in her hands, blade hooked around her fist.

'What in Hel is going on?' she demanded.

'Calm yourself, Mithrid Fenn!' Irien pleaded. 'This is nothing to do with me. I'm as shocked as you are.'

'You, the Lady of Whispers? Shocked? I find that hard to believe.'

Irien did not look hurt, but vexed. 'How quickly you turn against me when I show you nothing but hospitality and kindness.'

'Those are our friends down there! Aspala doesn't even have a sword.'

'And I might say the very same, Mithrid! And those people holding them, my dear,' Irien pointed past the girl's shoulder, 'are not my men. This is one whisper I haven't been privy to.'

'We have to get them out!' shouted Durnus. He was already working his way to the stairs they had entered by.

'It's too late.' Irien pulled him back. 'Once the fighters stand in the Viscera they cannot leave. They either die or they win.'

'But they are bound in chains! Surely it's obvious they don't want to be here?'

Irien shook her head with a solemn slowness. 'It doesn't matter. Some patrons scour the prisons to find their fighters. See there? Another man in the same chains. They fight for freedom, if only for a day or two of it, and a cheering crowd to send them off. Trust me. I would not lie to you. I—'

'Where is Farden?' Durnus yelled over them.

The stone in her heart turned sharp-edged. Mithrid said nothing as she turned and left. The booming voice of an announcer escorted her from the Viscera.

'To the three-hundredth and eighty-sixty Scarlet Tourney, the Bountiful Queen Peskora of Golikar welcomes you!' bayed an announcer.

'What can be done, Irien?' Durnus cried over the resulting roar. Explosions of smoke and sparks ran around the edges of the Viscera. The wooden bell tolled with short knells that sounded more like a drum being beaten.

Durnus gripped the railing so hard his fingers ached. He felt weaker than ever. Both Warbringer and Aspala looked to be fuming, but for some baffling reason they didn't fight or struggle. It was as if they knew the rules of the Scarlet Tourney.

Irien placed her wooden hand on his arm.

'The fighters don't seem to be happy about this late addition. Warbringer will pose a great threat. They might see it as unfair, and we will be able to extricate her if there's an uproar. As for Aspala...' Irien stamped her foot. 'I will see what can be done. At very least I will find out who did this, and how. I can promise you that, Durnus,' she assured him. 'Unless they are the first to fight today, I will arrange to visit them in their cells tonight.'

Upon the tower, Queen Peskora rose above the battlements. She was an incredibly tall woman and bald as a river pebble beneath her crown of copper gold. With her arms out wide, her emerald gown had the look of a tapestry, detailed with Golikan patterns of gold trees and roots.

'Welcome, one and all, strangers and friends, lords and ladies, contenders, patrons, and spectators of this grand event!' screeched the queen with a shrill and cracking voice.

Another mighty roar thundered through the Viscera. The endless petals and streamers fell in another downpour.

Durnus stared upon it all with hatred. The wonder and fascination had died a swift and brutal death. He could not tear his gaze from Aspala and the minotaur. They had spotted him, too. He held his hands out as if to plead for their calm. It was ridiculous advice, he knew, but it was difficult to be powerless.

The queen continued. 'Contenders of the Tourney! For the next five days, you will abide by all of the ancient rules. You will fight with honour! No vengeance will be sought from the outcomes of the bouts! And should you break the rules, the price is death by hanging for all to see.'

Almost every one of the fighters raised their fists and weapons and bellowed in unison. A dozen languages filled the air. Only Warbringer and Aspala stayed still. If Durnus judged the queen's expression correctly, it did not go unnoticed by those in the tower.

The queen screeched once more. 'May the Scarlet Tourney begin!'

To the heavy clanking of machinery, the cell doors around the Viscera opened. The lines of fighters dispersed as they chose. Some seemed preordained. Durnus saw the champion Irien had pointed out, Rovisk Dal'Bvara, pushing another fighter to the ground as he tried to choose the same cell. It raised another cheer and a great raucous laugh from the crowds.

Durnus was too busy watching Warbringer and Aspala being shoved into two cells side by side. Aspala managed to headbutt one of the masked strangers. Her beast-blood gave her a stronger skull than his wooden mask. He sprawled on the dust, unconscious, and had to be dragged away by his friends.

'I will have my guards seize those two men,' Irien hissed, clicking her fingers to the guards standing nearby. They vanished into the crowds without hesitation.

'You pay them well.'

'It pays merely to know me.'

'What happens to them now?' asked the vampyre.

Irien sighed. 'They're safe there, for now. The first names will be called for the first bout. Luckily, many of the contenders vie for the first fights. They can get them out of the way. Rest for a day, perhaps. The odds rise in the favour. Gold is earned. As a late addition likely with an unscrupulous patron, Warbringer or Aspala shouldn't fight today.'

'*Shouldn't.*'

Irien nodded, lips drawn and brow creased.

The announcer boomed again. He was a fat fellow with a deep voice to match. Durnus spied him below their parapet.

'Presenting Feen of the Sunter Isles against Lord Okram Marko of Bolsh!'

Durnus did not care for the fight, but the learned man within him needed to study his enemy. With Warbringer and Aspala in their cells, "safe" as Lady Irien called it, he could at least calm enough to see how this Scarlet Tourney worked.

Feen was a hunched fellow that looked as though he had washed up on a beach half-drowned and dragged through the tideline for good measure. His hair was threaded with black seaweed. His armour was a simple lattice of rusted iron and pale seashells. His two pickaxes had serrated teeth along their blades.

Okram stood admiring his fingernails while Feen postured and goaded the crowds. Wearing a gown of satin and silk, Okram looked more like a merchant than a fighter. He was as broad as a door, however, and as Feen got ready to charge, he calmly pulled two spiked gauntlets from his robes and slid them over his knuckles.

Feen hurtled at him. Quick as a hawk, Okram dodged the mad swing of the pickaxes and drove a fist into the side of Feen's skull. The man staggered away, bleeding from one ear. All energy was gone from him. He took another halfhearted swing, and Okram hammered his ribs and face again with a flurry of jabs and punches. The crowd went wild for the display. For every drop of crimson.

Bleeding profusely from a dozen wounds, Feen made it a dozen steps back towards his cell before he dropped his axes and fell onto his face.

And in that short time, the first bout of the Tourney was over. The dust and clay had been blessed with its first blood. To deafening roars, Okram shrugged, jabbed at the air some more, and bowed to the royalty above. Green-clad workers were already dragging Feen away.

Durnus glowered.

☙

In the dark beneath the Viscera, Mithrid found the mage. He was leaning heavy on a guard in wooden armour, spitting blood one moment and cursing loudly the next. A small group of bewildered citizens and workers stood around him, offering him cloths or shrugging at his demands.

'What do you mean nothing can be done? That is madness!' Mithrid heard him complaining.

'Farden!'

The guard saw a chance to break free of carrying the mage, and quickly placed him down at the edge of Krugis' stall, right where they had left him.

'Glad to see they didn't get everyone,' Farden hissed as Mithrid knelt by his side. Little of his pale skin could be seen under the dirt and mud.

'What happened?'

Farden took a moment to knead his eyes with split knuckles.

The guard tutted, feeling somehow important enough to explain. 'Didn't see much until it was all over. Found him and twenty dead folk back there. Says they attacked him. Their mistake it seemed. Looks like he got them all.'

'I told you, there were more! With masks and black cloaks. They attacked my friends, kidnapped them, and took them up there,' Farden shouted. He jabbed a finger at the Viscera's underbelly.

'Sure.' The guard rolled his eyes, replaced his helmet and stalked back into the mess of buildings. The others left also, gossiping to themselves. Farden and Mithrid were left alone alongside the hammering of the blacksmith.

'Are you hurt, Farden? This is a lot of blood.'

'Not all of it's mine.' The mage lifted an arm and slapped the knife on top of his knee. 'They ambushed us. Led Warbringer and Aspala off somewhere before pouncing on them. Must have been thirty, forty of them. I fought as hard as I could but I couldn't stop it.'

The grimace on Farden's face looked to be a deeper pain than just his injuries. He coughed and spat blood once more.

'We need to get you up. Can you walk?'

'It's that fucking Antor,' he hissed as Mithrid gripped him. Even without his armour, the man was bloody heavy.

'I know it's him.'

Mithrid was happy to have somebody to blame. 'It makes sense.'

'I'll skin the little bugger myself,' Farden muttered. 'Warbringer can eat what's left when we free them.'

After watching him wipe most of the blood and soil from his face, Mithrid put her cloak around the mage to make him look slightly less horrific. Only slightly.

Step by step, she led him back to the Viscera. It took twice as much time with the mage so injured, but at last they returned to Irien and Durnus. The lady's guards almost skewered him right there and then. He was almost unrecognisable, but to Irien's sharp commands, they took over from Mithrid and settled him down upon a couch spanning the rear wall of the balcony. He kept struggling to get up against their help.

Durnus was immediately at the mage's side. 'By Evernia, what did they do to you?' he asked, while Irien poured him water and ordered towels, and a healer.

'Where are they?' Farden barked. Mithrid was glad for the curtains that gave them privacy between the other balconies. Already the ruckus had drawn some eyes.

Durnus pressed him back into the couch cushions. 'Hidden away for now, but safe. Irien has guards chasing down the men that brought them in. We will get answers.'

'I don't care about answers. I want them out of there! Even if I have to drag them out of the Tourney myself!'

Durnus seized Farden by the shoulder as he tried to rise again. 'They cannot leave the Viscera under pain of death, mage. And you would be torn apart. Especially in your state.'

'It was that Antor! That detestable weasel of a man. It has to be.' Farden seethed through bared teeth.

'Quite possibly,' said Irien.

'Maybe you shouldn't have shoved him against the wall.'

'Not now, Mithrid!' snarled Farden. 'Where is he?'

Irien waved her hands over the Viscera. 'I will know soon, Farden. For now, we must wait. Even a patron cannot withdraw their fighter. They're stuck there without a decision from the queen. But don't forget, they're also far from defenceless.'

Farden shook his head. 'Aspala has no sword.'

'She doesn't need one,' Mithrid added in a cold voice. 'Trust me. I trained with her.'

'I will have Krugis work faster,' Irien said as she stepped away. 'And arrange food and healers for them if their mystery patron hasn't. Have faith in my children and their whispers, friends. I will have answers to this dire situation soon.'

'You never know,' said Mithrid with hope. 'They might just end up winning it.'

Neither the vampyre nor the mage felt her grim enthusiasm. While Durnus summoned what healing magick he could, Mithrid stood at the railing instead. The announcer read out the fates of the next fighters.

'Presenting Lady Nesime of the Diamond Mountains against Hrishnash of the Huskar!'

❦

Only blood and names marked the passage of the day. No sun held sway under the city of Vensk. Death was the meter of the hour. The cries of the defeated were the chime of regular bells.

There was little distraction in the bouts. Only mounting worry that the next names would be Warbringer's or Aspala's.

Mercifully, when the fanfare had sounded the end of the first day of the Scarlet Tourney, the last fights had lasted almost an hour each, until finally a throat was cut in a spraying arc of blood.

Fifteen souls had lost their lives in the Viscera that day, and still the crowds clamoured for more. Those who were not trapped in the queues back into the city crowded around the arena's edge to catch glimpses of their favourite contenders.

Rovisk Dal'Bvara had proven the hero of the first bouts, for reasons the crowd loved but Mithrid and the others had despised. He had toyed with his opponents like a sabrecat with a rabbit, wounding just enough to keep his foe fighting while he flourished and parried in grandiose manoeuvres. Now back in his cell, Rovisk posed and waved at the bars.

'All style, no substance,' Farden had growled.

Much to Durnus' consternation and the healers' annoyance, Farden had stayed standing at the railing. He had stared at every fight. Even now, as they stamped their way down the steps of the Viscera, he watched the fighters in their cells with sharp interest.

A ringing lingered in Mithrid's ears. The rumble of feet and voices and scattered cheers seemed like silence to her. One by one, the lanterns around the overhanging struts and highest tiers of the Viscera winked out. The queen vanished within her thin tower. The winch-lifts were at work again, bringing up patrons and servants to tend the fighters.

A broad doorway led down from the tiered seats into the Viscera's arena floor. It was guarded by a score of soldiers, half of them carrying pikes, the other long crossbows. Each of them wore royal colours of the Golikan wooden armour. Mithrid couldn't help but ponder what her axe would make of their wooden plates. The angry, fearful part of her wanted to find out. She silently urged them to put up a fuss, no matter the consequences.

'Halt there! Patrons, are you?' called the soldier in charge.

Irien tutted. 'Esteemed spectators, as it happens.'

The soldier looked them up and down. Her eyes narrowed when she saw the state of Farden. The blood had been wiped away but the bruises and cuts still remained.

'And who might you be?'

'Lady of Whispers. Golikan nobility and a far cousin of Queen Peskora of Golikar, and I wish to meet the fighters.'

The soldier shook her head. But Mithrid saw her eyes flashing back and forth and her palm creeping out.

'There's a price for access,' she said. 'Especially for you, Lady of Whispers.'

Irien sighed. 'Of course! You should've mentioned it sooner, good sir.'

Before the woman could argue, Irien slapped a fat leaf of silver into her hand and moved past her.

'Let them pass,' the guard hollered to the others.

Broad steps led them a zigzag path down to the arena. More soldiers lined the corridors here. They were not stopped, just stared at. It seemed like a Golikan pastime. One that Mithrid was starting to despise. She glowered back at them.

They were not alone on the floor of the Viscera. Workers scrubbed at blood and shit-stains and tramped fresh clay-dust over them. Other dignitaries and nobles and people rich enough had come down to tour the bars of the cells and stare at the fighters. Even the queen had emerged from her tower. Polished and gleaming soldiers surrounded them in a tight circle, square shields interlocked.

Unsurprisingly, Warbringer had drawn quite a crowd. Fondling their gold necklaces and hitching up their silks, they cooed like pigeons at the minotaur hunched over in the dark of her cell. Quite the opposite, in the nearby cell, Aspala bared her teeth and pounded her fists against the bars.

'Make way there,' Irien ordered imperiously. Farden and Mithrid stared down any that looked to object.

Warbringer arose when she saw them. 'You still alive,' she rumbled at Farden.

Farden nodded. 'Somewhat.'

'Thank Bezarish,' Aspala breathed. She had an eye so blackened it was almost swollen shut. Ropes had burned her forearms and wrists. 'We thought they had taken you too.'

'Who took you?'

'They not say. Told me if I refuse, you die,' said Warbringer. 'That we must fight.'

'I don't even have a sword.'

Irien clicked her wooden fingers again and one of her guards came forwards with a cloth bundle. She unveiled the gold metal beneath, still warm from the smith's forge. She moved towards the cages. The soldiers at their peripheries scowled and shook their heads. Irien approached anyway. Mithrid barely caught her handing over the silver bribe. The sword was back in Aspala's hands in moments. She withdrew into the cell to unveil it in whatever privacy she could get.

'Who is the patron of these fighters?' Irien called out. 'Who entered them?'

Not a soul answered. Irien yelled again, loud enough to attract royal attention. Mithrid caught sight of the queen turning around to stare at the disturbance. Her soldiers began tramping in their direction.

'Shit. My presence here might have been a mistake,' Irien said, quickly bowing. The others followed suit, no matter how much it wrinkled Mithrid. By the look on Farden's face, he felt the same.

The shrill voice arrived before the queen did. Peskora towered over Mithrid by at least a foot.

'So this is the fighter that would not honour me. And found the presence of my ashamed and banished cousin, no less. Even now it refuses to bow. Are you this beast's patron, my shamed cousin?' the queen asked of Irien.

'I am no beast,' Warbringer replied with a gnash of teeth.

The queen's soldiers bristled, lowering their sharp javelins at the minotaur. Shouts rained down from above from lingering spectators.

'To answer your question, Bountiful Majesty,' said Irien. 'We are not their patrons. We are looking for them, however, so we can complain—'

'Silence,' ordered the queen. She toured the bars of Warbringer's cage. Mithrid hoped the minotaur had the sensibility not to throttle the woman.

'I have heard complaints from patrons and fighters alike. Reasons why I should banish you from the competition. Unfair, they call it,' Peskora squeaked.

Irien clasped her hands. 'I would agree, Your Majesty. This is a tournament for those of human nature. Not beasts like this fearsome thing, clearly brought against its will. Just like its master here in the next cell. The bet-takers will not be happy with such sure odds. That's why we came to petition for their release.'

The queen stared Irien down until the Lady of Whispers bowed again.

'Strange, for a beast to be so adamant that it is not a beast,' said the queen. 'It seems human enough for me.'

Mithrid winced.

'No. You will be quite the challenge for our fighters. Quite the bloody spectacle you will be.'

Irien tried one last time. 'If I may, Majesty—'

'I have spoken!' Queen Peskora shrieked. 'They stay. You will go instead. Begone, cousin.'

The javelins turned in their direction. Mithrid found her fingers twitching; felt the cold sensation as her power surged.

'Mithrid,' Durnus warned in a whisper. She hadn't even noticed his hand on her arm.

With their tails between their legs and with glances over their shoulder, Mithrid and the others found themselves escaping into the colder air beyond the Viscera.

'Durnus?' asked Farden. The mage stopped, hunched and leaning in the centre of the walkway. He stared up at the complex tangle of city above.

'Yes, mage?'

'You're looking hungry.'

Durnus frowned until Farden elaborated.

'I think it's time you and I went hunting.'

Vensk was a city of darkness at night. The Golikans damn well seemed to prefer it. The moon was even less adept at puncturing the foliage. Wherever a glow-worm lantern didn't shine, shadows ruled.

'I'm tellin' you, the stuff won't burn. Chop it up into tinder and it takes an age to catch a flame. Spent hours tryin' to do it and this man just keeps laughin' at me. Took fifty silver leaves off me.'

'That's why you missed half the fights and can't afford a fuckin' ale right now, is it?'

'But it doesn't burn! What kind of tree don't burn?'

Antor Sleck shook his head. His neck complained as the heavy turban wobbled. The south was full of rubes, and in Tourney week, Vensk became full of them. There was plenty of money to made with cheap tricks, but Antor was done with cheap tricks. He had risen above them.

Raising his glass to the light, he threw back the syrupy wine the Golikans brewed from tree sap and arose from the bar.

'This tavern is filthy,' he remarked to the smiling wench behind the bar and tossed half what he owed at her. 'The wine full of silt,' he lied.

With no further explanation, Antor strode through the door onto a wide walkway that swayed gently with the hundreds of feet upon it. The contraptions made Antor feel sick.

That could have been the wine. It had been delicious but strong. There was already a tingle in his eyes. The glow-lanterns had an aura to them.

A passerby in a hood barged him. 'Mind how you go!' Antor blurted.

Damn it if he hadn't done it again: taken the wrong turning to his hired home for the week. He shouldn't have chosen somewhere so deep in Vensk. Ten years he had been coming to the Scarlet Tourneys and he swore Vensk's roads changed every year just to fuck with its visitors.

When Antor almost collided with a dead-end, he knew he had taken not one but several wrong turns. He turned to find the street empty and full of the faint mists that emanated from the Golikan pines at night. A bottle smashed somewhere in the gloom.

Antor clutched the dagger he kept deep in his robes. Golikans were all thieves at heart, so went the saying. He cursed the lack of light and went back the way he had come.

*There.* He caught a shadow ducking into another street.

Antor quietly wished he'd had the coin to pay for a whole day *and* night of a guarded escort. He hurried on, cloth shoes snagging splinters in the street. The footsteps he heard behind him vanished when he turned. Something flitted along the balconies of buildings towering above him. Antor blamed pigeons, but started to jog all the same.

With his breath loud in his ears, Antor took a swift right and chose a doorway to hide in, hoping to the Dawn God whoever chased him would run right past. Nobody and nothing came. Antor realised his breathing was like a forge's bellows. He forced himself to hold his breath, if even for a moment. To his horror, the breathing continued. Directly behind him.

A flurry of ragged cloth filled the doorway. A fist of iron grabbed him by his collar. Sharp nails raked across skin. His hat flew off as he was yanked from the dark. The world spun on its head, and not from the wine. The wooden planks of the street slammed into his face. All within a moment. Antor wheezed while limply fumbling for his dagger.

'Still got it, old friend,' Farden whispered as he rounded the corner.

Durnus ached to drive his fangs into the pale neck he strangled. He felt himself leaning towards the man. Felt his sharp fingernails digging in. He could smell the blood just beneath that thin layer of skin; feel the man's heartbeat pulsating in waves. He longed to drink, to kill. He could even feel the soul leaking from Antor's body like sweat and fear.

'Durnus,' Farden reminded him who he was.

'Stupid bastard near ran right into me,' Durnus hissed.

'Unfortunately for him.'

'I should have known it would be you. Not content with near choking me? Or insulting me? You now have to cause me physical harm?'

Farden placed his boot near to Antor's snivelling nose. 'Shut your face, Antor. We know it was you who took our friends.'

'You do, do you?' spat Antor.

'No games, man! Unless you wish for my associate here to put an end to your miserable, swindling life.'

'Would you please,' Antor choked, 'tell me what the fuck it is you're talking about?'

'Our friends. The Paraian woman and the minotaur you were so interested in. They were kidnapped. Forced into the Viscera. And who other than a jaded weasel like you, so desperate to get a patron, would want such a thing?'

'This is the first I've heard of this! I thought you had entered them yourselves. How dare you think I'd stoop so low! I'm insulted.'

Durnus clutched Antor's throat and made him squeak. A dread feeling crept into him. 'Why do I believe him?'

Farden was trembling with frustration.

'I haven't even got a fighter in the Tourney! You ruined that last hope yesterday,' Antor garbled.

'Let him go, Durnus. I hate to say it, but we have the wrong man.'

It took all his self-control to quench his vampyre's hunger. Since he had submitted himself to the vampyre's curse once more, the beast within him had been tempered, only emerging while feeding. Now, robbed of a meal, it was furious. It scared him to think it was not all vampyre, but now there was another beast inside of him, growing fast. Durnus had to wrench his hand from Antor's neck.

'Let this be a lesson to you,' Farden growled at him. They turned away from Antor, fists clenched, hearts heavy, and without a single answer for their troubles.

'You sons of whores!' Antor yelled.

Durnus whirled at the scraping of feet. He caught Antor's dagger too late: not before it had sliced his cheek.

There was no hope for the man now.

Before Durnus knew it, he had pinned Antor by his arms and bitten into his windpipe. Blood filled the vampyre's mouth, but he kept biting, crushing cartilage. Antor writhed beneath him, emitting nothing but a gurgling cry. Durnus once again dove too deep. The ravenous daemonblood within him was overpowering. The hunger was too intense. Sapphire vapour in the shape of a screaming soul seeped from Antor's pale, blood-spattered skin. Durnus felt its icy rush flood him.

Rough hands hauled him away. Antor's soul drifted back into his body, and his head lolled to the side. Blood bubbled around his throat as his last breath was spent.

Farden was wide-eyed, chest heaving, but silent. He had never been present for Durnus feeding before.

Durnus wiped his face with a trembling hand, expecting a furious tirade. Even with the power he felt in his veins, he felt a heavy sweat beading on his forehead.

'Farden, I… I intended to tell you about this… malady of mine.'

'Never mind that,' he said. Farden's voice teemed with emotion, but the mage was surprisingly restrained. 'What you just did… His *soul*, Durnus. I've only seen one other creature do that.'

'You know daemonblood runs in my veins, Farden. It always has. Hence my work to smother it with the vampyre's curse.'

'And yet you've never acted on it. Not in centuries! How long has this been happening?'

Durnus felt a righteous, cornered anger rising up. 'It started in Scalussen, if you must know. Normal blood was not working…' Durnus took a shuddering breath. 'Now it barely works for me at all. I feel the vampyre's cursing dwindling each day. My magick with it, dampened by daemonblood.'

'I told you not to toy with dark magick or with necromancy, and yet here we are! It's awoken something in you, damn it. Your true self. The one you've tried to forget all this time.'

Durnus recognised the look in Farden's grey-green eyes, now bruised and blackened around their edges. He saw the true disappointment in that stare, and it cut him to the heart.

'Farden—'

'I'll hear no more of it! Not now, not with our friends in danger. Not with my armour and magick still plaguing my mind. How dare you add to the pile of shit we swim in?'

'I am not the only one changing, you know. Where is *your* magick, Farden? Why are you hurtling towards the spear with no thought?' Durnus heard the poison in his voice. For a man with almost two thousand years under his belt, he still knew how to be petty.

Farden didn't rise to it. He was already walking away. 'We have work to do.'

# CHAPTER 16
## THE SILENT WITNESS OF STARS

*The mightiest of the Golikar trees were said to have sprouted from seeds brought from the fabled southern territory of Metisko. Fable has it the trees of Metisko wander hundreds of leagues to escape the wildfires that ravage their lands. The trees in the north have developed a different skill for avoiding fire, and that is to be practically inflammable.*
FROM 'A WOODCUTTER'S TRAVELS'

The sun was the enemy of their days. It beat down with merciless abandon. The sailors and mages sweat buckets. The interior of the ships sweltered. The only respite was the breeze and occasional spray from the bows, and night. The latter had thankfully fallen.

The sea was a black mirror, undisturbed by a single breath of wind. Any ordinary ships without wind mages would have floundered in the doldrums that plagued Paraia's coasts, but not the Rogue's Armada.

Even so, with the mages split between the ships, and after running so relentlessly, their progress was slower than Lerel would have liked.

The admiral stood alone at the wheel. With no waves, errant winds, and few currents to battle, she barely needed to steer.

The Cape of Glass was now long behind them. Every soul aboard, Lerel included, prayed that meant the leviathans too. Lookouts had spent days in the masts, watching, waiting, and baking under the sun.

The seascape was simple: dark rocks and white sand coves to port. Endless water to starboard. Ahead was a wavering coastline, devoid of life except seabirds and the occasional white-sailed dhow, hunting schools of rays by lantern and spear. The only settlement they had seen was a port town half a day behind, bordering a deep bay of turquoise waters. Lerel and the Rogue's Council, as Roiks had begun to call the heads of Scalussen, had suggested they dock and resupply. Elessi, however, had commanded they keep running south. Since then, the general had sequestered herself in her cabin with her thoughts and the inkweld. Only at night did she come to stare at the stars, when the others were asleep and questions were fewer, if any. Tonight she was late.

Lerel stared instead, counting stars she had spent a childhood staring up at. *Evernia. Thron. The First Dragon.* South of Emaneska, others shapes crept into the sky. Other gods and heroes of Paraian tales. There were too many she had forgotten; minor gods of beasts, hearth, whirlwinds, and the dunes. There were a thousand, each with a dozen different names. She remembered the famous and brightest ones, however: the Bane of Orestus, a scorpion spread across the sky. Bezarish the Holy. And Neringaë the sun goddess.

Aside from the constant air of salt and the hot tar caulking of the ships, Lerel could take a deep breath and smell the heat of the deserts wafting from further inland. Or the night flowers that bloomed in the shadows of dunes. Yelps from foxes and wolves chased them along the clifftops. The gryphon snored quietly behind her. It was peaceful. She took a deep shuddering breath. She ignored her aching body, and the flashing, visceral images of leviathan's jaws every time she allowed her mind to wander, and let herself lean against the wheel.

It wasn't long before Lerel heard the footsteps on the stairs. Bored, heavy steps. She knew it was Bull without turning to look.

'Warm night,' she said to him as he lumbered up.

'Strangely warm.'

Bull liked to stand at the wheel beside her as if he was steering. He wore the same morose face as he had since Scalussen. Half his day he stared east, as if Mithrid and Farden would come winging their way over the horizon on Fleetstar's back. He must have been the only body aboard the ships that was not exhausted with worry over the leviathans. Lerel stood back from her post.

'You take it. The wheel.'

Bull's eyes widened. 'Really?'

'Just keep her straight.'

Bull took the wheel with a reverence that suggested it was crafted from solid gold. He gripped the worn handles with his big mitts and stood as tall as he could. Lerel looked up at him and found herself smiling.

'There's nothing like sailing. Usually, that is.'

Bull murmured in concentration.

'You don't have a lot of fear in you, do you, Bull? Not a lot seems to scare you.'

The lad thought for a while. 'I'm scared of not seeing Mithrid again.'

Lerel smiled again. She had guessed. Both he and Hereni had taken a shine to the fire-haired girl.

'You ever lost somebody?' he asked her.

Lerel hadn't expected that. 'Plenty in all the wars we fought. Farden's uncle was one of the first that really hurt. He raised me like a father, see. Gave me a chance at the life I always wanted. Free. I grew up in chains like a lot of the Paraian people.' Lerel shrugged. 'Mithrid's not lost, though, Bull. And she's with Farden. There's nobody else better to have at your side than a Written mage. Or a minotaur, I imagine.'

Bull looked at her. 'You talk about Farden the way I talk about Mithrid.'

The chap had an annoying knack of noticing the simplest things.

'Perhaps I did, long ago. Our lives drifted apart.'

'Not too late.'

Lerel chuckled. Bull's powers failed him. It was a little too simple from the outside. She and Farden had loved each other once, maybe. They had never said it. They had never needed to. Unfortunately, not saying it had driven a wedge between them.

'What of Mithrid? You have feelings for her.'

Bull worked his gums, awkward. 'No. I mean... I don't know. I know I care more than I would for a friend.' He shifted attention back to her.

'Is that why you want to find Farden like Elessi does? Not that I'm complainin'. I'm all for it. I just hear some people saying it's the wrong idea. That we should be going ashore. Staying put.'

'First and foremost I keep this armada afloat. Beyond that I follow Elessi. This part of Paraia is dry desert and bandits anyway. There's no water here or supplies here. Running is the right choice. For now, at least.'

A flash of silver ahead of the *Autumn's Vanguard* brought all that worry crashing back. It was just a dolphin, bursting from the water and spinning like a top.

'Fuck me, that got my heart racing.'

'How are we going to kill those monsters?'

Lerel patted the lad on the back as she took back the wheel. She needed to feel the ship's rudder, as if for comfort. 'Dragonfire. Magick. Every arrow and bolt we've got. Maybe you'll get lucky with that bloody great bow you've taken a liking to. Shoot one right in the eye.'

Bull hummed deeply as if he relished the idea.

'If only we got some of those big bows you've got below, and put them across the top deck. We could turn them, shoot better than waiting for them to attack from the sides.'

Lerel blinked at Bull. 'Look who's been paying attention. A fine idea, Bull. If I was Eyrum or Hereni I'd be giving you a rank. If he doesn't, then I'll make you part of my crew. I'll be damned if I let Roiks pinch you for his crew,'

For the first time, Bull broke his dour marathon and showed off a grin.

'Go tell your idea to General Eyrum. Wake him if he's asleep. We'll have one on deck by dawn.'

Lerel watched the lad march off, faster than he'd come up the stairs. It was a fine idea. Likely not to make a difference for the speed the leviathans moved, but she'd take every edge she could get.

Ilios stirred behind her, and Lerel turned to find Elessi standing in a long cloak. 'Growing up fast, ain't they? He and Hereni. Mithrid, too, no doubt.'

'Hopefully not too fast. You're late tonight.'

'Wanted to let you two talk,' she said around a yawn. Elessi had deep bruises beneath her eyes. 'Good idea.'

'The ballistae?'

'That, and givin' him a rank. Captain, maybe. He's like Eyrum. Just does what's needed without thinkin'.'

'Any sign of the bastards?'

'Not a peep. For now.'

'I wish you'd stop sayin' it like that.'

'Any news?' asked the admiral.

'Farden's been quiet today. Yesterday they spoke of a tournament to the death. Somewhere in a place called Vensk. I checked your maps and some of the old books in the libraries.' Elessi removed a scroll from her cloak and let it fall open. She poked at a land by a sea Lerel had never sailed. Roiks, maybe. But not her. The distance between them was considerable. Across the Silent Sea, famed for hurricanes and pirates, around a long continent called Easterealm, and to the far north once more. It would take months. To add insult to insult, some idiot had sketched a bloody leviathan right in the middle of the Silent Sea, too. Lerel forced a disarming smile and kept quiet.

'At least we know where they are. And that they're safe.'

Elessi was peering at her. 'You can't pretend with me. I know you better than that, you sly old hag.'

'Still younger than you.' Lerel scowled back for a moment before spluttering into a laugh. 'Fuck, if Durnus didn't take them as far as he possibly could.'

Elessi sighed. 'We don't have a choice.'

'Towerdawn was right,' Lerel said, shifting the bookship further from the shore to avoid a spur of pillar-like rocks. 'We have to think of the cargo we carry. The survivors of Scalussen, the dragon eggs, and the spellbooks beneath us.'

'Spellbooks...' Elessi whispered.

'What is it?'

'Farden once told me that certain things, monsters, trolls, wild wyrms and the like, hunt magick. It draws them like the scent of blood. Maybe that's why the leviathans follow us.'

Lerel and Elessi both turned to look before the lookout high above screamed his warning.

'Leviathans to stern!'

In the distance, they saw them: near a headland they had passed hours ago. Merely a crash of water and a glimpse of a dark finned tail disappearing beneath the waves, but enough to put the fear of the gods in the armada. The lookout's cry shattered the peace of the night's sea. Sailors sleeping between shifts upon the main deck flew from their cots and hammocks.

Lerel bellowed orders without hesitation. 'All mages on deck! I want those sails full and this big bitch of a ship at top speed! Check that sail there!' She saw Eyrum on deck, wiping sleep from his scaled eyes. Bull was beside him, looking somewhat like the Siren's bastard son. 'get working. Lerel pointed at them. 'Get those ballistae on deck!'

Elessi clutched her arm as the *Vanguard* bucked with the increase in speed. 'What's in your mind, Lerel?'

Lerel shook her head to clear her tiredness. 'What I've been planning with the other admirals and captains. A trap. For now we keep up our pace. See if we can bore them.'

Elessi blew an uneasy breath. 'Here's hoping!'

Admiral Lerel gripped the wheel with her rough hands, and prayed to the old Paraian gods she was right.

꙳

Lerel's hopes were dashed by dawn. Every half an hour, the lookouts howled and pointed to a surfacing fin or flash of teal scales. Every time, the sea monsters had closed the gap between them and the Rogue's Armada. Wind magick and sails couldn't beat scales and fins.

Elessi had stayed by her side the entire night, watching the stars to keep from staring behind them for hours on end. The general had said nothing, letting Lerel lead the armada as she saw fit.

The twin islands of Phora and Kaleus now sat on their port. They were glorified sandbars, flat sprawls of grit and desert. A smattering of palms grew by the ocean's edge. Lerel ran the *Vanguard* close to them in the vain hope shallow waters might hamper the leviathans. It did nothing but make them show more of themselves. They thrashed the waters instead, sensing their prey was close. They were a mile away at most now. The fear was palpable across the ship. Their first encounter had scarred the crews deeply. Seasoned sailors hurled their guts in anticipation of the battle. White faced ballista crews hammered recklessly at their machines to get them ready.

Bull's idea had come to fruition within hours. Cranes lifted three ballistae from belowdecks onto the forecastle, midships, and aftcastle. Even now, behind Lerel, ship's engineers greased the mounts they had hastily crafted so the weapons could turn. Long iron bolts were being brought up in their dozens. Bull was getting to grips with the firing of the giant crossbows. He silently nodded to the instructions, though he stared at the machine like a page of foreign writing. Lerel bit her lip, but trusted him.

'Where's this trap of yours, Lerel?' Elessi finally said, when the leviathans were too close to bear. One had reared out of the ocean to unleash a blood-curdling screech. Lerel felt the *Vanguard* push even faster as the mage's tensed their spells. The vortex of wind they created around the bookship had begun to howl.

'No better time than now!' yelled Lerel. 'Halve sail! Ready, water mages! Prepare to turn!'

Bells tolled around her as the *Vanguard* signalled the rest of the armada. The line of ships, spread either side of her, began to turn hard. The smaller warships could tack sharper without mages, and they did so in unison. The ships' masts leaned half way to flat on the ocean, spars gently grazing the neighbouring vessels.

The bookships had water mages, however. Lerel felt the wind of the magick surging from the bookship's bow. The flat sea ahead of them churned in three separate whirlpools. Lerel and the other admirals drove their ships into them.

'Brace!' she cried.

The vortex caught the iron keel of the *Autumn's Vanguard* and bucked her sharply to port.

'Ready, battle mages!' Hereni could be heard ordering from the crow's nest.

Lerel heard Roiks crowing with laughter as he managed to turn the *Winter's Revenge* faster than she or Sturmsson. She and the latter shared a dry look as the mages halted their spells, lining the bookships bow to stern like a citadel wall, every hatch and port open, spells whining as the magick crescendoed.

The manoeuvre came not a moment too soon: the ocean was rent in two as a pair of leviathans broke the surface.

'FIRE!' Lerel roared.

Colossal jaws wide and screeching, they caught the full brunt of the barrage. Lerel cheered as she watched a fireball burst inside one of the leviathan's mouths. Scores of ballistae bolts struck their marks. Scales cracked. Blue blood stained the thrashing waters.

While one leviathan choked on smoke and its own blood, the other was so enraged it tried to attack the *Vanguard*. Hereni stood upon a platform, fire pouring from her hands. The leviathan recoiled at the blast of heat. Just in time for the other warships to complete their turns, closing an arc around the monsters and bringing their own broadsides to bear. Fire and lightning spells streaked across the waves-tops. Seawater raged into steam as the monsters dove back into the water.

Elessi yelled from her cover. Ilios stood by her, wings flared. 'Where is the third one of the fuckers?' she asked.

The admiral wished she hadn't opened her mouth. A great tremor shook the *Autumn's Vanguard* as it was struck from beneath. A blue tail surfaced to rear above the ship. Before the deck could be cleared, the tail fell with the weight of a tower. The ballistae they had placed on deck was crushed immediately. Spars and rigging were obliterated. The top deck splintered under the force. Displaced water surged back to drown the lowest ports as the leviathan withdrew its tail. The *Vanguard* and all aboard reeled. When Lerel had picked herself from the planks, there was a hole in her bookship two decks deep. The tail dragged rigging and a bloody smear behind it as it withdrew into the waters.

'We can't take any more hits like that!' she yelled. Bells ordered the fleet to hold its circle. Ballistae cranked furiously across every warship.

'Are you okay, Bull? Ready?'

Even now, the lad had no fear in his face. Just the pink of a tongue clamped between his teeth for concentration. He swung the ballistae back and forth, arms swollen. 'As ever!'

Lerel screamed in her mind. *Old Dragon!* She needn't have bothered: the dragons were swooping from the clifftops like crows to a carcass. They had seen the danger, and from above they could spy the monsters in the water.

*To your port, Lerel!* cried Towerdawn in her mind.

The words ripped from her instinctively. 'Fire to port!'

As the wounded leviathan reared once more inside their trap, the armada let loose. Its towering neck buckled while it uttered a pitiful screech. The dragons descended in force, blasting the monster with dragonfire. Hereni joined her fire spells until the smell of its burned flesh was heavy. When the steam and smoke were driven away by the dragons' wings, they found a charred leviathan tumbling like a felled tree. Its crown of spines fins had been burned to the bone. Its eyes were milky. A bolt stood out from its forehead like a horn. The splash of its fall doused the bookships, rocking them side to side.

The cheer from the armada and the dragons shook the air.

Roiks stood high on the battlements of the aftcastle of the *Winter's Revenge*. 'Take that you blue-blooded cun—Njord's balls!'

The two leviathans exploded from the ocean on either sides of the circle. One broke the spine of the warship *Thron's Hammer* in one blow. The other tore planks from the side of the *Revenge* as it reared up, painfully close.

Lerel watched on, helpless, as the monster's jaws plunged into the bridge of the bookship. Admiral Roiks and his officers disappeared in a storm of splinters. Those that escaped screamed as the caustic blue saliva burned to their bones. Again and again, the leviathan gorged itself on anything that moved before its weight could drag it into the water. When it was done with the bridge of the *Revenge*, blood and detritus pouring from its mouth, it turned with horrifying calmness to regard Lerel and the *Vanguard*.

Ilios screeched as he took flight, hovering between the looming, colossal face of the leviathan and the bookship. The leviathan roared at the challenge.

It was precisely the time Bull needed to aim his ballistae. The rib-shaking thump of the machine cut the noise. The bolt was too fast for her eyes to follow, but Lerel saw it strike: a direct hit to the centre of the leviathan's eye. The monster sank as violently as it had surfaced, thrashing the water in pain, and dealing the *Vanguard* a vicious parting blow amidships in its death throes.

The last remaining leviathan disappeared simultaneously. The cheers were stilted but heartfelt, immediately chased by the cries of wounded sailors and passengers. A quiet fell from the rage of battle.

Lerel hissed as she finally unpeeled herself from the deck. She hadn't noticed the gob of blue saliva burning its way into her arm. She splashed some of the water lying on deck on it, then ripped a strip of cloth from her shirt and wrapped it around her arm. She cursed under her breath. Ilios' beak tucked under her good arm, helping her up. She clasped the gryphon's feathers.

'You brave bastard. That thing could have swallowed you whole,' she whispered at the old beast.

Elessi was stumbling from the stairwell. She had a cut across her forehead. 'Bull! You did it!'

The lad rushed to help the general. 'Lucky shot,' was all he said.

Lerel staggered to the splintered railing and stared upon the mess of the *Revenge*'s aftcastle. Bloody seawater poured from the decks. The crew was still quivering with shock to do anything but idly drag the survivors to safety. Healers roamed the ruined decks.

'By the gods...' Elessi breathed as she looked over Lerel's shoulder. 'Roiks.'

'He's gone.'

'I'm sorry, Lerel. I—'

Lerel was already leaving. 'There's no time for that shit, General!' she snapped. 'Damage report!'

Shouts came from across the deck. '*Thron's Hammer*'s nothing but driftwood, ma'am!'

'*Sprite*'s busy sinking!'

A man with map of braided locks was busy trying to negotiate the stairs while wiping blood from his eyes. 'Got leaks aplenty belowdecks, Admiral! One of the libraries is flooding. We're taking on water by the bucket and struggling to seal it. Most of the water mages are spent, Lerel. Main mast and its clockwork is shot, too!

'And the *Revenge*?' she called to the nearby bookship. She was listing in the stern.

One of the surviving mates aboard Roiks ship was scarred by leviathan saliva. 'Wheel and steering's fucked! Dead in the water, Admiral! Officers are all dead,' he yelled back, offering a vague sweep of his hand across the bloody deck as if Lerel hadn't yet noticed the carnage.

'What does that mean?' Elessi called to her.

'It means, General,' Lerel said as she dragged the ship's wheel around. 'That we aren't running any more. That we're sitting seabirds now. It means we should start prayin' that we find a safe harbour before that last leviathan decides to finish us off.'

Wind-mages sluggish and sails half-ruined, Lerel's arms burned as she wrestled the ship's nose back towards south. She ignored the blood dripping down her ribs and focused on the tremble of the wheel.

# CHAPTER 17
## VISCERA

*They say that if you want to know the secrets you didn't know you had, you go to see the Lady of Whispers.*
OVERHEARD IN A DATHAZH TAVERN

The music of the Viscera was a simple tune.

Its melody was the grunting of exertion. The war-cries between blows. The hissing of blood as it sprayed the clay. The clang of blades and fists, steel against steel, gave the rhythm.

To Farden's ears it was a song he had heard played a thousand times in various styles by various skalds. It was the sound of war. Of death.

The rabid roars and cheers for every drop of blood spilled was new.

Farden heard no disgust, no sorrow. Just cries of joy for the winners. And for the losers, jeers as the servants dragged the bodies away. Curses at losing bets. Even most of the patrons Farden watched were angrier over lost winnings than the death of their fighters.

Wherever coin was involved, death became cheap entertainment.

Nine bouts had come and gone that day. The weather above the forest canopy had turned. barely a raindrop made it to the clay of the Viscera, but pipes and gutters in the Vensk streets above were more than happy to oblige. Umbrellas of silk and leaves had blossomed around the Viscera. Those rich or lucky or connected enough to have balconies had woven roofs lowered. Anything to ensure the show was not halted. The clay had now become mud. The fights more desperate and unpredictable.

Farden had given up plugging his ears for the announcement. He swore he was going deaf from it all. As usual, two names were shouted to the hordes. One of which sounded like five names.

'Presenting Gosh of the Destrix against Bastiat Jequel Ona Aqi Noroasen of the Island Kingdom of Ikani.'

Durnus was sat by the mage's side. 'Either there is a surplus of names on the island of Ikani, or they think far too much of them-selves,' he said.

Farden had barely responded to the vampyre's comments – or any of the conversation, for that matter – all morning. He had been busy watching every move of the queen and her soldiers. Every cell and servant. That, and he didn't want to give the vampyre any chance to talk about the previous evening. He still didn't have the strength to face it.

'I think the latter's correct, Durnus,' said Irien.

Irien was right: the feather-clad fool from Ikani danced his way from his cell bars, carpeting and cavorting in the most acrobatic of ways. Half the crowd seemed to appreciate the colourful chap, es-pecially given the blur of his swords as he taught the air a ferocious lesson.

His opponent, Gosh, was a tall and lanky chap with a perma-nent hunch. A whip with a bladed end was coiled in one hand. In the other, what looked to be a half-eaten sausage. He quietly finished his snack while Bastiat danced ever closer to him. When he was finished, he calmly wiped a hand across his chest, unravelled his whip, and let it fly. The bladed whip moved as a blur. Bastiat stood stock still for once.

'He's missed him,' Mithrid said, on her feet to get a better view.

Farden smirked. 'No, he hasn't.'

Bastiat's swords fell to the mud. Shortly thereafter, blood began to seep from his neck, and his head toppled as his body dropped to its knees.

The crowd turned wild for the display.

Gosh retrieved the head, took a galloping lunge, and threw it into the crowds. Blood sprayed in arcs. Farden scowled at those that danced it beneath it like rain beneath a drought.

'Charming,' said Farden.

Irien patted him on the arm to reassure him. 'That head will sell for a pretty coin tonight, no doubt. It could feed a family for a year.'

'Like I said yesterday, all show, no substance,' Farden spoke. His throat was so dry from lack of use he barely pronounced his words. He reached for the wine that never left Irien's side. Farden had wondered whether she shouldn't be called the Lady of Wines instead.

The dead were cleared and the bloody Tourney wound on.

'Presenting Rovisk Dal'Bvara against Hrishnash of the Huskar!'

Irien was their personal commentator. 'This should be interesting. Rovisk's first fight. He'll draw it out, but Hrishnash is no easy prey.'

The queen had thrown a flower from her tower to denote favour for last year's champion. Hrishnash sniffed it as if she were going to eat it.

'Farden fought a Huskar chieftain's son once,' Durnus commented idly.

'Correct,' grunted the mage. That encounter had won him his Scalussen vambraces, his first pieces of his armour. Habit made him feel his wrists. He found only clammy skin instead.

'They come to the Tourney every year to fight.'

Hrishnash of the Huskar was a formidable woman, short and wearing nothing but plates of krasilisk scales. She hadn't cleaned even her scimitar since her last bout. Rovisk, the Tourney's darling, meanwhile, showed off his mirror armour to every angle of the crowds. This was the champion's first bout. The hordes of spectators lapped up every pose.

Hrishnash swiftly grew bored of the display. With a wild cry and her sword above her head, she charged Rovisk.

For a moment, Farden thought the champion was done for. At the last moment, Rovisk pivoted on his foot. The Huskar's scimitar chopped down into the wet clay.

The sharp ring of their sword blades filled the Viscera. Fast and furious, with Hrishnash pushing Rovisk back step by step. Silence fell across the seats, from rich to poor and in the claws above. The crowd began to stand, one by one, as they fought to somehow see better.

The pace of the flurry of blows only increased. Side to side back and forth, their duel crossed the Viscera and back again. The swords clashed fast as racing heartbeats. Farden found himself standing to examine the swordsmanship.

Irien smirked at his crossed arms. 'Jealous?'

'Hardly,' Farden snorted. 'Besides, he's tiring her out. Pulling his strikes. He could have finished this a dozen times already.'

'Rovisk is a showman. He knows how to work the crowds.'

That was until the Huskar managed to land the blade on his neck, and drew the faintest line of blood. Rovisk bounded away, betraying his true speed. He came back at Hrishnash with savage abandon. He'd sliced his opponent in four places before he kicked her to the ground. Legs slashed, she wasn't able to get up. She lay lamed and growling at the champion standing over her. Rovisk held his sword over her neck and looked to the crowd for their decision. He even had the cheek to crook a hand behind his ear as if their roar wasn't thunderous enough. At last he looked to the queen above, who drew a line across her throat. The smile she wore as she did so was coldly broad.

'Rumour has it Rovisk is the queen's latest addition to her harem,' Irien muttered close to Farden.

Hrishnash took her death without making a sound. Hardly even a gurgle as the sword withdrew.

Rovisk toured the bars to mad cheers and chants of his name. He pointed his bloody sword at Warbringer and beat his chest. Farden couldn't hear what he bayed at her, but he bet whatever it was would earn him a gruesome death.

'Any word from your children on who is behind Aspala and Warbringer's capture?'

'Not since you last asked me half an hour ago, mage,' she smiled. 'I regret to admit it.'

The announcer interrupted them. 'Presenting Dooran of Dooran, son of Belerod of Haspia, against Aspala of Paraia!'

All of them now stood at the balcony's edge, eyes wide, hands clenching the ornate railings.

Farden saw Mithrid pour herself a cup of wine and drink it down in one gulp. He raised an eyebrow, and saw her lips muttering a prayer to somebody or something.

Dooran of Dooran came stumbling from his cell. Mithrid vaguely recognised his shirt of mail. He raised his hands to drum up some applause and cheers. He dropped his sword instead. Laughter rippled through the crowds. Apparently Dooran did not take kindly to that, and while he was gesturing to the layers of the Viscera, looking redder faced by the moment, Aspala reached him.

The woman was vicious. She kicked his knee sideways with a crack that they heard all the way in the balcony. That, for some reason, elicited a gasp from the crowds. He yelped as he fell in the dust. Aspala took his arm from his shoulder with a sweeping blur of her golden sword, shinier and sharper than ever.

Dooran of Dooran stared at his arm lying in the for a moment before he realised it was his. Aspala seemed content to walk back to her cell, but the boos of the crowd stopped her.

Irien explained. 'While I appreciate your friend's effort of mercy, the crowds do not.'

'Finish him!' cried Queen Peskora.

Aspala let her head hang. Shouldering her sword, she marched back to Dooran, who was busy scrabbling through the mud to get away. She gave him a warrior's death, at least, with the tip of her blade to the back of his skull.

Stilted applause followed Aspala back to her cells.

'Give them Hel!' Mithrid yelled across the Viscera. Aspala caught sight of them, which in turn brought the eyes of the hawk-like queen. Farden avoided her gaze, but instead stepped beside Mithrid.

'We don't want to draw any more royal attention, Mithrid.'

'Damn her. She had a chance to let them go and didn't.'

'And we don't want to see what else she could do. Don't get me wrong, I like wine as much as the next person, but there's one thing you don't want to be in a fight and that's drunk. Take it from me.'

Mithrid grumbled, but she put down the flagon for now.

The announcer howled again. It was curious to hear his voice starting to deteriorate with every set of names.

'Presenting Lord Okram Marko of Bolsh and the Broken Promise, Warbringer of Efjal!'

Farden shook his head at the attempt. 'This should be interesting.'

The man with the spiked fists emerged from his cell and stood close to the wall. Warbringer strode from hers to a strange mix of cheers and boos from those complaining about odds. She made a bee-line for Okram, who spent his last moments yelling up at the queen and clasping his hands as if pleading. When he realised he had no choice but to fight, he started backing around the wall of the Viscera, fists raised as the minotaur chased him. The closer she came, the more Okram panicked, finally freezing up just enough to scream as

Voidaran pasted him across the wall. The hammer hung from the masonry, stuck deep in the stone.

'I am Katiheridrade, the Broken Promise!' her voice boomed. 'The Warbringer! And I will send you all to the Bright Fields!'

'Evernia's balls. They're not helping themselves, are they?' Farden hissed.

Durnus' pale hand alighted on Farden's, and he couldn't help shrug away. The mage would later regret the action after seeing the disappointment in the vampyre's eyes, but the events of the previous night were still clear and uncomfortable memories Farden couldn't yet forget.

'Why do I feel I know that man?' Durnus said quietly, pointing past Farden.

'Presenting…!'

Farden didn't listen to the names. His gaze toured the crowd in the direction of the vampyre's sharp fingernail. The roiling masses of colours and limbs was an unrecognisable sea. Whomever the fighters were in this bout, they were obviously causing a stir. Only one group of people did not stare down into the Viscera's pit. They stood halfway along the same tier as Irien's balcony, wearing skull masks and vibrant blue and yellow furs, and they stared right back at Farden. There was a bald and beardless man in their midst, his face wide with a beaming grin.

'Because you met his son outside the Spoke,' Farden ground out his words. 'It's the High bloody Cathak himself.'

Durnus and Irien shared a glance. 'They are a common sight in Dathazh and Vensk, Farden,' she said.

Farden was already edging towards them. The pebbles were falling into place. 'And are they rich enough to buy two places in the Tourney?'

Irien's eyes were widening. 'Without a doubt. You wouldn't think it from their furs—'

'It's them.'

Mithrid pushed forwards after him. 'What?'

'I'll bet my fucking armour the High Cathak is the one behind the kidnap. The one behind these bruises.'

As if High Cathak Tartavor could hear him, Farden watched the fiend briefly don a mask of dark green wood, trimmed in a black hood. His grin was even wider when he removed it.

'Right you are,' Mithrid growled.

Farden barely beat her to the edge of the exit.

'Wait, Farden!' Irien snapped.

Farden and Mithrid pushed their way through the crowds to the music of curses and angry shouts from those they barged aside. The High Cathak made no attempt to escape. He waited with his cronies with arms open and that infernal smile on his face. It was a mask in itself: no humour was in it but for the dark enjoyment of watching the mage suffering. Anger and pain glistened in his eyes.

'A fine day for a Tourney, is it not, stranger?' he crowed to them when they were close enough to hear above the roar. The staccato meeting of blades below mimicked Farden's marching strides.

'You!' Farden yelled. 'You're the one behind this!'

'I am almost disappointed it took you this long to realise that,' the High Cathak responded. To the mage's surprise, the man walked out to meet them. Still with his cronies at his back, but he showed no fear. 'How intriguing to see you without your gold armour this time.'

Farden already had his knife in his hand, held low. He grabbed the Cathak by the collar of his furs. The other Cathak tried to seize him, but Tartavor held them back, much to Farden's surprise.

'I told you the Dusk God demanded a toll for your disrespect and trespass. And now you insult me further by taking my son from me. Payment is due, Farden of Emaneska. Yes, I know your name, and the names of your friends. You will watch them die one by one around you until you beg me for my forgiveness, and the mercy of the Dusk God.'

'I'll gut you right here and save myself the trouble,' Farden spat. The knife crept from his side to the man's chest, but it only reached halfway.

'Farden,' whispered Mithrid. The girl was close by, her armoured arm as solid as a wall behind him. Farden looked at her, realising he had drawn attention from the surrounding crowds. A number of the queen's soldiers had seen the fight brewing and were muscling their way down steps towards them.

Tartavor laughed. 'You cannot spill blood in the Viscera unless you are a fighter, Farden of Emaneska. You are no fighter. You are a coward and a cheat. A murderer.'

'He's right, Farden,' hissed Irien, now caught up behind them. She was carefully watching the queen, who once again was peering at them from her tower. 'This will not help the others.'

Farden hated every staring eye and muttering face. His knuckles had gone white with the restraint of keeping the knife out of Tartavor's belly.

'It would, however, entertain me greatly,' Farden hissed, almost nose to nose with the High Cathak.

'Break it up lest you want to lose a night in the gaols!' the soldiers were shouting.

Tartavor folded back into his Cathak. 'The Dusk God will be watching, Farden of Emaneska.'

Farden shrugged off Irien's hand as he barged back through the crowds. 'Foreigners,' somebody tutted at him. They were incredibly lucky he did not have his magick. His restraint was more than questionable at the moment.

As was Mithrid's, or so it seemed. Her face was as fiery as her hair, her axe has halfway from her belt. And yet, when they returned to Irien's balcony, it was Farden she seemed to blame.

'All of this because you had to kill his son,' she muttered. 'They're in there because of us. Because of you.'

'Aspala and Warbringer are in there because of *him*.' Farden pointed back at Tartavor. 'He chose to do this, because we trespassed in his woods and gave his son what was coming to him.'

Durnus held up a finger as he interjected. 'And for the dead man landing in the middle of his camp.'

Farden tutted. 'That was the dragon's fault.' He turned to Irien. She was already staring at him with her strange eyes.

'The High Cathak is smart as well as persistent. He can taunt you all he pleases here because of the rules of the Tourney. They are as unflinching as Queen Peskora herself. The last fool to break them interrupted a final bout by running through the Viscera stark naked. When it was announced he had escaped, Peskora promised to pursue the man to the ends of the earth until he was caught. Three days later, he was, and hung from his balls, naked.'

The words Farden had been waiting to spit out faded. Forgotten. 'What did you just say?'

'From his balls—'

'No the other part.'

'That she would pursue him to the ends of the earth.'

The mage paced back and forth, as if mashing the grapes of his idea. 'You said the Head of Sigrimur stays on that tower for the duration of the Tourney, Irien?' he asked, clasping her hand.

Irien nodded. 'That I did. Except for being locked in a vault within the tower at night.'

Without another word, Farden withdrew his hand and quickly made for the exit. He swept a cloak around him against the sporadic drips of rain. The beating of his heart now swirled in his head. He almost fell against a guard as he tottered away.

'Where are you heading, Farden?' Mithrid shook her head and reached for the wine. 'Off to make things worse?' she asked.

His shout was already half-lost in the crowds. 'Maybe!'

Irien shook her head as she watched Farden leave. 'I don't know how you're not grey in the head being around that mage.'

Durnus beat Mithrid to an answer, staring at her while he spoke. Whatever he and Farden had done the night before, Durnus was full of spit and energy, walking taller oncer more. The mage was quite the opposite.

'She has not known him long enough, milady,' he explained. 'Farden might work in chaotic and brutal fashion, his emotions might rule him, but his heart is pure. It is because of that emotion his magick runs so deep. Never have I seen a man care for his country or people, or justice as much as he does. Method to a madness, so to speak,' Durnus told them as he also reached for a cloak.

'And where are you going?' asked Mithrid. 'Cathak threatened all our lives to get to Farden.'

'I need to see a man about a minotaur,' said the vampyre, already beyond the balcony. 'And I would like to see them try me.'

'Curious creatures aren't they?' Irien smirked as she turned her attention back to the Viscera. An intermission was in session. Servants ran around the arena throwing fruits into the lower crowds.

'Which? Vampyres or mages?'

Irien grinned, reaching for the wine flagon in Mithrid's hands. 'Men.'

Farden raised his face to the sky once more, eyes closed, and let fat raindrops pelt his cheeks. He opened his mouth and tasted them on his tongue. Bitter. Dusty. Farden spat the rainwater over the rooftop's edge.

He looked out between the sharp blades of the treetops, where houses clung to increasingly skinny trunks. Tangled cobwebs of ropes and walkways kept them all sturdy, but Farden could still feel a faint sway of the giant trees beneath him. Above, the highest of the mansions and watchtowers roosted.

It seemed the moon was slowly rolling up the slopes of the black mountain. Rainclouds hid Eaglehold's peak. The top section of the moon was slowly disappearing.

Farden watched lightning crackle over the distant plains before spearing the earth with a blinding fork. Thunder came rolling several moments after, lazy and late, but no less formidable. Farden had often wondered whether storm giants only existed at sea, and whether some hid within mountain passes.

The mage closed his eyes and let out a breath. Farden had already tried ten times to reach the dragon since that afternoon, perched so long on Irien's rooftops his legs had gone utterly numb. It was worth the effort. Without Fleetstar, he had no plans left that didn't involve at least one of his friends dying.

He knew the dragon could be miles, leagues away by now.

Emptying his mind was hard with worry. *A clear and single thought, perfectly formed.* He focused on the dragon in his mind's eye, weaving across a black sky swollen with rain. A name crystallised. Farden pushed it into the dark with all his concentration, head trembling with effort.

*Fleetstar.*

The celebratory racket of Vensk far beneath him was a riot that was hard to ignore. He strained to fade it from his mind.

*Fleetstar.*

Farden shook his head. Eyes snapping open. He peered at the moon, using its silver shine to turn the rest of his vision dark.

Her voice floated through his thoughts. *What?*

Farden punched the air.

*It's good to hear your voice, Fleetstar.*

The voice was a slithering whisper, like old snake skin being crumpled.

*So you're not dead yet?* Fleetstar asked.

*Don't sound so surprised.*

*Then, I take it you need my help again?*

*That we do.*

*The dragon did not sound impressed. Is this why the vampyre dragged me all the way here?*

*He dragged us all here.*

Silence. Farden concentrated so hard he gave himself a headache. *It'll be dangerous*, he said.

*How dangerous?*

The voice was louder now. Between the streaks of rain and clouds that seemed in a hurry to be somewhere, Farden saw a dragon's shape pass across the face of the moon.

*The kind of dangerous that Towerdawn would roast me alive for involving you in.*

*Towerdawn isn't here, is he? When?*

*Tomorrow. As soon as my armour is fixed.*

*Leaving so soon?*

*We're not welcome here any more and I won't risk our necks another day. I'll show you.*

As he had been taught, Farden let his mind unfold with memories of the day in the Viscera. Of Aspala and Warbringer locked behind bars. Farden barraged her with his thoughts. An unintentional amount, perhaps. Worry and fear seeped along.

*And they call me mad*, Fleetstar whispered.

Footsteps clattered on the flat rooftop behind him. 'There you are,' said the Lady of Whispers. 'We've been looking for you.'

Farden nodded beneath his hood and let the patter of rain answer.

'What are you doing up here?

'Speaking to a friend.'

Irien came to sit beside him and peer over the edge of roof to the Vensk's glow. 'Your dragon?'

'Good guess.' In all honesty, Farden had been expecting one of Evernia's highly enjoyable visits, where she came to herald some new complaint of the gods. In all the history of Farden's fight against the dark history of Emaneska, the gods had only shown their faces when their own existence was threatened. Otherwise, they had been perfectly happy to meddle in his affairs from afar. Irien was welcome compared to Evernia.

'There's mind magick like that in the south,' said the Lady of Whispers. 'It's a skill I'd pay handsomely for. Pays to be astute in my business, and that is why the Cathak bother me. They worked alone and under my nose. Even my children were stumped.'

'I'm not holding it against you, if that's what you're worried about,' said Farden as he looked at her at last. She wore no hood, bearing the rain without care.

Irien squinted one eye. 'I wasn't. Though if I had known you would be this much trouble, I would have left you pondering the statue of Sigrimur and walked away. You're lucky I pine to see a dragon.'

Farden was about to apologise when she laughed clear and loudly.

'Admittedly, I've probably caused you further trouble. It isn't wise to be seen with me, being banished from the house of Golikar and all.'

'What is this queen's problem with you?'

Irien let the rain patter against her wooden arm. Clearly she wasn't bothered about rusting whatever clockwork sat inside its shell. 'Same as what cost me an arm. Queen Peskora and I grew up in the same circles and courts, you see, before her father became king. If there's anything that Golikar has too much of, it's not trees, but families. Matchmaking is a sport almost as bloody as the Scarlet Tourney. The lords and ladies this damned land teems with come sniffing around any noble that is coming of marrying age. Hoping to make a fine dowry at least, a shot at the throne in a generation or two at most.

'As soon as Peskora's father succeeded the king, anybody remotely related to her became the potential spouses of choice. The problem was that Peskora was maddeningly jealous. Queens and kings can marry as many as they choose to in Golikar. Now a princess, she claimed the same right, snapping up noble after noble. The families were more than happy to oblige given their new status and her father too old to care. But Peskora was clever, as well as vindictive and cruel. She never married them and simply built herself a harem. When she became queen, she decided she wanted the man my own mother and father had chosen for me. I despised the idea entirely. He did not. He was besotted with me. Naturally.' Irien smirked before her eyes turned narrow.

'The man was a fool. He ignored every one of my refusals until he rejected the queen herself, as if that made his love for me purer. He did it painfully publicly, too. Much like his execution. To Peskora's eyes, I was at fault, and after hanging him from Vensk's highest branch, she took my left arm. It was meant to be both, so that none could take my hand in marriage, but my father bankrupted himself saving me from my whole punishment. We were banished instead. I was twenty summers old at the time and a decade has passed since. Though I've made plenty of myself my hatred for Peskora still burns. And she for me. That's why I agreed to help you, and that's why she punished your friends.'

Irien's tone was disarming once again by the end of her story. Before Farden could speak, she nudged him with her good arm. 'I see you're no stranger to losing parts of yourself.' She nodded to his missing finger. Farden had been holding his hand and tracing the old wound without realising. It ached in the rain, and more so recently.

'A gift from an old friend,' he admitted with a sigh. 'Torn off during a fight for a kingdom long gone. Lost to empire.'

'And speaking of kingdoms and empires, what really brings you so far east, Forever King?'

Farden tensed. Instinctively, his eyes strayed to the crossbow on her arm, currently balanced against her knee.

'Oh yes, I've heard your story, even as far afield as Dathazh. The Forever King. The traitor mage who would defy an empire. The people's hero. I thought it was the story of some bard's song when I first heard it.'

'How long have you known?' Farden muttered.

'Since an hour after we first met. I didn't want to say as much before. Your reaction when I spoke of a warlord mage and the emperor was obvious. Better hidden than Mithrid's, but I would still stick to fighting, if I were you. You would not do well in my line of work. And you can relax, darling. I have no stake in your wars. After all, the hawks flying in from the west say that the war is already over. Rumour of a slaughter and that the north is aflame. I am merely curious to know how the famed mage and scourge of the Arka Empire comes to be here, looking for a stone head.'

'Magick. Durnus' magick, as it happens. We had a relic with us, what we call a Weight. An old tool of the Arkmages before Emperor Malvus. It's broken, now. Burned out and useless.' Farden knew how it felt.

'Why did you come here?'

'Thought you didn't care about the why?'

'I don't consider this to be business any more, Farden. Our fates are entwined now. And call me curious, seeing as the whispers I hear say that the empire lost dearly and the emperor is missing. Maybe dead. Seeing as the western sky burns through the night and ash falls on the Rivenplains, I would like to know ahead of time if that's what you're planning here.'

'The emperor besieged us. The rest of Scalussen was evacuated and we escaped at the last minute during the battle. We're here because Durnus found a map. The Head of Sigrimur and his last breath are part of the map. See, we didn't completely lie.'

Irien looked serious now. 'A map to what?'

'To something Emaneska desperately needs. Maybe even Easterealm too. That's all I will say.'

Irien leaned closer, gaze flitting across each of Farden's eyes as she examined him. 'Still don't trust me?' she asked.

Farden faced the skies, tasting the bitter rain once more. He chuckled as he shook his head. 'No. Not yet.'

'Will you tell me at least what you're planning for tomorrow?'

'Something loud and dramatic, as Durnus would put it.'

When Farden turned back, he found Irien had not moved. Standing even closer now. Still, her eyes roved his face. 'How old are you, to be called the Forever King? You don't look ten years older than me and I have thirty summers behind these eyes.'

'Old enough. Getting older all the time, it seems,' Farden sighed.

'Aren't we all?'

He pointed up to the clouds churning above, distracting her. 'You can consider this a down payment.'

Risking the lantern-glow of the watchtowers, Fleetstar soared dangerously close above the pines. Her wings were half-lost in cloud and darkness. Thunder masked their beat and her impudent roar.

Farden was gone by the time Irien turned back around, wide-eyed.

# CHAPTER 18
## PATH PAINTED RED

*The dark elves, when they walked the lands, knew all too well the vast
depths of magick. That is why they built great wells of magick to capture and
extort magick's unimaginable power. Inexhaustible, in essence. All it takes is
a vessel or conduit, one that is either large enough, or strong enough.*
FROM 'MAGICKAL MASTERY' BY WRITTEN SCHOOL TUTOR CADMIS
THE ELDER

The rain hammered the plains, bending the grass to its merciless
whims. It drowned everything in sight, from rock to grimacing shepherd. Flocks gathered around Lilerosk's walls under the tarpaulins
the wind hadn't ripped away. Bonfires were smothered by the persistent sweeping downpour. Those trapped beyond taverns and
houses and guard posts huddled together to endure the storm. They
were none the wiser to the pair of red-raw eyes that watched their
town from an overlooking hill. Eyes that held malice and murder behind them.

Malvus sniffed again, drawing in that familiar scent that he had
followed from the cursed wood to this wretched scratch of town. It
did not drift with the wind, did not wash away with the deluge. Even
the stink of sheep and unwashed shepherds could not cover it. *Magick*. Its aroma was sharp, metallic. Its trail glittered like a meandering river in each flash of lightning.

Malvus stretched out his hands and examined once more the
raw cracks on his skin between the runes of black and scabbed red.
Blood still ran from wounds that refused to heal. Even the daemonblood failed to close those. Even now, a fresh vial ran through him,

intwining with the magick in the most intoxicating way. He had called it pain before he had become... *this*. But now he had been drowned in pain, all he felt was power, coursing through every vein and burning to escape his drenched skin.

With a stretch of Malvus' fingers, fire ignited. Arcs of white flame rose and fell across his palms. Runes across his arm sizzled as they flared brightly. Raindrops burst into steam. The dark night was turned to day as he pushed the power to limits he had not yet explored. The wet grass beneath him was reduced to ash within moments.

Malvus looked back to the town. His head pounded, mirroring his racing heart. The rush of magick was invigorating.

*The mage was here*, spoke the voices again, so faint to be almost unmistakable from the howl of wind and the hammer of rain on his ragged hood.

*It stinks of his magick.*

*Consume it with fire.*

*Tear them apart for their insolence.*

The voices, like the burning within his limbs, had become a constant companion since leaving the farmhouse. Daemon or magick-borne, Malvus could not tell. He could not care. They were him and he they. They spoke with his voice, whispered the thoughts hence craved to speak to plainly. Finer allies than the god standing a dozen paces beside him. The god who flitted into the darkness half the days, only hunting alongside Malvus when it suited him.

'What's in your mind, Malvus?' Loki called over the howl of the rain.

*He doesn't trust you*, came another whisper. *You must kill him before he kills you.*

'Murder,' snarled Malvus as he met the gods curious eye. 'That and the smell of magick. Farden was here. Do you taste it too, god? Is this what the world feels like to creatures like you?

'I can feel it, but I can also feel that Farden and the girl are far beyond this runt of a town.'

'Any people that have given Farden shelter oppose me.'

He waited for Loki to contradict him. Lord Saker had been the only one with a stomach for what needed to be done. But the god surprised him with a nonchalant shrug. The rain ran down his face in rivulets as he stared, unblinking. 'You answer to none now, Emperor. These mortals matter not.'

Malvus chuckled deeply. 'I am no emperor any more, god. I am much more. I am nothing like these lands or any have ever seen. They will know my wrath and I'll pay no price for it to anyone. I am crippled by my frail and sickened body no more. I'm finally all that I dreamed. More powerful than armies and hordes. More powerful than Written and Scarred. More powerful than Prince Gremorin. Even you, Loki.'

Again, Malvus flexed his magick. No spell words tumbled from his mouth. No memorised mumbles of old words, just the raw innate nature of magick Malvus had always longed to understand. He had lost count of the times he'd cursed his parents for their weak bloodline. How many times magick awoke in this cousin or that distant friend. And now he was the very pinnacle of magick.

'The night is waning, Malvus. Time to put your magick where your mouth is.'

Malvus turned to the god, fire spitting from his hands. White runes shone across his chest, even his face. To Malvus disgust, the god did not flinch. Every drop of blood and magick in him ached to press on, to see what the god was made of, but Malvus managed to hold himself. The magick obeyed him sluggishly. Fire slunk back into his skin, making his tattoos shine. Malvus was left staring at the god.

Loki hoisted up a hood over his head. 'Remember who put you on this path, Malvus. I'm not your enemy,' he warned.

Malvus growled. He would be the judge of that. 'What is its name, the town?'

'Lilerosk, if I remember rightly. Why?'

'As that worm Toskig used to say, know your enemy.'

With that, Malvus turned to the wretched collection of ragged mages, soldiers, and other dregs they had gathered on the road. A stunted wood troll, madder than Hel. More fenrir. Even a wild vampyre, content to hover on the edge of their group.

With a crook of his hand, Malvus gestured onwards into the night.

❧

'You need your eyes tested, damn it! Drag me up out of bed for bloody sprites of your imagination!' Flocklord Boorin berated the drenched guard. He had been enjoying the finest dream of sheepskin clouds littered with shepherd's daughters when he had been rudely awoken. Fire on the hills, they'd said, but even after being dragged out into the wolfish gales, after soaking his best tunic and jacket right through, he'd seen nothing but an angry night.

'I swear it, Flocklord! Bright white fire!'

Boorin slapped the man around his leather cap. 'By Dawn, I don't want to hear about it! Ever since that bloody dragon appeared you've been skittish as lambs. This is the third time this week you lot have seen something out there. What was it last time? A strange-looking cloud? Bleeding Dawn!'

'Yes, Flocklord,' muttered the guard. The others around them upon the small tower beside the ogin bone gate bowed their heads. 'We're sorry to bother you.'

As the sound of a bleating sheep somewhere below, Boorin took one last look across the dark plains. He blinked, cursing his tired eyes. Between the driving curtains of rain, he swore he had seen the shape of an enormous wolf. He pushed a guard out of his way to stare out across the wooden battlements.

'Close the gates!' he screamed, more high-pitched than he would have liked in front of his men, but a huge black wolf sprinting towards his town was enough to choke him with fear.

'Close the fucking gates!'

Boorin began to flee. The steps were awash with rain. He clattered down them on his arse and squelched into the mud on his arse.

The curved doors between the ogin bone were still ajar when the wolf's snout crashed through them. Several guards tried to brace the gates, more in blind hope than in bravery. The wolf overpowered them in moments. Figures in dark and ragged robes swarmed through the rain, some screeching, others cackling, and others still methodically murderous. Puddles ran red as their swords went to work.

Fire turned the night to day as the guard tower was blown asunder in fire and lightning. Boorin was thrown against a wall by the blast. Those who hadn't heard the screams and shouts over the storm now flooded from the safety of their houses in confusion.

'Dragon!' some fool shouted. It mattered little that he was wrong. Lilerosk was soon drowned in panic as another of the wolves bounded clear over the wall. It broke a wooden shack clean in two as it crash-landed.

Boorin saw people thrown into the air, only to be snapped up by the wolves or to collapse heavy into mud or burning houses. He shoved himself up only to find his arm was broken. He was crawling with his elbows in the muck and sheep-shit when he saw the ogin bones cartwheel either side of him. One flattened the front of a tavern while the other turned a trapped crowd of shepherds into a bloody mess.

The flocklord turned around to see what evil had brought such ruin to his town. In his fear-addled mind, he stared upon the foul Dusk God himself: a figure cloaked in fire. Lightning forked from his spread hands. White script burned through his drenched wrappings and cloak. Death walked ahead of him. Destruction and fire he left behind him.

Boorin babbled every prayer he knew in a constant shrieking stream as the hulking figure approached. He was no man, no monster, but trapped somewhere between. The flocklord was ready to denounce Dawn itself when the grinning face of glowing white runes stared down at him. Boorin prostrated himself in the mud before him.

'I beg of you, my lord... my god... please spare me!' he cried.

The voice was deep and coarse. 'A man came here not too long ago. Of black hair and red-gold armour. There would have been others with him.'

Boorin clung forlornly to the possibility of salvation through correct answers. 'He did, lord. They betrayed us and we cast them out. Fiends, they were!'

A hand of searing heat alighted on Boorin's head. He quivered beneath it, trying to ignore the pain. 'But who welcomed them in the first place?' said the voice.

'I... I did?' Boorin gasped. 'Who are you, m—my lord?'

'I am death.'

Boorin's scream was short-lived as the fire consumed his skull, and lightning scorched him to his bones.

# CHAPTER 19
## THE LAST BREATH OF SIGRIMUR

*Daemonblood was a leftover from the wars of the world's formation. The loathsome creatures that escaped being turned to stars slunk into the darkness, and as heroes slew them one by one, a healer of unknown name discovered the curious properties of daemon's blood. Life and health, it bestows, even regrowing limbs, so long as one is able to stomach its initial effects. And, of course, its crippling addiction. Most that try to cut themselves off from daemonblood's temptation usually end up dying writhing in pain.*

FROM THE DIARY OF DURNUS GLASSREN, YEAR 903

Aspala pivoted on her heel. The whip cracked over her head. Breathless, she lashed out with her sword, slicing the blade from the whip. She seized it as she burst from the mud. Mercilessly, her opponent whipped at her with the remaining coil. Aspala's arm was cut to ribbons by the time she slid past the bitch on her knees, and sliced the backs of her legs to the bone.

Down came the boulder of a woman. Aspala finished her off quickly this time with her own whip-blade. She had learned. After all, this was the third time the queen had forced her to fight that morning. Before every bout, Mithrid had caught Peskora gloating in their direction. And every time Aspala had won, the queen had grown a shade redder.

Aspala raised her fingers to the crowd as she limped defiantly back to her cell. Her fleeting look to the balcony was too far away to discern, but Mithrid felt it stab her in the gut.

'Aspala can't take another fight! Where is Farden? Whatever he's planning, he better be doing it now.'

Irien had been watching the High Cathak since the third day of Tourney began. She watched him now even as she replied. The man looked livid that Farden had been absent half the morning.

'Below us, with Krugis the smith,' she said.

'Farden knows what is at stake. He is not heartless.' Durnus gripped the railing so hard Mithrid could make out every bones in his hands.

'He needs the armour as much as we need him, Mithrid.'

Farden drummed his fingers on the blacksmith's bench. Gods did he need to piss, but there was no time now. The announcer's voice – and now hoarse as a saw on stone – echoed through the underbelly, announcing Aspala's third fight that morning.

'That blasted queen,' Farden muttered to himself. Peskora was throwing her weight around, fixing bouts to teach them a lesson for Farden's indiscretion. The queen squeezed their time to a precious pinch of sand in the hourglass.

Farden rapped his knuckles on the bench, looking for Krugis behind the mounds of armour and monstrous tools around his forge. 'How's it looking, smith?'

The soot-painted man appeared, arms full of armour. 'By the Dawn God, you're a bastard, you know that? Barely begun to polish it.'

'Fuck the polish. Is it fixed?'

'As much as I could. Patched and reset the scales, fixed their fastenings. Most confounding stuff I ever did work on. Swore some of it moved around when I touched it, I swear. Now, there's the matter of Irien's promise…' Krugis explained.

Farden was not listening. He was pawing over his armour, checking, probing. The charring was gone. Almost all the scrapes and scratches, too. The metal was cold despite the heat of the forge.

He put the vambraces on first. He slid them over his arms with haste. He didn't even wait to add the gauntlets.

Krugis' jowls stopped flapping when he saw the metal scales flex and slither over each other as the pieces touched. Farden clenched his fist. The scales were less hesitant than before. None stuttered or scraped. He breathed a sigh of relief before snatching the other pieces and strapping himself into his armour one by one. The smith had even replaced the missing ruby eye of the wolf with a garnet.

Krugis scratched his armpit. 'As I said, your impatience don't come cheap. Neither does working with such fine and intricate armour. Haven't slept these past nights because of working on this. Put me behind in fact…'

'Uhuh,' Farden said. He felt the sweat gathering on his forehead despite the frigid metal. There was something that felt ghastly wrong. As if a piece of the armour was missing even though he counted it all.

Even wearing all the metal but his helmet, Farden felt none of the usual wintry touch seeping into his veins. The subtle magick of the Scalussen armour was missing. Farden felt his knees grow weak. Nausea swooped.

'So I'm thinking another hundred silver leaves—'

Farden slammed his fists on the bench. 'You said you'd fixed this?'

Krugis was immediately enraged. 'Yessir! Every scale of metal on that damnable suit.'

'I…' Farden put gouges in the bench as he withdrew his fists. 'Curse it!' He had no time to vent. No time to deal with the dread seeping through him instead of the cold magick he so despairingly longed for.

Farden began to run back to the Viscera.

❦

'There you are!' Durnus cried as Farden emerged on the balcony, tired, sweating beneath his armour. 'You look yourself again. Fixed?'

'It's almost time to go,' Farden gasped, ignoring the question.

'What in Hel we waiting for?' Durnus demanded. Mithrid looked as though the same question burned a hole in her, too.

Farden crossed his arms, quietly confident. 'You'll see. If I have the measure of this queen, as I think I do, you'll see.'

'And if you don't?'

'Presenting Rovisk Dal'Bvara against...' The announcer had to pause to be heard over the booming cheer. It left a ringing in Farden's ears.

'Against the Warbringer of Efjar!'

Farden nodded. 'She's going to regret this.'

Irien did not look so convinced. 'As much as I would love to see this outcome, and I truly would, I've never seen Rovisk lose a fight.'

Mithrid snorted. 'If I know Warbringer, I think you're about to.'

There was no strutting this time from Rovisk. Before he put on his helmet. Farden caught a furtive glance to the tower above, to his bed partner who had thrown him against this monster. The mage smirked. This kind of show he could enjoy.

Say one thing for Rovisk; the man was fast. He evaded War- bringer's first blows with a jump and a roll. Voidaran hit the mud so hard it sprayed in a great umbrella. Just long enough for Rovisk to unleash flurry of jabs, skewering the minotaur's bicep and thigh. If the prince had fought in the Efjar Skirmishes, he would have known how thick a minotaur's hide can be.

Warbringer backhanded him so hard every person in the crowd could hear the snap of a metal. Shock stalled the complaints. The cries of mercy and insults for the beast from the west.

Rovisk dragged off his broken helmet just in time to see Warbringer swinging Voidaran in a blur above her head. She let it go with a roar, and the hammer pulverised the wall Rovisk had just been leaning against. He managed another lucky strike, evading another fist and even nicking the top of one her horns as she bent to gore him. He even managed to score a deep cut across her chest, severing her necklace of bones and teeth.

Warbringer bellowed in his face at the insult. All his bravery withered in a moment. It staggered him long enough to bring Voidaran sweeping in an arc that broke his sword at the hilt. Warbringer knew no mercy for this pompous knight. Pink-flesh, she no doubt growled at him.

When she seized him by the breastplate and brought him close, the bastard swept a knife from his back. He managed to slash her face before Warbringer swatted the knife from his hand and shattered his arm at the same time. With her huge fist, she grabbed his throat and crushed it.

Rovisk Dal'Bvara fell dead on the Viscera mud.

It was the queen, shoving the announcer aside, who uttered the next bout without hesitation, before the servants could drag away his body. 'Bring out Aspala of Paraia! She shall fight this creature next! And if she does not you may shoot her where she stands!'

All across the Viscera, crossbowmen took aim.

'Farden…' Mithrid spoke in a low voice. 'You're not going to make them fight each other, are you?'

Farden felt a laugh bubbling out of his chest. 'Not at all, I just needed both of them out of their cages. It was only logical the queen would put our two friends against each other in time. She's cruel enough, after all.'

Mithrid's open mouth gave no words. It took her a moment to find some. 'I didn't think about that.'

A riot was brewing in the Viscera; the two fighters had touched weapons and taken a stand beside each other.

'Fight, damn you!' screeched Peskora.

'Farden?' Even Durnus was now growing cautious.

*Now, Fleetstar!* Farden roared in his mind.

Faint over above the booing and jeers of the thousands, Farden heard another commotion. Bells began to toll in the watchtowers of Vensk.

*Just in bloody time.*

Farden turned to the High Cathak, who was grinning at the supposed fate of Aspala and Warbringer. The bastard thought he had won, bless him.

'Irien, if I may borrow your crossbow?' Farden asked politely. The others watched intently, but he paused with his hands around her forearm. He looked expectantly up at the arse of Vensk. Screams in the highest row of spectators had begun to turn heads.

'It'll just be a moment,' he said.

No sooner had the words spilled from his mouth did a jet of orange flame explode over the roof of the arena. A white gold dragon spun fire in its wake as it appeared.

Tartavor was powerless but to look at the dragon, and as soon as he did, Farden raised Irien's arm, stared down the small bolt, and nodded. 'If you please.'

Irien fired with a deft squeeze of her fingers.

A cry of pain could be heard over the screams of the audience. Tartavor stared aghast and gawking like an owl at the arrow stuck high in his chest. He fell amongst his fellow Cathak, much to their cries.

'Now we go!' Farden cried, having to drag Irien away from gawping at the dragon.

Storm wind blasted them as Fleetstar swooped around the Viscera. She tackled the central tower with claws outstretched. The queen and her harem scattered before the crash of wood and masonry. Fleetstar snapped her fearsome jaws at soldiers until she had gnashed her way to the centre of the tower. There, she seized the cage containing Sigrimur's head and let her wings send them sprawling. Two of the queen's princes fell windmilling from the tower.

Fleetstar pirouetted and swept low across the mud. She practically crashed into Warbringer and Aspala, but with them both in her claws, the dragon climbed into the sky. Fool soldiers fired their crossbows with no care for the crowds screaming beneath. Thousands swarmed and fought in all directions to be free of the chaos.

It was over as abruptly as it had begun. Fleetstar escaped the arena to weave needlelike through the giant trees and left the Viscera reeling behind her.

When Queen Peskora emerged from the rubble, fine silks ripped, caked in blood and dust, she arose with a shaking finger pointed towards that foul Irien's balcony. But as she wiped her eyes and managed to peer through the smoke, she found the balcony abandoned. The strangers were already long gone.

Farden and the others barged through the bustle as quickly as they could without running. Fortunately for them, they had left before the bulk of the crowds, but in the path of the dragon, the lowest levels of Vensk were aflame with panic.

As soon as the cries of the Viscera were far enough behind them, they began to pound the cobbles in a mad dash for the river and the Ogin's Ford. Beyond the trees, a gusty day of driving rain welcomed them. They held their hoods and hands up to avoid its cold sting.

'I should have asked you to get us a carriage!' Farden yelled.

'Already ahead of you! I thought you might need to get to Sigrimur quickly. It's a glorified wagon, to be precise.'

Irien pointed at a man with two cows and a cart with canvas stretched over it waiting at the corner of the bridge. The man was already cowering from the skies, but at the sight of Warbringer, he scarpered in fear and left Irien to crack the whip and play driver. They were rattling across the cobbles in moments.

The giant shape of Fleetstar skimmed the towers of the bridge. The whole carriage shook to one side, causing Irien to yelp and the others to curse the dragon's antics. Aspala's howl could be heard clearly as Fleetstar winged her way to Dathazh with all haste.

With Dathazh empty from the Scarlet Tourney, and with the wave of confusion only just breaking across the river, they raced through the city gates with not a challenge. Every head was craned to the sky. They followed the shout of, 'Dragon!' wherever they heard it.

'We're here!' Irien yelled. Farden tumbled from the wagon alongside Mithrid. He quietly thanked the gods for his armour as he hauled himself up and into the narrow streets.

Sigrimur's Rest was practically abandoned. Rightly so, seeing as a dragon filled the space between the columns. Fleetstar looked cooped up and awkward, struggling not to knock over the statue with her claws or tail. A box was still clamped between her teeth. Aspala and Warbringer washed the water bloody as they waded to greet them. Aspala hung heavy in the minotaur's claws. The cut across Warbringer's brow and snout was crusted with blood. Her prized necklace of bones was clamped between her teeth.

'Took your sweet time, Farden,' Aspala complained.

Farden and Mithrid held her other shoulder up while Durnus checked her wounds.

'I'm sorry, Aspala,' the mage breathed. She looked dreadful, but alive. 'If it's any consolation, you did yourself proud.'

Aspala shook her head. 'Did Paraia and Scalussen proud. Fuck that queen,' she spat blood in the water.

'Say it was not in vain,' Warbringer rumbled.

The cage met the flagstones with a gentle clang. Farden, Durnus, and Irien rushed to it. The dragon had already cracked it with her jaws. It was quick work to wrench the thing open. They should have built it sturdier instead of prettier.

Durnus bent to retrieve the head of Sigrimur. White marble of incredible detail stared back at them. To Farden he had an ageless face. Eyes frozen shut in last moments of pain, face a grim mask. Hair wild. Some of its tendrils had broken off over the centuries. Some much more recently.

'What now, Durnus?' asked Farden.

The vampyre was walking with the head outstretched, facing it towards him. It was a peculiar dance to watch as he approached the statue. 'We listen to Sigrimur's last breath. I do not know why, but this feels right. Would you, Warbringer?'

The minotaur obliged, though even she had to reach to place the head upon the statue's severed neck. She held it there in place for a moment, worried to let go.

'Silence, all of you!' Durnus hissed.

Warbringer jolted backwards as the statue's eyes snapped open with a squeak of stone. Blue pinpricks of light shone forth. The head stayed in place. The marble flowed around Sigrimur's features as if he lived once more.

It was then the statue spoke with lips unmoving. It was no voice, but a breath held for a millennia, a death rattle. Wisps of faint, frosted vapour flowed with his voice, coalescing into a shape. A key of the most perfect crystal.

'*Fool's path you've chosen, headlong to ruin. Trace Vernia's glow to where a giant drowns and stand upon his brow. Bodies fall in faith betwixt the third dragon's tooth. There taste forgotten airs and lesser minds. Only the drowned shall know the sepulchre's secrets.*'

As soon as the riddle was uttered, the ghost-light of Sigrimur's eyes died and the key fell. Durnus managed to catch it in two hands, and with the sound of stone cracking, the head toppled forwards into Warbringer's grip. Durnus was already repeating the riddle to himself, committing it to memory as he stared at the crystal key. Farden was so exhausted he had already forgotten them. The voice had left a bizarre air in Sigrimur's Rest. Everyone present scowled as they pondered the words and the intricate relic in the vampyre's grip.

The key held no colour but the skin beneath it. About the length of Durnus' hand, it had a circular ring at one end and jagged teeth that were far too intricate for Farden's liking. He imagined a strong breath might shatter it.

'Well, I never,' Irien breathed. 'The last breath of Sigrimur was a key.'

'I do not know why I am surprised also,' Durnus said. 'It would make sense. Three tasks. Three keys.'

'In a quest where nothing else makes sense, I'll take it,' replied Farden.

'Then I wager we are looking for two more keys,' the vampyre mumbled.

The mage chuckled. 'We have fucking purpose at last.'

'We should leave. Discuss this on the road,' Mithrid whispered, reminding them of their company.

Farden turned to the Lady of Whispers. She was busy staring at Fleetstar, who had bowed her head to investigate the woman. The mage had to touch her arm to get her attention.

'You have what you come for, at last,' she said.

'And now you have met a true dragon, as promised. I hope it was worth it.'

'Many times over. Besides, it would have been worth it all just to see what this magnificent beast did to Queen Peskora.'

'I do talk, you know,' Fleetstar grunted. Irien beamed.

'And where will the Lady of Whispers go?' asked Farden

She regarded him with a fiendish look. 'I cannot stay here, that is for sure. Peskora will be coming for my blood as well as yours. But it was worth it to see the look on her face. Worth it to see a dragon such as this. I have many friends across the Easterealm and many whispers to trade. I have longed for finer weather for some time. Perhaps I shall go south, to warmer climes! I have plenty of whispers to sell in Normont and Lezembor.'

After the others had clasped Irien's hand and bid her farewell, Farden was left standing in the shallow water. 'Thank you for everything you did for us. Not just your hospitality, but your trust. You saved our skins.'

'Then I'll be sure to call on that favour. And perhaps we shall meet again on your journey,' Irien said, leaning close and kissing Farden on his stubbled cheek. 'She'll be coming after you now, you know. Watch your back, Farden the Forever King.' With that she turned on her heel and swept away across the waters.

'Are we ready?' Farden asked the others.

'Just one moment,' Durnus said. He was manhandling a fat purse into a haversack. It jingled loudly.

'What is that?' asked the mage.

'Coin. Golikan leaves, to be precise.'

Farden stared at the vampyre. 'Where did you get that?'

Durnus looked around as if the answer was obvious. 'I placed a bet.'

'You... you what?'

'I placed a bet on Warbringer versus Rovisk. Warbringer to win, of course. You are not the only one who can follow the threads of logic, mage.' Durnus patted his purse of winnings. 'Our quest now has funding.'

Farden laughed freely. He braced himself as Fleetstar's claws wrapped around his chest and ribs. The dragon lurched into the air, dragging roof-tiles and guttering down in clumps before she managed to escape into open air. The last Farden saw of Irien, she was half-hidden behind the shadow of a column, watching.

'East, Fleetstar,' he ordered, resting his hands against her scales.

# part three

## SHADOWS LONG
## & ECHOES DYING

# CHAPTER 20
## OF GRAVES & PYRES

*The Silent Sea is anything but. It is a battleground of hurricanes and mael-*
*stroms, ruled by pirates and monsters any description would fail. Woe betide*
*any stranger to its currents.*
FROM 'ON FAR-FLUNG SHORES' BY WANDERING WALLIUM

The iron keels of the bookships ground against the sand of the island.
Anchors were cast into the crystal waters with great splashes. It was
just in time. The *Vanguard* and *Revenge* were now listing slightly to
opposite sides.

Captain Hereni wiped the sweat from her forehead. Enough
came away to drip a small puddle by her side. She cast a scowl to the
blinding sun above them. Not a cloud bothered the cerulean sky. Not
a single ally to save them from the scorching Paraian heat.

Hereni stared out across the lump of an island. Its sand bars,
reefs and beaches might have spread for miles, but its core was no
bigger than Scalussen. A poor excuse for a mountain occupied its
centre. Jagged black spurs of rock leaned together. Birds of all kinds
swarmed around it in thick swarms. Sporadic forests of palm trees
surrounded it like an emerald tiara.

'Where are we, Lerel? Because it feels a lot like Hel to me,'
she yelled to the admiral, high above her in the bridge.

Lerel tried to laugh and coughed against a raw throat instead.
'An island off the Falcon's Spur. Be thankful we've still got some of
the breeze from the sea and land trading airs. And it'll grow a little
cooler the farther south we go.'

The so-called breeze was meagre now the mages' wind had died. Hereni spied some shadow further along the deck and moved between the bodies laying about the deck between the large wreckage. The mages were spent to the point of unconsciousness. The others who had managed to stay awake sat staring out to sea, where the leviathan still thrashed.

Lerel had led them on a merry and masterful maze through the sandbars and shallow waters. Hereni doubted few other captains in the world could have led nine ships, three of them colossal brutes, through such a mess of sand and crashing waves.

Beaching the ships was also risky, but as Lerel had informed Hereni, with mages they stood a better chance than the leviathan did at escaping. The monster knew it. It had stayed several miles back. It slapped its tail and screeched with rage as it waited for its prey to emerge.

As if even the *Autumn's Vanguard* sagged into exhaustion, one of the minor spars or rigging decided to snap, bringing down a sheet of black sail across half the deck.

Lerel rasped orders as she too descended from the aftcastle and moved across the main deck. 'If you can stand, then do so. Form crews to get this deck clear and the sails repaired! I need bailers and carpenters below urgently. Others need to help rescue any books or swamped survivors down there. Pass the word to the *Revenge* and *Summer's Fury.*'

'Aye, Admiral,' several weary officers chorused.

'Come with me, Hereni.'

The mage groaned as she ducked into a hatch with the admiral. The heat below was somehow worse in the tighter compartments and passageways. The breeze was nonexistent. Hereni flapped her mouth like a fish just to feel the air.

Several decks of smashed items and wounded, and otherwise sullen looking individuals, below, they found Elessi. She was in the top decks of the vast libraries within each bookship, helping a Siren healer who was busy tending Eyrum. Blood pasted both their shirts and baggy ship's trews. Sweat soaked them. The Siren kept struggling to get up, then roaring as he remembered his injury. Lerel sprang ahead. The same bolt of shock ran through Hereni, but she faltered in the doorway.

The Siren's right leg was gone. The flesh that remained just above his knee smoked and steamed as the leviathan's drool still ate away at him. The healer was daubing an oleaginous paste over his wounds to halt the bleeding and burning. Elessi was trying her best to keep the Siren on the table they had cleared. Hereni imagined she had started off pleading with him, but now she was cursing at him to bloody lie still.

'What happened?' Lerel said as she pressed Eyrum's shoulder down as best she could. 'Hereni!'

The mage recovered herself and leapt to help. She seized his huge forearm, barely even able to reach halfway around it.

'Fucking leviathan happened!' Eyrum seethed before falling back into his native dragonspeak.

Elessi grunted through the effort. 'He was fighting on the forecastle.'

'It came from behind me, spitting water and poison.'

Hereni almost left the floor as Eyrum slammed his fist down. She strained, looking around at the shelves of books instead of the wound. The infirmaries must have been overwhelmed. More injured lay on tables along the length of the library. More healers and survivors scurried around.

The paste now caked his leg. The bleeding had stopped, thank Evernia, but the pain still wracked him. The Siren healer pressed her hands to his forehead and whispered aloud. Hereni knew a spell when she saw it. It took several attempts, but it at last took hold, calming the Siren's pain to the point where he managed to pass out.

'Better for him,' the Siren said, before rushing away to the next victim.

Nerilan clattered her way along the corridor. She burst through the door with some more wonderful news. 'The leviathans burned a hole through your front deck.'

'That means the fuckers have managed to grind two bookships to a halt,' said Lerel.

Elessi hissed. 'And I count two of them dead.'

'Perhaps it is time you listen to us, General Elessi. We can't keep pressing forwards. That leviathan will drown us all before we are halfway to Farden.'

Lerel already looked done with this argument. 'There's a better time to discuss this, and that is later!' she yelled. 'We've been given a chance to take a breath. Let's not spend it at each other's throats. Or, you can all get the fuck off my ship and go argue on the beach.'

Elessi and Nerilan stared at each other but said nothing.

'The armada isn't going anywhere without repairs and supplies. Maybe you can help with those, instead,' Lerel hissed. Her voice failed her before her last word, and she left the library without excuse. Hereni knew that anger: one born of pain.

'She's right,' Elessi said. 'We go ashore.'

'Thank the gods for that.'

Hereni hadn't realised how much her legs had missed the feel of firm ground. Wet sand, to be precise, but still joyous. Hereni suspected it had a lot to do with the fact the leviathan was trapped in the sea. She felt safe again, as though she were back behind the black fortress walls of Scalussen.

Shivertread and Kinsprite flanked her, sniffing at the white sand. Ahead of them, the shadows of palms washed back and forth over the beach.

Bull was nudging at the shell of a crab picked empty by birds or fish. Its shell was a bright pattern of pink and white, and about the size of a child's shield.

'Sea spiders is all they are,' he was muttering.

The mage stretched her arms. Her crimson armour felt tight after days spent in sailor's garb. She rubbed her hands together and sparked a flame before quenching it. The magick flowed easily here. As strong as she had known in the north. She spread her fingers, letting them feel the wind of the power infused in every leaf and sandgrain. Learning to sense it as Farden does had taken her years. She felt its almost imperceptible threads washing across the island.

'I don't feel any magick besides us.'

Behind them, a small herd of crew members, Sirens, and survivors were busy kneeling in the sand, exhausted but finally safe. *For a while, at least, and for all they knew*, thought Hereni. She scrutinised every shadow between the palms, every bird that swooped too close. Many had called her a pessimist in her twenty winters. Paranoid even. But Hereni called it practicality. After all, she had learned firsthand and early what evils could dwell in an another's heart.

'I smell beasts. Pigs, maybe,' Kinsprite replied.

'Lerel and Elessi said we need water most. Sate your hunger later, you hungry beast.'

Kinsprite hissed before jumping into the sky. She flew above them in tight circles as if she were the carrion bird and they the corpse.

Shivertread wound his way across the sand beside her. His scales shifted hypnotically as they washed the colour of white sand, then striped as he passed beneath shadows. The dragon's wings were arched but not spread. One hooked over Hereni slightly to give her shade. His claws probed the sand like a stalking cat. The mage stepped in turn with him. A slight trail of flame wound around her fingers.

Bull brought up the rear and the crew of workers. His bow was sideways and an red-fletched arrow knocked.

'Hear that?' Hereni whispered to Shivertread.

The dragon's spines rattled as he twisted his head. 'No. What is it?'

'Nothing. No birdsong. No animal noises. Just these damned palms rustling.'

Shivertread's scales turned black as jet. Smoke curled from his nostrils.

The deeper they progressed into the forest, the thinner the palms became. Before long they walked in the raw heat of the sun again, across black rock and palm-leaf scrub. Dirt and sand mixed together underfoot. Ahead, the small mountain rose up from the island's gentle slope. A pungent smell of bird shite now wafted from its black rocks. The birds had been proven to be crows. Skinnier than the northern ravens Hereni knew. They flocked together in hundreds. Dozens already hopped around them, watching their progress through the scrub.

Kinsprite hovered over them. Several of the crows nearby exploded in a ball of feathers trying to get away from the dragon. The wind of her wings was strong and cold. Hereni barely listened, she was so thankful for the moment of cool. Her pale skin was already scorched around her neck. Skin flaked from her nose.

'There's some kind of settlement near you, just over that small ridge.'

'Anybody living there?'

Kinsprite shook her head. 'Looks long abandoned, but it's near a waterfall.'

Hereni and Bull almost had to hold back the crew of workers from sprinting ahead. The mage felt their excitement. She was parched as well. Caution overrode her thirst.

As they trod the hill of dead grass, Hereni saw the first skeleton. The crows had picked the bones spotless. The sun had bleached what was left. Even the sand had started to reclaim it.

The second lay just beyond, the third next to it. Hereni was counting past a score when she rose above the ridge.

Across the small plateau, half-buried skulls peered from the sand with one dark eye, or grinned at them with toothless jaws. Hereni saw no weapons left beside them or scars on the bones. The camp buildings hadn't been burned down, just left to rot and disintegrate in the heat. Nothing had overgrown them. What was left of a small garden of crops had withered to dust.

The clatter of a waterfall splashing on the far side of the plateau was all that mattered. The crew sprinted towards it. Hereni and Bull hung behind, still curious of the reason these mysterious people had all died together. With the sounds of an officer yelling orders in her ears, Hereni bent to look at a smaller skeleton. The draught of Kinsprite's wings brushed the sand away in gusts. One by one, a child's bones were revealed. Long gone was any muscle to give expression. It was the position of the arms that made Hereni pause. Even in death, though the bones had fallen into heaps, Hereni could tell the child had died with her hands around her throat.

'Hereni.' Shivertread was sniffing at the air. 'This island...'

But the mage was already sprinting to the waterfall. 'Don't drink the water!' she yelled.

It was too late. Cries already filled the air. One of the Siren helpers was clutching at his throat and retching. The tiny scales around his brows and cheeks were quickly fading to grey.

'Spit it out, man!' everybody was shouting. If they weren't, they were panicking, trying desperately to make themselves vomit the water they had just drank.

Two more crew sank to their knees with strangling cries. Their eyes bulged as if they fought to take breath.

'Kinsprite! Shivertread! Get them back to the ships! Every one of you, back away from that water. Put those buckets and pails down!'

Nobody needed encouragement to follow her orders. The dragons seized the afflicted and tore leaves from palms as they rocketed back to the ships. Hereni could still see the forest of masts beyond the palms. She kicked at a nearby skull, shattering it against the stone. Its shards fell into the waterfall, and tumbled across the narrow gully it had carved. With the black rock beneath it, the waters looked soiled by ink. Its pleasant splash upon the rocks was like the callous laughter of a murderer.

'Hereni,' Bull whispered.

Hereni realised the silence before she followed Bull's pointing arrow.

The crows that had been so content to flap and bicker around the mountain had fallen quiet and still. Every rock above was lined with them. There must have been thousands.

Hereni kindled flame around both her fists. Despite her worst expectations, the birds did not give chase as the workers fled back to the palms.

'Back to the ships,' she hissed.

The funeral pyres were lit as the sun dipped below the cursed mountain. Only a hundred bodies were taken from the ships. Five dead from the poisoned water. Hundreds more had been lost to the sea.

The pyres burned like beacon fires. The smoke drifted between the palms. The tens of thousands standing on the ships sang a low dirge that spread from ship to ship. The witches and snowmads said goodbye to their lost ones.

Standing in the shallows, Elessi looked upon the pyres with unblinking eyes. The heat of the flames failed to keep her eyes dry. Modren's pyre had been stolen from her. She watched the palm wood and bodies burning as if he lay atop them. Yet when she closed her eyes, she saw only the carnage of the day. Sailors smeared across the deck. Splinters still prickled her hands where she had clung on for dear and speechless life. Lerel had saved them from worse.

Elessi looked away, and stared into the darkness of the west where the ocean roiled in a fresh wind. The night that approached was full of clouds. The leviathan had disappeared from view, but she knew it still lurked. They had spilled leviathan blood. It was now personal for both of them.

Elessi felt the eyes of the crowds upon her. She offered no speech. She didn't have it in her. Anything she said would only have sounded like an excuse.

Her feet washed through the warm waters. Her toes sank into the sand. Lerel and Sturmsson were holding court on a falling palm. Towerdawn and Nerilan stood by. The dragon's scales were aflame with the pyre-light. The witches and yetin stood beneath in the darkness of the trees as if the heat bothered them.

'Go on then,' Elessi announced as she entered the circle. She spoke mostly to the dragon queen. 'Let me have it. Tell me what a mistake it was to press on. I've heard the crews muttering half the day. No doubt you have something to say.'

Nerilan had the class to stay silent. She shook her head and let Towerdawn speak for her.

'Lerel was just informing us there have been no suitable harbours for the armada until now. Whatever you decided, Loki's beasts would have still found us. We have suffered, but not because of you.'

Elessi let out a breath.

Lerel was jabbing at their small fire with a branch. Elessi saw her wink, brief and furtive though it was. By her side, the burly Admiral Sturmsson was nodding along while massaging his enormous beard. The words, 'Hold Fast' were tattooed across his knuckles. A refugee of Essen and the eastern half of the Arka empire, he commanded one of Malvus' warships in the early years of rebellion. He'd almost sunk Lerel's *Waveblade* before she rammed his vessel to pieces. He had surrendered, and after Malvus hanged the crew that swam ashore, Sturmsson swore allegiance to Farden instead.

'As I was saying, we can survive a day or two here with the supplies we have. After that, we have to move on, no matter what. We'll die of thirst here before we starve.'

'It's waiting for us out there,' Peryn whispered. She pointed past the dark waves crashing on the sandbars. Inside the witch's sleeve, a small finch cheeped. Lightning ran through the distant night in brief flourishes, highlighting the contours of clouds unseen and towering

Lerel chuckled. 'That's why we can sneak around the island when that storm hits. We'll escape behind the lea of the island, run south along the coast.'

'Are the ships ready to sail?'

'Enough as we need. The *Revenge* is in the worst shape of all, and now without a captain.' Lerel paused to swallow her emotion. 'The rudder's been rigged up to another wheel below. The other bookships can tow her. Best chance we've got if you asked me.'

'After you killed that sea snake today, I trust you,' Ko-Tergo growled. The poor yetin had spent most of the voyage vomiting, so for him to agree with sailing through a storm was remarkable. Elessi was jealous of the admiral in that moment. She bit her lip with regret.

Peryn spoke up again. 'The High Crone Wyved wants to know what comes after that.'

'Elessi will decide,' Lerel announced.

'Agreed,' boomed the Old Dragon.

Elessi kept her face stony as the decision was made without her. Some leader she was proving to be. The stress of the day poked at her irritation until it became anger.

As they filtered back to the ships, Elessi bent close to Lerel.

'You and I both know we saw several safe harbours coming here. I don't need you to stand up for me.'

Lerel looked her up and down, catlike eyes narrowed. 'I... Apparently you do, Elessi. We're fractured. We need a leader.'

'We have one. His name is Farden, and he needs our help.'

Lerel tutted as she brushed her aside to tend to her crew. 'He's not here, Elessi. We look to you, but you keep looking away.'

It was browbeaten and with curses on her breath that Elessi returned to her cabin, dragged open the inkweld, and scribbled a rough note. She didn't care if Farden was there or not.

'How did you do this?' Elessi spoke the written words aloud.

As the thunder broke open the western sky, she felt the sand scraping on the mighty keel of the *Autumn's Vanguard*. She saw the list of the ship in the leftover wine in a glass. Better, but the armada's finest still limped their way into a dark sky. Every crunch and scrape, every creak of quick patches, Elessi felt her hands trembling. She clutched them.

Elessi closed her eyes, and let fear rule her.

A prickle of pain shot through her neck, beneath the scars the daemon had left. She froze, willing the sensation to fade. It refused to when daemons were near. That would have meant their situation was even closer to hopeless. Fortunately, it seemed to be just a spasm of old and tired muscles. She massaged her tender scar and exhaled slow and shakily.

Above the island, where the coasts of the Falcon's Spur held fast against the ocean waves, the storm ruled. Rain battered the clifftops from every direction in the ceaseless gales. Not a creature dared to show its face above its burrow or den. Not a single bird could lift a wing for terror of being swept away. Not a soul braved the fierce night.

For a daemon had no soul to count.

Prince Gremorin sat upon a fist of slick black rock. His claws crunched and scraped, casting dislodged moss into the turbulent air. The crown of fire on his head crackled and hissed madly. As did his skin. His charred hide smoked and steamed where the rain lashed it. Every time he breathed, cracks of fire would sputter back into life.

Gremorin felt the tension in the air. He raised a hand to the clouds. The bolt of lightning crashed into his palm. Its white light ran through him, and he shuddered from its power.

The prince's many eyes squinted at the shapes far below him, black even against the storm water. Only the lightning showed them. Nine ships in a line, battling sandbars and rogue waves.

Though they only shone a handful of scarlet lanterns, to Gremorin they glowed with souls and magick. He tasted its stink on the air, and breathed it in.

Smoke billowed as the daemon folded into darkness.

# CHAPTER 21
## ENEMY OF MY ENEMY

*Darkness is the enemy of both dawn and dusk.*
OLD GOLIKAN PROVERB

The High Cathak Tartavor prised another sliver from the table with his knife and flicked it at the beetroot-coloured innkeeper.

'I have asked you repeatedly to stop that,' protested the man. 'These tables were carved by the grand artist Vang Ol himself, and they are very—'

'More drinks,' Tartavor pointed, momentarily forgetting his injury and cursing as pain shot across his chest. He felt the warm dribble of fresh blood seep down his ribs. Not to mention the tightness of his tender cheek, scorched by dragonfire.

The innkeeper recrossed his arms. 'As I've said. You haven't paid for the last hundred you and your kind have gulped down.'

Whatever thread of patience Tartavor clung to snapped. 'I said more drinks!'

'Look here, plains-scum,' the man started. He paused to leaned forwards and place his meaty hands on his precious table. 'The Tourney's over. Ruined. Vensk don't want no foreigners here no more. 'Specially ones that can't pay for ale and board—'

Tartavor slammed the knife into the innkeeper's hand. Before the man could bellow in pain, half a dozen Cathak grabbed him and wrestled him to the floor. The wife standing behind the bar with a broom screamed. Fists and boots rained until the innkeeper crawled bloody across the wooden boards.

'More drinks!' Tartavor barked before going back to his carving.

One of his captains, Novod, put a hand on his good shoulder. 'The herd can't stay here forever, High Cathak. What should we do? What's your orders?'

'My orders?' Tartavor laughed scornfully. They were without vengeance. They were without coin. And he swore the arrow-wound was turning sour.

Before he could summon up the wit for a reply, the door to the inn was kicked open. Soldiers of green Golikan armour swarmed inwards, yelling at the top of their voices and pointing their stupidly large crossbows. Tables clattered. Chairs flew.

Several idiots within his men decided to put up a fight. One threw a drunken punch before he was pinned to the wall by a dozen bolts like a tapestry to stupidity. Another was stabbed through the heart and left to bleed. The rest of the Cathak scrambled up against the back wall of the inn and held their hands up or over their faces. Only Tartavor was left at his table. No less than a score of Golikan soldiers surrounded him.

Within moments, the inn was packed to bursting with soldiers. Apart from the groaning of the dying, silence descended.

Tartavor eyed the crossbows with a sweaty unease. He placed the knife on the wood and shoved it out of reach. If this was to be the end, then the Dusk God would welcome him with open arms.

'What is the reason for this? What crime are we being arrested for?' he spoke.

Nobody answered him. The crowd of soldiers slowly began to part, starting from the doorway and spreading forwards.

Even leaning crooked on a golden cane, the Queen Peskora of Golikar towered above her soldiers. Beneath her usual finery, dressings and silks of gold covered up her injuries from the attack on the Viscera. A cut spanned her brow. Her other hand hung limp.

She cast a shadow across Tartavor and spent a moment examining him from head to toe.

'You,' she hissed. 'You are a High Cathak of the Dusk God.'

'Yes... Your Majesty,' Tartavor replied. 'Though the others would call me outcast.'

Peskora held the tip of her cane an inch from his face. 'It has been revealed to me that you are the patron who entered Aspala of Paraia and the grotesque beast known as the Warbringer into my Scarlet Tourney.'

Tartavor had committed enough people to the fires of the Dusk God to know a death sentence when he heard one. 'This is true.'

'Why?'

'Because of the one they follow.'

Peskora raised her chin to stare down her beak of a nose. 'The man of red and gold armour. The Emaneskan?'

Tartavor nodded. 'His name is Farden. Not only did he blaspheme our sacred grounds, he took my son from me and killed him in cold blood. I sought revenge, and I thought it fitting to force him to watch his companions forced to fight.'

Peskora sucked a breath through her bared teeth. 'You dare to use my Tourney for you own purposes?'

'Many do, Your Majesty.'

The cane struck him hard on the temple. He looked up at her then, turning the burned side of his face to her.

'It was a dragon that did this. The same dragon that attacked you. The same dragon that answers to Farden.'

Peskora rapped her cane on the floor. 'I do not come to hear what I already know. I come here because I wish to make Farden's head a new Tourney trophy. And those of any that follow him shall decorate my palace. My cousin, Irien, for example, shall be a new goblet. And that dragon? Once I eat its heart, I will have it stuffed. Do you understand me, High Cathak?'

Tartavor did not. Fortunately for him, the queen preferred the sound of her voice.

'You wish for the same, no?'

Tartavor ground out a reply. 'More than anything.'

Peskora signalled with a waggle of a bejewelled finger. Something worked its way through the crowd of soldiers. 'Join Golikar. Assist me in finding the mage,' she said, 'and I will allow you to take his life in payment for your son.'

Two soldiers carrying a wooden chest emerged. The table almost collapsed under its weight as they hammered it down before Tartavor. When it was opened, a pool of gold and silver leaves stared back at him.

'Summon your herds and the men of the Rivenplains. We leave at dawn,' ordered Peskora.

Gremorin watched the milky eye of the sun through the mists. It now hovered between two tall pines, one leaning precariously to one side as it clung to life in the bog.

The hour was growing late. For almost a day they had waited in the wretched marshes. Flies plagued them, drawn by their char and the steam the daemons' skin made as it sputtered in the fetid waters.

There was one allure to the marshes of the Wounds, and that was the souls. Barrows on firmer grounds, drowned souls still clad in rested armour, even travellers overcome, they all vomited their souls.

Around the prince, the daemons stalked the marshes, sizzling and growling here and there as they scared faint ghosts through the marshes. Their blue lights were barely visible in the light of day. Here and there the faint souls would be caught and devoured. It was the closest a daemon ever came to fishing.

The helbeast at Gremorin's side shrieked at the southern sky. Its front four claws raked at the marsh-mud independently.

'Be calm, girl,' Gremorin hushed it. He tasted the air with hair tongue to see what it was whining about. 'Loki is coming.'

His daemons spread in a line. A sorry few of them after the war. He had lost fifteen to the mages and minotaurs of Scalussen. Three more had drowned in the ice under Irminsul's fire. Barely a score remained of his kin. Even now, they stood hunched as if defeated, wings of smoke slack, shoulders hunched, claws hissing in the waters. Prince Gremorin's power was waning in the shadow of change and the light of these foreign lands.

Thunder filled the southern sky. The daemons craned their heads, clenched their swords. Storms did not worry them, but the wind tasted wrong. The smell of magick wafted with it.

As the sun grew dark, the mist swirled thicker, driven by the storm winds. Gremorin's helbeast snarled as they were enveloped. Smoke drifted from the daemon's skin. He had no love for its cold edge.

Gremorin drew his sword, staking it deep within the mud. Fire flushed through his skin. Char fell away with the wind.

'Show yourself, little god!' Gremorin yelled. 'We have waited too long for you!'

The black snout of a fenrir appeared between the mists. Frogs scattered with frantic croaks. Upon the beast's matted back sat Loki proud as ever. The god wore a little shine to himself since last they had met. Some mail beneath his damnable coat. The god had little company besides a few shuffling humans. They had been branded by fire and battle. Their minds glassy as their eyes. Gremorin could smell the scent of magick upon them. The helbeast at his side pressed itself to the mud and shrieked once more.

'How wonderful it is to see you, Prince Gremorin,' the god smiled his sickly smile, the one Gremorin longed to carve off.

'You are late, Loki.' he rumbled. 'We have waited the entire day.'

'Late is relative, Prince. Especially to those travelling south through these foul marshes to avoid the attention of a foreign empire. Golikar, I believe they call it. To me, I am in time. Early, you could say, given that I'm the first of my party to arrive.' Loki looked behind him to the growing darkness in the sky.

Gremorin bristled, spines rising, skin cracking red. 'Who else marches with you?' demanded the daemon.

Loki stayed silent and swayed with the movement of the prowling fenrir beneath him. It seemed tolerant of the daemons, but only just. It padded forwards. Water and flies scattered. The grotesque wolf dripped saliva as it brought its snout inches to Gremorin's face and rumbled deeper than the approaching thunder. The daemon snarled back, opening his fanged jaws wide. The fenrir recoiled at the blast of heat and cinders.

Loki sighed. 'It is a shame to see how few of you are there now, Prince Gremorin. All gathered in one place, I can see how many of your daemons Farden and Mithrid felled.'

His daemons stirred. Several dragged out their blades with showers of sparks as if insulted.

'Enough of your talk, silver-tongue. You cannot be trusted.'

It was Loki's turn to look offended. 'You are too impatient, Gremorin.'

'I have waited long enough! Twenty of their years we have waited on false promises and for a war that has never come. First Malvus and now a god of lies. You have promised us the world when even now it slips through your fingers.'

Loki's head swivelled around. Gremorin's smile cracked across the charcoal hide of his face.

'What are you talking about?'

'See? You are not as all-knowing as you pretend to be, god, nor as powerful. Scalussen and the Sirens still survive.'

'Do they, now?'

'Even now they are sailing south around Paraia. The daemon-touched woman and the oldest dragon leads them.'

Loki forced a laugh. 'No matter. They are inconsequential compared to Farden and Mithrid.'

'You underestimate them.' Gremorin wagged his claws. 'How unwise of you, little god. They have killed two of your sea monsters already.'

'How do you know?'

'While you have been distracted playing the new ruler of the Arka, I have been watching. Such grand souls deserve attention, especially when they have spilled the blood of my daemons.'

'Let me guess: you wish to destroy them?'

'Of course I do,' said Gremorin. The hissing and growling of his daemons came to an abrupt end when he added, 'But we are too few.'

'You sound... scared, Gremorin.'

In a breath of fire and smoke, Gremorin seized the fenrir by its lower fangs and dragged it close, jerking the god forwards.

'I have fought more battles than you have seen decades pass. I walked the ash of this world before you were a speck in your god-mother's eye. I have prowled the darkness and spent an age in the void above, and now that I have tasted flesh and fire again, I refuse to diminish. To scrape existence as a mortal when I was born to rule these miserable creatures. To drink the soul of the sun while gods weep beneath my claws.'

'And yet, you still need the help of a god to do it, Orion's Shadow,' Loki said with that infernal smoke.

'Give us what you promised!'

'And so I shall.'

The hesitation further enraged Gremorin, until lightning crackled over Loki's head, and interrupted his snarl. The wind took on a metallic taste. Magick swirled Fiercer.

Loki began to speak as the daemons stared at the sky.

'As I am sure you are painfully aware, there was once an idea. A prophecy, if you will, of a mortal so attuned to magick, such a conduit of power, that they could reverse the gods' curse that ended the war those thousands of years ago. With their bare hands, they could break apart the darkness of the void, undo the spell that trapped us all as stars, and bring daemon and god crashing back to the dirt in fire and chaos. You'll of course remember the first attempt: the girl they called Samara. She brought you back, but it was not enough. Her failure stranded your kind between sky and soil. Until now.'

While the prospect of that prophecy was enticing, the abomination necessary was quite the opposite. He, like the rest of his daemons, had felt the wave of magick pass through them not nights ago. He listened to them muttering in harsh tongues behind him.

'What have you done, Loki?'

'What needed to be done!'

Loki spread his arms wide as if he was a master of a circus. Behind him, the mist swirled as another fenrir appeared. This creature was unremarkable; it was the creature on its back that held every scrap of Gremorin's attention. The helbeast at its side whined piteously. He heard sizzling water and snarls as his daemons recoiled.

An abomination, it was, wrapped in ripped cloth and woollen blanket. The flesh that was bare to the elements was pale and tortured with blood and bruises, swollen with ripcords of muscle, and marred with script carved in needle and ink. The prince's burning eyes crept from one rune to the next, watching them sporadically flash with white light. The wind carried furnace-heat and the overwhelming stink of magick to the daemon's nostrils.

It was only when the creature raised its head and stared out from beneath its hood that Gremorin recognised the creature at last.

*It was Malvus.* Stretched and bloated, transformed, but those red eyes still carried the sharp daggers of a mortal mind set on immortality. Cruel eyes, now burning wide with a fiendish pleasure.

Gremorin saw the shine of daemonblood in that avid stare, and the stolen ichor of his kind disgusted him.

Marsh-water showered the fenrir as Malvus dismounted to wade through the bogs. He paid Loki no heed, as if he were nothing more than a herald for his master. Instead, he was transfixed by the prince.

Gremorin stood his ground, letting Malvus approach until he stood within arm's reach. He was unarmed, but Gremorin could still feel the magick prickling his hide. Daemons were not privy to wielding Evernia's. It was why they had forged the elves, and why mages like the Forever King posed such threat.

When Malvus spoke, his voice rasped like iron blades crossing. The runes spread across his face in no discernible pattern cracked and bled as he moved his lips.

'We meet again, Prince.'

'What has the little god done to you?'

'The magick of daemonblood combined with the power of Books. One in particular. Farden's.'

Gremorin snarled instinctively at the name. He hadn't realised he had taken a step back until Malvus laughed.

'How curious it is to be feared by a daemon. I spent my time on the Blazing Throne looking up to you, and now…'

Malvus stretched, coming up to Gremorin's chin. 'Even your own daemons can see it, can they not? Look how they quiver, how they look at you and question whether you could beat me. What kind of prince are you now before me?'

'This… this is madness! To mix daemonblood and magick as this in a mortal vessel is heresy! You meddle with powers even you do not know, Loki!'

'Speaks the daemon who helped create the elves. Who longed to be free of the sky for millennia. This is what you wanted, was it not?' demanded Loki, grinning still. 'Malvus grows in strength every day. It will not be long until he is capable of bringing down the heavens. Every daemon the gods trapped will be free, and my kin will look down and despair as we crush their precious world. They will bow to us and whimper for their lives before we set Haven ablaze.'

'All by my hand,' Malvus snapped at the end of the god's words.

'By his hand,' Loki recited with little feeling. 'Reinforcements, are what I am offering, Gremorin. You will have all the reinforcements you need to crush Scalussen and Emaneska just as I promised.'

'You will leave the mage and the girl to us,' Malvus ordered. Gremorin rankled at taking such commands from a mortal, even one such as Malvus. Fire curled from his jaws.

The abomination closed the distance between them. Black teeth and raw gums spread in a grin. 'Do you hear me, daemon?' he asked. 'Will you obey me?'

Much to the prince's hatred, Malvus' trap closed upon Gremorin. To fulfil the daemons' destiny, he had little choice but to accept, but in doing so he would kneel to a mortal. He could already hear his daemons muttering in discontent. His rule would be in question. Already it was clutched a thread between his black claws.

'Speak, Gremorin!' Malvus hissed.

Gremorin's shoulders blazed with fire as he sought to intimidate this upstart. He refused to be treated as a whip-slave by such a creature. Malvus did not wither. Instead, he lashed out with a fist and broke the daemon's sword in two with his bare knuckles. Its shattered blade fell to the marsh, quenched in the foul waters.

White fire scorched the air across Malvus' skin. Green light shone in rings around his hands. The prince roared against the pressure of magick. Malvus did not strike, but forced the daemon to his knees with his spells. The other daemons followed suit after their supposed prince.

The final insult came as Malvus stood over Gremorin. With his clawed hands, he seized the prince's crown of fire above his head and broke its spell into pieces.

'Your daemons are mine to command,' whispered Malvus, as they watched the other daemons kneel in kind.

Gremorin focused on the bubbling water seeping around his lower half and fought with every burning fibre to keep still. Never before had he stared death so closely in the eye. All balanced upon his next words. He spoke them not to the transformed emperor, but to the god upon the fenrir. The god with a paler face than usual, and a slight crack in his smirk. Gremorin's only solace was knowing that the god knew regret in that moment. Regret for what he had created. His only hope, that Loki might reap the ruin of his meddling before this was all over.

'As you wish, Malvus. As you wish,' growled the prince of daemons.

Malvus withdrew, smiling his wicked smile. As Gremorin watched him sniff the air, he tried to imagine the elation in his twisted, mortal mind.

'We move east,' he ordered. 'The mage is close.'

# CHAPTER 22
## THE SECOND TASK

*Broken are the pacts between gods and humanity. They are jealous beasts, consumed with their so-called sacrifice for our souls. If we had to burn in the fires of Hel to fuel their return they would not hesitate to light the wick.*
FROM WRITINGS OF JEKOL THE HERETIC

'Sabas! Sabas!'

Mithrid pinched her nose and prayed for patience.

'Yes... Sabas,' she repeated. 'But what is it? Can you eat it?'

The diminutive little shrew of a man babbled some more of his incomprehensible language. Mithrid shook her head again and mimed the horns. She hoped it would mean cow, perhaps sheep. She would even have taken goat.

The man laughed and nodded profusely. 'Sabas! Er...' The man put his hands on his head and stuck out his tongue. When that failed he barked.

'Dog?' guessed Mithrid.

Durnus shook his head. 'Dog? Dear me.'

'No,' Mithrid blurted. 'No, we don't want dog. What is that?' She pointed to another one of the carcasses that hung around the man's stall. Flies buzzed around half of them. A bucket of dead grasshoppers stared at her. Mithrid wished there was a fishmonger in the village. That, she was used to. In fact, she wished for anything but a butcher. This seemed the only stall that sold something remotely edible.

The shrew-man beamed a smile that lacked about half its teeth. 'Coelo! Coelo!'

Durnus held up one finger. 'That word I recognise. Yes.'

Instead of grabbing the coelo meat as expected, the man rummaged in a barrel. He untwined a chain of black sausages and hooked them around his arm.

'Not what we asked for, but I will take it.'

'Better than nothing.'

The man looked incredibly pleased with a silver Golikan leaf, and with their strange business concluded, Mithrid and Durnus began their walk back to the copse.

A fort of trees sat upon the vista of rolling fields, half an hour's walk from the ramshackle village. They'd had their fill of trees after Vensk, but it was wiser to keep hidden. After all, the entire queendom of Golikar was apparently out for their blood.

Mithrid dumped the ring of sausages onto a pile of leaves. 'Sausages. We've been assured they're coelo. Could be cat for all we know.'

'I'll take anything at this point,' Aspala whispered. She hoisted herself up onto her knees, her face a mask of pain. They had bound her wounds with a poultice of mosses and oily plants Durnus had recognised. She was far from death, but that didn't mean she hadn't hurt.

Warbringer snatched six of the links and stuffed them into her jaws. Nobody complained, least of all her. She had been silent since they had flown from Dathazh.

'Where are we then, Farden?' Durnus asked of the mage.

Farden was still bent over the vampyre's books, just as they had left him. The inkweld lay open and blank by his side. The crystal key of Sigrimur's breath sat atop it. A dappled pattern of morning sun fell on the tome he was examining: one of the maps Durnus had brought. The mage still looked like shit warmed up. His black eye and other bruises had only darkened. He moved even stiffer than before.

'By my calculations,' Farden began. 'That's what you always say, right?'

The vampyre grumbled as he stoked their campfire. 'I have been known to say it on occasion.'

'A day and a night of flying puts us just past the borders of Golikar, and somewhere near what's called the Wounds. Looks like that means the jagged coastline.'

'At least we know what Vernia's glow is. Evernia's stars, to be precise. Our goddess' constellation rises directly east. We should follow that.'

'Not *our* goddess,' Farden muttered. 'As for a giant, that must be a mountain, but there's no such mountain on this map.'

Mithrid could see where he was pointing. A featureless headland above a lump of land that some sailor had marked Hartlunder. No markings of mountains.

'Not that map. Perhaps we need an older one.' Durnus found a folded piece of parchment. It looked to have been ripped from a book long ago. 'A crude sketch, but the oldest map I could find. There is a rough marking there, directly east from Eaglehold. It looks like a mountain upside down. As for the dragon teeth, I have no clue. I am merely glad to see something other than those giant pines. Feels good to be in another land entirely and moving on.'

The others nodded in silence. The forests of Vensk had rolled on for what seemed like leagues, from dusk to first sunlight. Huge ravens had risen from their needle peaks to flap alongside the dragon and speak in their croaking voices. Fleetstar had almost seemed to understand them. Even now, the forests of Golikar were a dark band like a cliff to the west.

Farden reached for the inkweld, stopped, and then clenched his gauntlet. He still hadn't removed any of his armour. It lacked the polish Mithrid had seen in Scalussen, but it looked much better than before. And yet, for some reason, Farden seemed distracted. So distracted, in fact, he ignored the sausages beginning to sizzle in the flames, got to his feet, and left them to their cooking.

'Where are you going?' Mithrid asked him.

Farden did not turn. 'To think. You look after that key, Durnus. Keep it safe.'

The vampyre stared after him, nodding slowly. 'Leave him be, Mithrid. Farden likes to be alone after battle sometimes.'

'You let him be himself too much. I want answers,' Mithrid said, hoping that made the sense it made in her head. She stood and followed the mage to the edge of the scattered birch trees. She did not sneak, but tread quietly. Small scarlet birds trilled above her.

Farden sat upon a half-buried boulder that overlooked the grassland. He said nothing as she sat down in the grass next to him. For a time she said nothing, just quietly observed the cold and wet seeping from the ground into her trews. That's what she got for taking her armour off.

'If nobody has said yet, thank you for what you did in the Viscera. I didn't expect you to summon Fleetstar. I thought you'd forsaken Aspala and Warbringer. Thought you'd lost sight of what was important, though you got Tartavor in the arm rather than the heart.'

'I feel that isn't the last we've seen of him or Golikar.'

'You missing the Lady of Whispers?' she joked to break the stale silence.

'There are more important things to worry about than Irien,' Farden said. Mithrid thought she heard a tinge of regret.

'At least your armour is fixed?'

Farden bowed his head and nodded.

Mithrid knew the mage better than that. 'It's not, is it?'

'Superficially, maybe,' grunted the mage. He sounded dejected. 'The smith did a fine job, but there's more to this armour than simple craftsmanship and tempered steel. It still feels broken. Still feels... dead.'

'What does that mean?'

Farden took a shuddering breath. There was a concentration in it, as if he was fighting to keep his temper at bay. 'It means I'm dying, Mithrid. The Written will finally die out, and with me, no less. My armour's magick stops its wearer from ageing. Ever since I first found these vambraces more than forty years ago, I've worn this metal. It's a second skin to me, and it has kept me thirty winters old and away from time's claws. Yet, like my magick, it's fallen silent since Scalussen. Dead. Deceased. And ever since the battle, I feel as though the last four decades are breathing down my neck. I feel myself growing weaker by the day. Older by the hour. And if I feel weak, what does that mean for Scalussen? For us?' Farden's voice had become a whisper. 'For decades the responsibility has rested on my shoulders more than anyone's. Nobody can do what I can... could do. I believed my own legend: that I was unbeatable, even in the face of Malvus' hordes. I was so confident, I took on a volcano. I'm paying the price for that arrogance now, and so be it. But I won't let Scalussen, or Emaneska, or even this strange land pay for my mistake. I can't,' Farden kicked at the dirt, taking a moment. 'I would normally entrust these kinds of things to Durnus, but he has his own problems to worry about right now. I'm sorry for piling them on you.'

The word sounded foreign coming from the mage. As foreign as the shrew-faced butcher. Mithrid stared at the Scalussen scales before her. 'Don't apologise, Farden,' she said. 'What can we do?'

'Nothing I know of,' said Farden. 'But we are in lands I've never heard of, so all I can do is hope in Durnus' gamble. The spear is the only thing that matters now. Not me. Keeping Scalussen alive is all that matters. Hopefully Elessi is doing that. I haven't managed to raise them on the inkweld for a few days now.'

'Maybe the storm that hit Vensk went south and west,' she offered.

'Maybe.'

Mithrid had never seen the mage so resigned. In the short time she had known him, he pissed in the face of fate and circumstance, as she had aspired to do. Yet here he was, giving in. This was not the mage she recognised, and it shook her confidence.

'I want to train,' Mithrid said. The question had bothered her since Vensk, and she voiced it aloud. 'I keep wondering, what if the High Cathak had kidnapped me instead of Aspala? I doubt I would have made it two fights, and that scares me. I have all this power, and I survived Scalussen, but when there's no magick to fight I feel useless. I hate that feeling. If I am to be what I want to be, I need to be better.'

Farden was looking at her sidelong. 'Why?'

'So I don't die? Just one example off the top of my head.'

'That's not all though, is it?' Farden winked his black eye. 'You've got ambition in you, girl. Irminsul hasn't scared you as it should have. Any other soldier or mage would be grey behind the eyes by now after what we've done. Broken. You're not.'

Mithrid's words snapped at the heels of Farden's. 'Because I'm different. Because I'm convinced I'm made for more. I told you: Irminsul can't have been my only destiny, and now fate's done with me. I refuse to be a sidekick. I want to be… not *you*, but I want to *matter* like you do,' she replied, opening her hands and letting faint smoke blow in the breeze. 'I can't believe my part in this is over. You said yourself that something brought me to you. I have to matter. I have to play a part in all of this.'

'Fame and glory and power, is it?' Farden smirked.

Mithrid snapped her fists shut.

After a moment, the mage patted the knife at his side. Mithrid stared at it while he spoke.

'I will train you. Axes are best for Eyrum, but I still know some tricks,' Farden said. 'How is everyone faring? I forget to ask sometimes, with my head so full.' It was a clumsy change of subject, but Mithrid was glad for it. He had seen too deeply into her mind.

She sucked her teeth. 'Aspala is fine. Warbringer complained she didn't get to crack more skulls in the Viscera.'

'Classic minotaur.'

'Durnus seems in good spirits. Better than I've seen him so far. He bounces back fast, for being thousands of years old. I guess it's his... diet?'

Farden sighed. 'Something like that.'

'What's going on between you two? There's been a scowl on one of you since the first night of the Tourney.'

'Bad blood,' Farden said. There must have been some inner joke that the mage snorted at. Mithrid didn't get it. All the conversation had given her was unease. She had expected their time in Vensk would lay to rest some of the needles in her mind. She saw now that wasn't the case.

Their worries voiced and in doing so their edges blunted, the two looked out over the rolling hills of green grass and white flowers. The coast cut them to a savage edge barely ten miles or so from where they sat. The coastline looked like a child's frivolous cutting of a cake, sawing back and forth in peaks and troughs. The village was a sprawl of a dozen shacks along a chalky road.

As they stared, Fleetstar came swooping low across the vista. She cared not for the cries of the village. She swung above, and Mithrid could see the shark in her mouth as plain as the sun. Seawater and blood fell like rain.

'That bloody dragon,' Farden chuckled drily.

'Why do they call her the Mad Dragon?'

'Have you ever noticed how the dragons speak a certain formal way? That they follow tradition to the letter, and bow graciously to their Old Dragon?'

'I have, yes.'

'Well, Fleetstar does none of that. She does what she wants when she wants, as you might have seen. Nerilan has called her a child of Scalussen rather than of Nelska. The dragon population was growing until the war, but riders are still hard to come by. Takes a specific mind. Shivertread, Kinsprite, they're a younger generation but they follow the rules. They'll take a rider one day. Fleetstar is different. Individual. A lone wolf rather than a pack animal, and so they call her the Mad Dragon. Besides, Roiks taught her to swear, which Nerilan thinks is too human a trait.'

'Talking about them makes me wonder what the others are doing now.'

'Busy, it seems.' Farden knocked his fists together as he got up. 'And so we should be. Time is wasting, now more than ever.'

The sausages were dry, tough as boots, but edible. They chewed in silence, watching Fleetstar roasting pieces of her shark as she ate them. The dragon didn't share.

With their wounds dressed, the complaints of their stomachs quietened, and their flasks full of fresh water, they left the copse in a hail of leaves and twigs. Fleetstar seemed as eager to keep moving as the rest of them.

The hills of green grass blurred beneath them. Rings of old forts long conquered to rubble sat on the tops of the higher thrusts. Fleetstar weaved between their ruins, scaring peasants in fields, or skinny children tending flocks of galloping persnippen. Whatever had happened here long ago, a simple bucolic life had taken over. It was peaceful to watch such lands slide by.

Fleetstar followed the coastline, sometimes dipping below the cliffs to skim the whitecaps. Cliff-villages like that of Hâlorn huddled between crags, or hung from outcrops in baskets and ropes.

Miles fell away behind them. As did the sun, bringing with it a mist from the sea. It folded over the clifftops like a blanket of cotton pulled tight. The dragon's wings drew whorls in it.

Either Farden called for a halt or Fleetstar decided she was tired. Just as Mithrid's eyes were drooping, the dragon lurched into a descent towards a ruin reduced to a simple circle of stone blocks, head high. One solitary wall clung to the past and rose above the ruin. A square window looked both ways across the darkening grassland. Fleetstar chose a corner and immediately curled up, breathing hard from the effort of carrying them. She kept one cerulean eye open as the others made camp.

Mithrid was so used to a day of speed that the ground felt jarring. She tottered about, kicking feeling into her legs.

Durnus flexed his magick to light a fire of wood they'd taken from the copse. Mithrid's fingers tingled in its presence, and she had to hold herself back from reaching for it.

'Must have travelled another three hundred miles today,' Durnus said.

Farden cackled harshly at that. 'You were asleep the whole time, how would you know?'

'Not asleep. Concentrating on the riddle.'

'Doomriddle,' Farden snorted. The mage sat himself down by the fire as it began to burn brightly. After taking off his gauntlets, he found a fist-sized piece of wood in the pile, took Loki's knife from his pocket, and began to carve it.

After snaffling up a handful more of the raw sausage links from the haversack, Warbringer beat her chest. The minotaur would eat her way through their supplies before they found another butcher. 'Come now, fire-haired girl. Let us fight. Others too tired, look.'

Mithrid didn't expect to be granted her wish so early. Her arse cheeks hurt and her spine had taken on an impressive ache after an entire day sat on a dragon. At least Ilios had feathers and fur to sit on instead of stone-like hide.

'Er...'

Warbringer nudged her with her hoof. 'Up. No rest in war.'

'Well...'

Mithrid jumped back as the minotaur threw a hand at her. Claws thumped her on the arm, almost knocking her off-balance.

'Remember your training, Mith,' Aspala whispered. One of her eyes was propped open.

Mithrid thought back to the cold days upon the training yards, with Eyrum barking orders in her ear. And Hereni, catching her glances to the mage recruits.

Warbringer chided her with another cuff. 'Concentrate, pink-flesh. Too many minds in here.'

She no doubt meant to be gentle, but she rapped Mithrid's skull with a blunt claw, leaving the girl to pout and rub her scalp.

'Act. Don't think.'

Durnus held up a finger. 'That is not entirely the best strat—'

Warbringer silenced him with an angry snuffle. 'Owing you a blood pact not mean you are right, grey-skin.'

Mithrid settled into a stance and squeezed the handle of the axe in both fists. 'Don't you dare put me in that hammer of yours.'

Warbringer grinned sharp teeth before charging.

Mithrid had seen her fight in the Viscera. She knew the speed that hid in the minotaur's muscles as well as the strength. Mithrid knew she moved at half-speed, but even that was terrifying. Mithrid felt as green as she had her first and only time in Efjar.

Voidaran moaned as it sailed past her head. Mithrid had dodged just in time. Mithrid knocked the hammer away with her axe and circled the minotaur. She feinted for a strike and switched direction last moment. The trick failed. The minotaur grabbed the haft of Mithrid's axe and twisted her to the ground.

'Everybody expects first lie. Second lie, no.' The minotaur showed her, feinting like Mithrid had. The girl went to block the switch in direction, but Warbringer feigned again. Voidaran rested against Mithrid's ribs.

'Again!'

The clang of their weapons was a constant music between the ring of stones. The others watched. Even Farden, from his growing halo of wood shavings.

Warbringer's blows became harder each one that landed. Mithrid soon started to fear each swing as if it were real. The minotaur pressed her back and forth across the grass until Mithrid was drenched in sweat.

'A sword is still faster,' said Aspala, now far more awake. She stretched her sore bones as she sauntered over. Warbringer sat to eat while the Paraian began to circle Mithrid. 'Fast as a knife in most hands.'

In a gradual and almost ceremonial motion, Aspala handed Mithrid her golden sword. The scimitar was much lighter than she had expected. Perfectly balanced.

Aspala turned her back, arms wide. 'Try to cut my throat like Savask tried to do to you.'

Mithrid tried to grab the woman as a captive: one hand wrapped around her neck, and the sword menacing her throat. Aspala walked her through the steps in brutal efficiency, trapping Mithrid's sword-hand with one of hers, reached over to seize her collar, and shifting her weight down. No sooner had Mithrid's feet left the ground was she sprawling on it.

'Good trick,' she wheezed.

Aspala took back her sword and helped Mithrid to her feet. 'Might save your life one day,' she said with a wink of her mahogany eye.

Mithrid nodded as she tried to catch her breath.

'Allow me,' Farden said, drawing one of his borrowed Cathak swords and flourishing it in a figure of eight. Mithrid nodded and took as strong a stance as her dizzy head could muster.

Farden came at her with a simple cut. Mithrid blocked the mage's blade, but he reached over the arch of her axe to touch her on the shoulder. The girl hooked the sword away and swung a punch for Farden. She knew she had missed the moment his sword rang against the back of her cuirass. The blunt edge of the Cathak steel came near to her neck.

'You can get closer with a sword,' Farden lectured. 'More nimble. Deft.'

He twisted the sword in his hand and managed to land two blows on her arms before she could even shrug.

Mithrid's patience cracked. She tensed the muscle of her mind, spewing shadow from her spare hand. It enveloped Farden, and with the back of her axe, she swung for his legs to teach him a trick of her own.

Her axe stopped dead, shaking her hands from it and sending her sprawling. When her shadow cleared, Farden's boot had pinned the axe blade to the grass.

'Seventy years teaches you a thing or two.' He smirked before handing her axe back to her.

Durnus was pushing himself up. 'And several thousand teaches you a few more.' He rolled a sleeve as his fingers began to shine green with force magick. It seemed to take him some concentration that Mithrid hadn't seen before.

'If you are all helping her then so shall I! You must hone all your skills, Mithrid, and that means magick—'

'No!' Farden blurted, levelling his sword against the vampyre's spell. With the magick fizzling against the steel, he lowered Durnus' hand. 'Not tonight, I mean.'

Mithrid narrowed her eyes. 'Why not?'

Her question went unanswered, but she caught Durnus whispering to Farden. 'Your worries are unfounded, mage. Do not take me for a novice.'

'You dare do anything to her…' Mithrid heard him warn.

So it was that she felt a slight shade of unease as Durnus stepped into their makeshift training circle, marked by the clods Voidaran and her axe had carved from the grass.

'What schools of magick have you faced so far? Though my preference has been the subtler arts of space and healing magick, I know most.'

'Fire, force. Spark magick, too.'

'Something more tangible, perhaps.' Durnus weaved a shape above his open palm. Frosty light traced his movements. Mist swirled until a shard of glacier white ice coalesced in his palm. It shot out, smashing into the broken wall behind her.

Durnus had produced another shard and was spinning it around his fist.

Mithrid eagerly reached to strangle the spell. Shadow coursed around her forearms or stretched tentatively into the air. For some reason, the magick was difficult to seize. Slippery as the ice it formed.

Durnus unleashed the shard, and though it tumbled past her, her shadow did little to stop it.

'Stop this kind of spell at the source, like fighting the archer, not the arrow,' he said. He slid his hands apart and fashioned a short blade of ice.

Mithrid tensed. She had to close the distance between them to grasp the magick. Though Durnus blamed the spell, she blamed her-self. She felt rusty, though once she had ahold of the spell, she felt a fierce desire to crush it. The instinct did not feel like her own, but the feel of her power overpowering the vampyre's was stirring.

Durnus turned his cheek as the ice shard broke apart in his hand. He shook his arm as if he had trapped a finger in a door.

'Are you all right?'

'Unharmed, miss, thank you,' answered Durnus, voice waver-ing. 'Let's try again.'

'I think we should rest. Keep trying tomorrow,' Farden inter-jected. 'There's still so much we don't understand about Mithrid's power. What it draws from. Her potential. Her control.'

'I can control it.'

'Mith,' Aspala whispered.

Farden bunched his jaw. 'Enough.'

'So now you want to be a leader?' she challenged him.

The mage took a step towards her. Mithrid clutched her axe close.

It was Fleetstar raising her head, eyes snapping open, that halted their argument. She stared past them, to a gap in the ring of stone, where a man in a shabby coat had emerged from the mist. He was spinning a dagger around one hand, shielding his hands against the firelight with the other. Several others in similar patchwork clothing gathered behind him.

'A fine and cotton-headed evening to you travellers! How fortunate for you the Gentlemen Thieves have found you rather than another, lesser brand of criminal. Well, well, what have we here...?'

The bandit's voice trailed off as he saw exactly what he had before him. His dagger halted mid twirl.

Mithrid watched his peering gaze drag itself from the shine of their armour to the vampyre, who ignited two spitting fireballs in his hands. His next clue was Warbringer and Aspala pushing themselves from the fireside. The minotaur cast a horned shadow across the Gentleman Thieves.

If that wasn't enough reason, Fleetstar reared up, shining almost emerald in the yellow flames.

The bandit sketched a quick bow. 'You know, haha...' he said, laughing cheerily. 'I do believe we have the wrong campfire.'

His fellow bandits nodded profusely, tutting at their own stupidity.

'These ruins look all the same. Common mistake! Haha, well. We are immensely sorry to have disturbed you and we'll be on our way,' the bandit said with a salute. 'You have yourselves a fine evening.'

It was Aspala who began to laugh first, as she settled awkwardly back down in the grass.

'The wrong campfire, indeed.'

The mirth spread, next to Warbringer. Durnus quenched his spells and showed his fangs. Even Fleetstar uttered a hissing chuckle. Their laughter rang out across the hills.

'Rest, you fools. There will be time for testing ourselves soon, I'm sure,' Farden said, as he kicked some stones from his chosen resting place.

Mithrid sat hunched by the fire to eat as the others spoke of old fights and crossings with bandits. While those around her slowly fell asleep, one by one, she clenched and relaxed her fist over and over, spinning black threads around her fingers in ever more complicated patterns.

❦

They found their mountain shortly after dawn. Or, more accurately, what was left of it.

Farden had roused them before sunrise. They complained and muttered, but it was inevitable. Half-lit mist spiralled around the draughts of the dragon's wings as they flew towards the glow of the unbroken dawn.

Mithrid stared over the dragon's flanks. Between the threads of fog, she could see the beginnings of marshes and wetlands. Smaller, almost conical mounds poked through the mist banks. More burial barrows. Faint blue lights faded in and out between them.

'Ghosts, Mithrid,' Aspala explained over the rush of wind. 'Souls. They wander the desert just the same.'

Durnus, his eyes hidden by his dark spectacles, called back to them. 'Barrow wights, as Hereni would call them. The land she came from is plagued by them. Souls who have not been put to rest by fire, and so are forced to wander until their remains are put on a pyre.'

The vampyre stared at the ghosts just as avidly as Mithrid did. In Troughwake, ghosts had been a myth and fairytale. Of sailors drowned, calling others to the depths. Bogran had sworn he had seen one once. Mithrid had never believed him.

Other sights distracted her. Curving bones that rivalled the gates of Lilerosk. These were no ogin, but something perhaps even larger. Something of four legs than two. It looked as if the creatures had come to die together in great numbers. Great tusks still stood upright from their mass graves.

Dawn's amber light hurt Mithrid's eyes after the gloom. Black and ominous against the new sun, she saw the mountain.

In Troughwake, beetles often gnawed at the furniture. They had the annoying habit of gnawing into the legs of chairs or tables, until one day they would topple over, sending plates, vittles, and occupants flying.

So it was with this peak. Although Mithrid paled to think what size of beetle or creature could have done such a thing to a whole mountain, at some point in the past it had toppled over. Its jagged black slopes had gone from vertical to horizontal. Its summit now thrust out into the ocean like the bowsprit of a ship. Below, the relentless sea ate away at the mountain's corpse.

'That's a drowning giant if I've ever seen one!' Mithrid shouted.

'Drowned, I would say. Two thousand years have passed since Sigrimur.'

Farden pushed Fleetstar closer to the mountain than Mithrid thought wise. The mist had been burned away by the light of the dawn. There were scattered towns along the clifftops, and deeper to the north, where white mountains crested the horizon. Durnus shouted down to the dragon's claws, where Farden and Warbringer dangled.

Fleetstar, barely rested after yesterday's flight, had no complaints. Although the ground still squelched underfoot, she had saved them a slow trek through the marshes. A sloping swathe of wind-bent grass led an undulating path to the drowned mountain. Now that its rooftops were framed against the yellow morning sky, Mithrid could see a town perched on the mountains northern slope.

'Another strange town,' she said, neither thrilled nor worried.

'One we will not be spending any time in.'

Farden rubbed at the wrinkles of tiredness under his eyes. His bruises were turning green instead of purple. Something about the dawn light caught the new silver in his hair. The years were indeed racing to catch up. She could see it now, plain as daylight.

'Stand upon his brow,' Mithrid recited aloud.

'What would you call the brow of a mountain?'

Farden swung a cloak over his armour and hoisted the hood. He pointed with the butt of a sword before sheathing it. 'I say we start at its peak. See if we can see a dragon tooth from there.'

'A fine idea.'

'They didn't hide their tracks well, this cult,' Aspala said. 'These riddles are easy.'

'I have a feeling it is the tasks themselves that create the challenge. The risk, Aspala,' said Durnus.

'Sounds right. Nothing's ever simple for us,' Farden said, as he set out across the grass.

Leaving the dragon behind to stretch and sprawl to herself in the sun, they walked in single file. Conversation was stilted, if any. They spent their walk easing cramped muscles, and admiring the white, spindle-legged birds that prowled their way through the sea of grass like herons. Across the leagues of grassland, more persnippen grazed amongst huge coelos. Several of them fenced with their huge horns. The beasts seemed an even bigger breed here. Their horns were half the length of their bodies. They seemed mightily intrigued by the passing minotaur, and she with them.

'Unicorns, I have heard the people of the furthest east call these beasts. Or it might be unihorn, I forget,' Durnus lectured the silence.

By the time they had reached the first outcrop of town, dawn was a memory. Dusk had already begun. The distant giant pines of Golikar were a broad glowing band of green on the western horizon.

The towns were built of flint pebbles and mortar. Like the barrows of the marshes, they were conical, and seemed to be one huge chimney the way smoke drifted from holes in their points.

Where suspicion and doubt had plagued them in the Rivenplains, the people here seemed more than curious of the travellers. Ecstatic, almost, to have foreign faces among them. They wore clothes and brimmed hats of woven grass, and they stood in clumps to point and stare with smiles. Children ran to them to present flowers. Farmers approached with baskets of withered vegetables and flashed fingers for the prices.

'I don't think many folk come through this land,' Aspala said, as a muddy girl held up a wreath to her. The Paraian smiled and knelt to let the girl put it over her head. The girl cautiously reached to touch her horns. Aspala allowed her with a broad smile.

With a growing crowd in tow, they followed the chalk roads towards the cliff edges. The ocean roared far beneath. Mithrid dared a look over the grass-tufted edge. They dwarfed Troughwake's cliffs. She had to seize Aspala, much to her friend's pain.

'Sorry.'

Some centuries ago, when the mountain had fallen, it had crushed the cliff beneath it. The ground had swallowed the slopes. Grass had crept up its sides.

Larger villages sprawled across the black rock like lichen. Cairns stood high between the houses.

'Where from?' called a fellow in broken Commontongue. He walked alongside them, trying to barge through the throng of people that followed them babbling.

Farden raised his head. 'West.'

'But you not looks Golikan.'

'We aren't. Travellers from further west.'

The notion seemed highly impressive to the crowds, once he had translated.

'What do you call this place?'

'Mogacha. Mogacha.'

'So pleasant they named it twice,' Durnus said, drawing a snort from Aspala.

'And that mountain?'

'No mountain, traveller. Ossas. "Giant" in your tongue.'

They all shared a look between them.

'Feel?' The man put his hands to the earth. 'Ossas breathes. Ossas speaks. He still loves. Once tall. Monster from sea bite him. Poison weaken him. But he still fight. Thousand years and he still fight.'

'Monster, you say?'

'Monster… Wyrm. No…' The man clapped his hands as he tried to think of the word. 'How you say, dragon?'

Mithrid felt Farden's pace increase. They set foot to the dark rock of this fallen giant. It was there she felt the rumble in the rock through her boots. It came and went like the waves of the ocean, or rather like the breath of lungs unfathomably large.

They climbed the mountain's flattened slopes with ease. Mithrid found herself distracted by the scrub plants that grew amongst the rock. Strange herbs and purple berries almost lured her, but the brows of the giant called.

Where the mountain swept to its peak, huge fishing lines stood propped. People wound reels as large as cartwheels. Mithrid saw others slapping haunches of meat onto hooks as long as her arm. She wondered what in Hel they fished for.

The crowds hung back the further they pressed. Perhaps their interest waned, but to Mithrid it seemed more like fear, or they trod on sacred ground.

Farden led the way, determined as ever. Mithrid hung just behind him, watching the seascape reveal itself behind the black rock step by step.

An angry ocean stood beneath them. She could see the waves washing from the horizon. A dark bend in the blue in the distance, by the time they reached the coasts they reared up, their curved edges bristling with foam. They crashed against sharp islands before breaking somewhere beneath the cliff with a pounding thunder. Mithrid understood the giant's breath.

'You!' Durnus beckoned to the fellow who could speak Commontongue. The man seemed hesitant to join them. He did so in a comical, crouching walk, cringing every time the ocean hammered the cliffs.

'Where is this dragon?' Durnus asked.

The man looked perplexed. 'You not see it? There,' he said, pointing at the white needles of rock directly almost beneath them. They bent slightly inwards, just like fangs.

'Dragon's teeth,' Farden said aloud. Mithrid was already counting. Each island stuck vertically from the raging ocean. The third along was the proudest one. A long reef ran between them like a jawbone. With every wash of the waves, its rocks were revealed momentarily.

'This must be a joke,' said Durnus.

'What?' Warbringer asked. She was looking upon the ocean with a face that suggested it was made of shit, not seawater.

Mithrid remembered the riddle before the others. There, between the blue and white maelstrom between the waves, a small opening could be seen. A hole carved into the rock.

'Bodies fall in faith betwixt the third dragon's tooth,' Mithrid said quietly.

Farden scratched at his growing stubble. 'I'll echo Warbringer. What?'

'The girl is right. We need to go down there,' said Durnus.

'Do you have boats? Ships?' Farden asked of the Mogacha man.

He shook his head with emphatic speed. 'Much danger. Ships, er... die.' He mimed something breaking in half for good measure.

'A rope then.'

The fear had already hit Mithrid. 'I think it means we have to jump.'

' "Easy," you said.' Farden stared in accusation at Aspala.

'Farden does not do well with water. Almost drowned once,' Durnus quietly explained.

'Twice,' the mage grumbled. 'The second time I pulled it off.'

Mithrid's throat was inexplicably dry. 'It's the height that worries me.'

'There must be a rope.' Durnus was looking to the Mogacha when Farden started backing up. Mithrid saw the rarest of expressions on his face. One she had only seen once before. *Fear.*

'Farden…'

'Either you jump with me or you don't finish that sentence.'

Mithrid's mouth hung open. 'Me?'

'Aspala can't jump in her state. Warbringer?'

The minotaur laughed at the mage as if he was mad.

'Durnus?'

'I—'

'Then it looks like this second task is down to us. The Doom-riddle calls for faith, does it not?'

'Yes, but surely…'

While Mithrid was still trying to think of another excuse, the mage spat out a curse, counted to ten, and sprinted for the very peak of the mountain.

Mithrid watched him disappear, a figure of gold and scarlet plummeting like the steel-clad object he was. Just as it seemed he would be spattered on the bare rocks, the ocean swelled. He hit the waters with a colossal splash.

'Farden!' Durnus yelled. 'Godsdamn it!'

They waited for the next wave but all they saw was bare white rock. The eye between the dragon's tooth remained black and empty.

'I can't see him!' yelled Durnus.

'Fuck,' Mithrid hissed, crushing her fears into silence. 'Fuck. Fuck.'

Her legs moved with little thought. If Farden could do it, she had to as well. She knew if she hesitated she would never jump. Every piece of Mithrid's mind screeched for her to stay still, to be sane and stay on solid ground. Like Farden, she counted the waves, waiting for the pounding crashing beneath before she ran. If he could do it, even with fear in his heart, so could she.

Grit scattered as she bounded forwards. Cursing Farden's name as she reached the peak, she fixed her eye on the drowned cave and hurled herself from Ossas' peak.

It felt as though she left her stomach on the rock. She was sure her insides unravelled behind her; that was the only explanation for the sensation in her gut. Her breath clamoured to be free. Her arms windmilled furiously in the vain hope she could fly all along and had never tried. The ocean rose up to greet her as fast as a swinging blade. The bare rock was swallowed by a wave moments before she struck the water.

The impact had broken her legs, she was sure of it. Breath exploded in bubbles from her as ice-cold water seized her. Its bladed grip pierced every pore. It flooded her nose, mouth, and eyes.

The rock beneath her was a jolting surprise. It hit her in the breastplate before scraping past her. Panic surged as she felt herself sinking. She caught one last glimpse of the yellow day before a ring of dark rock swallowed her. Precious air escaped with her scream. The smooth rock refused to give her purchase as she continued to sink. A pressure was building within her skull.

A bottom mired in seaweed enveloped her. It only added to the panic. Mithrid felt a lasso of weed tighten around her ankle, and she thrashed to be free.

Over the roar of her bubbling scream, she heard a voice. It was muffled, incomprehensible, but undoubtedly human. Mithrid felt the emptiness of air beyond her grasping fingers. She burst upright, coughing seawater. Her hair had stuck to her face and filled her mouth. When she had stopped choking and managed to wipe it aside, she saw a wide cave before her. Stalactites of white and marbled stone hung above her. Purple crabs with limbs of spiders crawled their way across the walls and ceiling. Wet mosses of red and blue ran in spiral patterns, glowing with a faint phosphorescence. And beside her, a wet Farden looking at her concernedly.

'Are we dead? Is this Hel?' she asked.

'Hel looks a whole lot more lifeless than this, trust me,' Farden said. At the booming crash of something above, he added, 'We're in a cave in the dragon's tooth. You were right.'

'And if I was wrong?'

'Faith,' grunted Farden.

The cave did not end there, but meandered into a tunnel of the same weed-riddled chalk. Crabs clicked their way back and forth. Mithrid winced every time one crunched beneath her boot.

Farden had drawn his sword. He examined every crack in the stone with a tap of his boot, pressed on the walls, and generally acted wary.

'Traps,' he explained.

But for all the mage's caution, the tunnel was home to nothing but crustaceans. The air smelled stale. The water stagnant.

'Let's not linger here,' she whispered, as if afraid to break the silence with more than their footfalls.

The tunnel led them to another cave. The roof was crystalline, letting wavering blue daylight flood through. The mosses glowed in the corners. Ahead of them was a patterned floor leading to a ship's wheel upon a pedestal. The chamber was disarming save for some skeletons lying draped over rocks.

'Why do I not like this?'

'Probably the same reason as me. Ever seen anything like this before?'

'Never.'

Farden examined the floor with his toe. Somebody had spent time patterning the floor with shell-shaped flagstones. They seemed solid enough until Farden put his weight on one. The flagstone dropped down an inch with a clunk so very full of dread. Mithrid almost sprinted back to the water then and there.

'Bloody knew it,' Farden said, before seizing Mithrid by the arm and sprinting across the floor. Tiles dropped with a lurch wherever their feet touched. None fell more than an inch like the first, but it felt as though an abyss waited beneath. With alacrity they jumped onto the dais around the pedestal and clung to the wheel.

For a moment, nothing happened. They stared in their path across the flagstones until they heard it: the sound of rushing water. Unseen gaps in the wall began trickling, then spewing with seawater. Within a few breaths, the floor was already awash.

'All right,' Farden surmised with a certainty Mithrid did not feel. 'It's clearly a puzzle of some kind.'

'Runes,' Mithrid said as she pointed. No matter how hard she concentrated, she kept looking over her shoulder at the flooding chamber.

'Twelve of them around the wheel.'

'So a combination or a word. Are these numbers? What did the riddle say?'

' "Bodies fall in faith betwixt the third dragon's tooth. There taste forgotten airs and lesser minds. Only the drowned shall know the sepulchre's secrets." '

' "Only the drowned will know the sepulchre's secrets." This looks like a sepulchre, whatever that is,' Farden surmised. 'Check the bones!'

Mithrid and the mage went to it with a will, turning over the skeletons until they broke apart in their hands. 'I've got nothing!' she cried.

By now, the water was around their waists. Together they waded back to the wheel and hauled themselves out of the water.

'We have to think about getting out of here.' Farden was clearly gripped by the worry of drowning, but he slapped his hand onto the wheel and began turning randomly.

Nothing happened.

'Farden,' Mithrid said. 'I think we have to wait.'

'Are you mad?'

'Maybe the wheel has to be underwater?' She grasped at reeds. 'Or we do?'

Farden cast around angrily, looking for any clue but hers. 'Gah!'

On its far side, a shape shone like an arrow. Mithrid pushed herself up to snatch a breath. 'It's the water!'

Both of them submerged. Achingly slow, the runes upon the wheel began to glow in a sequence. Mithrid and Farden tried desperately to place feet and hands to remember their order.

Six, altogether, and by the time Mithrid's chest was burning for air, there was only a head's worth of space between the roof and the water.

'We've got one chance!' Farden yelled, his voice loud and without echo in the strip of air. Their faces looked haunting in the glow of the wheel.

'I remember them!'

'Fuck, I hope this works!'

They each took a huge gulp of air and dove. Mithrid took ahold of the wheel and rammed against it. Her strength was halved underwater. For a moment the wheel refused to move. Panic struck. Mithrid tried again and to her immense relief, it shifted. The first rune stuttered out as it met the arrow. Then the second. By the third, Mithrid's lungs had begun to ache. The desire to breathe was enticing. Bubbles popped from her lips. The fourth clanked into place. The wheel was beginning to stick. Now the fifth. Then the blasted sixth, taking a full turn of the wheel to reach. Her head began to pound with pressure and lack of air. Her throat gurgled as she fought to keep it closed and the icy water out.

The wheel stuck one notch before the last glowing rune. Even through the blur of the water, she could see Farden's wide eyes. Bubbles streamed from his mouth as he roared. In the muffle of submersion she could still make out his cursing. He braced himself against a nearby pillar and kicked the wheel savagely with his foot.

With a resonating boom, the wheel kicked into place and the water churned violently. Mithrid was swept around like a rag in a bucket. As her head collided with the flagstone floor, she couldn't help but exhale, and give into the darkness gathering in her eyes.

'Twice in two minutes you've almost drowned,' said a voice over her. 'Trying to beat my record?'

Mithrid fully expected to breathe in cloying water, to join the skeletons so the next unwitting morons who sought this cave could paw at her picked bones. Instead, spray hit her in the face. The water had made her numb. She realised the mage was propping her up. The water was still draining from the room and washing around her waist. Mithrid coughed to the point of almost vomiting. Farden patted her on the back. When she at last recovered and wiped a trickle of blood from her eyes, he was looking at her with a proud, if not relieved, smile.

'Only the drowned know this place's secrets. Bold guess, Mithrid. Luckily for us, you guessed right,' he said. 'Maybe you already are more than you think.'

'Not just a cliff-brat,' Mithrid wheezed. 'You could also say that's the second time I've saved your life.'

Farden pointed. 'What's going on there?'

Mithrid turned as if she expected an enemy. The ship's wheel was spinning in a blur. Spray shot from its handles. Its runes were all aglow, now a halo of light. The wooden core at its centre was unfolding, opening. Leaves of wood retracted over each other to reveal bubbling water. A crystal column of water stretched upwards. Something held still at its core. Farden clicked his knuckles and reached into the water. As soon as he had grasped their prize, the wheel stopped dead with a sharp thud. The water spilled to the stone floor. All magick died. Even the glow of the moss started to fade.

In Farden's palm lay another skeleton key of the most perfectly carved white bone. The intricacy bewitched Mithrid, and she was unable to stop staring at the loops and whorls and filigree of its ornate handle. To think this was ancient made a mockery of the modern wonders she had seen. Had the world stagnated? Regressed? She was desperate to know what was to blame.

'Mithrid!'

'Huh?' Mithrid had forgotten there was anything else but the key before her. Farden tore some of his tunic to wrap the key in.

'You weren't listening. I said you've got another problem to sort out. Getting out of here.'

'Erm. I'll bow to age and experience on this one.'

Farden narrowed his eyes in mock scowl.

It seemed Durnus had been working on such a problem. They could not swim up too far along the tunnel due to the fear of being swept away, or pounded to mush against the rock or cliffs. But before they needed to take another breath, a thick rusted hook clanged against the wall. Mithrid and Farden seized it gladly, and with the strength of an entire fishing crew, they were yanked into the fading daylight at a breakneck pace. Just in time, too.

A huge shark with a head like a black battleaxe burst the water behind them. Teeth lined the entire broad sweep of its face, from soulless eye to soulless eye, and they gnashed at Farden's dangling leg.

'Hurricane's balls, that was close!'

Farden nodded towards her wounded forehead. 'Must have tasted that blood in the water.'

Mithrid frowned, feeling the pain sting her. Within, the close shave with danger had left her shaking with guilty thrill. She spat blood that trickled into her mouth and watched it fall to the churning ocean behind them. She would wear this scar like captain's colours.

'Guess I better get used to scars. I'll have a mug like yours soon.'

'Scars mean nothing,' the mage cackled, as if she didn't get a joke. 'There's a fine line between showing you've stared death in the face and showing that you don't know how to block. The scars you can't see are what matter.' Farden tapped his head. 'You should know that as well as I do by now, and it's those I regret not saving you from.'

Mithrid's mental battlements cracked at that moment. Thoughts of Troughwake flashed across her busy mind. Of blood dripping into waxen puddles. Of dead hands still reaching for saviours that never came. Of her father. Irminsul's fire swooped after the memories. She shook her head with a growl, bringing another stab of pain. She felt a wave of guilt again, that she had not done enough yet. As if being adrift on their quest and all their hardship so far meant nothing. It angered her, made her want to push harder, faster. To outshine herself. None of their steps so far seemed good enough.

'You are both mad as hares!' Durnus was already chiding them, while they still hovered over the watery abyss. More sharks had gathered now. They could see their shadows in cresting waves. The cliff-folk were so used to fish on their hooks they actually tried to use nets with long poles before Durnus chided them. With a simple swivel of the long fishing pole, Mithrid and Farden were dumped onto the warm rock and left to recover their breath.

Durnus was a persistent shadow over them, framed by a sunset sky of fire orange and strange green edges to the clouds. 'Did you do it? What did you do?'

'Questions, Durnus,' Farden growled. 'Too many of them.'

The fire of their fight to survive was fading from them both. Mithrid's legs and lungs ached. Farden looked as though he had climbed the cliff back up. He groaned as he pushed out the bundle of tunic. 'Here.'

The Mogacha were getting too close for Warbringer's liking. She thumped the hammer on the rock at her hooves to make Voidaran cry out. With fearful whispers, they retreated.

'Better,' Warbringer said.

Durnus unwound the tunic and cradled the bone key with the utmost care. 'A second key.'

'Surprised?'

'Not at all. Did another verse of the Doomriddle come with it?' asked Durnus.

Farden and Mithrid stared at each other. She wracked her mind. 'There was nothing,' she replied, her tone like a question. 'I didn't hear or see anything. Did we miss something?'

Farden's mirth disappeared. 'I'm not going back down there.'

Durnus swapped his dark spectacles for others he had stashed in his satchel. 'Luckily for you, there are words inscribed in the side of this key. Minuscule, barely legible in even this light. Firelight might do it.'

'Then you better put that magick of yours to work and light a godsdamned fire. I thought I would have had enough of liquid by now, but somehow I'm now wondering if these Mogacha know how to brew or ferment anything. I miss Irien's never-ending supply of wine.'

'I bet you do,' Mithrid smirked.

# CHAPTER 23
## STORMFRONT

*Servaea was an island nation said to lie west of the coast of Albion. A grand nation of magick and commerce, incredibly long-lived, they rivalled the ancient Scalussen forges for their wisdom. All but in one matter: where they had chosen to build their capital, and that was unfortunately close to the volcano of Hegrabad. Its eruption was heard in what is now Essen. Those at sea survived, and as the decades since the disaster waxed, the survivors joined with the seafaring Arka. The Scribe of the Arka, inventor of the Written Book, is the last surviving Servaean known to scholars.*
FROM 'TALES FROM THE STREETS OF POWER' BY HARGRUM OLFSSON, YEAR 880

It turned out the Mogacha did indeed have knowledge of alcohol. Too much, if Farden was to be asked. He couldn't remember a headache such as this since the feast of Scalussen. Perhaps even years before that, when he'd drowned the sorrows of Kserak.

Wincing, trying to see which eye could focus, if either, Farden pushed himself up from his bedroll, and stared at a dawn he had never seen before. Almost everything he could see was ocean. The lands of the Mogacha curved north to disappear into sea fog, or to mountainous winter. Only one landmass sat south and west of them. Though it was some distance away, it shared the Mogacha's white cliffs. For a moment, still in last night's drunken haze, it looked far too similar to Albion for Farden's comfort.

Durnus was up, poring over the old maps and the elvish tome. The inkweld was closed. The Grimsayer, too, even though Farden thought he heard its mutter as he looked at it.

'What is that water?'

'The Bitter Sea they call it. This stretch of it at least. The Blue Mountain Sea is all of that,' Durnus gestured to the rest of the endless ocean. Storm-laden clouds ruled the horizon. 'The big land over there? That is what the Mogacha called Heart. One map calls it Hartlunder. Another map calls it Hartlund.'

'You learn all this from your Mogacha friend?'

'His name is Evorsk, and he is a collector of words, as he puts it. Scrolls. Books. Scraps from travellers.'

'How do you find these people?' Farden muttered with a shake of his head.

Farden looked across the others. Warbringer was snoring like a... minotaur, he supposed. Her barrel chest rose and fell to rival the grumble of the Ossas giant.

'Any luck with the bone key? Do we know where the third task lies?'

The last Farden remembered – somewhere between Aspala teaching the Mogacha an old Paraian war-song, Warbringer hammering stones into the dark night with Voidaran, or Durnus' heartfelt rendition of old eddas of Emaneska heroes long dead – he had seen the vampyre holding the crystal and bone keys to the firelight. Words had shone against his face and chest as if they burned on his skin, but somehow it was the keys that cast them in firelight.

'The riddle was in some bastardised elvish, mashed with an old dialect the cultist must have known. I hope I have translated its runes correctly using this tome. Fortunately, I brought a compendium of foreign tongues the Siren linguist Azber—'

'Durnus.' Farden massaged his temples. 'What did it say?'

'*Torrid waters fail to halt you, yet the highest price awaits. Turn where men fail to tread without sinking, with shadow in your right eye at dawn 'til roaring waters. West lies Utiru's wrath. Scarred sister's light burns the path, terror dark and crystal sharp. Cut the throat of your sweetest dreams or lose your mind.*'

Farden sighed. 'Well that seems... ominous. What is Utiru? A place? A person?'

'I think we shall find out soon enough. Where men fail to tread without sinking is...' Durnus frowned at his maps.

'Water.'

'The simple mind of the hungover triumph again.' The vampyre chuckled. 'With shadow in your right eye at dawn must mean south. We sail south.'

'I don't see a ship here, do you?'

'Not here.' Durnus pointed to a few white sails dotted across the expanse of ocean. 'We will need a captain. We cannot continue to press Fleetstar. Carrying all of us exhausts her, and you know we may need her like we did in Vensk.'

Farden reached for some of the roast vegetables and meats the Mogacha had shared in their hospitality. 'A ship it is. We'll have to look down the coast, back the way we came. Or head to Hartlunder and find a ship there. I won't go backwards. I'm not retracing my steps.'

'How does it feel with the armour back to normal? Has it helped your magick?'

Farden used the excuse of chewing on the cold food to ignore the question. 'Maybe I do remember a port several hours back, now that I think about it.'

'I know you heard me, Farden.'

The mage threw a carrot back in its iron pan. 'It's not fixed.'

'When were you going to tell me?'

Farden shot him a dark look. 'You going to play that game? Because I could ask you the same question.'

'Fine. We are fond of our secrets and loathe questions, a trait we have shared for decades. Perhaps it is time that stopped.'

'Krugis fixed the metal, not the magick.'

'Perhaps it will return with your own magick.'

'If either return at all,' Farden said. Whether it was admitting it to Mithrid the day before or the evening's spirits, he found his tongue looser. 'Meanwhile the years eat at me as if they're making up for stolen time. You know what ageing means for most Written. Inwick knew it. It is why I was so determined to find this armour in the first place.' Farden tested his aching arms and wrists. More of the colour had gone from his hands. Cracks had begun to appear between the scars.

'Modren was one of the only mages that the madness did not take. He may have been the oldest and sanest Written ever to live.'

Farden felt his throat tensing, and not from his sour stomach. 'I always thought Elessi was the one behind that. Rarely did I know a Written that took a husband or a wife.'

'Since we are speaking openly, for once, I thought you would find such a thing with Lerel once upon a time.'

'So did I.' Farden tried lying.

'Your magick will return, Farden. It has before. Give it, and your armour, time.'

'Time, Durnus, is what I am running out of.'

Durnus wagged a finger. 'We may find some better smiths in the south. Mages or wizards, perhaps.'

Farden knew it was the only advice anybody could offer, even his lifelong friend. 'I won't count on it. Irien told me magick is not treated with much love in the Easterealm. Golikar endured it because of the Skölgard Empire reaching so far east all those years ago.'

Durnus shook his head. 'Faith, mage. You jumped in faith yesterday, unless I am mistaking faith for a death wish?'

'That might be preferable at this moment,' Farden confessed as he tried to stand up. 'Evernia's tits, what was that we were drinking?'

'Fermented grain and coelo milk. Yogit, one called it.'

Farden's stomach clenched, and he considered the edge of the black rock.

'Do you wish to speak of my... condition, one could call it?'

Farden did not. 'I know addiction when I see it, old friend,' he muttered, taking steps a baby foal would have been proud of. A barrel of water sat nearby. He dunked his head into it without a thought and came up spluttering.

'That's more of that yogit, isn't it?' he wheezed.

The vampyre was trying to hide his smirk. 'They brought that barrel for Warbringer last night. That minotaur almost drank them out of their stores. Luckily the Mogacha saw it as a challenge.'

Farden found some water and doused himself. He blew spray while he watched the grass-hatted folk go about their dawn chores or gardening their crops, weaving, salting shark meat, or tending to beasts on the plains. 'A simple people. And I mean no disrespect. I envy them.'

Durnus nodded. 'We will get there once Malvus and Loki are dead. We can live a simple life.'

'No rest 'til freedom served,' Farden replied.

With their stomachs placated and parched throats wetted, the five foreigners began to say their goodbyes to the kind Mogacha.

Farden lost count of the number of hands he patted, something that seemed their custom instead of bowing. Evorsk made sure they went on their way with all kinds of packages of salted meats, dried seaweed cakes, and berry jams. Several leather skins of yogit were handed to Farden, who swiftly passed it to somebody else to carry. Even the smell was getting to him. He wondered whether the armour had secretly shielded him from hangovers all these years. That was an extra needle in the gut he did not need.

A scream cut the morning air, and though it turned a few heads, it did not seem to disturb the throngs of Mogacha. Farden looked around. It was no yell of a child. It sounded pained.

'What was that?' he asked of Evorsk.

He did not break eye contact with the mage. 'Mogacha,' he shrugged.

Looking past him, Farden saw another crowd gathered between some of the taller flint-cone houses.

'Farden,' Mithrid called after him. 'What are you…?'

The others were forced to follow as Farden kept walking. Another scream rang out. Farden walked faster. He saw stones in the hands of the mob. Stones flying through the air. The mage barged through the crowds, causing a stir amongst the straw-clad people.

It was immediately obvious what was happening. A man lay cowering against the wall of a house. He couldn't get too far; his hands were bound to a pole. He was cut in a dozen places, and before Farden could stop them all, two more chunks of flint struck him. One in the rib, one opening up his foot. Around the man, the dust and chips of flint whirled in strange shapes and spirals.

Farden took Evorsk by the shoulder. 'What is happening here, Evorsk?'

The Mogacha looked confused. 'This man criminal.'

'What's his crime?'

'Magus,' he stammered. 'Magick. It is not normal.'

Farden shoved Evorsk back into the crowds. He marched to the bleeding man while daring the crowd to throw another rock.

'Farden! We cannot interfere.'

'It not normal. Bad. Brings storm. Fire. Disease. This man wife stop breathing. He choke her. No touch!'

The crowd started baying for the blood they had been promised. Farden bowed his head, all affinity for the Mogacha dying a hard and sudden death.

'He's been born with wind magick, is all,' Farden hissed to the others.

The vampyre looked deeply concerned by the whole debacle. 'Magick is spreading here as it has Emaneska.'

'We can remove his magick,' Farden barked over to the crowd. 'Translate, Evorsk. Tell them we can remove his magick.'

Durnus looked around. 'We can?'

Farden continued shouting. 'We can fix him. He's not a criminal. What happened to his wife was an accident. Go. Tell them!'

Evorsk did as he was told. Perhaps he had noticed Farden's hand resting on his sword. Murmurs spread through the onlookers.

The mage levelled a finger at Evorsk. 'We fix him and you spare his life. Let him live. Agreed?'

The Mogacha needed little discussion to decide. They nodded and patted the backs of their own hands. It seemed agreed upon.

Farden stood close to Mithrid. 'Strangle his spells. Halt his magick. Hopefully the man will have the sense to learn to control it in the future.'

The crowd gasped as the dark shadow swirled around the girl's fingers. She moved quickly this time, barely seeming to concentrate before flexing her strange magick. Farden watched the swirling dust wind around the man die to nothing. He touched his hands together in wonder. Tears of relief sprang to his eyes. The man tried to hug Farden, but he held him at arm's reach. He tried hard to get the warning into the man with a look, as he would speak to Fleetstar. Somehow, he believed it worked. The man's relatives enveloped him, and with that, the mage was finished with Ossas and its Mogacha.

Leaving the others to be as polite as they needed, Farden made for the wavering plains of grass with a deep scowl on his face.

❦

Farden was right. A port lay several hours' glide back down the cliffs. It seemed to owe fealty to Golikar rather than Mogacha, neither of which Farden was now impressed by.

The excuse for a port occupied a narrow gorge in the cliffs. Zigzagging steps had been carved into the limestone walls. Piers had been built over a mottled pebble beach. A small town of shacks and trading houses sat in a crescent shape around nets for mending. A flock of fishing skiffs sat between two fat cogs with barnacles up their sides.

Fleetstar landed with a tired stumble atop the cliff, barely managing to avoid squishing the passengers clenched in her front claws. Warbringer and Farden rolled across the grass. It did wonders for the mage's unsteady stomach.

While they unpacked the saddlebags on the dragon and hoisted them onto their shoulders, Mithrid wandered across the grass, distracted by something. Farden noticed her leave, but was too busy staring at a nearby rickety sign. Its bleached wood said, 'Sculk Cove.' Farden didn't know whether that was a spelling mistake or an unfortunate name.

Mithrid called back to the others. 'Is that normal?'

Farden, hating sunlight that morning, was glad she stood and pointed west. Halfway to the horizon a narrow and dark storm front had gathered. A spear of black and roiling cloud spreading deep shadow across the plains. Rain obscured all beneath it. Lightning crackled through its vapours.

Farden and the others stood beside Mithrid and stared.

'Evorsk said this is a land of harsh weather,' Durnus advised, trying to stuff his books into his satchel.

Farden wasn't convinced. 'I've never seen a storm like that. Have any of you?'

Mithrid reached for the distant clouds. 'I think I can feel... magick.'

'Gods, do I wish I had another mage with me,' said Farden. 'Durnus, what can you sense?'

Durnus scrunched his face in concentration and copied Mithrid. 'I feel a cold wind amongst the threads of magick. The girl's right. There's magick in that storm.' He flashed the mage a look above his spectacles. His pale eyes were wide behind the black lenses.

'And it's coming this way,' Aspala whispered.

'Whatever it is, I don't like the look of it. Get down there and find us a ship. Sharpish, Durnus.'

Fleetstar stayed upon the cliff with Farden. Together, they watched the oncoming storm. It was likely to catch them shortly. She puffed smoke from her nostrils.

'You fear it's Loki, don't you?'

Farden couldn't tear his eyes from the clouds. The front was rising upwards as if clashing with another air, rearing up like the horn of an anvil. He could hear its thunder now, rolling across the plain. 'I don't fear Loki... and what have I said about reading my mind?'

'I can feel your worry like the heat of a fireplace, mage. You needn't worry about me, you should know. I am seeing more of the world than I ever thought existed. I don't want to stop.'

'That's what you want, isn't it?' Farden asked. 'All this time, I believed you were unpredictable. You're an explorer.'

'Towerdawn made a mistake when he told me of the dragons of old. The First Dragon. When we roamed the skies between oceans.'

Farden smiled, patting the Mad Dragon's scales around her jaw as riders often did. At first, Fleetstar flinched away from the gesture. She allowed him for a moment before sniffing at his armour.

'No magick in you still,' she rumbled.

'You can tell?' Farden didn't know why he was surprised.

'I never felt you so distracted. More than you ever felt in Scalussen. Are you sick?'

'Sick in the way all living things are, perhaps.'

Fleetstar tasted the air with her forked tongue. 'I'll be following. Try not to die in the meantime.'

The mage shook his head. 'You stay away from that storm, dragon!' he yelled after her.

Without reply, the dragon slunk into the rocky tors lining the cliff, where the grasses grew so tall they could even hide her bulk.

Farden's legs burned by the time he'd reached the pebble beach. Durnus had been busy swapping urgent words with three locals. The locals, as it turned out, seemed as dull-eyed as the fish lying in troughs and barrels. They chewed stalks of cliff grass like cows, preferring to mutter between themselves at great length before answering the vampyre's questions.

'There's a ship that'll maybe take you south,' they were explaining. 'Might have space for you. Tell you which one for a silver leaf or two.'

Farden couldn't see the glare behind Durnus' black spectacles, but he could imagine it just fine. He plucked one leaf from his cloak pocket and offered it. Each of them snatched at his hand. The grubbiest between them won it.

'Hurry it up, gentlemen. There is a storm brewing on the plains.'

'Yeah, yeah. That cog with yellow flags and some ugly bitch on its bow,' grumbled the grimy man.

The other two louts explained to Durnus behind their hands. 'It's his old wife, so it is.'

'She left him for another boat's captain.'

'So he carved the figurehead to look like her, see. 'Nother silver for the story?'

Durnus flicked another leaf into the air and left the three scrabbling.

'Yellow flags would be that one,' Farden snapped as he herded the others down the piers.

Aside from the bitterness of the locals, and the bad blood between him and his ex-wife, his label of ugly wasn't undeserved. The carpenter had given her a bosom that was practically inhuman, and a grotesque smile that ran from ear to ear. Her nose was bulbous. One eye was higher than the other.

'Gods,' Aspala winced as they stood alongside her on the pier. 'Poor woman.'

The name of the ship above read *The Seventh Sister*.

'Are we sure about this, Farden?'

The mage set his jaw. In the narrow window of sky above them, the blue was starting to succumb to the storm's grey claws. 'I feel we don't have the luxury of choice.'

Tar and old fish blood had dried in stains down its sides. The sails were patched so much it was doubtful any of the original material remained. A crew of individuals, six-strong and missing all sorts of ears and toes, leaned on the bulwark and stared down at the strangers. They seemed so at one with the rats that ran about the pier and anchor lines that one sailor even had one sitting on his shoulder, nibbling his pearl earring.

'Foul creatures,' Warbringer said as she stamped her hoof.

Even in his unsettled mind, Farden couldn't help but remember Whiskers. 'Lot smarter than you think,' he corrected her.

She was not impressed. 'But they taste like mud.'

Farden shoved Durnus ahead, being the least hungover of the bunch. 'Fine morning to you! Is this fine ship taking passengers?'

'Depends where those passengers want to go. Where they want to go depends how much they've got to spend,' said the man with a pet rat. It was only then that Farden noticed the rat's matching pearl earring. 'Rest assured. She don't look much, but she's faster than most.'

'South, past Hartlunder, maybe?'

A portly man spoke up as he moved the rat-man aside. 'There's a lot of south to Hartlunder. How far south?'

'To the roaring waters we've heard of,' Durnus bluffed.

The guess paid off.

'Chanark?' The sailor whistled a low note. 'For all of you?'

'All of us,' Farden grunted. 'Yes or no? We're short of time.'

'You'll have to share a cabin.'

'That's fine.'

'We can take you as far south as the Bay of Souls. Kedi Ada, maybe. Barges will take you the rest of the way to where you want to go.'

'How much?'

'Fifty gol—'

The fat sailor nudged the rat-man into silence. 'Seventy-five gold.'

Durnus made a good show of sighing, even rummaging in his satchel. Farden knew he had close to two hundred gold and as many silver in that winner's purse of his.

Farden would have laughed out loud had his face not been craned to the clouds.

'Sixty,' Durnus countered.

'Sixty-five.'

'Pay him what he wants, Durnus. Sixty-five, no questions asked, and we want to leave now.'

'Now?' one of them began to complain: a young runt with hair a copper shade. 'Tide's not right. Never mind the shit wind today.'

'I have a feeling that'll change.'

'What do you know, land-scrubber?'

Farden needn't have argued. The rotund sailor, perhaps the captain, had already decided. 'Deal!' he cried. He spat in the ocean to seal it.

Almost all the sailors nudged each other as if they had just won the Scarlet Tourney. There was a mutual round of smug smiles as they stepped aboard the frankly dilapidated ship, each thinking they had conned the other, and only one party being right.

'Hoist the sail then, lads!' yelled the captain as he busied himself counting his Golikan leaves.

Farden rushed to the stern. The cabin could wait. No sooner had he gripped the railing before thunder shook the air. Gloom-ridden cloud now filled the sky. Heavy rain began to fall. A smell of sulphur and metal found its way into Farden's mouth.

'Don't like this, King,' Warbringer growled. 'Remind me of storms that came to Efjar when Arka mages stood in force. All that magick. I can taste it.'

Farden shot her a look.

The *Sister* wallowed beneath them. Two of the crew poked the piers with oars. They had noticed the storm now, too. Instead of it concerning them, it seemed to bewitch them. The sails flapped uselessly without the wind. The sailors were quite happy to let momentum or perhaps strong intentions take the *Sister* out to sea.

It looked as though night had fallen above the cove. Cloud even began to creep down the limestone. The rain pelted now. Hailstones thwacked the deck. Children in the ramshackle village began to cry. It was then Farden felt the hairs on the backs of his arms rise. His nape prickled. An iron weight in his chest almost choked him.

'Durnus…'

The vampyre heard the tone in the mage's voice.

'Get us out of here now.'

Twisting his hands in a complicated yet surreptitious pattern, the vampyre hissed in annoyance. 'I have not done this in some time…'

'Now, Durnus!'

Durnus at last found the right spell. The wind magick buffeted them before the vampyre gave it direction. The sailors cried out as the *Sister* lurched with a billowing sail towards the gap in the cliffs.

'You land-scrubbers was right: storm ahoy!' the captain brayed from behind them. 'Get those lines sharpened up, damn it!'

The archway of stone swallowed them within short moments and spat them into a darkened day. The storm clouds spun overhead, whipping the waves into spray in its shadow. Farden and the others craned their necks to stare up at the clifftops as they escaped into the Bitter Sea.

'By Bezarish's arsehole, what is that?' Aspala yelled over the waves.

Farden was already staring at it.

A whirlwind of dust and darkness raged above the cliffs. The storm was powerless but to spiral about it. White and purple lightning burned streaks across the dark. The roar became constant. As they watched, the whirlwind approached the very edge of the cliff and then appeared to hesitate. A solid form could be seen within its vortex, unmoving. Barely a silhouette framed by the angry flashes of light. In stutters, the shadow raised its thick arms. With an ear-splitting thunder, a web of lightning spread across the dark clouds.

Farden crouched instinctively as a fork of crackling light struck the sea beside the Seventh Sister. Barely had he blinked its shine from his eyes than another pierced the waves on the opposite side. The heat was searing. Sparks crackled across the boat's iron fixings, charring wood or shocking the sailors into fits.

Durnus strained so hard to free them, the *Seventh Sister*'s bow actually began to rear from the water. It punished the spitting rollers like a flat-bottom scow. Mithrid held her head, eyes clenched as if the magick around her was becoming too much to bear. Aspala and Warbringer had seized the bulwark and were refusing to let go.

Only Farden stood defiant. He stood with fists clenched, staring directly into the eye of the unnatural storm, enduring every punishing crash of the lightning bolts though the next could have blown the *Sister* to cinders. Even once the wind had saved them from the storm's reach, and the others had righted themselves, he remained staring.

'Farden,' Mithrid breathed. 'What was that?'

'If my worst fears are true... an old enemy,' said Farden. 'The face from our nightmares in Dathazh.'

# CHAPTER 24
## A GOD'S RANSOM

*Some words are a poison better swallowed.*
OLD PARAIAN PROVERB

The escape from the Falcon's Spur had been a nightmare. There was no better description; simply a painful, drudged sail through battering seas and winds that tried their hardest to drown every ship in the Rogue's Armada one by one. The gods of Njord and Hurricane had been called out to and cursed in equal measure for days straight.

Three ships had fallen to the ocean's tirade. The *Windfang* had gone belly up in a rogue wave as those nosed past the island's shelter. *Forever's Blade*, an older ship still with a leviathan fang embedded in its hull, had lost its captain to a fallen spar. Turned on its side before the crew could claim the wheel, she was washed into a cliff and stowed in.

It was the Siren warship that cost the most to Elessi's heart.

Nerilan had ordered a dozen of the precious dragon eggs to be stowed aboard *Jaws of Nelska*. The ship had survived more than its share of northern storms, but it was the ferocious rocks of Paraian coasts that finally sunk her, with almost all hands lost. Only a score had been saved, and three eggs dragged from the angry ocean.

Now that the storm had abated, hundreds had been reported missing or outright dead. And every one of their names piled on Elessi's shoulders.

The hastily scribbled list trembled in her hands. The night winds were hot, even on the empty bow of the *Autumn's Vanguard*, but Elessi still shivered. It was not cold. It was a landscape of emotion, stretching from exhaustion to anger all the way to grief and back.

Gritting teeth to keep them from chattering, Elessi looked up at the diamond stars. More and more, each night she stood on deck, the less she recognised the sky. It seemed the heavens stretched and changed like the land beneath her. At first, she had come to watch them for solace. Not least because she and Modren had spent nights in the same way, but because they were as an anchor to her. As long as the sky stayed above and the old gods looked down, she had comfort. Elessi could still recognise not only the world, but herself.

One by one, Elessi began to read the names to the silent stars, hoping it would do the lost souls some scant good without pyres.

She had one last name to read to the list when she felt the scrape of wood and the presence behind her. Elessi had expected Lerel or Hereni to join her. She feared the company of any of the others. Even Eyrum, for she saw the results of her decision in his injuries.

When Elessi turned, she saw a familiar yet loathsome face in the shadows.

'Guards!' she yelled without thought.

Loki held up a fist before the shout had left her mouth. A gust of wind buffeted her against the railing, somehow stealing her words.

The god smiled broadly. 'I have come to talk, General Elessi. Nothing more,' he said, coming forwards to show her empty hands. His skin took on a pearlescent quality in the patterned moonlight bathing the decks.

The shock of his appearance still wracked her. Though he was their foulest of enemies, he was still a god. Elessi had never met one in the flesh. Something in her mortal mind urged her to prostrate herself. 'You snivelling wretch. The last time we spoke, you brought three leviathans down on us.'

Loki nodded. 'And you have survived them! Somewhat, at least. Killed two, or so my eyes tell me.'

The shock was fading. Elessi remembered the dagger in her belt and decided she didn't need guards. 'And it's cost us far too much,' she said, drawing her blade and stepping at him.

Loki looked disappointed. Hurt, even. 'I come here in peace.'

'I fucking don't.'

Before she could get within arm's reach, the god folded into nothing with a crackle of light.

The voice came from behind her moments later, further down the bulwark. 'Your anger is completely understandable, but as I said, I am here to offer a truce. No tricks. I should like to speak terms.'

Elessi shook her head. 'Your words are weapons enough.'

'Give me a moment of your time,' Loki hissed to her, 'and it may just save Farden's life.'

Elessi cursed. 'You'd best speak quickly and simply, god. Before I stab you myself.'

'My my. You've found some spirit since Scalussen, I see. I am almost impressed.'

She held the knife at the level of his throat.

'You and your armada can't survive these seas.' Loki looked around at the dilapidated state of the deck. 'That's plain enough from your. struggle.'

'Which is because of you. You summoned those monsters.'

Elessi saw Loki's patience wither for an intriguing and satisfying moment.

'Save yourselves,' he snapped. Carve a space from Paraia for yourselves here in this fine land, and I will be gracious enough and allow you to live,' He sounded proud to Elessi. If for no other reason, she could immediately understand why Farden loathed this creature.

'You seem to be really likin' this job of ruling,' she tutted, remembering Towerdawn's words on greed, and how even gods weren't immune.

Loki flashed a wolfish smile. 'I am a god, am I not? The only one upon the land in flesh and blood. That's why I have the power to promise you safe haven. No rest until freedom, was your battle cry. And look, here is freedom,' Loki spread his hand across the black seas, etched with moonlight. 'Here you can rest. The world is bigger than you know, Elessi. Forge your new Krauslung or Scalussen, or whatever you wish to call it, here in these warm lands. I bet you are bored of ice, no? Save your people from a worse fate on these harsh seas. In return, I will call back the remaining leviathan and, as promised, ensure Farden's safe return to you. You will have your king back. Your leader. More or less whole, but alive.'

'How generous of you. How can you promise that?'

'I have the ear of both the daemons and Krauslung. I can guarantee it. I may have set a certain interested party on his tail.'

'What do you mean, interested party?'

'Interested in removing Farden's head from his body, that is.'

'Gremorin,' Elessi guessed. The name still bored a hole in her mind most nights.

But Loki chuckled. 'My, no. Although the prince sends his regards, even Gremorin withers in its presence. And your dear mage Farden? Well, I'm afraid even he would not survive such an encounter either. But if you give up your journey, stay out of my way, I can intervene on Farden's behalf.'

'You lie. Farden can't be killed.'

Loki cackled harshly. 'Care to stake everything on it?' he dared her. Yet Elessi wasn't a fool. There was still flesh wrapped around this god. In the breeze he smelled of pines, of salt air, of every spice she ever tasted, but Elessi tasted the tang of sweat. There was more human to this god's form than he would have admitted. She caught the flicker of his eyes. It was the first time she had seen a crack in his perfect act.

Elessi crossed her arms, picking at her suspicions. 'Why would you help Farden?'

'You'd think I want the mage dead,' he said. 'But in truth, he is the only one who has ever understood me. He and I have a long history, and a fine path ahead of us, I am sure. Just ask Krauslung. The city has never been more at peace.'

Elessi felt the hooks of the god's words poking at her mind. She physically shrugged him away, stepping back. 'You lie.'

A silver bell appeared in his swift hands. The same bell he had summoned the leviathans with. Elessi's throat ran dry.

'Then risk it,' he threatened. 'You will lose both Scalussen and your precious mage. You can have both, safe and sound, or nothing. You should know better than to meddle in this affair,' he smirked in a simpering way. 'This is beyond you, General.'

Elessi looked up to the stars while she scoffed, organising which foul word would come first. When she looked back, Loki was gone. Just a sprinkle of ash drifting where the air wobbled in his wake.

The list Elessi still held in her hand crackled as she crushed it in her fist. She didn't stop until it was a ball that she hurled over the side of the bookship.

❦

It was strange to see snow in a land of grit and heat. And yet, above the verdant crowns of the palms, dark mountains shuttered half the sky. Black and brown were their slopes, but their summits were white as the mountains of the Emberteeth or the Tausenbar.

'What do you think, Hereni?'

With Eyrum still resting below, the captain had become the head of the mages and soldiers aboard the bookship. Lerel watched her sharp blue eyes scanning the bay. She had already examined every inch of it through her spyglass, but the mage had her spells.

The storm had blown them into a broad bay that stretched for a hundred miles north to south. On the maps, it looked to be a bite from Paraia's west coast. On its southern hook, another small bite had been taken. It was here the armada found itself, one eye watching the waters behind him, the other staring at what promised to be safe harbour at last. They had appeared to have lost the leviathan.

In the crook of mountains, a forest of palms and fig trees carpeted the foothills. A river cut a yellow beach in two. In a broad clearing, there looked to be a town of wood and stone towers.

What perturbed them was the smoke rising from them. Not the grey smoke of campfires but the unmistakable thick black smoke of buildings razed.

'Trouble, do you reckon?' Lerel asked.

'Looks it.'

The admiral looked down at the crew. Almost every soul stood aboard, both to escape the vomit-washed insides of the ship but also to see what sanctuary their strife and sacrifice had bought. Half of them, from witches to Sirens, looked up to the aftcastle where Lerel and Hereni stood. They waited for a decision. The fear of continuing on, of venturing back into the ocean, was palpable. Frustrated mutters were common in the crowd. Arguments broke out here and there before they were quashed by bystanders. The armada was fracturing fast.

Lerel watched Eyrum and Elessi appear from the stairwell behind the wheel. Their roles had reversed. The general lent her little arm to the giant Siren, who, to his honour, merely graced it with his touch. He leaned heavily on a pair of crutches that dug gouges in the deck. Bandages swathed him from neck to legs. The healers had to use their knives to save his life; his left thigh stopped at the knee. It cut her deep within to see the general so injured, and she was not alone. Lerel could tell the Siren raged inside with the struggle of even going a dozen paces, but she didn't dare broach the subject. Instead, she nodded to Elessi while Hereni took over supporting Eyrum.

Together, they walked to the edge of the aftcastle to look down on the decks and the glowing beach barely a mile away. The crystal waters showed them all manner of fish and rays darting beneath the ships' shadows.

Lerel didn't say a word. She had no idea whether Elessi was still deciding what to do or whether her mind was set. All she knew was that a mutiny might erupt should she order the ships on. But Lerel held her tongue; she knew her advice wasn't welcome any more.

'We will go ashore!' Elessi barked. Her voice was cold but clear. Resigned, almost.

The decks below cheered in muted fashion at the decision. Lerel surreptitiously blew a sigh of relief. Their supplies were in direr shape than the armada itself. Yet Lerel spied some who held back their celebration, preferring to mutter on in huddles.

Elessi barely looked at Lerel before turning away. Her visit was painfully brief. She patted Eyrum's arm before aiming for the stairwell.

'For how long, General?' Lerel shouted after her.

Elessi shouted back over her shoulder. 'For as long as you need, Admiral,' she instructed.

Lerel blinked at that. It was a jarring change in tone. She didn't know what was on Elessi's mind, but she could see it gripped her with iron claws. The general had a purpose, and Lerel wished she knew what it was.

Hereni's boots splashed in the crystalline shallows. The water that seeped into her trews was bath-warm. She turned to the others in the small longboat: a handful of her best mages and Bull, who had insisted on coming.

'Mages, with me,' she ordered.

The breeze toyed with her hair, yet that was all that moved upon the beach. Hereni shielded her hand from the sun to survey the stillness. Palms waved gently. Green and blue birds still cawed their warning songs as if danger still lurked. A lone Paraian vulegul wheeled ahead, keening softly.

Hereni and her half-dozen mages trod the wet sand, cautiously passing the tideline into the edge of the village. Shacks of palm wood were now smouldering piles of ash. Belongings had been strewn about, from buckets of fruits and vegetables to straw rabbits for children. Only one corpse lay amongst them: a young man with a wooden spear in his hand. The arrow that killed him was still embedded in the back of his skull. Hereni eyed its green fletching. It almost looked like Arka colours.

It was on the edge of the village clearing that she heard it: a low whistle she knew hadn't come from the circling birds. Another trill answered it from the other side of the clearing.

'Shields!' Hereni yelled. Bull ducked behind her. In the corner of her eye, an arrowhead rested over her shoulder, ready.

Magick punched the air just in time. Copper-tipped arrows clattered against their shields. The undergrowth thrashed as the attackers sprinted away with shouts.

No order was necessary. These mages were trained. Beside Hereni, they fanned out, trapping and catching several attackers one by one. Bull was left in the sand, head switching left and right.

'Bastards!' yelled the one Hereni had tripped. The scrawny boy of sun-tanned skin and fish-cloth squirmed under her boot. His shaved head was tattooed with geometric shapes. When a fireball burst into being in her clawed hand, he fell unnaturally still.

'You don't look like pirates,' he muttered.

'That's because we ain't, boy. Who are you?'

'I'm Sipid. Who the fuck are you?'

Hereni couldn't help but laugh. She liked the lad's spirit. 'People wanting fresh water and supplies is all we are. Explorers.'

'Really? This is no trick?'

'Yes, really. Do you have a leader? A lord?'

He squinted. 'Well, if you get your boot off me, I might tell you.'

'You aren't going to run?'

'No runnin' from a mage, is there?'

'Clever boy.'

Wary-eyed, Sipid got to his feet. The bow in his hands was ornate, older than he was. Sipid put two fingers between his lips and whistled piercingly. Hereni winced, but ahead of her, the under-growth of bushes between the palms produced figure after figure. Some even wore entire bushes on their heads and backs, and had yellow, brown, and green paints streaked across their faces. It was perfect camouflage.

'How many are you? What do you call yourselves?' Hereni asked as they found themselves swiftly surrounded. Her mages looked shifty, concerned.

The crowd split in two as their apparent leader was revealed.

Hereni had been expecting some grey-haired elder, or a proud, burly warrior covered in armour, but she mistaken on both fronts.

Their leader was a child, no more than ten winters old, perhaps. Though her people's complexions were dark and of olive hair, hers was the colour of Hereni's: a gold the same hue as the beaches behind them, so long it trailed behind her in a train of braids. A tiara of intricately woven copper threads rested on the flaxen waterfall. She had not a trace of fear in her eyes. Her face was so impassive as to be disconcerting. Even when she spoke in a thick Paraian that Hereni had never heard, her lips moved without engaging the rest of her face.

'*Jar Khoum*,' she said in a thin reed of a voice.

'Jar Khoum,' Hereni repeated, thinking it was a greeting.

Sipid translated for her. 'We are the Jar Khoum. And there are... enough of us.'

'*Inista, qe ana phero bakwa. Dal.*'

'We see the pirates coming every time. They can't catch us in the forests. They burn our houses, but we build them in a day again. Our real homes are spread throughout the palms and... other place.' Sipid said no more.

'And we are the Rogue's Armada. I am Captain Hereni, and we mean you no harm. We've only come here for shelter. Water. Supplies. Food,' Hereni said, raising her hands to the bright yellow berries sprouting from the branches above.

The child twiddled with one of her long braids. '*Hia wa ayala*?'

'She asks what have you to offer us in return?' said Sipid.

Hereni thought. 'Better arrows than copper, for one thing.'

She did not look impressed. 'Then take us to one who can bargain,' she said in jarringly perfect Commontongue.

Hereni raised an eyebrow. 'Back to the ships we go.'

The bell was incessant, calling her up. Elessi toyed with her dagger, spinning it across the wood of her desk while she waited for somebody to fetch her.

It was Bull they sent. The lad had sand smeared across his face. 'There're people living here. They talk so thick Lerel can barely understand them, but they want to bargain.'

'For what?' Elessi muttered.

'For their water and supplies.'

'Nothing is free in this world any more.'

'I think they might need us more than we need them, General. Said there were pirates that raid them every few weeks.'

Elessi prodded the dagger between the gaps in her spread fingers, daring herself to miss to feel something other than frustration. 'Pirates now?'

'That's what they said. They want to talk to the person in charge, they said.'

'Ugh,' Elessi sighed as she got up.

Within a moment, the hot sun of the Paraian coast was beating down on her once more. She looked left and right along the beleaguered ships. The *Winter's Revenge*, though still afloat, had not only grazed unseen reefs, but her repairs had failed and now her rudder had been gouged away. Her ample backside was slowly sinking. The sight of the proud bookship so ruined stabbed her in the heart. Few of the ships looked much better. Each of their captains watched the *Autumn's Vanguard* like hawks. The promise of safety hung heavy and uncertain.

The *Vanguard* had been nosed into the shallows. Her sharp iron bow carved into the sand and kept her steady. Elessi walked to the bowsprit as she had done in Krauslung, though this time at the speed of Eyrum.

Lerel and the other leaders were peppered across the bow. Below her, she saw a crowd of people so perfectly camouflaged in foliage and colours that she briefly thought the palm forest had snuck up on them.

Hereni stood beside a young boy and a child with a long mane of golden hair.

'Where is this leader of theirs?' Elessi whispered.

'Right there,' replied Bull. 'The little one.'

Elessi looked again at the small child. The fierce and broad white of her eyes was remarkable. She stood with her hands folded calmly behind her back. Her back was razor straight and her chin high, not merely because she had to look up at the bookship's prow. There was plenty of wonder in the rest of her people, but not her.

'My name is Elessi. I hear you wish to bargain.'

The child nodded curtly. 'The Jar Khoum have water, fruit, hogs, partridge and quail, coelo meat to trade.'

'And what do you want in return?'

The child stepped out from the crowd. 'Protection.'

'From what?'

She began to babble in her own language. Elessi saw Lerel wince, but the boy beside Hereni spoke up instead.

'Pirates. Though we've learned to hide and run every time they come, the pirates still take our lives, steal crops, burn our trees and buildings. We live constantly looking over our shoulders. Watchers on the mountains night and day. But you, with your ships and all your soldiers and dragons and mages, you can help us.'

Though Loki's warning had lurked in her head all day like a stone in a shoe, Elessi shook her head. These people needed none of Loki's interest. 'I'm afraid we've our own troubles to worry about. We can't help you. If anythin', we're a danger to you. We'll be leaving after we get supplies and repairs. And if you won't allow us, then we'll be on our way.'

Elessi heard the muttering spread through the crews of the huddled ships. She bit the inside of her lip. She watched Eyrum stare stoically ahead, following orders to the end. Hereni and Bull were with her, too, by their grim nods. Lerel looked expressionless. It was Ko-Tergo and Nerilan that muttered to their nearby cohorts. She heard their complaints drifting to her on the hot air.

*She'll sink us all.*

*How many more do we 'ave to lose, before we say enough, hmm?*

*Who knows where the king is? Is he even alive?*

*Words.* No armour could turn the blades of well-placed words. Elessi wanted to sink between the caulking of the deck. Her best efforts at keeping a last promise went unappreciated. Elessi's gaze started to fall, but a speck of colour in Hereni's hand fixed her. A green-fletched arrow.

'Who are these pirates?' Elessi yelled over the noise of discord.

'They are pale like you,' the lad pointed. Northern. From Galadaë and further.'

'Arka,' Lerel hissed.

'It doesn't matter,' said Elessi in a conspiratorial voice. 'We can't concern ourselves, Admiral. As soon as that last leviathan decides to explore this bay, we're sittin' pretty, like a buffet,' Elessi whispered. 'You said so yourself we're in no state for another battle.

That means we can't sit around waiting for pirates. And what of Farden and Mithrid?'

'And we can't keep losing ships, Elessi!' Lerel snapped. 'We have to think of ourselves for once!'

Elessi turned to the Siren at her side. Despite his great strength, even he trembled slightly from the strain of his new crutches. Dark stains had seeped through his bandages.

'Eyrum?' she asked in the vain hope he would be on her side.

'Looks like a paradise if I have ever seen one,' he said wistfully before blinking the blur from his eyes. 'Better odds here in shallow waters.'

Elessi bowed her head, letting her salt-encrusted silver curls curtain her face. Loki smiled at her from her thoughts, waving that infernal silver bell of his. His threat hung like a storm in her mind. She could have screamed right there and then, cursing the god's name and his ultimatum to the cerulean sky. The responsibility – the sheer cumbersome weight of choice – almost crushed her against the railing.

*Almost.* An old spark long-forgotten slammed Elessi's hands against the pockmarked wood. A refusal to cower.

'Fine!' Elessi yelled. 'If it means rest and repairs and fresh water, then we will help you as best we can. We'll promise that and that alone.'

The child in the shallows considered this for a moment before clapping her hands once. All tension across the beach dissolved into wide smiles from the Jar Khoum. The mutinous mutters behind her were stamped out – for now at least – replaced by thankful cries and somewhat of a mass exodus to the shallows.

Survivors and sailors threw themselves into longboats or simply hurled themselves overboard into the warm waters. Ship's officers tried their hardest to keep order and form teams for water and repairs, but even they succumbed to the sheer relief of safe land for the first time since Chaos Sound.

The Paraians amongst the Scalussen survivors greeted the Jar Khoum as if they were long lost cousins. Elessi even caught Lerel crooking an ear to hear their cheery words. Sea-hardened sailors grabbed fistfuls of the sand and cackled. Others ran straight for the palms, shaking large green fruits from their high branches.

'Lerel,' Elessi said, catching the admiral as she left.

She turned only slightly, looking sidelong at her. 'What?'

'I'm sorry for what I said to you. Because I do need your help, as it turns out. And because I don't think I'm going to be very popular come this evening. I hope you will speak up for me, if I need it. And if you haven't lost all faith in me.'

The admiral held her fierce glare. 'You didn't have to ask. I'd have done it for myself anyway, even if you hadn't apologised.'

Elessi shook her head. 'Then you're a better woman than me.'

'No,' Lerel replied. 'I'm just selfish like that.'

A smile cracked the admiral's stern face at last. 'What do you need?'

'Summon a council. Everybody that wants a say. First, we eat, and forget. Farden had the right idea in Scalussen. We've had the funeral. Let's give them a wake.'

Lerel nodded with grim satisfaction. 'Aye, General.'

Elessi watched her leave, wishing she could blurt her decision to her. Or Eyrum. Even simple Bull. But she pursed her lips and steeled herself. They had named her leader. She would damn well lead. It was always better to ask forgiveness than beg permission. Even when spitting in a god's eye.

'Bull,' Elessi whispered. 'Fetch me Admiral Sturmsson. Sharplike.'

'What shall I say for?'

'Tell him I have a favour to ask,' she hissed as she swept away.

❧

By evening, the beach was aflame. The village's ashes were cleared for the masses. It turned out that the Jar Khoum were not a mere handful, but a tribe composed of hundreds, perhaps a thousand in all. They set to welcoming their visitors with wild hollers and dances. Scalussen returned the favour as meagrely as they could.

Palms were hacked down to build long trenches of charcoal. Hogs, goats, and fowl appeared from the forest in the dozens and turned on spits. Ships' kitchens rebuilt themselves on the sand and boiled up broths and stews from everything and anything they had left in the stores. Smoked fish and lizards roasted to a crisp were passed around on sticks. Barrels of wine and ale were rolled from gangplanks and across the beaches.

It was a celebration of being alive. A defiant middle finger to the ocean that sought to drown them. A raised glass to both the dead and survived. It was a chance to sleep on solid ground, and a moment to drown all kinds of thoughts and sorrows in the liquor of conversation and the dribbling of barrels.

Once the sun had died behind the white fangs of the mountains, it took little time for the songs to begin. Songs of Paraia mixed with snowmad dirges and the keening of witches' ballads. The Jar Khoum seemed quite fond of keeping hounds, and, between stealing morsels from plates, they howled along in chorus.

Elessi walked barefoot along the beach. She had known naught but forests and mountains and ice for what felt like an age. To have a warm breeze on her skin even at night, to feel water so warm she barely noticed it washing around her feet, it seemed as though the storm had taken them to another world altogether. Her fur coat had been left in the cabin. Akitha had left her a thin dress of fine silver mail. A shortsword, too, just how Elessi liked, yet even that felt too heavy.

Though the mood was jubilant upon the surface of the fire-lit night. Worry lurked beneath the patina of feast and music. Stern watches had been set on every crow's nest and at the curves of the beach. Sleepy-eyed sailors worked shifts on the ballistae. Even amongst those on the beach, Elessi caught sour faces and tense huddles that fell silent as she walked by. They did not come from any particular tribe of Scalussen. Elessi saw mages that had served Modren, as well as Sirens she had known for years. Once the weed of discontent had been sown, it was near impossible to root out.

The bookships had been driven into the sand and beached. Between their huge anchor chains, long gangplanks ran from hatches lower down in the hull. Elessi sloshed past the brutalised *Winter's Revenge*, where hammering could be heard within. The *Vanguard* was quietly aglow with scarlet lanterns as carpenters inspected her broken decks. Dragons roosted in her masts.

It was the *Summer's Fury* she boarded.

Elessi gathered guards as she climbed the gangplank and strode across the deck. Suited in steel, they fell in behind her in silent succession. A dark maw of a hatch swallowed them. Stairs passed by her wet feet. The unoccupied and strangely empty layers of the *Fury* passed them by until they came to the expansive libraries. Lycans guarded the books of this ship. A familiar face of Roglurg showed teeth as she approached a wide, glass-lined room between the shelves. Elessi nodded to him and the piebald lycan bowed deeply.

Elessi had never been one for sensing the power of magick, only daemonblood. Even so, the gathered tomes and spellbooks gave off a thick air. It complimented the tension she felt upon entering the room.

The hushed yet urgent conversation died in her presence.

To the muted sounds of voices and music beyond the bulkheads. Elessi took her seat at the head of a long table. Normally festooned with books, space had been made for her summoned council. Only fluttering moth lanterns cast a cold glow.

The witches, snowmads, yetin, and the Siren queen stared at her from the far end. Beside her sat Lerel and Hereni. Eyrum and

Sturmsson not too far beyond them. The latter nodded to her deeply as she sat. The gesture drew Lerel's curious eyes.

'Thank you for calling this much-needed council, General.' Nerilan shattered the quiet, arms crossed and reclined in her chair. By the slight glow in one of her golden eyes, Towerdawn also joined the council from somewhere above. 'We have come too far already. Spent too long away from—'

Elessi held up her hand. As much as her heart thrummed, it felt satisfying to shut the queen up without care. Nerilan looked as though she had to physically swallow her words. She had seen Nerilan whispering to her allies all day long. Whatever torrent of complaints she had prepared could wait.

'I've spoken to Loki. He appeared on the *Vanguard*'s deck last night to parley with me.'

Splutters joined uneasy growls. Elessi continued before the complaining began. It had taken her this long to realise she was bored of their voices and complaints.

'Loki has given us an ultimatum. He wants us to stay put and not to interfere. He's given us free passage to build a new Scalussen here in Paraia.'

The lack of response was telltale and stomach-churning. Elessi could tell that wasn't what they expected from the god. After all, it had surprised her no end, as well. She pressed on.

'Loki said that if we stay here and make a home for ourselves, he'll allow us to live. He'll call the leviathan away, and what's more, he will promise the safe return of Farden and the others. If we don't, not only will Farden die, but all of Scalussen as well.'

The silence was damning.

Nerilan's painted nails dug hollows in her arms. 'And when were you going to tell us you've been parlaying with that god in secret? Accepted his offers? For too long have I let you order us—'

Elessi slapped her palm on the table, and only just managed to ignore how much it hurt. She pressed on to what she had spent half the day torturing herself with. '*I* called this council, not you, Queen Nerilan. I get you might misunderstand how this works, especially after our previous meetings, but this ain't a discussion.'

Peryn spoke for Wyved, who made a sign in the air. 'The High Crone says continue.'

Elessi thanked her with a nod. 'Though it disgusts me to say this, Loki is right,' she said. 'We can't all survive the journey to reach Farden. We can build a new Scalussen here, where it's safer. Where the leviathan will leave us be and Arka pirates will be our only worries.'

Ko-Tergo shed sand on the table as he gesticulated. Like most snowmads, he spoke more with his hands than his words. 'Though I appreciate you coming to your senses at last, General, do I hear right? You trust Loki's promises?'

'More accurately, do we trust his threats?' Nerilan said in an unusually deep voice. Towerdawn had spoken.

Elessi's face remained one of stone as she let them hear her decision. 'I would sooner slit my wrists than do what he says. That's why I've asked Admiral Sturmsson to clear all the survivors and dragon eggs from the *Summer's Fury*. By dawn, I'll sail this ship past the headland and south around the Cape of No Hope, across the Silent Sea, and give Farden and the others the help they'll no doubt sorely need. With any luck, we'll draw that last leviathan away with us.'

Nerilan immediately sat upright, eyes slitted in a glower. 'You'll... what?'

'You heard me. She's the least damaged and with a smaller crew and empty holds, she'll be faster than anything on the waves,' Elessi said, steadfast. She was sure everybody in the room could hear her heartbeat. She tried to imagine the weight of a hand on her shoulder, as Modren had often done when standing at her back. Elessi looked to Lerel as she elaborated. 'Loki might be the god of lies, but that's exactly how he's exposed what he truly wants. He might fear

Farden in some way, but he wants him to himself. What he doesn't want is this armada of ships and mages and dragons anywhere near his precious mage, and that's why he threatens us into staying. I'll bet it's because of the weapon Farden's looking for. It would throw a spear in the spokes of his plan.'

'You take a big gamble, Elessi,' warned Peryn. 'What if the god wants you to think exactly that, and is trying to further separate the survivors?'

The general didn't flinch. 'That's what it'll take to beat this god: a gamble. And I saw inside that god's mind last night. He made a mistake, a slip, and I saw it plainly as I see the relief on your face to be rid of me, Nerilan. Or your concern, Ko-Tergo. I know what you all see in me: no more than the wife of the undermage, a woman of work rather than of war. A general by name and consolation only. Then you underestimate me, because all the while I've watched how you people move and think, you leaders and you champions, you dragon queens. I've seen much and learned more. That is how I recognised that flicker of worry in Loki's face last night, and I'd gamble everything on that.'

'Admiral Sturmsson? You agreed to this?' Lerel asked.

Sturmsson waggled his bushy beard, his thick Essen accent coarse but confident. 'I did indeed. She's our general, after all,' he said, as if it was preposterous he should disobey.

'And how far have you got stripping the *Fury* down?'

'Half-done, Lerel.'

'Then you can tell your crew to stand down,' she replied.

Elessi felt her face grow hot. There was sweat beneath her hands. The admiral had chosen to betray her after all. 'What are you doing?'

'They'll sure to be exhausted after the day's work in this sun. I know I am,' Lerel shrugged, managing a sly wink that only Elessi saw. 'Those of my crew who've already eaten and rested can swap with yours, Sturmsson. Give yours a break. That way the *Fury* will be ready by sunrise.'

Elessi barely resisted the urge to slap her palm again and cackle in Nerilan's face.

'I'll even sail her myself,' added Lerel.

'Aye,' Sturmsson grunted. He looked somewhat relieved not to be facing the Silent Sea, and that both charmed and worried Elessi in equal measure.

Hereni thumped her fist on the table. 'I'm in.'

The dragon queen didn't look the faintest bit happy. 'Once again, you toy with our lives, this time by risking Loki's promised wrath!' Nerilan began to say, but she halted suddenly. Towerdawn did not agree, and she quietly fumed instead.

Elessi got to her feet, steeling trembling legs. 'I risk my own life, Queen. I know I'm right about Loki, and I won't sit here waiting for him to plot and scheme. Farden is in danger. We may all be Scalussen, but he is our Forever King, the last Written. Not to mention the safety of Mithrid. Durnus, Aspala, Warbringer, and your very own Mad Dragon. Fact of the matter is they need us just as much as we need them. Together we're stronger, and that's something I think you've forgotten. Why else would Loki be so concerned with keeping us apart?

'You should be happy, Nerilan; you're getting what you wanted. I'll even go as far as to say you were right. All of you. Though I did it to save us all, I pressed us into needless danger, even Farden and the others, by doing so. That's why those we've lost since Krauslung will lie on my shoulders until my dyin' day. Taking the *Summer's Fury* east doesn't make up for their loss, but it might just save the rest of us.'

Elessi took a breath. 'The survivors will be safe here with the Jar Khoum. Lerel and I, and anyone else who feels fit or fool enough to take the journey, will sail at dawn on the *Fury*. Those are my orders.'

Elessi shoved her chair back under the table, caught each of their eyes, and then made for the doorway. Lycans stood between its pillars, jet eyes fixed and staring at her.

The slow yet defiant clapping of Ko-Tergo stopped her in her tracks. She turned when Hereni and Eyrum joined in. Then, the admirals. Though the witches and Nerilan did not, they made no complaint. They nodded along to the clattering applause. Its echoes escorted Elessi along the passageway, her heart trying to climb up her throat and hands drenched with sweat.

# CHAPTER 25
## THE YAWN

*They say that in Lezembor's baths, a visitor does not just shed grime and dust, but secrets, too.*
OLD GRADEN ADAGE

Two days now, Farden had stood, statuesque, on the bilge-washed bow of the *Seventh Sister*. Not only to watch the north and the enclosing coastlines, but to mutter the name of the goddess of magick under his breath. Over and over. *And over*. Every hour that passed, the more that name turned from a request to a curse on his tongue.

If there was anything in particular the gods were useless at, it was being there when needed.

Farden looked down at the candle he had been carving into a stack of gurning faces. One angry. One sad. One laughing madly. It was all that kept the worry at bay. The figure on the clifftop waited for him every time he shut his eyes.

'What is it you're carving now?' Mithrid asked, to the rattle of the dice on the deck. Durnus had won every game since sunset the previous day, and still she kept trying. She hadn't figured the dice were loaded in Durnus' favour. That was the vampyre's true charm: looking helpless. Farden knew the truth.

'I never know. When I carve, I see nothing else, just each cut of my knife until a face appears. A fine way of losing my mind to something other than our problems.'

Mithrid leaned over his shoulder. 'That one looks like Loki. That one Malvus.'

The gold and silver knife Farden had taken from the Cathak corpse was a fine tool for carving. Sharp enough to slice each head from the candle one by one. The chunks of yellow wax landed amongst the dice game like the heads of the condemned.

'If only it was that easy,' he heard Mithrid whisper.

'No sign of the goddess, Farden?' muttered Durnus. The bags under his eyes were pronounced. More red flecks had gathered in his pale eyes. Scabs decorated his knuckles.

Farden looked at Durnus with a scowl that explained silently and perfectly how useless that question was.

'Anything from the inkweld?' he shot back an equally pointless comment.

'Nothing. We keep missing them...' Durnus realised Farden's point. The vampyre poked a fang with his tongue, and the mage watched the crew instead.

They might have been pungent and spent half their time leering at their passengers, but they seemed to know their winds and currents.

Aspala slept off her injuries below. Warbringer spent her time in the cabin also, guarding their discarded armour and supplies and likely hating every moment of being on the ship. Perhaps more so than Farden. Only the question of the dark figure following them kept the unease of being at sea from his mind.

Foam and seawater showered them as the fat cog nosed into an ocean roller. Farden winced as the water ran down the neck of his armour, and caught the captain's eye again. There was some heated discussion occurring on the aftcastle. Several of the sailors stood around the portly man, gesturing furtively. Their glances at their passengers on the bow were flitting. Suspicious. Perhaps it was boredom, or the lack of answers in his life, but Farden decided to investigate.

'Where are you going?' Mithrid asked. Always checking, always wondering, as she had since the Bronzewood. He was starting to suspect she didn't trust him. Or thought him going slowly mad. She might not have been entirely wrong.

'To see where we are,' he replied.

Durnus' map had given them a guess: somewhere between two countries called Normont and Hartlunder. The coasts had drawn inwards from the east and west as if the cog was a sword being shoved into a scabbard. A chokepoint of grey cliffs lay ahead. The striped layers in the rain-lashed rock lay at an angle as if somebody had shoved them. Strange, bat-winged seabirds followed their wake as if the *Sister* was a fishing skiff to steal morsels from. They tucked their wings and plummeted into the ocean waves beak-first at breakneck speeds. Under the waters, they swam as nimbly as any fish.

Whales had also followed them for a league or two. Not the piebald orca that Farden knew of the waters of the ice-fields, but beasts three times as long, grey and mottled as stone, littered with barnacles and scars. They lay upon the surface of the water like upturned ships, blowing giant bursts of breath with great roars, or engorged themselves on shoals of silver fish with lunging gulps with their sail-shaped mouths. Their sonorous songs resonated through the *Sister*.

The whales left them behind when the waves grew in height and chop. The closer they came to the chokepoint, the more severe the seascape became. It stirred the mage's stomach to gurgling complaints. Like the minotaur, he was no friend of boats and open water.

Farden's boots clomped on the moss-slick stairs. He could imagine Lerel tearing this crew to pieces for the way they stood about or clustered to gabble. She would have them on their knees for a week, scrubbing every inch of deck and bulkhead until the *Sister* looked new.

'For crew only! No passengers,' said the scrawniest one of the lot. He tried to bar Farden's path until the mage stared him down. He removed his hand and shrugged his jerkin as if it sat strangely on his shoulders.

The rotund captain eyed Farden sidelong, especially the Scalussen vambraces he still wore. Old habits were stubborn stains.

'Everythin' fine with your cabins?'

'Tolerable.'

A few of the sailors looked between them as if wondering what the word meant.

'Where are we, Captain?'

'Fast approaching the Irkmire Yawn. Thin bit o' coast between Hartlund and Normont. There's a fierce wind following us. Should whip us right through.'

Farden looked back over his shoulder to the western coasts, supposedly of Normont. Dark clouds filled that half of the horizon, masking every glimpse of Mogacha.

'Better get below, sire. Goin' to get awful wet and choppy up here. Wouldn't want any harm to come to our guests now would, we?'

As if to illustrate the captain's point, the *Seventh Sister* collided with a heavy wave and lurched to port. Farden had to seize a nearby line to keep from falling. His bones ached beneath his armour. Every day now a new pain or crick appeared in his ageing body, and refused to fade.

Farden eyed each of them, watching their pursed lips before he turned and left. He beckoned to the vampyre and Mithrid. The stairs, not least because they were worn and wet, gave him trouble. His ankles complained with every step. By the time he reached the lower deck, the others had caught up with him. Farden was irked to see the vampyre moving spryer than he was. To think Durnus had used a cane in Scalussen was bewildering. Farden momentarily pondered if he should try sapping souls like Durnus. He shrugged that thought away as quickly as it had come.

They found Warbringer and Aspala in a curious state. Farden reached for his knife at the sight of their broad and chary eyes. They seemed torn between their friends in the open doorway and something within the cabin. Even Aspala looked pale. Farden kicked at the door, splintering its frame. His ankle protested sharply.

Inside, they found nothing but a spiral of candle smoke churning in the corner of the malodorous cabin. The wicks spat and hissed. As Farden stared, wondering which magick had caused it, the smoke took shape. Limbs unfolded from the air. Hair cascaded. Edges were drawn in a pale light like dew on spider's silk. Colours shone in crystalline hues. Within moments, a woman's form coalesced in the flickering corner.

Only Durnus and Farden didn't shrink away. Mithrid even raised her axe to defend herself. But they knew the presence of a goddess when they saw it. The vampyre shut the door.

'Evernia, goddess of magick,' Farden breathed. That might have counted as the first time he was actually happy to see the goddess. She was naught but a bearer of ill news, a messenger of meddlers who spoke in riddles. Yet now, she would have the answers Farden wished for.

Before he could speak, another form began to grow from the smoke. Farden recognised its square jaw and build. It was Heimdall, the god who could see and hear from horizon to horizon. He could catch the whisper of a single hair falling, or glimpse the very threads of magick flicker through the air. Farden had not seen Heimdall's tawny-haired shadow for two decades. Like Evernia, his form still smoked at its very edges, glowing gently with a light the candles had no business casting.

'Two of your shadows. This must be an important visit,' Farden greeted them. He spared no bow, not even for the gods.

'We have come with a warning. Something follows you,' Heimdall spoke with a voice akin to tumbling boulders.

'A dark figure with a storm surrounding it. We know, we've seen it. But as usual, you're late,' said Farden. 'It has something to do with Loki and my Book, I know it.'

'Your Book?' Evernia twitched.

'Loki stole it,' said the mage, chewing each of his words. 'A copy of my Book that I myself made years ago.'

The goddess clasped her hands before her. Despite the stink of candle smoke, he could feel a cold breeze scented with grass.

'And you yourself have no magick either. How?' she asked.

Farden avoided her stare and paced around them. 'The how doesn't bloody matter. What matters is what or who this… *thing* is. Can you tell me that?'

Heimdall sounded tortured. 'Much to my displeasure, Loki still averts my gaze and my ears. Evernia came close to seeing with her own eyes. We do not know what he has forged or birthed, except a twining of daemonblood and magick. As such, it threatens us all. The very existence of Haven, Hel, and all between it.'

'Whatever Loki has done, he has created a force that bends the flow of magick for leagues around. I have never felt the like of which,' Evernia said.

Farden couldn't help but scoff. It had been long ago when he realised the fallacy of gods and humankind's dogged belief in their sanctity and sacrifice. They could be killed, born. Farden had even drawn blood from a certain god of lies. 'Even you, the goddess who created magick?' he asked.

'Even the Last War pales in comparison to this new danger.' Evernia tilted her head as though she had heard a distant scream. 'Magick…' It was a marvel to see the god hesitate. 'Was borrowed by the gods. It existed before us and may outlast us. I only harnessed the power of its song to give humans a weapon against the daemons and their elves. It was our right to do so, to save this world from such evils.'

'If this creature following us is made of magick, then I can fight it,' Mithrid blurted, standing tall beside the mage. 'I can kill it. That's what I was made for.'

Evernia regarded her for the first time. Farden might have been mistaken, but he would have argued he saw a slight frown upon the goddess' porcelain face.

'You have done enough already, Mithrid of Hâlorn,' whispered Evernia. 'Irminsul was a daring gamble. You know not of what you trifled with.'

'We did what we had to do,' said Farden.

Mithrid was more concerned with how a goddess knew her name. 'You know me?'

'We have watched you ever since you stepped onto the ice, Mithrid,' said Heimdall.

Evernia's eyes were like those of an eagle's, silently calculative and emotionless. 'You stoked the volcano and stopped Farden from consuming Emaneska in fire.'

Farden had to bite his lip to keep silent.

'That is what you were made for. That is what should remain your crowning achievement besides continuing to protect your king. I do not understand you, girl. You are not what was expected or foretold, and that is dangerous.'

Farden interrupted any complaint that might have been hovering on Mithrid's tongue. The girl looked fit to show some spit to the goddess. He saved her the trouble. Once again, the gods had proved useless. 'So what you're saying is you have no information for us? Something or someone of great power follows us, but you have no idea what? Wonderful.'

'We have not come to warn you of this creature, nor of the magick that follows you. We had to roam far and wide to find you,' spoke Evernia, regarding the cabin's occupants with slow drifts of her head.

Farden raised an eyebrow. 'I haven't been hard to find, surely? I've been calling for you for days. Even you, Heimdall?'

The stoic god had never learned the meaning of a facial expression. 'We have come to tell you a magick keeps you from my eyes and ears. The same magick that hides Loki.'

Farden heard Warbringer growl behind him.

Evernia's bare feet made no noise upon the deck as she approached.

'This trinket,' Evernia pointed to the knife in Farden's hand. Her fingers never touched him, but weaved shapes around his. 'It is of mortal making but it has a god's charm upon it. A spell. An unseen thread that reaches for countless miles through mountain and forest. Heimdall can sense it faintly now that we have found you.'

'He is tracking that knife like your own footprints,' Heimdall explained.

With a deep scowl, the mage stared at the gold filigree wrapped around the silver blade. Farden resisted the urge to march up to the deck and hurl the knife into the sea.

'So that's how he found us, no matter the distance we've travelled.'

'And why he will keep following us,' added Durnus. 'Until we have found the spear. It would appear we are doing his bidding after all. We should throw the knife away.'

Evernia drifted closer to the vampyre. 'The spear? Which spear?'

Durnus caught Farden's glance. There was a perturbed nature to the goddess' tone.

Evernia's hair rose up around her as if she was underwater. 'Which spear, mage? Speak.'

Farden crossed his arms in challenge. 'The spear of Teh'Mani. The God-Corpser. The Skyrender. The Allfather's spear that killed Sigrimur. Gunnir. Have you heard of it?'

'Of course I have, insolent mage,' Evernia hissed, light flashing beneath her pearlescent skin. All gods remember Gunnir. Built by the elves for evil until the gods recovered the weapon. It was that spear the Allfather entrusted to humanity as protection against those that escaped the sky. We realised it was not meant for mortal hands. It was hidden to keep it from greed and evil and it should stay hidden. This is why you are so far from the others of Scalussen?'

'And so it does exist!' Farden laughed. The sound was harsh in the diminutive cabin. He had his answers, no matter. 'It is good to know for sure at last, and the fact that you so clearly fear it is exactly what I needed to hear. That proves it's the weapon I need against Loki. Unless, of course, for some reason you don't want him dead?'

Evernia drew tall, haughty. Wind blew about the cabin like the vanguard of an oncoming storm. The light fell from her face. Shadows lengthened.

'That god has betrayed everything we have ever stood for. Once we were trapped in the heavens, we poured our all into new gods such as Loki, all of our faith and hope for mortal-kind. We gave him the task of raising the dawn, named him the Morningstar, and yet he has become our darkest failure. *My* darkest failure. He is the only one of the gods that walks in our true, full form, yet he works to destroy his own kind. He turns our world against us.'

Evernia spoke as a mother staring at her murderer of a son upon the gallows. Farden watched her with interest. The disappointment was raw. He had never seen such emotion in the goddess. Perhaps Loki was closer to her than the other gods. More offspring than brother.

It was Heimdall who saw to the heart of the matter. 'If Loki follows you, then his gaze is undoubtedly fixed on the spear. To unearth it would be to risk it falling into his possession. With Gunnir, Loki could rule every scrap of land between east and west. The daemons would fall at his feet. He could bring back the elves from their banishment. He would be unstoppable.'

'Then that is what he wants. That is his goal,' Durnus breathed.

Evernia was solemn. Heimdall spoke for her.

'He is determined to bring chaos to the lands. From his very lips came promises of carnage and a world aflame. Loki would watch us all burn. Mage, god, beast. Emaneska to this Easterealm. That is what he strives for.'

Farden swallowed his hesitation. 'Then all the more reason to find the spear. I will find it, I will keep it from Loki's hands, and with it, I will fix this world of its evil once and for all. If you want to stop me, Evernia, then you are welcome to try.'

Heimdall said no more and faded into the shadows in the corner. Evernia remained, battling to hold the mage's stare. It was a while until she managed words.

'Be careful, mage. Not merely because you hold the world in your stubborn hands once more, but fear what Gunnir may bring you, if you do succeed against the great odds of finding it. The cost of the spear's earning is greater than its wielding. Even the Allfather knew that. It broke Sigrimur, and it can break you.'

Farden made no reply as the goddess deliquesced into nothing but smoke. The others, save Durnus, were left staring at the dark corner and wondering whether they could trust their eyes. The vampyre just levelled a tired leer at him, as if the gods deserved a bent knee and a lit candle instead of Farden's rebellion.

☙

It was Warbringer who spoke first. 'Who was that?' she grunted. Her broad cow-eyes blinked unevenly. Her nostrils flared over and over.

'A goddess and a god, my good minotaur,' answered Durnus. 'Here to warn us.'

Farden scoffed.

Aspala piped up, drawing Mithrid's guilty attention.

'Did you just… did you just insult a god?' she asked.

'Two, most likely,' answered Farden, as nonchalant as if he had just slapped a peasant.

Mithrid was still staring at Farden's knife. It still hadn't left the mage's hand. Guilt wracked her. Though she still took Loki as an enemy by rote, the god had saved her life. She felt she betrayed her own life by speaking the truth, and yet it had gone too long without being voiced. Too important now.

'Farden,' she began, hesitant when the mage whirled on her. 'The knife is mine.'

She could feel the weight of Aspala and Warbringer's eyes. They were nothing compared to the fiery attention of the mage.

'Excuse me?'

'The knife is mine,' Mithrid admitted again. Confessions always came easier with repetition, no matter the crime they told. 'Loki gave it to me.'

'You better talk faster than that,' barked Farden.

'If I might interject,' Durnus said, trying to maintain the peace, 'though the question of our mysterious enemy might fox even the gods, their reaction to the mention of the spear is encour—'

Mithrid cut across him, talking only to Farden. The rest of the cabin might as well not have existed. 'In the battle with the steel dragon, I almost died. One of my friends I thought dead in Troughwake – one of Malvus' soldiers – she almost stabbed me. She would have, had Loki not appeared at the last moment, dropped this knife on my chest, and then disappeared. I threw it away on the Cathak's mountain, outside Lilerosk. The two Cathak found it, and shortly after that, you took it from them. I didn't want to say anything when you picked it up, in case you doubted me. Now, I've realised my mistake. We should have thrown it away or buried it long ago.'

Farden held up the knife, examining it in the light as if he wondered what Mithrid's blood would look like decorating it. As she was about to fill the silence with more explanation, he spoke.

'The god saved your life?' asked Farden.

'That he did.'

'Why?'

Mithrid shrugged. The question had never left her mind. 'How should I know what a god thinks? I'm just glad he did it, I don't care why.'

Farden stabbed the air repeatedly with his finger. 'Nothing that monster does is without some dark purpose. When in Hel were you going to tell me?'

'I don't know!'

'Loki's own knife,' Farden snapped.

Before Mithrid could answer him, there came a sharp rapping at the door.

The mage yelled in answer. 'What is it?'

'Some trouble you might want to see,' said a sailor from the passageway beyond.

'We'll discuss this later,' Farden whispered, shortly before whipping open the door to reveal the scrawny fellow that kept looking Mithrid up and down.

'What kind of trouble?' asked Farden.

The man chewed something black and viscous with an open mouth. 'The kind that needs all of youses attention.'

'Up there?' the minotaur rumbled.

The sailor said no more and slunk swiftly down the passage.

'Trouble, he says,' Aspala sighed. 'I'm looking forward to a time when there's no trouble, when we're not running or being chased. I feel like I've spent half my life doing that. I'm tired of running.'

'As do I,' muttered the mage. He glowered at Mithrid as he left. 'We'll speak of this later.'

The others gathered their things and went aloft one by one.

Mithrid enjoyed the feel of the cold air. The sky was a bruised blue, and the waves peaked in regular intervals that pounded the cumbersome prow of the *Seventh Sister*. The crew were spread about the ship, idly manning ropes and generally looking useless and work-shy as always. The captain, aloft by the wheel, halted them on the main deck with a hand.

'Stay right there, the waves are treacherous,' he forebode them.

Mithrid had decided the captain had the energy and semblance of a plump fish. One that was constantly gasping for air with jiggles of his chins. Even his skin had a slickness to it. Not scales, mind, but the grease of sweat and no soap.

'Then why are we on deck? What is it? Pirates? Leviathans, what?' Durnus called out.

The captain cackled abruptly. 'Trouble with your payment, it seems!'

Pulleys squealed above them. A net hidden in the rigging descended, wrapping them in its embrace. Mithrid thrashed at the coarse ropes that fell against her head. There was a moment of struggle before she realised the others had remained still.

'What's going on?' Mithrid asked, but the captain was uttering his ultimatum.

'We know that old man's got plenty more Golikan leaves. Coin that you thought you could avoid payin' us. If you want to spend another day alive and aboard my ship, then you can give us the rest of your coin, and we will be kind enough to cast you on the nearest beach without so much as a scratch. If you don't...' The captain pressed his fist into his palm, like dough wrapping over a dish. 'Well, we might be forced to 'urt you.'

Warbringer grunted in amusement.

'Is this how you treat all your passengers, Captain?' hollered Farden through the netting.

'Just the ones that have the coin or leaves to spare and the stupidity to flash it around. Pay us all you've got, or we'll knife you. Or throw you overboard for the whales to eat. I'll give you that choice.'

'How generous!' Farden brayed in an amused tone. Some might have called it fearless, but from Mithrid's perspective, she viewed it as reckless. Farden's hands were already on his twin Cath-ak swords.

'I'll give you one more warning,' he sighed. 'And then you'll get what's coming to you. We've worked too hard and travelled too far to have you bilge-stinking reprobates stand in the way. We've killed plenty fiercer than you.'

The other sailors looked to their captain for reassurance. Farden's threat had shaken them. Squeezed into a corner of pride and indecision, and eager to squish the sack of worms he had just opened, the captain blurted an order he would later – and very soon – regret.

'Kill them!'

'Durnus? If you please?' Farden yelled.

The vampyre seized the net with his skeletal hands. It seemed to take him a fraction more concentration than usual, but Mithrid felt the unpleasant pressure of magick on her skin. Flame sprouted from Durnus' fingertips like the wicks of candles. Despite the sodden nature of the ropes, the magick seared the net's tendrils. Mithrid grinned at the surprise on the crew's faces even as the cinders fell across her face. She saw the trout of a captain, who looked decidedly undecided about how his gambit was going, flapping his jaws as if he had forgotten his script. Mithrid seized her axe and stared down the nearest sailor, who wielded a bloody and hooked fish-knife.

'Come and try me then, you swine!' she threatened him.

The netting parted just in time for Mithrid to deflect the poor blow of the knife with the flat of the axehead. For a sliver of a moment she considered sparing the sailor, and then she remembered how the goddess had spoken down to her. Never mind that Mithrid had just met a goddess. *Dangerous*, she had called Mithrid.

Mithrid sketched her angst in blood.

She dragged her axe across his chest like a knife, sending him scrabbling. Mithrid whirled for the next foe, but before she could reach him, Warbringer batted him over the side of the *Sister* like a rotten apple. Mithrid chose another mark instead, beating Farden to the kill by hurling her axe over her head. It pinned the sailor to the bulwark by his shoulder. Farden's swords finished him off, stabbing two bloody holes in his belly and leaving him to squealing death.

Up the stairwells, they swarmed, pincering the captain and two of his crew by the wheel. Warbringer snapped one of their necks with a squeeze before Farden halted her.

'You realise your mistake now?' he demanded of the fool captain. 'This day could have gone very differently for you. But no, you had to be a fucking fool.'

Mithrid fully expected the mage to slaughter the remaining two, but Farden slapped the wheel instead to make them squirm.

'Sail us south or join your crew.' Farden pointed to the corpses splayed about the deck and smouldering netting.

'Right you are, sire,' the captain whispered as he bent himself to the wheel. The other sailor clasped its handles as if to appear useful.

'Much better,' said Farden, clapping the fish upon his sweat-damp back, and turning to face the bottleneck of cliffs the *Sister* faced.

Despite his threat of speaking more on the knife, Farden said no more to Mithrid. He stalked to the starboard side and balanced Loki's knife in his hands. For a moment, it looked as though he would let it fall into the ocean. Instead, he twirled it and seized its blade in his armoured fist. As he faced the light of the sun, Mithrid saw the worry plain as wrinkles. She had let him down, she knew that, but she felt innocent of blame. If the mage had any to level at her, she already had some words to fire back. *How was she supposed to know about the knife?*

For a time, Mithrid kept guard with Aspala at the wheel, staring into the back of his head and wondering what churned there.

'I can't believe I met a god today,' Aspala whispered when the silence had become too heavy.

'Farden seems to treat them like they're all Loki.'

It was Durnus that answered. 'The gods used him, just like many others have. They used all of us, to be honest. Elessi and I. It took Farden years to realise he was more than their machinations, that he was in control of his destiny. They chose him as their hero, but instead, he chose to be ours. Now, if you'll excuse me...' He said no more.

'Destiny,' Mithrid repeated the word under her breath. The prospect of hers was like a rope around her waist, tugging her willingly into a thick mist. She knew not where it led, but she had believed, deep within her, until now that it was somewhere important. Somewhere eddas are sung of. The goddess Evernia's words had been scissors to such rope, threatening to slice it. Frayed as her belief was, she clung to it all the more. Nowhere in the stories she knew did it say the gods were always right. And if one could lie, so could the others. So it was when the first stars appeared in the west, before the sun had set, Mithrid glared at them.

'Welcome to the Irkmire Yawn,' informed the ship's captain, with as much grandeur and ceremony as a semi-conscious toad. 'Foulest strip of water in all of Easterealm, besides the God's Rent. Giant whirlpool far out there in the Blue Mountain Sea. Once we're through the Yawn, it's plain seas and calm sailin'.'

Though he was a cheat and a would-be murderer, the man was not a liar. The Yawn was foul indeed.

As the two coastlines came to a pinch several miles wide, the currents jostled the *Seventh Sister* with violent purpose. All the angst of two meeting oceans caused whirlpools and towering standing waves. Spray fell like rain as wave after wave crashed against the cog's fat keel. Its flat bottom thwacked the sea every time it pitched and fell.

The captain worked tirelessly battling the wheel, mostly for his own survival, Mithrid presumed. She was glad Farden had given him the glimmer of hope.

Within half an hour of white knuckles and lurching stomachs, the *Sister* broke onto more predictable waters. According to Durnus' map, the Blue Mountain Sea spread before them, devoid of any coastline but the one that trailed off west and south. Hartlunder's slanted cliffs ran east as if fleeing the Yawn. Its dreary walls were all Mithrid ever saw of the country, and she wondered at the kind of folk who endured its dreary skies.

Farden, at last, left the bulwark. The knife was at his side now, along with his swords. 'Smooth waters from here, you said?' he demanded of the captain, pushing him from the wheel.

'Aye, that's what I said. Lest a squall blows in, Lezembor's just a day's stretch from here.'

Farden pointed over the man's pudgy shoulder. 'And what is that land? Friendly, is it?'

'Normont still.' The captain tried to turn but Farden shoved him ahead. 'It's wild but fair enough.'

'How far away would you say it is?'

'Couple miles maybe?'

'Then I hope you both are good swimmers,' whispered Farden.

It took an appalling amount of time for the captain to add two and two together. The trout of a man immediately fell to his knees. 'Please, sire! I ain't no swimmer!' he yelled.

'Shame,' Farden said, no delight on his face. 'This is what you deserve for trying to cheat and murder honest passengers. You're lucky I let you live.'

Warbringer muscled the last sailor to his captain's side. 'Over you go,' she ordered.

Mithrid looked to the others, who watched without expression. She saw no complaint in them, and there was none in her either.

'We'll do anything, we swear!'

All it took was one roar from the minotaur and the two men scrambled over the bulwark like pigeons fleeing a roost. Mithrid heard their splashes before they made it to the railing. The last she saw of them in the *Sister*'s wake was a flailing captain and a sailor splashing madly for land with no care in the world for his superior.

'Strange,' Aspala said, 'I thought so much blubber would float better.'

Mithrid thought the ship had hit a series of rocks until she realised it was Warbringer laughing, booming deep in her chest. Durnus joined with his papery snicker. Even Mithrid had to chuckle. The mage, however, did not break his sour expression.

'So,' Mithrid asked once the amusement had died. 'Does anyone know how to sail this mouldy thing?'

It turned out that none of them knew how to sail.

Not even Durnus, with a brain of millennia upon his shoulders, though he could name half the lines and parts of the ship itself, the act of sailing, even in a calm sea, was a comedy of errors. A miracle that the ship stayed afloat.

'Durnus!'

The shout came again, lifting the vampyre's head from the dead sailor's corpse he'd dragged into a cabin below, instead of hurling it over the side with the others. Both blood and soul rushed through his veins, though only one satiated his groaning stomach and shaking bones. Only one dizzied his mind. *Soul.* The blood was merely a taste of what the corpse gave him. Durnus' heart throbbed, not with the animalistic pleasure of a feeding vampyre, but of the more ancient blood within him. A power more than two millennia old, born of a great daemon cursed by all. His vampyre's form was weakening. All the spells and charms he had woven had failed. His former self resurging at last. For the first time, however, fear was gone. Only a feeling of gratification, and a lust for more.

Durnus drank deep, inhaling soul until his lungs ached. Shuddering as he breathed out, he let the body go limp. The loose threads of the soul drifted from his bloody lips as cobalt smoke. He wiped his lips and fangs and splashed water across his neck and borrowed shirt.

'Durnus!'

The mage's boots were pounding on the steps.

The vampyre was at the door within a blink. He surprised himself at the ferocity with which he opened it. He found the mage in the passageway, who was soon eyeing the corpse on the floor.

'Time to put yourself to use,' Farden said.

'Me? I tried to help earlier.'

'I bet you're stronger than I am by now,' Farden muttered. Durnus was about to protest and snap uncharacteristically, but he saw the gaunt edge of Farden's cheekbones, and found calm.

The mage was indeed ageing. Faster and faster each day, it seemed. Though seventy winters had passed since he had come screaming onto this earth, the Scalussen armour had stalled the wearing of the years somewhere around thirty winters. He had cheated death, but now it was collecting its debt. It broke Durnus' heart to see his friend so ravaged. Behind his eyes, Durnus saw the chaos whirling, no matter the quietly simmering exterior Farden wore. No doubt he stared back at Durnus thinking the same thing of him: troubled. *Scared.* He would be right.

Each of their daemons hung silently between them, unspoken. Durnus wracked his mind for something else and adequate to say. He realised all words were empty. Only actions could talk. His friend needed his help and nothing more, no matter the cost. Durnus took a step from the door and made his way to the stairs.

'Wipe your face,' Farden called after him. 'There's still blood on your chin.'

The deck greeted him with brisk wind and angry, flapping sails. The *Seventh Sister* was being blown sideways to the waves. Aspala was at the helm and doing her best to fight the winds.

The minotaur sat hunched on the steps of the bow.

'Warbringer is banned from touching anything,' Mithrid shouted. She was trying to tie a complicated knot around an iron cleat.

'It was accident,' she barked in defence.

'Hold that rope there,' Farden told Durnus. The vampyre did as he was told, and as Farden rescued a wild line, they finally managed to get the sail taut and under control. Slowly, they adjusted it until it caught the wind, driving them south and closer to the coast, flat keel slapping the whitecaps. Aspala kept the ship banked to a slight angle, making all of them lean.

For sailors as useless as they were, there was constant adjustment to be done. They hauled on all kinds of ropes until unarmoured hands were frayed. Durnus worked until he felt as frail as he had in Scalussen, but not a complaint was made in support of Farden.

Somehow, they kept the ship on course even as darkness claimed the sea. A waning moon and stars painted the slopes of the gentle waves silver. The wind had growing warmer by the mile even in the night hours. The rugged coastline of Normont fell away to sweeping coves of grey sand. Two islands stepped out into the Blue Mountain Sea, one small, its sibling much larger. They were far enough apart that Aspala and Mithrid – now helping to man the wheel – steered right between them. The Hâlorn girl had barely been herself all evening. The vampyre supposed the goddess' warnings had put them all in sombre moods. After all, Evernia told Mithrid she had no place in this quest, no purpose. Durnus would have despised the goddess just as she seemed to.

In the shallower waters of the channel, they came across barrels bobbing about, presumably tied to anchors deep below. Wrapped around their chains and staves were weeds that glowed milky green in the moonlight. Each barrel sported a sign and a long arrow that pointed in a general, broad direction thanks to how it wallowed about.

'Ingenious,' Durnus whispered. He pressed his fingers to the corners of his eyes, employing a swift spell to make out what the buoys said in the dark night. 'Lezembor, it says, and then a measurement that looks like two hundred. I am assuming miles.' Durnus kept reading as the cog sailed past each floating signpost. 'Kedi Ada, one hundred.'

'The place that the captain said he would take us,' said Farden, leaning against the mast with arms crossed.

As the *Sister* rounded the point of the smaller island, they saw the distant yet awe-inspiring glow of a sprawling city. Lezembor, presumably. Smaller settlements glowed all around the Bay of Souls. A larger stretch of glittering lights directly to the west beckoned.

'Where will we go?' asked Durnus.

Farden had already decided. 'I'm not venturing into another city again.'

Mithrid called down to them. Trying, somewhat, to appease the mage's distrust, Durnus wagered.

'But your armour's still broken,' she said. 'There might be a smith—'

'Nothing's worth the risks we faced in Vensk. If the Doomriddle says we find the third task past the roaring waters, then that's where we go. There's even less time to waste.'

'Agreed,' said Durnus, drawing unusual stares.

Warbringer had given up on trying to sail and was currently trailing a fishing line as thick as Durnus' thumb. He did not want to imagine what she intended to catch.

'What of cursed knife? Loki will follow us,' she advised.

'Oh!' Farden called to her, watching Mithrid from the side of his eye. 'I'm counting on it!'

'You have a plan, then?'

'You know me and plans, Durnus. They never turn out as expected. Why try? Win and not die. That is all I will hold myself to.'

'That does not fill me with the greatest comfort—'

Mithrid interrupted before he could get further. 'What are we going to do with this ship? I don't know about you but sailing through roaring waters doesn't sound fun!'

Far from comforting, Farden had no reply. Durnus watched him grip the wheel and set a stare almost directly south, where a dark and rocky coastline beckoned. Only a few campfires or villages gleamed along the whole stretch of land.

For hours they stood in relative silence, watching the strange new land come closer, and closer, and closer still without the mage changing course. A beach ringed with toothy rocks could be seen under the moonlight. Pearlescent sand and skinny grey trees stretched for miles. A lone fire burned on the beach. Three lithe figures watched the ship's approach with some alarm. One even started sprinting down the sand.

Durnus held on tight as Farden let the ship grind on the sand and pebbles. The noise was horrendous to his vampyre's ears, shattering the empty night. Thankfully, it was brief. The cog wallowed to one side, its fat bottom coming in use for once. Farden vaulted over the side and splashed heavily in the shallows. Durnus saw him struggle to get up, but before he could assist, the mage limped up the beach without him. The others followed. The splash of Warbringer soaked him. He hunched, dripping from his brow, and glared at her.

'It's warm,' Mithrid said in whispering wonder. 'The water's bloody warm.'

The strangers around the campfire were poised, short spears held low and cautious. Their skin beyond their cotton trews was dark like the rocks around them, and their eyes yellow in the night. Their arms and legs were painted with intricate spirals of glistening alabaster clay.

'We mean no harm,' greeted Durnus.

'Who ares you pale faces?' rasped one in a voice and accent quite unlike anything he had ever heard. The man had scars running from his lips down to his throat. 'Speaks!'

Farden decided to handle this negotiation and moved the vampyre aside. 'Would you like a boat? A ship, you could say?' he asked.

'Pale face speaks stranges,' the scarred man replied.

Farden jabbed a thumb at the *Seventh Sister*. 'We don't need her any more. If you want her, she's yours. It may need a clean, but...'

Suspicious looks were traded between the speaker and the silent. 'What bargains? What tricks?' he demanded at last.

Farden shook his head. 'No trick. No price. Just tell us where to find the roaring waters.'

The quiet man pinched his lips and whistled. Another sound to make Durnus wince. The third fellow, still full tilt across the beach, skidded to a halt. He began a loping return.

'This Bay of Souls,' continued the scarred. 'We's Chanarks. We's lives here. Always haves and always wills.'

'We would like to travel to the roaring waters,' said Farden.

The Chanark nodded sagely. 'Many faces, both pale and tan comes to sees. Most takes caravans road from Lezembors. War of norths and souths brews, but none comes yet. Chanarks wants none part.'

With caution, he approached. The other two skirted around their strange group to inspect the ship. Their hands wandered over the barnacles and dripping seaweed of the hull. They whistled low, reminding Durnus of the gryphon.

'We accepts,' said the Chanark. He came closer to Farden, taking a closed seashell from a pocket within his baggy white trews. Farden did not move, but Durnus could see the tension in his limbs. The Chanark opened the shell's halves to show an intricately carved little compartment filled with silver paint. With a long and spindly finger like that of a spider's leg, he daubed Farden across his forehead.

'You mays now pass upon the roads. Until Khandri's borders. Diamond Mountains,' he said.

The man waved his guttering finger from west to south, where a dark void in the sky spoke of huge and distant peaks. Always peculiar given his vampyre nature, but Durnus longed for daylight to see this new land by. The only upside to the trials of this quest was that he could finally look upon places only glimpsed in tomes and books. Places he had spent centuries wishing to visit. Too long, he had spent being a hermitous scholar, or as a servant of the Arka.

'The roarings waters ares south. Thundershores, we names them.'

Farden bowed deeply in Emaneska style, trying not to groan as he straightened. 'Thank you,' he said. 'Enjoy your ship. And if a fat man ever comes asking for it, do with him as you will.'

The Chanark weaved his hands in a bow of his own, and with the moon watching on, their brief meeting parted. Saddling supplies onto their backs and setting foot to the gritty sand of another new land, they walked onwards into yet another night filled with the darkness of the unknown. Another foreign road.

Durnus was not the only one who kept a furtive watch over his shoulder.

# CHAPTER 26
## GAUNTLET

*I am to be ever cursed for meddling, it seems. My experiments with perfect-*
*ing the vampyre venom, though arduous, were arguably and thankfully a*
*success. My blindness was cured by the vampyre's strength. I am immune to*
*the fire of sunlight at last, and the fangs I missed all those years as Ark-*
*mage, in my true form, have returned. But the frailty is a constant*
*hindrance. A curse in addition to the hunger for blood I was prepared for.*
*However, it seems my experiments with necromancy have had the opposite*
*effect, and awakened something... other. Older. I fear my true form has aris-*
*en despite the strength of the vampyre's curse, and that no other magick will*
*now dampen it.*
*I must resist the urges of my parentage, my daemon's blood. I cannot fail*
*Farden. I cannot fail Emaneska.*
FROM THE WRITINGS OF DURNUS GLASSREN, YEAR 925

'You sure about this, Elessi?' Lerel spoke, slapping a hand onto the
wheel of the *Summer's Fury*. Though carved by the same shipsmiths,
it felt distinctly different to the wheel of the *Vanguard*. Borrowed.
Belonged to another.

'I'm sure I've already made my decision, if that's what you
mean,' Elessi said, giving her a sidelong look. Despite the growing
heat of day, she still insisted on wearing her general's furs. 'Whether
it's the right one, I guess we'll see soon enough. There's no other
captain I'd trust than you, that's for sure.'

Lerel puffed out her cheeks. She reeled off their status to calm
her own nerves. 'One bookship gutted of everything except food and
weapons. Every ballista is loaded and manned. One hundred mages

and soldiers aboard. A hundred and fifty crew. Every one of them mad enough to join us.'

'And Hereni only asked for fifty good souls.'

'See? You're not alone.'

Elessi didn't look back to the beach. 'Feels it, seein' as we've got twenty or so thousand staring back at us, all a-wonder what in Hel we're up to.'

Lerel looked. Past the shallows, where the trains of bodies loaded the last supplies and unloaded the final cargo, all of Scalussen and the Jar Khoum watched the *Fury* ready to sail. The sun had only just risen, and yet the warmth was already growing to scorching. Umbrellas of palm branches wafted back and forth. Every surviving dragon had gathered, and they glittered like huge jewels in the bright sunlight. Their kaleidoscope of colours reached all the way down the beach. She saw Kinsprite and Shivertread flanking Towerdawn. They seemed to be arguing something. Older dragons like scarlet Clearhallow and Glassthorn watched with shaking heads. Nerilan was not to be seen.

What tore at Lerel's heart with the teeth of wolves, however, was Eyrum, standing defiant in the shallow waters, crutches repeatedly sinking in the sand as waves lapped at him. Sturmsson stood with him, a hand hovering to help but always shrugged away. Eyrum glared at them with his one eye, grey scales shining in the morning sun. It had been his decision to stay, but she could tell he loathed it. She ached to tell him he was wrong, that he was needed. But in truth, with Lerel and Elessi gone, Scalussen needed the general's mind to keep them from the mutiny she privately feared.

'What is this plan of yours, then, other than "go that way"?' She pointed out from the bay to the still slumbering ocean. She had to nudge Elessi to get a response.

Elessi cleared her throat of its tired grit. 'Draw the leviathan along with us and kill it in open waters, as we did the last two. Loki will have nothin' to threaten us with then. Scalussen will be safer than we are with the Jar Khoum. All Loki has are the daemons. There's no army left in Emaneska to raise, after all.'

Lerel nodded to every word without speaking.

Elessi had to ask. 'What're you thinking?'

Lerel laughed. 'That this is insane, but I believe it's the best chance we've got. Never liked having my fate in somebody else's hands, never mind the promise of that poisonous little cunt they call a god.'

Elessi spluttered, her severe demeanour at last cracking into a smile. Even Ilios trilled with amusement. 'That he is,' said the general, sighing as if finally understanding some riddle. Lerel had a mind to send her below to sleep, but there was no point trying.

Two figures came aboard below.

'If it isn't Bull the monster-slayer!' Lerel cried, raising a cheer from a crowd of sailors. Bull grinned wide, cheeks red and bashful. Hereni looked too busy for merriment. She stormed up the stairs to the bridge ahead of the lad, polished crimson armour clanking and a sword between her shoulders.

'Let's get this bookship moving!' Hereni announced with a clap of her hands. Despite the polish, the steel plate still bore scars of battle and leviathan spit.

'Aye aye, Captain!' smirked Lerel. 'What's your rush?'

'Got us a leviathan to kill and people to save, haven't we?'

Elessi rested a hand on Hereni's shoulder. 'That's the spirit we need. You ready?'

Lerel caught the fire in the blue of the mage's tired eyes. She smelled of smoke and char. 'Ready for what?'

Hereni had already answered with a curt nod. 'You'll see,' said Elessi.

'You know what? I've grown really tired of surprises,' Lerel sighed, as she felt the ship's heartbeat beneath her: the groan of wood and iron, the slight wallow back and forth with the waves, the footfalls of the sailors running with cargo. The bookship felt alive, and she was at one with it.

'Raise anchors! Make ready to sail!' she bellowed, making Elessi and Bull flinch away at her practised volume. Teams on the shore had already dug the keel free with the help of high tide, and began to push and pull at ropes. The *Fury* swivelled to face the endless west. Lerel's bosuns and mates, borrowed from the *Vanguard*, worked levers upon the three masts. Clockwork sang its rattling tune as colossal sheets of black canvas unfurled from the spars. Sailors bent to the capstans, hauling up the two thick anchor chains in with barks of rhythmic, 'Heave!'

'Wind mages, get ready!'

Across the ship, within the masts and on ramparts against the aftcastle, the mages took up their stances. Hands and lips weaved spells until the still, crisp air of fragrant palm and fire-smoke began to whip their cloaks and hair. Lerel felt the tingle in the air as they focused their magick between sprawled fingers, ready.

'Anchors up, Admiral!' came a report from the main deck.

Their departure seemed a sombre event. Tears ran down faces. Prayers to the old gods were rampant. That was until Eyrum grew tired and roared at the height of his lungs.

'For Scalussen!'

Cheers broke from the crowds. Dragons' roars and dragonfire filled the morning air. What had been funereal became the shouts of glory and honour. Battle-cries. The crew of the *Fury* joined them, from the sailors' cries to the gryphon's keening screech. The Jar Khoum must have been deafened.

'LET FLY!' Lerel joined their roars. The mages unleashed their spells, and the *Summer's Fury* leapt across the waters as if it had a damning thirst for blood and battle. With her holds and libraries emptied, the huge bulk was lighter, more nimble. That dawn, she was a warship, no longer a bookship. Lerel relished every tremble of the rudder.

A glisten of colour called her attention. Blue and silver scales pirouetted overhead, much to the whistle of the gryphon. Lerel thought Kinsprite and Shivertread were putting on a display before they landed with a scrape of claws on the rear of the ship. The *Fury* was built just the same as the *Vanguard*, with landing areas and eyries for a dozen dragons at a squeeze.

'What are you doing?' Elessi approached them, raising her hands as if to calm them.

'We are joining you on this mad voyage,' Shivertread replied as his scales flushed an obsidian hue. 'Our queen was not happy. Cursed us, even, but Towerdawn understood. On the condition we don't perish, of course.'

Kinsprite bowed her head low to the general. 'We owe it to Farden and Mithrid. And Modren. They saved us, maybe we can do the same.'

Elessi rested her hand upon the dragon's snout and nodded in slow cadence. Lerel wondered what words, if any, passed between her and the young dragon. Memories, perhaps.

It was over within a moment.

'We're glad to have you,' said the general, withdrawing her hand. She looked to her skeleton crew with a grim smile and shouted over the wind. 'No turnin' back now! Hereni, shall we?'

Hereni clapped her hands together and wandered between the two dragons.

'If you'll excuse me...' she said, nonchalant as ever. Few in Scalussen had as much swagger as that mage. Not a tattoo graced Hereni's skin, and yet many had thought her a Written because of her power. Not to mention the fact she had barely seen twenty winters. Lerel had, and always would, blame Farden for teaching her his ways.

'What're you doing?' Lerel asked, snatching looks over her shoulder. They were coming to the southern hook of the bay and her attention was needed.

'Gambling, as Nerilan would put it,' answered ELessi. 'I'm still of the opinion those leviathans were drawn by magick. We might not 'ave a pile of spellbooks aboard, but we've got wind mages. And our good Hereni there. Finest mage we've got this side of the map.'

While Elessi spoke, Hereni took a stand upon the very rear of the bookship and stared upon the wake and the beach they left behind. Already, Scalussen's survivors looked small.

Lerel turned the wheel and moved the ship around the headland, sending the *Fury* out into open, choppier waters. Her iron blade of a keel sliced the whitecap waves with barely a shudder. She glimpsed Hereni with her hands splayed.

With a whip-crack, two orbs of fire burst into life above the mage's palms, yellow as her locks. Hereni bowed her head, forcing the spell to greater levels. The flames grew in size, burning dark and crimson as she made them crackle and spin. There she stayed, arms splayed, spells burning fiercely in a meditation of power as Lerel guided the bookship south down the last westerly coast of Paraia.

The dragons spotted it first. Not a leviathan, much to the ship's relieved heart, but a green sail far on the southern horizon, where the waters were stained gloomy with cloud-shadows.

As soon as the other ship spotted the *Summer's Fury*, it turned tail and ran along the coast. The dragons watched with their sharp eyes, as did the lookouts and their spyglasses, but the ship was lost to distance and clouds.

'Reckon that might be the pirates the Jar Khoum talked about?' Bull asked. He was preening the scarlet fletching of his arrows, seeing how many he could stuff into a quiver before it became ridiculous.

The gryphon regarded him with the placid gold of his eagle's eyes. The trilling whistle that came from his beak meant nothing to

Bull, but the others had told him how smart Ilios was. A mortal mind trapped in a feathery body.

'I reckon so, too,' he said. Bull had been wary of the beast first. Not only was he the Forever King's beast, but even at half the size of a dragon, somehow the gryphon seemed more dangerous. Perhaps it was the unintelligible attention of his eyes, or the curved black claws that sprouted from every foot. A monster, Bull would have called him in Troughwake. Not now.

Out of arrows to check, Bull resigned himself to the waiting that seemed part of being aboard a ship. With nothing to do but keep watch, and with eyelids of lead thanks to a sleepless night of carrying cargo, Bull found his head drooping against his chest.

It felt as if he gave in for only a blink, but when he awoke, he was leaning against the broad grey and tawny feathers of Ilios' wing. The sun had moved halfway across the sky. The coasts had changed, now a sage green instead of the sandy yellow that had followed them for days. The gloom to the south had only darkened. Bull could see the foam of wind-chased waves.

The gryphon growled to the boy, nudging him awake. Confused, Bull watched Ilios trot across the deck. It was then the shouts made sense to his ears. It was Lerel, yelling at him.

'Bull! Sweet gods, shake the seawater from your ears, boy. It's here! It's worked!'

Bull tripped over his own big feet as he bounded upright. After adjusting his leather jerkin, his bow was quickly in his hand, an arrow in the other. 'A leviathan?' he asked.

'You bet your fluffy beard, boy!' Lerel bayed. Bull couldn't tell whether it was excitement or fear that animated her. 'The bastard has picked up the mage's scent. Look there!'

While probing the scattered hairs of his chin, Bull followed Lerel's finger and the cries of the lookouts. In the widening ripple of their wake, stretching miles behind them, Bull saw the blue fins he had come to hate so much, surging after them in sinuous motion.

Not a thread of fear held him back as he marched to the stern. He only saw a job to do. A task in the way of reaching Mithrid.

Hereni still stood at the edge of the *Fury*, now bent at the knees and arms drooping. With a cry, she finally gave in, letting her magick die and collapsing to her knees. Bull could feel the heat emanating from her armour as if she was a fireplace.

'Hurricane, mage. You'll burn yourself out before the battle,' he warned her. He tried to help and almost singed his fingers.

Hereni cackled between gasps. 'Worth it. Think I just set a record.'

'Don't speak too soon, Hereni. We still have to win this battle.' Lerel ordered. 'Not to mention we're drawing close to the Cape of No Hope. We're about to turn around Paraia, and the sea gods charge a high toll for that!'

'Let the storms come.' Elessi was striding across the bridge, eyes aflame and narrowed at the leviathan. 'This ends today.'

Lerel mock bowed to her. 'What's your plan then, General?'

'Kill it, nothin' more elaborate than that. Bull, I want you on one of the dragons. Shoot it from the air, aim for its eyes like you did before, you hear me?'

A rare shiver of trepidation ran through the boy. 'You want me to be a... dragon-rider?'

'Don't get too full of yourself and start sproutin' scales now, Bull. Kinsprite!' Elessi yelled as one of the dragons swooped near.

'Yes, General!' the dragon boomed. With gusts of wind, she landed next to Ilios, who trilled in complaint at his ruffled feathers.

'You keep this boy safe, understand?'

Kinsprite bowed solemnly and extended a wing for Bull to climb. A rider's saddle already waited on her spined back. Bull had not ridden a dragon since leaving Troughwake, and he did not hesitate at the chance to do so again. In his thrill, he took far too many attempts to strap himself into the saddle.

'Hereni, you and your mages make that fucker's life a seething Hel. I don't want it coming out of the water without a dozen spells hitting it in the face. Kinsprite and Shivertread, blast it with fire until the water boils. Lerel, you just keep this ship movin' and afloat.'

Lerel needed no more. 'Wind mages! I want to make this a running battle! Keep pushing and give me all you've got. Let's tire this beast out before we tangle with it!'

At last, Bull secured himself, and just before the dragon bounded from the rear of the *Fury*, he felt the bookship heave ahead. The sails bulged, testing every stitch and line.

The thrill of leaving the deck and the surface of the sea behind was enough to make Bull forget about the leviathan and their dire task all at once. He almost let go of his bow he was so entranced by the wind rattling the skin of the dragon's wing, the feel of her breath beneath him. For a blessed moment of freedom, he took his hands from the saddle's horn and let his arms feel the wind as if he were the only one flying. He laughed aloud, knowing Mithrid would have hated every second of it.

And so the race began.

The leviathan did not once rear from the water as it had on the last chases. It powered through the water, casting up a bow wave and spray as it chased the *Summer's Fury*. Hours passed, until the sun was beginning to die above the wild coast.

Bull hadn't let the monster out of his sight for a moment. His neck ached from looking over his shoulder so much while the dragons flew alongside the ship. Inch by inch across the miles they sailed, the leviathan had caught them up. It was now so close Bull could have counted its fangs if it dared to show any. The blue fin still thrust from the ocean. Instead of tiring, it seemed only to grow hungrier and more determined the closer it came to the *Fury*.

He heard Lerel's roar over the wind. 'This is it! Ready mages! Ready ballistae! Ready dragons!'

*Bull,* boomed a voice in his head. He was glad he was strapped in. The shock would have dislodged him.

'Was that you, Kinsprite?' he shouted over the wind.

*It was. Hold tight!*

Bull held on for dear life as the dragon swept up into the air, somersaulted on her wing, and swept towards the leviathan.

Bull's cold fingers struggled to nock his arrow to the bow. The wind battled him fiercely.

'Ready!' the dragon roared aloud. Her wingtip drew an arc of spray as she swung perturbingly close to the waves.

The leviathan chose that moment to erupt from the sea. Its mighty crowned head burst into view in a storm of seawater, jaws splayed and roar deafening. Bull knew fear for a sliver of a second, just as it looked like Kinsprite would be swallowed whole.

Bull almost forgot to loose his arrow. The seething fire exploding from the dragon's jaws reminded him. He fired by instinct, sending his arrow spinning into the leviathan's face. The dragon tore into the sky as the leviathan submerged once again.

'I missed!' Bull yelled.

As Kinsprite wheeled to chase the leviathan, the bookship opened fire. Arrows peppered the ocean, turning the leviathan's scales into a small forest of fletching. The arrows drew no blood, broke no scale. Spells turned the water into a churning mess of lightning and fire. Hereni led the volley, blasting the sea with her fire spells. Clouds of steam amassed in the *Fury*'s wake, and even so. the leviathan continued to chase them.

The dragons swooped together, hovering to blanket the leviathan's back with dragonfire. The sea bubbled now, but the leviathan was always ahead of the heat, pressing on after the ship.

Again and again, the dragons made their attacks until they ran themselves breathless with the effort. The leviathan was now practically gnashing at the *Fury*'s stern, only feet away. Hereni and her mages poured spell after spell on the beast, but nothing seemed to halt it. Bull saw the answer plain as the ocean before him. *The creature had learned.* Without emerging from the sea, the ballistae and spells were half as effective.

Bull caught sight of Elessi and Lerel as Kinsprite skimmed the *Fury*'s bridge. Their faces were not as confident as they were before. Lerel was baying at the mages for more wind.

Bull grit his teeth as they swooped. He saw the creature's fierce eyes just below the roiling wake as Kinsprite held level. Shivertread lashed out with flame. Bull waited, his hands trembling with effort at keeping his longbow drawn. The seconds dragged out, and yet still he waited. Even when the leviathan had sprung for a mad lunge at the stern of the *Fury*, he held off. Bull even waited for its jaws to sink into the rear cabins, for the pristine moment where the leviathan paused, still, and clinging like a bloodthirsty wrackle.

The string of the bow scraped Bull's cheek. The tension in his arms popped. He watched the arrow embed itself deep below the leviathan's eye. The creature let go of the ship immediately before thrashing into the water.

'Well done, boy!' cried the dragon.

Fallen back though it had, the leviathan was undeterred. Once again it began its chase, making up the distance quickly now that it had stalled the *Fury*.

'This isn't going how I thought it would!' Bull yelled.

'I think that feeling is mutual.'

Lerel was shouting increasingly high-pitched orders. Elessi was observing the ship's wake with arms crossed and face white as ice.

Bull felt a frustration growing within him. He began to fire madly at the leviathan. Half his arrows trailed behind in the ocean.

'Oh, what is this now?' he heard Lerel's cry across the water.

*Look ahead, boy.*

Bull's head shot around. Betwixt the churning sea and a bank of clouds that looked like the walls of Scalussen, he saw them. *Ships.*

At least six of them if his windswept eyes didn't lie. They had the same green sails as the vessel that had run from them. They were spread in a short line across the sea, stretching from the coast like a net.

'Who are they?' yelled Bull from the dragon's back.

The shout was muffled but unmistakable. 'Pirates!'

'Pirates!' bellowed Lerel. 'Now, of all times.'

Elessi could have screeched her curses to the blackened sky. She was about to, her throat brimming with anger, when an idea burst into her mind. 'This could work in our favour!'

Lerel stamped her foot on the deck. The admiral's conviction seemed to be collapsing fast. 'How the fuck, exactly?'

'I bet those pirates won't be expecting a leviathan as well as a ship,' Elessi hissed. 'We kill our magick and let it feast on the confusion.'

'You brilliant bitch,' Lerel said, admiring her madcap notion. 'It's better than nothing!'

Elessi wholeheartedly agreed.

The admiral bent her back to the wheel, turning the bookship directly for the centre of the pirate fleet and the stormy waters. 'Full speed, mages! Don't you let up on me now!'

Elessi hung on to the railing, her head flitting back and forth as she watched their enemies close in from either side. With the pirates' riding the storm-front at full sail, expecting a fine catch, they closed the distance as fast as the leviathan did. Thunder rolled at their sterns.

Running to the bow to look upon the sails of the pirates, Elessi saw the faded symbols of the Arka Empire in the day's last light. Even as freezing rain started to lash her face, she found herself grinning, the madness of the situation getting to her. At very least, she thought, they might fulfil the promise she had made to the Jar Khoum. Either that, or all of them would be at the bottom of the

Cape of No Hope within the next hour, a leviathan feasting in their remains. Elessi steeled herself. This is what she had chosen. This was her gamble. There was naught to do but cling on, and hope. Not a prayer to the gods escaped her lips or ran through her mind. This was her fate, not theirs.

Within half an hour, they could hear the beating drums of the pirates over the roar of wave and wind. Their ships had closed their net, drawing closer together as the *Fury* approached. The bookship aimed straight for the largest ship at the centre. They were motley vessels, patched and repaired over and over, bucking wildly on the towering waves, but they were formidable enough. More than enough, even for a single bookship.

Figures could be seen crowding the railings, enduring bucket after bucket of spray. Torch and brazier-fire shone orange on their readied blades. Grappling hooks spun in hands. Bows were trained. Elessi stared at them through her spyglass and urged them closer. Behind her, she heard ballistae crews standing by. She felt the magick swelling across the deck. The *Summer's Fury* was set for battle.

'Something's wrong!' yelled Lerel from the bridge, shattering Elessi's hope in one fell swoop.

Elessi ran as fast as her tired feet could carry her. Breathless by the time she reached the aftcastle, she gasped at the admiral, who only pointed aft.

After a day of chasing them ragged, the leviathan had turned tail and fled. The vexation scored Elessi deep. 'I...' she gasped. Terror fell like an avalanche. She had made the wrong decision yet again. The bookship was doomed on its first day. Imagined or not, she felt the eyes of the sailors and mages on her, silently blaming her.

The dragons dragged her gaze up and over to the pirate fleet waiting with open arms.

'Get ready to fight!' was all Elessi could shout, her voice cracking. 'No rest 'til just—

The mood on the pirate ships switched all too suddenly. She saw the figures on the bulwarks turn, saw bows dropped and heard distant shouts fill the air. Ahead of their ships, the waves began to bubble furiously.

'I thought we killed the other leviathans!' Elessi yelled to Lerel. The admiral had no answers, just wide eyes and a snarl frozen on her lips.

Hereni rushed to their side to see what was happening. 'We did!' cried the mage.

Whatever was happening, it panicked the pirates as much as the bookship. They were frantically trying to come about, as if scuttling out of the bookship's way. Without the leviathan in tow, it made no sense. Elessi blurted to the others without hesitation. 'What's going on?'

Every soul upon the *Fury* stared aghast as some... *thing* began to emerge from the roiling sea at the pirates' stern. First, the lance of an enormous bowsprit, coiled like a horn, burst from the waves. Behind it came the encrusted prow of a ship that almost rivalled the bookship in size. The rest of it rapidly surfaced in a detonation of sea-spray. Not a sail beyond rags hung on its huge and barnacled masts. Not a sailor or captain manned its deck. Elessi looked on, horrified to her core, as the planks of the ship's hull kept rising, revealing a flat expanse of what looked to be green rock. It enveloped its very keel as if the ship had sprouted from it.

Yet it was no rock. Ahead of them, the surface of the sea lifted as if the hand of a giant cupped the ocean to drink. Two of the pirate ships seemingly ran aground on the hellish ship's bedrock, capsizing immediately as the waters kept rising. Beneath its roiling surface, Elessi saw the honeycomb patterns of black stretching across the green like a tortoise's shell. Scarlet tentacles thick as trees surfaced, reaching up like the curled spires of a city, far above the bookship's mast.

'All hands, HOLD!' Lerel bayed over the roar.

The giant tentacles went to their brutal work. One of the pirate ships was pulverised into splinters while another was strangled until its two halves collapsed into the ocean. The *Summer's Fury* careened helplessly towards the maelstrom of tentacles.

For all the fear of the leviathan, Elessi felt herself paralysed by the scene she watched. She could only hold on for her dear life as Lerel manoeuvred the *Fury* between the storm of water and tentacles. Waves drowned the decks. Elessi heard the iron hull of the ship grate on the shell with a piercing scream. The whole bookship leaned to one side as it teetered on the edge of the creatures shell. In a stomach-swallowing moment, the *Fury* fell back to the ocean. By the time Elessi could bring herself to look, the bookship was in quieter waters, spinning on a wake not of her making. With bated breath, the whole crew stared at the carnage behind them. The monster reared from the ocean like a submerged island taking breath. Its squid-like tentacles had sunk almost every ship in the pirate fleet within seconds. Unperturbed, it left the sinking wrecks behind. As soon as it had appeared, the monster disappeared in the direction of the leviathan. The skeleton ship stacked on its shell was drowned once more.

The storm wound on as if it had all been some grand, shared hallucination. A silence overcame the crew. Even as the rain and wind thrashed them, one by one, hands were prised from ropes and railings.

Elessi turned shaking to Lerel.

'What…' she breathed, '… just happened?'

The admiral took a while to find her voice. Her knuckles were as white as the bone beneath. 'I don't know,' Lerel admitted, shaking like a leaf in winter gales. 'But I'm worried if I question it, it won't have happened.'

Unlike Elessi, she refused to look back and turned the wheel of the bookship closer to the wild shore of the Cape of No Hope. Compared to what they had just witnessed, the storm's frenzy seemed like a millpond.

It was with shaking hands and a trembling lip that Elessi drew up her hood, and watched the night swallow the strangest of days while the *Summer's Fury* set her bowsprit to the east at last. The Silent Sea beckoned to them with beckoning forks of lightning.

# part four

## TASKS EVEN GODS
## FEAR TO FACE

# CHAPTER 27
## THE THIRD TASK

*Many believe life to be exploring the known world around us and the limits of mortal threads. In truth, life is no more than surviving the world around us.*
FROM THE PHILOSOPHER FRENNETH

It had taken a whole night of travelling through dark sand-dunes and tors shaped like tree-stumps to find the roaring waters of the Doom-riddle. The Spinning Sea, or the Thundershores, as the Chanark had named them. The dawn brought their roar to their ears.

It appeared the shores were somewhat of an attraction to the sweltering region, that incidentally, was comprised of sand, pebbles, and hardly anything else. By the time Mithrid had walked far enough to hear the Thundershores, the sun was barely a thumb's length above the horizon, and she was already intensely bored of this newfound heat and dust. Under the morning sun, she found herself longing for the ice of the north. At very least, for the tepid winds of the Riven-plains. Her northern blood was not fond of this scorching sun.

From where they had beached the ship, the Thundershores were a straight shot due south. The strangers had walked unbothered for most of the night until they had come across the roads. There, they found the bustling caravans.

Given the uninhabited theme of the rest of the Chanark coun-try, Mithrid had been expecting nothing upon the roads. The sandy paths reminded her of the Sunder Road, but instead of a handful of wagons and traders, these roads teemed. Caravans of sheltered wag-ons and carts ran in trains miles long, back and forth across the road.

Some were so long, they tangled with other caravans and caused bitter arguments. Trade was so ubiquitous, half the caravans didn't wait to reach their destinations to set up shop and stall. They spread along the road in impromptu markets, hawking at the other passengers of the road with unrelenting ferocity. Kites crackled above their fabric roofs. Spices blew in the wind from dishes, yellows, reds and blues. All kinds of creatures hung from hooks, smoked or roasted. Garments and fabrics turned the road into a tunnel through kaleidoscope colours. There were even merchants selling replicas of the Thundershores by the dozen: small rings of carved wood and stone. Maybe it was the craftsmanship, but they did not look like much.

It had taken an hour to extricate themselves from the markets. The road was less busy but no less congested by wagons and beasts. Tall, straw-coloured creatures with humps on their backs gargled and groaned with every touch of their rider's switches. Coelos and the scaled persnippen birds were common, along with the lizard hybrids they had seen outside the Spoke.

As many people made the pilgrimage to the Thundershores as left with awe on their faces. Two columns moving in opposite directions ruled the road. Mithrid, Farden and the others fell in with the slow step of the caravans.

At last, they came to the ocean's edge. A line had formed for viewing, corralled by ribbons between sticks. A man in a violently green hat was shepherding people along one by one, taking coins for his service. Farden didn't bother with the guide, and instead, much to the man's vitriolic complaints, led the others towards the shore himself.

The ground beneath their feet rose up as if to meet the arch of cliffs. The closer they came to their apex, the more the wind howled, the louder the roar became, and the more Mithrid noticed the rumble under her feet.

Finally, squeezing between the crowds, they stood upon the brink of the Thundershores. Instead of a vertical drop as Mithrid expected, the cliffs sloped away in jagged intervals to the shape of a bowl. It spread into an almost perfect circle several miles across. Only one entrance to the bay existed, and it was a narrow mouth guarded by sharp rocks. Mithrid soon realised how the Thundershores had earned their name. The sound blasting her eardrums was enough of a clue. The cobalt waters within the circular cove whirled and churned madly. The spiralling waves smashed themselves against the rounded shores over and over, sweeping in a circle until they clashed with the fresh waters entering the bay.

Durnus seemed fascinated. The old man even began scribing notes in one of his books.

'Not impressed, Mithrid?' Farden grumbled next to her. He had not spoken to her since the *Seventh Sister*.

Mithrid had to admit she was. The haunting eye of water at the centre of the Spinning Sea was a dark sapphire and bewilderingly still. 'I am, but why do so many come? Ruins it.'

A willowy Chanark stranger clad all in yellow satin nearby decided to take it upon himself to answer. He too wore a green hat that clashed with the cloudless sky. 'It is the touch of the very God's Rent itself!' he said in accented but perfect Commontongue.

'I have no idea what you're saying,' admitted Mithrid.

'Far-travelled you must be! Worry not: we tolerate all and accept all, as long as they come in peace,' he explained. 'The great whirlpool beyond these shores is the God's Rent. Its grand churn echoes here in these Thundershores. It is as if you can hear the voices of the very gods themselves in its roar. Many come not just to see such the waters, but to pray, pilgrimage, some to offer their dead, believing the gates to the afterlife are here, at our feet.'

Mithrid looked closer around the ring of rocks and water. She saw all manner of groups within the crowds, denoted by varying shades of skin or different coloured cloaks or hats. There seemed to be a keen interest in headwear in the south of Easterealm. A dozen or so masked priests and conical hats wore all black. They must have been roasting. A stretch around the shores, another group in deep purple robes fed cotton-wrapped body after body to the punishing waters below.

Mithrid tried listening, but like the others, a constant air of urgency kept their minds distant. Farden's eyes persistently snuck to the west, as the riddle had dictated. The Thundershores were a signpost only, yet a poor one. The country of Chanark had proved itself nothing but a vast wasteland of bleached sand and rock, bordered by an endless range of distant mountains. Even the few settlements they had seen were flat, small, and tangled, with no architecture but plaster and adobe domes. The west was far too ambiguous, even with Durnus' map.

'Have you heard of Utiru, my good man?' ventured the vampyre, trying to put the stranger to use.

'You speak of Utiru the demi-goddess, yes?'

'Absolutely,' Durnus said, unflinching. Mithrid could have chortled.

'Her grave lies to the west,' he said, confirming the riddle's truth. 'A great er, rift – or canyon, as you say – lies in the Diamond Mountains. It is where she threw herself to die upon the shards of their peaks in rage. The tales tell of her displeasing the goddess of magick, Haspha, you see—'

Farden cut him off. 'Rage, you say?'

The guide bobbed his head, eager to have an intrigued ear. 'The canyon is near my town. Cursed, they say. Haunted. You can still hear Utiru's cries on certain nights. Where are you from, strangers? We've seen more and more of your sun-shy kind in recent years.'

'We are from places you likely have never heard of,' said Durnus, uncharacteristically impatient given his love for lore. Mithrid caught him glancing at Farden. 'Far to the west. A land called Emaneska.'

'You'd be right. Never heard of it! I would have said you were from Hartlunder if it weren't for your armour. Now, you should be careful journeying that way. South lies the Narwe Harmony, a great alliance of countries to the south grow restless and itch for war. Pale faces are coming down from Lezembor and further north, mining the richness of the Khandri's Diamond Mountains with no right or blessing from the Khandri or the Harmony.'

'*Ack, kansa behet al,*' hissed a nearby eavesdropper in Chanark paint. He showed his tongue to Mithrid and Farden.

'He says they – *you* to be precise – bring disease.' The guide held up his hands for peace and the man moved on. 'We Chanark are not part of their alliance and our borders do not touch the mountains. It is no war of ours, but not all think that. To go west will take you into Khandri territory. Pale faces are not welcome there, and your Chanark mark of welcome will not carry you far beyond our borders. You will have to barter passage, or run very fast,' the guide smiled before seamlessly switching to answer another visitor's question. The guide had drawn a small crowd of listeners. 'Why yes, several individuals *have* tried to swim in it, much to their regret…'

Mithrid and the others peeled away from the group, just in time for a woman to come bustling up to them. She seemed out of breath. Her vomit-green hat was askew. She babbled at them in another language before translating. 'You…' she gasped at Mithrid and the others. 'You can't just walk up to the edge and look without paying.'

Farden was uninterested in speaking with the woman. He walked on by, trudging down the slope while she buzzed around them like a fly. Only Warbringer seemed insulted.

'You not own this. You not build this. Why should we pay you for it?'

The woman stammered for an answer. 'Because… because…'

Warbringer was not done with her lesson. She spun Voidaran in her fist, making it cry out and driving the woman to back away. 'You can't ask for coin to look at sky, or walk upon the mountain. These were here before you and still exist long after you are gone.'

The minotaur's challenge did not go unnoticed or unheard by the queuing lines of people and pilgrims nearby. One man agreed with a wholehearted, 'Yeah!' and promptly broke the ribbon lines with his hands. The queues crumbled in moments, resulting in an uncontrollable surge to the edge of the Thundershores.

'Er... I think we better make ourselves scarce,' said Mithrid, as the conflict began to grow physical between the green-hats and those that wanted their coin back. Like the others, she stared in bewilderment. Crowds were strange and fickle beasts.

'They will learn,' grumbled Warbringer. 'Land not something to be owned.'

Feeling like being roasted alive was the order of the sweltering day. Mithrid had never known heat like it. A raw, incessant scorch that beat down as though she stood in a circle of bonfires. The dust and fine sand rose up to choke her. Every time she clenched her teeth, grit popped between her teeth. The black armour was smothering, becoming too hot to touch. Even when they carried their metal in sacks over their shoulders, walking was a drudgery. The shifting sand burned through their boots. Mithrid sweated in silence like the others. Only Aspala seemed free of such complaints, sniffing the hot air and striding ahead without a care, as if this was her home.

The country transformed from sand and scrubland to rolling hills. Skeletal trees that sprouted thorns as long as Mithrid's finger ran along the roads. They blossomed with oily black fruit as sour as salt, but they did offer one kindness, and that was their sage leaves cast a shade that they desperately welcomed. Skulls like they had seen in the marshes, big as wagons, sat encrusted with dry moss.

By midday, they strolled through a countryside covered in farms. Golden wheat grew in wild fields. The rest tilled vines in shallow craters dug from the barren soil.

Caravans and long trains of the humped beasts of burden crisscrossed their paths. Their flags were of Chanark and countries unknown. They received no bother except stares for the girl, mage, and vampyre. It was their pale faces the foreigners seemed suspicious of, though Durnus had gone grey rather than pale. Durnus asked each one of Utiru. Some laughed as they kept riding. Some cursed them for wasting their time and told them to go home.

One such passerby Mithrid would never forget. As they passed through a cheery village of marble-white buildings that shone blindingly in the sun, they found a disturbance in the road ahead. Carts and beasts were being herded to the road's gutters, giving way to a man who rode directly in the centre of the thoroughfare. His steed was a lumbering coelo, with its horn dressed in gold bands, beads, and silk sashes. Atop the ornate saddle, sat the man of spotted furs and gold chains connecting his nose, ears, and lip. He spun a wooden stick in his hands. Arms and chest also swaddled in gold, he was a bandit's wet dream, and yet due to what stomped behind him, Mithrid imagined he saw little trouble.

She thought them to be trolls at first. They were nine-foot tall at least, and their skin and bones were made of driftwood and splinters. Four of the beings altogether, walking in a line, their faces impassive whorls of wood studded with two glowing eyes and no mouths. Walking upon two legs, they moved with an awkward, lurching gait that was not exactly swift. In their hands were large wooden boxes wrapped in sheets. Warbringer could have been squeezed into one quite uncomfortably.

'Move aside!' barked their master, levelling his stick at the mage and the others.

For a moment, Farden looked as if he were about to teach the man a lesson in manners, but he relented silently and joined the others at the side of the sand road to stare. Children around their feet cheered. All but one of the golems moved its head to look at the crowds. His green eyes seemed dejected to Mithrid.

'Golems,' Durnus whispered. 'Creatures of rock or wood, made by magick. Like a troll but forged as one would a sword.'

'Which book did you read this in, Durnus?' Aspala asked.

'Farden, Inwick, and I fought one in Albion.'

Farden nodded. 'Built by a boy... a man named Timeon. Made it in my likeness, too.'

'Ouch. Must have been difficult to look at.'

While Warbringer guffawed and clapped the mage on his unarmoured back, Farden did not look amused. It was the third time Mithrid had failed to stoke some reaction from him. Now she had her proof he still harboured some resentment towards her.

Mithrid tutted and looked instead at the last golem to pass. There were sweeping and circular runes carved into its joints.

The spectacle had passed on, and so had they. Headlong, towards the growing band of jagged black that dominated the western skyline.

The closer they drew to the Diamond Mountains, they saw the faces of their fellow travellers change. Their first encounter with the northern interlopers the guide had mentioned was a band of them camped on a ridge beside the road. To Mithrid's eyes, they were oddly recognisable. Their armour was of steel plate, less ornate than Scalussen metal, angular and ridged to be almost like the carapace of beetles. Beyond that, from their square jaws and sunburnt skin, they could have passed for Albion or Arka with ease.

The strangers got up from their campfire to swig from wineskins and watch Mithrid and the others pass. They seemed equally confused as to where each other belonged.

'Lundish?' asked one of them as they passed. Mithrid had no idea what that meant. Like the others, all she offered in return was polite nods and smiles. They parted in silence and saw no more of them. They were not the last, however. Another group passed them not long after that, rattling south in wagons drawn by the scaled lizard beasts they had seen in the north. They snarled at the minotaur as if they could smell the blood on her horns from when she had gored one of her kin.

'Watch out, Khandri soldiers are about,' said one, sneering from the tent of his wagon, breathing pipe-smoke.

By afternoon, they had reached dusty foothills that crept from the mountains like broad buttress roots. The thorny forests spread up their slopes. From the hill Mithrid stared out from, she could see white scars of roads and towns spread across the undulating countryside. To the north, smoke arose from one of them. Not the campfire or chimney kind, but the burning things to the ground kind. Mithrid knew enough of war to recognise it immediately, and she wondered if it had been the guide's town.

At her side, Aspala sighed woefully, as if the sight had ruined the country for her. 'That must be the war they talked of,' she said.

If Mithrid peered, she could make out camps of bright yellow tents leeching over the mountainsides. Storm clouds gathered above them to the north. A wind was blowing towards it. The sight of the foul skies put a shiver through her spine.

Without discussion, Farden took a knee and shortly thereafter, collapsed into the dirt.

'What are you doing?' asked Durnus, taking off his black spectacles to better see the mage.

Despite the flush of his sun-scorched nose and cheeks, Farden looked increasingly dreadful. Somehow, the years rushing back to him at once took their toll in more severe ways. That's how it seemed to Mithrid's keen eyes. She watched him change daily. Fractions at a time, but it was getting faster. Time ate at him, just as the concern ate at her.

'Waiting for night,' said Farden.

'Why?'

'To cross the border with a better chance,' he replied, pointing to what looked like a watchtower Mithrid hadn't spotted yet. It sat upon the edge of a narrow river running a zigzag path south between the sandy foothills. 'And because I think I've figured the next part of the riddle. The scarred sister. Tyrfing once told me a story about the wars of gods and daemons before humans were created. You'll know the edda, no doubt. The gods made the sun to burn the daemons from the day, and when the daemons claimed the night, the gods created the moon. The daemons tortured it, leaving it scarred to this day. And so, the scarred sister's light.' Farden pointed to the half-moon already lurking between the peaks. 'Moonlight.'

Mithrid picked at dry lips. 'I wondered what you were chuntering about beneath your breath all day.'

'And if you asked me, that looks quite like a canyon.'

Aspala was right. Between the mountains, to the south of where they aimed, was a dark gap in the foothills. It forked deep into the mountainside, as if an unfathomable axehead had slammed into the ground aeons ago. Hardly a settlement dared to go near it.

Ducking behind the crook of the hill, they gathered some of the brushwood and built a fire to cook some of the supplies they'd retrieved from the *Seventh Sister* and kept from Mogacha. The sailors hadn't stocked much, but the captain had apparently had a great love of cured fish and cheese. It was a rich meal for their empty stomachs, but a little wine and the dry seaweed cakes helped it down.

Silence reigned in the last hours of the day as it had for most of their journey. There was plenty to say about their mysterious enemy as well as what lay beyond the third task. About Loki's knife, too, which burned a hole in Mithrid's mind. Yet nobody spoke. The mage had turned over to sleep. He snored fitfully. The knife hung on his belt. One arm was crooked over his sack of dead armour.

Durnus was studying the bone key again. In the light of the fire, and through its intricate carving, illuminated runes washed over his face. Warbringer had shut her eyes but looked to be praying to her strange minotaur god. Voidaran was clutched in her big paws. Aspala stood watch on the hilltop, painted a silhouette by the faint purple light of a sunken sun.

Without asking the vampyre, Mithrid reached for his satchel and brought forth the inkweld. The ink was desperately low, but she took a drip and wrote Hereni's name across the green pages. Durnus watched her with a raised eyebrow, but said nothing.

'I need to know they're still alive,' Mithrid whispered anyway. 'It's been days since we managed to speak to them.'

'We have checked the Grimsayer. They're alive.'

'I don't care.'

'They have likely done what Farden said and found safe harbour and are biding their time, staying safe while we complete this quest.'

Mithrid wrote the mage's name five times before she gave up.

'Are we worried about those storm clouds gathering in the north. They've only come closer.'

'Worried, yes. Not fidgeting with what I could call excitement.'

'Not excitement. I have been next to useless on this journey until the second task. I don't care what the goddess said. Maybe this is the part I play in all of this.'

'Do not be so concerned with the idea of fate, Mithrid. Fate can be a scapegoat of responsibility for lives lived poorly, or evilly. And in those whose hearts are purer, delusions of grandeur, or worse, madness trying to figure what one's path is. Life is the journey. Fate, if there is such a force, is the destination. To focus on the latter erases the former. As a scholar, I prefer to believe in coincidence, in happenstance, and in consequence. Even chaos can be beautifully prescient. Each breath can become a storm, in time.'

'I disagree,' said Aspala, crunching back down the slope. 'Fate is a goddess of Paraia. All of us have destinies that she decides for us.

For some, it is dying on the battlefield; others, the gutter. Others still become kings or killers.'

Durnus mused, rubbing the stubble that was sprouting across his chin. 'What kind of world is that where we have no choice?'

Grit shifted as Farden rolled over and sat up to look at the moon, now bright over the silver mountains. 'Leave the philosophy for another day. We have work to do.'

Perhaps it was the wine, but Mithrid blurted. 'Are you ever going to talk to me?'

The mage regarded her with sleepy but narrowed eyes.

'Why should I when you lied to us, Mithrid? Lied to me, to be precise.'

Mithrid clenched her fists. She'd rehearsed her lines. 'I didn't lie. I just didn't say anything about it.'

Farden scoffed. 'You've grown up more than that to still use such childish excuses.'

That scorched Mithrid. She felt her age under the gaze of the others watching.

Farden was not done. He spoke as he put on his armour piece by piece, punctuating his words with clangs and grunts. 'You said nothing when I found that knife, and that in itself is a lie. You could've put us all in jeopardy by keeping that back. But what offends me the most is that fact the foul bastard saved your life.'

'Farden?' Even Durnus looked shocked.

'Don't misunderstand me,' the mage said. His anger was the cold and calculated kind. Mithrid almost wished he would shout so she could vent the pressure she felt in her heart.

'I'm happy he did and ashamed to say I wasn't there instead. But why, Mithrid? Why is Loki so interested in keeping you alive?'

'I've asked myself many times. I don't know.'

'And that,' Farden growled before turning away, 'is what worries me.'

'Then why not just throw it away!'

'Because you'll get your wish soon enough, Mithrid. Your wish to prove yourself!' he yelled over his shoulder.

It had not gone as Mithrid had hoped, but there was no talking about it now. With questions spinning in a hurricane within her, she donned her armour despite Aspala's unneeded help and slogged down the hill after the others. The argument was dead, and she had lost. The mage was right: she had lied, but his punishment turned her guilt turned to anger. *How dare he, after all he had done wrong?*

Gauntlets creaking, Mithrid followed in guilty, raging silence.

The night was far too light for running outright across the landscape. Aspala and Durnus led the way, their eyes leading them down paths between the hills, sticking to scrub and goat paths. The dark was full of the yapping of foxes and owls. High above them, a shape swooped low. Fleetstar, blending perfectly with the night.

They had reached the river when shouts broke the calm. Clashes of steel made them hunker in the river's shallows, the cool water burbling against their legs.

Farden used the distraction. He sloshed through the river with wild abandon, breaking across the banks and into Khandri territory. Though the land looked no different from before, the air was different. Taut like a glass pane creaking beneath a heavy weight.

Over the next few hours, they wandered in furtive dashes across the land. Quiet villages slept on as they passed by unseen. Hounds were the only creatures that caught their scent, yapping at the night. By the time their masters had come to see what disturbed them, Mithrid and the others had already scampered on, further up the mountain slopes.

At last, they stood at the maw of Utiru's canyon. Only there did they pause to catch their breath and stare at their surroundings.

Above them, the canyon's gates stretched to the night sky. It was wider than it had looked in the distance. A hundred soldiers could have marched side by side. Dirty crystals spouted from the ground in clumps. Veins of them glittered in the crags of the rock. Most came to a sharp and angular point. Mithrid touched one as gently as she might a petal. Yet its cold glass cut her finger so keenly she only noticed when the blood came.

'Damn it,' she hissed.

'Scarred sister's light burns the path,' Farden said to the silent canyon mouth.

As they stood and waited, the moon crept along its nightly path. Its light washed down the canyon walls inch by inch. When it bathed the crystal veins, some of them began to glow with a colourless light and lit a rough path that weaved its way across the canyon's north wall.

'In we go.'

Walking in the half-light of the moon and the crystals, they entered the canyon. The crystals only grew in number and height as their path narrowed. Soon they were forced to duck under fallen arches of the giant geodes, or step delicately through fields of their clumps. Nothing stirred amongst the crystals. Not an insect. Not a bird. The only movement came from the occasional tumbling stone from the dragon on the cliff above, keeping watch, as always.

The light led them down a branch of the canyon where they had to walk in single file. It was not long before they stood at the entrance of a cave. A black hole lined with crystal, leading downwards into the rock. A cold breeze emanated from it. Mithrid swore she heard a voice float with it. Words she had never heard before.

'You hear that?'

'Just the wind, Mithrid,' said Farden, though his tone was far from certain.

'Are we going in there?' Warbringer cleared her throat. She scratched at the thick tufts of hair along her jaw.

'Where else would we go?' Farden said. 'You're not afraid… are you?'

The minotaur snuffled in insult. 'Katiheridrade is not afraid of anything.'

'I don't like the look of it,' Aspala said.

'I'm sure the Cult of the Allfather trusted in that very reaction,' Farden replied, before drawing his second sword and sauntering into the dark.

Waves of light glittered along the wall, throbbing like blood through veins, leading them deeper down. The entire tunnel was crystalline. Sharp spears of the quartz poked at them from the walls. Every footstep cracked like glass. Echoes refused to die, and still the wind blew across Mithrid's face. Getting warmer. Getting staler.

A clicking sound gave them pause. Weapons were raised. Voidaran sighed next to her ear. She looked back at the minotaur to see her wide-eyed, and her face a stark monochrome in the soulless light.

A corner in the tunnel gave them their answer. A crystalline spider the size of Mithrid's splayed hand tapped a ponderous path across the wall. It looked half-broken, stumbling on a missing leg. As the others gave it room, Mithrid leaned close to stare at its sparkling hide, but it dashed away from her shadow and scuttled down the tunnel wall.

'Follow it,' whispered the mage. They did so with a scuttling of their own, furtive, and barely keeping up with the rapid little insect.

It didn't guide them far until the tunnel changed. The inhospitable borehole became blunter, straighter, polished, even. Perfect, unmarred crystal lined the walls, so thick and deep as to look as if they walked in a tunnel of glass beneath a dead and empty sea. A floor of fine sand sighed under their boots. More of the spiders clinked across the walls and ceiling, gnawing at the crystal. The walls held the faint echoes of moonlight, and as they passed, reflections emerged to follow them. Everywhere Mithrid looked, her own green, wild eyes stared back. She menaced one reflection with a sword only to have it menace her right back.

'Only mirrors, Mithrid,' breathed Aspala.

But as Mithrid turned away, she saw her reflection pause for just a moment. She whirled around, but the murky visage mimicked her perfectly once more.

'There's some foul magick at work here,' she said. It was a guess. Mithrid felt nothing but the ever-present wind, and the eyes of her reflections watching intently.

Farden quickened his pace. 'I'm inclined to agree.'

Their shadows became maddening all too quickly. Mithrid stared at the others in the mirrors to escape her own, but even they tricked her. Between a blink, she saw Warbringer standing on a land-scape of burning marshes. Even she startled at that. In Durnus' mirrors, a glowing crown of fire hovered above his head. He looked wan even in that cold light. The vampyre gawked, just the same as Mithrid.

She noticed Farden standing stock-still in the middle of the path. He stared at her. Not directly, but via the walls. In his mirror, she saw a man of a hundred winters, bearded and grey, lost in the snow. But Farden ignored his visage. Mithrid turned to see what had stolen his attention, and lost her breath when she saw herself in grand black armour wreathed in shadow, and sitting on a throne ringed with flame. Beneath her, a fortress of white marble burned.

'What is that, Mithrid?' Farden barked.

'It's not me!' A city screamed below. Mithrid could hear their cries, taste the char on the wind.

Aspala was hammering on one of the mirrors, trying to reach a woman on a desert of endless dark sand. 'What's this place doing to us, Durnus?' she yelled.

The irascible clicking of the spiders' crystal claws increased in volume. It became a constant rumble.

'Gah!' she reeled away, swatting at her own arms as if she had unwittingly let go of her magick. Mithrid covered her ears, muscling ahead down the mirrored tunnel in the hope there was an end to this hallway of fractured nonsense. Spiders scattered in her path. One she even crunched with her foot.

'Mithrid! Wait!' came the shouts behind her.

It was then she saw Malvus, grinning in a mirror, dressed in all his finery and untouched by war or fire.

'Mithrid!'

But she was already swinging her axe.

The crystal shattered beneath her honed blade. A great crack spread across it. Malvus died away to reveal a shattered version of herself. All other reflections died with it. She wrenched her axe free and held it in two hands, heaving with breath.

'I do not think that was wise, my dear!' Durnus shouted. The others swiftly gathered around them as the rumble grew to the roar of a crashing wave.

Spiders, scores of them, spewed down the tunnel. They covered the walls, the ceiling, the floor. Durnus broke the air with a shield of magick as Warbringer roared. Mithrid began to spin her axe as Eyrum had taught her. Aspala stood ahead of her, sword flat and crouching low.

Just as the flood of spiders was about to fall upon them, the light sputtered out. The scarred sister's light failed them at their darkest moment. Mithrid couldn't help but yell in sheer panic. She felt the spiders crawling up her legs, their crystalline legs stabbing at her armour. One stabbed at her scalp and she sprang into the dark to get away from it. She swung her axe to and fro through the pitch black, crashing through heaps of them until she staggered on their dead corpses in the dark. The shouts and yells of the others filled her ears along with her own screams. There, covered by a hundred needle-like claws, she thrashed the air with her magick, but to no avail. Hot blood streamed from cuts across her body. Her panic became a blinding red maw that consumed her, and buried her there in the darkness.

# CHAPTER 28
## UTIRU

*The gods and daemons were not all that roamed the primordial aeons. Others creatures were born of the spark of life. Some that glowed with virtue. Others foul, full of trickery. All older than memory.*
SOURCE UNKNOWN

Sand filled his mouth. Blood, his eyes.

Farden retched until he could draw a breath without vomiting or choking himself. He reached out to wipe his face and found the claws of a spider beneath his hands. He recoiled sharply, and his body was swift to remind him of every cut, bruise, ache, and pain.

Farden shuffled away with a pained growl, but felt rock at his back. He reached out and groped another wall far too close to his face. In misery, he scrubbed sand across his face. From the resulting sting, wounds scored his scalp and cheek. Chin, and neck, too.

The mage could have cried with joy as he realised the light had returned. Faint, barely enough to see by, but immensely preferable to the pitch black. However, he had somehow buried himself in a gutter of rock.

*And spiders.* Farden shifted to find another crystal spider lying dead beside his head. Another fell atop him. He forced himself upright, keeping back a yell and brushing more of the foul creatures from his body. He was littered in their corpses, and somehow that had saved him. Almost retching once more, Farden crawled from his pit and looked around. He was still in that cursed hallway of mirrors. All that lay around him were the brutalised bodies of dead spiders. Not a hide nor hair of the others could be seen in the gloom.

'Mithrid!' he whispered as loud as he dared and could manage. Only a timid echo answered him. Farden dropped his forehead into the sand and immediately regretted it. He touched his wounds one by one. The Scalussen armour was not completely useless. He had been saved being lacerated to death, at least.

Beyond the dried blood, his head throbbed. Farden had taken enough nevermar and quaffed enough ale in his time to know the difference between losing a bucket of blood and being poisoned. The spiders had a venom, he wagered. In their needle legs or jaws, he didn't know, but that was the cause of the void in his memories. The last thing he remembered was the rushing surge of horrid insects. Farden knuckled his eyes but the shadows of the nightmare refused to fade. *An image of himself as an old and wizened man. Durnus with the crown of a daemon prince. Mithrid as queen of the Arka.*

Those ghosts could wait.

Much to the protest of his headache, Farden shook his head as if to shake his mind into sense, pushed himself to his knees, and dragged himself to standing. Loki's knife was still at his side, much to a mixture of displeasure and relief. One sword was nearby. The other, for some reason, at the mouth of the ongoing tunnel. A lone spider tried to scuttle away from him, but Farden sliced it in two with a crunch.

Already, the reflections had returned to follow him. Farden held the handles of the swords by his eyes to block their silent stares. *Not this time.*

Mirror after mirror tried to show him another taunting facet of his imagination. When that failed, Farden glimpsed scenes of his past. Even a nine-year-old Farden waved at him from one mirror. It was all he could do to shake his head and break into a hobbling run. He felt as though the tunnel had already aged him ten years. He didn't dare wonder how long he had been unconscious.

Thankfully, the mirrors did have an end to them, yet it came in the form of a void of a cavern. Spiders clicked ponderously across the sand, some tiny as a coin, and others the size of hounds or worse. The walls and ceiling were unseen, vanished by distance and dark. Only a faint glow, leftover from the crystals behind him, cast a puddle of light. It was all Farden needed to see the horrors before him: the single feature of the cavern.

Bodies. A score of them, hanging in midair just at the edge of the darkness. Suspended by their heads and faces, they dangled from silver threads that disappeared into the gloom above. A webbing masked them, but Farden could still tell their mouths were open mid-scream, as if the threads came from within them. Most were emaciated or withered of bone and wax skin. Four were fresh, dangling lower than the rest. Mithrid, Durnus, Aspala, and Warbringer hung there like fresh kills, twitching irregularly.

The mage, throat dry as the sand beneath him, clicked his neck from one side to the other and took a step into the cavern. The smaller spiders scattered from his careful footsteps. Even the larger ones, who Farden attacked carefully and with swords crossed, shied away from him. Their mandibles chuntered. One even screeched before scuttling back into the gloom. By their choreographed movements, he got the impression a deeper, singular mind was behind theirs. Farden groaned as something enormous boomed in the darkness. The sand shook under his boots.

As the mage turned full circle, light scattered about the cavern's reaches like the glitter of a storm cloud. Farden glimpsed stalactites like towers hanging above him. Great webs spanned between them. And where the light couldn't shine, he saw the very mind he sought. Black legs bent and curled in the cavern's corners, thick as Golikan pines. A great void of a bulbous body commanded the darkness. Skeletal, spiny limbs reached above him, and from them hung the bodies.

Farden tried not to flinch as a giant leg slammed into the sand not ten paces from his right side. In truth, his tired body hadn't the energy. It was a struggle remaining vaguely upright and the swords off the ground.

Another limb pounded the earth on his left. With a sound akin to the cracking of spines, the body lowered itself. A grotesque figure came into view: a vaguely female form, protruding from the very face and mandibles of the spider. Where the enormous spider ended and the figure began, her skin became a milky white, shimmering as if clad in some vile saliva. Six arms spread from her skeletal shoulders and ribs, held in all directions and each holding what appeared to be a mask. Her neck, disturbingly obtruded, held a skull of a head, wrapped in strands of flesh. Eyes of black regarded him calmly. A lipless mouth sneered. Silken strands drifted as hair. As she bent close to greet Farden, the bodies above lowered, like a drooping gallows. In all his life, only a hydra had ever come close to defying her size.

As Farden stared, haunted to his very core by the face, she held one of her masks across her face. One of faded gold, a single eye, and a snarling mouth.

'*Kochika*,' she hissed, filling the cavern with her voice as if every damn spider spoke with her.

Farden did not understand. He pointed a sword at the nearest of his friends. Mithrid, her face enveloped in silk. She twitched ever so slightly. Farden fought the panic back down his throat. He hadn't been eaten immediately, which was always a good sign.

'Are you Utiru?' he yelled. Introductions seemed a fine place to start.

The creature removed her mask and chose another, one of porcelain this time, or so it seemed. It had two eyes and a smiling expression, but otherwise looked human.

'Utiru,' said the creature. 'A name I have not heard in a long time. A name of the new stars.' There was no wistful sigh to her voice. No tone of any kind. The simple cold statement of unflinching fact. 'Why do you seek her?'

Farden remembered the guide's words at the Thundershores: a demi-goddess, he had called her. And he knew all too well the pride of gods, and their need for the power of belief and prayer. It seemed as sharp a weapon as any against a monster as vast as this. 'Er... we have heard great stories of you! We crossed the world to see if they were true.'

Utiru weaved back and forth, still holding the mask to her face. In the darkness she shuffled her legs with thunderous noise. 'And now?'

'Your majesty knows no bounds. Your size is... endless! And yet, for all our awe and wonder, you've attacked us and stolen my friends.'

'All know the meaning of the spider's web,' she whispered. 'To enter it willingly is no fault of the spider.'

'If you let them go, we will tell your story far and wide. People will chant your name. Sing about your mercy.'

Utiru came close, faster than Farden could recoil. She hovered an inch from his sword, watching through her porcelain mask. Studying. Farden strived to keep to his act. He wracked his mind, repeating the Doomriddle's last verse over and over. Between every glance he looked for any sign of a key.

'Utiru cares nothing for mercy. She offers nothing but paradise. The deepest and brightest and most blissful of dreams. Your greatest wish fulfilled. Your friends thank Utiru even now. They will sleep an age in my web. In return for your honour, I will allow you to leave. You are polite for a mortal. Leave now before I decide otherwise.'

'No,' Farden said.

Crystal spiders crept from the shadows, clustering around Utiru's huge, skeletal legs. She rose above him. The creature switched her mask to a third face: another of wood, human still but crinkled in a frown. And yet still, there was no anger to her voice. Cold, she remained.

'Greatest wish, you say? I bet you can't show me mine.'

'You challenge Utiru not,' she replied. Again, no emotion spilled from her. Her voice remained flat. The bait tangled, untouched.

Farden got down on one knee. He did not let go of his swords. 'I want that,' he said. 'My greatest wish. Give that to me.'

Utiru came closer still. Farden barely resisted the urge to strike there and then. 'You submit yourself willingly.'

Farden hoped to the very gods he loathed that he was right about this. 'I do.'

Utiru gripped his neck with her cold and clammy claws. A thread of silk was wrapped around his chin, and then his face. Farden fought to restrain himself as he felt the silk fill his mouth. Before darkness enveloped him, he felt his feet lifting off the floor.

❦

Fresh air struck him in the face. Cold, that morning, sign of winter's touch. The heat was already fading from the countryside. The leaves were turning golden. Geese flying in their arrowheads made a fuss above as they sought the south. A river burbled nearby.

Farden sighed as he looked across his tangled branches of a small vineyard. He placed his hands upon the fence. His scars were rosy in the early sunlight. His bare arms and chest felt warm.

He took another breath, taking in the scent of soil. A bird trilled in a tree beyond the river. Rain lingered in the distance.

The mage heard a clattering of dishes behind him. He did not turn, he only smiled.

'Farden!' yelled a woman. One he both knew, and did not at the same time.

A presence hung beside him. A dark shadow across the vines. He did not mind it.

'Fine morning,' he said, voice still raspy from sleep.

'Peace and silence,' said the shadow. Dark arms reached out, one holding his shoulder, the other picking a grape from an ambitiously curled vine. Claws squeezed it. Blood-red juice dripped. 'To be left alone. Your greatest longing.'

The words jarred Farden. He looked again at the rolling hills of empty grass and found a mist had swallowed half of them. The shadow put another hand on his other shoulder.

'Is it not? A woman by your side, a hearth and field to tend. And look.'

Farden looked unbidden, down to his bare skin. The skeleton keys tattooed upon his forearms were gone. He felt no fear standing shirtless. He felt the sun's warmth on unburdened skin.

'Farden!' called the voice again. He turned, past the skeletal legs clustered over him to a cottage of thatch and river stone. A willow tree hung over a small garden. The door hung upon. The chimney belched smoke and a figure bustled inside.

For a moment, the mage teetered upon a smile, upon a, 'yes.' He remembered a cavern. The bulbous body of a monster crouched in the dark. A blink turned the willow tree to horror. Bodies hung from its branches. Silken webs covered the garden. The shadow's claws tightened.

'Do not fight it,' it whispered.

Farden steeled his jaw. A force willed him to look inside the cottage, but he battled it, once again daring to look down. A sword lay in his hand. His other lay empty.

'You're wrong, Utiru,' he replied. 'You've shown me my fate, not the journey, as a friend of mine once said.'

Claws sank into his skin. An earthquake began to shake the hills.

'Because if I truly want this,' Farden continued. 'Then there's blood and pain and shit that stands in the way. This has to be earned, not given.'

Fire burst on the hills. Corpses littered the vineyard around him.

The faintest hint of annoyance entered the voice in his ear. 'You speak madness.'

'Maybe I do long for chaos, as Mithrid tells me. And what is chaos without a weapon to wreak it? I want the key,' Farden spat, convincing himself even for a moment. He stretched out his hand, thinking only of the spear and Loki's limp, lifeless body. Of himself wielding it as a god. A crown of fire upon his head and a blazing throne at his back.

A weight snapped into his hand. Farden opened his eyes to see a key of cold and polished obsidian lying in his palm.

The shadow at his back faltered, falling away from him. Farden whirled on Utiru, finding that masked face hissing, arms raised and claws spread.

'Cut the throat of your dreams,' he uttered before the steel flashed in the morning light.

Grey blood sprayed his face as Utiru screeched. The countryside folded into the darkness of an endless well, whisking Farden with it. He howled once last time for good measure.

'Cut the throat of your dreams!'

Vomiting silk, Farden awoke to find himself falling. Legs kicking, arms whirling, he slashed at every thread he passed on his plummet. Fortunately, Utiru had not dangled him too high.

Farden struck the sand with a wheeze. It took him a moment to recover himself enough to check the cold object in his palm. The key of stone lay there, unassuming, somehow inconvenienced by the whole affair.

Warbringer retched beside him, trying several times to get to her feet before she had prised the silk from her face. She roared, almost bringing her warhammer down on Farden before realising she stood, once again, in reality.

Durnus had also fallen, leaving Aspala and Mithrid dangling above still, thrashing about in the throes of Utiru's pain. The masked creature was no more. All six hands clutched at her throat.

'What do we do now? How do we fight this thing?' bellowed Warbringer as she reduced a huge spider to shards. Utiru's legs stabbed at the sand around them. Farden ducked and rolled, sweeping the vampyre with him.

'We have to hope they heard me!' he cried.

❦

Mithrid stood in a tent of emerald cloth. Soft carpets lay beneath her bare feet. Braziers crackled softly, wafting the smell of sandalwood and spices. She stretched, feeling unexpectedly joyous. Then, she heard a murmuring behind her and spun on her heel.

Before her knelt Malvus Barkhart, bruised, bloodied and beaten. A rag had been stuffed in his mouth. A dark shadow of six limbs stood behind him, two hands on his shoulders. A smiling porcelain mask tilted its head to look at her. Mithrid knew no fear.

'It is time,' it said, and she nodded solemnly.

A knife was at her belt. Malvus watched her unsheathe it with muffled curses and promises of all kinds. There was nothing between the blade and his death but moments, and he knew it. Mithrid tested the steel with her thumb.

'For your father,' the mask whispered.

A voice hollered from beyond the green canvas.

*Cut the throat of your dreams.*

Mithrid echoed the voice's words. 'I know that from somewhere...'

The masked shadow tensed, arms raising up, hooked claws menacing.

474

'Kill him!' it retched. The dark shuddered and gargled at her side. In a swooping moment of horror and realisation, Mithrid swung the knife without hesitation and slit the creature's throat.

❦

The ground punched Mithrid in the face as she crumpled to numb legs.

'What in the fuck…' she garbled, after she coughed up most of her insides.

'Come on, Aspala!' somebody cried. 'Yes! She did it!'

Mithrid looked up to see a colossal, deformed spider reeling in pain. Its screeching was deafening. For some reason, Aspala was tumbling through the air, limp as a discarded sock. Mithrid was still trying to figure where the tent had gone. It had all felt so… real.

Warbringer caught her with as much care as the iron muscle of a minotaur can offer.

'I think it's time we left!' yelled Farden as he dragged Mithrid up from the sand. She reeled, dizzy. To her fright, a giant claw stabbed the ground in front of her, barely feet away. Spiders the size of cats reared up at her. She kicked two in the face before she was hauled onwards.

'Move, Mithrid!'

She needed no encouragement. Plenty of dragging and holding upright, it seemed, but she was utterly on board with fleeing whatever nightmare she had awoken from and into.

'Was that you?' she shouted at Farden over the sound of the spider crashing about the cavern. Rocks fell around them. Durnus held a shield spell over their heads as best he could.

'It was. That creature Utiru feeds on happiness. Deny it, and she has nothing to feed on!'

'Then I'm glad I slit her throat.'

'In our dreams, maybe. We won't have long before she comes after us, I think!'

Farden was irritatingly correct. Utiru came after them with a cold and calculated vengeance. Though they had cut her throat in the dream, grey blood still spattered the sand around them as she raced from the gloom at terrifying speed. Shards of crystal shattered around them as they dove into the tunnel of mirrors. Blinkered by their hands, they ran back the way they had come. Their reflections raged silently, mouthing every curse and flinging every gesture at them. Their hold over them was no more. Mithrid gladly put them behind her, occupying herself by kicking or slashing at every spider that nipped at their heels.

'Keep going!' Farden cried as he faltered behind. His swords slashed in vicious arcs as he freed himself of spider after spider.

Mithrid ran back to help him, reversing roles as she now dragged him onwards and upwards. They could hear a roaring ahead, that of a dragon calling their names. Light surged through the crystal walls.

Breathless, they burst from the tunnel. Mithrid had to grab ahold of the minotaur to keep herself from tumbling onto a patch of dagger-like crystals.

'What is in there?' bellowed the dragon.

Farden fell against her wing and heaved out his words. 'Remember what we did in that mountain in Albion?'

Though it meant nothing to Mithrid, Fleetstar apparently knew exactly what Farden had in mind.

The dragon unhinged her jaws and opened them wide, almost matching the mouth of the tunnel, and filled the crystal hole with dragonfire. Glass shattered alongside the howl of flame. High up above them on the cliff-face, fire sprouted from fissures. When Fleetstar recoiled, the crystal had either been charred black or was glowing softly.

'What was in there?' she asked, as she watched the others slowly stumble about, hands pressed to their temples.

'Do you like spiders, Fleetstar?' groaned Farden.

'No. Dragons despise them.'

'Then pray you never know.'

'The things we saw in there... I saw myself in ages long gone. A prince among...' Durnus began to say, and soon realised he had no desire for the answer.

Farden said it anyway. 'Daemons. Just as I saw myself without my Book, bearded and grey. It proves they are lies. Lies of the great spider.'

'How big?'

Farden ignored Fleetstar, instead letting his gaze linger close to Mithrid, unable to quite look at her. 'I have to believe they are lies,' he muttered.

It took perhaps an hour for all of them to feel remotely normal enough to press on. Mithrid had no idea how the others felt, but her mind reeled, flitting from thought to thought, image to image. Reality blurred with memory and imagination. She had to touch the crystals and test their sharp edges once more to feel alive. *Real.*

'Fuck that cave,' she muttered after some time, over the monotony of crunching boots. 'Fuck those spiders. Fuck this quest.'

Nobody answered her for a while. Mithrid needed to hear the others' voices. To know if any of them had dreamed of murder. 'What did you see, Aspala? In your dream?'

'I...' Aspala shivered uncharacteristically. 'I was with my mother.'

Warbringer spoke up. Her voice broke at the edges. 'I saw my clan. Saw Efjar gleaming with cook-fires and younglings.'

Mithrid was still breathing hard. 'Farden?'

The mage took a while to answer. 'I saw what I needed to see to help me cut Utiru's throat.'

'How did you know it would work?'

'She made a mistake tangling with my rat's nest of a mind. There's not much happiness here,' Farden offered with a wry smile.

'Thank you for saving us,' Mithrid offered. It sounded some-what foolish, as if there had been no other choice, but Farden nodded all the same. The mage still couldn't face her. The mirrors' reflections had scarred him just as they had her. All she could think was why. Was that truly who she was? *A murderer or warlord in the making? A queen?* Trickery or not, a divide had been driven between the mage and her.

Durnus caught Farden as he stumbled, but he shrugged away. 'And did you get the final key?' asked the vampyre.

Farden produced a third and matching skeleton key of jet or obsidian. It seemed more roughly hewn than the last two. 'Somehow,' he admitted. 'Didn't think it would work, but here we are.'

Durnus retrieved it from him, but it took reaching the canyon's mouth to find enough moon and starlight to see the key's script by. There the dragon preened her scales while the others took some time to gather themselves.

Mithrid hovered over Durnus' shoulder as he studied the key. A script ran along its ridged spine. It was in a language Mithrid had no hope of understanding, but she trusted the scholar of a vampyre.

'*Madness you may have survived but darkness calls you on. South, go you, to Gunnir's birthplace. Nothing but the wrath of the gods awaits you behind cursed doors. The final payment to claim Gunnir awaits. The highest price,*' Durnus read.

'Is that it?' Farden said, hands on his knees and breathing hard. Whatever he had done to free them had exhausted him. He kept a lookout while the others gathered around the key to see.

'Does that mean anything to you?' Mithrid asked.

Durnus shook his head as he brought out his elvish tome. 'Not much beyond the word south, and that Gunnir's birthplace must be where the clan of Ivald forged the spear. I presume we must find Ivald's forge, but south of here, the map becomes no more than a rough sketch. Labels are few. Several markings are spread across the desert in that direction. All of them are Khandri names I have never seen before. Ezera. Hasp. They could be cities or countries for all I know. Several are around the coast. This one might say Khanat. One lies at the very southwestern tip of this scorched country. Azanimur, I think it says...' He rubbed his tired and scarlet eyes. 'All utterly unhelpful.'

Farden coughed hard and repeatedly into his hands, bringing a glisten to his eyes from the effort. Whatever he saw in his gauntlets afterwards, he was sure to keep it hidden. 'Keep those keys safe, Durnus. We go south.'

'We should rest, surely,' suggested Mithrid, feeling a strong need to stare into a campfire and burn out the memories of the evening. The mage didn't seem so convinced. He was already pointing himself south.

Farden tottered three steps before lightning carved the sky in two. He whirled to the north, where a bank of mist rolled like a humongous arrowhead across the plains of scrubland. Towns were swallowed as it swept forwards at great speed. Farden pushed past the others to look upon the sweeping storm. Mithrid joined him. A darkness swarmed at its centre. She swore she could see a great beast galloping in the shrieking flash of the storm's lightning. It gained on them quickly.

'Get on the dragon,' Farden growled.

The others did not argue. All except Mithrid. She stepped out onto the hilltop and narrowed her eyes at the storm.

'This is no time for your arrogance, Mithrid! I saw what was in those mirrors just the same as you.'

Mithrid didn't answer. She reached out to the storm with crooked fingers and sensed the magick sparking within its clouds. The hairs upon her neck stood on end. She could feel the figure bent double upon the beast's back. Shutting her eyes, she could almost see him shining in the dark, an incandescent rage.

Magick punched the air as Durnus threw out a shield. Not a moment too soon. A fork of lightning struck it not seconds after. 'It is time to go!'

'FARDEN!' the storm spoke with a thunderous voice. At the centre of the sweeping clouds galloped a fenrir wolf. The figure on its back raised his arms wide, dragged the beast to a halt and jumped to the dust. Lightning crackled around him as he strode towards them, unrelenting.

'Mithrid!' Farden's hands seized her arm. 'Get on the fucking drag—'

'It's Malvus!' she cried, shrugging him away. This was no smirking creature of a mirror, or the prisoner of her dreams. This was a man changed and transformed. The magick peeling from him in waves was enough to dizzy her, as if she had learned nothing since her first day in Scalussen.

Colours burst in Mithrid's eyes as another bolt of lightning struck the sand far too close for comfort.

'Do you not recognise me, Farden? Or you, girl?' boomed the creature marching towards them, seemingly enraged by the lack of recognition. 'You will scream my name and beg for mercy before the sun rises on your corpses!'

The voice. No matter how changed it had become, it still held the same vehement spite. The same haughty assuredness that only an emperor learns. 'I don't know how, but I know it's Malvus!' she yelled. 'He carries your magick with him, Farden.'

Farden was shaking his head over and over. 'No…'

Another lightning bolt struck the cliff, leaving a grinning Loki in its wake. He was utterly out of reach, even from the dragon's fire, but Mithrid could see his smile all the same.

'Old friends meet again!' the god crowed. 'I had hoped to let you get further, of course, but this will have to do. He is rather impatient, you see.'

Farden slammed his vambraces together in habit, even though he had no magick to wield. 'What have you done, Loki?' he bellowed. 'What in Emaneska have you meddled with now?'

'What should have been done years ago! The Books of Written – most notably a certain Forever King's – and daemonblood entwined. Enough to bring the skies crashing down as they should have years ago. And the perfect vessel, if I might add,' yelled Loki. 'Oh, and Mithrid? I'm expecting much of you.'

Farden snarled as Malvus showed himself piece by piece as the distance shrank, in every crackle of lightning. Jet runes covered his swollen, chalk skin. Every inch of him between the rags had been tattooed. Even his face, now devoid of hair and half of it a bloodthirsty grin. Muscle contorted across his shoulders and arms. He stood as tall as the minotaur and almost as broad.

'He has made an abomination!' yelled Durnus, trying his hardest to maintain the shield. 'We have to leave! You cannot fight him without your magick.'

'But I can,' hissed Mithrid, and before she could question herself, she was marching out to meet him.

'Mithrid!' Farden chased her.

She matched Malvus' stance, arms spread and power sprawling around her. She unleashed the shadow aching to be free of her skin. Aching to be of use. It swarmed around her in arcs and coils, spinning ever faster as she and Malvus grew closer.

Despite his momentary surprise at dealing with the girl before Farden, Malvus accommodated her challenge willingly.

'You have chosen to die first, I see. Very well.' Fire spells detonated like thunder in Malvus' palms. The frenzied magick railed at Mithrid, blowing her shadow across the scrubland like a ragged pennant. She snarled against the roar, drinking in the power she felt, and readied herself to face the magick.

The stream of fire hurtled towards her, faster than expected. Mithrid barely caught it, levelling a wall of black shadow against the searing white heat. Her heels dug furrows in the sand. The heat scorched her fingers and face, but she held fast. It took every shred of effort to battle the onslaught. She almost pitched forwards when Malvus ceased the spell. He chased his own flames, his fist glowing with a bright green fire. Now that he was close enough, Mithrid flung out her shadow, strangling the spell until it shrieked like a gale. Lightning sparked as Malvus battled her, sheer force against sheer will. Shadow against sputtering fire.

However Loki had transformed Malvus, he was still the foul soul he always was. Between the rush of black shadow and magick, he managed to kick sand under her guard. Mithrid spun away, blinking furiously. She caught the fist too late. The impact was like a hammer. A searing pain ricocheted through her body. The ground was unyielding, and Mithrid arose breathless but defiant to the core.

Malvus bore down on her, claws raised and lighting churning in a blinding orb. She threw out her hands in panic. Malvus choked as if she had gripped his very heart. She snarled as she squeezed. Face to face, they came in their struggle, Malvus rasping in his tortured voice, Mithrid trying desperately to keep his claws from closing inwards. His breath was foul, rotten teeth dripping saliva as he spat curses at her. White light burned through the tattoos across his face. Mithrid felt her eyes blurring as she dared to look upon them.

'You peasant! You don't deserve these powers!'

'Neither do you!' she strained.

It was Voidaran that broke their stalemate. The warhammer clouted Malvus square in the face. Any normal creature would have had their brains splattered across the grit, but Malvus spat a tooth and wiped black blood with a fist. His face shone with white script.

Two fireballs forced him backwards in quick succession. Along with the mage's swords, cutting two deep gashes in the bastard's ribs, but Malvus repulsed them with a shield spell. It was so powerful Mithrid somersaulted through the air before landing wheezing on the hillside.

'We can't stay here!' Aspala yelled. 'I believe in you, Mithrid, but he has the strength of a dozen Written behind him! Live to fight for glory another day, damn it!'

Aspala's shrieking tone cut through Mithrid's fury. Flames billowed as daemons began to emerge from the storm's shadow. Ragged soldiers, too, dregs hailing broken weapons and limbs, doggedly drawn by the magick. Trolls and other fenrir howled as rain began to fall upon the dry plain. Mithrid bellowed at the unfair fight.

'Aspala is right! Today is not our day for revenge, Mithrid!' Farden yelled in her face.

As much as she hated him in that moment, he was right. With a cry of rage, Mithrid bounded for the dragon beside the others. Durnus' spells barely kept them safe while Fleetstar launched herself from the hillside. She had to wheel around forks of lightning before soaring vertically into the air, riding the storm winds Malvus had summoned. Every one of them watched the foul creature diminish beneath them until he and Loki were lost to light and distance.

Mithrid shivered in the grip of the dragon, and not just with the cold of the high winds. The battle still ran through her veins. She cursed every moment, questioning silently why she hadn't been faster, stronger.

It was to such a churning mind that Mithrid subjected herself until the first pale signs of dawn, breaking over the sea to the west. Fleetstar swooped downwards to taste the heat of the deserts that sprawled beneath them, and to chase the herds of goats that covered the patches of dry grassland.

Not a word had been traded. The mood lay heavy between the passengers. Heads remained bowed and breaths heavy. And yet it became violently apparently the night of horrors was not done with them yet.

The bolt appeared as if from nowhere, slamming into her left wing. Mithrid felt the impact through her bones and the tightening of Fleetstar's claws, as painful as the roar that split her ears. The iron arrow struck the dragon with such force that it forced her into a plummeting roll that left Mithrid choking on her own heart. The ground spun beneath her as Fleetstar tried desperately to keep flying. Only her curiosity in the landscape had saved them from a greater fall. Crescent-shaped dunes grew larger at a horrific pace.

Fleetstar had the sense to let go of Mithrid and Farden before she struck the summit of a dune. The last she saw before the cloud of sand smothered their eyes was a cartwheel of wings and a thrashing tail. The others had the sense to unstrap themselves to avoid being crushed. They tumbled like cargo from an overturned cart.

The heavy groan of the dragon filled her ears. Mithrid tried to right herself, but her hands refused to stay put in the thick, fine sand. She could feel its grit scraping beneath her eyelids.

'Well… shit,' she croaked.

'That's the spirit. Up you get,' said Farden. He looked as though he'd had some experience traversing a dune or two. He helped her upright, and together they staggered for Fleetstar.

The others were shaking sand from their ears and still trying to find their balance.

Fleetstar was enraged. One wing was splayed across the sand like she was an injured bird. Blue blood dripped from the wound. The arrow had torn a hole in the skin and scored her muscle deeply. She snapped her jaws at Mithrid as she tried to approach. Even Farden couldn't calm her.

'Who?' Fleetstar snarled, more animalistic than Mithrid had ever seen her. 'Who dared to fire this disgusting thing at me?'

'I don't know, but I'll let you eat however many of them you want. Durnus! We need some magick here.'

The vampyre went to work while still coughing sand. His black spectacles had been smashed into two pieces but somehow, both halves still hung from his ears. He set his hands to the iron arrow, melting it with heat spells to save her from the pain of the barb.

Fleetstar roared flame as they took the arrow out. Mithrid hovered about, helpless. She kept a lookout instead, and set her foot to the shifting wall of the sand dune. She hated it within seconds. Sweat dripped from her nose by the time she reached its peak, stared into the dawn-lit desert, and saw the answer to Fleetstar's question rushing towards them.

'We have company!' she yelled shortly before rolling back down to the valley in a dizzying flurry. She almost vomited on Fleetstar's claws before Warbringer hauled her up.

'How many? Who?' she barked.

'Too many, and I don't know. They don't look Cathak, that's for sure. Soldiers!'

'From the frying pan into the fire, and then into the furnace,' said Farden in a bitter tone.

'Then let us hope not to Hel.'

The mage spun his swords low by his sides. 'At least it will be good to see my uncle again!'

The soldiers' approach could be felt in the sand before it was seen. From left and right they came like a pincer, spears low and diamond shields forming fierce walls that bristled. Their pointed helmets each sported an arrowhead. The orders that kept their formations knit as tightly as tapestries were a constant stream, and in the harsh tongue they had heard at the border. Several knights in gold armour marched between the rank and file of chainmail and leather. Their helmets were plumed with dyed bristles of hair that ran down their backs. They had no visors but masks of mail that hung like beards. Their swords were shaped as though the smiths had decided to make a scimitar halfway through a longsword.

The dragon chewed fire as she reared to a lopsided upright and opened her maw for all to see. The archers in the crowd drew their bows, making Mithrid tense, but no command came.

'Easy, Fleetstar. You'll get us all killed!' she hissed.

'Though it pains me greatly to say this,' Farden said with a dramatic sigh. 'I think this is the second defeat of our night.'

To Mithrid's surprise, it was the vampyre who looked as though he had to be restrained. 'We were so close!' he seethed.

She glimpsed a crimson colour in his glacial eyes that had never shown itself before. Perhaps it was burst blood, but before Mithrid could decide, Warbringer stepped in front of Durnus to keep him civil.

'Who are you?' Farden demanded of the soldiers. 'And what do you want of us?'

Mithrid twitched, feeling magick in the crowds somewhere. She wondered if Malvus had already found them again, but it had a stranger edge. Its cause was one of the knights. He had black details of birds across his golden armour. He stared at Aspala as though she were a traitor before marvelling at Warbringer and the dragon.

'It is you who trespass upon Khandri lands, northerners!' he brayed. 'You will lay down your weapons and come with us in peace, or in pieces.'

'Come with you where?'

'Why, to our Lord Belerod. He has been expecting you.'

'Lord who the fuck now?' Farden spluttered. Something about the name was familiar to Mithrid. 'We will not give up our weapons. Warrior to warrior, you can respect that.'

The knight cackled. 'Warrior to warrior, you should know what being outnumbered looks like, and when to shut your mouth and do as you're told. Weapons. Now!'

The formations closed inwards with a menacing stamp of their feet. Arrows landed in the sand at their feet with puffs of sand.

Mithrid looked to Warbringer. She held Voidaran over her shoulder as if she were about to flatten anyone in sight. Farden shook his head at her emphatically. 'Please, Katiheridrade,' he whispered, somehow pronouncing her true name where Mithrid had failed so many times.

'Would you give up your armour?' she growled back.

'I need you alive. This is no fine death. I will not let you or your clan down. I promise.'

Mithrid threw her axe down to catch the minotaur's eye. Aspala, though it clearly pained her, added her scimitar to the pile.

It was with a solemn muttering that Warbringer surrendered Voidaran. Both she and the hammer sighed deeply as she dropped it to the sand. Even the knight had to stare back at his men as if to wonder how they would carry it.

'And we were so close,' Aspala hissed, as Khandri came forwards to bind them.

Mithrid saw the mage staring at her from the corner of her eye, but she refused to look even when shackles slid around her armoured wrists. She knew somehow it would be full of blame.

The knight ripped the satchel from Durnus' shoulder and threw it on the ground. 'We know of your spellbooks and sorcery. You can't trick us, old man.'

Durnus bared his fangs, making the man recoil. To Mithrid's horror, the inkweld fell from the satchel and opened on the sand. It was only when she was being hauled away she saw the script tumble across its pages. It said one word only.

## MITHRID?

'Wait! No!' Mithrid yelled, but they gagged and hooded her before she could put up any complaint.

# CHAPTER 29
## A WARLORD'S EMPLOY

*The secrets of a golem's construction lie in the stone and the correlating*
*spells used. Each stone has its own tune that the magick must sing also.*
*Limestone, for instance, can suffer from weak binding. Basalt has a tend-*
*ency to snap under complex spells. Sandstone will crumble at the faintest*
*error. But granite not only holds the magick, it is sturdy to most bindings,*
*even after collapse.*
FROM A MANUAL ON HASP "WINDTRICKING"

Rage was a wonderful emotion. All-encompassing. Blinding. Singular. No mortals were themselves when rage soured their hearts and
minds. A wonderful excuse for all manner of evil. A moment when
the skin of civility is peeled away to show the animal within every
creature.

To that analogy, Malvus might as well have bared raw flesh to
the night air.

Loki stood by and watched with curious intrigue as Malvus
once more levelled his spells against the cliff face. Rock and crystals
shattered and tumbled to the sand in a torrent of debris.

'He was within my grasp!' Malvus bellowed again. 'Barely
feet away. Curse that whore of a child and her magick!'

'What did the girl's touch feel like?' Loki asked.

Malvus flexed his hands. Dark veins between his tattoos
bulged. 'Poison,' he breathed. Loki could smell the stink of him from
a dozen feet away. 'To be normal and useless as before. I will crush
her skull!' Anger bubbled up within him again, and Malvus tore a

stone from the earth. He hurled it across the wasteland. Gremorin and his daemons had to move to avoid its path.

'Why did Farden not use his magick?' snarled Malvus. 'Why does he seem weak? Years older, as never before?'

The same question had been asked in Loki's mind. It had intrigued him. Bothered him, in truth. *The mage was still necessary.* Weakness was precedent to failure.

The silence got to Malvus.

'Why are you not concerned, god?' he yelled. 'Do you doubt me? Trick me!'

Malvus' chipped and dirt-ridden fingers came reaching for the god, but Loki shifted to the side before he could grab him.

'I do neither,' Loki replied, playing calm. 'As for why I do not seem concerned, I am not. Not in the slightest. Farden's magick may have been lost to Irminsul's fire, I would wager, or perhaps the girl's magick. Or the Weight that brought them here. But it doesn't matter in the least. He is weaker; you are stronger. This was a skirmish before the true battle. And that lies south, by what I can sense.' The fools still carried his knife with them.

'Why would Farden be here? You keep your answers closer to your chest than ever before, Loki, and your tongue has been uncharacteristically still this whole journey. While my ears welcome it, I'm starting not to trust it.'

Loki forced a smile. 'Quietly confident in you. And as for Farden's plans, I do not know. Perhaps he is fleeing as far as he can from you,' he lied, much to the furtive satisfaction that broke the husk of rage on Malvus' scarred face.

'You are almost ready, Malvus, to bring the skies crashing down. Your power is almost at its peak.'

Malvus reached to the storming heavens as if to test his powers. Light scorched his skin as the runes and script illuminated. Muscles rippled. Tendons stood stiff as cords beneath his skin. He seemed to stretch the air around him. Loki felt a rare prickle of pain spread through his body.

'Promises,' Malvus breathed, when the spell failed him. Instead, he twirled fire between his fingers. The flames licked the air dangerously close to the god. His voice was deep as a daemon's. Harsh as Irminsul's fire. 'Promises are worth nothing without their payment, little god. Farden's blood will drip from my hands when we next meet, or yours will. And the sky will fall upon your shattered corpse.'

Though Loki hated the daemons' name for him in Malvus' mouth, he knew to stow his complaints. He could hear the crescendo of his plan rising like thunder with every mile south they journeyed. A masterpiece he had orchestrated over years coming to a clashing conclusion, private and performed solely for him. But Malvus and Farden wavered the harmony. Sowed discord. And Loki could not have it.

'To the mage's blood,' Loki grinned to Malvus as he poked at that incalculable rage once more. At least that was predictable.

To the crackle of lightning, Malvus broke out across the wasteland, daemons leaving cinders and smoke in their wake.

*Water.*

Farden had never longed for it so badly in all his life.

He poked his lips between the bars of the rattling cage, gasping like a fish at the breeze. His tongue felt like the sole of an old boot.

The desert taunted him. Every dune looked the fucking same.

The mage had given up wondering how the Khandri knew where they were going. They could have been walking them in circles in some slow, cruel torture. There wasn't a landmark in sight. No roads behind the one their caravan of soldiers and wagons forged.

The landscape was so monotonous, in fact, and his mind so delirious, Farden was slowly becoming haunted by the thought he was secretly back in Utiru's clutches, and everything he had seen so far was part of her trick.

*Water.*

Farden rasped the word at a passing guard once more, only to have a hand thwack the bars. To their credit, the Khandri hadn't actually laid a hand on any of them besides the dragon.

The mage and sprawled on the cage floor instead. At least there was shade in the cage. He stared at the ceiling of their simplest of abodes and felt the thrum of his wheels under his cuirass.

'Are you all right, Farden?' Mithrid asked.

'Me? Dying rapidly as ever,' he replied cheerily. 'I'm surprised you noticed me. A day and a night we've been in this cage and you've spent all of it looking north. I wonder why.'

She shifted her gaze back to the desert. 'I wasn't strong enough. I could have stopped him.'

Farden shook his head. 'You couldn't. Not with the daemons and the creatures he's dragged behind him. Your thirst for vengeance could have got yourself killed.'

'Next time,' she muttered. 'I will break him.'

Aspala's voice was quiet and subdued. 'Think he'll keep coming?'

'Of course not. Not while I, or you, still draw breath. Or Durnus. He doesn't like him either.'

The vampyre nodded, eyes closed. The heat was sapping him. His strength had ebbed since the cavern. He rocked back and forth slowly, fangs raking blood from his own lips. 'Threw me in a prison once. Our best hope is to find the spear and use it to kill both Loki and Malvus at once.'

Mithrid thumped her head against the steel bars. 'I was thinking our best hope was me.'

'Sometimes, I wish I had never told you that you were a weapon,' Farden sighed.

'Not only do you think me a liar, but you doubt my abilities now, too?'

'I don't doubt you, Mithrid. I worry. I know the path you walk on.'

Durnus hissed softly. 'The very weather follows him. I have never seen the like of his tattoos. He outnumbers and overpowers us. Even with your magick, Farden, and with you at his side, Mithrid, I would bet on Malvus against us. And that speaks to Loki's unthinkable meddling, not to your power. You saved us the other night, that is for certain.'

Mithrid grumbled, dissatisfied.

Farden sighed. If it was all a dream, at least nothing mattered any more. He could almost see Utiru's appeal. 'You'll have your chance, I'm sure of that,' he told her, sitting up as shouts came down the Khandri lines.

'The inkweld fell to the sand when we were bound. I saw writing on it, saying my own name. What if it's lost? How will we find the others?'

'A problem for after we find the spear, I'm sure,' sighed Farden. Pushing his head to the bars again, he saw greenery at last. He cheered for the break to the monotony. Or, at least he tried to cheer. It came out more like the wheezing of old bellows.

'What is it?' asked Aspala. Farden had thought her asleep. She had spent the entire time curled up at the edge of the cage, knees to her chin and hating every moment of captivity.

'I see palm trees. Water, maybe, though I've sworn I've seen water on every flat bit of sand we've passed.'

'Mirages,' Aspala nodded knowingly.

A sharp whistled made Farden turn. The knight with the mask of mail had ridden up alongside them on an armoured persnippen bird.

'Only your best behaviour, you understand? Lord Belerod does not abide cheek!'

Farden smacked his chapped lips. 'What about impudence? Impertinence?'

The knight thrashed his reins so hard the giant bird unleashed a garbled squawk. 'No insolence of any kind, or we will make good on our threat.'

'How could I forget?' Farden looked behind them, where Warbringer and Fleetstar had been given their very own cages and an extra helping of shackles. The coelos that pulled them along the sands looked exhausted. Alongside their cages, however, two wagons escorted them. Atop each one was a ballista, similar to those of the bookships. Cradled in their taut strings was an iron arrow as tall as he was. The same kind that had already speared Fleetstar once.

If Farden stared at her too long, he felt her frustration and pain washing through him, so heavy to be a rush of nausea. And yet, somehow, the spark of connection kept him awake, and hopefully reassured the dragon in some way.

Warbringer knelt in the shade of her cage. With her heavy brows and her brooding stare, she looked more dangerous than Farden had ever seen her.

'I have been thinking,' Durnus muttered. His eyes had crept open. Without the dark spectacles the knights had broken, Farden saw a faint tinge of red to those eyes, at utter odds to the glacial hue he had known for decades. Dark veins gathered at the collar of his robe.

Farden squinted against the sun. 'Always a bad sign.'

'I have been thinking about the Doomriddle's first promise to us. *Three tasks every god and mortal fears to face await. Three duties yet fulfilled of blood, breath, mind, and soul. Three cursed keys to three doors to be left locked evermore.* The blood, breath, mind, and soul. Those words have played on my mind for days. I did not want to believe them before, but now, I cannot escape them.'

Aspala sniffed at Durnus. 'What are you talking about?'

'The blood is what Sigrimur shed. The breath you had to hold in the second task. And we almost lost our minds to Utiru.'

'Speculation, Durnus.'

Durnus snarled back at him. *'The final payment to claim Gunnir awaits.* What else could be demanded of us next but the sacrifice of a soul? One of us will be expected to make it.'

The vampyre's words were damning, as though a noose had just been tied about each of their necks. Danger had followed them every step of the way, but it had never been so certain or foretold. They all traded sour looks as if pondering which one of them the spear would demand.

Mithrid shook her head, adamant and seemingly incensed. She worked away at her hands, grinding her gauntlets together. 'No. We've beat every task so far. We can beat this one.'

The girl's confidence wilted in the silence that followed. Farden watched her, recognising the fury roiling inside her. The frustration at the double-edged blade of the fate she believed in.

Farden dug up some reassurance for them, even though it felt hollow for him. 'Let us escape these jaws first before we think about what Gunnir wants from us.'

The sandy buildings the caravan passed at first didn't look like they belonged anywhere near the abode of a grand lord. They were ramshackle, seemingly deserted but for a few hooded villagers. Goats sat or stood or butted heads on their square and ramparted roofs.

'Where are we?' Farden asked the knight still trotting at their side, keeping watch.

'Nowhere important, or that would educate you.'

'Belerod doesn't live in a palace or fortress?'

'Normally, he does. He is a prince of Narwe, after all. Lord Belerod has several palaces, but now he is heading to war. With your northern lands, no less. You ravage our towns and mine our mountains. Now you will pay the price.'

'We're from Emaneska. Far away from your Diamond Mountains and your problems. We are simply passing through.'

'Tell it to my lord.'

'Oh, I will,' Farden threatened, but before he could antagonise the knight more, a glitter demanded his attention.

*Water.*

Farden hurt his cheeks he pressed his face to the bars so forcefully. The pool of blue water spread between the buildings before curving around the dune. Palms bent shade over its banks.

It was here the encampment began. Tents sprang from the sand, interspersed by more trees. Gold of hue, they were square-face and pointed, but there the simplicity ended. They were sculptures of canvas and rope, some reaching even two stories like houses. The caravan weaved between their ropes and sweeping awnings. Some parts of the tent settlement were completely covered in canvas as if to forge great halls.

It was a camp of war, no doubt. Soldiers occupied every tent. Swathes of smiths and armourers clogging the hot air with cinders and clanging. Somewhere between the canvas forest, beasts lowed at the watering hole.

What captured Farden's eye – besides the palm-wood barrels of water and wine – were the engines of war. Similar to the machines they had built in Scalussen, though not runecrafted for strength. Instead, they were built larger, thicker, and from more iron than he thought possible.

A fanfare blared at the head of the caravan. The jolting of their wagon slowed as voices yammered back and forth about them. They had come to a courtyard of canvas and rope. A strange crowd stood about, sipping from tall, thin goblets of coloured glass. Men and women alike were dressed in golden silks of varying finery. A goat-faced man played a lute with a wand of string. It gave a haunting whine that a nearby drummer tapped nonsensically to.

Farden understood what this was. He had seen enough in his time. It was a lord's court, and no court was without its fawners and wealthy contributors, even if all they fawned over was a person who usually loathed them in return, and all they contributed was their addled presence.

The court of Lord Belerod seemed no different. A multitude of attendees hovered about in clumps of conversation and nibbled from gold platters. They whispered as the wagons were drawn into an arc before a dais. Yet despite his court's glitter, the lord's lair seemed strangely functional. His burgundy tent was entirely open on one side. Its awning was splayed in the blue sky like skins being left to cure. Braziers of ornately carved stone burned on either side of a sweeping map table. A middle-aged man with a shaved head and a broad but trimmed granite beard stood waiting upon them. His mahogany skin bore a constant frown. Generals in gold armour whispered at his back. Soldiers, too, but Belerod had no need for them.

As the bolts were knocked from the cage hinges, and the bars fell away, Farden examined the two stone golems that loitered either side of the dais. These were far beyond the beasts that they had seen on the roads, instead masterfully carved. Their grey, almost blue stone, was veined with mica and quartz. Their shards and plates of stone echoed the muscle and shape of human lines. One was carved to look as though it wore armour. The other had claws curved like blades. Each must have been twelve-foot tall at the most. Their grim faces and piercing blue eyes regarded the prisoners with the curiosity that mortals reserved for insects.

'It is about time!' Belerod yelled. His accent was strangely reminiscent of deep Paraian, past the Dune Sea. His Commontongue was perfect.

'Presenting Lord Belerod of Wind-Cut, Haspia. Master Windtricker. Envoy of the Narwe Harmony,' yelled the knight as he poked them from the cage.

Belerod swept forwards. His golems were well trained and stepped with him. Beside them, the lord looked like a glass half-empty. His tone was gruff, yet it had a welcoming tone that surprised

Farden. Though he spoke to the others, he stared avidly at Fleetstar. They had not let her or Warbringer from their cages. Their belongings and weapons clanked on the ground in sacks. All except Voidaran. The soldiers had refused to handle it. Instead, it lay strapped to War-bringer's wagon.

'I apologise for the mode of travel,' said Belerod. 'It is not the most comfortable, my golems tell me.'

Farden cut straight to the point. 'You could apologise for shooting our dragon, while you're at it.'

Belerod nodded. 'Though necessary, I regret to harm the creature, and I trust it is nothing permanent. The Narwe have some of the finest surgeons known to history.'

The Mad Dragon blew smoke. 'You'll not touch me!' she snarled. 'Necessary? You mongrel cur. I'll roast you alive.'

Farden half expected her to do it. The crowd of courtiers had the gall to gasp and gossip at the sight, as if they were an audience to some impromptu theatre.

'It speaks! How pleasing,' Belerod said. Though his brain had forgotten to tell his flat lips, he was clearly exuberant. He moved around them, striding back and forth like a captain drilling recruits.

Farden lifted his chin. 'You didn't have to do anything but give us passage through your land. We have no time to waste on our journey, and it would be in your best interest to let us go. Sooner, rather than later.'

'You're right about that,' muttered Mithrid.

Belerod chuckled, and even then his lips. 'How else was I to meet you?'

'Meet us? Why?'

'By politely asking?' ventured Farden.

'Ah,' Belerod grinned. 'You were correct, Lady of Whispers!'

Farden's head snapped around with a click of bone. He felt the heat prickle his cheeks.

Sure enough, from the crowd emerged a familiar face: Lady Irien, draped in white cotton and a gold silk sash. Her arm made her unmistakable. There was no smile on her face now. No glimmer of her constant amusement whatsoever. Her hair still stood in its ridge. Gold trailed from her ear and around her throat. She stood upon the sand between the court and the prisoners. Her stare crept to Farden. It might well have been the gaze of a frog for all the emotion and insight it offered.

'In what way, Lord Belerod?' she asked, both voice and eyes frosty.

'They are fine characters indeed. Full of spirit and strength, just as you informed me. This one in the red and gold looks older than I recall. How the Easterealm has aged you.'

Farden tilted his head. 'Have we met before?'

Belerod entwined his fingers as he now examined Farden's armour. He marvelled at the interlocking scales. Farden caught Belerod's proving fingers between his manacled hands. The nearby knights darted to intervene but Belerod shook his head. The mage felt a strength in the lord's arms that said he was not just a planner of wars, but once a fighter, too. Farden released him unharmed.

'Oh yes,' Belerod crowed. 'There is the anger, the rebellion. I saw you in the Viscera, good sir, and not only did your friends here perform admirably in such weighted bouts, but I must praise you for the most sudden way in which you brought the Scarlet Tourney to a close. That nest of vipers and gamblers deserved every drop of blood that was spilled.'

Though he strained his mind to the point of pain, the mage could not remember this man; not from crowd nor from the contestants. 'Lord Belerod...' he muttered.

'And you are Farden and Durnus of Scalussen, sorcerers both,' Belerod announced their names in kind, sweeping back and forth their line. 'Mithrid of Hâlorn, if I pronounce that correctly. The Warbringer, the Broken Promise, and Aspala of Paraia. It is an honour to have you here. We shall have food brought for you. Song, if you wish. I treat all the guests of my court and my children of stone with the utmost respect. Unless they displease me.'

Farden felt his lips crack as he smiled. He hadn't the strength for another enemy. *Not now. Not when we are so close.* He hoped he had made enough already. 'In that case, I suppose now's a good time to remove these shackles, no? Though while your hospitality is much appreciated, we can't stay long.' He raised his shackles, but neither the soldiers nor Belerod made a move. Irien winced.

'Ah. I feel I've misunderstood,' Farden said.

'I feel you have.' Belerod's puckered mouth broke its form, breaking into a vicious little smirk, like a rat discovering a cheese larder left open. 'I am an artisan, you see. Like the Lady of Whispers here, I appreciate fine artefacts. I recognise quality, skill, and crafts-manship when I see it. After seeing what you did to the Viscera, I knew I had discovered a number of rare specimens that I not only needed to meet and study, but that would strike fear into the hearts of my enemies. Like my Wind-Cut golems, no less. But a true western dragon? My! The northerners will quake in their fortresses. Not to mention a minotaur. Two mages and fighters both. And you, Aspala of Paraia, who murdered my youngest son to the cheer of the Scarlet Tourney.'

Farden's head switched to the other side. If there were any more revelations he would soon break his neck.

'I what now?' Aspala shook her manacles.

Belerod stepped to examine her. She was taller than he was, especially with her horns now fully regrown, but the looming shadow of the golems somehow gave the lord the edge. The one with sculp-ted armour growled.

'Dooran of Dooran was his name, son of Belerod of Haspia, or so they dubbed him,' Belerod said, much to the sighs and slow, sad shakes of his courtiers' heads. Fawners all.

The name was slowly dawning on a memory. Farden remembered a hesitant fighter dropping a sword.

Belerod jogged their memory for them. 'My sixth boy and a fool for entering the Tourney, I said! But alas, Dooran was not born with his father's smarts. I blame his Borian whore of a mother.'

Farden scowled. He was not alone, though the court muttered in defence of their lord, not in criticism.

Aspala bared her white teeth. 'I was put into that arena against my will, do not punish my friends for my—'

Belerod held a finger to his lips. 'Fortunately, the goddess Haspha smiles upon me. I have many more sons to replace him.' Several knights spread around the circle of tents thumped their breastplates, including the fellow that had captured them between the dunes. 'You gave Dooran a clean warrior's death, and for that I will spare your life. And I do not punish you; I am rewarding you with a proud place in my army! Honour and glory. Blood and chaos, as Irien tells me you crave. She has been quite useful here in the south. Her knowledge of the north will make this a swift war.'

'Now, I think it's you that's misunderstood,' Farden tutted. He wished he had the moisture to spit at the lord's feet.

Belerod continued as if the mage hadn't spoken. 'Under my command, and fighting under the banners of the Narwe Harmony, you will bring death to your pale brothers and sisters. The northern marauders burn village after village in our foothills. Our ancient mines are being sacked and raided, and already, they send a fleet of ships down the coast. War for the Diamond Mountains has been declared, and I will deliver a first blow that will send the north reeling.'

'We will not fight for you,' scoffed Durnus. 'Not for some jumped-up warlord and a war we do not belong to.'

Aspala looked wild behind the eyes. A knight had to seize her manacles. 'I refuse to be caged!'

'Let us go, Belerod, and you'll be better for it.'

The man did not look the least bit hampered by Farden's threat. 'Allegiances and friends are a double-edged sword, my new warriors. This is why I advise against such fancies, and trust only what I can build with my hands and the winds. It is simple: I will kill one of you, and then another, until those who remain agree to do my bidding.'

The simple evil of the matter silenced them. The lone wolf had no such problems, but Farden had the weakness of companions, and frankly, a heart. As the golden knights grabbed their manacles and led them into the camp at Belerod's behest, he found Irien in the crowd and bored a hole in those bewitching eyes. He cursed himself for believing her charm. He should have recognised the wolf in her, too.

Belerod was a peculiar captor. Despite the chains and swords at their back, he acted the grand and accommodating lord as if imprisonment was a favour he were paying them.

'Ten thousand Khandri have joined my cause. Thirty thousand Hasp,' he boasted. They had not wanted a tour of the camp, but he provided one anyway.

Farden got the feeling he was a man of minor beginnings. The kind that felt the need to hammer home their status with proof, as if it were constantly in silent question. Most chose jewellery or treasures. Others palaces or politics. Some the path of the learned scholar, but Belerod had chosen war.

Belerod's mind was a wicked thing, and one that Farden slyly took hints from. He was no simple noble who fancied himself a warrior, but a warlord and a general. And an engineer or inventor, too, judging by his golems and contraptions of murder. Farden saw complicated ballistae capable of firing racks of arrows at once. Catapults sat ready and loaded with spiked balls of steel connected by chains. He wondered if the northerners had weapons to match, or if they were due for a bloodbath in return for their trespass. It was no war of Farden's.

There was magick in the war-camp, too. Much to his ever-present anguish, Farden could not feel it, but he saw it between the tents. Mages using wind magick to stir whirlwinds against shield walls. Toned individuals mixed potions and powders that puffed with smoke, like the witches of the ice fields.

Other creatures and captives besides them lingered in cages, waiting to be of use in Belerod's war. And of course, there were the golems.

Belerod's pride burned most fiercely for his granite creations. Ten more of the intricate beasts were scattered through the camp between siege machines and chariots.

'Twelve, I have built so far. A thirteenth, possibly my finest, is currently under construction in my homeland of Haspia to the east.'

'How does one build a golem?' said Durnus, somehow treating it exactly as a tour.

Despite his magnanimous sentiments, Belerod was reticent with some secrets. 'With old magick and patience. These golems, however, are carved with the winds of Haspia. There are none like them in all the world.'

Annoying as it might have, Farden was inclined to agree.

'Of your dragon and minotaur, what does it eat? Does it sleep?'

Nobody answered the warlord, least of all Fleetstar and War-bringer. The dragon just charred the bars of her cage with restrained fire.

*Stay calm. I'll get us out of here*, Farden whispered in his mind. She did not respond, but she recoiled from the bars all the same.

'Very well, hold your tongues. I am a quick learner. I am most fascinated by the concept of dragon riding.' Belerod extended his hand to the dragon to feel her scales, but Fleetstar snapped her huge jaws at him. The knights menaced her with swords.

'All in good time, as with all things,' Belerod said confidently. 'And at last, here are your quarters. The dragon will come back to my court with me, under my watchful eye.'

'You best not lay a finger on her.'

'While you are in no position to threaten me, Farden, rest assured. I will do no more harm to my property. Unless I am forced to.'

Fleetstar whined as they parted them and dragged her cage back the short way they had come.

Their "quarters" were tall, glorified cages, similar to what they had seen in the Viscera. Four of them altogether, each side by side and sharing bars. A tent stretched across the sprawl of iron to hide them from the sun. And, to Farden's joy, there was water.

It might have surprised the others to see him striding behind his bars, but as he dunked his head into the trough of oasis water, he couldn't care less. Farden drank like he was drowning.

Belerod bid them no goodbye as he swaggered away, clearly pleased with his swift and seamless acquisition. For the first time, Farden knew somewhat of how Hereni or Mithrid felt, or any of the soldiers and mages Malvus had stolen into his armies. It was too swift. Too helpless. The only difference was that they were not as helpless as Belerod perhaps imagined. *Not quite.*

Farden submersed himself again.

*Water.*

# CHAPTER 30
## BETRAYAL'S TOLL

*There will always be war. So long as man has more or less than his neighbour, there will be war.*
EASTEREALM PROVERB

Crimson wine splashed the golden sands at Irien's feet.

'To Haspha, goddess of magick,' Belerod intoned.

From every damn glass of wine, he spilled a little to the earth for the goddess. It was a waste, and as he grew drunker, the offerings came closer to splashing her. The warlord was toasting his new additions, as saturated as the red sand.

'As I was saying, you've done well, Lady Irien,' Belerod continued over the braying of the bowed lutes and chatter of other courtiers. A sickle of moon put a sheen to Belerod's already shining scalp. 'You shall be handsomely rewarded when we march north. Lands in Lezembor. Caskets of gold.'

A knight bustled from between the silk-clad crowd to interrupt. 'An envoy approaches from the coast, my Lord Belerod. They are of the northern fleet our spies spotted.'

Belerod dismissed him with a wave. 'They shall not bother me tonight! Tonight is for celebration.' He took a swig of his wine, dribbling a good deal of it in his beard. 'You spoke truthfully. They are tight-knit exactly as you described. Friends true and all. The fools. Compassion is a weakness in war, Lady Irien, as I am sure you understand,' he said in his usual practical tone. The only emotions the man seemed to understand was victory and anger.

'War is business,' Irien answered with a broad smile. She felt Belerod's stare upon her as she watched the soldiers continue trying to pick up the minotaur's hammer. Most curiously, the golem refused to touch it. Haunted, they called it. Beyond their game, the dragon crouched and smouldered in her cage. Her blue scales appeared silver at night. Nothing broke her stare. Not a burst of flame from the fire-eaters. Not any of the braying laughter from the courtiers. She watched Belerod with a predator's focus.

'How pleased I am that our paths crossed. A highly profitable encounter for both of us, I would wager. I have new weapons for the war, and you have successfully avoided Golikar's wrath. I confess, I doubted your intentions at first and suspected a trick. But I see a fellow soul of practicality in you. As you said,' he chuckled. 'Business.'

Irien raised her wine. 'Business.'

She held her smile as long as she could while she got to her feet. 'Even the nights here are too hot for me, it seems! I believe I'll take a walk to shake some of the sand from me and find a breeze.'

'I see.' Belerod watched her over his flute of wine. Irien bowed deeply, bade goodnight, and walked slowly through the crowds, even pausing to speak her wishes to others she knew amongst the court.

Irien made sure to drift past Fleetstar's cage as she wandered into the night of campfires and noise. Irien did not break pace; Belerod's gaze burned in the back of her skull.

The dragon shifted her enormous eyes only momentarily, long enough to murmur, 'Traitor,' before Irien was out of earshot.

'What are you doing?' Mithrid had grown bored of the silence.

Farden had been propped at the corner of his bars since sunset. 'Watching. Waiting.'

'Waiting for what?'

'Currently? An end to these questions,' Farden said with a sharp look.

The vampyre appeared lost without his books. Weakened without feeding, it seemed. Durnus' grey skin looked clammy and his eyes were raw from the sun. He sat in the cell diagonally from Mithrid, dejected and slumped, yet breathing hard as if he simmered with outrage. They couldn't exactly ask for a fresh body for the vampyre. The food on his plate had gone uneaten until Warbringer snuffled it up.

'What's the plan?' she asked him.

'Up to Farden,' he growled. 'Dragonfire and swift feet, I presume. Otherwise, Belerod will take us back north, or Malvus will come for us, and all of this effort will be for nothing.'

'Out of the question,' Farden said. 'This is now the final stretch. A race to Gunnir. Loki knows we are close. I won't let him swoop in like the vulture he is.'

Mithrid had given their plight plenty of thought. She counted each problem on her fingers. 'But Belerod has our weapons, the Grimsayer, and map. The inkweld fell to the sand and might be lost or stolen. And not to mention, the cursed keys were in Durnus' satchel! What if Loki has already—'

The mage looked smug.

'What?'

Farden hooked a thumb beneath the collar of his armour and hooked out a thin chain. Crystal, bone, and obsidian poked above the gold metal.

'You bastard!' Durnus snapped, angrier than Mithrid expected. His fangs were proud in his snarl. He rattled his iron bars. 'I have been torturing myself thinking they were lost, broken by the knights!'

Farden looked at him, abruptly concerned. 'I took them out of your satchel when Mithrid came rolling back down that sand dune. I can't tell you how oddly heavy and uncomfortable they are.'

As Durnus slowly fell back to his arse, she pressed them harder. 'Our weapons and the inkweld are still a problem.'

'Full of problems and no solutions. Come on, Mithrid, what do you propose? You fought in the siege just as we did.'

'Durnus uses a shield spell, we crouch behind Fleetstar and dash into the night.'

Farden and Durnus shook their heads. 'How far would we get, with the whole camp behind us and a wounded dragon that can't fly? Unless you plan to burn another fifty thousand men and women just because they're in your way.'

'Seems like a plan you'd be all for,' Mithrid hissed. His doubt and lack of trust were not just grating, they were becoming insulting. The Forever King's glamour had dulled to rust and dirt.

'Durnus is weakened, as am I. These bars would take some fire to break through. The guards, what few there are, would notice.'

'So... what? How do we escape? Or have you given up?'

'We need be sneaky,' grunted Warbringer, doing foul business in the corner of her cage that none of them dared look or sniff at.

'Warbringer is right,' said Farden. 'That's why we wait.'

'Some race,' Mithrid huffed. Patience was a skill she hadn't trained in. She tried to copy the vampyre's cross-legged approach, eyes half-closed in meditation and calm breath. She lasted moments before being distracted by passing guards. Braziers burned around cages as if they were quarantined. The light hid the tents beyond.

'I don't know how you do it,' she confessed.

'Imagine a battle in your mind. That is how I passed the time in the cages of my past. Imagined every slash and dodge, different ways to catch a man off-guard and spill his insides. Your muscles might be shackled but your mind is not.'

Mithrid nodded. She had done plenty of that since the fight with Malvus. But before she could imagine three different ways of ramming a sword down his throat, Farden hissed something she couldn't make out.

'And it seems we do not have to wait long,' muttered the vampyre.

❦

'About time,' Farden hissed.

The hooded figure walked the murk between the pools of brazier light. The shaded tent kept the moon and firelight from them. Noises of dancing and songs kept the soldiers distracted. Belerod was so confident in his bars and his mastery of his captives, he hadn't set much of a guard. It felt the perfect trap, but Farden had seen the victory smirk on the warlord's hairy face. That kind of man was drunk on success.

'If it isn't the Lady of Whispers?' he greeted her, arms crossed and voice a whisper.

Irien paused to stare at him in the half-light of the flames. 'You look... older, Farden. Years looked like they've passed you by, not a week and more. What has the road done to you?'

'Just a few bruises and cuts, is all. And if you came here to insult me instead of to explain yourself, then you can turn around right now and fuck off somewhere else.'

Irien pressed herself up against the bars to meld with their shadow. Farden stepped away. Mithrid and Durnus stood, like a haughty council for Irien to appeal to, despite the fact she only looked to the mage.

'After we fled Dathazh, I came south. Like I said, I had plenty of whispers to sell in Lezembor. I was on the cusp of the city when Belerod's caravan crossed my path. He and I have had dealings over artefacts in the past. He'd no doubt seen me with you, and as such, asked if the Lady of Whispers knew of a way to get an audience with you. A meeting, is what he called it.' Irien winced as she heard her own words aloud. 'I didn't expect him to do this.'

'What did you tell him?'

'Your names and of your homes. Nothing of this quest you seem to have survived. Only that there was a likelihood of you coming south.'

'How did you know?' Mithrid chipped in.

'I didn't. A guess that I thought could buy me into his good graces while I found more ways to leverage enough gold to either stay on the winning side of this war, or avoid it altogether. I know a lot of the north's secrets. And you can wipe that look off your faces. I left a lot of my wealth behind because of you.'

'Because of an agreement you proposed,' Farden corrected her. 'What? Didn't you have enough of the dragon in Dathazh?'

'I swear to you, Belerod said nothing of his plans! And now it seems I am a prisoner of his also. An advisor, at least until it suits him to get rid of me. You and I are in the same position.'

Mithrid snorted in disbelief. 'Yet you're the one on that side of the cage.'

'For now.'

Farden let her conscience eat away at her, what little she had of one. Self-preservation drove her, no doubt. He had hoped for more, and as such, he let her stew. Petty, perhaps, or the only chip he had to bargain with.

'So are you going to let us out of here or what?' he grunted at last.

Irien tutted. 'Of course. I was beginning to wonder if you wanted to argue all night.'

But she didn't move, merely looking to the north and muttered to herself.

'What in Hel are you doing?'

'Hush, mage. All will become apparent momentarily.'

Irien didn't finish her sentence before a fountain of white sparks shone over the faraway peaks of the tents. Hot sparks, palmwood, and canvas never mixed well, especially in desert climes. Shouts of danger chased the whooping of drunken soldiers as the flames crawled up the palms and turned their leaves to torches. Tents began to crackle.

'That's the problem with these southerners,' Irien said, her face orange in the light of the flames that now billowed. 'They enjoy mixing all kinds of magick powders and tinctures together to see what happens. Sometimes, or so they whisper, an accident or two can happen.'

'Where are you going?' hissed Farden. Irien strode away as if her work was done.

A flood of soldiers swarmed past the other side of the cages. Golden knights surrounded Lord Belerod as he came to check upon his prizes before rushing on to the fire. Farden and the others shrugged or waved nonchalantly, not having to pretend they were innocent. Irien had thought this through.

As soon as Belerod had passed, Irien was back at the bars with hands full of gold cloaks. She slid a thin and serrated blade from the wrist of her wooden arm. The Lady of Whispers was full of all kinds of surprises.

The cages each had four locks of varying sizes spread across their latches. It seemed the Lady of Whispers was not unused to picking locks, either. She poked the blade into the keyholes of each one and worked away until they came apart with reticent clanks. It took far too long for Farden's liking, even with Warbringer snapping one lock from her cage with her bare hands.

As soon as each door was open, some inner mechanism clunked free, and the doors of the cages opened in clockwise order. Ingenious, but Farden had no time to marvel. He was first from his prison, and he wasted not a second in seizing Irien by the throat. The mage pressed her against the iron, and squeezed just enough to let her know this was not for show.

'You give me one reason not to snap your neck for your betrayal right now.'

Irien's eyes flared, not afraid and far from angry. Almost daring him. 'Belerod tricked me just the same.' She thrust her chin out. 'And because I know you're done with killing, Farden. I can see it in your eyes. Even in the Scarlet Tourney you had no taste for it. You couldn't kill Tartavor for his trickery and you won't kill me for an honest mistake.'

Farden could see Mithrid in his peripheries, watching and listening intently. Though he let Irien go from his fist, he leaned closer to her, almost touching noses. 'Fail to get us out of here, and I might show you how wrong you are.'

A dark shadow came over them as Warbringer loomed. 'If I may?' she asked, before brushing Farden aside with her big paw. She also seized Irien, and she had no qualms about throttling the woman. Warbringer lifted her three feet off the sand and slammed her against the iron. Irien croaked and pried ineffectively at the minotaur's thick mitts.

'Warbringer...'

Her question was simple. 'Where is my Voidaran?'

Irien couldn't so much answer as point and pat her with assurance. She was dropped to the ground and left to sprawl against the bars. 'Well, that's one experience I never expected to have,' she rasped.

Farden scoffed. 'And if you don't want to see what comes after, I'd get moving.'

Irien flashed him a hurt look, but she led them on all the same, at first, along with the bustle of soldiers to the fire that had set the palm trees on fire, and then, curving back around to the court of Belerod. Hoods up and looking precisely more or less like Khandri and Hasp soldiers, nobody gave them a second look, even the hulk of the minotaur, swaddled under four cloaks

Belerod had not yet returned, and it looked as though plenty of his courtiers had scurried after him. The remaining few dozen were too drunk, fat, or lazy to follow. To Farden's fury, Belerod had parked Fleetstar's caged wagon directly in front of his dais. Handfuls of the rich folk stepped around Fleetstar's bars, daring themselves closer while the dragon whipped her tail against the iron and snarled. They would giggle and whoop and skip away in their fright.

One skipped right into Farden's armoured fist.

The man fell away, his nose mashed into his bloody face and mouth too full of loose teeth to scream. The rest fled before the imposing silhouette of Warbringer. She took one look at the game being played with her hammer by the drunken soldiers and began to charge. She didn't stop until she had swept Voidaran into her hands and swung it directly through Belerod's map table. The wood exploded under the force, as did one soldier who unfortunately chose to cower instead of run.

Their weapons and belongings were spread across another table like spoils of war. Mithrid seized her axe and held it close before fighting for the satchel with Durnus. The vampyre snatched it away, pawing within before letting out an enraged bark.

'The inkweld is gone!' he cried.

'I told you!' Mithrid hissed. They must have left it behind in the desert.'

At least the Grimsayer remained, sat open and still. Belerod had clearly not been smart enough to figure its value. The purple elvish tome was shown the light.

'How are we going to find the others?'

'Another bridge to cross at a later hour!' Farden yelled back.

While he reached for Loki's knife, one of the Khandri swords lying forgotten nearby caught his eye: the ones shaped like a question mark. The blade had an impeccable balance and finer steel than his borrowed Cathak swords. He hooked it over his shoulder and yelled to the others. Their definition of sneaky had changed somewhat; the camp was already in uproar.

'Help me get this cage open, Warbringer!'

'No!' Irien hissed.

'What do you mean?' snarled Fleetstar.

'The whole camp is abuzz with the idea of a caged dragon in their midst, but to see one strolling between the tents is another thing altogether. We keep you in the cage until the edge of the camp.'

Fleetstar cursed in guttural dragonspeak but otherwise pressed herself against the bars as Warbringer picked up the yoke of her wagon and heaved. Her hooves dug troughs in the sand, but the brute force of Warbringer got the wagon to gather momentum and begin rattling south. Not for the first time on this accursed quest, Farden found himself thanking his stars for a minotaur.

None of the passing soldiers and camp slaves did more than gawp at the passing dragon and nudge their comrades as they sprinted to the fire. It seemed Irien's distraction had caused quite the blaze. She must have guessed Farden's thoughts as he stared over his shoulder, for she shrugged.

'All of Golikar is out for your blood, say the whispers that come down from the north. The seas are full of Golikan ships looking for a minotaur and a red-gold man.'

Farden held his tongue.

'What is it you're chasing, I wonder? What is worth so much that you would have the entire Easterealm up in arms just to get to it?' Irien asked. Again, as Farden clung to silence, she pressed him. 'Is it something to do with her? Mithrid?'

That got his attention. 'What do you mean?'

'She's got a fire in her, more than I ever saw in Vensk. You, however, keep checking her with every other look, making sure she's nearby. You look... scared of her, Farden. What happened between you two?'

'Nothing I care to repeat or speculate about. All that matters is the present and getting out of here. Going to find the forge of Ivald...' Farden bit his tongue as they passed another hurrying patrol. Irien bid some Khandri greeting to them and waved a hand at the fire.

'Did you say Ivald?' Irien said, seizing him by the hand.

'Why?' Farden could see Durnus had heard them, hovering close. 'Have you heard of the clan of Ivald?'

'Ivald wasn't a clan. He was an elf. *The* elf who forged the Allfather's mighty spear. The same spear the Allfather later gifted to Sigrimur when he was a man, only to then betray him by killing him and turning his flesh to stone. What most don't know is that Ivald was Sigrimur's father. That's why some of the oldest songs paint Sigrimur as half-elf. Even part of his name, *imur*, used to mean elf in some dialects. That is the truth only we ancestors are told—'

'Then, do you know where Ivald's forge was?' Durnus interrupted.

Irien puffed out her cheeks. 'In his fabled stronghold I suppose. Sword of the Elves, the songs call it.'

'Sword of the Elves,' whispered the vampyre as he hurried along, robe flowing behind him. Foreign words trickled from from his lips as he though aloud. 'If *imur* means elf... *Imur. Kiliz* is sword in a similar dialect. *Yara*, to cut, *azin* means blade...' Farden heard it at the same time Durnus did. The vampyre dug into his satchel and frantically rifled until he found the map of the east. 'Azin Imur. Azanimur. It is not a Khandri name after all, it is elvish. The forge must be—'

'Halt there!' came an order from behind them. A gold knight was following them, his sword already unsheathed and ready.

'Rather not!' snapped Farden, as he tried to lend his own strength to the wagon. To his dismay, there was no discernible difference. The edge of the camp could be seen at the end of their undulating path. The open desert, falling away into a lowland of scrubland and salt-pan.

Farden clutched Irien's arm. 'You've kept your side of the bargain,' he said. 'Go now, while you can. It's our turn for a distraction.'

Even then, in the panic and rush of escaping, Irien found time to grin and seize his vambrace with her wooden hand. The contraption was strong. 'That sounds like forgiveness to me,' she said.

'It's not,' Farden said. He did not shrug her free but let their diverging paths do it for him.

'Whatever the south calls you to, do me a favour and stay alive,' Irien said before vanishing between the tents. 'I have a feeling our paths are entwined, Farden, King of Scalussen.'

'If I see you again, Lady of Whispers, it will be too soon!' he called after her.

'Farden!' Mithrid yelled after him. He caught the others as they weaved a zigzag path between tents and woodsmoke. With the knight lost behind them, Warbringer broke the bolts of the cage with several swings of Voidaran. Fleetstar was soon free, snarling at them as she stretched her wings. She yowled as the pain caught her left wing. It hung limply at her side, and she slammed the wagon with her tail in anger. A wheel collapsed, broken in two.

It was a simple drunken soldier that brought the camp swarming after them. Farden saw him all too late. He lounged against a tent, cross-eyed with wine but still able to recognise an angry dragon, even in his state. Whether he sounded the alarm or did it for drunken fun, he raised the horn he held in his hands and blew it.

'Fuck!' yelled Farden, before breaking into a stumbling run. The others bounded after him.

'Can you glide, Fleetstar?' Aspala yelled by Farden's side. She managed to catch him as he tripped upon a tuft of sand. He nodded thanks to her in silence. Her face, framed in the firelight of the burning palms, normally serious, seemed alive with the energy of the escape.

'I may be able to,' rumbled the dragon. Sand flew from beneath her claws.

'It looks like we may have no choice!' yelled Durnus. There was now a growing number of soldiers chasing them.

Farden kicked over a brazier and set a tent ablaze. Goats scattered from inside, providing a wonderful and chaotic reaction. Mithrid followed suit with another, and as they ran, she spun shadow behind them. Even despite all his reservations for the girl – deeply closeted fear, even – she was a fighter.

The edge of the camp appeared all too suddenly. They burst from between two tents into the colder air of the desert. Guards stood about between braziers, arrows nocked and looking bemused.

'Can I burn the camp now?' Fleetstar growled.

Farden set his hand to her neck. He could already feel the inferno roaring within her chest. 'Be my guest!'

Fleetstar opened her jaws wide, sending the guards running for their lives. The dragonfire reduced several of them to ash before she paused for breath. The sand turned to brittle glass wherever her flames of gold swept.

When the first arrow thumped into the sand at the mage's feet, he knew their upper hand was swiftly crumbling. 'We need to run!' he ordered. Durnus threw up a feeble shield as the minotaur dragged him and Mithrid onwards. The plateau of sand reached out into the night before falling down into the lowlands beneath.

*Fleetstar!* Farden bayed in his mind. He had to throw his hands against her and push the thought through those stubborn scales. Whether it worked, or it was the sight of a monstrous ballista trundling out from between the tents, but the dragon almost knocked him flat as she turned.

Once again, Aspala was there to hold him up.

'Keep the others safe,' he yelled. 'Don't worry about me!'

'You forget, King! Without you, there is no Scalussen,' she snapped.

Something hissed past his ears, and Farden watched as a black streak hammered into the sand perilously close to the minotaur. Another arrow clanged from Mithrid's armoured back, knocking her into a spreadeagled roll. Warbringer hauled her up and tore into an all-out sprint for the plateau's edge. Farden stowed every ache and pain and pushed himself as fast as he could go. Fleetstar thundered past him even so, skidding lopsidedly and almost knocking Durnus into the night. Mithrid was aboard, hunkered low as another iron bolt whistled into the darkness. Now the vampyre. Warbringer seized the dragon's front claws. Farden pushed Aspala on ahead of him. His legs were leaden in the sand. He was tiring fast, and yet he did not slow. An arrow ricocheted from his arm. The shock rang through his armour like a bell. Aspala turned as she sprinted, and as she did, her dark eyes widened. Before Farden could turn, she seized his out-stretched arm and with a vicious heave, sent him sprawling.

Even before he had crumpled into a heap, he knew.

The sound was unmistakable. Of steel puncturing flesh and bone. Of Aspala's gasp.

Farden scrambled upright, sand stinging his eyes as he hurled himself after the woman. An iron bolt had skewered her, pressing her into the sand. The bolt ran her through the stomach. About two foot of iron and bristled fletching protruded from her back.

'Aspala!' Mithrid screeched. She was fighting to get off Fleet-star's back, fighting Durnus tooth and nail. She shouted over and over to be free.

Aspala fell to her knees just as Farden reached her. Blood already dribbled from her lips, but she was wild-eyed. No shock lingered on quivering eyes, just a cold determination. As Farden ducked more arrows, fired wildly into the darkness, he watched her drag the rest of the bolt through her with a blood-curdling roar. Crimson stained the sand black in the starlight. It left a horrendous wound in her belly, but she clung to life with a fierce determination.

Aspala fended off his attempts to pull her to the dragon. They were so desperately close.

'We have to go!' he yelled at her. 'Up you get, soldier! You've seen worse.'

But Aspala would not be moved. Digging her sword into the sand, Aspala pushed herself to her feet with inhuman effort. 'It's time for you to leave, King,' she gurgled. 'Ever since that cave of mirrors, I cannot stop thinking of my mother. Now I know I'll see her soon enough. Give me a warrior's death, as I've always wanted. As I promised you.' The smile spread across her bloody lips.

Farden could not leave her, and yet Aspala slowly wound her arms out of his grip, and raised her sword to her forehead in salute. He could see dark shapes swarming across the sand towards them. Gold armour glinted in the now-distant brazier fire.

'Go!' she grunted, pushing him away before menacing him with her sword. 'Do not force me to make you. Do what you promised us all, King!'

Farden raised his sword to her, lingering as long as he dared. It was with a heart struggling to beat and an enraged shout that Farden was forced to turn and run for the dragon.

'No rest 'til freedom served!' she bayed to the stars, before crossing blades with the first of Belerod's soldiers. The man's body fell to the sand headless.

'We can't leave her!' Mithrid screamed in Farden's face as he clung to Fleetstar's back.

'She won't leave!' he bellowed right back. 'It's too late, Mithrid!'

Fleetstar gave the girl no further chance to complain. With a lurching flap and roar of pain, she launched herself over the slope of the plateau and careened into the night. Her wounded wing was barely kept aloft, but the dragon burned with more than just fire. A monstrous determination kept them aloft and gliding.

It was with grinding teeth and tears that they watched Aspala fade into shadow. A circle of corpses was growing around her. The ring of her golden scimitar filled the night like the mad tolling of a bell. The last they saw of her, before the ridge stole them from view, the Khandri and Hasp were rushing her with shields. Her guttural roars chased them across the dark and silver sand.

'Escaped, you say?'

The Khandri soldier bobbed his head again, hands clutched in front of him like a servant begging a boon. 'They escaped, Lord Belerod. All save one. The one that killed your son.'

A scimitar landed on the steps of the dais. Its gold had been painted red with blood.

Belerod twiddled the knife, drilling a small hole in the table's varnish. The court held its breath as they waited the warlord's judgement. The sound of grinding stone came from behind him as one of his golems shifted its weight.

He saw the figure weaving through the gathered, hooded and confident. Belerod raised his knife, ran the blade along his hairless scalp, and then hurled it.

The soldier fell to the sand to hushed gasps and whispers, eyes cross and staring at the knife embedded between his brows.

As the corpse was hauled away, Belerod turned to the shadow that had fallen over him.

'And what do you have for me?' he asked her. 'Oh, Lady of Whispers?'

Irien sat down beside him with a smile. 'I was right. Just like I suspected in Vensk, Farden is looking for an ancient weapon. One that, if I know my ancestor's history, is worth more than mages and dragons. More than your golems, perhaps.'

'Lies,' Belerod spat. He extended a hand and a servant immediately filled it with a flute of cold wine.

Irien chuckled. Her wooden arm rested on her knee, fingers tapping ponderously. 'The smithing and crafting skills of the ancients has yet to be matched.'

'But they shall in due course,' scoffed Belerod. He had no respect for those who had fallen to history's ravages. His empire, his Harmony, would last a thousand years when he was finished. 'What kind of weapon?'

'Sigrimur's spear Gunnir. A weapon of great power and fit for the gods, or so say the old songs.'

'And where is it?'

Irien pointed a wooden finger. 'It was said to be destroyed or lost to the ocean. Nobody has ever found it, but Farden and Durnus are trying to prove countless scholars and skalds incorrect. He is going south to search for a place called Azanimur, where the spear apparently lies.'

Belerod had studied every map of the Harmony. He dug through his memories as a scribe might peruse a library shelf. 'At the far edges of Khandri is a ruin of that name...' Belerod drew another knife from his belt and waggled it at her. 'I will not let my prizes escape my clutches willingly and chase them hundreds of miles for pure amusement. Mine or yours. That weapon will be mine.'

Irien fixed him with an unwavering gaze. 'You will not regret this, Lord Belerod. You and I shall have what we want at last.'

'And what, pray, is your great goal, Lady of Whispers?'

She tapped her nose. 'A shame you had to kill one of them. That was not what we had planned...' Irien began.

'My lord!' came a cry. One of his knights came wading through the court with little care for who he barged or how forcefully. 'My lord! The northern envoy has arrived.'

The evening had distracted him. 'What envoy?'

'The, er, envoy we told you of earlier. Our spies report their fleet of ships have landed off the northern coast, near Chanark. Thousands of soldiers have come ashore, despite a storm sweeping south. They are Golikan, they say, Lord.'

Belerod exploded to his feet. 'They invade our lands!'

'No, Lord, they come to ask for passage south across the deserts. Their queen Peskora waits for an audience with you. She refused to speak in more detail to a mere, er... *dusty peasant*, in her words.'

'Passage, indeed?' Belerod glowered at the man. This was highly unexpected, and if there was one thing Belerod hated in the world was surprises.

'The Golikan queen, did he say?' Irien asked, trying to play nonchalant, but already he could see the stiffness of her posture.

Belerod ignored her and instead marched to the edge of his dais to greet the northerners' arrival. Warm winds ruffled his beard and robe. A dozen of them entered before the Golikan queen. Hands on hips, Belerod stared at their intricate wooden armour and their stocky crossbows.

Queen Peskora was a pale woman of some height, little girth, and even less hair. Her armour's varnish gleamed. A waterfall of pendants of silver and gold hung around her neck, glowing softly with a green dust. She would have cut quite the formidable figure had it not been for her injuries. She relied heavily on a golden cane. Her other wrist was bound in dressings beneath her armour. A cut scored her brow like a second frown.

Beside her was an older man of weathered skin and many years, and furs dyed yellow and blue. He sweated profusely, and his shoulders were lopsided. One side of his face had been burned quite recently. *By dragonfire*, Belerod strongly suspected.

Though this man lowered his head, Queen Peskora refused to bow in Belerod's presence, just as he had refused in hers.

'Lord Belerod of Haspia,' she greeted him. 'I recall you from the Scarlet Tourneys.'

'That is my name. And you are Queen Peskora of Golikar. And you, sir? I don't recognise you.'

'I am the High Cathak Tartavor,' said the sweating man.

'And what is it that brings you so far south with no invitation, if not for war or the diamonds of our mountains?'

Peskora looked impatient. 'We have no interest in your mountains. You have a pest upon your lands. And if the burning palms and tents I saw during my approach are any indication, you have already experienced it. His name is Farden. I seek vengeance on him, as is my right. I hear he's fled here, and I would ask for permission to take my army after him.'

'A whole army for one man,' said Belerod. 'My, my.'

Queen Peskora's gaze snuck past Belerod. 'And while I am here, I will take the head of that woman behind you.'

Belerod turned to find Irien smirking defiantly.

'Hello, cousin,' she whispered back. 'And here was I, thinking you'd come all this way just for me.'

Peskora chewed her painted lip.

'The Lady of Whispers is under my protection, sadly,' Belerod replied. 'And as for your original request, it will come with a price.'

Belerod could see the anger flitting across the queen's face.

'A toll?'

'You can have the mage to do with as you please. His dragon, minotaur, and his belongings are mine,' he uttered. 'We will march alongside you as a guide.'

Peskora and her fur-clad ally flashed a fiendish grin. *Fools*, to not know the price of their own prey. 'A fair deal. I accept,' she said.

'As do I,' added Tartavor.

Turning his back on the queen and the Cathak, Belerod returned to his ornate throne of a chair while they were ushered from the court. After he had taken a swig of wine, the warlord rested his hand on Irien's wrist of flesh and bone and began to squeeze. His tone was measured. Quiet. Conversational despite its threatening words. 'You had better be right about this weapon, Lady of Whispers. Otherwise, I will hand you over to this queen that seems to admire you so much.'

The woman was resolute. 'If you go south, Belerod, you will not regret it. Farden has become weakened. Durnus looks sickened or plagued. And Mithrid is a wild force. They will not be able to stand in your way.'

Irien kept her smile until Belerod turned away and stared across his whispering court with a satisfied expression of his own.

'We march at sunrise!' he barked.

# CHAPTER 31
## AZANIMUR

*The daemons forged the dark elves from their spite, the corpses of
lesser gods, and tortured magick. It is no wonder they bathed in destruction and death as much as their masters! The elves were so cruel
to our ancestors that many stories paint them as the primary evil behind the daemon's war with the gods, and the slavery of the first humans. They inherited cunning from their creators, built machines of
foul intent, and summoned creatures from the void of the other side.
Yet for almost two millennia since elves and daemons were banished
to the sky by the gods, it was the elves we feared more. That is why
parents threaten wayward children with the claws of an elf in the
dark should they not behave! Why their wells of magick were destroyed, why their grand fortresses were cast to ruin, and all trace of
them burned away! Many believe the elves linger between their daemon masters within the stars, but I warn you, not all dark shadows of
this world fell to the gods' wrath that day. Not all.*
FROM WRITINGS OF THE HERETIC FALSO

Silver sands were soaked crimson by the morning sun. The dawn felt
cold to all the endless deserts but the handful of travellers who
hunkered close to a dragon's back.

Fleetstar's claws clipped the dunes. The rising heat gave them
another few miles of soaring before the pain grew to be too much,
and the momentum of their glide, too little.

At last, Fleetstar landed, saying nothing but growling plenty in pain. Nor spoke the others. They removed themselves from the dragon's scaled back and clutches, as cold and stiff as the stone automatons that had stood at Belerod's command.

Mithrid wasted no breath. She put her numb legs to the sand of the boundless landscape and started walking. Her mind was just as numb as her limbs, and though they gradually awoke with use, no amount of concentration could make sense of her mind. The dawn burned a glare into her left eye as she stared at the rippling horizon.

Not a shout chased her. Only the others, walking in single file and matching silence. Although their purpose was clear, their time was no doubt shortening by the second now they travelled by foot. Mithrid felt it. The few times she spared a glance for the north, the others were staring too, where a dark, distant band of a sandstorm lingered. Farden faced ahead, a concerned look on his face that Mithrid neither wanted nor needed. No doubt he had some lesson for her. Some apology or explanation that changed nothing. She knew the best medicine for death: blood.

Mithrid was growing to realise that was her fate. The reasons came with each stomp across the sands. Not glory, but death. To either take lives or have them snuffed out around her. *Her father. Remina. Littlest. Inwick. Modren.* And now Aspala. The old friend of blame tried to sink its fangs into her, but they were blunted. The mirrors were right: she would see the world burn again for them. That was what they deserved and what she owed them.

Under her punishing pace and an even more torturous sun, they surged through the dunes and white salt flats, where the heat made illusions of lakes all around them. By noon the landscape was growing rugged again. Red sands grew striped with yellow, and then blue, until they walked a rainbow path. Scrub bushes hunkered low in rifts and hollows, as if wilted and baked in the heat. Their purple flowers held no distraction for any of them, even Mithrid.

Not a beast dared brave the heat as they did. A few hawks and vultures paraded above, but not a track but theirs disturbed the sand. The night, however, held all manner of life. Harsh noises and scampering shadows kept their necks sore from turning. Mithrid saw nothing bigger than a wolf. Even then, she did not break pace, holding her axe out low and her hands clawed around shadow.

And still, not a word broke their mourning or exhausted silence. Not a pause to their headlong journey. Even Farden, who looked half-crippled and switched between riding Fleetstar and walking, stayed silently plodding. The mage's eyes were still clamped on the southern horizon. Durnus' head was bowed, but Mithrid glimpsed his glowering eyes, yellow and red in the light of a second dawn.

'Are we close, Durnus?' Warbringer asked. Her back was bent beneath her hammer. Sand clung to every patch of her hair and skin.

Durnus refused to meet their looks. Instead, he looked to the pursuing storm in the north. It now swept from east to west, bruised dark. 'I hope so,' he muttered.

They had no supplies to cook, no inkweld to scour, and nothing but the armour and clothes on their backs and the few flagons of water they had stolen while rushing through Belerod's camp. Wasting their lead by halting made no sense to any of them, and the decision went unspoken for another whole day, until the third dawn brought them a peculiar chill wind.

The rainbow sands had long faded to burgundy and now grey. Almost black. The sharp heat dulled with it. Clouds streaked the sky, their bottoms dark and heavy. The meagre sun that fell between them brought no heat. It was bliss compared to the sweltering desert and the labour of walking.

The clouds above slowly thickened. The smell of salt came with the wind. The grey land rose up to what looked like the crest of a hill. Black rocks of granite and volcanic glass poked from the sands in scattered, angled shards, like spears against a charging horde. They slipped between them with ease and climbed the ridge of grit. There, the snow began to fall, turning afternoon to evening. Sleet, to be more accurate, so cold it felt like it sliced Mithrid's hot cheeks.

As Mithrid reached the crest of the hill, she realised it was no hill at all. The pounding of waves grew thunderous as she approached a sheer drop down to a shattered beach of razor rocks and sea-spray. The grey waters were wrapped in the sleet, but from the size of the waves that rolled from the ether, Mithrid felt the trepidation of standing on the precipice of the world.

A sharp ridge of rocks defied the waters to reach a tall turret of stone that braved the ocean's onslaught. She got the impression more of it had once existed. The island's sides had been eaten and hollowed by waves, leaving a crooked castle to perch precariously above the maelstrom. Ruins lay crumbled and fallen into the water. Not a single light or flame glowed in the ruin. It looked haunted, never mind deserted.

A crash of armour sounded behind her as Farden fell from the Mad Dragon's side. Mithrid didn't move to help, but before Warbringer could reach him, he had crawled upright. Farden looked like death: haggard in the cheeks. Yet more silver had found its way into his jet hair. The bruises of the north still had yet to fade. His hands, free of their gauntlets, were of scrunched paper. Each scar was a purple welt. His nails broken and grey.

He stumbled to the edge to stare at the castle, wordless for some time while he propped himself up on his stolen sword.

'Is this it? Is this what we've struggled for?' Farden asked. His voice sounded thin.

'Died for,' Mithrid corrected him. Hers was little more than a dusty croak. He levelled a glare at her.

'Azanimur. The Sword of the Elves,' Durnus breathed. 'Ivald's forge.'

'At fucking last.'

With no more to add, the mage made his way back down the slope, his boots crunching in the half-settled snow and dun grit.

Durnus looked put out. He was not alone. 'Where are you going?'

Farden didn't reply. All he did was draw the knife Loki had given Mithrid.

She marched after him. 'Where are you going, Farden?'

The mage walked a hundred paces until the ridge was almost lost in the haze of sleet and cloud.

'Speak to me, damn you!' she yelled at last.

Farden whirled on her, brandishing Loki's knife. 'You save that anger for somebody who deserves it, Mithrid. You'll need it all too soon, I'm sure.'

He raised the blade, making her hand flinch around her axe before he slammed it into the ground. Only its ornate golden hilt protruded from the grit.

Mithrid stared at the knife until a flash of lightning stole her attention. It came from the west, and yet she heard its rumble to the north. She understood nothing but her own impatience and thirst to deal death.

❦

'To Aspala,' Farden said as the others gathered around him and the girl. He raised their last flagon of water and dribbled some of it on the cold ground around the golden knife hilt. 'To a true warrior, a friend, and a believer.'

'Aspala,' the others murmured. Mithrid shut her eyes and refused to open them. She looked seething, not soothed over paying respects.

'What are we waiting for, Farden?' Durnus hissed. 'The spear is within our grasp.'

The vampyre was shivering. His sharp nails repeatedly dug into his folded arms. Farden told himself it was the cold, over and over, and not Durnus' daemonblood burning to be free. So much dangled by so fine a thread, Farden worried even the wrong thought might snap everything he had gambled so far.

'Redemption,' was all he gave them. Every second that passed, his stare bored into the skies, waiting and watching. And hoping, while he felt the cold seep deeper into his armour and bones.

The dim clouds had swallowed the coast to the west, bringing an early night with them. The sandstorm closed in from the north. Snow had begun to carpet the desert of rocks and grit. Wave after wave pounded the beaches and cliffs behind them, counting the moments down until every knuckle was white.

'What of the Doomriddle,' Warbringer growled, 'and its promise of death?'

Nobody answered her, least of all Farden. The riddle's words had plagued his mind since Durnus mentioned it. By their unresponsive clearing of throats, the others had suffered the same malady.

Lightning coursed through the sky, reaching towards them. He did not need his magick to taste the acrid char to the wind, the metallic taste on his tongue. By his side, Mithrid took a step, teeth bared.

'It's time,' Farden grunted. 'Time to put an end to this, at last.'

Farden dragged his blade through the dust. Hoarse orders spilled from him. 'Fleetstar. You will take the others to the Sword. Durnus, you will take these keys and find the three doors. Be quick, now.'

'And what about you, Farden? You will be stranded here.'

'Bait.'

The daemon's fire within Durnus showed itself for a brief moment. 'Explain yourself, mage,' he grunted. 'You are in no condition to fight Malvus alone. You look fit to drop at any moment.'

'As your king, I don't need to explain and we don't have the time.'

The daemon's spite shone through Durnus' eyes for a moment. It made Farden's heart stutter to see it. They stared, and saw the truth of each other: two men, each crumbling from within in such similar, yet different ways. Neither could help nor heal the other.

'You shun your title the whole way here, only to order me around at the last moment?' Durnus hissed.

Farden had to turn away. 'Find that door, Durnus. Have Fleetstar speak to me when it's done.'

'You can't just—!'

'Warbringer?'

'I will fulfil my vow,' Warbringer boomed as she manhandled Durnus away. He fumed, fangs bared, but Farden saw the fleeting worry in his glare.

It looked as though the minotaur could also see the change in Durnus, however much he hid it. 'To grey-skin and to you, King. You kept your word.' Warbringer lowered her horns in a shallow bow, Voidaran touched to the rings of her snout. Farden returned the gesture, sweeping as grand a bow as he could despite the constant bonfire of pain in his body.

'You had best join us, mage,' hissed Durnus before he was gone, as pebbles and sand tumbled around their feet and hooves. 'Both of you.'

Farden turned at last to Mithrid. She was a white-lipped pillar of black armour and hair blowing around her face. Green eyes stared through that scarlet fire.

'Don't you dare,' Mithrid warned. The tirade that had been building for days spilled from her. 'Don't you dare send me with them. The spear is nothing to me now. I just want Malvus for myself, with nothing but my magick. I know I'm strong enough, and you can't stand in my way any more. I won't let you. I can't stand your doubt, Farden. You filled my mind with glory, with possibility, both here and in Scalussen. Now, for you to hold me back, to distrust and loathe me after…'

Mithrid could have driven the axe into Farden's face right there and then. A small piece of her even tried.

Farden was *laughing*.

'What in Hel are you doing?' Mithrid spluttered at the cruelty. 'Are you so broken that you have lost your m—?'

'*You*, Mithrid, are exactly the person I want by my side.'

'What?'

Farden took a deep breath and tasted the electricity in the air. 'You are destined for power and glory. As much as it may concern me, I believe that wholeheartedly. And despite Loki's tricks, I do not doubt you, Mithrid. I definitely do not loathe you. I've been holding you back until the time was right. Your lust for revenge does not just drive you, it defines you. You long for blood and death, but not to avenge the lives of the lost as you think, but to, in truth, make yourself feel better. You seek revenge to have control over what you cannot control. Death comes for us all, and chasing vengeance for every corpse and loved one becomes selfish. I say this because I, too, let it consume me. It breaks my heart to see you fall into the same ruts as I have. I don't know *better*, but I know what you feel. I lost everyone, even those who didn't die.' Farden clutched at the gauntlet, where she knew he lacked a finger. 'The temptation to give into it still lingers, as I may have done in Irminsul. Even now, the same fire still burns inside me. For Modren. For Inwick. For Aspala. But for the rest, too. Those still alive and depending on us. I can only warn you about this path, but right now, I need that pain and fear, Mithrid, all that rage and selfishness storming inside you. Because here, now, you are the only person that can hold Malvus back long enough. Evernia was wrong.'

Mithrid found no spit in her mouth. Her tongue rasped, dry. Farden had floored her with his honesty. All the anger she held for him vanished. 'Long enough for what?' she whispered. 'What right time?'

Farden waved his sword from the storm to the sand. 'You'll see soon enough.'

'And Loki?' she asked.

'Ever since that mountain of shale and mist beyond Lilerosk, I knew Loki had sent us here. The knife only confirmed it. Every path we've trodden, every struggle. Every sacrifice. It's all been Loki's doing. He needed us to find the spear and its resting place. Malvus, like us, is his tool.'

'And you sound unnaturally calm about that. I thought you despised being a pawn.'

'You better hope Durnus is right one last time.' Farden grinned and slammed a fist against the wolf on his breastplate. 'If Loki wants the spear, then he can have it.'

Before Mithrid could respond, more laughter rang through the rushing air and snow. It was not Farden's this time, but familiar all the same.

A shape drifted from the haze. Coattails crackled in the growing breeze.

Mithrid leapt forwards, but Farden's sword blocked her path. 'Not yet.'

'Who is that?'

'That would be Loki, God of Lies. The Morningstar.'

Loki flitted from place to place, the air snapping with magick. He wove a jagged path towards them as he spoke. His voice reached out beyond the wind's touch, as if he circled them instead of approached. Mithrid held her axe high and ready. Ice flooded her veins as she sought her dark magick.

'That it would be, Farden Forever King! And Mithrid Fenn, still alive, thank goodness. Tell me it is not just you two that survived? What a shame that would be.'

Farden's face fell once again deathly impassive. 'A shame indeed,' he called back. 'And where is your new pet? The abomination you've created out of our fallen Malvus?'

'So very close.'

'Aren't we all?'

'How far you've come from Scalussen!' Loki crowed. 'Just as I trusted you would. Through fire and even Hel you would walk for your friends, Farden. It was charmingly pathetic until now, when I needed such an obsession. And with that vampyre's keen mind, and this fierce young woman by your side, I knew you would do me proud.' Loki cast a casual gaze around across the snow and spears of rock, and laid bare his true purpose. 'Tell me: where is the Spear of Gunnir?'

Farden shrugged. 'No idea.'

Mithrid spoke up, determined to have her piece in this. 'We're lost, sadly. All this way for nothing.'

From his furrowed brow, it looked to Mithrid as if the God of Lies had never been lied to.

'Ever the defiant jester, aren't we, Farden?' Loki snapped though he feigned a grin. He stood not a dozen paces from them now. Mithrid strained every muscle to stay still.

'Three tasks. Three keys. Three doors. That's what the elvish book mentioned. Why else would you have come all this way? Why else would you battled from Dathazh to Mogacha, run so far south, it's become almost north again, only to come all the way to this place? You are a poor liar, Farden.'

Farden was fiendish. 'Unless we wanted to draw you as far away from your precious Krauslung as we could. To waste your time, perhaps.'

'All because you thought yourself too smart, that we would meekly do your bidding without realising your plan,' Mithrid yelled. 'We knew what you've wanted all along.'

Loki curled his hand. The knife embedded within the sand scraped in its grave for a moment before flying back to the god's grasp. He grinned effortlessly. Behind him, a fierce glow permeated the gloom. Fingers of lightning, red, green, and blue, stretched over their heads to the reverberant ocean.

'Petty mortals! I am bored with you. Cling to your pathetic rebellion if you must, Farden and Mithrid, I'll take the three keys now, or I shall pry them from your dead bodies once Malvus is done with you. I've seen your lack of magick, Farden, and how weak you truly are. I have the upper hand, at last.'

Mithrid had never heard the mage's voice as cold. His words were the razor edges of flint.

'You won't live long enough to lay a finger on either of us, Loki.'

'Farden, King! Mithrid Fenn!'

Their names were uttered in rolling thunder.

Mithrid tensed as she saw Malvus emerge from the curtains of snow. No fenrir paced beneath him now. His own great strides closed the distance between them. The snow melted before his mere presence. Every rune on his foul body was lit brightly and burned through the soiled rags that still clung to him. The very shine of him hurt Mithrid's eyes. She persevered, not daring to look away.

Tendrils of black shadow flittered around her, poised. The mage beside her did not shrink. Sword and axe were raised and quivering only slight, gold and black steel glinting in the light of magick.

'Don't hold back,' he growled to her.

'Wouldn't dream of it, old man!' Mithrid yelled.

Malvus wasted no time with talk, as Loki was so fond of doing. He raised his hands and sent a wave of magick coursing across the ground, scattering snow and pebbles.

The onslaught drove Mithrid's heels through the sand. Her magick billowed inches from her fingertips. She barely kept the storm of fire and lightning at bay.

When Malvus broke the spell, Mithrid reeled. She snarled, spinning a shield of shadow just before Malvus hammered her again. Green lightning sought to pry her shield away, wind spells buffeted her. Her knees felt weak already. Farden was behind her, looking grim and determined.

Mithrid remembered his words, and roared as she thought of Irminsul, and how she had dragged up every dark memory to fuel her. She thought of Aspala, dying alone on a dune at the hands of foreign soldiers. Shadow streamed from her. Malvus' magick shrivelled for a moment. Across the stretch of snow, he bellowed her name as her power stung him.

'Mithrid Fenn!'

It was not enough. Her best shot, powered by all her fury, had barely touched him. The doubt raced through her, usurping the cold touch of her powers.

Behind her, Farden said nothing, merely staring north and east as if this battle was boring to him.

'He's too strong, Farden! Even stronger than before!'

'You don't need to fight him for long.'

'What?' she spluttered. 'I need to kill him!'

'Tell your witch to surrender, Farden! And I will make your deaths quicker than you deserve!' Malvus beat his chest. Magick poured from him now. It washed across the snow and black rock like a tide. Even the touch of it pounded in Mithrid's head. Her shadow shrank away, spiralling around her arms instead.

She picked at every scab in her mind, dragged up every pool of blood in Troughwake, and even then, she barely held back his next barrage of spells. The onslaught forced them to the foot of the slope, towards the precipice. Loki lingered behind Malvus, where his retinue of broken soldiers, fenrir, trolls, and daemons had appeared.

Mithrid saw Gremorin, standing without his crown. Blood roared in her ears. 'Tell me you have another plan, mage!'

Farden said nothing.

'You are too weak, Mithrid!' Malvus bayed over the inferno spinning in his hands. The heat was palpable even from a stone's throw. 'And you, Farden! Cowering behind a child. You are no champion, no marvel any longer. I can feel how weak you are! Your true might lies in my skin now. I have become the pinnacle of power, forged by magick and daemonblood. Face me, you cur!'

Fire poured towards her like the breath of a dozen dragons. Mithrid fell against Farden as it railed against her wall of shadow. With gritted teeth and sweat pouring down her face, she pushed against Malvus' might. Pain surged through her as the spell scorched her hands.

And still, the mage did nothing but stare at the dust-heavy sky that loomed perilously close.

'What in Hel are you doing, Farden?' she bellowed.

But Farden was already standing tall before her, sword out and the fire swirling around his boots in the wake of the monster's spell. A smile had spread across the mage's face. To Mithrid's confusion, the thunder of the magick had yet to subside. Snow and shadow spinning about her, she stared after the mage.

'Malvus!' Farden roared.

Malvus grinned, spread his glowing arms wide as if to embrace an old friend. 'At last, you greet your death as a man.'

'It's a fine army you've brought, Farden called. 'I so happened to bring one of my own.'

Malvus looked around at the empty wasteland and cackled, lips spreading grotesquely wide as if he had ripped his cheeks. 'Your tricks will not work on me!'

Loki had noticed the same rumble as Mithrid had. No thunder. No magick. A dark band had appeared in the fog-wrapped hills to the northeast. 'Malvus!' shouted the god.

At last, Malvus' singular attention, as distracted by vengeance as Mithrid had been, turned as the horns began to blow.

Farden beamed.

'What the fuck?' she gasped.

'Redemption, Mithrid, and in the hands of our enemies no less!'

Mithrid watched, enraptured, as the dark band swarmed down the hill. Soldiers. Thousands of them. Beasts crested the hilltop in close pursuit. Armoured coelos with banners streaming behind them. Chariots drawn by galloping birds. Even Cathak cows, bred for battle. And three colossal beasts with forts built upon their backs, tusks the length of a ship's mast, and strange trunks that reached the floor. Their bellows were louder than any battle-horn. The pebbles shook around her as the armies swept towards them.

Mithrid saw Harmony gold and the green banners of Golikar riding together. Mithrid considered every slashed throat, every slight in the Tourney, even the burning of Belerod's camp.

'You planned this all along,' Mithrid breathed. 'Didn't you?'

'That I did.' Farden laughed coldly and with a shake of his head, as if he were a tired builder, at last looking upon a finished work of toil and sacrifice. 'Tartavor and Oselov gave me no choice and Irien's warning about Queen Peskora following me to the ends of the earth gave me the idea. I knew Loki had created something to stand in our way. We needed protection. I stirred up enough trouble to have it all come after us. And now, by the looks of it, my gamble has paid off. We have an army of our own, thirsty for blood.'

All this time, she had thought him mindless. Reckless. But there was method to his barefaced madness. Despite her doubt, the Forever King was as sharp as ever. Mithrid stood, weak but already feeling bolstered. 'Just one problem: aren't they thirsty for our blood?'

'Malvus doesn't know that, does he?' Farden answered. 'And I'm sure he'll be happy to introduce himself!'

Just as predicted, the furious creation ordered his daemons readied. Their thirst for souls and carnage could always be counted upon. Fenrir bounded to meet the enemy ranks. Malvus clawed at the air, bringing lightning bolts down on the front ranks. It was all the excuse the army needed to unleash arrows upon the daemons. If they had ever seen such beasts, Mithrid did not know, but they did not falter. She saw the daemons ploughing into spears and soldiers with almighty roars. One daemon was immediately impaled on a colossal tusk. A fenrir clawed curiously at the giant beast's side while archers filled its face with arrows.

'Curse you, Farden!' Malvus bellowed across the wasteland. Mithrid flinched, expecting a charge, but the god at Malvus' side had other ideas. Loki yelled something at him over the clash of battle.

Malvus raised his hands to the sky. 'Witness what true magick looks like!'

'Is he doing what I think he's doing?' cried Mithrid.

'If Evernia was right, then yes!'

Mithrid was already reaching, but her shadow crumbled before the blistering waves of magick. She took a step, but Farden held her arm. 'But we have to stop him! He'll tear down the sky if we don't.'

'I've seen it happen before,' he muttered, dark memories crowding behind his eyes by the look of his glower. Had he not just magicked an army from the snow and sand, she would have shrugged him free. It took her all to hold still.

'Only the spear matters!' Farden said.

She watched the mage mouth the dragon's name as he called out to her. *Fleetstar.*

The ruckus of magick and battle triumphed over the battering waves. All that could be seen of the clash was the lightning that scored the sky above the castle. One bolt even struck a chunk from the highest turret and sent it spinning into the foaming waters. Seabirds fled in flocks.

Durnus could feel the pressure against his skull. Magick from the outside. Ravenous hunger and bilious anger from within. His thoughts were a tangle of worry for the mage and Mithrid, never mind the battle of his own heart.

Warbringer's shout shook him free. 'Durnus!'

Once again, he peeled himself away from staring at the obsidian cliff behind them and pressed his fingers against another mould-encrusted wall. Fleetstar spouted fire into the hallways, burning moss and years of vines from the vampyre and minotaur's path.

The search was desperate yet fruitless. The ruin held all manner of hollows and dark spirals into the darkness within the rock. Dilapidated caverns of halls above dripped sea-spray. Snow fell through open roofs and turrets. The black stone held old murals, once chiselled and painted but now fallen to two thousand years of decay and wear. Durnus knew the feeling.

For all the stone doors that remained on hinges, most already lay open, as if the inhabitants had dashed to leave this stronghold. The others needed only a barge to open, or did not fit any of the three keys.

Much to Warbringer's dislike, the search led them down into the darkness. A broad spiral stairwell, large enough for the dragon, escorted them to halls hewn from the bare rock and carved into ornate coiling architecture. Great vaulted ceilings lay in darkness. Durnus sparked a light spell and found statues of steel looming from pedestals or lying face down on the stone. The seawater permeated from somewhere, leaving a film of muck on the floor. The only sound became the steady muted crash of the waves. Durnus could feel their rhythm in the soles of his feet.

Forges lay silent past the statues. Complicated machines of crystal and iron cogs lay broken around them. A stone table lay at the centre of the greatest and final hall. A dim shaft of light pierced the roof above, bringing the day's feeble light and the occasional snowflake floating down. The table looked half an anvil, half an altar. Workbenches and broken kilns lingered in the shadows at a respectful distance like a hushed congregation.

The daemonblood fought against the magick in Durnus' veins, but he pushed through the sharp sting beneath his skin and expanded his spell. The white light in his palm reached the edges of the round room. Warbringer and Fleetstar were already searching them, but the rocks were smooth as parchment.

'I see no door,' said Warbringer. She cast around in stomping circles. 'What we do, Durnus?'

But the vampyre was staring at the table. The more he considered it, the more it looked like an altar, not an anvil. Durnus approached it, stepping across rings of patterns carved into the floor. He spread his fingers across the dust and scattered snow. The altar was flat and unmarked. The vampyre frowned. He had expected something more than bare stone. He cast around, probing every edge before he lay the first key on the altar. There was no effect. Then the second, and third, and still nothing.

'What is in your mind?' Warbringer demanded as she loomed over him. 'This is no door.'

'Sacrifice,' he said aloud, speaking the persistent echo in his mind. 'What if this is an altar. What if...'

'Durnus!' the dragon roared. 'Farden is calling for us!'

'Gods damn it!' Durnus felt urgency becoming panic.

'Move, grey-skin,' Warbringer ordered. 'You not use your eyes as you should. Mind too full. Too busy. This an anvil. No altar.'

Barely before Durnus could scatter out of the way or protest, Warbringer swung Voidaran over her shoulder and down onto the stone with a painful clang. The hall refused to give up the echo.

'What have you done!' Durnus yelled.

His words were still falling on her when the anvil began to split into pieces. Not under the force of the hammer, but into perfectly divided segments. A star-shaped void appeared beneath Voidaran's touch to the scrape of stone. Stale air belched free. Choking dust rained.

Durnus and Warbringer recoiled as the pieces kept recoiling. The intricate floor's rings spun beneath their feet, almost tripping them into the hole before they could reach the safety of the hewn floor. They clattered to the dust.

On their knees, with the dragon peering over them, the vampyre and minotaur stared down into a perfect bore through the obsidian rock. It fell thirty feet before it ended in another spiralling floor. This one was smaller, made of crystal and set within a thick ring of plain stone. Peculiarly, statues ran along its sides, not fallen, but perfectly horizontal and at peace on their plinths.

'I go. Catch you,' grunted Warbringer. As always, the minotaur's words were not discussion but narration of the actions she was already undertaking. She was already on her hooves and aiming for the stone below.

Warbringer fell barely five feet before she slumped against the sheer side of the pit. Durnus had to rub his aching eyes.

'By Thron's balls,' whispered the dragon above him.

Warbringer stood upright, level with the statues and completely perpendicular to the floor Durnus stood on.

'Dark magick,' the minotaur growled.

'Tell Farden we've found the door!' yelled Durnus, as the light above began to fade dark, and furious crimson. Taking a breath, he jumped headlong into the pit.

# CHAPTER 32
## EVERY GOD & MORTAL'S FEAR

*Three tasks every god and mortal fears to face await. Three duties yet fulfilled of blood, breath, mind, and soul. Three cursed keys to three doors to be left locked evermore. If that be your fate, your errand, the first task lies in Eaglehold's roots before the serpent's shimmer, by Gunnir's last blood. Hear the last breath of retribution's lesson. Follow its call to your screaming end.*

*Fool's path you've chosen, headlong to ruin. Trace Vernia's glow to where a giant drowns and stand upon his brow. Bodies fall in faith betwixt the third dragon's tooth. There taste forgotten airs and lesser minds. Only the drowned shall know the sepulchre's secrets.*

*Torrid waters fail to halt you, yet the highest price awaits. Turn where men fail to tread without sinking, with shadow in your right eye at dawn 'til roaring waters. West lies Utiru's wrath. Scarred sister's light burns the path, terror dark and crystal sharp. Cut the throat of your sweetest dreams or lose your mind.*

*Madness you may have survived but darkness calls you on. South, go you, to Gunnir's birthplace. Nothing but the wrath of the gods awaits you behind cursed doors. The final payment to claim Gunnir awaits. The highest price.*

THE DOOMRIDDLE, WRITTEN BY THE CULT OF THE ALLFATHER

Clouds billowed in concert to Malvus' clawed and clasping fingers. A whirlwind blew around his boots, half-sunk into the sand under the weight trying and failing to crush him.

Daemons bayed and howled around him, keeping the intrusive army at bay with their claws and fire and blackened swords. Arrows swarmed around Malvus. Either they were caught in the wind or burned up in the heat that was now turning the sand to molten glass beneath him. And still, Malvus toiled to tear down the sky.

The voices wailed in his pounding head.

*Burn it all.*

*Bring it down.*

*Then make them all bleed!*

Malvus indulged them.

He knew not what he grasped for, except the very stars themselves. He could feel them like burning coals of light in the maelstrom above him: searing hot, yet worth every bolt of pain. The bones of his legs screeched in protest at the effort it took to stay upright. His muscles were aflame beneath his skin with the weight of his spell.

'Keep pulling, Malvus! This is what you strived for! Not some mage's head, but the very sky and stars themselves!'

He saw the god from his sweat-filled peripheries, grinning as madly as he was. Fists clenched, cheering him on.

Malvus felt the spell reach its crescendo at last, blasting past the clouds and the very firmament to where he felt the daemon struggling in the void. It ached to be free, and Malvus sought to break its shackles with all his might, focused and pure. To destroy the ancient spells the gods thought unbreakable. *How wrong they were.* Malvus tore them down with an inhuman roar.

The resulting uproar was so loud the battle fell still for a heartbeat. The daemons were slowly being overwhelmed and pushed back. One of the giant bastion beasts was charging straight for them, crushing its own ranks in the madness with tusks and tree trunk feet. Yet even that dumb creature turned to face the sky as the clouds burned red and the air split in two.

A star wrapped in fire and brimstone punched through the storm and crashed directly into the bastion's back. The castle exploded in flame as the beast was floored, immediately gutted. Wings of black shade and a tail of fire emerged from its smoking corpse. Hundreds of soldiers sought to flee while thousands more kept pressing them in.

Malvus' amusement was a shrieking cackle. Despite his fingers cracking under the strain, he seized the next star, and the next. 'Even the gods will bow before me, Loki! Beginning with you!'

But the god was not listening. He was staring beyond the army. Beyond the fallen daemon. He was looking to Farden and Mithrid, who stood defiantly in the face of the chaos.

Loki began to stride towards them, knife low and purposeful.

'They are mine, Loki!' Malvus boomed.

❦

Mithrid's whole body trembled. The sky was falling before her eyes, and with it, every shred of confidence in her power crumbled. This was beyond her. This chaos was of edda and song, not a reality she could grasp.

Farden hissed in her ear, as loud as he dared over the noise of battle. 'Finally! They've found the door!'

Mithrid wrenched herself away from gawking at the pandemonium. 'And just how were you proposing we get to them?' she asked, voice cracking.

'We don't. Now, we've forced Malvus' hand we keep Loki away from the spear until the last moment,' Farden snapped back. Mithrid was still glowering at him, a single eye narrow. 'Trust me.'

'I would, except Loki is coming straight for us.'

Mithrid spoke true. The god was striding towards them, head craned and eyes searching the sky beyond them.

'I feel it, Farden!' he cried. 'I feel your dragon's voice in the air. I feel the magick long lost and unfelt. Did you think you could trick me, mage? My puppet strings stretch across Emaneska and back to places you've never dreamed. My hooks have been in you for years, swallowed by your flesh and bone. You cannot pull the wool over my eyes. I am inescapable!'

Farden clomped down the slope, sword spinning. 'Keep him from leaving!'

'Where is your magick, Farden!' challenged the god. This was a different Loki than she had seen. No coy wit any longer. No charm and flitting eyes. He shone with magick of his own. He clenched a fist, shattering a nearby thrust of stone into shards that pelted their armour.

Mithrid reached for him with her shadow. He held it just beyond his reach, but Mithrid felt the strain in him.

'It's not possible,' he sneered. His form wavered. The air buckled around him, yet he could not escape.

'Damn you, Mithrid Fenn! I should have let you die.'

'Yes,' she said. 'You should have!'

Mithrid was pushing him skidding through the snow when the daemon fell to the dirt between them. Fire and rock exploded in her face. She felt herself flipping through the air. Sky and sand pirouetted until one of them chose to drive the wind from her. Blood dripping from a cut in her face, Mithrid tried and failed to push herself up.

Beyond her quivering hands, the ground fell away. She watched the snow scatter in the wind and dance around her fingers. The roar behind her was a whistle to her ears. Only her breath could be heard, shallow and short. The iron waves below came at their leisure, unperturbed by the matters of gods and daemons and mortals. Fearless, ceaseless. Never-ending. Mithrid stared at it while her eyes dropped.

The glint of fire kept them open. A flame, soaring through the haze of snow far out to sea. Another chased it. A large shadow lurked between the haze.

'Farden…' Mithrid croaked.

The mage's voice made no sense. 'She found us! That wonderful, crazy woman found us!'

Before Mithrid could push herself up, she felt cold metal fingers grab her by the collar and haul her up. It was Farden. The urgency in his face looked like madness. It must have been madness, for he forced them towards the edge of the cliff. The sea's maw opened.

'Farden!' cried the god behind them, wreathed in fire.

Mithrid howled as Farden threw them over the edge. Like the ground beneath her, all trust in him vanished in that second. She reached for his throat even then.

A surface of solid muscle and fur knocked the breath from her lungs. The keening eagle's cry brought reality crashing back to her.

*Ilios.*

Mithrid's fear of heights and all things winged disappeared entirely in the face of her startled relief. She seized Ilios' fur in a tight grip, and, as the gryphon swooped for the ruined castle at a violent degree, she grinned.

'The fire! The signal!' Mithrid yelled to the mage, perched in front of her and grimly clinging on. 'You saw it! Scalussen came for us after all!'

'Trust in Elessi to disobey me!' cried Farden.

But Malvus still lived, raining star after falling star upon Belerod, Peskora, and Tartavor's armies.

The lurching of the gryphon ripped her attention away. Ilios rolled over a low beam, following the scene of dragon or minotaur, no doubt. Relief withered. Fear came rushing back as Ilios barrelled through corridors barely wider than his wing, and in a somersault, plummeted down a spiral staircase. As Mithrid became convinced the gryphon would dash them to entrails on the stone floor, he flared his wings and swooped into a cavern of a hall. Broken forges lay beneath them. Statues crowded around pillars. Ilios wasted no time in exploring, and before Mithrid could make sense of that hall, they had darted into another and another, where Fleetstar waited with her head stuck down a hole in the floor. She roared at the sight of the gryphon, whose claws scraped patterns on the flagstones as he skidded to a halt. Mithrid and Farden tumbled across his wing, and almost fell straight into a pit that was the fatal kind of deep.

Mithrid must have hit her head harder than expected. Durnus and Warbringer were stood below before a circular door of crystal. Yet somehow they were not on the floor, but they stood upon the wall. Even the flames of their torches were slanted horizontal.

'Jump!' yelled Durnus.

Mithrid spat in disbelief. 'Fuck that!'

Farden's penchant for hurling himself from precipices knew no bounds, but as she watched, he did not fall down, but to the side, crash-landing on his back with a wheeze. In the pale light shining through the crystal door, the mage's hair and beard looked grey. It jarred her, but not so much as the pit's bizarre spell. Mithrid almost vomited, even though she had managed to land on all fours.

With her hand under Farden's arm, they ran to reach the others. Durnus had the crystal key halfway into an elaborate portal. Spiral script ran around the door in concentric rings.

The sound of a whip cracking broke her concentration. Gryphon and dragon roared above as Loki came barrelling through the air. He slammed into both the mage and Mithrid with the force of a catapult.

Though she struggled like a sabrecat, Mithrid felt inexorable hands pin hers, and cold steel at her neck.

'Slowly now, Mithrid,' Loki whispered in that sickly voice of his.

She arose gradually with the god close at her back, the knife firmly in his grip, and the others' weapons pointing at her.

'I'm sorry, Farden,' Mithrid muttered. The mage visibly seethed.

Durnus stretched out a hand, but no spell blossomed. He tried again, wincing. Voidaran made no noise when Warbringer twirled it. Even Loki seemed momentarily perturbed when he met Durnus' empty hand with his own.

'Well! A curse lies on this place, it would seem,' he whispered. 'No magick can exist here. It should make for an interesting resolution to this stalemate, should it not? All of us on equal footing, at last?' Loki chuckled. 'And so here we are, at the end of your long road. After all your toil, you still end up doing my bidding and landing in my clutches.'

'You vulture!' Warbringer boomed.

'Open the door, my good Durnus, or I shall slit this girl's throat and that will be the end of her story. Let's finally see what you worked so hard for. Let's see Gunnir together, shall we?'

Durnus didn't move.

'Do it,' Farden ordered. Mithrid caught the surreptitious shake of his head and kept still. She remembered what the minotaur had taught her. 'Do what he says.'

'Wise words, oh King.'

In her ear, Loki whispered again.

'Be good, Mithrid, and you just might live to see your friends again before I wipe them from the map.'

Durnus pushed the crystal key into the mouth of the keyhole to the faint musical scrape of glass. Muttering something to himself that sounded suspiciously like a prayer, he turned the handle and elicited a resonating boom. Light rippled through the intricate glass of the door as it came apart, splitting along faint lines that had been invisible before. Whatever magick of machinery moved the panes, it was slow and silent.

Farden had no time to marvel. He watched every shift of Loki's gaze. He matched every tread of his foot, never dropping his Khandri sword for a moment even though his arms burned.

Beyond the door, the tunnel continued down to a door made of what looked to be bone. Rings of ribs and jawbones decorated this one. Ghoulish faces stared down at them. The script between them had become ever more frantic and imperfect, now chiselled as if in a hurry. At the door's centre, a star of knuckles, and a keyhole for the second key.

Loki couldn't resist working his serpent's tongue. Why it wasn't forked, Farden did not know. He pushed faster, and Loki sped up, too. It was all he could do not to lunge at him. *Loki was so close, and without his magick…*

Farden felt the cough rising in his throat. He fought it back but to no avail. Pain lanced across his chest, almost bending him double. Farden spat to the side, spotting the stone with dark blood.

'My, my. I have never seen you so weakened, Farden. The road has ravaged you. Ravaged you all, it seems, has it not? I see Aspala is not amongst you. A pity. I liked her.'

Mithrid struggled briefly before remembering the steel at her neck.

Above – or at least behind – them, dull booms could be heard, and Ilios' plaintive whistling. Daemons and spells were beginning to fall on the castle.

'You and Durnus have changed much,' Loki continued un-fazed. 'Weary in contrasting ways. What happened to your magick, Farden, or the blessings of your armour? Don't tell me… you're broken? By the gods, what a shame. No wonder I can see more years on your face. You're the Forever King no more, it seems. And Durnus. I see the daemonblood in those raw eyes of yours and feel the shadow in your veins. And after all the times Farden warned you not to engage with soul magick and necromancy. Can you be called a vampyre, or even a man, any more? You are no less a mongrel than Malvus.'

With fangs bared and wielding heroic restraint, Durnus put the second key to work. Once again, the door split into six segments. A foul breath of ancient air leaked forth with a sigh as the bones slid into the rock.

'One more key. One more door,' whispered Loki.

The final door lay another stretch ahead. No statues waited here. More faces, not of bone, but carved black obsidian. Each was as tall as a man, in varying stages of frozen screams. Their glasslike faces looked liquid in the torchlight. Their wide and pained eyes seemed to follow them.

Farden could see breath before him. Cold misted his armour. Colder were Loki's words.

'I wonder how you lost your magick. Most curious, unless you've developed a taste for nevermar once again, Farden?'

'No such luck. Irminsul's fire was fierce.'

'I would rather wager it was our good Mithrid here.'

'And I'll strangle the magick and life out of you the moment your back is turned,' she hissed.

'Fine advice that I shall listen to. But I think I've stumbled on the answer, no? Who else could do such a thing? No witch. No daemon. No shadow of a god.'

'Oh, how I will enjoy cutting your tongue from your mouth, Loki,' Farden showed his teeth in a mock smile. The god's poison flowed so easily he had grown almost used to it. He and Loki did not break their stare, not even while Durnus produced the final key. Its rough obsidian matched the circular door, indistinguishable from the walls around it. A final, hastily scribble of a warning circled the keyhole.

Loki read it aloud. ' "Your screaming end awaits",' he said with a confident chuckle. 'Then what are we waiting for, my friends?'

Durnus gave the mage a look so blank as to be worrying. 'Farden?'

Farden took a deep breath. 'Open it.'

Still, the vampyre hesitated. Loki drew blood from Mithrid's neck. 'I'll slice her head clean off right here, Durnus. Open it, like Farden said. Open it!'

Durnus bowed his head as he entered and turned the key. Another boom shook the walls and stone under their feet. This door did not split evenly, but cracked along jagged lines. Splinters of obsidian were spat to the floor. Most disconcertingly, the rumbling and quivering did not stop.

With bated breath, he watched the door shatter before them. Icy breath stole his away. A void of a room awaited them, reticent to give up its shadows to the torches. At its centre lay a shaft of light that no sun or moon or star gave. Hovering at its centre, held by no altar or chain, lay the Spear of Gunnir.

A sinuous curve of ornate steel and silver, frost millennia old decorated its metal. It floated an inch from the flagstones and spun slightly in its column of light. Slightly taller than Farden, the spear had the wicked blade of a glaive, pockmarked with runes and forks of lightning entwined in silver. Gunnir had a ring to it. A music. A whisper like the Grimsayer that somehow could be heard over the increasingly loud rumble above them.

Farden brought up his sword and tried to keep the point from wavering. 'Give us Mithrid, and take the spear. You've won, Loki.'

'Farden!' Durnus hissed.

Loki cackled heartily. 'My! You should have been bards and skalds, both of you! Do you think I haven't studied the same elvish scripts? The same riddle? I was the one who brought it to you, remember? "Of blood, breath, mind, and soul". It warns you from the outset that the spear demands a sacrifice,' he lectured. 'And if I am wrong, then you will have no trouble bringing it to me.'

Farden, Durnus, and Warbringer exchanged glances. It dawned upon Farden that the god might have won indeed. That this, after all his planning, his strife, had been part of Loki's plan the entire time. *It was all too easy for him,* he snarled under his breath. All too simple for a god.

A chunk of black glass fell from a height untouched by the torchlight, and smashed at the foot of Warbringer.

'We haven't got all evening, it would seem!' yelled Loki. His grin was mad with glee. Farden half-raised his sword to strike, but once again he held Mithrid tight and pressed the knife deeper. All the while, he circled closer to Gunnir. Farden matched him as if duelling. Durnus, too, weaved a path.

Loki roared at them. 'Choose now, you mortal worms!'

'Stay back, Durnus!' Farden warned him. There was an avid glint in his eye that clutched Farden's heart in ice.

'Go ahead, Durnus!' Loki urged him.

'There's no other way, mage! One of us has to choose. It was always going to be this way!'

Another crash of glass sounded behind them. A section of wall had peeled away. Shards skittered around Farden's feet.

'We're running out of time.'

'You shut your fucking mouth, Loki! And you, Durnus! Back away! Don't you dare!'

Durnus' hand reached towards the spear, the veins of his arm black in the pale light.

As Farden lunged to bat his hand away, Loki finally made his move. Mithrid had been waiting for him to do exactly that.

Seizing Loki's wrist like Aspala had shown her, she reached behind her head and grabbed the god's golden locks. Loki screeched like a wraith, but as he reached for the spear, he found the floor greeting him instead. Mithrid sank to her knees and drove his nose to the stone. Warbringer pounced to hold Loki down.

Farden's hand found its mark, seizing Durnus' wrist at the last moment. But as he pushed, he found it rigid as an iron railing. Farden's gaze moved down his old friend's arm. There, firmly in his grip, was Gunnir.

To Warbringer's bellow, Farden grabbed Durnus by his collar, holding him to prove he was still alive. He stared into his reddened eyes, and clasped him by the back of the neck to feel the frail warmth to his skin. The vampyre looked no different. Durnus even showed his fangs in a smile.

Hope surged through Farden. 'See, you were wrong, Durnus! Gunnir doesn't need a sacrifice!' he cried.

And yet, with the subtle yet inexorable shake of Durnus' head, Farden's hope met a crushing end.

'I can already feel it, old friend,' said the vampyre in a whisper.

'No! You bastard! You selfish bastard!' Farden yelled in his face. He pulled and pulled at the vampyre's hand, but there was no dislodging it.

When Farden looked up, his eyes were half-closed and calm. 'It is done,' Durnus whispered. Farden watched, aghast and useless, as the pale skin of his face began to crumble away to nothing but fine sand.

'This was my choice, Farden. I made it long ago, and I would see my own way to Hel instead of losing my mind to the daemon-blood fighting to claim me. This death has been coming for a while, and if it can be of use…' The vampyre shuddered. 'Then so be it.'

Durnus' left jaw had almost disappeared. Farden could feel the skin of his neck crumbling beneath his hands. Tears sprang to the mage's eyes. Durnus reach out a hand already half gone.

'You never failed me, Farden. Not once. For a man who never had the chance at a life of normality, one with wife and child, you were a son to me.'

'I never meant it,' the mage babbled. 'What I said on the mountain. You saved us all by putting us on this path.'

'Who knew,' Durnus smiled again, one eye now disappeared. 'After all this time. It was me who was the hero. Perhaps now they will write an edda about me at last.'

Farden caught the flash of movement behind him; heard Mithrid's scream.

'Farden!'

Before Farden could turn, before Durnus had fallen completely to dust, he felt the vampyre's last thread of strength seize his hand and thrust it onto the cold of Gunnir. Durnus' last whisper drifted into the dark.

*Save them.*

A mere blink later, Loki's hand seized the spear. The god and the mage found themselves grimacing at each other for the briefest of moments before Loki began to cry out in pain. The rumbling built to fever pitch. Ice exploded from the spear, slicing Farden's brow. The steel grew hot in his hand, almost unbearably so. Rocks exploded left and right of him. He could see Mithrid and Warbringer shouting to him but the roar was deafening. The cavern was collapsing. He stared down at the god, rising above him as Loki knelt, seething in his desperate attempt to keep hold of the spear. Farden realised what Durnus had done. Gunnir was Farden's, and his alone. He squeezed the spear with all his remaining strength. Its heat ran through his veins, surging up his spine and swelling in his skull. Not just Gunnir's power, but a flame long missed and absent.

Farden went rigid. Magick sparked and crackled into life within his bones, seeping into him with jarring convulsions. White firelight raced across his back. And there: the flurrying prickle of ice. Of Scalussen cold and Scalussen steel. Of old blessings. Farden felt the pain beginning to recede as his armour rattled violently. Light escaped from the scales.

Farden held Loki's wide and furious eyes, and grinned.

'Beat you,' he said.

The concussion knocked Farden to his knees, but it hurled the god spinning against the obsidian wall. The force brought half of the cavern tumbling down atop him.

Mithrid and Warbringer were staring at him with a mix of wonder and fear. He was levelling the point of the spear at the half-buried god when light pierced the gloom. Not Farden or Gunnir, but light of a waning day and growing fire. The ceiling beyond the tunnel of doors was collapsing. Ilios trilled frantically.

With the daylight, the hold of the tunnel's spell broke. Farden felt the magick rush from him, clashing with Mithrid's in two opposing waves. Together, they charged the god, but not before there was a burst of glass shards, and Loki, once more, vanished.

'CURSE IT!' Farden bellowed, and with his voice, an unexpected stream of searing light poured from the spear's blade. The obsidian disintegrated before its power. A smoking hole was left in the rock.

'I'm sorry, Farden,' Mithrid began, tears scarring the dust and blood across her cheeks. 'For Durnus—'

'Durnus saved us all. Let's do him the honour of making his sacrifice count,' Farden snarled. 'It's time we left!'

With a resounding bell-toll, he slammed the spear's haft on the stone and the air split before them.

Malvus was the agent of slaughter. The master of magick.

The sky had almost been emptied.

As the final daemons fell to the frozen earth, the armies of gold and green scattered, broken and defeated. Daemons' claws dripped with gore as they stalked the fields of wounded. The rest were fleeing over the hill, chased and devoured one by one. Malvus' arms collapsed in the grit. Heat emanated from him in great waves. Light ran across his tattoos in rapid succession.

*Farden.*

*Mithrid.*

*Kill them both.*

Malvus bellowed their names as he pounded the sand and snow beneath him. The slope was a cliff. He could see a horizon of ocean between the sleet. He remembered a riddle of snow, distant, belonging to his old body. He dismissed it as nonsense, and ignited an orb of fire in his clawed hand. His head drummed with pain, but he spurned it all for the mage and the child.

'Where are you, Farden? You owe me a death. I will peel your skin from your—No!'

A huge Scalussen ship of black sails sat in the ocean, near to a wave-battered and smoking ruin. No daemons stirred in its rubble.

Malvus let the fire rage white-hot as he took aim at the ship. A piercing cry halted his arm halfway cocked.

Claws slashed his face as a huge gryphon exploded from the edge of the cliff. Malvus reeled, blood in his eyes. He managed to clear his vision just in time to see a hammer swinging for his face, at the end of it, a bellowing minotaur.

The impact sent him sailing back down the slope.

Malvus found himself face down in the snow, spitting bloody teeth. His jaw was broken in two, but it did not stop him spreading his fingers across the ground. The very stones around him cracked under the force of his magick. Green and white fire blazed across his arms and shoulders. The gryphon reared before him as he stood. Curses streamed from Malvus' shattered mouth. The wind around him howled as he brought his spells to bear.

Lightning speared the earth before him. A rift cut the air. Figures of steel strode forth; red, gold, and black. Malvus' spells fell dead as he stared, somewhat dumbly, at Farden raising a silver spear towards him.

The arc of light struck Malvus in the chest, blasting him a dozen paces before he crashed to the unforgiving cold once more. His rags had been burned away. Smoking burns spread from his groin to his neck. Even the runes beneath had fallen dark.

Before the light could reach him again, Malvus screeched as fire consumed him. He bent it into a vortex, a shield before him. Farden struck him again, and the spell held.

Two dragons, black and blue, raced across the sand with the jaws wide and flames streaming.

Malvus screeched as their fire joined his. It seared him to the bone, yet even as he felt his own flesh burning, his power grew even brighter. He flung out his hands and let his inferno fill that cursed wasteland.

Farden met the wild firestorm with a splayed hand and a shield spell that made Mithrid's ears pop viciously. With his other hand, he kept Gunnir pointed at Malvus. He shook with the effort. The light threatened to blind her. She held up her shaking hands to shield herself. Her shadow trailed behind her like smoke before a gale. Gunnir's power railed against her skull like the minotaur's hammer.

'It's you, Mithrid!' Farden shouted to her. His face was one of sweat and strain. 'It's you that can beat him! Fighting magick with magick won't work!'

Mithrid shook her head. 'If even the spear can't kill him, what can I do?'

'Damn it, Mithrid!'

Farden barked to Warbringer instead. 'Get to the ship! We will meet you!'

*The ship.* The word stabbed Mithrid in the heart. 'Hereni,' she uttered aloud. All this time, she had fought for the dead, dredging up their corpses to warp her shadow. *She had forgotten the living.*

Mithrid clapped her hands together. Shadow whirled, bending the fire and even Farden's shield before her. He shouted after her, but she heard no words.

*She had forgotten those beating with blood and fire like her. On the ship below them. In the mage next to her. Even in those upon their arduous road, and all to claim power over the dead. To speak for the hand of fate when it was really her selfishness that called for blood.*

Mithrid snarled with the effort. She couldn't see Malvus through the inferno, but she kept pushing all the same.

*The dead could not be saved, yet her friends – her family – they still could. They were worthy of such selfishness.*

Mithrid found him. The bloodied creature opened his mouth in a scream she could not hear, not cared for.

*She thought of Elessi. Of Bull. Of Lerel.* Of how Malvus would see them all dead and devoured just the same as the bodies across the plain beyond. There, with the fire scorching her steel and skin, seeking to reduce her to cinders, Mithrid let go of the hooks of revenge that she had woven into her skin. This was about survival. This was no longer about vengeance but victory.

Shadow poured from her hands, arms, even flowed with her cry of struggle. Her magick crashed against Malvus' spell like the ocean behind her. Again and again, she pushed him, watching his flames shrink until he knelt in the sand and screamed her name.

Mithrid felt the magick deep within his screaming bones and wrenched it from him. The shield of fire shattered, and Gunnir's light reached him at last.

She looked on with grim satisfaction as Malvus was pierced by the light. It near deafened her as the sheer force of Gunnir's power ran him through. Leaving him slumped upon his knees and staring at the glowing hole in his gut.

Mithrid drew her axe. Her boots chose a slow and careful path towards him through the snow and cinders. Malvus, even with his last breaths, tried to goad the girl of Hâlorn.

'You are more of a monster, it seems,' the broken emperor gasped, reaching a crooked finger to point at her.

'At last, you pay for what you've done, Malvus, and the world will be safer for it. Your body will rot here, perhaps food for the gulls or even the daemons. Hel is too good for you.'

In full view of the gathering daemons, Mithrid swung her dark Scalussen steel.

The head of Malvus Barkhart fell to the snow with a thud. Blood seeped from it, both red and black as tar. Mithrid stared while Malvus blinked one last time at the cold ground pressed to his cheek.

A hand rested on her pauldron. The spear of Gunnir whined in Farden's hand as he spun it. The daemons were watching on. Mithrid saw the charred and bloodied hulk of Gremorin standing closest. Hundreds of daemons stood at his back, and even with their numbers, they made no move. They recognised Gunnir, and by their snarls and curses, they felt its fell magick.

'Leave!' Mithrid yelled at them. 'Or die here today.'

One by one, the daemons made their choice. They began to vanish in bursts of lightning and brimstone. Soot and smoke drifted with the snow, and as their thunder died, and the air calmed, the faint ringing of a ship's bell could be heard.

'It's done,' Farden breathed, shuddering. She could hear the grief catching in his throat. The Scalussen armour rattled slightly against hers at the tremble in the mage's arm. Tears streaked the muck of his cheeks.

'Let's go home.'

Snow eddied as Farden opened a rift before them. Unseen hands dragged them into a blinding void.

The waves counted every moment Farden and the others didn't return to them. Only Warbringer upon Ilios' back and an exhausted, injured Fleetstar had escaped the clifftop. The minotaur's head had yet to leave her chest. A great sorrow went unspoken.

Elessi's knuckles aches, wrapped around the railing of the *Summer's Fury* as they were. 'I didn't come this far, battle leviathans, pirates, storms, and fucking Siren queens to have them die at the last hurdle. I refuse.'

Warbringer broke her silence. 'He has the weapon. He has Mithrid. He needs nothing more.'

'And Durnus?' Elessi voiced a question she had come to fear to ask. A shadow crept over her heart when the minotaur turned away. She noticed the satchel upon the minotaur's far shoulder, and fought back the closing of her throat.

Below, wood and caulking splintered beneath the force of the spell that ripped through the silence of the deck. Foul heat and the char of scorched meat wafted.

'They're home!' Lerel breathed, simultaneously sagging against the *Fury*'s wheel. 'You did it, Elessi.'

Two figures stood hunched upon the decking, surrounded by a breathless circle of soldiers, sailors, and mages.

*Only two.*

Elessi was already sprinting down the steps. The admiral chased her.

Farden looked burned by time and peril. Grey hairs dusted his black hair and haggard beard, and he had collected far more cuts and bruises, but he was alive. The same old stubborn light shone in his grey-green eyes. An ornate spear lingered in his hand. Close by his side, Mithrid's hair hung lank with sweat and blood. She puffed her cheeks in a relieved sigh.

'Durnus?' Elessi's voice cracked. 'Aspala?'

'They gave their lives,' whispered Mithrid.

Beside her, Farden's legs folded inwards. He crumpled to the deck. Elessi rushed to him.

'We beat him. He got away, but we beat him at his own game,' Farden was muttering, heaving with breath. It took a moment for him to regain his senses. 'I knew you'd come. Where is the rest of the Armada? Don't tell me—?'

Elessi squashed his fears rapidly. 'They're safe in the west. In Paraia. They didn't want to make the journey, so I took it upon my-self—'

'Ourselves,' interjected Lerel.

'—To take matters into my own hands, not listen to you or anyone else, and do what was needed. And I'm bloody glad I did.' Elessi tilted her head proud. Salt and snow encrusted her silver curls. 'Nerilan was not a fan of my ideas, but it's a longer story than I care to tell now.'

'Trust you to defy a dragon queen,' the mage snorted. 'But to speak the truth, I wouldn't dare trust anyone else. I'm glad you came.'

'What else was I supposed to do? I promised Modren I would look after Scalussen. All of it. That meant you as well,' Elessi replied, and the simplicity of her words gave her all the justification she had searched for since Krauslung.

Farden held her stare. They had not seen each other since the undermage fell to Gremorin. Words were chewed over and swal-lowed, left unspoken.

'Besides,' Elessi said, dusting her hands. 'I'm not going to put up with ruling in your stead. It's far too bothersome. I only came all this way to put you back to work.'

Farden tried to smile but it was a withered thing. He put his chin to his chest instead.

'Is that the weapon? The one you came all this way for?' Lerel asked.

'The Spear of Gunnir,' Farden replied. 'And it had fucking bet-ter be worth every mile.'

'Mithrid!' came a cry across the deck.

Mithrid turned. The dizziness of Gunnir's spell was trying its best to strike her down, but she made out Hereni rushing through the crowd of Scalussen. Bull scrambled after her.

Mithrid didn't know strength propelled her. On fawn's legs, she staggered to meet her. She thought she had come this far for Malvus' head, but when she saw the mage, she knew there was no other finishing line but her. The mage did not stop her as Mithrid grabbed Hereni's cheeks in her bloody hands and kissed her until she lost the energy to stand.

'If our bet still stands, then it looks like I beat you to the book-ships after all,' Hereni said with a grin.

'I didn't doubt you'd come for a moment.'

Mithrid felt eyes upon her. Bull hovered nearby, the beaming smile on his face slowly fading. She stumbled towards him. He did not turn away, but his embrace was stiffer than hers. Bull bowed his head.

'You look like you made Troughwake proud,' Mithrid said.

'And you look like shit,' he sparked a feeble smile before he stepped back into the crowd. Mithrid clung to Hereni. The relief she felt earned a sour edge.

Elessi had raised Farden to his feet. Lerel stood at his side, clasped under his arm.

'What now, Forever King?' Elessi asked. The ship's deck waited, uncomfortable. They had seen the sky fall. That rattled even the hardiest of spirits. Mithrid felt her eyes drooping as she watched Farden propped himself up on Gunnir.

Magick swirled at the base of his skull once more. Unbridled. Un-hindered. Farden felt almost drunk on it. The power of the spear and his armour thrummed through his body, and yet his mind was frail. Torn. Dizzied with lost choices and words he had failed to fit into those last moments. He gripped the spear as if it was Durnus' hand. What strength he had he put into standing was fading fast.

'How far a journey is it back to the others?' he asked.

Elessi and Lerel looked at each other with dour faces. 'Is there not a quicker way? Something this spear of yours can do?' asked the admiral.

Farden felt Gunnir's weight. He could not help but wonder whether Durnus dwelled within it, as souls lived in Voidaran. He had to believe it, or else he had no trust in what he was about to suggest.

'This worked as a Weight twice now. Maybe I can transport the whole bookship…'

Despite Farden's words sounding like lunacy, desperation won them over. A map was dragged from the aftcastle. Lerel pointed the others' whereabouts, far to the west and deep in the hook of Paraia. Farden began to concentrate on it.

Elessi rubbed her wind-chapped lips, 'And if you're wrong?'

Farden grinned madly, setting the crew whispering and seeking things to hold fast to. 'Then this whole endeavour will be for nothing.'

Mithrid moved closer, Hereni at her side. 'I trust you,' she told Farden, speaking her mind as well as his. 'I trust Durnus. Wherever he is.'

Farden held the spear in front of him. Vicious point to the snow-dark heavens. He raised it up, hoping it was a prize. One worth all the death and blood that had been spilled just to touch it.

'Hold on,' he growled, and every soul on board did as he commanded with wide eyes and gritted jaws.

# CHAPTER 33
## HOME

*Faith is not a mantle one can wear with ease. It is heavy work, and tiresome. The urge to take it off will be strong, but to reap the benefits, it must be worn at all times. There is no more righteous a path to greatness than absolute faith.*
FROM THE BLESSED MANUAL OF THE EASTEREALM GOD, THE ARCHITECT, BRESU, VERSE 24

Wine-dark in the grave-light of the sun, the night sky had been mortally wounded. All of Scalussen had gathered to stare up through the still palms. Voices were made whispers.

Two thirds of the stars had been swept from the firmament, leaving scattered constellations that belonged only to the old gods and half-remembered legends. Their slow dance seemed stilted and sombre. No moon showed her face that night.

Eyrum made his way inch by inch across the crowded shore and between the buildings of fresh wood and paint. It was quite the unique torture trying to keep his crutch from sinking into the sand every time he leaned on it. He would have refused it, but none around him, neither Scalussen nor Jar Khoum offered help. All were enraptured by the ominous sky. Even the fires hunkered low and cowed.

Eyrum made his way for the gold glint of Towerdawn. He was greeted with wary glances from the Old Dragon and Ko-Tergo. Only the witches refused to look, bowing heads to the sand. Their birds made not a sound.

Like Eyrum, many of them had fought in the Last War, when the sky had fallen for the first time. They had won that day by the skin of their teeth. This night looked lost already.

'It is a fell omen,' muttered Queen Nerilan. 'A sign of doom. A sign of mistakes made!'

For centuries, Eyrum had belonged to the Nelska. Centuries, had he served its people, its Old Dragons and their queens. Never before had he wanted to physically harm one. His restraint was of iron. 'Enough, Queen!' Eyrum blurted instead.

His queen regarded him sharply with her golden eyes. 'You forget yourself, General. You are a Siren first, and you will respect your queen!'

'No,' Eyrum replied proudly.

The Old Dragon by her side rumbled softly. Not a growl, but not encouragement. Nerilan drew up to her full height and still failed to reach Eyrum's chin.

'Elessi was right. I am Scalussen,' he pressed on. 'We are all one, and to continue to deny that does nothing but drive a rift between us, as Loki would want. You've been ceaseless in your doubts, and I, for one, can't take it any more.'

Nerilan's sharp reply drew stares from the crowds around them. Gazes were torn from the empty skies and fell upon the Siren queen. 'None of you can see what I can!' she snapped. 'You are content to be lost and homeless while our own land sits under the control of a god. You sing victory when you should lament defeat. And instead of acting, you cling to hope for the return of that foolish Elessi and a king that abandoned us when we needed him most. Foolish. We are sheep to Loki's wolves, and it disgusts me to see the Sirens stoop so low. And now this! Daemons in their hundreds, fallen only Thron knows where. This is what we get for our mistakes and for trusting in Elessi! I will do what I should have done outside Krauslung and take control.'

Eyrum snorted. 'Do as you must. Spark a mutiny, then. But just know that I will not follow you. Neither would many others, I would guess. I follow those with faith in their hearts, not fear.'

Nerilan slammed her glaive in the sand. 'I will have you in chains for your insolence and treachery, Eyrum!'

Eyrum threw his crutch aside and stuck out his bare and grey-scaled wrists. He stared at her, willing her to do it, to prove that she had fallen by the wayside of their endeavour.

Towerdawn reared upright and drew breath to speak, but it was Ko-Tergo who intervened. The yetin was sniffing the air. 'Smoke on the wind. Char. Blood.'

'Daemons,' thundered Towerdawn.

Alarm rippled through them. Jar Khoum began to scramble into the palm forest without a single order being uttered. Scalussen soldiers and mages ran alongside them.

'Come with us!' Sipid yelled to the Siren as he beckoned them into the forest.

Ko-Tergo seized Eyrum around the waist and heaved him towards the mountains. The Siren could feel the yetin's body already beginning to grow. He felt the hammer of the creature's heart against his ribs. Within several strides, Eyrum barely touched the sand.

Vicious wind swirled around them. Sand whipped his face. Eyrum held onto a palm tree and turned to look back at the stragglers who sprinted or hobbled in all directions from the black ocean beyond the fire.

Eyrum could smell it now: faint sulphur and the stink of scorched flesh. Ko-Tergo tugged at him, barking gruffly, but the Siren wouldn't move. Instead, he hauled his axe from behind his back and held it high.

A fork of lightning carved the night a blinding wound. Eyrum felt the wind change direction in the snap of fingers. Palms bent sideways as a screeching rose to a banshee's pitch. The rift of white light tore wider. The Siren clasped his ears.

Cloudless thunder rocked the beach. Lightning burst in a flash that turned the entire coastline to daylight. He saw no more: a shockwave of sand threw Eyrum against a tree. Breath driven from his body, he choked on a mouthful of beach before he managed to avoid suffocating. He could hear panicked yells. With his good eye still clogged, he threw himself and his axe blindly at whatever foes stood before him.

The clang of metal meeting metal reverberated through Eyrum's body. The axe was almost shaken from his hands. With a frantic hand, he rubbed the sand from his face and found a wall of iron plates standing in his way. Runes had been chiselled across them.

Confounded, Eyrum stared up to a gigantic wooden hull. As he recognised bulwarks and black sails, he heard the cheers and yells of surprise.

Crushing palm trees and the Jar Khoum village, the *Summer's Fury* rested on the land, lopsided and planks still shattering under her own enormous weight.

Eyrum dropped his axe. An unbridled yell broke from him unbidden. He could not wait to see the look on Nerilan's golden face.

Farden collapsed on the deck once more, spent and shaking. Gunnir steamed quietly in his hand. He glanced around, desperate to see where he had crashed the bookship. By the sand drifting through the air and the smell of campfires, he had missed the ocean. The air was hot and humid in his lungs.

At his side, Ilios vomited with a whine. He was not alone. Half the crew lost their guts under the force of magick and nausea.

Lerel staggered to the railing, pale as the snow. 'By Njord's arsehole, you did it, Farden! You missed the water and broke my ship by the feel of it, but we're home.'

'Where is this home you've found?' he gasped.

With Mithrid and Hereni insisting on helping, Farden dragged himself to her side. A pearl beach curved into the cloying night. Waves whispered softly across it. Palms swayed in the dust cloud and swirling eddies of the spell. Swarming from the forest came the survivors of Scalussen in their thousands. They cheered and hollered at their return. Mages let off light and fire spells. Minotaurs roared and performed odd dances of celebration for their Warbringer, who stood like a statue at the bulwark. Voidaran was stretched to the starless sky.

Below, he saw Eyrum, wounded sorely and missing half a leg. Ko-Tergo, in full white yetin form, was his crutch. The High Crone Wyved knitted thick patterns in the air with their flocks of sparrows and finches that sang as if it were dawn. Nerilan stood like a rock in a stream of bodies, arms crossed and face impassive. Whatever he had missed, the queen looked wonderfully inconvenienced by their return.

'A dark night made brighter by your return!' boomed the Old Dragon, as he alighted on the deck with an enthusiastic thud. He bowed his head low to the mage, golden eyes closed. 'And you have returned our dragons to us, more to my heart's content. We were wrong to doubt you, Elessi.'

Elessi, looking as tired as Farden felt, managed a smile but not a word except to Farden. 'A long story.'

The dragon chuckled. 'With a fine ending. It is good to see you, old friends.'

Farden did his best to bow back without stumbling onto his face. 'The feeling is wholeheartedly mutual.'

Towerdawn was immediately intrigued by Gunnir. 'So this is what drew you to lands forgotten? What has added years to your face?'

Farden held it before him, but the dragon shrank away respectfully.

'Does Loki live?' he asked.

Farden had not the energy for wasting a moment of thought upon the god of lies, nor his infuriating knack for escape. There would be time enough for justice. Rest called to him at last. 'That he does,' was all Farden said.

Mithrid spoke up. 'Malvus lies dead and defeated, once and for all. We can take some comfort from that.'

The dragon's serpentine head swung across the deck. Golden orbs pierced the shadows. 'I do not see Durnus or Aspala,' he growled in a sombre tone.

The silent shaking of heads was enough to silence Towerdawn on the matter. 'There will be time enough to speak of it all. Of lost friends and enemies survived, and the stars extinguished. Tonight, Farden, Elessi, Mithrid, we can rest. The war against the empire is finally won.'

Farden could not remember hearing a sentence so beautiful before.

Though his legs were fit to crumble, he stood by the bulwark as the gangplanks were lowered and the *Fury* slowly emptied. The crowds enveloped the crew and the others who had survived the east and the ocean. Mithrid looked back at the mage before she was whisked further up the beach. A simple nod was traded between them, and that was all that was needed.

Farden found Lerel lingering at his side. Her eyes had always held a feline glint to them, especially at night. He held her curious gaze, watched her lips toy with the idea of a smile.

'I hope you're not planning any other long excursions any time soon?' Lerel asked.

'If I can help it. I think my feet might murder me if I tried.'

Lerel tapped at the ruby eyes of the wolf on his Scalussen breastplate with her rough and sea-worn finger. 'The lone wolf, home at last,' she mused. 'A little greyer perhaps, but whole, thankfully. Are you coming? Your subjects await to cheer their king's return.'

'Shortly.' he replied in a quiet voice, barely heard over the noise of his kingdom.

Lerel held him by the cheek for a moment before striding down the gangplank, grinning wildly at a gesticulating Admiral Sturmsson.

Farden clenched his jaw. He let the voices fill his ears as he lay Gunnir flat in his palms and studied its spiral runes and etching, so perfect he became lost within it. Once more, its power crept through his body in wave after subtle wave, like a second heartbeat.

*Farden,* came the whisper, not as clear as a dragon's call, but louder than the muttering of the Grimsayer. He stared at Gunnir with narrowed eyes until he heard it again, just as soft. The whisper of a pyre's ashes in a breeze.

*Hello, old friend.*

The mage found a smile cracking his weary face. Necromancy had its benefits after all.

# EPILOGUE

There was no carrion like the remains of a battlefield.

Crows and white ravens vied with seagulls to tear at the broken and mauled bodies. The giant carcasses of beasts lay infested with swarms of the cackling, arguing birds.

Wolves and dogs had come from the deserts to have their fill, finishing off the few survivors the daemons had left behind. The ones that crawled by inches through the slush and snow and blood, gasping for breath and cursing the masters that brought them to this wasteland of carnage.

Queen Peskora was one such soul, clinging onto the life that ebbed from her body to the dripping of her blood. A daemon had driven a spear through her before biting the head clean from High Cathak Tartavor. Not a single one of his Cathak tribe had survived the battle. Her detestable cousin and Belerod had fled them in an enclave of his golems. Peskora's own soldiers had routed, abandoning her, running screaming with their backs aflame.

The snow fell upon her face in skittering flakes. She blinked, listening to the crunch of bones in nearby jaws. Hours had passed since the last magick had scorched the ground.

Peskora dragged herself onto her belly as a crow came to peck at her eyes. The wound in her stomach complained, squelching blood. The rest of her body had fallen numb with cold. She stared at the empty field, where the creature lay beheaded.

Not a single bird or beast touched the body. Her vision was clouding, but she could still see where a dark rift hovered in the air, dark as night and smoking softly. Though the mage and the cursed witch of a girl had disappeared, long gone and escaped, their magick remained.

The queen made it several feet before her body failed her feverish determination. The whine of the wolves made her flinch. A corpse-cold wind blew across her bloodied scalp. Spears and discarded swords around her wavered.

One eye now closed, and with the echo of her heart becoming nothing but a shiver, she stared at the rift. She scraped snow from her face once, twice, to make sure it was not a trick of death.

There, a foul hand curled around the ragged lip of the rift. Mottled grey and green was its skin. Six fingers flickered in the air as if tasting the blood on the breeze. A plain of steel wasteland lay beyond. Abject and constant night streaked with the green spirals of unknown stars.

The fluttering of her heart halted, and Peskora remained staring, lifeless, as a fell-dark face of golden eyes emerged from the shadow.

SCALUSSEN WILL RETURN IN

SCALUSSEN CHRONICLES BOOK THREE

Join Ben's Elite Circle to stay notified, get sneak
peeks, and see behind the scenes:
WWW.BENGALLEY.COM/GET-INVOLVED

# MORE FROM BEN GALLEY

# Did you enjoy
# Heavy Lies The Crown?

If you enjoyed this epic adventure, then feel free to tell a friend,
spread the word on social, or leave a review on Amazon and
Goodreads. Your support keeps an indie author like me writing.

Follow me on social to stay up to date with new books, competitions,
fantasy stuff and news:
WWW.LINKTR.EE/BENGALLEY

You can also visit my website for all the details on my fantasy
books and series:
WWW.BENGALLEY.COM

Join my **Elite Circle Patreon** for weekly behind-the-scenes content,
access to books a month before release, exclusive
merch, and weekly chapters:
WWW.PATREON.COM/BENGALLEY

## THANKS FOR READING!

Made in the USA
Columbia, SC
22 August 2021

44074760R00350